A GLASGOW TRILOGY

George Friel (1910–75) was born and brought up in a two-room flat in Maryhill Road in Glasgow, the city where he was to live and work all his life. Educated at St Mungo's Academy, he was the only one in a family of seven children to go to university where he took an Ordinary MA, before training as a teacher at Jordanhill College. He married his wife Isobel in 1938 and the couple moved to Bishopbriggs where they resided for the rest of their days. When war broke out Friel served in the RAOC before returning to teaching, a profession he gradually came to hate and distrust, although he never lost his concern for children. He became assistant head of a primary school before retiring in the early seventies. Such experience became the basis for his novels.

Friel's first novel was *The Bank of Time* (1959). In all his books he determined to write about the everyday lives of ordinary people from his own working-class background. His rather dark sense of humour and a rigorously intellectual style did not make him a popular author, although *The Boy Who Wanted Peace* (1964) sold well after its appearance on television. *Grace and Miss Partridge* (1969) was followed by *Mr Alfred M.A.* (1972), perhaps his most powerful novel. *An Empty House* appeared after the author's death from cancer in 1975. His short stories were collected and published posthumously as *A Friend of Humanity* (1992).

GEORGE FRIEL

A Glasgow Trilogy

The Boy Who Wanted Peace
Grace and Miss Partridge
Mr Alfred M.A.

Introduced by
GORDON JARVIE

CANONGATE
CLASSICS
90

This edition first published as a Canongate Classic in 1999 by Canongate Books Ltd, 14 High Street, Edinburgh EHI ITE, © Estate of George Friel. *The Boy Who Wanted Peace* copyright © George Friel 1964; *Grace and Miss Partridge* copyright © George Friel 1969; *Mr Alfred M.A.* copyright © Isobel Friel 1972; Introduction copyright © Gordon Jarvie 1999. All rights reserved.

The publishers gratefully acknowledge general subsidy from the Scottish Arts Council towards the Canongate Classics series and a specific grant towards the publication of this volume.

Set in 10 point Plantin by Hewer Text Ltd, Edinburgh. Printed and bound by Caledonian Book Manufacturing, Bishopbriggs, Glasgow.

British Library Cataloguing-in-Publication Data
A catalogue record for this book is available
on request from the British Library.

ISBN 0 86241 885 2

Contents

Introduction

Arguably, the writing of George Friel (1910–75) is far more widely known today than it was during the author's lifetime. His short stories were finally collected and published in book form in 1992, a mere eighteen years after his death and more than half a century after their author had originally planned to publish a collection of stories. His first novel, *The Bank of Time* (1959), finally made it into paperback in 1994 – a wait of only thirty-five years. The appearance of this collection of his three greatest novels may now accelerate the slow process of popularisation of a still-neglected literary canon.

In his lifetime, Friel was a prophet without much honour in his own country. He found it very hard indeed to get his work published. His inscription to a good friend inside the copy of his novel *Grace and Miss Partridge* (1969) nicely summarises some of the frustrations he encountered getting his work into print:

In explanation of the long delay

I wrote a story in 63
about a partridge in a bare tree.
I typed it clear in 64
and tried my publishers once more.
Back it came in 65 –
Ah well, I said, I'll still survive.
It lay unread till 66
till Mrs Boyars[1], promising nix,

1. Marion Boyars, of publishers Calder and Boyars, who were the publishers of four of Friel's five published novels.

asked to see it again in 67,
accepted it – so all forgiven.
I got no proofs till 68
and that was November, rather late.
Printed at last in 69,
so now it's yours as well as mine.[2]

The novel in question was not written by an unknown
writer. It was to be George Friel's third published novel,
and it followed the minor triumph of *The Boy Who
Wanted Peace* (1964), a book which received wide acclaim
from mainstream critics and fellow writers, and one which
was compared favourably with *Brighton Rock, Lord of the
Flies* and *A Clockwork Orange*, among others. And yet the
publisher prevaricated.

The author, for his part, was no trimmer before the
winds and fads of literary fashion. He was the uncompro-
mising realist who also penned the lines:

Seven times I wrote this story,
Not for cash or fame or glory,
Just to get the telling right
Though it never see the light.
If it's printed I confess
Truly I could not care less.[3]

All of Friel's writing is based on Glasgow, its new
housing schemes, its industrial wastelands, its blackboard
jungles, the nooks and crannies of its closes and sandstone
tenements. No writer can paint this landscape with more
laconic authority or grim humour. Friel tried to describe
this world 'like it was', unvarnished and unidealised.
Defending himself from the accusation that his fictional

2. In an unpublished MLitt thesis, 'George Friel: An Introduction to His Life and Work', by Iain Cameron (Edinburgh
   University 1987).
3. Author's private papers, National Library of Scotland.

world was bleak and depressing, he asked rhetorically, 'What am I going to do? Put my head in the sand and say that everything is lovely? Surely a novelist, even in Glasgow, if he is writing about contemporary life, must tell the truth as he sees it. If I could see a lot of sweetness and light in Glasgow I would be happy to write about it: this is life. If you say what is going on then something might get done. But if you play Mr Glasgow and pretend that it's a fine warm-hearted city then you are kidding yourself, kidding the public, and pledging the future to no reform.' (Interview in *The Guardian*, 24 March 1972.)

After Glasgow, a second key theme of George Friel's fiction is the world of Scottish education. If they read no other fiction in the course of their studies, all trainee teachers should read the novels of Friel. They tell us more about the Scottish school system of the 1950s and '60s than any history book could – and, by extension, offer us much to ponder regarding the kind of school system we have today. When the psychiatrist asks Mr Alfred why he doesn't like the new methods and new schemes of work in his profession, Mr Alfred explains: 'Well . . . all that's said in their favour is that they're new. I don't like that. It's not a reason.' (p. 584) What would Mr Alfred – in his own literary way, a champion of traditional values – make of the current orthodoxies of Scottish education, after a further quarter of a century of relentless novelties?

Like Friel, many modern Scottish writers have been teachers by profession. One thinks of Sorley Maclean and Norman MacCaig, Robin Jenkins and Iain Crichton Smith, to name but a few. But unlike any of these writers, the world of school is uniquely central to Friel's novels and stories. School in his fiction is a metaphor for the uneasy relationships between the adolescent and the adult world, whether individual or institutional. At the individual level, Percy Phinn is the not-quite adult leader of the Brotherhood in *The Boy Who Wanted Peace*, whose authority over the gang rests on the fact that he is bigger and older than his schoolboy rank-and-file; likewise Miss Partridge's potentially sinister hold over Grace; and Mr Alfred's more innocent infatuation with Rose Weipers.

Friel tried for an authentic picture of the school system he worked within. He had no wish to demonise or idealise it. Sometimes the picture he painted went too close to the bone for the apologists for the system, and he was certainly no friend of political correctness. It seems fairly clear that Friel blames the system for failing to face the facts of the situation it had to cope with. As he rambles semi-coherently at the apocalyptic end of the book, Mr Alfred finds a piece of chalk in his pocket, and this sets him off:

> 'Talk and chalk,' he said. 'That's me. Out-of-date. The child is master of the man. New methods. Visual aids. Projects. Research. Doesn't matter half the bastards can't read. Do research just the same. Discover Pythagoras' theorem for themselves. Could you?' (p. 575)

Or again:

> 'You must never say a child is stupid,' said Mr Lindsay. 'There are no stupid children, just as there are no bad children.'
>
> 'But there are,' said Mr Alfred. 'Whether you believe in original sin or believe in evolution, you can't deny there's wickedness and stupidity in the world.'
>
> 'You know that and I know that,' said Mr Lindsay. 'But the top brass won't admit it. They've never worked nine to four, Monday to Friday in a classroom. They talk as if there was only a shower of little Newtons and Einsteins who haven't had a fair chance because you didn't teach them right.' (pp. 543–4)

Miss Seymour, 'airy-mannered, brisk-moving, swift-speaking and fully fashionable', sums it all up:

'Spelling and grammar don't matter . . . just as long as they write something. Creative activity, that's what counts . . . What you see there is what the inspectors want. This is the day of the child-dominated classroom.' (pp. 545–6)

It is in this strange world that Mr Alfred is drowning:

Mr Alfred didn't like it. He wanted to teach. But nobody wanted to learn. He knew it was his job to make them. He tried. He failed. It was like talking into a phone with nobody at the other end. (p. 543)

It is not only Mr Alfred who illustrates the challenges of teaching. Mr Daunders, headteacher in *The Boy Who Wanted Peace*, is another well-sketched character. Like Percy Phinn, Mr Daunders too wants 'peace and quiet to sit in the sun and read' (p. 167). He spends much time lamenting his fate:

. . . he sighed at the destiny that had condemned him to be a headmaster in a small primary school in one of Glasgow's wild-life reservations, a pocket of vandalism, a pool of iniquity. (p. 68)

The school in Tulip Lane provides centre stage for the action of *The Boy Who Wanted Peace*; here Percy's late father had been janitor and his mother was a cleaner; in its basement, among the old Sunshine Readers and boxes of stage props, is concealed the robbers' loot; Percy himself is a former pupil and his gang are pupils of the school. Similarly in *Mr Alfred M.A.*, Collinsburn Comprehensive, Waterholm Comprehensive, and the vandalised annexe of Winchgate Primary are key locations. It is no exaggeration to say that the smells of childhood – of school corridors, playgrounds and classrooms – haunt and pervade the pages of two of these three books.

It is maybe not entirely surprising that one of the young
George Friel's literary heroes was James Joyce. Appropriately enough for a son of first-generation Donegal
emigrant parents, George's notebook sketches indicate
plans to write a Glasgow version of Joyce's *Dubliners*
(1914), and in some respects his short stories of the
1930s stand comparison with Joyce's classic collection.
In the novels represented in this publication, there are
explicit references to *Finnegans Wake* (1939) in *Grace and
Miss Partridge*; and to Stephen Dedalus in *Mr Alfred
M.A.*, as well as a quote by Mr Alfred – he 'had silence
and exile, but no cunning' – from *Portrait of the Artist as
a Young Man* (1916). And at the end of Mr Alfred's story,
the scene in the mental hospital with the two psychiatrists
is straight out of the work of another James Joyce fan –
Samuel Beckett. It is to the work of these writers that
George Friel's fiction seems most akin, rather than to that
of his Scottish contemporaries.

Some of the wordplay of Friel's writing echoes Joyce
and Beckett in its economy and exactness, and occasionally
in its poetry:

Still, with his usual politeness he answered insincerely, or with his usual insincerity he answered
politely. (p. 392)

A ruffled hen laying a complaint and making a song
about it. (p. 406)

Tordoch . . . became a waste land of bracken and
nettles surrounded by a chemical factory, gasworks,
a railway workshop and slaghills. At that point the
town council took it over for a slum-clearance
scheme. They built a barrack of tenements with
the best of plumbing and all mod cons and expected
a new and higher form of civilisation to flare up by
spontaneous combustion. (p. 408)

[Gerald Provan] grinned, hands in the pockets of his tightarsed jeans, kicking the kerb, radiant with the insolence of an antimath idling out his last term at school. (p. 414)

Wanting to kiss Rose. Rose upon the rood of time. Red Rose, proud Rose, sad Rose of all my days. Rose of the world, Rose of peace. Far off, most secret and inviolate Rose. (p. 468)

The linguistic distinction of Friel's writing is consistent. Anyone picking up *Mr Alfred M.A.* is duly warned to be on the alert in the two pages of the book's opening chapter:

She had always to be protecting [her son] from the malice of the world. (p. 387)

The anapaests of his bawling were hammered out by his punches. (p. 388)

. . . confounding her mother and her brother in one strabismic glare. (p. 388)

Friel can also be linguistically jocular, as when he describes the thug Gerald Provan in the nice zeugma 'wearing new jeans and an old smirk' (p. 456), or the educational spokesperson (English, of course) 'leaving no stone unturned till she nips us in the bud' (p. 439). Or:

He said he was sick and tired of all the feuding and fighting that was going on in the school and he was determined to stamp it out. He nearly said with a firm hand. (p. 429)

As one of the characters points out regarding Mr Alfred: 'Half the things he said were quotations' (p. 429). This is a very Joycean tendency, and can be both effective and amusing: '. . . there was a breathless hush in the lane that night and Mr Alfred knew his moment had come. Cowan lunged, Turnbull dodged, and Mr Alfred spoke out loud and clear' (pp. 415–16).

The downside of Friel's linguistic interests is most apparent in *Mr Alfred M.A.* It is in this work that he seems to flaunt obscure words in a manner at once ponderous and irritating, a point that was taken up by Auberon Waugh. So we have 'He sprawled raniform', 'invulting arms', 'a newly acquired claudication', 'aposiopesis', 'palaestra', 'silent catatropia', 'nuzzer', 'the gamekeeper's tetragrams' (the famous four-letter words in D. H. Lawrence's most notorious fiction), 'the autochthonous tribes', 'imbibitions', 'a mammose wench . . . flushed with hebetic vulgarity', 'a perlustration of the city', 'a nuchal smack and an auricular threat'; and many more. All these words and phrases are appropriately defined in the *Shorter Oxford*; but it seems a pity to have to stop and look it up quite so frequently. Arguably, this is a sub-Joycean feature of George Friel's writing style.

A more topical aspect of Friel's writing style is his pioneering effort to capture in print the speech patterns of Glasgow demotic. In his use of 'mamurrer' (= my mother), 'Feudcleanyurears' (= if you'd clean your ears), 'Hoosnagang' (= who's in a gang), Friel is a precursor of Tom Leonard, Stephen Mulrine, Bill Keys, Adam Mac-Naughtan, Margaret Hamilton and many later writers. Friel had a good ear for vernacular speech, and might well have made a reliable contributor to Michael Munro's *The Patter: A Guide to Current Glasgow Usage* (1985). He also put down one or two interesting markers anent the use of Scots as opposed to standard English in schools. When, in *The Boy Who Wanted Peace*, the young Garson is interviewed by the headteacher about an insult which had provoked a fight with Savage,

> . . . he couldn't use Savage's words. He answered in the book-English a bright Scots schoolboy uses when he talks respectfully to his teachers. 'He

accused my mother of eloping with a Negro,' he said. (p. 102)

Savage had actually said something slightly different: 'Yer maw ran awa' wi' a darkie' (p. 87). Similarly, in *Mr Alfred M.A.*, when the teacher grabs Gerald Provan to haul him before the headteacher, Provan says: 'Take yer hauns aff me'.

> His dialect vowels were themselves a form of insolence. Normally a boy spoke to his teacher in standard English. (p. 429)

Nowadays we tend to ask the question: Was this policy of linguistic cleansing wise?

There are of course numerous other themes and topics in this rich fictional canon awaiting the reader's exploration. There is the violent world of graffiti-land, of the Glasgow gangs and their significance in the society which spawned them. The death of Poggie in *Mr Alfred M.A.* and of Donald Duthie in *Grace and Miss Partridge* are important events, and here again Friel tries to tell it like it is – arguably with more insight than the sociologists manage. Then there is the whole business of sanity and madness in all three novels. Is Percy quite right in the head? Is Miss Partridge? Is Mr Alfred? Is it society that is mad?

Finally, there are the great apocalyptic scenes of Annie Partridge and her 'spectres' (pp. 334–43) and of Mr Alfred and his doppelgänger Tod (p. 574 et seq). These seem quintessentially Scottish, in the tradition of Scott's Wandering Willie, James Hogg's justified sinner and R. L. Stevenson's Tod Lapraik. It is hoped that this new edition of three important novels will renew interest in a significant contributor to Scottish literature of the twentieth century.

Gordon Jarvie

BIBLIOGRAPHY

The Bank of Time (Hutchinson 1959, Polygon 1994*)
The Boy Who Wanted Peace (Calder and Boyars 1964, Pan 1972,
    Polygon 1985)
Grace and Miss Partridge (Calder and Boyars 1969)
Mr Alfred M.A. (Calder and Boyars 1972, Canongate 1987)
An Empty House (Calder and Boyars 1975)
A Friend of Humanity: Selected Short Stories (Polygon 1992)

*indicates work currently in print

THE BOY WHO
WANTED PEACE

A NOVEL

Hugh O'Neill and Shaun O'Donnell, two big broad Glasgow Irishmen who claimed to be descended from Niall of the Nine Hostages who was King of All Ireland when the ancestors of the English aristocracy were grubbing for nuts in the forest, bumped into each other getting off the same bus at Parkhead Cross just as the pubs were opening. The sky was blue, the syvers were littered, and there was the clinging smell of decaying refuse that goes with a warm spring evening in the East end of the city. They were parched, hot and sticky after a hard day's work, and with a little jerk of the head and a question in their royal blue eyes they understood each other at once and went into the Tappit Hen for a brotherly crack over a quiet drink before going on home for their tea. They were only a couple of workers from the Yards who built more ships talking shop of an evening at the bar than ever they built in a year's work, but their conversation on this occasion may throw some light on the events that began the same evening, though they themselves were of course unaware of the coincidence.

'What'll ye have?' O'Donnell asked since he happened to be the first through the swing doors.

'A glass and a pint,' O'Neill answered, raising one hand high to salute the barman. The shade and coolness of the place were pleasant to him after the heat and dust outside. He liked pubs especially when they had just opened. At that time they were as dim and quiet as a church. A man could be at peace there with a drink in front of him, and the gantry was a kind of altar. Certainly it held on its glass shelves the expensive liquid that made life bearable and sometimes even enjoyable – uisgebeatha in the language of the Gael, the water of life in the language of the Saxon.

'A glass and a pint!' O'Donnell repeated in alarm, his Irish eyes reproachful. 'Do ye think I've been robbin' a bank? Ye'll have a half and a half-pint and like it.'

They stood in reverent silence till they were served.

'Funny you saying robbing a bank,' said O'Neill. 'I was just reading in the paper there coming in on the bus. See the Colonel's deid.'

'Oh aye, the Colonel, aye, so he's deid, is he,' said O'Donnell. Not until he had put a little water in the whiskies did he try to understand what they were talking about. He frowned. 'How do ye mean, the Colonel?'

'The Colonel I mean,' said O'Neill. 'Him they got for the Anderston bank robbery. He's deid.'

'Oh, I see, God rest his soul,' said O'Donnell with routine sorrow in his flat voice.

'The paper was saying he died in jail,' said O'Neill. 'Well, no' in the jail exactly, it was in the infirmary, but he was still in jail of course because it was eight years he got.'

'Funny,' said O'Donnell. 'That other bloke they got for the Ibrox bank robbery, he died in jail last month as well.'

'Aye, it makes ye think,' said O'Neill. 'He was a Canadian.'

'No, he was an Australian,' said O'Donnell. 'Or his pal was an Australian or wan o' them was an Australian but no' a Canadian.'

'No, he was a Canadian all right,' said O'Neill.

'No, an Australian,' said O'Donnell, finishing his whisky and elevating his beer.

'Ach, ye're thinking o' the Ibrox bank,' said O'Neill. 'That was the Major, no' the Colonel. The monocled Major they called him. 'He was an Australian but it was his pal that died no' him. But the Colonel was a Canadian so he was, it was the Major was an Australian.'

'That's what I'm saying,' O'Donnell complained. 'He was an Australian, him or his mate. Wan o' them.'

'Funny how these blokes come to Glasgow,' said

O'Neill. He shook the dregs of his whisky glass into his beer.

'Ach, there's a lot o' folks come to Glasgow for the country roon aboot,' said O'Donnell. 'They've heard o' the bonnie, bonnie banks o' Loch Lomond.'

'It's no' the banks o' Loch Lomond they fellows came for,' O'Neill retorted, pouting over the half-pint he was raising to his lips. He sipped and went on. 'It's the Royal Bank and the Clydesdale Bank and the Commercial Bank and the Bank of Scotland and the British Linen Bank, that's what they came for. Ye know, there's been a wheen o' bank robberies in Glasgow in the last five or six year. Just you think back.'

'Ach, I don't know,' said O'Donnell. 'See the Bhoys is doing well the now. Were you there on Saturday?'

'Aye I was there,' said O'Neill. 'But they're no' that clever. The polis aye catch up on them sooner or later so they do. The trouble with the Bhoys is they never keep it up. They go away and let the Thistle or the Thirds beat them when ye least expect it.'

'I don't mind so long as they beat the Rangers,' O'Donnell replied nonchalantly, offering his mate a cigarette. 'Here! But the polis are no' that clever either. They get them but they don't get the money.'

'Ye're right there,' said O'Neill. 'It says in the paper there's thirty thousand pound still missing. But the Bhoys has got youth on their side, that's mair nor the Rangers have. You can see it in the paper there for yourself.'

O'Donnell looked at O'Neill's paper.

'Funny,' he said. 'It was just the same wi' the Ibrox robbery. Forty thousand it was they didn't get. But I'd never take the Bhoys in my coupon.'

'Oh naw, neither would I,' said O'Neill. 'And then there's Napper Kennedy. Maryhill. They got him in Dublin but they never got the money. Oh naw, I'd never take them in the pools. Ye canna trust them.'

'They got some of it did they no'?' said O'Donnell.

'Somebody left a suitcase in the left luggage. It was his brother wasn't it in the Central Station?'

'Aye, they got five thousand,' said O'Neill. 'Nothing much. There was mair nor thirty thousand they never got yet. And there's Charlie Hope, him that done the Partick bank. He never got as far as Dublin. They got him in his club in St Vincent Street. A bridge club he called it, some bridge club. But they got damn all else but the smell o' his cigar. That was another thirty or forty thousand job. They boys have something to come out to so they have.'

'Ach, they'll never get near it,' said O'Donnell. 'What I say is, the Bhoys ought to spend money on a good inside forward. They've got a lot o' good young yins but the young yins need an auld heid. They'll no' even get gaun to the lavatory without somebody on their tail.'

'Ach, I don't know about that,' O'Neill shrugged. 'They've got ways and means I'll bet you. They don't go to all that trouble for nothing. Where would ye get a good inside forward anyway? They've spent good money before this and it's been money wasted. They're better sticking tae what they've got.'

'Trouble, aye it's trouble all right,' said O'Donnell. 'Eight or nine years they get, every time. But you're right enough I suppose, some of their best servants was players they got for nothing.'

'Well, so what?' O'Neill asked. 'Would you no' do eight or nine year to come out tae thirty or forty thousand?'

'Aye, if I was coming out tae it,' said O'Donnell. 'But that's what I'm arguing, they'll no' come out tae it. The minute they touch it they'll be lifted.'

'But they've served their time, haven't they?' said O'Neill. 'They canny put them in jail twice for the wan offence.'

'That's murder you're thinking of,' said O'Donnell. 'Robbery's different. Sure they'd take the money from them, wouldn't they? They'd never let them get away wi' it. That would make it too easy. I'd do it myself for eight or nine year.'

'But suppose somebody else has been keeping it to feed it back to them when they come out, ye know, in regular payments, quiet like.'

'Who could they trust to keep thirty or forty thousand for them?' O'Donnell asked derisively. 'Would you trust anybody wi' that amount o' money if you were inside for eight or nine year?'

'I don't know,' said O'Neill thoughtfully. 'I've never had that amount o' money. Maybe ye could if ye made it worth their while. What'll ye have?'

'Just as a matter of interest, how many is that now?' O'Donnell asked.

'It's only yer second,' said O'Neill. 'You put the first wan up when we came in and that's all we've had. Do ye want the same again?'

'Naw, no' the drinks, the bank robberies I mean ye're talking about,' said O'Donnell. 'Anderston, Ibrox, Maryhill, Whiteinch, that's four at least.'

'Oh, there's been a lot mair nor that,' said O'Neill. 'And tae think it's a' lying somewhere! They're a' inside and the money's outside. Thirty thousand here and forty thousand there and the same again and mair. It would break yer heart just thinking about it.'

'Aye, it would be a bit of all right finding even wan o' they stacks. Will ye be up seeing the Bhoys on Saturday?'

'Aye, ye could find it but would ye have the nerve tae spend it?' said O'Neill. 'Och aye, I'll be there all right.'

'I'll see ye here at two o'clock then,' said O'Donnell. 'I like seeing the Bhoys when they're doing well.'

'But I'll see ye before then,' said O'Neill. 'Ye'll be in here the night aboot eight, will ye no'?'

'Och aye, sure,' said O'Donnell. 'The Bhoys is drawing big money the now all right.'

'Forty-five thousand there last Saturday,' said O'Neill.

They took no more after O'Neill had returned O'Donnell's hospitality. They were two steady working-men, and they went straight home for their tea after their second drink. They knew they would be back in the same pub in a couple of hours. And besides Glasgow's plague of bank robberies there was the state of the Yards on the Clyde to discuss, and there was the Celtic football team to talk about. For two Glasgow Irishmen that was a topic as inexhaustible as the weather to two Englishmen.

That same evening, in the Bute Hall, the Glasgow University Choral Society and the University Orchestra gave a performance of Bach's B Minor Mass. It was damned with faint praise by the music critic of the local paper, a sour Scotsman who complained of the acoustics and found the choir's hundred and eight voices too light for the place and purpose. O'Neill and O'Donnell, like most people in the city, didn't know the Mass was being sung by the University Choral Society, so they weren't present. They were back in the Tappit Hen before the Sanctus. But among those who did attend the Bute Hall was the unwitting hero of this true narrative, a culture-hungry teenager who had failed in his eleven-plus examination and come to life at sixteen, just after he left school. He was working as a packer in the Scottish Cooperative Wholesale Society in Nelson Street, but he knew he deserved something a lot better. He went about his daily chores with a dagger of bitterness against a system that had refused him a higher education just because he didn't happen to pass an examination when he was only twelve. He tried to educate himself. He went to the public library every night and brought home books on philosophy, psychology, economics, and the history of art from the cave-paintings to Picasso. He found his pleasure in the very act of borrowing them. When the girl stamped the date-label and filed the title-slips with his tickets he was sure she admired and respected him. Nobody else in his unjust position would have had the courage and intelligence to borrow such books. He had always to take them back before he had time to read them, but he felt that even having them in the house was something. To see Kant's *Critique of Pure Reason* on the kitchen dresser alongside the first volume of Marx's *Capital* was a great consolation to him. You never knew who might come in and see them. It only annoyed his mother. She had no patience with him.

'It's high time you took them books back,' she scolded him every time she dusted the dresser where she displayed her grandmother's two brass candlesticks, the four large seashells she had brought home from her holiday at Millport the year she was married, a photo of her mother in a white-metal frame, a snap of her brother when he was a sergeant with the Argyll and Sutherland Highlanders in Singapore, an enamelled tray showing two pastoral lovers beside a rustic bridge, and her bottle of cough mixture. 'How can I keep this corner tidy if you clutter it up with books? And they're all overdue and I never see you open them anyway.'

'You don't see all I do,' he answered, looking down on her from a great height.

'There's sevenpence to pay on each of them,' she complained the night he was getting ready to go to the Bute Hall. 'You might as well buy the damn things, the money you spend in fines. Do you think I've nothing to do with my money but give it to you to pay for all the books you keep past their time?'

'Money, money, money! All you can think of is money!'

He was peevish with her. She was always nagging him since his father died a month ago.

'Somebody's got to think about it,' she said, her head high, acting the calm lady to his bad temper. 'Of course, you're Lord Muck of Glabber Castle, you're too high and mighty to bother about money. I'd have thought now your poor father's dead at least you'd try and help your mother. You've only one mother in this world, you know, my boy.'

She wiped her eyes with a dirty hankie, and went ruthlessly on.

'Your poor father's no' here any longer to look after us now, ye know. Him dying the way he did. Puffed out like a candle. Wan minute he was there, the next he wasna. It's something I'll never get over. The day after his brother was killed. No' that he was any good. But your poor father was a good man. Do anything for anybody. Worked hard all his days. Then just to die like that, down in the cellar all by himself. And then they tried to tell me it was his heart. Funny he never complained about his heart before. Of course him and Sammy was twins. They was born together and I suppose they had to go together. Well, near enough. Sammy was killed on the Friday and your poor father was found dead the next day, couldny ha' been more than a couple of hours after he heard about it. Makes you think. You ought to be helping me, no' annoying me the way you do.'

She sniffed wetly, and his nerves jangled at the sound of air through mucus.

'I'm helping all I can,' he said dourly. 'But I never get a bloody word of thanks for it. Don't forget it's me pays the rent for the house.'

'You're lucky to have a house at all to pay the rent for,' she snapped, her nose clear again for a minute. 'Don't forget we lost a good house rent-free when your father went and died.'

'Some house,' he gibed, surveying her as if he was estimating her height and weight. How could he, so tall and handsome, come from such a shrivelled thing as this crabbit woman with grey hair, mournful eyes, a flat chest and skinny legs with black cotton stockings? It was another injustice. He should have had a beautiful elegant mother with shapely legs and a bosom like the advert for a shaving soap, not too much and not too little, a mother who would inspire him to write the poetry he knew he could write if only he could get peace and quiet. 'A janitor's house in the school playground! That's a fine house! Living right in the middle of the slum where he worked.'

'It was a bigger and better house than this,' she shouted. 'Who could I bring here, a room and kitchen up a dirty close with a stairhead lavatory, and a single-end on each landing? You never think what a come-down it is for me to have to go out to work and be a cleaner in the very school where your father was the janitor for fifteen year, aye, and his job was jist as important as the headmaster's I can tell ye. He saw them come and he saw them go, and they'd all have been lost without him. He kept them right. And now I've got to be a cleaner there and live in a room and kitchen that looks right on to the four-apartment house I had rent-free in the playground. It just shows you how life treats you.'

'You're just after saying we're lucky to be here,' he stabbed quickly back, gloating over her cracked temper. 'Lucky that big fat drip Nancy went to Canada. Ha-Ha! That was a bit of luck all right. If ever a dame got on my nerves it was her with her very coarse veins. A real intellectual topic of conversation she had!'

'You'll please me if you speak of your Aunt Nancy with proper respect for your elders,' she said stiffly, on her dignity as a lady again. 'If your Aunt Nancy hadn't got the factor to agree to us getting her house I don't know where we could have went I'm sure. And just having to flit across the street from the school was a big saving. If we'd had to pay for all our furniture getting took somewhere across the river it would have cost us a lot of money I can tell you. But you never think of that. You've a mind above money, like.'

'You aye come back to money, don't you?' he said. 'You'd think that was all there was in this life, money, the way you talk, you've no idea of art and philosophy and – and—'

He was stuck for a moment for another subject, to let her see what a superior mind he had.

'And poetry and the drama,' he added quickly, remembering the card above the shelves in the far corner of the library. 'You've never lived. I've lived, so I have. I've read the great poets, it's more than you ever done. You, you've no idea of culture.'

'Have you?' she asked him very coolly, cutting him deep. 'You couldn't even pass your qually and you try and kid me about culture. You never read the half of the books you bring in here.'

'Ach!' he snarled at her.

'Another thing,' she pursued him cruelly, turning from the cracked, mottled sink where the window looked across Bethel Street to the ancient school where her husband had worked. 'It's high time you stopped hanging about the backcourt and going across there to the playground every night. If you could just see yourself! Be your age. It looks daft, a big fellow like you playing with wee boys at school.'

'I'm not playing with them,' he answered proudly. 'I'm helping them. They come to me for advice. Cause I'm older and cause I know more than they do. I'm trying to learn them. If I'd had somebody to guide me the way I guide them when I was their age I wouldn't be where I am today, so I wouldn't.'

'A crowd of scabby gangsters,' his mother muttered. 'There's no' a shop in the street safe from them.'

'Okay they've got a gang,' he admitted generously. 'And what's wrong with having a gang? A gang is only the expression of the primitive need for a community. You read any book on child-psychology, that'll tell you. People feel they must belong. I mean ordinary people. And these lads aren't even ordinary. They're a lot of poor dirty neglected children with nobody to shower love on them.'

'Shower,' his mother sniffed, having trouble with her nose again. 'They're a shower all right. Shower o' bastards.'

'Their parents have no interest in them,' he went on, making a speech at her, 'and they've no interest in their parents. They were born in the jungle and their whole existence is one fierce struggle to survive. The only law they know is the law of the jungle and they're beginning to learn its disadvantages. So they come to me and I try to learn them to live according to the law of law and order. They see you've got to have someone to appeal to so they come to me. I'm their referee. They rely on me for to see justice done. I'm the lawman. I'm the judge. Cause I stand above it so I can see it. Boys are like Jews, they're different from the people round about them. And where would the Jews have been if they hadn't had Moses to give them the Law?'

'Ach!' his mother derided him. 'Playing wi' a lot o' weans and ye call yourself Moses!'

'They're not weans,' he shouted. 'They're innocent children. And Christ has said unless ye become as little children ye shall not enter the Kingdom of Heaven.'

'Oh, it's Christ now, is it?' cried his baffled mother. 'You'd gar anybody grue so you would the way you talk. Moses! Christ!'

She returned to the dishes in the basin in the sink.

At that point in their friendly discussion he banged out of the house, scampered down the three storeys to the close, went into the littered smelly street and walked across the city to the University. He liked passing through the Main Entrance in University Avenue. He felt he was entering the land he should have inherited. He often walked through the University to comfort himself. When he crossed the Arts Quadrangle and approached the Bute Hall he felt happier and lighter. All his grudges dropped from him. He was where he ought to be. If the girl in the library could see him now she would think he was a student all right. A university student, that was the life.

Bach's music didn't get over to him, but he was pleased to be sitting there while the choir and orchestra went through it. His attention drifted peacefully. Music always made his mind wander. That was why he liked to go to orchestral concerts. He felt liberated. So while the sopranos got lost in 'Cum Sancto Spiritu' he plunged contentedly through the jungle of his grievances.

All he wanted was peace, peace and quiet, and he couldn't get it. He wanted to be free from the need to earn his living so that he could be a poet like Shelley or make documentary films like Peter Scott or be a novelist like Tolstoy or even a television personality. He knew he had other talents too. He had helped to prepare and move the scenery when the Drew Rowan Youth Club put on a pantomime, and he enjoyed being back-stage. He knew he had a good sense of the theatre. He could produce plays, or he could travel round the world with a cine-camera and do a series about strange places and peculiar peoples. There was nothing hard in what David Atten-borough did. Anybody could do it. All you needed was money. Anything was possible if you had the money to give you the leisure to do it. He could be an authority on modern art. Nobody else in Packing and Dispatch had read the amount of stuff he had read on Picasso and Henry Moore. Shelley and Wordsworth had enough money to write poetry without having to work as well. If they had been a janitor's son like him they wouldn't have had the chance. If he had the money he could buy a house on some lonely part of the coast in Devon or Cornwall, and it would be peaceful enough there to be a poet. To be a poet you had to see things as children saw them, all fresh and unspoilt, like the smell of apples or the colour of the sky when the sun was setting behind the Campsies in summer or the touch of a cat's fur or the taste of a glass of milk and a buttered roll. And because he liked to be with kids and listen to them blether so that he could keep roots in the world of his childhood people laughed at him. They said he was soft.

They had said he was soft since the first day he went to school. He blamed it on his name. He hated it for years. Percy was a sloppy name. It was too uncommon in the tenements, too Kelvinside, too English, to get respect. It was worst in the qualifying class, where even the teacher made jokes about it. She kept on saying he was slow in arithmetic and backward in reading and poor at spelling and hopeless at composition. Her daily crack was to tell him he must persevere.

'Ah, here's Percy again,' she said to the class every day when those with no sums right lined up for the strap. 'He tries very hard. He's very trying, is our Percy. It's a fine old English name, Percy. So is Vere.'

She raised his hand a little higher, straightened his palm, and addressed him as she strapped him.

'Well, Percy, you must Percy Vere. That's all.'

And every day the boys and girls preparing for the eleven-plus examination laughed at the same joke and laughed at him. It was the girls' laughter hurt him most. It fell from Heaven like the merriment of angels looking down on the antics of a clod-hopper who couldn't get his big feet out of the mud. He grew sullen at Miss Elginbrod's daily joke and one bright morning in May he challenged her. The room was stuffy in the early sun. Miss Elginbrod always kept the windows closed because she disliked draughts. His head was hot and he didn't know what the sums were about. It was trains one minute and marbles the next, then it was rolls of cloth, then it was tons and quarts. One minute she was saying you add the speeds, then she was saying you subtract them. She kept on hopping about. You were just beginning to think you were bringing pounds to pennies when she made you bring pounds to ounces. She never gave you peace. So for the thousandth time he had only two sums finished out of the five, both wrong, and for the thousandth time she shrugged over him.

'Well, Percy, you've just got to persevere, that's all.'

He faced her, rather round-shouldered because of his height. Even then he was much taller than other boys of his age, and it made him look gawky.

'Please, miss,' he said, and then his nerve failed.

'Yes?' said Miss Elginbrod, looking at him with patronizing patience, swinging the strap in a practice smack. 'Is there something you don't understand?'

Her question gave him back his determination to oppose her.

'I don't understand why you call me Percy Vere. My name isn't Percy Vere, it's Percy Phinn.'

An earthquake unpredicted by the eight o'clock weather

forecast shook the class. A cyclone of laughter lifted the roof and a tornado of girlish screams whipped the walls apart. He felt himself naked to the wind and weather when he had expected to stand there proud and respected in an awed silence. He was frightened. There was never a mockery like this, clawing at him on all sides and tearing him apart to eat him up.

For causing a disturbance in the class Miss Elginbrod gave him three hard ones with her strap, not the thin one she always had in her hand but the thick one she kept away at the back of her desk out of sight until she was really angry. And when she had done that she said he had been insolent, and gave him another three.

When he was reborn at sixteen he looked back on his past life and blamed Miss Elginbrod for his failure in the examination. She had discouraged him. She ought to have seen he was a case of late development like Sir Winston Churchill. She ought to have seen his true merit and given him love and understanding. She wasn't fit to be a teacher. People like her would have failed to see Shelley's gifts when he was a boy at school. She had never even told him he had the same name as Shelley. She just made a joke of it. That proved she was so ignorant she didn't know Shelley's first name. He had to find it out for himself after he had left school. The discovery excited him. He stopped hating his name. He became proud of it. It made him something of a poet too. He read up on Shelley. In a biographical dictionary in the public library he found a sentence that he copied out and learned off by heart. 'Percy was a boy of much sensibility, quick imagination, generous heart, and a refined type of beauty, blue-eyed and golden-haired.' He hadn't only the same name as Shelley, he had the same colour of eyes and the same colour of hair – though his mother said his hair was 'like straw hinging oot a midden'. But his mother had no sensibility, no quick imagination. It was a mystery where his had come from. And he was a rebel too, just like Shelley. It was for being a rebel that Miss Elginbrod had given him six with her Lochgelly strap. Well, he would remember her, and when he was famous as a poet or a producer or an authority on modern art she would be ashamed of herself. But to get fame he would have to get leisure, and to get leisure he would have to get money. It always came back to money.

'If only!' he dreamed while the choir exulted in the Gloria. 'If only I had enough money to live without having to go out to work every day. If only I had a private income like Shelley and Wordsworth. I could get peace then I'd show them. If only I'd got a fair deal out of life I could play my cards better.'

While Percy Phinn was attending Bach's Mass a search-party was out from the gang that bowed to him as patron, chairman, and final arbiter. They were frightened, and they wanted advice. Some of them laughed at Percy behind his back, some of them argued he was 'dead clever', but they all agreed he would never do them a dirty trick and they were all scared of him a little, especially when he fixed them with his big, sad eyes and lectured them on the good life. And now they needed help from somebody clever, somebody older, somebody they could trust. It could only be Percy. That was the unanimous decision, taken in full assembly in the cellar. But they couldn't find him. He wasn't in Johnny Hay's billiards-room (billiards was the one game where he showed any talent), he wasn't in the public library, he wasn't in the house, he wasn't at the corner watching the big girls go by, he wasn't in the playground refereeing five-a-side football, he wasn't at the swings pushing the kids higher and higher, he wasn't anywhere. He had simply vanished. It showed how clever he was. They were baffled. They had never heard of the Bute Hall or Bach either. They were only ten or eleven years of age. Hughie Savage, the oldest of them, was not quite twelve. He couldn't read very well, but he was shrewd and he could write out a three-cross double with no difficulty. He was far cleverer than his teachers ever suspected, and his line of humour was to put on a la-dee-da voice and speak in what he thought was an English accent. He had a big head on a bull neck and his ears stuck out like a couple of cabbages.

The scattered groups of the search-party returned by

arrangement to the cellar at half past nine. When they were all present for the second time that evening Savage took the chair and reported Percy's disappearance. The chair he sat on was a high-legged one with a broken back and a foot-rail. It was the chair Miss Elginbrod had sat on when Percy was in her class, but the back spars and the shoulder-rest came off one afternoon when she threw a cheeky boy across the room. He fell against it and knocked it over. When he got to his feet he kicked it apart in a fury while Miss Elginbrod whipped him round the legs with her strap. She sent it to the janitor for repair, and the janitor put it away in the cellar till he could find time to look at it. Death found him first, and the chair had lain there ever since, in the cellar below the school, the secret headquarters of the gang that Percy sponsored.

This was no picayune cellar. It was a sprawling low-roofed vault stretching below the main building and out under the playground, where it ended in an unexplored boundary of evil darkness. Not even Frank Garson had ever touched that far-off invisible wall, and when the Three High Clavigers of the Bethel Brotherhood ordered him to make a map of the cellar because Miss Elginbrod had praised his drawing and handwriting he left his sketch open at that side and along it he wrote in a scroll *Here Be Rats*. A door in the basement, at the end of an L-shaped line of wash-hand basins, opened to a dim and dangerous staircase that went steeply down to the bowels of the building, and that was commonly supposed to be the only door to the cellar. But because of the gradient on which the school was built there was another door to the cellar in Tulip Place, a blind alley round the corner from Bethel Street. It was a small, inconspicuous, dark-green door, hacked by many initials, and behind it was a chute. That was where the coal for the boilers had been delivered before the school changed over to electrical heating, and then the door was locked for good and forgotten.

Percy had a key to it from his father's days as janitor. Three other keys were cut from his and given to the three oldest members of the Brotherhood. The cellar became their church, the scene of enrolment, expulsion, and initiation rites. It was to be entered only from the blind alley after the school was locked up for the night. Percy found a word for the keyholders who alone had the power to permit entry. He got it when he was grazing in a dictionary in the reference room of the library. He called them the Clavigers. To be a Claviger in Percy's gang was the highest rank you could reach. He gave himself the title of Regent Supreme because the boys knew those two words, but he went to great trouble to explain to them what they meant apart from their occurrence in a television advert.

Over the undated years the cellar had become a junk-house, a dark neglected dump where people threw things they didn't know what to do with. Scores of old registers, tied in tape and going back for decades, were stacked against a wall and crowned by bundles of ancient group mental tests and verbal ability tests, pupils' record cards, report cards and medical histories. Nobody had ever dared destroy them. Such documents are intimidating. They have their own over-weening life. To burn them would be as brutal and immoral as committing murder. And you could never be sure they wouldn't be wanted one day. Somebody might ask for the date of birth or the father's name or the IQ of a pupil who had left years ago and was now in Barlinnie Prison for house-breaking. It would never do to reply, 'The records have been destroyed.' The whole point of keeping records is that they are kept after they are kept. Otherwise why keep them?

Scattered alongside these sacred but forgotten documents there were blackboard compasses, blackboard rulers, pointers, pyramids, cones, cylinders and spheres, a carton of inkwells with the bakelite rims chipped off by vandals so that they fell through the hole cut for them in the pupils' desks, the broken pole of a dead traffic warden, a punctured hose, brooms, spades, shovels and rakes, brown paper piled four feet high with the salvaged string wound round the sheets, a pail of stucco, a barrel half-full of washing-soda, empty bleach bottles put aside to be filled with ink made from a powder, political maps of Europe, Asia and Africa dating from before the First World War, a coal-scuttle and a stirrup pump. On one side of the outmoded boiler was a woodwork bench with a vice that wouldn't screw up tight, and on the other a ziggurat of broken dual desks. In front of the desks was an old piano with occasional dumb keys. It had been put there twenty-two years ago, when an insistent music-teacher asked for and got a new piano. The janitor filled in the correct form to have the old one uplifted, but somehow nothing was ever done about it. On top of the piano was the large hand-bell that had been rung to assemble and dismiss the school before the electric bells were put in. It was a heavy bell, solid brass, and Savage said it was worth at least a fiver as scrap metal, but Percy wouldn't let him hawk it.

Across the cellar from the broken desks, under a tangle of legless chairs, educational publishers' catalogues, pre-war copies of the *Scottish Educational Journal*, and five dozen derelict reading books called *The Sunshine Way*, were six tea-chests, three along and two deep, containing the costumes and small props used in the annual school concert. But there had been no annual concert for five years, and in that time there had been two new head-masters and Percy's father had died of a thrombosis, so that nobody in the school knew exactly what was in them.

There were two weak ceiling lights in the cellar, but the Brotherhood preferred not to switch them on during council meetings. They lit six candles, using the bleach bottles as candlesticks, and the dim unsteady light, with flickering shadows on the walls receding into the damp darkness where the rats were, gave a proper obscurity to the arguments of the assembly.

'I vote we carry on without the Regent,' said Hugh Savage, Chief Claviger, whose Christian name was locally pronounced 'Sheuch'.

'No, I object,' said Specky, Second Claviger, sitting on

the inverted coal-scuttle to the right of Savage's chair. He was a brassy, blethering confident boy, wearing thick convex glasses with thin wire frames, a Schools Health Service issue, and he talked like a book.

'Well, we'll vote for it,' said Skinner, Third Claviger, sitting on a drawing-board placed across the pail of stucco. He was always called Skinny in affectionate abbreviation of his surname. It was only a fortuitous anomaly that he happened to be a chubby child.

The Three High Clavigers faced the ruck of the Brotherhood, obedient troopers who sat, knelt or squatted on the grimy stone floor. Savage was the strong arm, Specky was the brains and Skinny was the kind heart. In that cavernous gloom they looked like three subterranean judges addressing a jury of sooterkins.

'I'm in this,' Frank Garson shouted from the front row. 'It was me that found it. You can't decide, Sheuch. You've got to wait for Percy. That's the rule for urgent business.'

'Don't you call me Sheuch when I'm in the chair,' Savage checked him crossly. Then he leered forward. 'Anyway, how can it be urgent if we've got to wait for Percy? And you should be in the dock, so you should, but I move that Probationer Garson's expelled. Come on, get him in the dock!'

Garson was pushed and pulled by four of Savage's faction and forced to stand behind a dual desk on the left of the chair.

'What's the charge?' he screamed.

'You broke the first commandment,' said Judge Savage. 'All for one and one for all, united we stand but divided we fall. That's Percy. Percy's a poet, ye know.'

'That's our motto,' Garson objected hotly. 'It's not a commandment.'

'Doesn't matter, you still broke it,' the judge answered swiftly. 'You wanted to keep it all for yersel'. If Specky hadn't have been with you we wouldn't have knew a thing about it.'

'That's not true,' Garson shouted, wriggling in the dock

between his jailers. 'Specky wouldn't have knew a thing about it if I hadn't told him.'

'That's right,' Specky admitted, standing up to address the judge. 'I said it was a matter for the Brotherhood and he said we ought to tell the cops but he never said he wanted it all for himself.'

'No, of course, he wouldn't say it,' Savage complained. 'But that's what he meant to do all right. Get the bell and expel him!'

'You can't do it like that,' Specky whispered, horrified.

'That's wrong,' Skinny called out, indignant.

The campanologist, so named and appointed by Percy to perform the rituals of admission, expulsion, summoning and dispersal, grabbed the bell from the piano and Garson darted at once from the clutch of his warders and struggled with him. The bell rang irregularly as they wrestled for it.

'A barley, a barley!' Skinny yelled in distress, and the contestants stood frozen. The assembly murmured against the brawl, condemning the decision that had provoked it. Savage saw he hadn't the support for an expulsion and tried again quickly.

'I propose an equal division then. Right here and now. Elect two tellers and share it out without Percy.'

'Twenty tellers couldn't count it,' Garson protested vehemently. 'And if they could you couldn't spend it. I said the cops because I saw it was too much for us but when Specky said report it I agreed because he's a Claviger and I'm not, but I meant report it to Percy, I never meant you, you big ape!'

'Who's an ape? You're an ape,' said Savage. He had a talent for repartee.

'I still say you can't decide without Percy,' Garson argued. 'Not on an urgent matter, not without Percy.'

'Yes, we can,' Savage overruled him. 'It's an urgent matter. You're just after admitting it. Percy said we had to decide urgent matters for ourselves, it's important matters we're supposed to tell him.'

'But this is important,' Garson said. 'That's what I'm saying.'

'You're just after saying it was urgent. Is it urgent or is it important? Make up your mind, you can't have it both ways.'

Savage grinned in the anticipation of victory and called out to the assembly, confusing them by the phrasing of his command.

'Hands up those who agree it's urgent.'

But before he could seize the victory he felt was within his grasp the troops were suddenly paralysed with fear. Someone was coming down the chute from the door in Tulip Place.

'It's Percy, it's Percy!' Frank Garson yelled in relief as a tall round-shouldered youth slouched into the range of the candlelight.

'What's going on here?' a mournful voice asked, a voice that had only recently been broken and sounded as if it was still being mended. 'I just thought yous was in here when I couldn't see a soul anywhere outside.'

Frank Garson rushed at him and clung to him.

'Help me, Percy! Save me! They're going to put me out of the Brotherhood. We were all out looking for you. We need you, Percy! We need you! Sheuch's trying to confuse me because I said it was urgent so he said we could decide it for ourselves but I said it was too important to decide without you, and he said I couldn't have it both ways, but if it's urgent it's important too, isn't it?'

Percy rocked on his toes and heels at the question and decided not to answer it.

'What were you putting him out for?' he asked, scowling round the meeting to remind them he had the seeing eye and they had better tell him the truth.

'Where'd ye get to?' Savage asked, boldly facing the seeing eye. 'We've been looking for you all night, so we have.'

'I was at a concert listening to a choir singing,' Percy answered in his faraway voice, his sad eyes dreamily focused on the furthest wall where the rats lived. 'It was rare, so it was. If we could get that piano there tuned I could start a choir with you lads if we could get somebody to play it.'

'That's just what I've been saying for years,' Savage agreed insolently.

'Scottish education, ach!' Percy snorted in bitterness.

'Percy, please!' Frank appealed to him, shaking his arm. But Percy was beyond his reach, mounted on his high horse again.

'They're supposed to learn you culture and how to live and they don't give you anything about philosophy or music. They never learn you how to write music for example. All they hammer into you is sums and spelling. If I could just read music I could form yous into a world-famous choir so I could. See the Vienna Boys' Choir?'

'No, where are they?' Savage asked eagerly, looking round the cellar with dramatic jerks of his head. 'Are they here the night?'

'They're only boys like you except that they speak German,' Percy explained, snubbing the Chief Claviger. For some time he had regretted ever appointing him. Savage seemed too coarse a type to do his job properly. 'But they've had a chance yous have never had because the Germans have always had a great love for music. The world's greatest composers are Germans like Batch and Baith-hoven.'

He rocked, toe to heel, heel to toe, dreaming how he would love to be the salvation of these poor neglected urchins by introducing them to the good things of life.

'Oh, Percy, listen!' Frank pleaded, clutching him, shaking him.

They were all clamouring at him, everybody shouting at once, demanding attention, trying to explain. He came sadly out of his dream. He gathered there was something worrying them. He submitted wearily to the duty of helping them and dismissed Savage from Miss Elgin-brod's chair with a peremptory gesture and sat there himself. Nobody would ever say he shirked his duty. And he liked to sit where Miss Elginbrod used to sit. It was a kind of mild revenge. He put himself in the pose of Rodin's 'Thinker' as he had seen it on the cover of a book he got for sixpence on the barrows in Renfield Street, and waited patiently till his supreme position got silence. He liked silence even better than he liked music. That was why he didn't like his mother. She was always nattering.

'Gi' me a report,' he growled.

'Frank, Frank, Frank!' the Brotherhood chanted. 'He's the one that knows! Let him report!'

Savage huffed away from them, kicked a stack of old examination papers containing, though he didn't know it, his father's score of five out of forty in mental arithmetic thirty years ago.

'A frank report, eh?' Percy smiled down at them from his throne. 'Frank is always frank. That's what you call a pun, lads. I had nobody to tell me these things, that's why I like to tell you. Shakespeare was very fond of puns, and I like a good pun myself, so I do.'

'I like a pun too,' Savage muttered to the dusty sheets. 'A pun o' chocolates.'

Frank Garson went back to his place behind the lid of a dual desk, but this time without two warders holding him. He was the only child of a motor-mechanic who worked in the garage at the far end of Bethel Street, an intruder in a gang that respected his intelligence but distrusted his cleanliness. He seemed a cut above them because his father had a good job, and they couldn't understand why he was so keen to be a member, even ambitious to be a Claviger. It made them suspicious. But they all liked him in the end because he was always straight. His mother had deserted his father for a West Indian bus-driver four years ago, and he could remember her only dimly as a bright-eyed woman with comforting arms and a good kissing mouth. He remembered also a cosy smell, quite different from the smell of chalk that accompanied Miss Elginbrod. But he could never talk of his mother. A boy whose mother had run off with a coloured man inherited a shame, and the fact that he was clever, clean and loyal, and that his father was a non-smoker, non-drinker and churchgoer, merely made him more of an oddity to his mates. Their fathers were drunken, idle and cruel, but they knew their mothers just had to put up with it. What kind of a mother then had Frank Garson that ran away from a good husband? Frank knew she was condemned, and he carried her guilt always with him. Dark-haired, rosy-cheeked, innocent-faced, and well-spoken except when excitement made him stutter a little, he would have suited a choirboy's collar.

'The new janny,' he began, conquering his stutter in the hush that respected his report, 'he doesn't know where anything is, so he asked me to help him because the janny in Comelygrove asked him for the lend of the gipsy costumes we had in our school concert when your father was the janny because the Comelygrove are going to do a gipsy cantata at Christmas in the Bellfield Halls and he didn't know where they were but the janny in Comelygrove knew we had them all right, so the new janny asked me to look for them in the cellar because anything you can't find must be in the cellar he said. So I asked Jasper, that's the teacher that came when Miss Elginbrod retired, you've seen him, he comes here on a mo'bike and he's got big bushy eyebrows and a blue chin, that's what we call him, that or Bluebeard, but his right name's Whiffen, and he let me come down here at two o'clock to look for them and I came down through the basement, the janny opened the door for me and then left me, and I found them in the tea-chests over there.'

He stopped, his mouth working. He felt his stammer coming on, and he fought against it.

'End of Part One,' Savage called out from the rear. He put on a television advert voice and chanted as he performed a Red Indian war dance round the back and flanks of the assembly. 'Use the new super duper scientific formula automatic aw-tae-buggery Freezing Point. Never go without a Freezing Point. In a man's world a girl needs a Freezing Point. Washes whiter than black and prevents flavour blur. Get one now, get one tomorrow, get one last week. The time is out of joint till you get a Freezing Point. And now back to Maverick.'

'I think you've got far too much to say,' Percy reprimanded him severely. 'And stand still when the court's in session.'

'Well, tell him to get to the point then,' Savage answered shrilly.

'That's the point,' Frank hammered the desk, hating Savage. 'I found the c-costumes, Percy, and I found something else too, a lot more, in the tea-chests. I gave the c-costumes to the new janny but I didn't tell him what else I'd seen. I wasn't sure if I'd seen right so I told Specky. You see there was a big spider came scuttling down the side of the tea-chest when I took the costumes out and I got a fright.'

'Feart for a spider!' Savage commented in disgust. 'Feart for a spider and he wants to get a key one day! That's the kind of probationer you get nowadays. Before I could get into the gang at all I had to get the Chinese Rub and I had to break seven windows in the scheme and steal a hundred fags and—'

'I stopped all that,' Percy interrupted him, frowning at the mention of the barbarous rites used before he civilized the gang. 'That's nothing for boasting about. And I'm still waiting to hear what all the excitement's about.'

'I hit it with one of those shovels,' Frank explained, keeping his own course doggedly, 'and I knocked it on its end, the tea-chest I mean, and a lot of rubbish fell out, paper hats, you know, and decorations and that wand the fairy princess used and I saw a lot of money.'

'A spider, a big big spider,' Savage mimicked Frank's soprano. 'And he lost the heid. I wonder what he would have done if he'd saw one of the rats from the other end up there.'

'What do you mean, a lot of money?' Percy asked anxiously. There seemed no escape from dreams of money and talk of money.

'Pound notes and five-pound notes,' said Frank. 'I told Specky. And bags of silver, paper bags and cloth bags, you couldn't count it. I told Specky at playtime and we came down here after four by the door in the basement to make sure. I couldn't believe it, I thought maybe it was stage money, but there was too much of it. You couldn't spend it in years. You remember Miss Elginbrod put on a play about a millionaire that tried to give all his money away in an Alpine village but nobody would take it because they were happier without money. That's why I thought it was stage money at first. Then I wanted to tell the cops and Sheuch says I was going to break the law you gave us but I would have shared the reward with everybody here, honest I would, cross my throat and spit!'

He went through the actions in his excitement.

'But Specky said no, report it here,' he concluded, exhausted by his ordeal. 'He'll tell you that's how it was, you ask him!'

Specky rose from the coal-scuttle, bowed to Percy, turned and bowed to the Brotherhood and went into the witness-desk as willingly as Frank left it. He was going to enjoy this. He liked speaking. He would show them how a formal report ought to be made.

'Probationer Garson reported to me at afternoon interval,' he began benignly, 'that he had seen millions and millions of pounds under the costumes in the tea-chests. He requested me to accompany him in a further visit to procure verification. Immediately following the dismissal of afternoon school we therefore descended together to our present location via the door in the basement when the janny's back was turned and I personally inspected the receptacles indicated. I ascertained they contained money and I came to the conclusion that the money was genuine currency. However, I differed from Probationer Garson in my estimate of the amount. According to my calculations there are not millions and millions of pounds there at all. There are only—'

'I didn't mean millions and millions as millions,' Frank

interrupted him resentfully, clenching his fists to keep his temper. 'I meant a lot, that was all.'

'At a tory estimate,' Specky proceeded, pleased at the chance to use a long-hoarded synonym, 'I would say there are only thousands of pounds dispersed in three of the six receptacles referred to.'

'What's the game?' Percy asked, wondering whether to be angry with them for trying to kid him or just laugh it off. 'What are yous up to now?'

'It isn't a game, Regent Supreme, sir,' Specky replied respectfully. 'It's true, I'm afraid. When I had made a provisional count of the contents of the first receptacle and then discovered that there was another two also containing money I abandoned the count and summoned an Extra-ordinary General Meeting in virtue of the powers vested in me as High Claviger. Chief Claviger Savage proposed immediate equal division of the money but I vetoed that in accordance with the constitution as laid down by the Regent Supreme, that is yourself, sir.'

'You couldn't divide it,' Frank complained direct to Percy, appealing to him with his hands clasped in prayer. 'And even if you could you couldn't spend it. We'd be found out, bound to be! We'd all be in trouble. Please, Percy, tell the cops! Please!'

'I myself told Chief Claviger Savage equal division was out of the question,' Specky said with condescending calm to belittle Frank's hysteria, 'but he wouldn't agree. He even proposed to expel Probationer Garson for treason but I opposed that too and said it was a matter for the Regent.'

Percy bowed in regal acknowledgement. He was trying to think, and the chattering in front of him only confused him. There seemed to be something ominously true in what Frank and Specky were telling him, and in that case he must take charge and be cool, calm and collected. He mustn't get excited, and yet he felt his leg tremble under the weight of his elbow as he resumed his thinker's pose. The chattering became a clamour.

'Silence!' he shouted, in a temper with them.

'Permission to speak, please!' Skinny called out, his right hand high.

Percy grunted permission. He must keep patient and listen and try to think at the same time. It was difficult for him. Why was it, he wondered, that some folk were born with a quick brain, shrewd customers, fly men; and better folk needed time and privacy to work things out? Where was the justice or equality in that? But he knew enough to know that silence can be mistaken for wisdom and that nothing is so infectious as panic. So he held his tongue and put on an air of indifference.

'The majority decision of the Clavigers was to refer the matter to you,' Skinny started, taking Specky's place behind the desk, 'because your father had charge of the cellar and you're your father's heir, so if the money in those chests belonged to your father then legally it's yours, and there was nobody else looked after the cellar, so it must have belonged to your father.'

'Ach, don't be daft, Skinny!' Frank shouted. 'You've seen what's there. Percy's father never had that kind of money, never, never, never!'

Skinny turned from addressing the chair to argue with his subordinate.

'How do you know? That's for Percy to say. Percy knows what his father had, you don't. Percy's the boss, it's no' you!'

'Well, I like that!' Frank screamed. 'It's me that's been arguing Percy's the boss, and now you try and tell me!'

Percy felt the first throbbings of a headache. It was the frequency of his headaches, beginning just after he left school, that made him suspect he was an intellectual. They were probably due to the abnormal activity of his brain.

'You've always said you should have had money if you had your rights,' Skinny turned back to the chair, 'so maybe this money is your inheritance, maybe that's why you could never find the money you knew your father ought to have left you if you were to be a great man because that's where he had hidden it.'

'Yes, could be,' said Percy, too overwhelmed to dispute the point. 'Let me see what yous are all talking about.'

He came clumsily down from Miss Elginbrod's chair and the Clavigers dragged the three lower tea-chests out of the darkness into the candlelight.

'That's how they were, with the three other chests on top of them,' said Frank 'and there was all those costumes on top of the money but we put everything back just as it was to keep it hidden.'

Specky, Skinny and Savage pulled out concert costumes, Christmas party decorations and brown paper from the first chest, and Percy stooped over it when they gestured him to look inside. He fumbled out a bundle of notes with an elastic band round them and flipped it through with dumb awe.

'Those are all fivers,' said Frank helpfully. 'But there's singles as well there, and the bags with the half-crowns and the florins is in the middle one.'

Percy slouched round the other chests and examined them perfunctorily. The money was real. There was no doubt in his mind. And when the three chests were emptied of all the rubbish crammed in them to reveal the money underneath he saw that the bottom of each was covered with notes an inch deep. He felt slightly sick, much as he had felt when an old man in Packing and Dispatch had taken him into a pub and made him drink a pint of beer one night after they had been working late, and there was a quivering and a fluttering in his stomach.

'Cover it up again,' he said, stricken with responsibility. 'Hide it just as it was! And let me think! Let me think!'

'Oh no, Percy, no!' Frank whispered in dismay. He had seen the glint of greed, and he was afraid.

Percy ignored him, and the Clavigers hastily and willingly obeyed the order.

'Now put the chests well back, away back at that wall where the rats are,' Percy commanded firmly. 'We'll need time to think. I want to think about this.'

'But the rats might eat the money,' Skinny objected. 'It's only paper after all.'

'Some paper!' chuckled Savage.

'They'd have to eat their way through all those dresses and things first,' Specky commented, shrugging.

'And we'll be back before then!' Savage cried. He showed off his good young teeth like an animal showing its fangs as he leered in triumph at Frank Garson. 'Lovely lolly! All the lolly in the world there! And we'll be back!'

'Yes, we'll be back,' Percy admitted.

He felt a vague but none the less substantial right to the money. Even though he hadn't found it himself it had been found in his father's territory and he was his father's heir. Indeed, it had been his territory too. Many a Sunday he had been sent down to the cellar to look after the boilers in the days when the school was still heated by steam pipes. Many a Saturday he had spent sweeping it out and making it tidy before it became a neglected dump. It was merely accidental that someone else had found what was in those tea-chests. But the right didn't lie solely in the finding, it lay just as much in claim to the place. This cellar was his. He wondered where the money came from, but passed on at once. He had met somewhere in his grasshopper reading the remark that science consists in asking the right questions. That meant there were questions it was stupid to ask. For example, where this money came from. There was no answer. Why ask a question that couldn't be answered? The right question was what to do with it. But first he must frighten the Brotherhood into obedience.

'Gather round!' he yelled in his Regent's voice, and sat again in Miss Elginbrod's broken-backed chair.

'This is a very serious matter,' he declared. 'There'll have to be a solemn vow of secrecy. Yous have all got to swear not to say a word about it to anybody and take a blood oath.'

'That's the idea! Great!' Savage cried and rubbed his hands together and gloated.

Percy felt the glow of inspiration. It came to him some-

times when he was instructing the Brotherhood, a warm
feeling round his brow and a tingling in his scalp, and he
wished it would come oftener, it was so mysterious and
thrilling. He took a safety-razor blade from his trouser-
pocket, a blade he carried in a metal holder, and lightly and
bravely he cut the ball of his thumb.

'Kneel before me one by one,' he commanded. 'And
repeat after me.'

They came to him in single file and he bent and dabbed
the blood from his thumb on their forehead.

'I promise not to tell,' he incanted.

'I promise not to tell,' they repeated after him.

They waited in groups round the cellar after the oath
had been taken, and then Percy told them they were all to
come to a special meeting at eight o'clock the next evening,
and they wouldn't lose by it. They left the cellar by the
chute and scattered silently from Tulip Place. Percy
ushered them out one by one and locked the door when
they were all gone. He stayed there for a moment before
hurrying down the chute and running over to the wall
where the rats were supposed to be. He had never seen a
rat there in his life. He dragged out one of the chests and
whipped away the rubbishy garments above the money.

Some of the notes were dirty, and some were fairly
clean; some were creased and some had never been folded.
He took a long time just looking at them, flipping them
over and flipping them over but keeping each bundle in its
elastic band. He noticed they were all from the same bank,
but the numbers were all mixed up. It would be safe to
pass them. He tried to work out just how much was there.
If he counted what was in one chest and multiplied by
three he might get a rough idea of the total. But Frank
Garson was right. He couldn't count what was in one
chest. He kept on losing the place. He would need a bit of
paper to write on and keep the score. He attacked the
bundle of fivers and tried to do it by short methods:
twenty in each bundle was a hundred and ten bundles
were a thousand. But when he came to count fifteen,

sixteen and seventeen bundles he wasn't sure if seventeen meant the bundle he had just counted or the one he was just going to count. He gave in and gave it up. He knelt over the chest, his arms thrown across it and his head on his arms, and he wept.

He could have coped with buried Inca treasure and found delight in a sunken galleon or a pirate hoard. He could have revelled in plundering an Egyptian tomb and taken the jewels of Ophir in his stride. Gold in Arizona or diamonds from Africa would have been a thrill within his range. But so much ready wealth in the commonplace form of pound notes and five-pound notes frightened him. It was too stark, too simple, too easy. He knew it was too much as well, but it was his. Not for a moment did he think otherwise, even as tears rolled down his cheeks where a fine floss still waited its first shearing.

'Oh, God help me!' he moaned. 'Please, God! Help me!'

The special meeting was a nervous, frightened affair. Even Savage was slightly scared. Percy spoke so long and so mournfully on the dangers and responsibilities of their position, his brooding eyes seeming to see right into their trembling souls, that he gave them all the jitters. At one point they would mostly have settled gladly for five bob if that would let them out of it, but then he spoke of the freedom before them if they were obedient and faithful, and they saw a lifetime of happiness ahead.

'Now, to avoid any suspicion and to make sure yous are not found out,' he said, 'I'm only going to allow yous a little at a time, and yous'll get it only for a particular purpose, something you want right away, and you'll tell me what it is, otherwise you won't get it, so that nobody'll ever find you with a lot of money on you. Now, I can't always be watching yous, and there's three of you got a key to the side door and any of yous could slip down through the basement during school hours if you were willing to take the risk of being caught by the janitor, so we'll make a gentlemen's agreement to do it my way and never go behind my back to take any of it on your own.'

He explained a gentlemen's agreement to them, and to begin with he limited them to the silver. It kept them from buying anything big enough to arouse comment from the gossips at the close-mouth in the tenements round about, and it kept the younger members happy enough. A couple of half-crowns was wealth to them. But he knew he was only postponing the problem of what to do about the folding money. He heard a murmuring against him in the higher ranks of the Brotherhood. Skinny supported him, but Savage was niggling and Specky was slippery.

'Ah, but look,' Skinny argued when Savage wanted to remove the paper money in handfuls, 'we made a gentlemen's agreement. You can't break a gentlemen's agreement, that's the whole point about a gentlemen's agreement, you can't break it, that's why Percy made us make it. Percy's right, you know, Percy's shrewd.'

'To hell with Percy!' Savage spat.

'You'd only spoil everything any other way,' said Specky. 'I hate to admit it, but you've got to. But what he ought to do is give us more or put one of the chests aside for us and nobody else.'

'Gentlemen's agreement!' cried Savage. 'Where's the gentlemen? Him, he's only a janny's son. Mind you, my old man's a gentleman all right, he hasn't worked for fifteen year. Us three could empty those chests in a week. We could stash it somewhere else. We're the only ones with a key, we could slip in any time at all. Nobody would know.'

'Percy would know,' Specky pointed out so quickly that Savage saw he had thought of it himself already. 'Then the rest of them would get to know and they'd start coming in through the door in the basement.'

'And if you make it a free-for-all you'll only get us all caught,' Skinny complained. 'Somebody would clype. I bet you wee Garry would go to the cops. It's only because Percy's took charge that he's keeping quiet. Oh, he loves Percy! He thinks Percy's wonderful! Take away Percy and it would be a disaster. Garry would shop us in an hour.'

'I'm afraid that's right,' Specky conceded sadly. 'You've got to keep the agreement, for a bit anyway. Percy's right enough in a way. Ye canny give pound notes to folk like Pinkie and wee Noddy and Cuddy.'

'What could they buy?' Skinny asked earnestly. 'If they started spending big money where could they put whatever they bought? Folk would be bound to notice. What could Noddy put in a single-end for example?'

'Him?' said Savage flippantly. 'He's that stupit he'd buy a grand piano and try and hide it under the kitchen sink. He's real daft about music. Give him a tune he's never heard before and he'll play it for you right off on the mouth-organ.'

'He's got a super one now all right,' Skinny remarked. 'Made in Germany. He got one made in Germany because Percy said the Germans were the best in the world at music like the Spaniards at football.'

'Percy patted him on the head when he said what he was going to buy with his ration and told him he was a very wise boy for putting it to a good use,' Specky said, and shook his head at the memory.

'Ach, the Rangers could beat them any time,' Savage bridled.

'Don't talk wet,' said Specky. 'They never even qualified to meet Real Madrid, sure Eintracht slaughtered them.'

'They were lucky,' Savage said, and waved his hands in front of Specky's face to wave the topic away. 'A ten-bob mouth-organ's all right for Noddy, but I want mair nor that. I want ready cash in my pocket.'

'Aye, it would be rare,' Skinny said.

'Instead of this percy-monious weekly ration,' Specky said brightly, looking round for a laugh but the word was unknown to his comrades, and he sighed at the company he had to keep.

Percy was worried. He knew what they were thinking, he could guess what they were saying. He slept badly, wondering how to control them, and the solution came to him in disturbed dreams. But he didn't tell them he had dreamt of the solution, he told them that what he had to do was revealed to him in a dream. Maybe it was because his mother had laughed at him for comparing himself to Moses, but he had a dream about Moses and found help in it. He dreamt he was on a mountain top and the clouds were all around him and he couldn't see anything but a grey mist that chilled him to the bone. Then suddenly the mist was gone and there was a risen sun and everything was made clear to him though he couldn't put it into words. He went down to the plain by a winding stony path, running sure-footed like a mountain goat, full of zest for the new way of life revealed to him. He found the Brotherhood anxiously awaiting him and he raised his hand and blessed them and they were sheep and he was their shepherd, and somehow he was holding a crook in his hand though he hadn't been holding one before.

A sheer coincidence gave substance to his vague dream. Turning the pages of the same dictionary where he had found that claviger meant a keyholder he saw the word 'bethel' and stopped at it because it was the name of the street where he lived. The dictionary said that bethel meant a Methodist church and came from the Hebrew *Beth-El*, the House of God. The discovery set him trembling with excitement, for he knew that as a poet he must believe in the magic of words, and it came to him in a flash of inspiration that El wasn't only the God of the Hebrews, it was also in one of its forms the sign for the pound note. It was more than a coincidence to him. It had a meaning. It was a revelation, completing the revelation of his dream. The street called the House of God contained the cellar that contained the pound notes, and the pound notes were El and he was the prophet of El just as much as Moses was. He felt the burden of the elect upon him.

He intimidated the Brotherhood by the force of his will for power over them, by the nagging of his cracked voice, by the solemnity of his face. He gathered them in the cellar and spoke to them like a preacher.

'Yous has all been poor neglected boys all your life, without a good suit to your name or a good pair of shoes, but God has a special care for the poor and underprivileged, and sometimes He reveals Himself to them, like He done to the Jews. He chose the Jews and that's what He's did to you, He's chose you to get the good of this manna from Heaven to help you in the desert, 'cause you see this life is like a desert. He chose you, He didn't choose boys

from Govan or the Gorbals or Maryhill or Partick or
Whiteinch, no, He chose you. Just think about that. Just
think what that means. It might have been anybody and it
was yous. Now that proves you are the chosen people, only
you need a lawman like the Jews had Moses. Well, I'm
your lawman, and you have got to do like I say or else.'

He believed they had been chosen because he believed
he had been chosen, and they had to believe it too. There
was a halo round his head, a vision in his eyes, authority in
his voice. They were only children, he frightened them –
especially when he threatened what would happen if they
committed the sin of disobedience. The youngest weren't
sure if he meant they would go to hell for ever or go to jail
for ever. He made them all take a new and more elaborate
blood oath, and when they had taken it they had to make
the sign of the El. He showed them how to do it. They
drew the index finger of the right hand across the eyes
from left to right, up over the brow in a loop, and down the
line of the nose to the chin. Then they traced another loop
to the left and came back along the jawbone and up to the
right ear. The sign was completed by drawing two parallel
lines across the tip of the nose and upper lip. It was the
sign of the £ drawn on their face, the symbol of the god
they were now to serve.

He had written the oath on a little card he held in his
hand, with a bar between the phrases to keep him right as
he read it out.

'Repeat after me,' he said, and they repeated the
phrases.

'I solemnly swear – I solemnly swear – not to reveal –
not to reveal – the place of the treasure – the place of the
treasure – to anybody – to anybody – and I solemnly swear
– and I solemnly swear – not to speak of the treasure – not
to speak of the treasure – outside this cellar – outside this
cellar – nor to touch the treasure – nor to touch the
treasure – without permission – without permission – of
the Regent Supreme – of the Regent Supreme.'

They took the oath standing. When they knelt down he

said the rest for them, making it sound more frightening than they could ever have managed in their own unguided treble.

'And if I break this oath may the Brotherhood break the bones of my thighs. If I speak of the treasure outside the cellar let my tongue be burnt with a soldering iron, and if I touch the treasure without the Regent's permission may the hand that commits the offence be eaten by the rats in the cellar and may my arms be paralysed, withered and shrivelled till they drop off like a dead leaf from the trees in autumn.'

He made the Clavigers take the same oath, to remind them that they were his subordinates and they too could touch the money only with his permission.

Zealous, sincere and worried, oppressed by his responsibility for them and for so much money, he never thought what he himself might do with it. He was too busy driving them far beyond a mere gentlemen's agreement, imposing on them a religious attitude, a true piety, towards the uncounted wealth.

He was surprised how quickly and easily he got it all going the way he wanted. He declared the word 'money' tabu. They were never to use it to say what was in the cellar. They were to say 'El'. He told them it was the only safe word to use. The other word would give away their secret and bring a terrible punishment. He said they would all get scabies, chickenpox, dysentery and measles if they ever used it.

Savage was just as frightened as the rest of them by Percy's talk, but he couldn't entirely conquer his natural flippancy, even for blood oaths, candlelight, hymn-singing and bell-ringing. Halfway through one of Percy's early sermons on the almighty power of El he nudged Specky and whispered, giggling, 'If you want anything, go to El!' He chanted audibly a counting-out rhyme used by Glasgow children, an obscure rhyme from an unknown source, supposed by local antiquaries to be of Druidic origin.

El, El, Domin – El,
Eenty, teenty, figgerty – fel!

Percy heard him and was shocked. He knew there was
danger to them all in irreverence. Their secret would be
safe only if he could make them appreciate the sacredness
of what they had found. They must be made to understand
that the finding of the money imposed a great piety on
them. He must bind them to an unquestioning respect for
himself as the person who had first led them to the land
where El had appeared to them. They must have faith.
They must be made to see it was a divine revelation, and
they must obey him as its medium.

He thought of expelling Savage, but he was afraid it
might make him an enemy, a spiteful Ishmael who would
go to the pagan world outside the cellar with a story of
hidden treasure and come back with a band of freebooters
to invade the sanctuary of El. The fear of it kept him awake
at night, fretting. It was no joke being in charge of a crowd
of children. So he spoke to Savage privately and told him it
was a matter of policy to make the Brotherhood respect the
holy name of El. If they didn't, it would mean complete
lawlessness and nobody would win. They would all lose
everything.

'Aye, I see fine what you're after,' Savage answered, and
grinned with an atheist's insolence at the gangling Regent.
'You're right enough. You're a fly big bugger, aren't you?
It's the only way to keep these stupid bastards in order.
But you don't expect me to believe all that tripe about El
revealing himself to us because we're a chosen people, now
do you?'

'Why not?' Percy asked coldly. 'I believe in El, why
shouldn't you? You think you're too clever maybe? Let me
tell you, there are more things in Heaven and earth than
are dreamt of in your philosophy, Horace. And just let me
warn you, you'd better believe in El in front of the
Brotherhood or I'll cut you off from El altogether.'

He made them make the sign of the El at every meeting

and rang the bell three times before they filed forward for their weekly allowance. Inspired by his position as their guide, philosopher and friend he made up a hymn for them to the tune of *The Ash Grove*, careful to work in his own name as an essential item in what he called the 'relevation' of El.

> Down, down in our cellar, where rubbish
>   concealed him,
> When daylight is fading, we bow unto El,
> And promise to follow the one who revealed him.
> So sing Percy's praises and ring out the bell.

After that they chanted with gusto to the tune of 'Boney Was a Warrior', 'El is our salva-ti-on, rah, rah, rah!' They particularly enjoyed the 'rah, rah, rah' bit, and Percy was thrilled to have a choir of his own even if it wasn't just as good as the Vienna Boys'.

For nearly a month he lived more delighted with the success of converting the gang into a reverent congregation than with his lordship over the money. He was proving himself a poet at last. He was a sacred bard whose job it was to create and maintain the religious secrets of his tribe. All he bought for himself was a plush-covered copy of Shelley's poems, and a portable typewriter to type his own poems for publication once he got them written down. Later on he could get whatever else he wanted, there was always tomorrow. Meanwhile he kept the Brotherhood in order, he accepted only reasonable demands for money, and he advised them how to spend what they asked for. Still excited with the miracle performed for them, the boys didn't think of asking for much. Like Percy they found their satisfaction in dreaming of the future, when they could have whatever they wanted. Like him, they enjoyed the secrecy and the mystery of it, they loved the hymn-singing and the bell-ringing in candlelight, the sense of belonging to a chosen people when they made the sign of the El. It was better than going to church. They

could understand it. They could see what they were asked
to adore and they felt it concerned them and the real world
they lived in. The Clavigers stopped murmuring and
bided their time.

'Ach he's out of this world altogether,' Specky said
pityingly. 'He's round the bend. He's carrying on like a
real Holy Willie.'

'Aye, he's round the bend all right,' Skinny agreed
sadly. 'Do you know I don't think he's touched a penny
of it for himself.'

'No, just a few fivers,' said Savage. 'There are nae
pennies in it. Nothing so common. I bet he's been shifting
it in wads every night in the week when we're no' there.'

'Oh, I don't believe that,' Specky said reproachfully.

'How would we know if he wasn't?' Savage demanded.
'Tell me that and tell me no more. Don't forget it was
never counted. To this day it hasna been counted. He
could dae what he likes wi' it. He could tell us in another
month it was all done, and we couldn't argue. Ye know, he
had a bloody cheek making us give him back our keys.
Clavigers! He likes big words. I bet ye he likes big money
too.'

'Well, after all it was him that gave them to us,' Skinny
said. 'They were his to start with. It was him got them cut
from the key his old man had.'

'You know, I could apply my boot to my posterior,' said
Specky. 'I should have got one cut before I gave him mine
back. I should have anticipated some such manoeuvre on
his behalf.'

'You mean you didn't expect him to do that?' Savage
asked, and grinned, his animal teeth on a victory parade.

Unable to resist showing off he thrust his hand into the
back pocket of his tight studded jeans and showed them a
new key.

'I thought of it all right,' he boasted. 'I used the loaf. It's
time you brushed up your IQ, Specky.'

'You can't brush up an IQ,' Specky tutted at him. 'An
IQ is the result of the primitive formation of your

inherited characteristics from your paw and your maw. You can't do a thing about it.'

'Well, you could dust your brains then, couldn't you?' Savage retorted, shoving the key away in his back pocket again. He was content to wait. He had a key. He had the whip hand.

The silver was done. There wasn't a half-crown or a florin left. They had all been squandered on sweeties, cigarettes, lemonade, playing cards, slot-machines, comics and the pictures. Percy burned the pokes and faced at last the problem of what to do about the folding money. He thought of changing handfuls of notes into silver and keeping the gang going a little longer on a diet of half-crowns, but he was nervous about going into a bank with the notes in case he was asked questions, and to go round the local shops, changing singles and fivers here and there, would only cause talk. Anyway, he saw he couldn't keep them much longer from real spending. They were all getting peevish with him. He made up his mind to start them off on pound notes. He thought he could trust them, but he warned them just the same.

'Yous don't want to look too affluential,' he addressed them from the chair in the candlelight. 'And you shouldn't buy anything conspicious. You have got to be very careful from now on.'

'A fine thing if we've got the money and canny spend it,' Savage commented at the foot of the throne.

'Of course you can spend it,' Percy scolded him, resenting the comment. 'There's nothing to prevent you from spending it if you want to spend it. All I'm saying is you've got to be careful and don't spend it on things that would get you asked awkward questions. Yous want to detract attention from yourselves.'

'And just buy sweeties like?' Specky asked. 'Boy-oh-boy! Twenty shillings' worth of lollipops! Nobody would ever dream of asking what you were doing with all those lollipops, not much.'

It was beginning to dawn on him, as on some of the others, that there wasn't much they could do with so much money. They would be better off with less. It would be easier to spend.

'Don't be funny,' Percy snapped at him. 'It takes brains to be funny. And you fellows should be helping me, you're the Clavigers, not niggling and nattering and trying to be sarky. I don't like folk that are sarky, and I don't like folk that nag.'

He gave out the pound notes grudgingly and hoped for the best. In a little while he found they weren't spending them, they were accumulating them and little groups were pooling their resources for purposes they kept secret from him. They began to demand a twice-weekly ration, and he gave in to them for the sake of peace. He was in the cellar every night to satisfy himself everything was all right. Then various members of the Brotherhood began to turn up every night too and tap at the side-door till he had to let them in. Once they were in he had to let them have something before they would go away. He felt he had lost the place somewhere, but he didn't see what he could do about it.

He gave up his job without telling his mother and spent his days at the Mitchell Library pursuing an elusive something he thought of as his studies. He looked particularly for books in one volume that would tell him what he wanted to know. He read Wells' *Outline of History* in a hop, skip, and jump, and from Russell's *History of Western Philosophy* he wrote out the names of the philosophers. He made notes on what he tried to read, haphazard notes, not always coherent or legible, but still notes. It made him feel more like a real student when he sat in the Mitchell Library and took notes. Odd items of information stuck to him, items as dead and separate as flies on flypaper, but for all that he was learning. Sometimes his eyes ached and he wondered if glasses would make him look more like a student or if he wouldn't suit them.

It was a great pleasure to him to sit amongst the under-graduates and look at the legs of the girls from Queen Margaret College when they sat across from him with their knees crossed. It made him feel he was a student too. He went home every day at the usual time after a cheap lunch in a small back-room restaurant near Charing Cross, and every week he took the amount of his wages from one of the tea-chests and handed it over to his mother. Some-times he thought of buying her a present or making her a gift of a hundred pounds or so, but he always decided not to bother. In the first place, she didn't deserve it, the way she was always finding fault with him, and in the second place she would only ask questions, not scientific ones, but the wrong ones, like where did you get all that money. He admired himself for not having given up his job at once. It proved his consideration for others. He had been so busy getting the Brotherhood organized under the protection of El that he hadn't had time to think of himself.

'I suppose some folk would say I should get my head examined,' he said to himself proudly, scratching it. 'But worldly matters are beneath we poets.'

The thought reminded him he had meant to write poetry if ever he had time. He bought a beautiful big book, half-bound in leather, like a ledger except that it wasn't ruled off for cash entries, and he meant to start writing poetry in it. But he had to hide it from his mother, and that made it hard for him to get a chance to write in it. He didn't seem to have any time at all to himself, even though he wasn't working. The Brotherhood found employment for him. They made him their errand-boy: because of his age it was he who had to go into town and buy what they wanted. They were quite changed from the weeks when a pocketful of silver was enough for them. They outflanked him: they didn't want the money as money, they wanted things. And he had to go and get them.

'We could buy a ball and strips and start a team,' said Cuddy. 'The Brotherhood Rangers. The Bethel Thistle, eh? A dark blue jersey with an orange lily.'

'Is that all you can think of?' Percy cried, despairing of his chosen people. 'Football! Can you no' think of anything else but football? Do you never think of culture? You could buy Shakespeare's plays or a season ticket for the SNO. And who would you play? Tell me that! There's no league for a street team for lads of your age, and folk would ask where you got the money for a strip.'

'That's all you can say,' Noddy complained. 'Whatever we want to buy you say folk'll ask questions, that's what you keep saying. Have we no' to buy anything?'

In the end Percy went into town and bought them a strip. He bought them two strips, and three balls, and two dozen pair of football boots. But they never wore the strips or the boots except at night in the cellar, when they played a brawling game of five-a-side. Percy kept the jerseys, pants and stockings in his own house every day, telling his mother they were the strip of the school football team (the school hadn't a team), and he was their trainer.

In a big shop in Renfield Street he bought a ukelele one week and a guitar the next because Noddy insisted money ought to be spent on his musical education. He took a bus to Shawlands one afternoon and bought a tape-recorder because somebody thought it would be fun to have one, and another afternoon he went across the river to Maryhill for a transistor set, and while he was there he bought himself an electric razor. It was high time he was shaving every day. He told his mother the foreman had got it as a Christmas present, didn't like it and gave it to him for nothing. He had to tell her something. He couldn't go into hiding every time he wanted to shave. Another day he went over to Govan and bought a record-player. Much of the stuff he was sent to buy wasn't meant to be anyone's particular property. The tape-recorder, the record-player, the transistor, the television were everybody's and nobody's. They were bought because of a general will for them, and they furnished the cellar as a club for the Brotherhood. They were kept in the cellar and used there and nowhere else. The electricity required was got by using an adapter plug in one of the light-sockets. These items were not only kept in the cellar, they had to be hidden in case the janitor came across them, and Percy lost sleep worrying they would be found in spite of all his precautions. He worried too when he saw every member of the Brotherhood wearing a wristlet watch. Some of them had a pocket-watch as well, and he was sure they would attract attention. They had cameras too, Leicas and Voigtländers and Zeiss Ikons, but they didn't dare use them.

Friday nights were a great comfort to him. He had been beaten in his attempt to limit the spending of the money but he was determined not to yield on the Friday night service. He was grateful nobody opposed him. It was quite the opposite. In their orgy of spending they seemed to enjoy the Friday night with more zest and reverence than they had shown when he had sent them away with five bob each. They weren't just obeying him from force of habit, or doing casually what they knew he wanted done. They were doing it because they wanted to. They had taken over his creed and ritual and made them their own.

By their very submission to him they corrupted him, like a country that by accepting a dictator gives him a legal authority and wider scope for fanaticism. He had set out to be their leader, and he had become their slave, and he followed the code of his masters. He wakened to wants he had never known when he was only a packer in the Coop in Nelson Street. If his boys could find things to buy, then so should he to keep up with them. He bought a leather pocket-book so as to have something to carry pound notes and fivers in, for although he rationed the Brotherhood he never went out without twenty pounds in his pocket. He bought binoculars that cost him forty pounds, two expensive fountain pens to write his poems with and a dictionary of quotations to give him a short cut to a knowledge of English poetry. Lying in bed one night he had foreboding he might have to leave in a hurry and travel far in search of peace and quiet, so he bought a big briefcase, in genuine pigskin, and hid it in the cellar

against the rats' wall. It had three compartments and he
kept a suit of pyjamas and his shaving tackle, carefully
wrapped, in one compartment. The other two would hold
thousands, he was sure. He bought a pair of skates and
went to the ice-skating at Crossmyloof, more to see the
pretty girls there, and try to pick up one of them, than
because he was keen on skating. He bought a fishing-rod
and basket, and boots and waders and a jacket and hat to
match, though he knew nothing about fishing and didn't
know where to go fishing anyway. But he had read that
fishing was a solitary and peaceful sport, fit for thoughtful
men, and he hoped he would find time to be solitary and
peaceful some day.

He bought himself a new suit after he stopped working
because he believed a gentleman of leisure should be well
dressed, and when his mother made a scene about it he
said he had been saving up for it for a year. She snorted
sceptically and said no more, so he bought another couple
of suits and shirts and ties to go with them. If he was smart
and well dressed he might have a better chance of getting a
girl, and a poet whose life was dedicated to the pursuit of
beauty shouldn't be wearing shabby clothes.

Seeing Jasper's motor-bike parked in the blind-alley
aroused him to a new want. Why shouldn't he have one
too? He bought one. After all, Shelley had a boat. A poet
must move with the times, and Shelley would certainly
have had a motor-bike or a racing-car if he was alive today.
What's more, he would probably have written an ode to
Speed. He began one himself, just to do what Shelley
would have done, and wrote the first three lines in his
leather-bound log-book.

> O wild Speed, be thou me, impetuous one,
> Driving my thoughts around the universe,
> And let the engine of my spirit run . . .

He didn't know where or how he wanted his spirit to run,
so he left it till he could get peace and quiet to finish it.

Meanwhile he was busy learning to ride the bike. He had a skidlid and L-plates and a manual, and Frank Garson's father gave him a few tips. He parked it in the blind-alley every night, at the same spot as Jasper's bike was parked during the day from nine to four.

'How do you come to be having a motor-bike?' his mother asked.

'I won it in a raffle,' he said, very short with her.

She looked at him with her mouth hanging open. She was used to his being insolent and sarcastic to her, and she wouldn't give him the satisfaction of arguing when he gave silly answers to serious questions. But this one sounded so casual it might well be the truth. But it couldn't be true, for it was clearly absurd. She was baffled to silence.

He was parking the bike in Tulip Place one Thursday night at half past ten, before it was quite dark, after a thrilling practice run to Balloch and the banks of Loch Lomond, when a man came out of the close across the street and jabbed a finger in the small of his back. Percy jumped. In a moment's searing intuition he saw the hoard discovered, the owner identified, and himself in jail. The early summer evening seemed no longer beautiful, but ominous, and the sun he had seen setting behind the Campsies was a signal of the doom he had come back to meet.

'D'ye know Mr Phinn?' the stranger whispered, his scrubby face close against Percy's smooth chin. The electric razor was doing a very efficient job.

'Mr Phinn?' Percy asked hoarsely.

'Mr Phinn,' the stranger said, nodding his head like a hand-puppet.

Percy was frightened. He didn't see a square man in a belted raincoat, stained and shabby, with a curly-brimmed felt hat down over his eyes and a scar from the wing of his nose to the bend of his right jawbone. This was no Glasgow bauchle. What he saw was a looming super-natural figure that he identified with a deity he thought of as Nimeesis.

'Well, I'm Phinn,' he said cautiously. 'Percy Phinn. You see, I'm named after Percy Shelley the poet. You don't mean me, do you?'

He didn't think anyone would ever think of him as Mr Phinn, any more than you would think of Shelley as Mr Shelley, and he was puzzled. But with him that was the same thing as being frightened. The stranger shook his head, the horizontal movement as puppet-like as the vertical one had been.

'No,' he breathed vigorously into Percy's face, and Percy recognized the smell of whisky. His father used to drink that stuff. With the speed of lightning, for thought is swift even in the slowest, he wondered if it would be worthwhile buying a bottle of whisky to find out what it was like, decided a bottle of wine would be a more appropriate drink for a poet, regretted he had never thought of buying a bottle of wine for communal wine-drinking at the Friday Night Service, feared his buying days were over, and simultaneously found an answer to the stranger.

'Well, I'm Mr Phinn if you like,' he offered, prepared to sacrifice himself to save his boys.

'I don't like,' said the stranger.

'Ye'll jist have to like it I'm afraid,' Percy said bravely, but he felt his belly trembling and his left leg was quivering, 'there's no other Phinn about here. What Mr Phinn do you mean?'

'Who's the janitor in that school there?' the stranger asked, and thrust his head towards the building behind Percy.

'Oh, you mean him?' said Percy, and sagged in relief. Nobody could question the dead. 'That was my father so it was. Is that who you mean?'

'Well, what do you mean there's no Mr Phinn here?' the stranger demanded irritably. 'Has he been shifted? You're after saying your father's here. Do you mean he's been shifted?'

'No, he's no' been shifted, but he's no' here now,' Percy said brightly. 'He's dead.'

'Are you kidding?' the stranger whispered, his face so close to Percy's that they looked like two Eskimoes making love.

'What would I be kidding for?' Percy answered indignantly. 'I wouldn't be kidding about a thing like that, would I? I can show you his grave if you don't believe me.'

'Oh Jesus Christ!' said the stranger and bowed his head in grief.

Percy was impressed by the piety of the ejaculation.

'Did you know my father?' he asked tenderly.

They stood looking at each other under the single gas-lamp in the drab lonely alley called Tulip Place by a poetic Town Council, and the summer twilight gathered into darkness.

'Naw, I never knew him,' said the stranger impatiently, then slowed to a fonder utterance. 'Och aye, I knew him well.'

'I see,' said Percy uneasily.

'You see that door there, does that door lead to a cellar?' the stranger asked, jabbing a finger abruptly at the scarred door across the pavement.

'Oh aye, that was for the coal,' said Percy. 'But it's never used now.'

'You've got a key for it, have you no'?' the stranger said with a smile so ingratiating that it put Percy in a new panic.

'Oh no,' he disclaimed hastily. 'That door's never used now, it was for the coal you see, but you see they don't use the boilers now, cause it's all electric, so there's no key for it, ye canna get in that way at all, it's no' a door really, it's all bricked up inside, so you see a key's no use. Because of the bricks. Ye canna get in that way. It's all bricked up.'

'You mean it's bricked up?' the stranger glowered. 'Then how do you get in? Tell me that!'

'Well, there's a door in the basement,' Percy admitted, 'in the school I mean, but it's never used, you see, and nobody's got a key to it. You see it's no' a cellar now, it's just a rubbish dump and nobody has ever any call to go in there, and it's overrun wi' rats, you see.'

'I see,' the stranger said patiently. 'Did your father ever mention any of his pals to you, doing a favour for them like, you know? Did you know your Uncle Sammy?'

Before Percy could decide on the best answer they heard someone plodding along Bethel Street. They turned together in alarm and looked at the corner. A policeman was passing on patrol. Percy knew him. It was Constable Knox, the local bobby who had often taken a wee rest in the cellar in the old days and had a cup of tea with his father. He raised a hand in greeting as Constable Knox passed and the policeman acknowledged it with a nod so dignified it was almost imperceptible. Then when he turned again to cope with the stranger Percy found he was alone. He was just in time to catch a glimmer of a raincoat scurrying through the close on the other side of Tulip Place. He set his motor-bike safely against the kerb and galloped home on a wild bronco of alarm.

CHAPTER SIX

He made quite sure the stranger wasn't in Tulip Place or
Bethel Street the following night before he went down to
the cellar by the side door. He was glad it was a Friday
night, for that meant every member of the Brotherhood
would be present to attend the Friday Night Service. He
had taught them to refer to it as the FNS, and they were
drilled to accept the penalty of forfeiting a week's money if
they missed it. He let them in cautiously, opening the door
no wider than was needed to admit a sidling entrance, and
after the Creed and the hymn, before they came forward in
single file for the share-out, he made a little speech. It was
understood that any announcements he had to make would
be made between the singing of the hymn and the distribution of the grace of El, so when the choir had finished
the hymn and the campanologist had rung the bell three
times to emphasize the end of that part of the service, he
stood before Miss Elginbrod's chair and addressed them
solemnly with the scarf of a Rangers' supporter draped
round his shoulders like a stole.

'I've got an important announcement to let yous know,'
he said, and looked from left to right and back to front
before going on. He had read that a pause could be used
with great effect in public speaking, a pause and a look, so
he paused and he looked. There was silence. Gratified by
the hush he went on. 'The holy sanctuary of El is in danger
from the prying nose of a stranger. An enemy. Yous all
know that in this world which is a vale of tears we are
continuously besieged by enemies seeking for to devour
us. El is ours and we are El's and it's our duty to behave so
as to keep it that way. Now you have got to be told that just

the other night, not far from this place where we meet to
pay our respects to El, I was detained by a man who was
certainly a spy sent here by them we've got to beware of.
He proclaimed for to have knew my father but he made a
strong depression on me of having an interest in how to get
in here. So if yous ever see a bowly-legged man anywhere
in Tulip Place or Bethel Street yous is not to knock at the
door. Wait till he goes away. And if he doesn't go away
don't come anywhere near the door. He only wants to find
the way in, and if he ever does we've all had it. You know
what happened to the Incas of Peru when the Spaniards
discovered Montezuma's treasure.'

They didn't, but the way he said it made them understand it wasn't a good thing for Montezuma.

Savage lurched from squatting at the right foot of the
Regent Supreme, bowed insolently to the Brotherhood,
and turned half-right to speak to the chair.

'What should we no' come in by the door in the basement then for?' he asked. 'There's nobody could see us
that way if we came in through the playground and went
down to the basement.'

'Of course you would be seen,' Percy said impatiently.
'Yous would have to go in by the main gate, wouldn't
you? And yous would have to cross the playground right
in front of the janny's house. He'd be bound to see you.
It's no' dark till after eleven o'clock these nights. Or else
he'd hear you. I know. I lived there long enough. Just
take my word for it if you don't believe me. And anyway
the door in the basement's kept locked. The new janny
keeps it locked. And I never managed to get a key for it.
So you see you just couldna get in that way. And even if
you could you would never manage it, no' without getting
caught.'

'Aw, I see,' said Savage, and squatted with such a
pleased smile that Percy was puzzled. And being puzzled
he worried.

But it was time to go on with the business of the evening
and he let Savage rest. He stood before the first of the

three tea-chests, signalled the campanologist by making
the sign of El in mid-air, and when the bell had been rung
the Brotherhood came forward to the chest and knelt down
to whisper their request.

'Four fivers,' said Noddy, making the required sign on
his brow as he humbly knelt at Percy's large crepe-soled
shoes.

Percy frowned. How quickly times had changed since
they were content to ask for a small sum for a particular
purpose! Now they asked for an absurd amount and never
thought of telling him what they wanted it for. They had
panted through an orgy of spending, asking for things
instead of money. And he had agreed. He had even been
their errand-boy. That was his mistake. He saw it too late,
and stood frowning at Noddy in disapproval. This was a
new phase. They had tired of buying things they couldn't
use and couldn't hide. Now they wanted money again, not
for anything special but just to have the money itself as
power in their pocket. He had given in to them too long, he
had let the gentlemen's agreement lapse. It was high time
he made a stand.

'No,' he said firmly. 'That's far too-too much for you.
You just want it. You don't want it for anything.'

'I do,' said Noddy. 'I'm saving up for a piano.'

'And where would you put a piano if you had one?'
Percy demanded. 'You'd have the whole street talking.
You'll get one, and like it.'

'One fiver,' said Noddy humbly.

'One single,' said Percy meanly, and handed him it.

Noddy took the pound without arguing, but he muttered behind Percy's back. Savage listened to him. Savage
courted him.

'Are you saving up hard?' he asked Noddy on the stairs
the next morning. They lived up the same close.

Noddy nodded. He wasn't given to saying much.

'It'll take you a long time to get enough for a piano at
Percy's rate,' he suggested.

'Aye, so it will,' said Noddy neutrally.

'And if ye're saving up what are you doing for spending-money?' Savage asked sympathetically.

Noddy brought his shoulders up to his ears and showed off two black-palmed hands. He said nothing to mean nothing.

'Here I'll give you a few bob for spending,' Savage said, lording it over the dumb urchin, and gave him two ten-shilling notes. 'Percy isn't the only prophet of the great god El, ye know. Just you see me tonight at seven outside the pictures and I'll give you something to help to get your piano.'

He gave him twenty pounds. He had been entering the cellar secretly at midnight for a week past and taking away money in handfuls from the third and last of the tea-chests, the one that was stowed away in the farthest corner of the rat-wall, the chest Percy seemed to think would do for their old age. Some of the money he hid up the chimney in the back room of his house, where a gas-fire had been fitted into the place once filled by the cradle for a coal fire. Some of it he hid inside the derelict air-raid shelter, built before he was born and never pulled down, that filled the hinterland of the tenement where he lived. Some of it he hid on the roof of a glue-factory where the gutter came within reach of the flat top of the washhouse in the back-court. Some of it he put inside an old pair of wellingtons under his bed and stuffed sheets of newspaper on top of it. He was careful never to carry much of it about with him, but he had between four and five hundred pounds he could get at quickly, and he set himself up as a rival to Percy. He liked giving money away. It made him feel big.

Noddy put the twenty pounds into his own hoard, and kept the two ten-shilling notes in his pocket as spending money. He was delighted with them, so delighted that he had no desire to spend them. Two bits of paper were twice as good as one, and he valued Savage's gift of the two half-notes more than he valued Percy's donation of a single pound. The ten-shilling notes were beautiful. He would sit looking at them, marvelling at the curly lines round the heading, Bank of England, and puzzling over the words 'Promise to pay the Bearer on Demand the sum of Ten Shillings', with more curly lines round the last line. What did it mean, *Promise to pay Ten Shillings*, when this bit of russet and dirty-white paper was itself ten shillings? He stared hard at the seated lady on the left with a long pole in her hand and wondered who she was. And beneath her was a long number and beneath the number there were the words *Ten Shillings* in a frame with curly lines all round it. Up at the right there was the same number, and a fancy design with 10 Shillings in the centre. On the back, inside a lot of feathers or dead leaves, it said 10/- twice. So there was no doubt it was ten shillings. Then why promise to pay ten shillings for it? Or what was 'on demand'? It hypnotized him. Probably no one had ever looked so long and so hard and so often at a mere ten shilling note as Noddy did that weekend.

He was still at it when he was back at school on the Monday. He had one of them under the desk when Jasper was at the board trying to teach the division of fractions.

'Three-quarters divided by one-half equals three over four multiplied by two over one,' he jabbered, scribbling with the chalk as he went through it, 'equals six over four equals one and a half.'

He turned to look at his class. They were staring at the blackboard with a glazed look, stunned, stupefied and speechless, all except Noddy. His eyes were equally glazed, but not at the four-line transmutation of three-quarters into one and a half. He was admiring one of his ten-shilling notes.

Silent in his rubber-soled shoes, Jasper prowled over to the faraway boy. He wore rubber soles as an economy measure, for on his salary he couldn't afford two pairs of shoes and a motor-bike as well. He was a poor man. Noddy hadn't heard a word of the gabble at the blackboard, but now he heard the silence and looked up sharply to see what was wrong. He was too late. Jasper pounced.

'Where did you get that?' he breathed in horror, holding the note reverently by the corner while Noddy cowered, fretting the fingers of his empty hands.

'It's no' mines,' he answered swiftly.

'Go and stand in the corner, Mann,' said Jasper. 'Mines is things you go down. Coal mines, copper mines, gold mines. The correct possessive pronoun is mine. I'm sick and tired telling you that. I might as well talk to a brick wall.'

Noddy exasperated him much as Percy had exasperated Miss Elginbrod half a dozen years earlier. He couldn't help picking on Noddy, the boy pulled at him like a magnet. He pushed him into the corner with his face against the wall, and snorted at him, 'Hum! Hm! Mann! Some man!'

And then he said, as he had said so often before, for Noddy had an ugly face with a broad flat nose and a scowl like Beethoven's, 'You're no more like a man than a monkey.'

He stood behind the boy, turning the note over and over. It seemed real all right. He was taken by a sudden anger that this unwashed urchin should have ten bob in the middle of the month when he himself hadn't much more.

'There's something fishy about this and I'm going to find out what it is. Where did you get it?'

'Found it,' said Noddy, over his shoulder.

'Where?' Jasper asked, caressing his blue chin between thumb and forefinger.

'Forget,' Noddy said in a half-hearted whisper.

Jasper brought the headmaster into it. Mr Daunders was an experienced man. He had a talent for questioning pupils who were found with more money than they could reasonably be expected to have. The school was full of midgie-rakers, petty thieves, pickpockets, raiders of their mothers' lean purse, breakers of gas-meters, milk-round embezzlers, robbers of weans sent on a shopping errand. What else could you expect in a Glasgow slum where the

buildings had been condemned thirty years ago and were
still standing as warrens where smalltime criminals pro-
liferated?

'Leave him to me,' he told Jasper. 'I'll get to the bottom
of this.'

So Noddy stood on the strip of carpet in front of the
headmaster's desk, and the headmaster sat behind the desk
and played with a bone paper-knife. The offending ten-
shilling note flat in front of him, Mr Daunders looked
calmly and benignly at the suspect. He saw an undersized
boy wearing a ragged grey jersey and torn jeans tucked
into a pair of wellingtons, a flattened, frightened dirty face
and dark eyes as uncommunicative as the eyes of a wild
animal.

'That's far too much money for a wee boy like you to be
carrying about,' he began pleasantly. 'Where did you get
it?'

'Mamurrer,' Noddy mumbled.

'Your mother gave you it?' Mr Daunders interpreted.
Noddy nodded.

'Why?' said Mr Daunders.

'Go a message,' said Noddy.

'What were you to get?' Mr Daunders asked.

'Forget,' said Noddy.

'I see,' said Mr Daunders. 'And where were you to go
for this message?'

'Doh-no,' said Noddy.

'I see,' said Mr Daunders. 'Your mother gave you ten
shillings to get something you've forgotten in a shop you
don't know. That's not a very good answer, young man.
Now just tell me the truth.'

'Muncle gay me it,' Noddy offered.

'Why?' asked Mr Daunders.

'For ma birthday,' said Noddy.

'I see,' said Mr Daunders. He drew open a card-index
box at his right hand, flicked to Mann, Nicholas and took
out the card. 'And when did your uncle give you this
rather generous birthday present?'

'Lass night,' said Noddy.

'I see,' said Mr Daunders. He waved the index card gently. 'And can you tell me why your uncle should give you ten shillings for your birthday last night when your birthday was five months ago?'

Noddy couldn't. He said nothing.

'Did he forget about you for five months?' Mr Daunders asked.

'Yes, sir,' Noddy whispered respectfully.

Mr Daunders sighed.

'No, I don't believe you're telling me the truth yet,' he said sadly. 'Now I'm not accusing you of anything, I'm not saying you stole this money, I'm not saying a thing against you. I just don't believe you're telling me the whole truth. I wouldn't be doing my duty if I didn't make inquiries when a boy is found playing in class with a ten-shilling note he can't explain how he got.'

Noddy clenched his toes inside his wellingtons and said nothing.

'All right,' said Mr Daunders. 'Suppose it was your uncle. Is that your father's brother or your mother's brother?'

'Ma murrer's,' said Noddy. He hadn't seen his father for a couple of years. His mother always visited Barlinnie alone.

'I see,' said Mr Daunders. 'Then what you're saying is that Mr Mann gave you ten shillings for your birthday five months late. Well, better late than never. Is that right?'

Noddy granted the point with another nod.

'You're sure?' Mr Daunders asked. 'Quite sure?'

Noddy nodded.

'But how could he be Mr Mann if he's your mother's brother?' Mr Daunders asked softly.

The soil on Noddy's plain cheeks was irrigated by two parallel streams.

'Ah now, there's no use crying,' said Mr Daunders, a forefinger raised. 'You tell the truth and you'll have no need to cry. Once you tell me the truth you'll have nothing to worry about.'

Noddy thrust one hand into the pocket of his jeans to grope for the other ten-shillings note and draw comfort through his finger tips from the touch of it.

'Come, come,' said Mr Daunders. 'You don't stand before your headmaster with your hand in your pocket. Stand up straight with your hands by your side.'

Then he saw something dart through Noddy's alien eyes, a passing fear, a swift alarm, and the hand seemed unwilling to come out of the pocket. He saw he had missed a move.

'Turn out your pockets,' he said. 'Let me see just what else you're hiding.'

He sighed and tutted over the second ten-shilling note and put it on top of the first.

'And who gave you this one?' he asked wearily.

'Ma murrer,' said Noddy.

'To get messages?' Mr Daunders suggested.

Noddy agreed in his usual way.

'And she gave you the other one too?' Mr Daunders prompted. 'Not your uncle, your mother. Your mother gave you them both?'

Noddy nodded.

'But she'd already given you one ten-shilling note to get messages. Why did she give you two?'

'Case Ah loast wan,' Noddy tried bravely.

'No', said Mr Daunders. 'That won't do, Nicholas. I'm not saying you stole this money. But I don't think you're telling me the truth.'

'Please sir, si truth,' Noddy wept.

The interrogation went on from six minutes past eleven till seventeen minutes past twelve. But Noddy wouldn't say Savage's name, or Percy's, or mention the cellar. He was bound by his oath, and he was more afraid of the consequences of breaking it than of Mr Daunders. If his arms were paralysed and withered and shrivelled and dropped off like the leaves from the trees in autumn he would never be able to play the piano. He might as well be dead as have no arms. Nothing Mr Daunders could do would be as bad as losing his arms. He prayed to El to give him strength and he called out to Percy in the lonely darkness of his soul, and he gave nothing away. Mr Daunders tied him in knots, unravelled them, and tied new ones. Noddy didn't care. It always surprised him how grown-ups dug into a story that wasn't worth listening to. He said he had saved the money, he said he had found it, he said his mother had given him it, he said his uncle had given him it, he said his mother had given him one note and his uncle the other, he said he had saved one and found one, he said a big boy who had left school had given him them to keep for him, but he didn't know the big boy's name, didn't know where he lived, where he worked, or what school he had gone to. He said he had just happened to put his hands in his jeans and found the two notes that morning in class and he had no idea how they got there.

'Two ten-shilling notes, that's one pound,' said Mr Daunders thoughtfully, smoothing the notes on his desk. 'Well, I still think it's a lot of money for a boy like you to be carrying about. Especially when you're not very sure how you come to have so much.'

He stared hard at the ragged dirty urchin and shook his head in defeat. A brief smile jerked at Noddy's frog-like mouth. He was thinking of the daftness of all this fuss about a couple of half-notes when he had hundreds of pounds in fivers and singles stowed away safely to buy a piano when his mother got a new house in the scheme. It would be a rare surprise for her. But he couldn't buy a piano so long as they were living in a single end. He kept his hoard in a waterproof bag inside the cistern in the stairhead lavatory, and his mother thought he was suffering from diarrhoea, he went to the closet so often, but he was only making sure his piano-money was still safe. He loved counting it.

Mr Daunders recognized that the twist in Noddy's enormous mouth was a smile, and he frowned severely.

'There's nothing funny about it, you know,' he said.

'You were crying earlier on. I don't see why you should be smiling now. I'm going to keep this money and I'm going to send for your mother, and I'll get to the bottom of this yet.'

Mr Daunders called in Noddy's mother right away. She was a cleaner in the school, so he had no trouble getting in touch with her. He waited on after four o'clock till she came in for her evening's chores. But it didn't get him anywhere. She stood in his little room, a timid foot and no more inside the door, with her working-overall on and scarf round her head in royal fashion, a big-bosomed, enormous-hipped, thick-ankled woman. That this hulk of womanhood should be the old block of a skelf like Noddy made Mr Daunders think of the mountain that gave birth to a mouse, and as he remembered the phrase he sighed at the destiny that had condemned him to be a headmaster in a small primary school in one of Glasgow's wild-life reservations, a pocket of vandalism, a pool of iniquity. He had a painful stab of longing to have done with back-ward and delinquent children and be a retired headmaster living his own life, following his own interests. He had an elegant eighteenth century edition of Horace with the mad Christopher Smart's prose translation facing the Latin. He always took it with him when he went on holiday, but somehow he never found time to open it. Now he couldn't even remember where it was that Horace had spoken of the mountain in labour giving birth to a mouse. 'I must read Horace again when I retire,' he thought, even as he was talking severely to Mrs Mann.

Mrs Mann had her own distracting thoughts. According to the book of words only widows were supposed to be employed as cleaners in Corporation schools, and she wasn't technically a widow though she passed for one in so far as she didn't have the support of a husband. A

husband in jail for robbery with violence wasn't a resident
head of the house. She felt entitled to her job, but she was
afraid Mr Daunders was going to tell her she was sacked.
When she understood he was talking about her son she felt
quite happy and smiled encouragingly to the headmaster.
Mr Daunders frowned at her. He knew quite well she was
no widow, he knew where her husband was. He had hoped
his knowledge might be used as a lever to extract information from her. But she had no information for him. Yet she
was the only person who gained from the interview.

She challenged Noddy that night.

'I was hearing you was found wi' more money than
you're supposed to have,' she said, slapping his face to
begin the discussion on the proper terms. 'Two ten-shilling notes, eh? Now where the hell did you get two ten-
shilling notes?'

Noddy said he had found them in a midgie in Ossian
Street. There was a bank at the close. The bank must have
thrown them out by mistake. They were in an envelope.

'Ha-ha, a likely story!' said Mrs Mann her fingers
splayed on her hips. She didn't think of asking for the
envelope as Mr Daunders would certainly have done.
'And what did you never think of telling me you found
them for if that was how you got them?'

'Ah never goat a chance,' Noddy mumbled, crouched in
a corner of the kitchen near the sink, his right hand over
his ear. Mrs Mann darted swiftly and smacked his left ear
and Noddy changed guard.

'Ye hid nae intentions o' tellin' me, ye little bugger!' she
screamed, and then smacked his right ear. Noddy put both
hands up.

'Ah hud,' he said. 'Ah've never saw you since Ah fun
them. Ah only fun them this moarning.'

'And whit wur ye gaun tae dae wi' them?' said Mrs
Mann, pursuing her beloved seventh son as he edged
round the kitchen past the dresser and the coal-bunker,
along the valance of the recess-bed, up to the fireplace, and
behind the ruptured armchair that flanked it.

'Ah wis gaun tae gie ye hauf,' said Noddy, willing to give up one of the bits of paper for the sake of peace.

'Oh, ye wis, wis ye?' said Mrs Mann sceptically. 'Well, come on then! Let's see ye hauf it!'

'Ah canny, he's goat them both,' Noddy wept in vexation.

'Oh, the bastard! So he hus!' cried Mrs Mann, and shook her fists at the whitewashed ceiling above the pulley where her shift and a pair of bloomers were drying, her head thrown back and her bleary eyes staring wildly.

And just as Mr Daunders had waited for her at four o'clock she waited for him at nine o'clock the next morning after she had finished her morning chores. She was humble, garrulous, apologetic, over-explanatory and nervous, but quite firm. Noddy had taken the money from her purse. It was a terrible thing to have a son that would steal from his own mother who had always done the best she could for him, but he was only a boy and he wasn't very bright, he just liked to play with bits of coloured paper, so if she could have her money back, she paused and leered in expectant servility.

Mr Daunders knew when he was beaten. He gave her the two ten-shilling notes, and since she was an honest woman and a good mother she didn't keep them both. She gave one to Noddy.

'There y'are, ma son,' she said tenderly, and threw him across the kitchen in the excess of her affection. 'There's your share like you promised me. And the next time you find anything jist you let me know and don't go causing a lot of bother keeping things tae yersel. Ye've goat tae let yer mammy know. Yer mammy's yer best friend.'

Noddy took the note silently. He didn't know what he wanted to do with it, but it was good to have it in his pocket again.

'Ah ye're a guid wee boy,' his mother grinned, and she rumpled his long uncombed hair. Noddy jerked his head away and scowled. Any show of affection distressed him.

He was even more upset to find he was in the bad books

of the Brotherhood. The news of his interrogation had spread with the speed of foot and mouth disease, and he was brought on his knees before Percy at the next Friday Night Service. Percy was frightened. First the stranger and now Noddy's two ten-shilling notes. He saw them as two straws that suggested there was a wind rising somewhere, but he didn't know where to look for it.

'I gave you a pound note,' he said severely to Noddy. 'How did you come to be caught with a couple of ten-bob notes? Tell me that.'

'I changed the note you gave me,' Noddy declared, primed in advance by Savage. He tried to rub one of his knees as he was forced to remain on them by Specky and Skinny while the Regent Supreme examined him. It was a most uncomfortable position. He wasn't used to it. Looking at the squalid urchin Percy had an idea. He must get them all to kneel during the Friday Night Service.

'What did you go and get it changed for?' he demanded with the soul-searching stare in his mournful eyes again.

'Because,' said Noddy. 'Let me go, let me up! Ah never told nuthin. Ah swear it, Ah kept the oath. You ask old Daundy. He'll tell you Ah never told him nuthin.'

'What did you change it for if you're saving up?' Percy persisted. 'You're sure nobody else has been giving you grace?'

'Course Ah'm sure,' Noddy complained, rubbing the other knee ostentatiously. 'Let me up! Ah've got a sore knee. Sure you're the only one with a key. Who else could it be?'

'If I find any of yous fellows coming in here behind my back,' Percy addressed the congregation threateningly, 'I'll burn the whole lot, so I will. Have you no respect for nothing? I made you make a gentlemen's agreement, I taught you about El and how powerful he is if you keep him secret, and now you go flashing ten-bob notes in the school. I don't like it. If there's the least danger of strangers getting a lead into the sanctuary of El we'd be

much better to burn the chests and all that's in them. I'm
warning yous.'

'Don't be daft,' said Savage, squatting at the right foot
of the Regent. 'You're the only wan wi' a key. Whit are ye
worrying aboot?'

'All right,' Percy said grudgingly. 'I'll let it go but I'm
telling yous I don't like it, I don't like it one little bit, so I
don't but.'

Savage smiled, and Percy passed sentence. Noddy was
condemned to forfeit payment for four weeks for being
caught in possession of the money they had all sworn never
to be found with. Noddy wasn't bothered. It was enough
for him that he could get up off his knees. He relied on
Savage for the month that followed. Savage had promised
to give him double his ration if he didn't let Percy find out
where the ten-shilling notes had come from.

His mother wasn't bothered either when the other
cleaners talked about her son being up before the headmaster for stealing money.

'He never stole it, he found it,' she said, choosing to
concede at last that she had heard them talking behind her
back and under her nose. She shook out a duster as if she
were a torcador at a bullfight, her torso swivelling on her
enormous hips. 'And I may say for your information if
you're interested that my Nicky is a good son to me.
Anything he does steal he brings straight home to his
maw. He's always been a good boy, I don't care what yous
say about him.'

'There's nobody saying anything about him,' said Mrs
Phinn, gaunt and chilling.

'Not bloody much,' said Mrs Mann. 'Dae yous think I
don't hear ye? Dae yous think I'm bloody-well deaf?'

'I was only saying I wish my Percy could find a couple
of ten-shilling notes and give me one of them,' said Mrs
Phinn from about three storeys above her.

'Him,' snorted Mrs Mann. 'Your Percy couldna find his
way frae here tae there withoot tripping ower his big feet.
Him! He couldna gie ye a kind look, he's that bloody sour.

Ma wee fella's aye cheery anyway, I'll say that for him. He doesna go aboot wi' a face that wid turn milk.'

'He was never a midgie-raker anyway, my Percy,' said Mrs Phinn proudly. 'He was never a lobby dosser like some weans that never see their faither.'

The vernacular struck home and Mrs Mann could only grunt contemptuously. The janitor was coming along anyway to break it up. She couldn't deny Noddy had been a lobby dosser more than once in his short life. A lobby was the word for the long stairhead landing found in older tenements, and a dosser was a person who slept there. So a lobby dosser was a waif, stray or vagrant who took shelter at night in the common stairway of a tenement and went to sleep in the lobby. Noddy had done it often, playing truant and staying away from home for nights on end. But he was always discovered by some man leaving at five or six in the morning to go on the early shift in Singer's or Beardmore's. Yet he never learnt. He would do it a week after he had promised never to do it again. There wasn't all that much difference between sleeping on the stairhead in a strange close and sleeping under the old coats on top of the boards in the recess-bed in his mother's kitchen.

'Come on, my darlings,' Mr Green bustled them jovially. 'You're not paid for standing there arguing the toss. It's time you did some work. I bet you I've got the biggest blethers in Glasgow for cleaners. So she says to me so I says to her. Yap-yap, morning and night. Come on, get cracking.'

They shuffled off, but he came after them with a hand up, remembering.

'Here, wait a minute! Who's got my key for the cellar? I had it hanging up on its nail in my room, and it's not there now. Do any of you know who took it?'

'We've no occasion to go near the cellar,' said Mrs Phinn, her pail with a shovel in it in one hand and her brush in the other. She was the self-appointed spokeswoman for the cleaners because she was the late janitor's widow, but she was far from being the oldest cleaner, and her assumption of seniority didn't increase her popularity with the other widows. 'Nobody here touched your key.'

'Well, somebody's took it,' Mr Green insisted. 'A key doesn't just go for a walk all by itself.'

'Why should we touch your key?' Mrs Phinn asked him straight, putting down her pail and brush and folding her arms across her flat bosom in a position of rebellion. 'We never need to go down there.'

'Maybe no,' Mr Green granted. 'But I've got to get down there, and soon. I've been trying to get down since I came here. I'll need to get a weekend there and clean that place up. I opened the door once and shut it again quick. I'm keeping that place locked now. I don't want Tom, Dick and Harry wandering in there. I'm fair ashamed of it. It would scunner you. It's a real Paddy's market, I'm no' kidding.'

Mrs Phinn glared at him through her NHS spectacles.

'Aye, it's all very well for you,' Mr Green said jovially to avert a quarrel, 'but your man left that place in some bloody mess, so he did. Christ, it's even got a piano in it! How the hell he ever got a piano down those stairs beats me. And what a stupid place to put a piano anyway!'

'Where else was he to put it?' Mrs Phinn asked indignantly. 'That's where he put everything there was no room for. That's where he was told to put things when Mr Gainsborough was headmaster. That was years before your time, of course.'

'Aye, and before Noah's time too by the look of the place,' Mr Green muttered, rather less jovial. 'Did you ever take a look at it? I bet you you'd find St Mungo's report card down there.'

'St Mungo would never have been at this school,' said Mrs Mann, only half-joking. 'He'd have went to a Catholic school.'

'If you think my husband's to blame for the state of that cellar, I'm quite willing to work on Saturday and tidy it up,' Mrs Phinn declared, standing straight and noble between her pail and her brush that leaned against the door of a classroom.

'Oh, so you're after some overtime, are you,' Mr Green clapped hands, rubbed them, and smiled. 'I couldn't put you through for overtime. The Office would never wear it.'

'Not for overtime, for my husband's sake,' Mrs Phinn answered, and drew surplus mucus up her nose in the way that always annoyed Percy. 'If you think you can run him down. He was a janitor before you were born.'

'I'm not running anybody down,' Mr Green soothed her. 'I'm only passing the remark that the cellar's in a bloody mess. Many thanks for your kind offer of course. Nevertheless, notwithstanding, I'd better see to it myself. The trouble is the key's lost.'

'I know all about that piano,' Mrs Phinn said aggrievedly. 'My man told me all about it. He filled in a white requisition to have it uplifted and he was still waiting for them to come when he went and died.'

'Oh, well, ye canna blame him for that,' Mr Green said kindly.

'Maybe wan o' the boys has took it,' Mrs Mann suggested. 'Ye know whit boys is like.'

'Oh, I know,' said Mr Green, nodding his head and tutting. 'They found a kid here the other day with forty-seven keys in his pocket. They pick them up and steal them and borrow them and get another one cut and then they try them on the shop doors and up closes where they think there's nobody in. Oh, ye canna be up to them!'

'Well, I hope you find your key,' said Mrs Phinn, stooping to her pail of sawdust. 'But we can't stand talking to you all night. Some of us has got work to do.'

Mr Green found the missing key back on its nail in his cubbyhole two days later. He never found out that Savage had pinched it and had a duplicate cut in Barrowland quick.

'I'm fly, you see,' Savage boasted to Specky and Noddy. 'I didn't steal that key. I just took a lend o' it and put it back before wee Greeny had time to miss it. You see the idea is you've got to make sure you're not suspicious.'

'So you've a key to get in by Tulip Place and you've a key to get in through the school,' Specky nodded in admiration.

'You're going to cause a lot of trouble,' Skinny muttered sadly. 'Percy'll find out sooner or later.'

'It was for Percy's sake I done it,' Savage grinned. 'I think he dreams mair nor he sees. But maybe he's right about somebody watchin the door round the corner. So I can get at the money—'

'You're not to say money!' Skinny cried, anguished.

'Well, I can find the road to El through the basement then,' Savage amended unctuously. 'Is that better?'

'And how do you get past the janny's house?' Specky asked. He was offended that an ape like Savage had managed to do more than an intellectual like himself.

'I put my sannies on,' said Savage. 'I know when wee Greeny and his wife are watching the telly, and I just creep across the playground. It's as safe as the Bank.'

'How much have you taken?' Specky asked bluntly.

'Enough,' Savage laughed at him. 'Do ye want to come in? Percy's daft. Ye canna leave it all to him, can ye? I've got enough put away for life.'

'Well, don't you ever boast to Frank Garson or he'll shop you to Percy right away,' warned Specky. 'I think he's suspicious already.'

Mr Green wasn't suspicious.

'Just one of those things,' he said to his wife when the key turned up. He never made mysteries out of the inexplicable, he never brooded over how, why and where-fore. He simply put aside every anomaly in daily life as 'just one of those things', and went on living his busy life. So far as he thought about the return of the missing key at all he supposed one of the cleaners had taken it in mistake for another, forgotten about it, and put it back in its place rather than own up after he had asked questions about it.

He went down to the cellar alone on the Sunday afternoon, not meaning to do any work, just to estimate how much work would be needed to put the place in order and get rid of the lumber – once he was sure what was lumber and what wasn't. As on his previous visits, a glance was enough to depress him. He went sadly up the narrow steps, shaking his head and far from saying a prayer for the repose of the soul of the late Mr Phinn.

'What a janitor!' he muttered as he locked the door. He felt he had an enormous cupboard there, with countless skeletons. 'It must have been worrying about that place killed him.'

He was quite unwilling to tackle the job of tidying the cellar himself in spite of what he had said to Mrs Phinn. He took her at her word and got her to come in the next Saturday afternoon and work for nothing. To help her, he drafted in another cleaner, Mrs Quick, promising her a few bob out of his own pocket. Mrs Mann heard of the job and offered her services too for a mere tip. Mr Green didn't mind. He knew Mrs Mann was just being nosey and hoping to come by pickings, but he couldn't see what pickings there could be in a cellar full of school rubbish. He stood in at the start of what he called jocularly Operation Underground, gave the three cleaners a general idea of what he wanted done, and when they were started he stealthily slipped upstairs and went out for a pint.

The cleaners were good workers. By shifting the position of the various items, putting like with like, marshalling everything along the walls and sweeping and mopping a central area they created an illusion of tidiness. The cellar certainly looked different when they were finished, and to that extent they had made an improvement in it. Mrs Mann found the three tea-chests hidden behind a rank of broken desks along the darkest wall where the roof of the cellar descended to meet the rising floor halfway under the playground, and rummaged in the first of them. Maybe there was something would never be missed.

'Nosey!' cried Mrs Phinn, scowling from the centre of the cellar, and drawing the back of her rough hand across her sweating brow. She had a sudden jab of pain when she saw Mrs Mann kneeling over the chest. It reminded her of the way she had found her husband, sprawled just like that, stone cold dead over the very same chest.

'How are we to know what's rubbish and what's not if we don't look?' Mrs Mann asked hoity-toitily over her shoulder. 'That's what wee Greeny's paying us for. He wants to know what he can throw out and what he can't. You've got to be nosey to do the job right.'

She plunged into the crate again and surfaced with the fairy wand. She flourished it towards Mrs Phinn and in the voice of a pantomime fairy she chanted. 'And now I banish the wicked witch! Begone, bugger off, you ugly old bitch!'

'Ach, that's the school concert stuff,' Mrs Quick cried with a wave of her broom.

Mrs Phinn's scowl narrowed to a glare. It was the sorrow of her life that she had been the belle of the district between seventeen and nineteen, lost her good looks and her figure, and finished up, she well knew, an ugly old bitch. The worries of marriage, the strain of making ends meet and coping with a husband who kept bad company and drank too much, had ploughed her youth's fair field with furrows of bitterness.

'It's an awful pity they stopped doing a concert every year,' said Mrs Quick. 'I used to enjoy them. They used to do some rare pantomimes and a kind of variety show. And they were good for the weans and a'. It learned them good to speak right.'

Mrs Mann put the wand across one of the broken desks and dived into another tea-chest, her broad bottom level with the edge of the chest as she delved deeper, her head and torso inside. She came up again and turned round with a top hat in her hand.

'Oh, I remember that turn!' Mrs Quick squealed in delight. 'There was wan o' the girls came on dressed like a man and she wore that tile hat. Oh, she was a rare wee dancer!'

Mrs Mann crowned herself with the top hat, picked up
the fairy wand again as a walking stick and swayed to the
swept centre of the stone floor singing in a broad Glasgow
voice.

> I'm Burrlington Berrtie,
> I rrise at ten therrty,
> An' go furr a strroll in the Parrk!

She did a little jig with an ease and lightness surprising
in a woman of her colossal bulk, but she was used to it. She
performed those steps every year when she marched
behind the flute band in the Orange Walk on the Twelfth
of July.

'You're going back some!' Mrs Phinn commented
coldly.

'I used to hear ma maw sing that song,' Mrs Mann
explained amiably. 'She'd be about your age.'

'Ach, yer granny's mutch!' Mrs Phinn retorted contemptuously. 'You stand there and do a song and dance act but it's
me that's doing all the work and getting nothing for it and
you're doing nothing and getting paid for it. It's no' fair.'

Encouraged by Mrs Mann's entertainment Mrs Quick
delved into the third of the chests and dragged out a
brocade jacket.

'That's what the Baron wore the year they did Cinderella,' she screeched, and tried it on.

'Baron Figtree!' Mrs Mann howled, clapped her hands,
took a front-stage pose and declaimed a couplet from an
old Glasgow pantomime.

> Tomorrow's my grandmother's wedding day.
> Ten thousand pounds will I give away.

'Hooray, hooray, hooray!' Mrs Quick took the cue, with
a triple change of voice to suggest the discordant applause
of the lads and lasses of the village. Mrs Mann bowed and
went on.

On second thought I think it best
To stow it away in the old oak chest.

'Boo, boo, boo!' Mrs Quick responded as before.

'When yous two has stopped acting the goat,' Mrs
Phinn cut in with clearly enunciated superiority.

Her two helpers leaned over the tea-chests, laughing as
only fat women can. That Mrs Phinn had no joy in their
turn increased theirs. Mrs Quick wiped her eyes with her
duster.

'Well, come on, Jessie,' she wheezed. 'We can tell him
this is a' the old concert costumes and he can burn it or
date whit he likes wi' it.'

'Shove them up against the wa', Maggie,' said Mrs
Mann. 'The three o' them. Then we can tell him they're
a' the gither.'

Mrs Mann kept the top hat. If she couldn't pawn it
Noddy might be able to use it when he dressed up for
Hallowe'en. It would maybe earn him a few extra coppers
round the doors or on the street. She was always thinking
about money.

'We could tell some o' the weans there's a lot of good
stuff down here for when it's Hallowe'en.'

'Aye, they could get some rare fancy clobber here,' Mrs
Quick agreed, thrusting the top layers of the chests down
hard to make them look tidy.

'I don't suppose it matters there's no false-faces,' Mrs
Phinn muttered. 'Your Nicky wouldny need one.'

'Ho, ho,' Mrs Mann replied, pushing the third of the
chests alongside its mates. 'Very clever, I must say.'

Percy was the first to see the cellar had been entered. He came down by the chute on Sunday night, making his usual visit to what had become a sanctuary to him, and stopped at once when he reached the floor. He thought he was going to faint. For the first time in his life he understood what it meant to get a shock. Something seemed to have hit him in the midriff, his heart went vaulting and then tumbled, his legs were paralysed, his head was a clamour of alarm bells, his eyes were in a mist one moment and as sharp as an eagle's the next, his palate was parched and his tongue was stuck to it, his brow felt chilled, and he nearly wet himself.

When he recovered from the seizure he galloped over to the chests, almost tripping himself on his splay feet in his excitement. His torso was so far ahead of his legs that he seemed to mean to get there by bodily extension rather than by running. He saw the concert props and costumes weren't quite as they had been left. Some that had been in different chests were now in the same chest, some that had been underneath were now on top. He leaned over the first chest, pulled out skirts, hats, jackets, trousers, cardboard capstans and festoons of coloured paper, and delved to the bottom. The money was still there. And so with the other chests. Whoever had been in the cellar and swept it out and moved the chests hadn't disturbed more than the top layers. The transistor, the tape-recorder and record-player, the TV and the uke and the guitar were still safe against the farthest and darkest wall of the cellar, the rats' wall, behind a façade of planks, pails and the barrel of washing-soda. So much for the thoroughness of the cleaners' cleaning. He knelt beside one of the chests with his hands clasped and said a sincere prayer of thanks.

'Oh, blessed El, I thank thee for not allowing thyself to fall into the hands of the ungodly,' he panted, his mouth against his finger-tips.

He thought of moving the money, but he didn't know where else he could put it. If it had survived one attack in the cellar it could survive another. The cellar still seemed the safest place for it, and the proper place too, since it had been found in the cellar. He was unwilling to find a new site for what had always been safe in the place where it was discovered. The cellar seemed its natural and even sacred place because that was where El had chosen to reveal himself. Even the distribution amongst three chests had a mystical meaning to him. He couldn't bear to tamper with fortune by shifting anything.

He called an extraordinary assembly at once, held a special service, and declared an extra dividend in thanksgiving for the safety of El. The Brotherhood didn't mind the special service, they liked singing together, and they took the extra share-out gladly enough. But looking down from his throne Percy noticed signs of a strange unin-terest here and there, an air of forced swallowing. There came to him suddenly the memory that he had helped the woman in charge of the dinner-school once when he was a boy, and she had given him a double helping of ice-cream after the diners were all gone. He took it eagerly. It was three or four times as large as the largest ice he had ever had before. Then she gave him a second plateful, just to be nice to him, and he got through it only because it was impossible to refuse ice-cream. But he was sick afterwards, and it made him think less of ice-cream in the future.

'It was only the cleaners, ye know,' Savage explained wisely after the service. 'The way you talk you'd think it was evil spirits had raided the place.'

'Maybe you don't believe it, but the world's full of evil spirits,' said Percy.

'Oh aye, I believe that,' said Savage with flippant solemnity.

'I know it was the cleaners was in,' Percy tried again. 'I'm perfectly well aware of that, but the point is what made them come down here. Nobody's ever been down here before. If that wasn't the promptings of evil spirits, what was it? Go on, you tell me! And what's more it's a miracle they didn't find anything. That shows we're being looked after. You've got to believe in destiny, ye know. Kismet. Kay Sarah, Sarah.'

'It was wee Noddy was telling me his maw was in here Saturday afternoon,' Savage answered conversationally, refusing to ask who Sarah was. He knew Percy was just dying to explain it to him. 'He knew by the Saturday night everything was okay. His old girl never mentioned a thing. Your maw was down as well. Did she no' tell ye? Jees, that would have had ye worried stiff if she'd said to ye, I'm going down the cellar to clean it out!'

Percy snubbed him silently. He hadn't known his mother was in the cellar on Saturday. He had missed her in the afternoon, but he hadn't asked where she had been and she didn't tell him. It made his head ache to think of the danger they had been in. His headaches were becoming a daily plague, and he blamed them on the strain he was under, being responsible for the safety of thousands of pounds and the welfare of a horde of ungrateful boys. And so it would go on till something happened. Something was bound to happen. But he couldn't imagine what it was. He lived in fear of a knock at the door. Every time he passed a policeman he felt nervous. He dreamt nearly every night of the stranger who had accosted him in Tulip Place, and waited patiently for his bad dreams to come true. The stranger must reappear. He knew there was no escape from him. He felt all alone and powerless. It came back to him that he had wanted to have a lot of money so that he could get peace. And now he had less peace than ever. He had the money, but his mind wasn't free to write poetry. But would Shelley have written any poetry if he had to look after a street-gang? He made up his mind to start tomorrow and organize his life better, so as to find time and peace to begin writing a poem. But it was always a case of starting tomorrow. He groaned, sitting on Miss Elginbrod's chair, and put his head between his hands, his elbows on his knees.

'Headache?' piped Savage brightly in a commercial TV voice. 'Be good to yourself! Take a Scrunchy-Lunchy. Six good points for sixpence. Makes you one shade lighter. Scrunchy-Lunchy's good for weans, puts an end to aches and pains. Take a Scrunchy-Lunchy tonight and tomorrow you'll—'

'Oh, shut up, you!' Percy snarled at him, turning on his Chief Claviger, taking his hands away to reveal a frustrated face with big bewildered eyes. He hated vulgarity. It added to his distress that he was coming to hate Savage, yet once he had liked him. He had meant to polish a rough diamond, and now he hated the look of it.

Savage was delighted. He had got Percy really annoyed.

'Aw, keep the heid,' he said amiably, and went away.

Drunk with power at having got the better of Percy he caught up on the other members of the Brotherhood at the corner of Tulip Place and entertained them with an imitation of Frank Garson. He couldn't stand Frank Garson, and he couldn't leave him alone. He had always to be making a fool of him because he kept his face clean and spoke politely. His star turn was to put on a West-end voice and repeat something Garson had said. The incongruity of chaste correct speech coming from Savage's loose mouth gave the Brotherhood an uneasy amusement and they laughed guiltily when he imitated a girlish walk to go with his imitation of Garson's girlish voice.

'It was Ai who found the money, but Ai don't want any share, ow now, thenk you. 'Sa metter of fect, Ai think Ai ought to inform the polis.'

He picked up a phone from mid-air, dialled a number in the same place, and squeaked, writhing like a striptease dancer, 'Ello, ello, Sat Whitehall 1212? Ken Ai hev a wurrd with the Chief Constable, pulease? Ello, ello, ello! Satchoo, Chief Ai jist want to report there's an awful lot of boys here has an awful lot of money. Kin Ai claim a reward for telling you?'

'Ach, wheesht,' said Specky, past being amused. 'You'll make jokes about money once too often. Somebody'll hear you.'

'You know Percy's rule,' Skinny accused him. 'And it's a wise rule too. We promised never to mention money outside.'

'I'm fed up wi' him and his great god El,' Savage retorted lightly. 'Money's money the world over, and ye might as well admit it. Kidding yerself it's something mysterious and supernatural, the way Percy talks, it's daft. Where's wee Garson? I want to see him. Did ye notice he's still no' taking any money?'

They ambled on together, a little gang of them, till they caught up with Frank Garson crossing the waste land between the Steamie and the back of Bethel Street, a desolation of hard earth and dockens.

'Oi, Garsie!' shouted Savage, a domineering note in his voice.

Garson turned obediently and waited. He was always polite, even to people who were rude to him. Savage came close up and flipped his finger tips against the waiting boy's nose.

'When are you gaun tae start taking yer share o' the lolly?' he whispered, smiling maliciously.

It vexed him, it provoked him deeply and sharply, that Garson stuck to his position that they ought to report the finding of the money and wouldn't take any part of it. Garson knew he would never go to the police on his own, especially when they had the money so long, but Savage didn't know that. He was afraid Garson would turn informer and he wanted to incriminate him by forcing money on him. Being a reasonably intelligent youngster, Garson saw what Savage was up to and he had the wit to see that taking a little would make him just as guilty as

taking a lot. He determined from the beginning to take
nothing and he was nowhere near yielding now. He would
keep his hands clean against the day of reckoning that
would certainly come. But he went to the Friday Night
Service every week because he enjoyed the strangeness of
it in the candlelight. Percy's sermons and the hymn singing satisfied a longing for communion with his mates. He
was lonely, and he needed the Brotherhood, he was still so
young.

'Are ye feart somebody catches ye wi' a pound note in
yer pocket?' Savage persisted against the silence facing
him.

'I just don't want any money,' Garson answered simply.
'That's all. I think you're all making a terrible mistake.
And you'll be sorry one day. You'll see.'

'Then you shouldn't be coming to the cellar at all,'
Savage argued, pushing him away. 'You've no right to be
coming to Percy's Friday Night Services. That's only for
folk that believe in El, like Percy says, it's no' for heathens
like you that believe in nothing.'

He turned and grinned to the gang that had followed
him in pursuit of Garson, amused at his use of Percy's
language and wanting them to be amused too. They
watched with dull faces.

'I go to them because I want to,' Garson said boldly. 'I
don't have to defend myself to you. I've a right to go. It
was I who found the money.'

'I tellt ye, I tellt ye!' Savage crowed triumphantly to the
gang. 'Oh boy, oh boy! It was Ai who! Oh brush my shoes,
Cherlie! My maw's a duchess!'

He flicked a finger tip against the tip of Garson's nose
and asked abruptly, 'How is yer maw noo? Dyever see
her?'

The flick in the nose angered Garson. It was surpris-
ingly painful. It made his eyes water. In an instinctive
response he hit out at Savage and missed him. Savage
cackled and danced round him.

'Haw, haw! Ye couldna hit a coo on the erse wi' a banjo!'

Garson lunged again and missed again.

'Haw, haw, ye hivna got a maw!' Savage chanted the rude rhyme, and sang on malevolently, 'Yer maw ran awa' wi' a darkie.'

'She didn't!' Garson screamed in a frenzy. Yet it was all he had ever heard said, and his denial was an act of faith in the ultimate goodness of the universe. If he accepted common gossip as the truth then the world was bad, but the world couldn't be bad. It was good, Percy was good. His father was good. School was good. The stories he read were good. He tried to grapple with Savage, to catch him and choke him, but he was far too slow, and he was blinded with tears of anguish. Then as he blundered and lurched this way and that way, Savage stood stock still and faced up to him.

'Come on and I'll fight you then,' he said, suddenly grim and blood-thirsty.

The Brotherhood formed a ring with a rapid manoeuvre worthy of well-trained troopers, and the surplus members climbed on to the top of the pre-nuclear-age air-raid shelters to watch the fight from there and cheer the winner from a ringside seat.

Garson blinked, trying to see his enemy clearly through tears that reflected a cruel world. He had a brief intuition that the people were evil after all, and if that was how it was there was no use fighting. He was beaten before he started. He was no fighter anyway. He was smaller, slighter, far less of a brawler by build and temperament than Savage. But he had to fight even though it was useless. He would die honourably. He shaped up clumsily, nervously, and while he was still making up his mind whether to lead with the left hand or the right Savage punched him right on the nose with one hand and then bang on the eye with the other.

Garson yelped and wept, and Savage hit him in the stomach. He put his hands there to console the shock and Savage smacked him on the ear. In a few seconds he was a quivering helpless morsel of inadequate boyhood. Blood came down his nose over his lips and he was squeamish at the salty taste of it, the water brimming over his eyes kept him from seeing right, and the bells ringing in his ear made him lose all sense of balance and direction. He stumbled and flailed. Still he wouldn't give in. He wouldn't turn and run. He didn't know where to run to. He kept on trying to fight, but he had no idea of fighting. Savage was radiant with the lust of punishment. He had no mercy. He was a wily battering ram, and Garson was the young lamb bleating at the slaughter.

Skinny filtered silently through the rowdy mob as soon as he saw it was a case of murder, and ran for Percy. He found him with his big feet in Tulip Place and his head in the clouds. He was thinking about the stranger. He was always thinking about the stranger. But now he was beginning to feel safe again, it was so long since he had seen him. He was rather proud of his plan for making sure nobody entered or left the cellar if there was anyone odd hanging about the corner: one of the Brotherhood stayed outside at every service and if he saw any stranger he was to play in Tulip Place and keep kicking a ball against the cellar door as if he was practising shooting and collecting rebounds. That was the warning. A simple signal that no stranger could recognize for what it was, Percy was sure. So far there had been no need for the sentry to kick a ball against the door. Perhaps the stranger had gone away for good. Perhaps he was in jail. He looked a real jail-type. Whatever he was he didn't seem to be a danger any longer.

Last to leave the cellar, the dreaming lord of uncounted wealth, Percy paid off the sentry and ambled down Tulip Place in grim meditation, welcoming the headache it gave him as the price he had to pay for being a thinker. It was all very well looking after a crowd of ungrateful schoolboys, but it was time he did something for himself too. He had his career to think of. All this time gone and he hadn't even got around to finishing that Ode to Speed he had started.

'Savage is killing Garson!' Skinny yelled, grabbing the Regent by one gaunt wrist and shaking it madly.

'Whit are ye talking aboot noo?' Percy grumbled crossly. He left the island in the Mediterranean where he had a patio or hacienda or something like that, he wasn't sure which, but he had in mind a big house with a verandah, and came unwillingly back to Tulip Place.

'He's fighting him and Garson canny fight,' Skinny explained in a hurry. 'It's blue murder so it is. Come on and stop it, Percy! Please! Afore he kills him. Ye ought to see the state he's in, it's terrible!'

'Whit way could you no' stop it?' Percy demanded, forced to trot as Skinny, still clutching his wrist, turned and raced across the street, through a close, across the back-court, and over to the waste land beside the Steamie. 'Or Specky? Fat lot o' use there was making yous somebody. You never use the authority I gave you. How would it be if I just let yous all do whit ye like? Tell me that.'

He grumbled all the way, but Skinny said nothing. He let Percy grumble. He saw no point answering such daft questions. How could he ever stop Savage hitting anybody he wanted to hit? There were things you just had to give in to and put up with, like the brute force of Savage. He had taken a big enough risk running away to fetch Percy. He could only hope that in the excitement nobody would notice it was he who brought Percy along and that he would be safe from the later vengeance of Savage for spoiling him of his prey.

The Brotherhood opened to let Percy get into the ring and he splay-footed indignantly over to Savage, who was kicking Garson in the ribs as the boy cowered on the ground with his head in his arms and his shoulders shaking with sobs. Percy hit Savage an open-handed smack across the face, so hard that the sound was clearly heard by the spectators on top of the air-raid shelters, and they gasped an 'Oo-oo-oo!' of mingled delight and alarm at the violence of the blow.

'You chuck that!' Percy shouted angrily. 'Or I'll give you a kicking, so I will. You're nothing but a big bully. You think you can settle everything by force. Whatever you're fighting about fighting proves nothing. I've tellt ye that before. Can ye no' take a telling?'

He glared down at Savage, heaving with temper, and Savage rubbed his cheek and grinned up at him amiably. He wasn't bothered. His lust was satisfied. A smack on the face was a small price to pay for leaving Garson a bloody weeping humiliated victim on the ground. His father had hit him harder often for nothing.

Percy shook him at the throat, almost lifting him off the ground, and Savage wriggled and wrenched himself away.

'It was nothing,' he said innocently. 'Keep the heid, Percy. The wee fella wanted to have a square go so I gave him wan and he couldny take it, that was a'. You don't need to start shouting the odds aboot it.'

Garson got on his knees, then on his feet, and brushed himself with trembling hands, little soft white hands that couldn't have punched a bus-ticket. His lower lip was going as if he had a permanent stammer and he was still crying.

Percy wanted to comfort him, to stand up for him, to avenge him. His brain was in a mist of pity. But he had sworn never to have favourites in the Brotherhood because that would only cause strife and jealousy. He swallowed his loving anguish for the unfriended boy till the bitterness of it made him grue. Then he spoke out harshly, shaking Garson as he had shaken Savage.

'What do you want to go starting fights for? You know damn fine you're no' a match for Sheuchie Savage, ye wee fool!'

Garson suffered the shaking patiently as long as it lasted, and the moment he was released he turned and went away. The mob opened an alley for him and let him pass along without a whisper of sympathy or a hand raised to console him with a pat on the back, and he went off shaking his head as if Percy's large hand was still at his collar.

'Ye're a horde of ruffians!' Percy cried in exasperation, feeling he had let Garson down but not knowing what else he could have done.

'Yous that was watching and made no attempt to stop it, yous are just as bad as Savage, only worse. We've got all this – all this—'

He paused and the Adam's apple in his scraggy neck moved up and down, but it was a crisis to him and he had to say it.

'All this money. Aye, all this money. Yous know damn well what I mean. We've got all this money and yous canny live in peace. I give yous up! Come on, get away home all of yous! Scram! Come on, run, run, run! Every one of yous, beat it!'

Normally the false plural slipped from him only now and again. He had learned it was wrong, and he was trying hard to stop using it. But he was too angry to think of his grammar.

He waved his gang away with open hands like a farmer's wife shooing hens, and those on the ground dispersed slowly, resenting his command to run, and those on the roof of the air-raid shelters jumped down and mixed guiltily with their brethren. In a few moments Percy was all alone in the waste land.

'Hate!' he muttered unhappily. 'It's only brought hate. Those two hate each other. It could have made them so happy if they would only be reasonable. I should have made them make it up before wee Frankie went away. I should have made them shake hands and be friends. It's an awful job, making yourself responsible for folks that hasn't been brought up to what's right.'

Mr Garson was a lonely man, a dour man. He wasn't given to complaining and he suffered many daily injustices rather than make a fuss, but when he came home from the garage that evening and saw his son's black eye and puffed lips he was just a little bit angry. He was willing to take it as natural that boys should fight now and again, but this hadn't been a fight, it looked more like assault and battery. He wanted to know what had happened, but he couldn't get anything out of the boy, so he shook him by the shoulder in an impatient attempt to make him speak. The boy winced and yelped.

'Take your shirt off,' said Mr Garson sharply. He hadn't grasped him all that roughly, there was no need for such a cry of pain unless the damage was as great elsewhere as it was on the face. He suspected it was, and he wanted to make sure.

Garson stripped grudgingly to the waist, embarrassed to be half-naked in the kitchen under the glowering eye of his unfriendly father. His shoulders were bruised, and his flanks were black and blue where Savage had kicked him.

'You tell me who did that to you or I'll give you worse,' said Mr Garson, quite cold.

The boy would have told him gladly if he had been thawed by a warm sympathy, he would have enjoyed weeping out the name if he had been consoled and pitied, but the cold threat froze him.

'I'm warning you,' said Mr Garson with a frightening sincerity, 'You'd better tell me.'

The boy had a brief fantasy of his father fighting Savage's father to avenge the family honour, but he knew that was absurd. His father was too proud even to speak to Savage's father, far less fight him in the back-court or the waste land. Nor would he rush out to look for Savage and smack his ear. That was just as absurd. He just wanted to know for the sake of knowing. All right then, why shouldn't he tell? He kept his silence for a little longer till he didn't feel quite so frozen inside and then he told.

Mr Garson took time off from the garage on Monday morning and went to the school. He didn't know what he wanted exactly, he certainly didn't want vengeance, but he did want to make a protest and get some kind of assurance it wouldn't happen again. He thought he was likelier to get that from the headmaster than from the parents. Mr Daunders promised to look into it, he offered to have Savage brought in right away and invited Mr Garson to remain and see the boy for himself. Mr Garson said he would rather not.

'So long as you promise me to make sure he gets a lesson, I'll leave it to you,' he said respectfully. He was only a motor-mechanic, and he looked up to Mr Daunders as an educated man.

'I'll give him a lesson all right,' Mr Daunders promised cordially. 'We could do with more pupils like your boy, always clean and smart and industrious, but you see every school has its Savages and that's what makes our job so difficult. It's one long struggle against the jungle here.'

They parted at the door of the headmaster's room, both talking at once in polite expression of mutual trust.

'I'll leave him to you,' said Mr Garson.

'You can safely leave him to me,' said Mr Daunders. 'I wish we had more decent parents like you, Mr Garson.'

He sent for Savage at once and lectured him on the immorality of bullying. For all his confident promises to Mr Garson he wasn't sure of the best way to handle it. He was a good man, a reasonable man, unwilling to damn any boy till he had tried hard to save him. He saw little sense telling Savage it was wrong to think that the use of superior physical force was a good thing, and then going on to give him a lathering with a Lochgelly. It was the use of force he had to discredit. He spoke sternly but reasonably. He tried to make Savage see the dangers of living by jungle law. Savage slouched insolently, his black leather jerkin, with the zip unfastened, bulging out in front of his broad chest. He was a big boy, but Mr Daunders was a man. He looked down on him.

'I've told you before not to wear that belt,' he said severely, 'Take it off. You don't need it.'

Savage took off an Army webbing belt and rolled it in his hand. Many a fight he had won with it.

'Where did you get that jacket, by the way?' Mr Daunders asked curiously. He knew quality when he saw it, and he knew that Savage's father could never afford the price of it. 'I haven't seen you wearing it before.'

'My Granny bought me it,' said Savage.

'For your birthday?' Mr Daunders asked, a vague memory of something he had heard before putting an ironic edge on his question.

''Sright,' Savage nodded willingly, leering up as Mr Daunders looked down. He understood too late what the headmaster was staring at. The bulge of the jacket exposed the lining.

'And what's that you've got in there?' Mr Daunders asked gently, simply gesturing to the lining of the jacket. He was too careful ever to touch a boy's clothing.

Savage's hand flashed to the four pound notes he had pinned inside the jacket that morning.

'Let me see it,' said Mr Daunders.

Savage knew when he was caught. He unpinned the notes and handed them over. He wasn't bothered. He had plenty more.

Mr Daunders scowled at the notes. He didn't like it at all.

'What are you doing with these pinned in your jacket?' he cried in bewilderment. It was always the same. One inquiry always led into another you hadn't expected. You started to question a boy who had simply played truant and before you had finished finding out where he went, you were on the track of a series of thefts from shops and lorries.

'That's where Maverick keeps his money,' Savage stalled.

Mr Daunders wouldn't admit to a scruffy schoolboy that he too followed the adventures of Maverick.

'Whose class is he in?' he asked judicially.

'He's no' in a class, he's on the telly,' Savage explained.

'That hardly tells me what you're doing with four pound notes pinned inside a very expensive leather jacket, does it?' Mr Daunders murmured.

Savage said nothing.

'Where did you get this money?' Mr Daunders asked wheedlingly. 'Come on, you'll save a lot of time, and save yourself a lot of trouble if you tell me the truth. Where did you get it?'

'Wee Noddy gave it to me to keep for him,' Savage answered. He was quick in his own way. He knew it was safe to mention Noddy, because Noddy wouldn't give anything away. He couldn't, because he couldn't speak. To tell about the cellar was far beyond Noddy's powers of speech.

'Who?' said Mr. Daunders, just as unwilling to admit he knew nicknames as to admit he knew Maverick.

'Nicky Mann,' said Savage, 'in Jasper's class.'

'In whose class?' Mr Daunders asked gently. He knew quite well who Jasper was. He had often commented on the amazing knack schoolboys had for giving a teacher a nickname. Jasper was an admirable name for the blue-jowled, villainous-looking young man with the lock of jet-black hair always falling over his right eye.

'Mr Whiffen's,' said Savage. 'Nicky Mann in Mr Whiffen's class.'

'Oh no!' Mr Daunders groaned, his compulsive act of judicial ignorance over. He had to face it.

'I'm keeping this money,' he said. 'Send Mann to me.'

He knew he had blundered the moment Savage crossed

the door. He should have kept Savage incommunicado and had someone else fetch Noddy. But he was tired. Tired of evasive, deceitful, dirty-faced schoolboys. He had another spasm of longing for his retirement and his Horace.

Noddy arrived, briefly but efficiently warned by Savage, and Mr Daunders knew he was beaten before he started.

'I never,' said Noddy.

'But he says you gave him it,' said Mr Daunders.

'I never,' said Noddy.

'Where did you get it?' asked Mr Daunders.

'I never,' said Noddy.

'Are you saying Savage is telling lies then?' Mr Daunders asked.

'I never,' said Noddy.

'Well, where do you think Savage got it?' Mr Daunders asked.

'I never,' said Noddy.

'You're not answering my question,' Mr Daunders said. 'Just listen to me. Now—'

'I never,' said Noddy.

Mr Daunders gave in. He had to admit it was impossible to get a statement from a boy who was inarticulate, but that was only what Savage had seen before him.

He kept the four pound notes, though he wasn't happy about it. He insisted on seeing Savage's parents, but it was no use. They never answered his letter inviting them to call, for Savage made sure he got his hands on it first. The loss of the money didn't bother him, he had plenty more. He was more concerned to keep his father out of it.

Mrs Mann was no help either. Noddy told her no more than he told Mr Daunders, and she was too cautious to claim the money. She had a nose. So had Mr Daunders.

'It smells very fishy to me,' he told his chief assistant, a superior person from a Border family with the double-barrelled name of Baillie-Hunter. 'There seems to be a lot of money floating round this school just now. Miss Nairn told me she found McGillicuddy with a pound note inside his reader. He was apparently using it as a book-mark.'

'He always reminds me of those odd mountains in Ireland,' said Mr Baillie-Hunter, sniffing languidly. 'McGillicuddy's Reeks.'

'He does smell a little,' Mr Daunders conceded. 'You see, they never wash all over, and they sleep in their shirt, these boys.'

'And McCutcheon had money last week,' said Mr Baillie-Hunter.

'Yes, Mr Whiffen caught him passing a ten-shilling note to Morrison when they were supposed to be doing their sums,' said Mr Daunders. 'And Miss McIvory found out Somerled was paying McIntosh and Crombie five bob a week each to do his homework for him. One of them did his arithmetic and the other did his grammar. There he was, getting his homework right every time and couldn't get a thing right in class. The deceit was as gross as a mountain, open, palpable. They've no craft, these boys. His mother was up to see me only yesterday. Quite cross because I hadn't approved him for a full senior secondary course. She wanted to argue he was a clever boy. Always got his homework right. She damn soon changed her tune when I showed her his dictation book. Forty, fifty and sixty errors in dictations of less than a hundred words.'

'Oh, we could never send him to a senior secondary school,' said Mr Baillie-Hunter, appalled. 'Why, he doesn't even know his tables.'

'Ah, they're a great lot!' Mr Daunders sighed. 'I don't know what I did to be sent here as headmaster in my declining years. I might as well be in the CID, the things I've got to investigate. And what am I to do about this four pound? It isn't mine, and I'm damn sure it isn't Savage's. Do you think they could be selling what they steal? There's a sort of gang there, you know, Savage – he's the ring-leader, I'm sure – and Noddy and Cuddy and Cutchy and Somerled. Wherever you find trouble in this school you find they're mixed up in it.'

'What about Tosh and Crumbs?' Mr Baillie-Hunter asked.

'No, they're not in it,' Mr Daunders was sure. 'They're just a couple of sycophants. Anyway, Somerled was paying them. He wouldn't be paying them if they were in the gang. They would have their share of whatever money's going. Whatever it comes from.'

'Gambling?' suggested Mr Baillie-Hunter.

'I hardly think so. What kind of odds with the money a schoolboy has would let Savage win four pounds?'

Mr Baillie-Hunter finished his mid-morning coffee with his headmaster and returned to his class for a poetry lesson. He was reading to them 'Lord Ullin's Daughter' and acting it well, changing his voice to be the chief of Ulva's isle, the boatman and Lord Ullin, and even the raging storm itself. He ended solemnly in a good rolling Scotch voice.

> 'Twas vain! The loud waves lashed the shore,
> Return or aid preventing.
> The waters wild went o'er his child,
> And he was left lamenting.

He indicated the rise and fall of the waves by an undulation of his right hand, and in the sorrowful hush that followed his dramatic reading he looked round the class with gratification. He knew he had a good delivery, and he found a certain pleasure in giving such a touching rendering of corny ballads that children were thrilled to unshed tears. He expected to see here and there a hand furtively brushing a wet eye. Then he exploded at the dry-eyed inattention of a boy in the back row.

A minute later he barged into Mr Daunder's room and slapped down a dozen or so bits of paper on the head-master's desk.

'I just found Wedderburn playing with – with these,' he gulped, agonized.

'What are they?' said Mr Daunders, putting the stock

book aside. He had an annual return to make to the office, and he was puzzled to see the stock book showing him as having a piano more on hand than he thought he had. For any other item he would have balanced the discrepancy in the usual way by putting '1' under the 'Consumed' column, but he wasn't sure he could properly claim to have consumed a piano.

'They're bits of a five-pound note,' Mr Baillie-Hunter moaned. 'All the bits! Wedderburn was playing with them.'

'Oh, Jesus Christ!' Mr Daunders breathed devoutly, a pious ejaculation for divine assistance, his elbow on his desk, his brow on his hand, the stock book and the mysterious extra piano forgotten.

'He was doing it as a jig-saw puzzle,' Mr Baillie-Hunter complained miserably. 'You see, it's all there! Somebody has cut it in little pieces. You see how clever it is.'

He fitted two or three of the geometric fragments together. 'It was just a jig-saw to Wedderburn, it wasn't money, it was a puzzle. He says he found it inside his poetry book. You see, I don't let them keep their poetry books. I give them out when I take poetry. So anybody could have left them there if he's telling the truth. And he knows we can't prove he isn't.'

'We'll have to get to the bottom of this,' Mr Daunders muttered, and rubbed his palm wearily across his aching eyes. 'This can't go on. Ten-shilling notes, pound notes, a five-pound note. Where is it going to end?'

He brooded.

'Yes, as I told you, I've got a very strong feeling there's too much money floating around this school. Do you know, I've had about a dozen parents up lately. Complaining. Their children can't sleep at night, or when they do they have nightmares. And they're off their food. They seem to think Jasper's frightening the weans. Then they say, "Oh it must be all these sweeties they're eating between meals." But they can't tell me where the money's coming from to buy sweets to that extent. They talk as if it was my job to stop them eating sweets!'

He brooded again.

'Garson!' he cried, slapping his desk so hard that the phone tinkled for a moment or two. 'I've got it. Garson knows the answer.'

'Garson wouldn't be mixed up in anything dishonest,' Mr Baillie-Hunter objected indignantly. 'Garson's a good boy. He grasped decimals right away.'

'Maybe so,' said Mr Daunders. 'But he's in on this money epidemic I'm sure. That's why Savage gave him a beating. Garson knows where all this money's coming from, and he was going to talk. I'll make him talk all right! You get him in here now.'

But Garson wouldn't talk. He still believed that what Percy was doing was wrong, he was still afraid a day of reckoning must come, and he still wanted no part of it. But he was quite clear in his own mind that the discovery of the hoard would never come through him. He had his own code. He was loyal. Loyalty was all that was left to him, even though it was loyalty to a gang that had never completely accepted him. He was worried about Percy most of all. He believed Percy should have taken his side against Savage and not been so neutral, but he still loved him. Percy was the leader and the organizer. He was the eldest. Whoever had to pay one day, Percy would have to pay most. And he wasn't going to have Percy's punishment on his conscience. Since it had to come sooner or later let it come later, through the inevitable gathering of circumstance, not because of any words he ever spoke. He had been long prepared to cope with an interrogator who knew much more than Mr Daunders.

'Now you didn't just fight about nothing,' Mr Daunders kept at him, stubbornly drilling through his stony silence. 'Something must have started it. Tell me what it was.'

Garson recognized it was time to answer. His fingertips went to the bruised and swollen bone under his eye.

'It was a private matter,' he said.

'How private?' Mr Daunders asked. 'You can surely tell me. I'm trying to help you.'

'My family,' said Garson, warmed to a confidence by the old man's kind wheedling voice.

'What do you mean, your family?' Mr Daunders pushed at him.

'He-he-he insulted my mother,' Garson answered, his rosy cheeks rosier, his engaging stammer appearing for a moment. 'So I hit him and he hit me back, and we-we-we started to fight. It was a fair fight.'

'I see,' Mr Daunders murmured, as embarrassed as the boy. He felt he had blundered. He should have known better than to go on once Garson mentioned his family. You never knew what scandals you were going to stumble on if you asked too many questions about a boy's family in this school. He remembered the muddle he had failed to sort out when he tried to discover why a boy was called Addison, his mother was called Mrs Mappin, and the man she was living with, whose name was on the doorplate, was called Tanner. Mr Tanner called one morning after it was proposed to send Addison to a special school, a school for the mentally handicapped, and Mr Daunders tactfully queried his relationship to the boy.

'Oh, I'm one of his parents,' Mr Tanner answered lightly. 'In a sort of way, you see.'

'I see,' said Mr Daunders, wondering who Mr Mappin was if there ever was one, and what had happened to Mr Addison.

The trivial incident had been a lesson to him, but he still felt he should probe Garson. He still felt there was more to the fight with Garson than a schoolboy's routine insult to a classmate's parent. He remained convinced Savage was afraid of what Garson knew and had given him a beating to keep him quiet. He believed if he kept on asking questions he would come to the real sore, distinct from the wound about an insulted mother though perhaps connected with it.

'And what did he say about your mother that annoyed you so much?' he tried.

Garson looked at him and trembled with a strange pity.

The man seemed to want to be shocked. He surrendered. He would repeat just what he had suffered and let this grown-up suffer too. Why should he bear the cruelty of the world alone? But he couldn't use Savage's words. He answered in the book-English a bright Scots schoolboy uses when he talks respectfully to his teachers.

'He accused my mother of eloping with a Negro,' he said.

'Oh dear,' said Mr Daunders sadly. He knew a dead-end when he came to it. But he couldn't stop worrying away like a dog at a bone. He turned the topic over and attacked it another way.

'You're sure it wasn't because you knew something about Savage that he doesn't want anyone else to know?'

For all its directness the question missed the target. Garson certainly felt guilty about the money, but the money meant Percy and the whole Brotherhood, not specifically Savage. He answered with a candour that was totally convincing because it was genuine.

'I don't know anything about Savage.'

'He's not afraid of anything you know?'

That came a little nearer. Garson was uneasy for a moment. He wondered if Old Daundy could possibly have got on to the money in the cellar. He put the idea away. If he knew about the money in the cellar he wouldn't be wasting time asking a lot of silly questions. As for the question just put to him, he couldn't see why Savage should be afraid of him when the rest of the Brotherhood knew all he knew. Surely Savage knew he would keep the oath as faithfully as the rest of them.

'There's nothing I know that other folk don't know,' he answered carefully. 'Savage has no reason to be afraid of me.'

Mr Daunders let him go, but unwillingly. He felt he had neared the brink of the abyss where the mystery was buried.

It was a day of interrogation for Garson. His father started too after their silent evening meal together. From the casual way he spoke the boy guessed he had been thinking about it all day.

'You never told me what you were fighting about anyway. What started it?'

What made grown-ups ask questions they wouldn't like to hear answered, the boy wondered. He had had enough. If he could tell Mr Daunders he could tell his father. It was only right people should get what they asked for.

'Savage said my mother ran away with a darkie,' he said sullenly, and waited for it, ready to cower. And indeed his father's hand went up before the words were fully spoken. The boy moved round the kitchen table to safety. His father put his hand back in his pocket and let him be.

'That's not true,' he said walking from the kitchen sink to the kitchen door and back again, rubbing his nose, rubbing his lips.

The boy watched him alertly and waited.

'It's not true,' his father repeated. 'That's gossip. I know what they say. But it's not true. Your mother didn't run away with anybody.'

'What did she do?' the boy demanded, his battered face twisted to choke the tears that the memory of Savage's taunt brought back to his eyes. 'Why is she not here?'

'Aye, as far as you're concerned she just disappeared,' his father muttered, still walking up and down, still rubbing his face and thrusting his fingers through his hair in a private misery. 'That's all I know myself.'

'Why?' said the boy, determined to keep at it. He was going to find out something he wanted to know, he was sure of it. People had asked him too many questions. It was his turn.

'Because she – because she wouldn't do what I told her,' said his father. He was started, his tongue was loosened after years of silence. He had to tell himself now, not just his son. 'She took a job on the buses. She was a conductress. I didn't want her to. But I let her do it because she said she needed the money for new this and new that. I don't know what the hell she didn't want. She wanted new curtains, that was all to begin with. Just work for a wee while, she said. Then she wanted a washing-machine, then she wanted a television, then she wanted a fridge. It was going to go on for ever. I told her to stop. Her place was in the house. But oh no, her place was wherever she liked. She liked being out working. The house was just dull, she was nobody's skivvy. She was going to go on working just as long as it pleased her. I ordered her. A man's the head of his own family. But she wouldn't obey me.'

'You sent her away!' the boy saw the truth of it, and he was gripped by a hatred of his father's masculine authority.

'I told her to come back into the house or leave the house,' his father admitted.

'And where does the darkie come in?' the boy asked, feeling a black cloud between himself and his father.

'There's no darkie,' said his father wearily, resting from his walking up and down and standing with his hands wide apart on the kitchen table as he looked across at his bitter son with unhappy eyes. 'Your mother's driver was a West Indian, that was all. She was always on the same shift with him. They got on but that was all. He's been in this house since your mother went away. He tried to help. He's got his own wife and family. She never ran away with him. That's nonsense. People said that because they were pals but it's not true. Any conductress on the buses is pally with her driver.'

'But you must know where she is,' the boy complained. Now the darkie was explained he didn't matter. What mattered was that his mother had been allowed to stay away. 'You could find out easily enough. You could find her depot and get her address.'

'She changed her depot.'

'You could find out.'

'I'm not going to run after anybody,' his father shouted. 'She made her choice. She wants to work, well, she can work. If she wouldn't agree her place is here, then this is no place for her.'

He stared down at the table, his eyes on a dirty plate of ham and eggs.

'I'm sorry,' he conceded to his son. 'Maybe she's sorry. I don't know. But there's some things can never be put right. But that's a lot of nonsense about a darkie. There was nothing between them. Just because she left me when she was working with a coloured driver some people liked to make up a story and they ended up believing it themselves. But it's only a story. That wasn't the trouble. Your mother never had that fault. It was just she said she could help the house by working and I told her she could help it better by being the housewife. I told her if I couldn't keep a wife I didn't deserve a wife. My mother never had to go out to work. And she had a hard time of it. My father never had the job I have. That's what it was about.'

'I want my mother back,' the boy cried, but only to himself. He couldn't say it aloud.

The father waved a hand over the dejected tea-table.

'Come on! You get this table redd and get these dishes washed and stop greeting.'

'You did what was wrong,' the boy muttered, moving to his chore with the speed of a snail. 'I'm not greeting.'

'Maybe I did,' his father answered. 'Well, you're damn near greeting. You'll have to learn not to. It doesn't get ye anywhere. Maybe I did, but sometimes you've got to do what's wrong to be right.'

The boy stopped listening. He was thinking. What kind of a house was this, where he had to do the washing and cleaning and shopping and make up the laundry and do the cooking? If his mother had stayed at home he could have lived like other boys instead of having to live like a girl. A rebellion was gathering in him. The road to open insurrection appeared before him as he lay snivelling in bed that night, and when he was doing his paper-rake the next evening he loitered on the stairhead and looked at the advertising pages of the *Evening Citizen*. If his mother had gone away because she wanted to get more money then a promise of plenty would surely bring her back. Money seemed to be the eternal question and the universal answer.

He was the only member of the Brotherhood still working after school hours. Everybody else had given up delivering papers, milk, and rolls, and going round with the fruit-lorry or the man with the float of coal-briquettes. Why should they break the law forbidding schoolboys to work, just to earn a few bob, when they had pounds for the lifting? They despised the tips they had once gloated over, but Frank Garson still depended on them. His father gave him little, and what he gave him he gave irregularly. The boy had no grudge. He handed over his wages every week with pride. He couldn't help being faithful. It was the way God had made him. But he kept all his tips. They were his own the way he saw it.

And now he pouted thoughtfully, childish brows furrowed, as he read the small ad rates. His father never bought an evening paper, so he felt he could proceed in safety. The prices interested him. It was like sending a telegram. Intimations (Births, Marriages, Deaths) two and six a line; Property, three shillings. Holiday Guide, three shillings, Situations Vacant, three shillings, Personal (Private), four shillings, and Personal (Trade), four and six a line. He wrote his appeal four times on a sheet of jotter-paper before he got it right, and asked Percy to let him use the portable typewriter to type it out fair. He knew Percy was too much of a gentleman to ask what he was typing. He did it in the cellar, alone in a corner, before the start of a mid-week service. GARSON, he jabbed with one finger, and went slowly on, searching the keyboard grimly for the necessary letters. HELEN, he assembled. *Come home. Admit was wrong. Money no bother. Frank has loads. Bob.*

He knew his father's Christian name was Robert and he supposed his mother must have called him Bob, but he couldn't hear her in his mind. She seemed to belong to that other world he had lived in when he was young. Now he was old, living in a real world, a hard, solid world where things were enemies. He felt he was trying to call up a ghost. But for all his doubts he went to the *Citizen* office alone, wandered round fearlessly till he found the right counter, and tholed the squint glance of the clerk who counted the words. It cost him sixteen shillings. He paid it with a pound note Percy had thrust on him to make up for not giving him better support against Savage. He took it as a gift from Percy. It came privately from Percy's pocket, not from the chest in front of the Brotherhood, so he claimed before his conscience that he still hadn't taken any share of the hoard. It would be time enough to demand his rights in it when his mother came home.

Helen Garson was working the Yoker–Auchenshuggle route with a new driver two nights later. Her husband was right when he had told their son the West Indian had nothing to do with her leaving home, but she still kept up with her old driver. She had to have some friends, and she visited the West Indian and his wife about once a month and had the distraction of sitting for an evening with a happy family where she felt welcome. Apart from that, she was a lonely woman, determined to like living alone. She bashed on, doing her best not to grieve for her man and her boy and her old home in Bethel Street, and she was doing as well as could be expected until two things upset her.

The first thing was Percy got on her bus about ten o'clock at the Hielenman's Umbrella, and the sight of him reminded her of Bethel Street and that reminded her of all she was stubbornly forgetting. He wasn't alone. He was escorting a girl, a long-legged, wide-skirted, pony-tailed, large-breasted, gum-chewing, big-eyed teenager. She knew him at once but he didn't know her. He was only a boy at school the last time she saw him and now he was like a young man, so stylishly dressed that he looked slightly odd. He sat in the back seat upstairs, holding his girl's hand and their brows touched as they mooned together the whole journey. She grued a little at the sight of them, for she was an anti-romantic, and the girl seemed to her anyway a stupid-faced doll who would be none the worse for a scrubbing and a haircut. Percy wore the gawky look he had always worn, but he was wearing it with a difference now. Instead of the gawkiness of a backward schoolboy he was showing the gawkiness of the male animal reaching towards the female for the first time and not quite sure how to set about it. She was glad to see them get off at Partick Cross. They linked arms when they stepped on the pavement and she sent a sniff of contempt after them.

'He never was very bright,' she thought as she rattled upstairs and down, breezily collecting her fares and tyrannizing the passengers as only a Glasgow bus-conductress can. 'He was aye kind of glaikit and he doesn't seem to have improved any. Seeing a girl home at his age! And where did he get the money to dress like that? I bet he hasn't got two pennies to rub together. I don't know how they do it nowadays, courting before they're right out of school. And he's left himself with some journey back home too, the silly fool! It's no' a girlfriend he's got, it's a penpal, staying that distance from him. The things they'll do when they think they're in love! Ah well, they'll get a rude awakening one day and hell mend them. All they think of is sex, they're sex-mad, these kids nowadays. The way she sat pushing her breasts up to him, must have been pads she was wearing, the little bitch. Ach, they'll learn one day, when they've rent to pay and light to pay and coal to get and weans to feed and clothe.'

She was so annoyed with Percy for coming on her bus and raising ghosts that she made up for it by tearing him and his girl to pieces all the way along Dumbarton Road to the end of the line.

Then at the lying-in time there the second thing happened to upset her. It was worse than the first, much worse. She saw her son's small ad in the paper. It was just a piece of bad luck, for she never bought an evening paper. She happened to see this one because on the last lap of the journey she left her bus for a moment and bought two pokes of chips, one for her driver and one for herself. It was a bad shift they were on, and they had got the habit of buying chips to give them a filling bite between the end of one run and the start of another. The Italian who owned the fish-and-chip shop always served her at once, no matter who else was waiting, and she was back on her bus before the passengers knew she had left it. She handed the chips in to the driver. They would keep warmer in his cabin than on her platform.

When the empty bus lay at the terminus she sat downstairs facing her driver, and since he was the strong silent type she occupied herself reading one of the sheets of newspaper Enrico had wrapped round the two pokes.

'That's last night's paper you're reading,' her driver remarked detachedly, recognizing a headline.

'You don't expect him to wrap the chips in tonight's paper, do you?' she answered crossly, and turned the page.

She gazed amongst the births, marriages and deaths, delving into the chips with coin-grimed fingers while her driver ate his way steadily through the other poke.

'Harry didn't put much salt on them the night,' he commented.

'You're hell of a talkative all of a sudden,' she retorted. 'Just you go get them tomorrow night then and you tell him that!'

'I don't like a lot of salt,' he said, after brooding over her answer.

'I see there's an awful lot of shorthand-typists wanted,' she muttered.

'Ach, they're no' well paid they girls,' he said. 'You're getting more than them, even without your overtime.'

She turned from the situations vacant to the ads for second-hand furniture, vacuum cleaners, fur coats and tape-recorders.

'What do people buy all these things for if they're that damned hard-up they've got to sell them?' she asked peevishly. 'They buy them the one day and want to sell them the next. Aye, they're all as good as new according to the advert. Aye, I don't think!'

She was just going to crumple the paper and dump it in the litter-bin at the bus stop when she saw her married name in small capitals at the foot of a column.

The whole thing was a sheer fluke, a pure accident, a

fortuitous concatenation of circumstances. That Enrico
had happened to use that page to put round the chips and
that she happened to see the ad at all, was the kind of
coincidence that happens every day in the real world that
God created but is condemned as far-fetched in the work
of a novelist, as if God wasn't the greatest novelist of all.

She frowned. She scowled. She stared. She read it three
times and squinted over at her driver. He was lighting the
remainder of the cigarette he had started at the other end
of the route. He didn't seem to be watching her and she
didn't tell him what she had seen. She wasn't a woman
given to confidences. She tore out the ad roughly and
stuffed it quickly in her pocket.

'Are you going after another job?' her driver asked
casually.

'You don't miss much, do you?' she answered, crum-
pling the paper viciously.

In a little while she was busy collecting fares again as her
bus weaved east, and when the top deck was full and she
had five standing downstairs she stopped anybody else
from boarding, barring them with the lucid command
always given by Glasgow bus-conductresses in such circumstances, 'Come on, get off!'

She was too harassed to think any more of Percy, who
had anyway been displaced by the advertisement she had
seen, and she didn't know that when she passed Partick
Cross he was standing with his girl in the back-close of a
grey tenement north of her route. The back-close is that
part of the close that lies beyond the stairway to the flats
and leads to the back-court. Since it usually turns at an
angle from the front-close and can't be seen from the street
it is the site of countless Glasgow courtships and seduc-
tions. Some write of beds and sofas, some sing of the green
cornfields and acres of rye, some tumble panting in the
hay, but Glasgow's sons and lovers have the back-close.

For all he had a pride in possessing the refinement of a
true poet Percy was insensible to the drabness of the
setting. He was in a state. It didn't matter that the midden

was only fifteen paces away across the back-court nor that the brown paint of the close was chipped, peeled, and scarred with obscure incisions by the pocket-knives of schoolboys. He was exalted. He had been aching for a girl and now he had one. He had one all to himself, all alone, against the wall though not against her will. He was trembling on the brink. His curiosity was as wide and burning as his ignorance, but it was the way girls dressed disturbed him more than the girls themselves. Indeed the girls he saw every day left him inwardly as cold as a Scots summer. It was advertisements for nylons, brassieres and girdles made his heart quicken, toilet soaps and deodorants told him of breasts and armpits, and foam petticoats under wide skirts whispered to him a warming suggestion of the unseen thighs above the calves and the instep arched by high heels. They all created a mysterious world of elegance, freshness, cleanliness and softness that he longed to enter and embrace, a world not inhabited by the girls he saw every day. But Sophy had long legs and a wide skirt, she had a bust like a girl in a television advert, her hair was glossy, she smelt of soap and something else, so it was Sophy he wanted.

Of course, his curiosity concerned anatomy as well as underwear. Faces never moved him, for the face was always visible. But he would saunter slowly past the window of a ladies' gown shop in Sauchiehall Street, squinting in a fluster at the naked wax models of women, and pretend he wasn't looking at the breasts, belly and thighs at all, his big feet pointing north and south as he ambled west. Not sure of what he had seen he would turn back at a decent distance and stroll past the window again, his head hot with guilt, but he never dared stop and stare and get it right once and for all.

And now at last he had a girl of his own. Now at last he could come to grips with the problem and be satisfied with the answer. He had survived the first stage of saying goodnight at the bus-stop. He had been given a pass-mark and allowed to enter the second degree of saying goodnight at the close-mouth. Tonight Sophy seemed ready to let him graduate. She let him edge her into the back-close and when they were there she put her handbag on the ground to leave her hands free if he tried to make love to her.

She was a very junior waitress in a cheap restaurant, a rough eating-house where he went for a midday meal when he first gave up his job. Then he began going there for morning coffee because it wasn't so busy before lunch, then for afternoon tea too when it was quiet again, and he could sit and look at her in peace. She couldn't help getting to know him by sight, and when she moved around and Percy sat admiring her bright legs and her hips under her black dress she answered him with a little smirk of a smile over her shoulder. He spoke to her at last with all the confidence in the world, depending on the money in the cellar to see him through all difficulties. Without telling her a direct lie he let her think he was a student. He thought that would explain why he could spend so much time just sitting around. He let her see he had money by tipping her absurdly every day and making a show of opening his wallet to pay his bill so that she could see the wad of notes inside.

Naturally she agreed at once to go out with him, but for all his money he never took her anywhere special. He had the money all right, but not the knowledge gained only from experience how to spend it. He was intimidated by the uppish look of expensive places, with a commissionaire at the door, and he never dared cross the threshold. A frugal eater and a non-drinker, he could move only within a narrow circle of cafes and cinemas. It didn't bother Sophy. A cinema in town and a box of chocolates were luxury enough to her. She wouldn't have been comfortable drinking cocktails in a hotel lounge. Percy suited her, except when he told her he was a poet. Still, she got over it quickly. She supposed a boy had a right to at least one oddity and she believed poets were great lovers. She waited for the great lover when they embraced in the back-close.

As for Percy, he had dreamed of this hour and this solitude so long and so often that the reality of it was but a dim substitute for the ideal. Yet because it was the nearest he had come to his desire he felt himself on the verge of great deeds and great discoveries. He believed he was thrilled, and he was. He was wandering in the pathways of the moon, guided by a celestial light that illumed her remote beauty while he drowned in the deep mournfulness of a love not yet made known and satisfied. He gazed at Sophy's brow and cheeks and the curve of her throat and his worship grew and grew. He was in bliss. The light of consciousness went out and his heart vibrated in a fecund darkness that promised the unutterable satisfaction he deserved.

With an inscrutable smile Sophy spoke.

'Did you ever think of writing a pome about me?' she asked in a voice as if some tender soul imprisoned within her was asking the question. After all, she was only seventeen, though she had been kissed often enough. 'I mean, when you're writing your pomes do you ever do one to me? Just how you see me, I mean, when you sit watching me serve the tables and saying what you think about me?'

'Well, I did start something,' he admitted, red-faced but encouraged by her interest in his work. 'It's a sort of song. You know, what Rabbie Burns used to write, that kinda thing.'

He chanted huskily.

'*Doh, soh, me, re-doh.*'

After a nervous swallow he went on, incanting his composition to her in the development of a simple melody.

> Darling, you must know
> How I dream of you
> Morning, noon and night,
> You make the world seem bright,
> Fill me with delight.
> Sweetheart, kiss me gaily

As I play my ukelele,
Then just hold me tight,
Hold me tight and love me right,
And be mine tonight.

'That's lovely,' she beamed the brightness of her smile
in the dim corner while his hands fidgeted up and down
her flanks. 'I like the way it rhymes. You could sell that.'

'Oh, I don't write for money,' he said proudly.

'But it doesn't say much about me. I mean, it doesn't
describe me. I'm just not there, am I?'

'Well, that's not the point,' he defended his lyric. 'You
see, a poet writes about his emotions, not so much what he
sees like, it's what he feels. That's what matters to him,
what he feels.'

He felt her hips and back with wandering hands and she
squirmed in a movement ambiguously encouraging and
disapproving.

'Yes, but there's not many girls with hair like me, or my
complexion,' she suggested. 'Then there's my eyes. Did
you never think of writing about my eyes, for instance?'

'No, it wasn't so much your eyes,' he answered, a crease
in his brow as if he were thinking.

'Well, what was it then?' she persisted. 'What was it first
attracted you to me?'

'It was the way you walked, you know, the way you go
round the tables,' he said. He didn't want to say it was her
legs. He talked around it.

She made a low humming sound of acknowledgement,
staring over his shoulder at the scribbling on the opposite
wall as if she was trying to read what was there.

'Did you ever hear of Shelley?' he asked. He felt he had a
duty to educate her. 'He was a great poet if you like, a
rebel. That's what I am. I don't agree with the world as it
is today. I mean to say. I've read all his works. Do you
know him?'

'No, I can't say I do,' she conceded. His hands were at
rest now he was going to teach her all about Shelley, and

she wasn't sure if she would have preferred his tongue to be at rest instead.

'There's a smashing wee pome of his I learned off by heart,' he said relentlessly. 'Would you like to hear it?'

'I don't mind I'm sure,' she said patiently. She had been out with all kinds of boys in her short sweet life. She had learnt to be accommodating.

'See!' he declared abruptly, and she was reminded of a Scots comic she had once heard say, 'See? See me! I don't like fish!'

He gulped and went on in a canting voice.

> The mountains kiss the heavens
> And the waves clasp one another.
> And the moonbeams kiss the sea.
> What is all this kissing worth
> If you don't kiss me?

'That's nice, I like that,' she breathed, and they kissed. He wasn't very good at it and she felt he needed practice.

'That's Shelley, that is,' he broke off. He couldn't kiss and talk and he had to talk. He was getting scared at his own state. He was there on the brink, afraid the dip would be too cold. Talking would put off the embarrassing need for action. 'It's called love's philosophy.'

'Oh, yes, of course,' she answered intelligently.

'It goes on,' he said.

And he went on, his hands on her hips inside her open coat while hers dangled daintily over his narrow shoulders.

> The fountains mingle with the river
> And the river with the ocean,
> The winds of heaven mix for ever
> With a rare emotion.
> Nothing in the world is single,
> All things by a law divine
> In one another's being mingle,
> So why not you with mine?

He ended throatily, appealingly.

'I don't like that,' she said severely, staring beyond him again. 'I don't think it's very nice.'

She wriggled. He was pressing too hard against her. She squirmed loose and stepped past him, right shoulder forward, her body very straight and her head up as if she was doing the side-stepping movement in a reel.

He managed to grab the tail of her coat just as she reached the bend in the close under the gaslight. She was halted. Percy tugged and she pulled and they wrestled. They finished up panting in the back-close again, only this time they were against the opposite wall. So Percy won. Or Sophy let him win, for who would dare argue that the parallelogram of forces represents the resultant of a lovers' scuffle?

'Don't be daft,' he complained, standing over her with his long arms on either side of her drooping shoulders so that she was barred from escape. 'What did you want to run away like that for?'

''Cause I didn't like what you were insinuating,' she said firmly.

'I wasn't insinuating nothing,' he answered, all hurt. 'It was Shelley I was saying.'

'I still don't like it,' she tossed her head.

'But there's nothing wrong in it,' he argued. 'It's perfectly natural. That's what Shelley was saying. If two people love each other like you and me—'

His arms came closer in his eagerness to confine her.

'I wish you'd lay off the subject,' she muttered, scowling darkly in the dimness.

'Why?' he demanded, and his arms went round her like the coils of a boa-constrictor. Inspired by a confused recollection of a novel by Lawrence he had tried to read he was proud of his wholesome maturity and maleness and he longed to reach the dark roots of her being and quicken her. 'We should act according to our impulses, it's the only natural thing to do, if a man's to be a man.'

'I thought you was a nice boy,' she complained, struggling again.

He was worse than he had been. The wrestling-match at the bend of the close had raised his temperature to boiling point and he was in a state again.

'Oh, Sophy, please,' he groaned, an asthmatic bull in a grassless meadow. 'I think you're wonderful. I love you. I want you.'

She didn't even pretend to be impressed. She sent a little signal of scepticism through her nose, a maidenly snort of disbelief, but he blundered on. He felt he was face to face with death, the death of his hopes for an initiation with Sophy. He didn't want to die, ever, and he was panic-stricken in case he died wondering.

'Come on, be a sport, let me!' he pleaded, as hoarse as an NCO after his first day taking a squad in the square.

He wound round her to crush her squirming body in a heroic hug, but she ducked, side-stepped, and stood free of him. He was bang up against the scarred brown paintwork on the wall while Sophy stood at his side with one hand on her hip and the other caressing her pony-tail. But he still wasn't beaten. He was only provoked. He went on blundering.

'I can make it worth your while,' he declared, staggering from the unwelcoming wall. He delved into the pocket inside his new sports jacket (best Harris tweed, heather mixture pattern, fourteen guineas in Carswell's), fumbled with his pocket book, opened it trembling, and brought out a five-pound note, another five-pound note, waved them before her astounded young eyes.

'You can have them! You can have them both! I don't care, there's plenty more where they came from!'

He was teetering there, certain he was going to gain her, and then her little hand darted. First in a vertical flash it scattered his precious wallet and then it came back on the horizontal plane and slapped him hard across the face. (Mrs Maguire on the ground floor stood with the teapot over her cup and breathed nervously, 'What was that?')

Percy put his hand to his cheek as if to make sure it was really his face she had smacked.

'Well, I like that!' Sophy flared. 'So that's the kind of girl you think I am! Just right here and now, eh? Just like that? Do you think I'm mad? And if you've got that kind of money to throw away what the hell are you bothering about me at all for, tell me that! You don't need to come slobbering round me if you want to buy it. You know where to go or it's high bloody time you did. Well, I like that! You and your po'try. And I don't know what you're doing with all that money anyway, a fella that's no' working. I've a good mind to tell my brother about you.'

Her inflated little bosom heaved, she flared and sputtered at him. Then she picked up her handbag and marched off. No side-slip this time, but a military quickstep, and Percy was left alone with his smarting face. He stood bleak and frozen in the twilight of the back-close, heard Sophy's high heels tattoo upstairs, heard her knock at her door on the second storey of the three, heard the door open and the door bang. She was gone, gone for ever. He nearly wept. But perhaps her brother was in. There was no time to waste in tears. He picked up his wallet in a flurry, put the fivers back inside as he hurried through the front-close and ran to the nearest bus-stop.

It was all very well for Shelley. He could say it and get it printed in his immortal works and even in the *Golden Treasury*. But Shelley didn't have to deal with these narrow-minded waitresses who had no appreciation of love's philosophy. He worked hard on a grudge against Sophy as he waited splay-footed and nervous for a bus to come, one hand inside his jacket fondling his wallet as a talisman. He didn't care which bus he got so long as it took him away from the scene of his Waterloo. He suddenly felt hungry, and a shattering thought lashed his already turbulent mind.

'I'll have to find somewhere else to eat now!' he lamented to the bus-stop standard, and tutted to the night air at the nuisance of it. He felt himself wronged and humiliated.

After the way she had mentioned her brother he would have to disappear for good so far as Sophy was concerned. He had made a mistake.

'Ach, maybe she was right,' he thought generously arguing against his fabricated grudge, for he took a pride in always seeing at least two sides to any question. 'Maybe it was a mistake to offer her money. But I was desperate. I should have kept it till after.'

By the time he was speeding home on the bus his brain was empty. It was tired of fretting about Sophy and the absurd failure to seduce her. The stranger drifted in to fill the vacuum.

'Oh, dear! There's him to worry about!' he remembered in misery. 'He's a menace, he is! I wonder where he's got to.'

Stumbling on a rhyme he brooded about a poem in which a stranger was a danger. He thought out the first two lines.

> Within life's vale of tears I face one danger
> That makes my blood run cold, a questioning
>   stranger—

But he couldn't go on. His headache began to bother him again, his stomach quivered, turned, tied itself in painful knots. He was frightened again. Sophy's brother and the stranger merged into one cloud darkening his future, disturbing his peace of mind.

Mrs Phinn's daily duties as a school-cleaner were in two spells. She went in at six in the morning before the school opened and worked till a quarter to nine, and she went back at four o'clock in the afternoon when the school was dismissed and worked till six in the evening. She did it with a grudge. She hated being a poor widow who had to do a menial job for a few shillings to pay her way, and a hardup way it was. She resented being under the eye of the janitor for clocking in in the morning and clocking out at tea-time, because she despised him as an interloper. He would never have got the job if her husband hadn't been found dead in the cellar the day after his brother was killed in a car-crash on the Glasgow–Edinburgh road, the no-torious A8. And he didn't strike her as being a janitor in the true tradition. He wasn't like her husband, serious, clever and experienced. He was a flippant, scruffy, in-expert little man, always calling in a plumber or a joiner for jobs her man would have done himself as a matter of course. And he knew next to nothing about janitor's stock or janitor's requisitions. He could never say, as her hus-band had said in all truth, that although he was only the janitor he was just as important to the school as any headmaster. Her husband knew his job. This fellow didn't. He didn't even know his place. He was chatty with the headmaster and familiar with the cleaners.

'Well, with some of them,' she complained to Percy, not that he was listening. 'That Mrs Winters in particular is never out of his room. I don't see how she can be doing her job right, the time she spends sitting in there drinking tea. They think I don't know. She's some widow, that one.

Made up to kill. Out at six in the morning with her powder
on thick and her lipstick on like a chorus girl. I don't know
what he thinks he's up to. She's no' as young as she makes
out to be. Her hair's dyed for one thing. And he's got a
wife of his own anyway. She calls him by his first name.
Imagine that! None of the cleaners ever dared call your
father by his first name when he was on duty. But this little
upstart never wears a hat. Your father used to polish the
badge in his hat every night. He looked the part. He knew
how to hold himself. He knew how to speak to cleaners.
But all these things is dying out now. Everybody's equal.
It's all wrong.'

She crossed to the main gate at six o'clock the morning
after her son had kept his chastity and her body trembled
with longing for the sleep the alarm had broken. Yet it was a
fine summer morning, the sky above the tall tenements was
blue and unclouded, and the pigeons were already talking to
each other in the high roof of the sandstone school. She
grudged feeling it was good to be alive after all, but she felt
it, and her awakening senses granted to her weary body that
it was better to be up and doing on such a lovely morning
than lying in a lazy bed. She was just coming really awake,
approaching the gate, when a man at the corner of Bethel
Street and Tulip Place whistled to her. She was affronted.
She was wearing old stockings, her bare head showed her
greying hair, and anyway six o'clock in the morning, even if
it was a lovely morning, was no time for a man to be
accosting a woman. Her head reared and her small thin
body stiffened, dignity and alarm fighting for control of her.
She glanced obliquely at the whistler, just to see what kind
of man he was. He came quickly towards her, beckoning her
over anxiously. She stood still and waited. She wasn't going
to walk to any man. Let him come to her. The janitor would
hear her if she screamed.

'Mrs Phinn?' he asked civilly.

She didn't deny it.

'I'm the man that drove the car,' he said. 'You know,
Sammy's car.'

She looked at him hard. She didn't believe in ghosts at any time, certainly not at six o'clock on a summer morning.

'He was killed,' she said. 'They both were killed, Sammy and the man that was driving him.'

'Aye, on the Friday, but I mean on the Thursday. It was me that drove the car on the Thursday, that's what I mean, on the Thursday night.'

He smiled wisely to her, showing two yellow fangs, but she was more taken by a pink line from his nose to his jawbone, the scar of a razor-slash.

'I don't know what you're talking about, I'm sorry,' she answered, her head up and back from him as if he was a bad egg she had just cracked.

'Who are ye kidding, missis?' he complained, not so civil now. 'You know damn fine what Sammy was up to the Thursday night afore he was killed.'

'He was up to no good if I know him,' she snapped. 'He always was up to no good.'

'He was up to a lot of good that night,' the stranger smiled again. 'And he saw your man on the Friday morning afore he went to Edinburgh. You know that, don't you?'

'I'm afraid I don't,' she snubbed him. 'I can assure you my man wanted as little to do as possible with his brother even if they was twins.'

'Did Hamish no' tell you what he did with it all?' he kept at her.

'All what?' she asked impatiently. 'I've got my work to go to, I can't stand here wasting time talking to you, when I don't even know who you are anyway.'

'I've told you who I am,' he said, his hands out with the palms up. 'I'm one of Sammy's crowd. It was me drove the car, and I got nothing for it. No, he tells me to wait, just wait. It'll be all right in a month or two. Then he goes and gets killed and here's me still waiting. Somebody must know. You must know. Because Sammy saw your man right after it.'

'I assure you I don't know,' she insisted, very dignified with him, talking with a bogus accent to let him know she was a respectable woman who knew nothing of her criminal brother-in-law. 'I can assure you I've no idea what you're talking about.'

She looked towards the gate and wondered if she could run that far and get into the school before this strange man assaulted her.

'Don't give us that,' he said roughly, his palm lightly under her elbow, ready to clutch her if she moved. 'You must know. Look, Sammy was coming back from Edinburgh when he had that smash, wasn't he? And he'd been to see the jelly-man, hadn't he? Don't argue. I know. And he gave him fifty quid on account, but that was in fivers from another bank. So he's still waiting too. The bloke with him that was killed, he went inside with Sammy, but he had nothing on him when he was killed. There's nobody had nothing. So where is it? It's a hell of a lot of money to be lying about.'

'If you're trying to insinuate that my brother-in-law stole some money and gave it to my husband to keep for him, you're mistaken,' Mrs Phinn locuted at him. 'And I can assure you I know nothing about any money. Do I look as if I had anything to do with money? Do you think I'd be out here at this time in the morning going to sweep floors if I had any money?'

'That's no' the point,' he countered. 'You couldny use the kind of money I'm talking about. It would only scare folk like you. You wouldny know whit to do wi' it. All you've got to do is tell me what Sammy fixed up wi' Hamish and I can take it off your hands and give you plenty o' money you'd be glad to use.'

'Money, money, money!' she cried. 'I've told you. If you're trying to tell me Sammy Phinn passed a lot of money to my man you're up the wrong close. As a matter of fact many's the time my Hamish lent his brother money, money he never got back.'

'Oh aye, they were thick,' the stranger granted. 'Your man was good to his twin. Sammy told me that himself.'

'Aye, they were twins but quite different,' Mrs Phinn said proudly. 'My Hamish was a good man. He was never the gambler and the drinker and the thief his brother was. It was Sammy broke old Granny Phinn's heart. In and out of jail, in and out of jail.'

'Look, missis,' said the stranger aggrievedly. 'Stop kidding me. You know fine it was Sammy did the Finnieston bank that Thursday.'

Mrs Phinn let out a little scream and her rough hand went to her flat chest and then fluttered to her mouth in alarm. 'Sammy Phinn never did a bank in his life,' she cried. 'He wouldn't dare. Wee sweetie-shops and pubs was his level. A bank! He could no more have did a bank than fly in the air.'

'He did that one all right,' the stranger answered. 'The sweetie shops and the pubs all went to experience, missis. A man's got to learn. He took a year working on it. Got it organized.'

'I don't believe you,' said Mrs Phinn.

'He brought out forty-five thousand pound,' the stranger bashed on, clutching her elbow now though she was too shocked to move. 'He had it in two suitcases and there wasn't more than three quid in his pocket the day he was killed. It's a lot o' money, missis. It canny just have walked.'

'I'm sorry I can't help you,' Mrs Phinn panted. She was frightened. 'I never knew a thing about forty-five thousand pound, I can tell you that. And what's more I don't want to know about it. I'd rather have a clear conscience and my night's sleep than all your money.'

'You keep your conscience and I'll rest content wi' the money,' the stranger bargained. 'The point is I haveny got it. I think you've got it. Sammy had it all in two suitcases when I drove the car away that night. But we couldny stop and divide it at Anderston Cross at two o'clock in the morning, could we? Sammy said we was just to wait till things got quiet. He got out of the car at the Saltmarket and I know he took a taxi your way. I heard him. He went

to see Hamish wi' the money. The next thing I hears he's
deid and there's nae money on him. Nothing in the bank,
nothing in the post-office, nothing in his digs. Missis, this
is serious. Hamish must have said something to you.'

'No, I'm afraid you're wrong,' Mrs Phinn told him
sincerely. She was beginning to think the man was
mad, and she felt less frightened. He could be humoured.
'Hamish never mentioned that kind of money to me, and I
can assure you—'

'You're a bloody assurance society, you are!' the stranger interrupted her peevishly. She was sure there was a
mad look in his eyes the way he glared at her.

'Yes, I can assure you,' she sailed on, not at all put out
by his rudeness. She was used to the way Percy talked to
her. 'I can assure you my man wasn't the sort of man to get
mixed up in bank robberies. Bank robberies! For goodness
sake! Huh-hm!'

She gave one of her special snorts, the violent kind that
jarred Percy's nerves.

They glowered at each other, neither yielding, and Mrs
Phinn jerked her elbow free from the stranger's clutch.

'Why don't you just go home and go to your bed?' she
suggested. 'You've been watching the telly too much.'

'Oh, Jesus Christ!' the stranger cried in pain. He seemed
on the point of weeping.

'Now, I don't like blasphemy,' said Mrs Phinn. 'I'm not
accustomed to it. If you must swear go and swear somewhere else.'

The stranger stared at her, shaking his head sorrow-
fully, and she was sure she saw tears glisten in his crafty
eyes.

'Missis, are you mad?' he whispered. 'Come on, don't
act it! This is serious. I'm only talking to you for your own
good. I was just the driver but I'm entitled to my share. I'll
play fair wi' you but there's other folk starting to wonder
and if they get on to you they'll chiv you as soon as look at
you. I'm telling you, missis.'

'I'm sorry, I've got my work to go to,' said Mrs Phinn

calmly. 'I told you, I've got to work for my living. We canny all go about robbing banks and living in the lap of luxury. Forty thousand pound! Did ye ever hear the like!'

'Forty-five thousand pound,' the stranger corrected her dourly.

She looked at him pityingly and tutted.

'To a penny?' she asked sarcastically.

'I was talking to your son the other night,' he said abruptly. 'A big fella with splay feet.'

'You can leave my son's feet out of it,' Mrs Phinn objected with dignity. 'He canny help his feet. At least he's no' a wee Glasgow bauchle like you.'

'Aye, all right,' said the stranger huffily. 'I'd rather be a Glasgow bauchle than a big drip like him. Oh, la-de-da. Called after Percy the poet says he. He could do wi' a haircut at that.'

'He never told me,' said Mrs Phinn.

'That's funny,' said the stranger. 'Maybe it's him that knows and he's keeping something back from you.'

'My boy's a big simple soul,' said Mrs Phinn proudly. 'He wouldn't do anything that's wrong. He was never brought up to it.'

'I could see he was kind of dumb,' the stranger agreed neutrally. 'He talks a lot but he doesn't say very much. He's not all that bright I don't think. That's why I never told him what I'm telling you. I wanted to see if he knew anything first. But I don't think he knew a thing.'

'He knows as much as I know then,' said Mrs Phinn.

'Unless he was acting it?' the stranger suggested.

'I can assure you he had nothing to act about,' said Mrs Phinn.

The stranger brooded into Mrs Phinn's thin sour face before he spoke again.

'You see, missis, when Sammy left us at the Saltmarket he told us he'd cellar the money till it was safe to divide it. Aye, he was the boss. He liked acting the big shot. Wouldny trust us. No' to spend it daft-like right away I mean. No, he'd take care of it. Don't yous worry, he said.

Ye can trust me. I'll cellar it safe and sound where it'll
never be found. Now what did he mean, cellar it? The only
bloke Sammy saw when he left us was your Hamish, and
your Hamish has a cellar in the school there, hasn't he?'

'My Hamish is dead,' Mrs Phinn reminded him with a
widow's proud sorrow.

'Aye, but the cellar's no',' the stranger commented.

'Yes, the cellar is,' she retorted. She was a contrary
woman. She wasn't going to have this layabout telling her
about the school cellar. It had been the bane of her
husband's last years, it was in such a state, and she wasn't
going to have it talked about by any stranger. 'That cellar
hasn't been used for twenty years or more. It isn't a cellar
at all now, not since they stopped the steam heating.'

'But there's a door there in Tulip Place,' the stranger
waved a hand. 'That's the door to the cellar, i'n't it?'

'That door?' said Mrs Phinn, sneering at his mistake.
'That door's blind. There's a brick wall behind it. Has
been since the school went all electrical. That's where they
delivered the coal in the old days.'

She didn't know her contrary mixture of fact and fiction
was a repeat of Percy's story to the stranger, and she didn't
understand why he seemed to sag and surrender. She
supposed his early morning fit of madness was leaving
him.

'Ach well, I can only keep on trying,' he muttered,
fishing out a cigarette end from his pocket and lighting it
with his head to one side and his lips pouting. 'I'd ha' been
on to it sooner only I had to go to Manchester for thirty
days.'

'Oh, I see,' she said sympathetically.

In the local idiom 'to go to Manchester' meant to go to
jail. She knew that. Her husband had often told her of
children who told their teacher their father couldn't sign a
form for free meals or free clothes because he was in
Manchester. The locution saved everyone embarrassment.

'What did they get you for?' she asked softly, just to let
him see she knew the language.

'Loitering with intent. You see, a man like me. A known character. Wan o' Sammy's crowd. But the crowd's no' the same now. We miss Sammy. He put it on a bit but he'd got something. There's no denying it. He took a year rehearsing the Finnieston job, his first real big job. He had a great future, so he had, the same man. Then he had to go and get killed, the stupid bastard. But he had something, oh aye, he had something!'

He smoked and looked over bitterly at the grim three-storeyed school.

'Forty-five thousand pound, that's what he had,' he muttered. 'It canny just have went up in smoke.'

'Come on, Mrs Phinn! You're late!' a voice called through the mild morning air. The janitor was at the front gate, blithe and debonair. Without his hat on, Mrs Phinn noted disapprovingly.

'I'm just coming,' she sang out sedately.

'You can see your boyfriend when you've done your morning's work,' the janitor shouted over to her jovially.

Mrs Phinn glared at him, the stranger scuttled swiftly, and the pigeons on the roof quarrelled noisily. It was a lovely morning. She went into the school, took off her coat, tied a scarf round her head, and started to tackle the classrooms on the top flat.

She saw Percy at tea-time. He came ambling in, splay-footed as usual, round-shouldered to keep his head clear of the ceiling, and looked remarkably untired for a youth who claimed to be doing a hard day's work every day. He sat playing with an Alsatian pup he had bought after he bought his motor-bike. He told his mother it was a stray that had followed him home, and she kept on looking at the small ads in the evening paper in case the owner advertised. There might be a reward for returning it.

'Even ten bob,' she said. 'It's always something.'

'Ten bob!' Percy smiled cunningly. He had paid fifteen pounds for the pup. It had a pedigree. More than I have, he thought bitterly when the dealer told him, and he felt it was another injustice.

'Who would pay ten bob for a wee thing like this?'
He chuckled at his private joke.

'Aye, you bring it here but it's me that's got to feed it
and look after it,' his mother complained. 'It's me that's
got to take it out for a walk every morning when you're no'
here and I could be having a lie-down on my bed. I'm up
before six every morning, don't you forget.'

'You don't give me much of a chance to forget it,' he
muttered, pretending to throttle the lively pup. He called
it Boatswain.

'That's a daft name for a dug,' said his mother.
'What does that mean? Boatswain! Did ye ever hear
the likes!'

'That was the name Lord Byron gave his dog,' he told
her from the chair. He liked giving information from his
chair. It made him feel professorial. 'But you wouldn't
know that, would you? I don't suppose you've never heard
of Lord George Gordon Byron. You never think of reading poetry, do you? You've never lived, that's your trouble. Me, I've read them all, Shelley and Byron and – and –
and eh Keats, and I've read Shakespeare, so I have, and
I've read—'

'I have so heard of Lord George Gordon,' his mother
cut in, angry with him, before he could think of another
poet he had read. 'I seen him in the telly last winter. He
was in a serial. It was about folk breaking into prison.'

'Breaking into prison!' he sneered. 'You break out of
prison, you don't break in.'

'These folk broke in,' she insisted. 'Lord George Gordon was in it. He was against the Pope. So was your father,
in case you forget. You see I have so heard of Lord George
Gordon. I'm not as stupid as you like to think. I seen the
serial I'm telling you.'

'What serial was that?' he challenged her rudely. 'Lord
Byron was never on the telly. He never gave a damn for the
Pope.'

'That's what I'm telling you,' his mother answered.

'Just tell me the name of it,' he nagged at her. 'Tell me

what it was called, go on, tell me. You don't know what you're talking about.'

'Barnacle Rudge,' his mother decided after a few moments' brooding over the frying-pan on the gas-ring. She was frying a couple of eggs, and she had some chips in deep fat, for Percy's meal.

'Never heard of it,' said Percy and rolled the pup over, bent forward from his chair.

'I missed bits of it,' his mother admitted. 'Maybe I couldny tell you the story right but I know what it was called. I know what I seen.'

'You couldny follow a serial,' he taunted her. 'You'd never remember what happened the week before. Sure you canny even remember when it's the day for my laundry. You'd have me looking like a tramp if I didn't remind you.'

'Huh-hm, your laundry!' she snorted, and Percy frowned and fidgeted. 'I wish that was all I had to worry me, your laundry.'

Percy had the pup on its back and he throttled it lovingly.

His mother simmered. She could keep it in no longer. They were seldom very cordial and they were never given to confiding in each other, but his manner annoyed her, she didn't like dogs, and she wanted to take the conversation off her failings and give it another direction.

'A funny thing happened to me this morning,' she started.

'Ha-ha!' Percy gave a staccato imitation of a ham-actor's laugh.

His mother clenched her teeth, counted ten and went on.

'A man stopped me at the corner of Bethel Street and Tulip Place.'

Percy's large hand loosened its grip on the Alsatian's throat.

'A man?' he said throatily, and he felt his stomach turning over.

'A wee bauchle,' she said, spooning fat over the eggs. 'Wearing a dirty coat. I don't know what he wanted a coat for, a lovely morning like it was this morning. Looked as if he slept in it. To hide his rags I suppose. A right Glasgow ned.'

Percy gaped up at her. His thick underlip hung even lower than usual and the neglected pup squirmed on the carpet beside the empty fireplace and barked for attention.

'He was trying to tell me it was your Uncle Sammy done the Finnieston bank,' she said, and snorted again. 'You remember the Finnieston bank? They still haveny got who done it.'

'Uncle Sammy never done a bank in his life,' Percy objected indignantly. 'He never done anything bigger than McIlweeny's pub and he was caught coming out. Him? He couldny do a bank. He hasny the brains.'

'That's what I told him,' said his mother, turning to the pot with the chips. 'And he says your uncle gave the money to your father to keep for him, and then your uncle was killed in that smash on the Edinburgh road, and your poor father collapsed in the cellar the day after that. Ach, the man was stark raving mad!'

Percy tickled the pup again, his head down.

'You never told me he'd been speaking to you too,' his mother threw at him sharply over her shoulder as she drained the chips in a wire basket.

'Him? Speaking to me?' Percy said as if he was puzzled. 'Och aye, I remember. There was a man stopped me one night in Tulip Place and talked a lot of tommy-rot about the cellar. I sent him away. I wouldny waste time talking to a man like that.'

'He asked me about the cellar too,' said his mother. 'I just told him it was never used at all now. That cellar broke your father's heart. I'm sure that's what drove him to an early death. A man in his forties to die like that, hinging ower a big box o' rubbish. He couldny get that place straight. I don't care what they say. He never had heart trouble when he worked in Sybie Street school. It was the sight of that cellar. He couldny do a thing with it. I just told him the door in Tulip Place was bricked up. I'm no' going to have the likes of him quizzing me about the place where your poor father took a shock and died. He must have lay there for hours before we found him.'

'That's what I told him too,' said Percy.

'Come on, your tea's out,' said his mother, and Percy went to the table followed by his pup. He settled it masterfully at his feet and tossed it the crust of his bread. He didn't eat his crusts.

His brain worked so slowly that for a long time after it had received disturbing information his face remained stolid, slightly vacuous with its thick under-lip hanging loosely. His mother had no inkling he was frightened. He bent his head over the plate, stuffing his face quickly, but all the time his head was throbbing painfully in confusion and dismay. Forking his chips greedily in threes and fours he comforted himself. The stranger was a bird of ill-omen, that was sure. But he had no right to the money. Nobody had any right to the money. Nobody but the person who had a right to the place where it was found. It was nobody's money, so it was his. Uncle Sammy could never have had anything to do with such countless wealth. Uncle Sammy? Uncle Sammy was a fly man that couldn't keep out of jail. He could never have been the goose that laid the golden egg. No, no, a thousand times no! Ah, sweet mystery of life, and this was a mystery too. Poetry dealt with mysteries and so did poets, and he was a poet. He was still the chosen of El. And he had been very fair dividing it amongst the under-privileged children who hadn't a decent pair of shoes to their name. It had been given to him for a purpose. He had been true to the purpose revealed to him. He would give in to nobody. Nobody would frighten him. His stupid mother and the bauchly stranger wanted to bring the money back down to earth and explain it. But it didn't belong there. It wasn't to be explained as easily as that. It came from heaven. You had to have faith.

He gobbled his egg and chips in a flurry of fear and washed at the kitchen sink.

'I've got nervous dyspepsia, that's what I've got,' he thought into the towel as he dried his face. 'It's an awful responsibility to carry. But you've got to face your destiny. I'll see it through, so I will.'

'Are you not shaving the night?' his mother asked slyly. 'You usually shave before you go out after your tea. What's up? Are you no' seeing her the night?'

'I'm not seeing anybody,' he answered, quelling her with a look. Her question reminded him of Sophy, and that was an offence.

'Where are you going then?' his mother asked.

'Out,' he informed her concisely.

'Ach, I bet you're going to meet some girl! I don't know what a fellow your age is bothering about girls at all for. You're far too young, and without a penny in your pocket. I don't know how you do it.'

He let that go. He wouldn't boast about what he had in his pocket. The elect don't boast they've been chosen. As for girls, he wanted to forget them after last night. He was beginning to remember that once he had wanted nothing but peace, peace and quiet.

'Funny how you get too busy to do what you meant to do,' he thought, pleased at his understanding of human nature.

But now it was high time to make sure he found peace. Sophy had let him down and the stranger was getting too near. He was heart-sick and disgusted at seeing wealth passed to outsiders in defiance of the oath to El, he was bitter at the way the Brotherhood had abandoned the religion he had tried to teach them. It was time to go away.

He walked round the town, a slim torch in his hip-pocket, loitered in the Central Station, felt himself superior to the humanity oozing around him there, and when it was getting dark he went back to Bethel Street. He slouched up and down Tulip Place for quarter of an hour till he was sure there were no watching eyes in the blind-alley and slipped into the cellar.

CHAPTER TWELVE

Earlier that night Helen Garson was waiting across the
street from the garage where her man worked. She was
there before five o'clock, still wearing her uniform. But
she was on an early shift, and finished for the day. She
preferred to watch and wait till her man came out rather
than go home and change and call at his house. She had
long persuaded herself she would never go back there. He
came out fifteen minutes late.

'That's him all right,' she recognized disapprovingly.
'Never could stop sharp. Many a good meal he wasted.
Unpaid overtime, that's what he does, but you can't tell
him anything.'

She beckoned discreetly with one arm up and a slight
side-to-side movement of her hand, a royal admission that
she was there to be seen and welcomed. Bob Garson was
aware at once of the green uniform across the street. Every
time he saw a bus conductress he was reminded of his wife,
and he would have kept his head down and passed on,
burying the memory as he always did when he saw one,
but the little wave of the hand halted him in a twilight of
two minds at the graveside. He looked, he saw, he recognized. You would never have believed a man could be so
embarrassed at being stopped in the street by his own wife.
After all, he had courted her, he had married her, he had
slept with her, he had begotten a child on her, he had seen
her in her underwear and less, and now he was blushing
and awkward at the sight of her on the Queen's highway in
the hardly glamorous coat and skirt of a female employee
of Glasgow Corporation Transport. But she was that kind
of woman. It didn't matter what she wore. She was always

herself, a rare womanly presence. He stood on one side of the street and she stood on the other. It was where they had left off: a test of wills. She waited and he waited. She beckoned again, with the index finger of her right hand crooked and signalling. For all the silence of her summons it might as well have been the song the sirens sang. She won. He crossed over. Yes, he was scowling, he was quite unamiable, he hadn't a word to throw at her in greeting, his heart was black and his face was red, but though he was no Caesar he had crossed his Rubicon. But he didn't know that when he made a brewer's lorry stop at the pedestrian crossing to let him over.

'What's Frank been up to?' she asked coldly.

'I don't know what you're talking about,' he answered, iceberg to iceberg, but of course we are told by those who know that kind of thing that two-thirds of an iceberg lie below the surface.

'That's a fine one!' she cried indignantly. 'You ask me to come home because of Frank and then you try to tell me you don't know what he's been doing. Well, I'm telling you straight, I'm not coming back home. I mean I'm not coming back to your house, till I know what it's all about.'

'What what's all about?' he looked at her strong wilful face with a grudge. But he couldn't hold her eyes, and he looked down. That was no better. Even in that thick coat and graceless skirt she looked well. He knew she had a good figure, and he resented that too.

'You tell me,' she said boldly. 'It was you that started it.'

'It was you that started it,' he echoed her. 'You left me of your own free will and as far as I'm concerned you can stay away.'

'So that's your story now, is it?' she nodded wisely. 'You want me to crawl, do you? I'll see you in hell first. You think because you put a bit in the paper I'm going to come running back to you? Aye! Come back, all is forgiven! Who do you think you are to start forgiving anybody? You're going to forgive me, are you? So I've to admit I was in the wrong! Oh no, Bob! Oh, no!'

Her thoughtless use of his name tingled him, puzzled him, confused him.

'What are you trying to do?' he asked, bewildered. 'What are you talking about, a bit in the paper? You think you can kid me, do you? You think I'm still—'

He stopped and scowled at her. He had come too near saying part of their trouble, that she had ruled him because he so much wanted her that he always had to have her. It was his way of solving all differences. But it wasn't hers. She wanted to win arguments by withholding herself. At that point, hating her for playing on his weakness and even despising his weakness, he denied himself, denied her, and told her to come into the house for good or leave it for good.

'You'd cut off your nose to spite your face,' she told him when he took that position. 'You'd rather do without me altogether than let me go out to work.'

'It's not a question of my nose and my face,' he had shouted at her that last night. 'It's a question of who's boss in this house. If you think because I—'

He stopped then as he stopped now. He wouldn't say it, he wouldn't admit it. She was taking what he called an unfair advantage, standing there so straight and confident, so well-made and womanly even in that uniform he hated.

'It's you that's trying to kid me,' she threw back at him in anger. She always was a spitfire. 'If you didn't want me back why did you go to all that trouble of putting it in the paper?'

His healthy honest face, almost stupid in its bewilderment, made her throw out an explosive sigh of exasperation. She fumbled inside her tunic at her right breast while he watched her hand with sad memoried eyes, and shoved the newspaper cutting across to him. He took it and read it. He read it twice, and he was still out of his depth.

'I never put that in,' he frowned. 'I don't know anything about it. Frank was in a fight a couple of days ago and I thought that's what you were talking about. He was all kicks and bruises. Because of you.'

'How because of me?' she demanded, straighter than ever. 'I haven't even seen the kid for four years.'

'Well, you know whose fault that is,' he charged her.

'Yes, yours,' she countered immediately.

He preferred not to answer that.

'One of the boys in his class said you ran away with a darkie,' he chose to answer instead. 'And he thought he had to stand up for you. But he got the worst of it. That was all.'

She laughed and cried all at once.

'A darkie!' she said, nearly hysterical. 'Oh God! I wish that was all that was to it. I've lived without a man for four years.'

'I wish I could believe that,' he muttered sourly.

'That's your trouble,' she spat fire at him again. 'You've got a bad mind. You liked to kid on you just had to be head of the house and I should stay at home, but there was more than that to it. You didn't trust me. You were jealous. You liked to think that every man I worked with was making love to me. Why can't you grow up? The world's not like that at all. The men I worked with had their wives and family and they were perfectly happy. They liked me and I liked them and that's all there was to it. But not for you, oh no! You had to make more of it because you've got a bad mind. You wouldn't trust me, that was your real trouble. Oh, I saw through you all right!'

'You should have said that long ago,' he defended himself weakly. 'I would have trusted you if you had only told me you didn't want another man.'

'I shouldn't have needed to tell you if you had sense at all,' she answered impatiently. 'I married you, didn't I? Who else would I want? I'm not a filmstar, I'm a girl from Fife. When I marry, I'm stuck with the man I married. I know all your faults and I've no doubt you know mine. You told me them often enough. But I never looked for a man since the day I left you. I never left you because I was bothered about a man. That's got nothing to do with it and you know it. But you like to kid yourself.'

'Oh, but Helen!' he muttered, so embarrassed by her bluntness that he evaded it. 'That boy took a terrible beating. I saw his side. He was kicked, Helen, he was kicked something shocking. Standing up for you.'

'That's got nothing to do with it,' she brought him back to the issue. She jabbed her finger on the cutting he was still holding. 'That's got your name.'

'Aye, but it's not mine,' he said, quite firm with her on that point. 'I never asked you to come home. I never put that in the paper.'

'Then it was Frank,' she said quickly. 'What does he mean? He's got loads. Is that a disease, or has he won the pools?'

'Don't be daft,' he retorted impulsively. 'A boy of ten wouldn't know how to fill in a coupon.'

'Well, what does it mean?' she insisted.

'How should I know?' he countered in the traditional Scots way, answering one question by another.

They stood in the broad evening sun, arguing like any husband and wife where the wife has a perfectly good point that the man can't answer, and the woman keeps at it and the man tells her she is talking nonsense, and they didn't see till later that they were on speaking terms again. So long as you keep quarrelling you're still speaking. Their argument brought them together on the normal terms of married life, and it was a long time since either of them had been so worked up about anything.

'It's Frank,' said Mrs Garson. 'I'm sure it's Frank. It was Frank I'm telling you. It was him put it in the paper.'

'Don't talk soft,' said Mr Garson superiorly. 'How could it be Frank? Where would he get the money to pay for putting adverts in a paper? Damn it, he couldn't even write an advert, he's only ten.'

'Aye, but he's a clever boy,' his mother claimed. 'At least he was, unless you've knocked him stupid. He took after the Grahams, no' the Garsons.'

'The Grahams!' Mr Garson despised them with his tone. 'Like your big sister Nessie that could hardly read or write. The postcard she sent us from Saltcoats. We've had no rain. Kay-enn-oh-double-you. Oh aye, she was a rare scholar!'

'Maybe she didn't spell so good,' Mrs Garson admitted. 'But she made a damn good job of that wee paper shop she got out of the compensation-money when her man was killed at his work.'

'Aye, she did all right. And she never thought of coming to see her nephew, not once. She couldn't even send him a Christmas card.'

'What do you expect? And since when were you ever bothered about Christmas?'

'She could have sent him some wee thing, the boy's got nothing.'

'You put me out the house and then you think my big sister's going to run after you and your boy! You've got some rare ideas you have. You'd make a cat laugh you would!'

'Your boy,' Mr Garson cut in before she finished.

'He's yours too,' said Mrs Garson. 'Or is that something else you don't trust me for?'

'I never said that,' he answered, shocked at her. 'But if you're going to suggest things—'

'There, see what I mean?' she appealed to him against himself. 'A wee bit sarcasm and you canny take it. You start thinking things. You must have an awful life with a mind like yours!'

'With a wife like you,' he answered dourly.

'I've told you all I'm going to tell you,' she said sharply. 'I told you I married you and that's enough for me. If you can't make sense of that and see what I'm telling you then you're even thicker than I thought you were.'

'Well, would you come back?' he asked. He knew quite well what she was telling him, but he liked making himself sour and suspecting her of all kinds of duplicities.

'Would I come back?' she echoed him in a voice of overacted astonishment. 'You're after arguing you never asked me. You're after telling me to stay away for good.'

'Because of the way you approached me,' he said defensively.

'You're getting away from the point,' she stalled. 'There's that thing I tore out of the paper. If that wasn't Frank, who was it? I want to see him. You've kept him from me long enough. I want to see him.'

'Now?' he nearly shouted, as if the idea was outrageous.

'Well, I don't mean next Christmas,' she snapped at him.

They moved off together, hardly hand in hand, but both at peace, quite reconciled. After all, they were both Scots. There is nothing puzzles the Scot more than the Englishman's claim not to wear his heart on his sleeve. To a Scotsman, the Englishman wears his heart like a breast-pocket handkerchief, stuck in front of him for show, and flaunts it in public too. To the Garsons, their crabbit conversation had been a warming bout of making love, and their final snarl at each other had given them all the confidence of the final kiss that knows it isn't final because the best is yet to be.

The only thing that still bothered them was the small ad in the *Citizen*. They were straining at the leash to get home and see Frank and sort the whole thing out.

'Damn cheek, putting our names in the papers,' muttered Mr Garson. 'Anybody might have seen it.'

'He was doing it for the best,' said Mrs Garson. 'He was always a sensitive boy.'

'You never thought of that when you left him without a mother's care,' said Mr Garson.

'You never thought of that when you wouldn't let me see him unless I gave in to you.'

'You didn't make much of an effort.'

'Ach, my mother died when I was eight, and I lived,' Mrs Garson remembered callously.

And chatting in that way, with true Scots friendliness, they walked the short distance from the garage in Bethel Street to the tenement where Frank was making tea, twenty-seven Ossian Street, three-up the far-away.

The boy was frying sliced sausages and eggs for his father's tea, and he was hot-headed with anxiety as he stood at the gas-cooker in a corner of the kitchen. He had begun his evening routine at the usual time, right after he finished his paper-rake, but his father was late. He didn't know what to do for the best. If he took the frying-pan off the gas his father would walk in when the sausages were cold and the eggs sloppy. And if he kept the frying-pan on the gas the sausages would get charred and hard and the eggs would get all brown and burnt round the edges, and that would be when his father would walk in. It was the way of the world. You couldn't win.

He tried a compromise. He held the pan above the blue flames of the gas-ring and kept moving the sausages and eggs round and round in the pan so that at least they wouldn't stick to the bottom. He was doing all right, quite engrossed in his compromise as an end in itself, a task with its own interest, watching the sizzling fat and the changing colour of the sausages, when the kettle on the other ring came to the boil. The lid moved in the angry, turbulent way that attracted the attention of James Watt as early as 1759, though it isn't generally known that he had been anticipated by Robert Hooke, but Frank Garson was no Watt. He was only a ten-year-old schoolboy in a panic, trying to prepare the evening meal for his father in a motherless, wifeless house. He slapped the frying-pan down on the gas-ring again and lowered the gas under the kettle. Another problem reared its ugly head. If he brewed the tea at once it would probably be too strong by the time his father came in. If he didn't brew it the water would inevitably be off the boil altogether before his father came in. The real trouble was his father didn't like to be kept waiting. He was a just man according to himself, but an impatient one according to those who knew him. The sweat on the boy's brow glided down his nose and down behind his ears. It wasn't just his anxiety nor even the heat from the cooker. The summer evening was still hot, and the kitchens in the tall tenements were all stifling airless boxes of irritating heat.

He was coping with a simmering kettle and a sizzling frying-pan, willing to be happy enough with either if only the other weren't there, when his father and mother walked in on him. His father never knocked or rang. He always had his key. That was what seemed to make his entrances so abrupt.

'Oh my godfather! Are you still using that thing?' the boy's mother cried at once. She deliberately ignored her son and crossed to the old gas-cooker, tutting at it as she took charge. She wouldn't let any man see that the sight of her only child moved her at all. But the cooking facilities were a subject of comment and attention.

'It was you that bought it,' her husband reminded her dourly.

'Aye, eleven years ago,' she retorted. 'Things has changed a bit since then or haven't you heard? Holy Christmas, even my landlady's all-electric.'

She brewed the tea deftly, soothed the misunderstood sausages and eggs, elevated them with a flip of a fish-lifter, served them skilfully on a couple of plates, and kept nagging her man.

'You've no idea, Bob! You're content to live like your grandfather. You've never heard of the wind of change blowing through the kitchens of Britain. I was always surprised that a man like you, so clever with cars and bang-up-to-date on models, and you just never bothered your backside what women can get nowadays.'

'Frank, here's your mother come to see you,' Mr Garson answered, very stiff, annoyed at his wife's reference to cars. He had no car, nor was like to have one, but he could tell the make and model of any car a hundred yards away, and it was hardly a thing to be sneered at if he could take a motor-engine apart and reassemble it. He knew his job, that was all. But fridges and tellies were a piece of nonsense.

The boy hovered a little distance from the conquered

gas-cooker. If this was his mother then that grimy contraption was no longer his concern. He had no wish to defend his claim to it. But he was shy when his father spoke to him. This woman in the green uniform of a Corporation bus-conductress wasn't so much his mother as a person like someone he remembered, a long long time ago.

As if to introduce herself his mother ruffled his thick waving crop of chestnut-brown hair, a gesture of affection not unlike the spasm that had seized Noddy's mother when she came home with the two ten-shilling notes she had wheedled out of old Daunders. Like Noddy, Frank Garson jerked his head away, distressed. Yet his scalp tingled, and he wondered what to do to reach her.

The three of them sat at the table in a silence as solid as the walls of Edinburgh Castle. The head of the house was hungry and he wolfed in, but he tried to break through by asking his wife to have something to eat.

'No, I'm all right,' she said calmly. 'A cup of tea's all I want.'

She had taken off her coat and her blouse was smart, her ungracious green skirt with the thin red stripe hidden as she sat at the table between her husband and her son. The latter squinted at her as he ate. He was too young to have nervous indigestion, but the state he was in wasn't likely to do his digestion any good. His heart was going so emphatically he was sure it must sound like the alarm clock in the other room, his middle was the site of a civil war, and his palate was as parched as if he was a man with a hang-over. He kept on squinting because he liked the look of this strange woman. Before he has the possibility of a sexual appreciation even a boy of ten has an aesthetic appreciation of a woman, and Frank Garson warmed to his mother. This was no sour dame with specs and a flat front like Percy's blighted mother, this was a woman like the kind you saw in photographs in the papers. This was like the woman he had dreamed he had kissed when he was in Miss Montgomery's class, a woman that was at one and the same time Miss Montgomery and wasn't. Not once but three times, and the dreams puzzled him when they came back to him the next day, recalled by a word, a sight, a sound. He had left his seat in class, walked out and kissed Miss Montgomery, only of course it wasn't Miss Montgomery, it was somebody else who was Miss Montgomery. But what had he to do with kissing? The memory of the three dreams allured and repelled him. He felt he had been brave, he felt he had been ridiculous. What would his classmates have said if he had told any of them he had dreamt he had kissed Miss Montgomery? But not of course Miss Montgomery, because she was really Mrs Joyce and her husband was a captain in the Merchant Navy and she was a fit wife for a ship's commander, so well dressed and beautiful. Had he been ridiculous or just gallant? It baffled him, and although it was only yesterday he had been Miss Montgomery's lover it was also a thousand years ago, another world, another person.

'Take your time,' said his mother. 'You're shoving that down your throat as if you hadn't seen food for a week. You're not chewing it at all.'

He put his eyes on his plate and he chewed.

'And another thing,' said his mother. 'You've got some explaining to do, young man.'

It was only with those words that he remembered the silly advert he had put in the *Citizen*. He had made up that advert in a mood, much as a man might utter an oath in privacy, and no more than that man had he expected to find his words having any influence on the real world he couldn't escape from. He was frightened. The civil war in his middle was settled by a truce that merely raised new problems. His heart slowed. His brain left its confusion of his mother with Miss Montgomery and settled on a simplified memory of Percy. He would be better to say nothing. His mother was back and he was sure she wouldn't go away again in a hurry. He didn't need to say anything to keep her. He had an old loyalty now to remember. He would admit the advert and pretend it was only a trick to get her to come back.

That's what he thought. But when his mother slapped the newspaper cutting on the table in front of him he saw he wasn't going to be coaxed to admit it was his work. He was being told. He heard the rumbling of approaching disaster. He felt very small and unready. He had a passing memory of the time he had tried to pick up a full-size football with one hand. It was far too big for his grasp, he had to let it drop. And so it was now. He would have to let go. Yet even in the rout of his plans he noticed it was his mother leading the attack. His father just sat there and glowered.

'Your face gives you away,' his mother said sternly, and he felt his face hot with the blush of known guilt. 'It was you, wasn't it?'

She pretended to be asking him but he knew she was telling him. He nodded, afraid that if he spoke he would start crying, and he wasn't going to cry in front of any woman, especially not this one.

'What do you mean, loads?' his mother demanded, her finger jabbing three times at the simple word, her other elbow on the table, her face close against him, intimidating him.

'A li-li-lot,' he answered with difficulty. He always had trouble with his 'l's, his throat was all tightened with anxiety, and people who frightened him always brought upon him the fear that his erratic stammer would win and make him ridiculous.

'What do you mean a lot?' his mother persisted. Her face was so close now, she was staring at him so hard as if she was trying to hypnotize him, that he was drowned in the dark-brown depths of her eyes, and a wisp of her hair touched his brow. But though her eyes and hair were soft her voice was hard. 'When did you get a lot? Where? Have you been doing the pools?'

He smiled unsurely, then he saw she wasn't being funny at all. She was still grim. She really meant it.

He wiped the smile off his face with a jolted reflex and shook his head.

'Where did you get the money to pay for putting an advert in the papers?' his father asked suddenly.

'Out my tips,' he said quickly, glad for a question he could answer reasonably.

'Not out of the loads of money you say you've got?' his mother suggested, and he wilted under the dry irony of her tone.

'No, I – I – I haven't got loads,' he admitted in crumpled misery.

'Then why did you say loads?'

His mother kept at him, and he suffered for a moment a strange fear that she wanted to be told he really had loads of money so that she could claim her share right away as his mother. Then he saw it was his fault, not hers, if that's how it was. He had hinted at money to get her back. So why should he be disappointed if she came back and asked for some? It was only what he had planned. He hung his head in shame at his own muddle. His plan had been a mistake from the start, and he learnt then that to use certain ways of getting what we want means that what we wanted wasn't worth having. But he wouldn't believe that of his mother.

'Why did you say loads?' she was repeating, hammering at him.

She grabbed him by the hair and shook his head to make him look up and answer her.

He broke. This woman blasted his loyalty to Percy. His loyalty to the Brotherhood he knew was already withered. He had never heard of *la femme fatale*, all he knew was that this woman was ruling him, that he felt himself an inferior part of her, and had to give in to her, because the whole is greater than the part. He wept a little and came out with his story through little sobs. It had to come out. He was sick with keeping it in. Maybe now he could sleep at night without bad dreams and take his dinner with some pleasure in what he was eating. It was like putting down a heavy load he had been carrying too far without a rest.

'I haven't got loads but I know where there is loads because it was me that found it in the cellar, in the cellar in the school. I said we ought to tell the police and I thought Percy would agree but he didn't, and he's giving it out to the gang every week but I wouldn't take any. Everybody was getting money so I thought why shouldn't I get a share because it was me that found it, but I didn't want it for myself like them, they've been spending it on rubbish and things they can't use, but I could take hundreds for you if it's money you want. You went away to get money, so if it's money you want I can get you hundreds, or thousands if you like. I can get it if you want it, cause I know there's still loads left in spite of Percy. I know. I've seen it. But I don't like it. I still think the police ought to be told. You don't know what's behind it.'

He stopped. He couldn't speak any more. His sobs and his stammer beat him.

The husband and wife looked at each other anxiously, each seeming to expect the other to have the solution.

'Has he been keeping all right?' Mrs Garson whispered across the table, her clutch on her son's thick hair slackening to an absent-minded caress of his skull.

'There's never been a thing wrong with him since you went away,' Mr Garson answered aggressively, provoked at the insinuation that the boy was mad and he didn't know it.

Mrs Garson put one hand across her son's forehead. It was fevered all right, but hardly the fever of delirium. She was a woman, she was an intelligent woman. She had intuition. She could recognize when the truth was passing by, whatever odd garment it was wearing at the moment. She kept at the broken boy, determined to make him whole again. His life was more important to her than her own. She was only the tree. The fruit was more important. She couldn't be at peace till she had made sense of him. She nagged at him, patiently, kindly though sometimes a little harshly, but always bearing down firmly on the issue. Her husband sat admiring her with a silent grudge. He could never have done what she was doing, but he saw she was right. She kept at the boy. She bullied him, she loved him, she smacked him, she caressed him. She was a good mother to him. She went over and over his story with him, sobering him with her careful questions. Even Mr Daunders could have learnt something of the art of interrogation from her. She even got out of him the story of how Savage had picked on him for not taking a share of the money and then dragged her name into it before the fight that turned out to be a massacre.

'So there's the fight you were trying to tell me about,' she said indignantly to her husband. 'You didn't dig very deep, did you?'

'Well, damn it all,' he retorted, just as indignant as she was. 'Boys are always fighting. How was I to know there was—'

He searched his boyhood for a cutting phrase.

'Buried treasure!' he finished sarcastically.

'There's no use talking like that,' she turned on him. 'I think you should take him round and see the police.'

'I'm not going near the police, I can tell you that,' her man answered quickly. 'I'll go to the school with him tomorrow morning if you like. I don't mind seeing old Daunders. I've met him before, he's all right, but I'm not going to no police.'

He fiddled with his knife and fork across his dirty plate.

'Thousands and thousands,' he muttered. 'I'd like to see it.'

There was silence except for the boy's diminishing sobs.

'Stop snuffling and redd the table,' said his father abruptly. 'Come away ben, Helen, I want to talk to you.'

The routine job soothed the boy's nerves and he put a kettle on the gas to get hot water for the dishes. It was good to be alone again, and he felt strangely happy at the way he had been left alone. He could hear a murmuring of earnest conversation in the other room, the clish-clash of two people disputing but not on bad terms. At least they weren't quarrelling.

He was drying the knives when his father called him. His parents were standing close together in the lobby between the two rooms, behind the half-open front door.

'Your mother's going away now,' said his father. 'Say goodbye to her.'

He looked up at her and said nothing. She clutched his hair and shook his head again.

'It's time you were getting a haircut,' she said. 'You might have pinched the price of a haircut out your cellar instead of cheating the barber. Well, I'll be seeing you.'

'Go and get your dishes done,' his father muttered and pushed him back into the kitchen.

'I've done the dishes,' he answered, grudging the way he was dismissed, but he had to go, with that strong hand thrusting him.

Yet as he returned to the sink he was aware over his shoulder that his parents were still standing there together. He had a quick glimpse of them coming together in a swift hug and he knew they were kissing.

'Will she be coming back?' he risked later in the evening, an impulse letting him say what an hour's brooding hadn't given him the courage to say.

'Who's she?' his father asked primly.

'M-my m-mother,' he took the rebuke nervously. Sometimes the 'm's were as unpredictable as the 'l's.

'Well, you don't just call your mother she. You speak of her with some respect. You say my mother, you don't refer to her as she.'

His father rested a moment after the strain of that lecture on etiquette. Then he answered the question.

'Of course she'll be coming back. But not tonight. These things take time. She's got – I mean your mother's got to settle things up where she's living. But you'll see her at the end of the week. It'll be all right, don't you worry. Now about this story of yours, you've got to come with me tomorrow and we'll see your headmaster and we'll go into it and—'

His father blethered on, but he wasn't listening. The money seemed of no importance. He was glad it was out of his hands.

'Your mother'll be there too,' his father was saying. 'She can speak better than I can. She's good at explaining things. You know, your mother could talk the hind leg off a donkey once she gets started.'

'Will she be staying here, I mean will my mother be staying here?' the boy felt bold enough to ask. He was amazed at the difference in his father. He had never seen him so light and cheery. He remembered an encyclopedia he had seen in the school library. It showed the mammoths that once roamed over Europe before the coming of the Ice Age, and then it had drawings showing the retreat of the Ice Age. His father, once so huge and cold, now seemed a new and smaller continent, a Europe after an ice age.

'Well, maybe not here,' said the altered man. 'I was just telling your mother. They're building an awful lot of petrol stations the now on all the main roads out of the city. You know away up between Springburn and Bishop-briggs, aye and on to Kirkintilloch? There's nothing but petrol stations on both sides of the road. Well, I know one of them, but it's not out that way, it's more the Stepps direction, and it's actually got a house above the station. How would you like to live in a place like that? You see, this place never suited your mother. It was far too small, and she couldn't be doing with buildings all round her. Your mother was born in the country. She wouldn't mind living out in the wilderness again. And then you see she'd have space for the kind of things she wants. I can get that job there with the house above it, with two bedrooms too, mind you, I can get it if I want it. There's nothing I don't know about cars. I could manage a place like that with my eyes shut. Anybody would do for the pumps, but what they want is a man that would know what to do in an emergency, a manager. That's me.'

He had never heard his father boast before. He listened, fascinated. But he wasn't so much concerned with his father's ability to cope with a service and filling-station as with the prospect of escape. If he had to go to the police, if he had to tell old Daundy all about the cellar, it didn't matter any more. Once it would have frightened him, but not now. Once he would have feared the vengeance of the Brotherhood, but now he could leave the Brotherhood behind him just as easily as he had stopped reading the *Beano*. As for Percy, he found he had no feeling. Yesterday he would have died for him. Today, he wouldn't cross the street to speak to him. So sudden is the death of a boy's love. And his mother would be there. He hadn't felt the least bit jealous when he knew his father was hugging and kissing her like a man and woman on television. On the contrary, he was pleased. It made his father a better and surer means of bringing his mother back than all that business about the money. He didn't want to go through with that. Now he was up against the test he had blundered into, he still didn't want to touch the money. He was at peace that they hadn't asked him to get the hundreds and thousands he had said he could get. He could trust them. He would sleep tonight all right.

'Who is this Percy fellow anyway?' his father was asking him.

'Oh, he's a nice big fellow,' the boy answered vaguely. 'But he's a bit up in the clouds most of the time. You see, he's a kind of poet.'

'It's a very true saying when you come to think about it,' Percy told himself as he went carefully down the chute, his little torch stabbing the darkness with a long dagger of light. 'Familiarity breeds contempt. They've forgot they ever made a gentlemen's agreement, so they have. They don't even bother to come to the Friday Night Service any more, well, most of them anyway, there was only four there last week counting me, and when they do come they just mumble through it and want to get out quick. They've no respect for anything now. And you can't trust them. I don't trust Savage for one. He's sleekit, that fellow. I wouldn't be surprised if he was getting in somehow and shifting it. Anyway there's some of them getting money behind my back. Well, it doesn't matter to me now, I'm finished with them. I've wasted too much of my time on them already.'

The cellar was eerie with so much throbbing darkness fighting powerfully against the thin yellow line of his torch, and he shivered a little. But that was his nerves, not the cold. He had never been farther away from his front-close than the banks of Loch Lomond, and now he was set to go to Land's End. It didn't seem possible to go any farther, short of leaving the country altogether – and that would have meant getting a passport, but he couldn't get his own passport till he was twenty-one. So Land's End it had to be.

'My Ultimate Thool,' he called it.

From Land's End he would travel along the coast. He could buy a mo-bike when he got there. When he found a good spot far from anywhere he would buy a little cottage.

There must be hundreds of cottages in these lonely parts of England. He would find one where the sun was warm, the sky was clear, and the waves were dancing fast and bright. Then he would settle in and write a play for television. Not for the money. He didn't need money. But it would be great to see the words on the screen: Specially Written for Television by Percy Phinn. That would be one in the eye for old Elginbrod if she was still living, the old bitch. He had thought of a good title too. *Rabbits With Ostrich Feathers*. He liked that. It was striking, puzzling, original. All he had to do was get to Land's End, find a cottage, get peace and quiet, and think up a plot.

He strode like a conqueror to the corner where he had hidden his briefcase, checked his pyjamas and shaving tackle, and advanced boldly on the tea-chests. He pushed the first two aside and attacked the third, the one he had always kept in reserve. First he broke one bundle of twenty fivers and stuffed the notes into his wallet so as to have plenty of money easy to get at on his journey. Then he began to fill the briefcase. It was only when he had stowed away a couple of dozen bundles that it struck him the chest wasn't as full as it ought to be. He was nearly at the bottom already. He stopped, frowned, and brooded.

'Somebody's been here,' he decided cautiously. 'There should be a lot more than this.'

It gave an extra push to his eagerness to pack up and go. Things weren't right. He had felt it for a long time.

He speeded up filling his briefcase. Two thousand five hundred, two thousand six hundred, two thousand seven hundred. And he still had room for as much more. If need be, he would fill up from the other chests. Meanwhile, he went on trying to empty the one he was at. At two thousand nine hundred he heard a rustle. He wasn't sure where it came from. He froze, his hand halted between the chest and the briefcase, a large hand holding a bundle of five-pound notes in an elastic band. He stayed frozen, listening and counting. He had never heard his heart beat before, and the sound frightened him. It didn't seem right that his life should depend on that sound going on and on. He was in a panic, poised between time and eternity. A creak, and then another rustle.

Was it a draught? There was no wind in the cellar, there couldn't be, the summer night was airless. A rat? But there were no rats.

He shoved the bundle of fivers into his case, covered what was left in the chest with handfuls of old clothes and paper chains and pushed the chest back into its corner. Then turning suddenly like a cowboy quick on the draw firing six rounds rapid from his trusty forty-five he raked the cellar with his torch. Bang at one wall, crack at another, swift shots into the corners. His messengers of light swept the cellar clean. They caught something – a foot, a leg. He raised his aim and dazzled the eyes of a familiar face.

'It's you!' he cried, nearly foaming with fury. 'I might have known!'

'Hello, Perse, old boy,' said Savage pleasantly, coming out into the open from the jungle of broken chairs and *Sunshine Readers*, wearing his black jacket and jeans and putting on his comic English accent to disarm his enemy. 'Robbed any good banks lately, me old cock sparra?'

He had a torch too and he flashed it into Percy's eyes, an insolent retaliation that made Percy really mad. Oh, he was angry now all right. He was ripe for murder. Miss Elgin-brod wouldn't have been surprised. She would have said it was all in his medical record: enuresis and hysteria in the infant department, treatment at the Child Guidance Clinic for anti-social behaviour when he was in the juniors, proposals to commit to a special school when he was in the seniors. What could you expect, she would have asked. But a youth doesn't need to have a medical history to be capable of murder.

Savage flashed Percy up and down, teasing him. Percy shoved his torch in his pocket and barged at him. He hit him on the wrist with the edge of his palm and Savage's torch clattered to the stone floor.

'You little rat!' he screamed, wrestling with him in darkness. 'You've been stealing the money, that's what you've been doing! You think I don't know!'

'And what were you doing there?' Savage croaked weakly with Percy's claws at his throat. 'Just taking it out to give it an airing?'

He fought back wildly and brought his knee up hard against Percy's crutch. Percy yelped in an extremity of agony and fell on the floor. Savage jumped on him and kept punching him on the nose and mouth. But for all his height and strength he was only a boy trying to fight a young man twice his size. His defeat was only a matter of time.

Percy took the punches woodenly till the sickness brought on by that knee bashed in between his legs left him. He bided his time deliberately. He knew he was bigger and stronger. He heaved Savage off, scrambled up, and while Savage still rolled on the floor he kicked him in the legs, on the ribs, on the arms, and when Savage squirmed over he kicked him hard on the bottom and between his shoulder blades. He was beginning to enjoy it.

'Yuh big bastard!' Savage screamed, sprawled out like a frog.

He wriggled along the floor and got to his feet clear of Percy's size ten shoes with the thick crepe soles.

'I'll get ye for that,' he said, fierce in the darkness, whipped off his Army webbing-belt and swung it. The brass clasp came viciously down, just missed Percy's face and hit him where his neck joined his shoulder. Percy sagged with a new pain, and now there was hate in the darkness, a lust of hate between them. They were both panting with eagerness for the ultimate violence, as inflamed as two lovers in darkness. Percy rushed in close to get under the range of the flailing belt and Savage wrapped it round his neck and tried to throttle him. Percy groaned, pulled at it, and heaved. Then he used his knee the way

Savage had done to him and Savage fell writhing and
cursing on top of a fallen column of *Sunshine Readers*, his
belt lost, both hands at his crutch. Percy knelt over,
clasping him between his thighs and grabbed him by
the ears.

'I wasted months ower you, tae try and teach you for tae
be decent,' he cried bitterly. 'Months, and months, and
months!' He banged Savage's head on the floor.

'But ye had nae idea!'

He banged it twice again, and some *Sunshine Readers*
slid under Savage's head.

'Ye're nae use, to anybody!'

He had lathered himself into a fury and went on pulling
Savage's skull up by the ears and then bashing it down to
the rhythm of his words.

'Savage by name and Savage by nature. You spoiled my
gang, you ruined my plans, you'd take the good out a bad
egg, so you would, you rotten little bugger. And you've
been raiding the money. Admit it, admit it, admit it!'

Savage moaned, and a sound like a death rattle came up
from his bared quivering throat. Then he was quiet.

Until then Percy wanted to do what he was doing and he
didn't care what happened to Savage. He was living
entirely in the present moment, giving Savage no more
than Savage had asked for. He was the righteous man
punishing wickedness. But the moment Savage stopped
struggling and lay silent, he overflowed with regret for
what he had done. He was sorry, truly sorry. He slapped
Savage's face, a pale flower in the darkness, once on each
cheek. There was something almost tender in those two
little slaps.

'Come on, stop acting it,' he said severely. 'You're all
right. Quit the kidding. Don't come it, Hughie!'

Savage said nothing.

Percy shook him by the shoulders instead of by the ears,
wheedling at him as if he was just trying to waken a heavy
sleeper. The body stayed limp, let itself be shaken, gave no
answer.

'Oh, my God,' said Percy.

He thought he had killed him. He was willing to admit he had gone too far after all. Whatever his faults, Savage hardly deserved to be murdered for them. Anyway, murder would be an awkward business. It might mean he would never get to his cottage at Land's End.

That was enough to make him move, and move quickly. He groped for his torch and sent the yellow line ahead of him across the cellar to the chute. He was halfway up when he remembered.

'My briefcase!' he cried. 'My cottage.'

He scampered down again, stepped over Savage, grabbed his case, and locked it, standing on one leg, supporting the case on the thigh of the other leg. He was too anxious to get away to think of taking any more money. Up the chute once more he went, his key at the ready. He was just going to put it into the lock and open the door when the door moved in towards him. He was paralysed for a second, then he stepped to one side so that he would be hidden behind the door when it was opened.

A little man in a belted raincoat and cloth cap came through the doorway, stood at the top of the chute and jabbed a flash down into the cellar. It was the inquisitive stranger. Percy recognized the way one foot was turned in a little. It was a time for action, and Percy had never believed that a poet was incapable of action. He swung his briefcase hard against the nape of the stranger's neck, rammed his knee into the small of his back, and pushed him down the chute with every ounce of his strength. The stranger stumbled, tripped, crumpled, and rolled down like a sack of potatoes, crashed at the foot and lay there. Percy dived through the doorway, brought the door to behind him and locked it swiftly.

'He never got a glimpse of me,' he assured himself as he ran down Tulip Place. 'He hasn't a clue what hit him. They can lie there, the pair of them. A couple of rogues. Money, money, money, that's all they could think of.

They'd no respect for it, nothing they needed it for like me. They just wanted it. Sheer greed!'

He didn't go home. He loped far away from Tulip Place and Bethel Street, crossed the river and remembering he was a poet he stopped on the bridge for a moment to admire the beauty of the neon ads reflected in the night-dark water. At an open-all-night public convenience near Glasgow Cross he washed his face and combed his hair, removing all signs of his fight with Savage, but he couldn't do much about a dark blue bruise under his eye. Returning to the upper world he struck over towards Charing Cross.

'It's rotten with wee hotels over there,' he told himself. He liked talking to himself, it helped him to work out his plans. 'I'll get a room there for tonight and my breakfast tomorrow and get the ten o'clock to London and I'll find out where to get a train to Land's End. I'm no short of money, that's one good thing.'

He had never slept a night out of his own bed before, and when he stood at the desk in the Kelvin Hotel near Clairmont Gardens he chattered compulsively to hide his nervousness.

'I'm just up from Leeds,' he said. 'Down at my grandmother's funeral. Eighty-seven she was. Going back to Aberdeen first thing the morrow. That's where I live, you see. My train was late getting in. Missed my connexion. Lucky I've got enough money on me to pay for bed and breakfast.'

The night-manager looked at him with weary heavy-lidded eyes. A good look. You never knew when the police would be in the next day asking for a description. There was something odd about this big fellow. Very odd.

'Yes, sir, quite so,' he murmured neutrally, and pushed the register over.

Percy took the offered pen and hesitated. He hadn't thought of this. The manager saw the hesitation, slight as it was, and made a note of Percy's height, colour of his hair and eyes, suit and briefcase, and the big bruise on the right cheek. Percy put the pen to the page.

'Percy Bysshe,' he wrote in the ugly back-hand that used to madden Miss Elginbrod.

The night-manager swivelled the book round with a movement that had all the deftness of routine and glanced at the name.

'And your address in Aberdeen, please,' he said suavely. Bysshe. Who ever heard of such a name? Obviously made up. 'We have to have it in the register, you see. By law. Just in case.'

He stopped, quite enjoying intimidating this lout with the black eye who had given him a lot of gratuitous nonsense about his granny in Leeds and a home in Aberdeen in a voice of the purest Glasgow.

'Oh aye,' said Percy. 'Of course.'

Once more he hesitated. But no dapper little twerp in a dark suit and grey tie, with sleepy eyes and a Kelvinside accent, was going to frighten him. He was no ignorant teddy-boy from a housing-scheme. He was a poet on his way to a poet's cottage. And he had read a bit in his time too. He knew that the motto on the Aberdeen coat of arms was Bon Accord.

'27 Bon Accord Street,' he wrote. Maybe there wasn't actually a Bon Accord Street in Aberdeen, but Bon Accord was Aberdonian enough to serve his turn.

He had done quite well. But then he spoiled it. He read out the address and stressed all the syllables of Bon Accord equally.

'Is that how you say it?' said the manager from somewhere up in the ceiling, far above Percy. 'I thought Aberdonians pronounced it Bunnaccurred.'

He made a dactyl of it. Percy struggled mentally with the two rhythms. He liked the manager's way of saying it. It flowed.

'Oh aye, they do, of course they do,' he said, grinning like a friendly collie. 'I just said it the other way so you'd recognize it, cause you see these names in print and you never know how to say them till somebody tells you and my writing's not very good. You see I write a lot and it's kind of spoiled my writing. Bunnaccurred of course. Bunnacurred. It's the town motto, you know. It means good accord.'

'Really?' said the night-manager.

The night-porter came up to the desk to take Percy's case and show him to a room.

'Oh no, no thank you,' said Percy, holding the briefcase up and away. 'I'll hang on to this if you don't mind. It's got my grandmother's jewellery in it.'

He couldn't sleep. The bed was too good, it was too clean and comfortable, he felt himself in too strange a world to settle to sleep. Then in the darkness of the strange room he couldn't help thinking of Savage again, and he tossed and turned anxiously. He couldn't believe he had actually killed him, for that was the kind of thing that happened to other people. But even if Savage was lying dead it could never be proved he had murdered him, and since it couldn't be proved then he wasn't guilty. All he had to do was get up sharp in the morning and get away. He had come where life had taken him, and he had still farther to go, he had to get to Land's End and live in exile. When at last he fell over he dreamed of the river all in black running silently through a deserted city, and he was floating down the river in a little boat that wasn't sea-worthy, stalked by a stranger who was dead and alive, harmless and dangerous, cunning and stupid. And he was frightened.

The hotel was wrapped in silence like an old woman in a shawl. Only the light in the entrance hall and another in the little office still burned. The night-manager and the night-porter stood on either side of the desk, conversing in whispers.

'There's something funny about him,' said the porter, exbatman to a lieutenant-colonel in the Royal Scots Fusiliers.

'Odd,' said the manager, whilom major in the Army Catering Corps during the Second World War.

'You remember that couple last month,' said the porter.

'I'm not likely to forget them,' said the manager.

'Honeymoon couple, all the way from Brighton. Only it was them that did the smash and grab in Romford.'

'The mistake these people make,' said the manager, 'it's a simple one, but they all make it. They think if they come to a quiet little hotel in a backwater like this they'll never be noticed. Whereas of course it's just in a small place like this that we do notice them. That insurance manager last year, the minister and his church organist before that, and that fellow from Ipswich that did in his wife the year before that, and all the rest of them, they all come slinking in here as if they'd come to the end of the line where nobody would ever find them. And an hour after their case is in the papers we're on to them and on to the police.'

'I wonder what he's been up to,' the porter whispered, jerking his thinly thatched dome to the staircase where he had led Percy. 'He doesn't look the violent type, mind you.'

'You never can tell,' said the manager. 'We had a cook once in the Middle East, he looked like a cut-down Mr Pickwick and he put a butcher's chopper through the skull of a mess waiter that was always trying to kid him. He got fed up being kidded, that was all he would say.'

'Well, some of these blokes that are aye at the kidding would get on your nerves,' the porter commented, condoning the murder. 'We had a captain once in my regiment and he was always trying to take the mickey out the RSM. He couldn't ha' done a stupider thing. The upshot was—'

'Yes, I know,' said the manager smoothly. 'You told me. He was beat up in the Schipperstraat in Antwerp and he never knew who did it but he never cracked another joke till he was demobbed.'

The manager withdrew to his little office, and the porter ambled to his corner for a snooze.

And while Percy in the storey above them rose and fell in troubled waves of shallow sleep, like a cork bobbing on the Clyde, Savage still lay still on the stone floor of the cellar. Abandoned by Percy, never missed by his family, he just lay there, a couple of *Sunshine Readers* for his pillow. No comfortable room in a hotel for him, no snow-white sheets and a soft bed, and yet he had just as much money stashed away in an air-raid shelter as Percy had in his briefcase.

Even the stranger hadn't stayed to help him. One look frightened him away. He was only winded when he fell down the chute and he got on his pins cursing and swearing, determined to turn this damned cellar upside down. For all his watching he had never seen anybody go in by the door in Tulip Place, but he had never believed the Phinns' story that the door was only a blind. A lock-smith friend made half a dozen keys for him, one of which was almost bound to fit the conventional lock on such a door as he had described. He had got the keys that morning, and waited till it was quite dark before trying them. The third one was the lucky one. When it opened the door he felt he was Aladdin entering the cave. The way he was shoved down the chute the moment he put a foot across the threshold convinced him someone was trying to keep him out of the cellar. Which in turn proved that the cellar was the right place, as he had suspected all along.

He too had come furnished with a torch, a bigger and better one than Percy's or Savage's, and he used it to probe the extent of the cellar when he staggered to his feet. He was ready and willing to take all night to searching it. But when he saw a schoolboy in a black leather jacket and jeans lying huddled against a pile of rubbish his heart came up to his gullet, turned over, and fell to the pit of his stomach.

Whether the boy was dead or dying was no concern of his. It was enough there was a body lying there. He had his own pride in his intelligence, and his guess was that two other folk had found the money before him and one of them had done in the other.

'Just my bloody luck!' he moaned. 'Just that bit too late. The bastard that wired me must ha' been on his way out with the lot. So help ma Bob!'

He flashed a beam of daylight brightness on Savage, up and down him and round him, and bent over him a little. He thought he heard breathing but he couldn't wait to make sure. He didn't want to get involved. To hang around murder or manslaughter or whatever it was would put him out of the way of the money for ever. He left Savage lying and scrambled up the chute, practically on all fours, back to his kennel in a motel near Bridgeton Cross.

The sun rose again in a clear sky, promising another hot day, and Percy rose with it, not refreshed but not fatigued. He washed and shaved slowly, wallowing in the luxury of his first morning in a hotel. He was all set for his flight to London and from there to Land's End. His scalp tingled, as often before, with a thrilling sensation that fate had marked him out for something special. He was no commonplace non-entity from a back-street. He had a destiny, and he had the talisman of his briefcase. He wasn't sure how many thousands were in it, for the fight with Savage had confused his memory, but he was sure he had enough to arm him for a long time against an unfriendly world. He thought he could live for years on what he was carrying, and he couldn't think past that.

He had his breakfast in a corner of a heavily quiet dining-room, a gaunt clergyman and his chubby wife in another corner, two debonair commercial travellers in a third, and an elderly couple who looked like Punch and Judy living in retirement slobbered softly in the fourth corner. The centre was a desert of white tablecloths and glittering cutlery. Grapefruit or porridge, toast, and bacon and eggs. Percy chose the grapefruit because he had never liked porridge and then he had difficulty scooping out a spoonful. He let it go half-eaten, but made up for it on the toast and bacon and eggs.

The night-manager was still on duty and when Percy passed the desk on his way out to Charing Cross and a bus to the Central Station he sent a weary glance from under his heavy-lidded eyes, and a little smile flickered under his pencil-line moustache.

'Good morning, sir,' he said gently. 'Pleasant journey to Aberdeen.'

Percy splayed manfully on.

'Morning,' he muttered audibly, and inaudibly he said, 'Sarcastic little nyaff. You'd think he didn't believe I was going to Aberdeen.'

It was just turned nine o'clock on a bright summer morning in the middle of June.

So bright was the morning that elderly men went to work without a hat and without a waistcoat, young girls bloomed at the bus-stops in sleeveless frocks and bare legs, glad to leave off their stockings because it meant they didn't need to wear a girdle, schoolboys who had sat their term examinations played truant along the banks of the Canal as far north as Bishopbriggs and Cawder, and the city reeled in a heat haze filled with the choking smell of dust and tar. The cruel sun put a limelight on the decaying front of slum properties where housewives eighty feet above the gutters sweated in a love-longing for the country and listened to the pigeons moaning, all in the blue unclouded weather.

Before nine o'clock Mr Daunders had two phone calls. The first was from Miss Nairn's mother to say Miss Nairn wouldn't be in because she had flu.

'Flu in the month of June!' Mr Daunders muttered callously when he put the phone back in its cradle. 'Flu in weather like this! What will they think up next?'

He sat chafing at his little desk and tried to work out a way of dispersing Miss Nairn's class amongst the other teachers without coming into collision with the non-cooperative element. He had nearly finished allotting the last half-dozen of Miss Nairn's forty-eight pupils when he had his second phone call. Mr Whiffen said he wouldn't be in till some time after ten or eleven because his widowed mother had taken a bad turn during the night and he had to wait in for the doctor to call. There was no one else.

Mr Daunders sneered at the phone sceptically when he

cradled it again, and sat at his desk to work out what to do about Mr Whiffen's forty-five pupils.

'He probably means he won't be in all morning, if I know him,' he snorted. 'Now what's the best thing to do? I don't want to disperse another class. I've nowhere to put them even if I did. What I could do is shift an infant-teacher into Whiffen's class for the morning, and put six girls from the top class into the infants. It would serve. They could keep them quiet or play games with them. Oh, if I could just find peace and quiet to sit in the sun and read my Horace! Aye, the far Coolins are calling me away!'

He went out to the playground at nine o'clock to see the school in and strolled back in the sunshine to his room. Maybe he could get peace for an hour or two now. But when he entered the corridor where his room was he saw a man and a woman waiting at his door. He hadn't his glasses on and he peered. He sensed trouble. He relaxed a little when he recognized Frank Garson and his father. They wouldn't be bringing trouble. They were nice people.

'Beautiful morning,' he said pleasantly, raising his grey felt hat to the lady. 'Can I help you, Mr Garson?'

'This is my wife,' said Mr Garson. 'She thought we ought to come and see you. I kept the boy back, to come with us, I hope you don't mind, but you see it's him that's the reason for us wanting to see you. It's him that knows what my wife thinks you ought to be told. He's got a story about the cellar.'

'The cellar?' said Mr Daunders. 'Come in. Come in, Mrs Garson. You mean the school cellar?'

'I'm afraid so,' said Mr Garson unhappily, and threw an appeal at his wife to take over. She knew he hated talking. That was her line, and this was her idea. His wife raised her head high with pride, taking her cue, knowing this was her hour, and started talking calmly, fluently, clearly, with a don't-you-dare-interrupt-me firmness.

Mr Daunders hunched at his desk and played with his

paper-knife as she talked. Apart from the fact that he prided himself on always letting other people have their say and believed he had a cool, analytical brain that could extract the essence from any amount of blethering, he was in no state to interrupt. As soon as she mentioned money hidden in the cellar his head was a battlefield of different pains struggling for supremacy; a dogged steady ache holding its ground like fire-baptised infantry grimly obstructed the sudden sallies that thrust deep into his skull like a combined air and tank force blitzing the infantry.

'I knew it, I knew it, I knew it,' he muttered, not interrupting her, merely making a light marginal note to her narrative as she described the share-out. He ploughed his grey hair with clean-nailed fingers and turned to the boy when the mother finished.

'Just how much would you say was there?' he asked sadly.

Frank Garson knew he had to go through with it now it was started, but he wasn't enjoying being an informer. He looked at his headmaster dully and said nothing.

'A hundred?' Mr Daunders bid.

The boy shook a heavy head.

'A thousand?' Mr Daunders raised his bid.

The boy looked at him as if he was daft.

'Ten, twenty or thirty, I don't know,' he gave a grudging answer.

'Thousand?' Mr Daunders' eyebrows went up. 'You mean thousands, you don't mean just ten or twenty pounds?'

'Thousands,' the boy insisted softly.

Mr Daunders sagged over his paper-knife.

'Now, think, my boy, think!' he admonished him magisterially. 'Maybe there's not much between ten and twenty pounds, but there's a big difference between ten thousand and twenty thousand. As for thirty thousand, now just think! Thirty thousand is twenty thousand more than ten thousand.'

The boy didn't dispute it.

'You surely know better than that how much you saw,' Mr Daunders said plaintively.

'It was an awful lot,' the boy said helpfully.

'We'd better go down and see this cellar,' said Mr Daunders bravely rising.

He sent for the janitor to bring the key, and they all went down through the basement, Mr and Mrs Garson, Frank and the headmaster, and Mr Green the janitor leading them with the key in his hand like a mace-bearer leading a royal procession. Once the door was opened Mr Green switched on the ceiling lights and ushered them all in. He was glad he had the foresight to put a team of cleaners on to tidying the place. His conscience was clear. He didn't mind who inspected the cellar.

'It's a bit dusty,' he said pleasantly, 'but I try to keep it in some kind of order. It was just a dump before I came here. What was it you were wanting to see, Mr Daunders?'

The headmaster wasn't disposed to tell the janitor more in the meantime than he had to.

'It's only something this boy thinks he saw down here,' he said remotely. 'Just wait by the door, Mr Green, please, if you don't mind.'

But before Frank Garson had time to cross the cellar and point out the tea-chests they all saw Savage lying on the floor. Mr Daunders cried, 'Oh, my God!' Mrs Garson screamed, Mr Garson frowned, the janitor came forward from the door, eager for sensation, and Frank Garson fainted.

The mother attended to her boy and the janitor attended to Savage. Like all janitors he was a bit of a plumber, electrician, carpenter, glazier, accountant, wages-clerk, and first-aid expert.

'He's all right,' he said on his knees. 'He's breathing. He's knocked out or fainted or something.'

Mr Daunders hopped bird-like round the kneeling janitor and the prostrate boy.

'Phone for an ambulance,' he cried anxiously, 'phone

for the police, get his mother, take him up to my room, get a doctor, quick!'

'Well, give us a hand then,' said Mr Green, slightly aggrieved at the number of orders.

Mr Garson thawed far enough to help him to carry the boy upstairs. Frank Garson came to and followed them with his mother's right arm round his shoulders, and Mr Daunders guarded the rear from further alarms.

'Just remembered,' panted the janitor as he laboured up the steep staircase from the cellar to the basement while Mr Garson grunted with Savage's feet against his midriff. 'This is the school doctor's morning, the monthly medical, you know. Maybe he's in by this time.'

All Mr Daunders' orders were obeyed, not all at once, but in due order. They laid Savage reverently on the floor in Mr Daunders' room, they fetched the school visiting doctor from the medical room, they phoned for an ambulance, and they sent the school milk attendant to fetch in Mrs Savage. The call to the police Mr Daunders put off for a while till he had time to take his bearings.

The doctor said it was only a case of concussion. Mrs Savage said the boy hadn't been home all night but she hadn't worried, because it wasn't the first time he had run away and he always came back, and the ambulance took him to the Royal Infirmary.

'Now,' sighed Mr Daunders, hunched at his desk again. 'Where are we?'

'Look, Mr Daunders,' said the janitor shrewdly. 'That boy was in a fight. Cause I saw his belt lying beside him when we picked him up. You know that belt you told him not to wear, that Army belt with all the brass studs in it, it was lying near him. I bet you he took it off to swipe somebody and got the worst of it. But I don't know how he got into the cellar, there's only me got a key to it.'

He was in on this and he wasn't going to be kept out. No standing by at the door for him, he was on the inside now. After all, it was his cellar. You couldn't have boys lying

unconscious in his cellar, and then try and tell him to wait
outside please. No, thank you.

'There's something queer going on,' he said. 'You mark
my words.'

'Let's go back down,' said Mr Daunders patiently. It
couldn't be kept from the janitor. There was no point
trying. 'Are you all right now, Frank?'

The boy nodded, standing in front of his mother with
her hands on his shoulder, nestling into her like a frightened sparrow.

'Yes, he's all right now,' said his mother. 'That would
have given anybody a shock, so it would. He might have
been dead for all we knew. But we want to get this story
cleared up one way or the other.'

They all went back to the cellar, with Frank as the
fingerman. One chest was empty, the next had three
hundred and fifty pounds, and the third had two hundred
and seventy. The janitor was astounded, Frank was humiliated, and his parents and Mr Daunders looked at him
with respect. To them, his story was proved. He had
merely mistaken hundreds for thousands, a thing any
schoolboy might do at the sight of a lot of money.

'Good God, what an amount of money!' cried Mr
Green, and rubbed his chin with itching fingers.

'Somebody's been at it,' Frank Garson whispered.
'Somebody's shifted it.'

'Was there more?' Mr Daunders asked softly.

'A wheen mair, I mean a lot more,' the boy told him,
almost angrily. 'And there was money in the chest that's
empty. I know. I tried to count it once. And I saw it at the
last Friday Night Service.'

'The last what?' Mr Daunders frowned.

'This boy Phinn was starting a new religion,' Mrs
Garson explained. 'That's a part of the story I didn't
make clear when I was talking to you.'

'Yes, of course, this fellow Percy Phinn was the ring-
leader, wasn't he?' Mr Daunders remembered. His head
was giving him hell. 'I'd better send across the street for

his mother. I know her. And I'll have to phone the police. I'm sorry, Mrs Garson, but I'll have to.'

'I don't mind,' she answered proudly. 'My boy's hands are clean.'

'Leave those chests just as they are, Mr Green,' the headmaster addressed the janitor formally. 'Lock the door after us and give me the key. I want things left just as they are for the police.'

He sent the Garsons home. The parents said they were afraid of reprisals if their boy stayed on at the school. He told them to get a medical certificate for him.

'Nerves, general debility, anything you like,' he said. 'It doesn't matter. There are only two weeks left till the end of term. And he's sat all his examinations. It doesn't matter. He would be safer away till all this is sorted out. You're quite right.'

'We're moving anyway,' Mr Garson chipped in so unexpectedly that Mr Daunders turned to him as to a dumb stranger who had suddenly acquired the gift of speech. 'I'm getting a job outside the city, and I'm going to put the boy to another school after the holidays.'

'An excellent idea,' said Mr Daunders. He was too concerned about the police calling at his school to care very much where Frank Garson went next session.

'There must have been nearly a thousand quid there,' said Mr Green chattily when the Garsons were gone and Mr Daunders stood at the phone dialling the police.

'Would you mind running across the street and asking Mrs Phinn to come over and see me for a moment?' he said, freezing him.

Mrs Phinn came over in her slippers and an old black dress that was torn under one arm-pit. She knew nothing of any money. She was only a poor despised widow, forced by poverty to work as a cleaner in the school where her man had once been the janitor, and a far better janitor than Mr Green would ever be, a janitor headmasters could turn to for advice. All she knew was Percy hadn't been home all night, and he was a good son and he had never stayed away all night before. Where was Mr Daunders hiding him? What was he trying to do to her?

'You know more about him than I do,' she said aggressively. 'Bringing me over here to ask me a lot of questions. And you know the answers, I can tell it the way you ask me. What are you trying to make me say?'

She didn't do Mr Daunders' headache any good, and he was glad to get rid of her without telling her very much.

'We thought you might be able to help us, that's all. It's nothing much, not really. No more than I've tried to tell you, if you'd only listen. There's been some money hidden in the cellar and some boys said Percy knew something about it. We're not accusing anybody, we just wanted to have a word with your son.'

Mrs Phinn was as keen to get away as Mr Daunders was to let her go. She didn't want to listen to any talk of money in the cellar. The moment he mentioned it she remembered the stranger in the raincoat. She was sure it meant real trouble now, and all she wanted to do was bury her head in the sand of her own corner till it was all over.

'I always knew that big stupid lump would get into trouble one day,' she muttered, banging the door behind when she got home. 'Him and his books, as thick as his head. Ideas above his station, that's his trouble. And where the hell has he got to? Well, he won't break my heart, I'll make sure of that. And me sticking up for him, telling folk he's a good son. He's been a dead loss since the day I weaned him!'

Mr Daunders relaxed for a moment or two in the blessed silence of his room when Mrs Phinn had gone.

'I suppose I'll have to phone the Office too,' he thought, sighing in misery. He had always made it his policy never to bother the Director of Education. 'See what they think. They may want a formal report. I don't know what the procedure is in a case like this. But that cellar is Corporation property, so I suppose the Office has a legal interest in the money. Found on their property. I wonder whose it is? But I can't see that I'm responsible in any way. Oh dear, what a mess! By God, I'll enjoy this summer holiday. A fine quiet month in Skye, far away from it all!'

While he was waiting for the police to arrive he sent for Noddy, Specky, Skinny, Wedderburn, Cuddie and Cutchy – all the boys mentioned in Mrs Garson's account of what her son had told her, and all the boys he had found with too much money at one time or another. He saw them one by one, keeping them incommunicado till his interviews were complete. He questioned them cleverly, he wheedled and coaxed, he shouted and whispered, he threatened and promised, adjusting his technique to the temperament of the boy. He learned nothing. Maybe they weren't very bright at the general analysis of a complex sentence or the decimalization of money, but they knew when the wind was in the east. They had their own grapevine. They didn't know Savage had been found knocked out in the cellar, but they all knew Savage was absent. They had all seen Garson waiting with his father and mother at the headmaster's door. They didn't know why. But they all knew Garson hadn't gone to his class after that. They saw their cue and they took it. There is nobody shrewder than a backward schoolboy. It may be an awkward fact, but it is still a fact, that when a boy has a battle of wits with his headmaster, even if that headmaster is an Honours graduate in Latin and Greek with a pass in the classes of Logic and Metaphysics and Mental Philosophy, the boy wins every time. He isn't tempted to parry and equivocate, he doesn't feel any desire to show off and come back with a clever answer. He is a brick wall, and you can't see through a brick wall by logic alone. You need a window.

Mr Daunders dismissed the last of them and prepared a memorandum for the police. Two plain-clothes men called just before the morning interval and made Mr Daunders' little office look tiny indeed. He sat at his desk rather than stand up beside them, five feet seven against six feet one and six feet two. They made notes in a little notebook as he went through his narrative.

'Looks like your boy Savage had a fight with this fellow Percy in the cellar last night,' said one of them, thrusting his notebook into the inside pocket of his jacket. 'They had a fight over the money. Let's have a look at it, please.'

Mr Daunders took them down to the cellar, and when they saw it they glanced at each other and nodded.

'Yes, we know where this came from,' said the one who hadn't spoken before.

'What we want to know is how it got here, of course,' said the other.

They climbed the steep staircase to the basement again and went back to the headmaster's room. Before lunch-time they had questioned all the boys Mr Daunders had tried to question. And Noddy, Specky, Skinny, Wedderburn, Cuddy and Cutchy who had stonewalled Mr Daunders' bowling, didn't raise a bat when the two plain-clothes men got to work on them. There's nobody like a plain-clothes man for getting a Glasgow schoolboy to come clean. Stringing a teacher along is all part of the natural order of things, but he doesn't like taking a chance with a detective. The law-man always wins. The telly had taught him that, even if it had taught him nothing more.

'Looks like this fellow Percy is our man,' said the taller detective when the three of them were alone again. 'I don't think he knows where it came from. It looks like he just found it. But it seems pretty certain he organized these lads to spend it and then blew with the rest of it. He's probably got thousands. We'll push off to the infirmary and see if this boy Savage is fit to talk to. I think he guessed what Percy was up to and they had a fight about it.'

'Oh, this Phinn fellow won't get very far,' said the other plain-clothes man. 'We've got a good description. We'll pick him up by tea-time. You can't escape the police today. Telephones, radio, television. Wherever he goes he'll be recognized. He hasn't a chance.'

'No,' said Mr Daunders. 'There's no escape, is there? Not for any of us.'

The two plain-clothes men took leave of Mr Daunders

graciously. They were polite and unexcitable. They knew they were on the winning side.

'Of course, Callum,' said the one to the other on the way out, 'we don't know that Phinn will be able to tell us how it got there.'

'No, that's true, Ewan,' answered his mate. 'But he must know something surely. Anyway, before we go to the infirmary let's get his description out. London, Dublin, Belfast, Liverpool, the Channel ports, the works.'

Percy felt fine travelling first-class to London. He would have treated himself to travelling by air but he didn't know if you had to book in advance, and he had no time to find out. The train was so quiet he had a compartment to himself, and he sat back enjoying his solitary comfort. This was the life. This was the beginning of his long-desired peace and quiet. Between Glasgow and Kilmarnock he was thrilled with the speed of the train and gazed through the window with childish interest at the circular sweep of the countryside as it rushed past him. He felt the blue unclouded sky above the fields was blessing his journey and he marvelled at the way the train was devouring distance. He had never been so far from home before and his journey was hardly started. He fetched out a little diary with a map of the British Isles on the front fly-leaf and studied his route.

'Morning coffee,' intoned a man in a white jacket, sliding the door half-open, and then passed on lurching smoothly to the roll of the train.

'Sure thing,' said Percy brightly.

He took his briefcase with him. Maybe he wasn't a poet, maybe he was a promising young executive on his way to a conference in London. He put a distant look in his eyes as he sat alone at a table for two, his precious briefcase snugly between his side and the window. The waiter would recognize he had problems on his mind, business problems, and his case contained the documents he had to study.

'White or black?' said the waiter, two jugs at the ready.

Percy found it a difficult question. He had never been

served that way before. All his mother ever made was tea and all Sophy ever gave him was espresso coffee. He wondered which was the more sophisticated choice.

'Black if you don't mind,' he said at last with ungainly assumption of nonchalance.

He fumbled badly taking a couple of biscuits from the tray offered him and grew cross with himself. Anybody carrying the amount of money he was carrying had no call to get nervous. Then he made a problem out of the tip. The bill was one and six, and he had a florin and a half-crown handy. Sixpence seemed too mean a tip, too Scots for a poet on his way to Cornwall, so he put both coins down and waved away the change like a pasha dismissing an unsatisfactory dancing-girl.

He spent the time between morning coffee and lunch brooding about it. Maybe he had tipped him too much. There was something in the arch of the waiter's shaggy eyebrows. He had read in a magazine that the proper tip was ten per cent of the bill. Ten per cent of one and six was quite a sum for him to work out in his head. The only answer he could get sounded absurd and the calculation reminded him of Miss Elginbrod so he gave it up. Anyway, a poet was above arithmetic. There was that great French writer he had read of who used to tip the waiter at the Ritz extravagantly. If he had over-tipped he was in good company.

Lunch came along accompanied with more problems. He felt clumsy with the soup spoon, awkward with the knife and fork, ill-at-ease with the dessert spoon. He would willingly have settled for his mother's stand-by of mince and tatties followed by a cup of tea with no saucer. But there was no tea to follow. It was coffee again.

It was afternoon tea finally shattered him. He was bewildered by the accent of a waiter he had seen from a distance at lunch.

'Teakike aw taoust?' he asked, bowing over him with a large tray balanced in one hand and a serving-fork in the other.

Percy didn't recognize the language. The cockney diphthong echoed and echoed in his head till in sheer fatigue it resolved itself into a good round long 'o'.

'Toast,' said Percy severely, resenting the accent.

He was left with his toast, a little china teapot and a small jar of apple jelly. The train barged on, exulting in its freedom, and it gave a heave and a sway like a wild mustang every time Percy lifted the teapot and tried to pour himself a cup of tea. He got more tea in the saucer than in the cup, and when he raised the cup and tried to find the rim with his lips drops of spilt tea fell on his lap. He decided to do without a cup of tea and eased some jelly from the jar with his knife. He nearly had it safe on his toast when the train did another bucking-bronco act, and the quivering jelly slid off his knife, missed his toast and his plate and landed plop on the white cloth. He scooped it off hastily and felt the cockney waiter's eyes squinting at him. To assert himself and demonstrate his natural dexterity he lifted the teapot again. It was worse than the first time. He didn't only miss the cup, he missed the saucer too. The waiter came over with unostentatious grace, murmured, 'Excuse me, sir,' removed the swimming saucer and dripping cup, and came back with another cup and saucer. Silently he poured Percy a cup of tea from the little pot without spilling a drop.

Percy was humiliated. He felt all his self-esteem and all the confidence built by the money in the briefcase evaporate like moisture under a blazing sun. And the sudden evaporation chilled him to the marrow. He began to feel afraid.

When he stepped off the train and walked through Euston Station the weakening of his confidence cracked to a complete failure of nerve. What had seemed a vague and distant future, fit material for daydreams, was now a precise and immediate problem. It was all very well saying he was going to Land's End, but just exactly where and how would he live when he got there? What would he do? He had fallen from the clouds and had to pick his way on

the ground. He didn't like it. There was no breakfast,
dinner and tea, no laundry and rent, no strangers to meet
and no bills to pay in his daydreams. But they were all
worrying him now, little daily chores he would have to
face, and he didn't feel fit to cope. It wasn't enough just
having the money. He had to get organized.

He took a taxi, his first taxi, to Victoria. He had picked
up the idea somewhere that Victoria was the right station
for the west country.

'Oh, blimey!' said the taxi-driver when Percy paid the
fare with one of the fivers he had shoved into his pocket in
the cellar. 'What's this? A soap coupon?'

'That's a perfectly good five-pound note,' Percy told
him severely, rebellious at his flippancy.

'Yus, but taint an English fiver,' the taxi-driver retorted. 'It's the foreign exchange you want, mate. I don't
reckon on changing fivers every trip, not Scotch ones,
anyway. Is that all you've got?'

'Yes, it's all I've got,' Percy admitted, and his head was
hot and his face was red. To prove he was telling the truth
he fished out the handfuls of fivers he had stuffed in his
pocket.

'Whatja bin doing? Robbin a bank?' asked the taxi-
driver pleasantly. 'Youghta changed all that foreign
money before you came down here, son.'

He changed the note with a grudge, and when he had
turned round in a curve hardly bigger than the arc of a
Scots threepenny-bit and dashed back into Victoria Street
he left a very worried Percy outside the Station.

'I never thought on that,' he meditated, alone and
bewildered. 'I should've got travellers' cheques, so I
should. But then I'd have to have banked it, wouldn't
I? And I couldn't just walk into a bank and bank thousands
in fivers. That would have put the ba' up on the slates, that
would! I should have studied banking instead of reading so
much philosophy. I might have found a way round it
then.'

He turned his back on the station and trudged along

Victoria Street, making trivial purchases here and there
and changing a fiver each time. Between the difficulty
caused by his accent and the strangeness of the currency
he tendered, he had a rough time. He was made to feel his
notes were being changed this time as a favour, but he
wasn't to do it again.

He became so confused he forgot he had taken a taxi to
get him to Victoria, and kept slouching on away from the
Station. When he came to Parliament Square and Westminster Bridge the tea-time rush was at its thickest. He
stood at the pavement edge, afraid to cross the road. He
was a Gulliver among the Brobdingnagians. All these
smart, elegant young men, these slim swift girls, seemed
a superior race. Glasgow was a village in comparison, and
he wished he was back there. By the time he had walked
round Parliament Square and managed to get across to
Westminster Bridge to look at the Thames he was lost. He
wasn't sure if Victoria Station was behind or in front of
him, to his right or his left. Half an hour in London had
shattered him. He fought back bravely for a moment by
going up to one of the smart elegant young men in black
jacket, striped trousers and bowler, with a rolled umbrella
in hand, and asked him how to get to Victoria Station. It
was only another defeat. The elegant young man couldn't
understand a word of Percy's broad Glasgow and Percy
couldn't understand a word of the elegant young man's
Lambeth. (In fact all he said was, 'I'm sorry, I don't speak
French.')

More by good luck than guidance he got back on his
tracks again and his weary splay feet took him slowly back
along Victoria Street. He was tired, hot and sticky, but he
didn't dare take a bus because he didn't know which one to
take, and he was sure he wouldn't know where to get off
anyway. One thing was certain, he wasn't going to ask any
of these foreigners to direct him a second time. Nobody
could make out what they were saying. You asked them a
simple question and you got a lot of gibberish back.
Walking was safer.

The Station frightened him when he saw it again. It was
a jungle of people. He could never fight his way through
there. He didn't even try. He kept on prowling, thinking
he would rest in a hotel for the night and enquire in the
morning how to get to Land's End. A small place in
Wilton Road took his fancy and he sidled through the
glass door into a hushed house with thick carpets. A
dapper little man behind a highly polished counter greeted
him in a benevolent whisper, and Percy nervously explained he had left Aberdeen in a hurry on an urgent
business matter and hadn't had time to change his Scottish
fivers to English ones. He showed a handful to prove he
could pay for a room. 'Would you accept these . . .' He
faded away like a radio with a defective valve.

'Oh, yes, of course. That's quite all right,' the dapper
little man said courteously. With an ear accustomed to
divers accents he got a working idea of what Percy was
trying to say. The only thing that puzzled him was why a
youth with an unmistakable Glasgow voice should say he
had come from Aberdeen.

He pushed the register across, and Percy signed his own
name, too worn out to think what he was doing.

He lay on top of his bed for an hour, his shoes and socks
off, wiggling his toes to cool his fiery feet. London's
pavements were hotter than Glasgow's. He slid into a
little doze and disorderly pictures of Savage passed over
his exhausted brain. Then slowly, for all his morning
coffee, his three-course lunch and his afternoon tea, an
appetite uncoiled in him and he had a craving for a fish
supper. Surely in a big city like London he could buy a
poke of fish and chips somewhere. He certainly didn't
want dinner in the hotel. What he had seen of the dining
room when he was being shown upstairs to his room had
been enough for him. He didn't want a snow-white cloth
and a spread of gleaming cutlery. He just wanted a poke of
fish and chips, and maybe a cup of tea.

He heaved himself up with a sigh and sat on the edge of
his bed, shoving his fingers through his straw-coloured

hair and yawning. When the long groaning yawn was
spent he bent down to pick up his sweat-damp socks from
the floor.

'I should buy another pair of socks, that's what I should
do,' he thought, groping wearily.

There was a knock at his door. He froze, still bent down,
one hand clutching one sock. He straightened slowly,
holding his breath.

'Aye?' he called out hoarsely, puzzled.

Two men came in. Two tall, broad-shouldered men,
clean shaven and alert, bareheaded, one just a little grey,
the other red-haired. For all his sheltered life Percy knew
two plain-clothes policemen when he saw them.

'Ye didn't take long, did ye?' he said, his bare feet on the
carpet with the toes clenched.

He looked at them plaintively and began to cry. He was
tired and fed up.

'Percy Phinn?' said the grey-haired man.

'Is he dead?' Percy asked, still clutching his sock. The
sole was hard where the sweat had dried. His answering
one question by asking another was involuntary. He
wasn't deliberately stalling. He was worried about Savage.

They didn't know what he was talking about. All they
had was Percy's description and the information that he
would probably be carrying a lot of money that wasn't his
own. It was all the hotel-manager had too when he phoned
them. Percy didn't know he was famous at last, just as he
had longed to be, named and described on radio and
television. He hadn't thought of his flight being public
knowledge by tea-time. What he thought was that only
murder could have brought the police on to him so
quickly.

'Is who dead?' the grey-haired man asked gently.

'Savage,' said Percy with a quivering lower lip. 'You
know about Savage. Did I kill him? I never meant to. It
was an accident.'

'We just want to ask you a few questions,' the policeman
said soothingly. He preferred to let the question of Savage

lapse till he learned more. 'May I see your luggage, please?'

Percy began to cry again, with such childish abandonment that they had to take time off to comfort him. They weren't cruel men. They didn't enjoy seeing a big fellow like Percy in such a state.

'Come on, come on now! Pull yourself together!' said the red-haired man. 'If you'd killed anybody we would know about it. We just want to have a chat with you. Come on now, you're all right now!'

Percy watched them take his briefcase and open it. His sobs died away. He put on his socks and shoes and stood up, willing to go. He knew he had lost the briefcase for good. It was like having a bad tooth pulled. Courage screwed to the sticking point, panic in the pit of his stomach, and then the grinding loss and the relief, the consolation of knowing he would be better off without it, the suffering over.

He felt very important being taken away in a police-car, and when he sat in the police-station answering questions he was anxious to be friendly. He wanted to impress these two kind gentlemen who had treated him so courteously. They gave him a cup of tea. They even got a fish supper for him. He was grateful. He owed it to them to make it clear he was no dumb delinquent from a Glasgow slum. No, he was an intelligent youth with a good command of English. All the doubts that had obscurely budded within him during his journey south in the Royal Scot, all the dim misgivings that had thrown a deathly shadow over his self-esteem, the frightening sensation of being a Lilliputian in Brobdingnag when he left Euston Station, all these made him eager to surrender. But to surrender with dignity. The bubbling stream of his fluency surprised himself, and he was proud to be so clear and honest.

The two policemen listened so attentively he was sure he had captured their interest by his gift for expression. Partly they had to concentrate to understand what he was saying in his outlandish voice, partly they knew there was a time to stop asking questions and just let him ramble. He rambled. Behind him another policeman sat at a small table taking shorthand notes, but Percy was so taken up with his defence that he didn't even notice him.

'Mind you, I see the fallacy,' he said. He liked the word. It was an honest admission of error. 'I like to give in to a fair thing. Money won't make you a poet or a philosopher. You've got to have genius or well anyway talent and when you have it you've still got to work. To use it, I mean, to make anything of it, you've got to work. You just can't run away with money. What did I want the money for anyway? Well, I'll tell you. I wanted to get peace and quiet. Peace and quiet to be a poet or something. Aye, but then when you've got the peace and quiet you've got to make use of it, you've got to do something, you've got to work. Money'll give you leisure but the leisure's no use if you haven't got the genius. And when you haven't got it, money's no substitute. I had been reading a lot of Shelley, cause he's got the same name as me, the same colour of hair, and he had the money to do what he wanted, so I thought if I had the money I could do what Shelley done. But you see that's the fallacy I was telling you about. The money itself won't do it, you've got to be born to it. It's all a matter of birth. You've got to be born to the use of money just like you've got to be born with genius. You take the folk that win the pools. I read an article once and it showed that ninety-nine-point-nine of the folk that win the big money in the pools never come to anything. Mind you, I didn't want the money for materialistic purposes. No, what I'm telling you is I've got spiritualistic values. I wanted the money to get peace and quiet, to write my poetry, you understand. And then coming down in the train today it dawned on me I hadn't a pome in my head. I've wrote nothing since I found the money. I'm not a poet, I'm not a philosopher. You've got to be born to these things. It's all a matter of hereditary. There's no use kidding and swanking. My father was only a plumber and then he was a janitor and my mother worked in Templeton's carpet factory before she was married. You see, I'd need a different hereditary, but then I wouldn't be me, would I? Mind you, I'm clever enough, I'm not stupid, but money won't make you a poet, will it? It won't even get you peace and quiet when you're not born to the use of it.'

'So you found this money?' said the grey-haired man.

'No, I never found it,' said Percy quickly. 'One of the Brotherhood found it, and it was reported to me because I tried to learn them and I had to take charge of the money for their own good.'

'Did your father ever mention it to you?' asked the red-haired man.

'Oh no,' said Percy, almost laughing at the idea. 'My father never mentioned anything to me. He was a sort of quiet man. He never spoke to me much.'

'Well, where do you think it came from?' asked the red-haired man.

'Now, that's a good point,' said Percy eagerly. 'Now, you might think this a bit far-fetched but I feel very serious about it. I believe it came from God like the manna to the Jews in the desert. We were all in the desert. We never had a thing. And I believed God chose me, 'cause God does choose people, doesn't He? I mean, you can't deny it, can you? You take Moses.'

The two policemen looked at him steadily, showing no inclination to take anybody.

'Do you know El is the Hebrew word for God?' Percy asked them in the tone of a person who is sure the answer is No. 'And El is the sign of the pound note. You know that much, don't you? Well, I believed the God of Moses had revealed Himself to me under the form of El. I had a regular service every Friday night, I taught piety to the Brotherhood, but they fell away, just like the Jews did with Moses. I was the only one that was true to God. I believe in God, you know. I'm not an atheist. I'm not one of your juvenile delinquents. I've studied things. Maybe my God's not your God but He's still God, and

I'll grant you your God's God too. But my fallacy was . . .'

He was off again in a circle, and the policemen let him talk till he dried up. In the morning they took him back to Glasgow.

Savage came to just about the time Percy was having lunch on the Royal Scot. He was foxed for a while to find himself in a clean bed all to himself, wearing a night-shirt he had never worn before, and he sniffed curiously at the strange smell of the place. It was an odd stink, like strong soap. Then it all came back and he knew where he was. When the nurse who saw he was conscious at last brought in a policeman to see him he was too crafty to talk. He pretended he had lost his memory.

'Don't remember,' he mumbled in reply to every question.

He stayed in hospital all that day, and slept there that night, still pretending to be very groggy. There wasn't a thing wrong with him, but he knew the policeman would come back and he wanted time to think what to do.

'Hey, hey!' he called his nurse over with rude insistence at breakfast time. 'I've got to get up, I've got to get outa here. My memory's come back. I've gotta go and tell the polis what I know. They're waiting for me to help them.'

He was so eager, and he looked so innocent and well, they discharged him. But he didn't go near the police, he didn't go home, and he didn't go to school. He wandered round the fruit-market, stole a turnip just for practice, strolled over to the docks and bought a hot pie and a cup of tea in a poky little café in Anderston. He felt thrilled with the delight of freedom, happy with a plan that was funny enough to make a cat laugh. He sang to himself with the joy of it, hopped and skipped, chuckled and rubbed his palms together. Life was good and the sky shared his pleasure, flung wide over him without a cloud in it.

He turned up in Bethel Street at tea-time and the bush telegraph went to work so quickly that he had most of the Brotherhood at his appointed meeting-place within quarter of an hour. They came in ones and twos across the waste ground between the Steamie and the back-courts of Bethel Street, silent, worried, waiting the words of wisdom from the great Savage, Senior Claviger of the Bethel Brotherhood.

Specky came forward with his right hand high.

'Hail!' he said with an ingratiating smirk.

'Hail!' Savage murmured, his hand barely lifted. 'Whadya know?'

'Garson shopped us,' said Specky.

'He did, did he?' said Savage. He sneered briefly. 'Don't worry. I'll get that little lilyfaced come-to-Jesus bastard yet. I'll tie his guts round his neck, so I will. Don't worry. I'll sort him all right.'

Skinny was only a step behind Specky.

'Whadya know?' Savage greeted him too impartially, lounging against the wall of the air-raid shelter.

'It's in the papers,' Skinny said mournfully. 'And it was on the Scottish news on the telly there the now. They've got Percy. He's been arrested. They got him in London last night. Imagine our Percy in London!'

'Scotland's secret weapon,' Savage murmured lazily.

'He stole all our money and done a bunk,' said Skinny. Savage grinned wisely.

'The game's up,' said Specky. 'The cellar's finished. There's been cops there all day. You'd think the school was a police-station, the bobbies that's there.'

'You don't want to worry about the cellar,' said Savage.

'Well, we canny get in there now,' Specky complained.

'So what?' Savage asked, very uppish with him. 'There's nothing there now.'

'No, it looks like Percy cleaned it out,' said Skinny.

'I cleaned it out,' Savage boasted quickly. 'I've got ten times more stashed away than Percy took. I'm the boss now, Percy's a dead loss.'

'But the game's up,' Specky repeated. 'We couldny use it now. The cops is on to it. They'll be wanting to see you. They've seen us, all of us, even that nit Noddy.'

'What did yous tell them?' Savage asked.

'What could we tell them? You canny kid the cops. We told them everything.'

'Except where it is now,' Savage answered, grinning round at them all. ''Cause yous don't know. I know.'

'Well, we spent it, didn't we?' Skinny asked, looking at him dubiously.

'We spent nothing,' Savage derided him by his tone. 'I told you I had it stashed. What did we spend? A couple of hundred? Five hundred? What do you think?'

'I've no idea,' Skinny admitted.

'We spent nothing, nothing to what's left, nothing to what I took away,' Savage shouted at him, almost angrily.

He waved them to gather round and led them into the derelict air-raid shelter on the margin of the waste land, impatient to show them what he had hidden and to assert himself as their true boss because of the power he still had, the money he still had. The Brotherhood clustered in the cool dimness inside four brick walls, the floor only tramped earth, and listened to him offer them all the money they wanted. He was greater than Percy, he was smarter. He knew the cellar wouldn't be safe for long, he had been shifting the money for weeks and weeks, he had more than they had spent, ten times more than Percy took.

'There's loads and loads of it left,' he told them. 'I'm willing to share and share alike, and we can keep it for years and nobody'll ever be able to pin a damn thing on us. Yous willing? I'm willing!'

They wouldn't give in to him. They listened, but said nothing. They were frightened. They wanted no part of it any longer. He knew they were right. They were only behaving as he expected.

'Okay then!' he cried viciously. 'Nobody else'll get it.'

He dragged out a chisel from the back pocket of his jeans and prised away four bricks from the wall near the

tramped earth. When he straightened he had a bundle of
fivers in his hand and he tore off the band, scattered the
notes loose on the floor and then kicked them together
with his foot, collecting them into a little pyramid. Specky,
Skinny and Noddy, Cutchy, Pinky and Cuddy, and all the
rag tag and bobtail of the Brotherhood watched him
silently, suspiciously.

'Anybody want them?' he challenged.

Nobody moved, nobody spoke.

'Okay then,' he said once more, wagging a finger. 'Yous
don't want it, I don't want it. Okay then, nobody else'll get
it.'

He brought out the stump of a candle from his pocket,
showed it round on the palm of his hand, and when they
had all seen it he lit the wick with a loose match. The
Brotherhood watched him sullenly, suspiciously. They
didn't believe he would do it. He waved the lighted candle
round and above his head till the flame seemed to form a
continuous circle over him like a halo and grinned at the
grim eyes staring at him.

'Burn it then!' he cried in an ecstasy of destructiveness
and tossed the candle on to the little heap of notes.

A long-drawn gasp, like the involuntary sob of a sick
man in mortal pain came from the circle of spectators and
Savage laughed at them, a wild screech of joy.

The notes caught fire slowly, but when they burst into
flame the wax of the candle melted in the heat and yellow
tongues leapt high from the floor. The Brotherhood drew
back a little. Those flames looked dangerous. But Savage
was still cool. He went back to his cache and fetched out
bundle after bundle after bundle of fivers till they thought
he would never be done, all the money he had shifted
secretly from the cellar since the day he had his own key
made. He fed the flames carefully for a while with loose
notes, a few at a time to keep the fire burning brightly, but
he got impatient, he had so much to burn. He began to
throw on whole bundles, without even taking the band off,
and there was more smoke than flame.

Fits of coughing spread like an infection and Savage kindly raked the smouldering heap with the toe of his shoe to encourage the flames to leap out again. He chuckled happily as he tossed a last fistful on to the new blaze.

'That's the lot,' he turned and addressed the Brotherhood. 'Any complaints?'

They said nothing, but the dourness in the faces softened, dull eyes became brighter. They sagged in relief from doubt and anxiety, they breathed freely again like a patient who finds his illness wasn't mortal after all. Savage knew he had won. He was their master. He was the unchallenged leader of the pack, he could do what he liked with them. He threw his arms up, leapt like a ballet dancer high in the air, clicking his heels, and screamed to the roof.

'Yip-ee! Yip-ee! Yip-ee!'

He was inspired by the greatness of his action and went capering round the fire, whooping Red Indian war cries, his palm bobbing against his open lips, then down on his hunkers doing a Cossack dance. The frozen Brotherhood thawed completely in the warmth of his enthusiasm. Murmurs rustled through them like a wind in high corn and their feet itched to dance with their leader and their throats ached to howl with him.

Making a mockery of Percy's short-lived deity Savage began to chant the immemorial counting-out rhyme of Glasgow's back courts.

> El, el, domin-el,
> Eenty-teenty, figgerty-fel,
> You – are – OUT!

He pounced on Specky, and Specky opened his mouth wide and let out the most blood-curdling screech ever heard in any shelter. He circled round the flaming money in his own version of a Comanche dance and drunk with Savage's insolence he too chanted.

> Eenty-teenty, figgerty-fel,
> Percy's in a prison cell,
> I saw the cops and widny tell,
> You – are – OUT!

He tigged Skinny in his planetary course round the sun, and Skinny joined the dance, contributing squeakily.

> El, el, domin-el,
> Robin Hood and William Tell,
> Lawman, gunman, shot and shell,
> You – are – OUT!

He claimed Noddy in transit, but Noddy scorned to add to the chant. The only music he loved was what he could wheedle from a mouth-organ, what he hoped to coax from a piano one day if he succeeded in keeping the money he had hidden in the lavatory cistern. Still, to prove he had the true party spirit, he did a cartwheel, walked on his hands for twenty paces, and tumbled his wulcats. The rest of the Brotherhood surged exultantly forward and soon they were all in the fire-dance, whooping and hopping in a circle, right hand on the right shoulder of the comrade in front as they all swayed to the rhythm of *El-el, domin-el*.

Savage broke off at a tangent and ran to a corner where he kicked away a pile of causies, bent down lithely and came up with the big brass bell, the old school bell Percy had forbidden him to hawk. It was his now. Returning to the blaze he sergeant-majored the dancers, bawling out to inject the flagging chant with new strength.

> El, el, domin-el,
> We've lit the candle, now ring the bell!
> Garson shopped to save himsel',
> Let the bastard rot in hell,
> He – ran – OUT!

He rang the bell three times, and the Brotherhood halted and bowed their heads in mock reverence at that reminder of Percy's ritual.

'Yip-ee!' screamed Savage and whipped them on again. They picked up the steps, roaring together rhythmically, 'Yah! Yay! Yah-yah-yah!' Savage herded them as an out-rider, ringing the bell at every third step.

He rang it too often. And the ringing of the bell led to the end of their burial service for the god El and in a few moments they were scattered like leaves before the wild west wind for the stranger in the belted raincoat was crossing the wasteland just as their dance round the burning money was at its noisiest. He too was fully informed by press and radio of all that had happened, but when he learned that Percy had been lifted with about three thousand pounds on him he was far from satisfied the game was over. There was too much more still to be accounted for, too much for a gang of schoolboys to have spent in three months. He swore, and swore to find where the rest of it was.

In the afternoon he had asked at the hospital for Savage, pretending to be an uncle worried about the condition of his nephew. When he was told Savage had left in the morning to go to speak to the police it was just something more he didn't believe. Savage and not Percy now seemed to have the key to the mystery. By tea-time he was prowling round Bethel Street, Ossian Street and Tulip Place, hopefully looking for schoolboys. The trouble was he didn't know what Savage looked like. But he couldn't just go away and do nothing. He had to keep looking for schoolboys, because until he found them he wouldn't find Savage. One of them might say something, one of them might lead him somewhere. But there were no schoolboys to be seen. He had never known the area so empty of boys. He stopped hanging about the back-streets and went through the closes in Bethel Street desperate for some boys he could quiz. There was no point hanging about near the cellar. Nobody would go into the cellar now.

Anyway it wasn't likely the money was still there. If Percy had run away with so little, somebody else must have already shifted more. And that somebody else was Savage. He was sure of his deduction, proud of his shrewdness, but it didn't bring Savage any nearer.

He went into the back-court, but there were no boys there either. He went sideways through a bent railing into the waste ground and blundered over towards the Steamie, and that was when he heard the bell ringing in the air-raid shelter. He stopped, looked and listened. He saw a thin trail of smoke coming out of the entrance, he heard the hubbub of boyish trebles, and then the bell again, and again. He moved over stealthily, peered in cautiously, saw the blazing paper on the floor, the boys dancing round it, an acrobat doing somersaults, a midget all topsy-turvy walking on his hands, whirling dervishes, howling wolves and laughing hyenas. But boys for all that. That was all he wanted. Boys. He had come to the end of the line. He knew it. He dashed in like a commando attacking an enemy outpost single-handed.

Then he saw it was indeed the end of the line. He saw the flames leaping from the bright apex of the pyramid and on the slopes, curled with the heat, already licked by eager tongues, he saw the fivers and recognized the imprint of the bank. They seemed to be drawing the flames to themselves like a magnet, and nothing could save them.

As quickly as the stranger recognized the banknotes Savage recognized the stranger Percy had warned them about. He held the bell by the clapper, raised his free hand to hush his brothers, and stepped forward boldly to confront the intruder, a savage chief despising the white man come in quest of native wealth.

'You're too late, Mac,' he announced insolently. 'That's the lot there. We couldn't use it, you're not going to get it.'

He saw no need to mention the fifty fivers he had inside his leather jacket.

The stranger gawked, his throat working as if he was going to be sick on the spot.

'You stupid bastard!' he moaned, and dived at the fire trying to save something, burned his fingers, and yelped.

Savage laughed. The Brotherhood laughed.

The stranger knelt by the victorious fire and whined up at them.

'Yous didn't know what you were doing. Yous were too young to get a chance like that. You hadn't the brains to make use of it. There was enough there to set a man up for life. You could have had heaven on earth wi' what was there, and you've burned it, you've burned it. You set all that money on fire! Oh, Christ, yous are mad!'

The Brotherhood gathered round, looking down on him, and then their unconcerned laughter changed to a silent awe when they saw tears rolling down the stranger's cheeks. They looked away, too embarrassed to watch a grown man weeping like a wean and wringing his hands. The stranger jumped to his feet and went berserk. He dived in amongst them, hitting out viciously, and they yielded ground, retreating to the exit. Then on a common impulse they made an about turn and scattered, leaving him to rake amongst the ashes for at least one whole fiver out of thirty thousand pounds. He didn't find one.

And while he crouched alone in the air-raid shelter sobbing and cursing, O'Neill and O'Donnell were having a cool pint in the Tappit Hen.

'Did you see what was in last night's paper?' said O'Neill. 'It's jist what I was telling you a couple of months back.'

'Ach, they get swelt-heidit, some of the young yins,' said O'Donnell. 'They play a couple of seasons and then they think they're worth a lot of money so they ask for a transfer. But he's no' the first that's had a quarrel wi' the Celtic and the club aye gets on without them.'

'No' him,' said O'Neill. 'The weans that found the money I mean. Though mind you I was wan o' the first to say he was getting in bad with the club. I seen it coming.'

'Oh aye, I seen it,' said O'Donnell. 'Imagine a lad of

seventeen finding it and dishing it out to a crowd o' weans.
Of course he had a grievance. They dropped him for the
semi-final remember. But you notice they're no' saying
where it came from.'

'Maybe they don't know,' said O'Neill. 'That would be
a laugh, eh? And I telt ye, that's only wan o' them. There's
mair to come yet. You see, it was a matter of discipline, he
broke the training. He's no' the first star Celtic have
dropped before a big game, and anyway they went on
and won the Cup without him. A boy of seventeen is all he
was, kind of glaikit from what I heard. My good-sister
knows his mother. She used to live up the same close.'

'His mother's an Orangewoman, she was heartbroken
when he signed for the green and white,' said O'Donnell.

'No' his mother, the Phinn wan's mother,' said O'Neill.

'Ah but he was clever, you've got to admit it,' said
O'Donnell. 'I've saw him travel the whole length of the
park and so help me God you'd think the ball was tied to
his laces. He was a real artist, ye canny deny it.'

'It's like these modern weapons,' said O'Neill. 'Power in
the hands o' folks that's no' fit to use it.'

'He used it all right against the Rangers the last Ne'er-
day game,' said O'Donnell. 'But isn't it damnable the
now? All ye get in the papers on a Saturday night is golf
and tennis and cricket. Who the hell's interested?'

'No' him, the weans,' said O'Neill. 'All that money.
They could never spend that amount o' money. That's
what I'm trying to tell ye. Power in the hauns o' folk that's
no' fit for it. If it had been you or me it would have been
different. We could have retired. D'ye know the money
spent on armaments every year would let a man no' need to
work mair than two days a week?'

'I still say the Celtic could do wi' mair like him,' said
O'Donnell impatiently. 'And anyway tell me, what would
you do if you hadn't your work to go to?'

'I suppose you're right,' said O'Neill.

GRACE AND
MISS PARTIDGE

A NOVEL

In the tenement where I was born there was an old maid lived all alone in a single-end on the top storey. We always called her Miss Partridge to her face, but behind her back she was Wee Annie. I remember her as a sourfaced, greyhaired, flatchested, lowheeled, roundshouldered, undersized crabbit thing, anywhere between fifty and a hundred, though maybe once upon a time she was pretty. Her clothes were as grim and Presbyterian as herself. She frightened me. I used to have nightmares about her. She would be chasing me with a funny big hat on her head and a broomstick in her hand, like the ugly old witch she was, and I had to waken up to escape. I would be at the edge of a cliff, and the only way I could get away from her was to jump over, but I couldn't jump because I was paralysed with fright. So I cried out, 'Help, help! Somebody, quick, waken me!' And calling out like that I wakened myself.

She didn't like boys, and we couldn't get playing in peace in the backgreen for her shouting at us over the staircase window. We knew she was just being malicious, for her own window looked on to the main road like the window of any other single-end in the block. She couldn't hear us at all if she stayed in her own room, and nobody else up the same close with a kitchen window right above our games ever said a word of complaint. It was sheer badness made her come down to the half-landing and hang out the window there to bawl curses at us for the noise we were creating.

No, she didn't like us, but she liked little girls. It was gruesome to see her sour face uncurdle to a leering sweetness when any of them came near her claws. She stroked them and squeezed them and tickled them and ruffled them, and fed them with buns and sweeties. She never ate sweets herself. She bought them just to give away to her favourites. She took them upstairs for a biscuit and a glass of milk, and if they were very young, round about the age for starting school, she counted the steps aloud in a weird chant as she climbed up three flights clasping their hand. They came out with their nose wrinkled, distastefully holding by the rim a piece of bread and jam or a buttered Abernethy biscuit, made straight for the midden in the backgreen, and chucked Wee Annie's gift into the ashcan.

The summer all this started was the summer Angus Erskine and Donald Duthie came to our close. Wee Annie left the door of her single-end ajar one evening that bright season and crept downstairs like a cat to the half-landing and leaned out the staircase window. The girls had taken over the backgreen since teatime, but we didn't mind. We sprawled on the wash-house roof and listened to the singing games, 'O What is Mary Weeping For', 'Queen Mary, Queen Mary, My Age is Sixteen', 'I Sent a Letter to My Love', 'The Big Ship Sailing through the Eely-Alley-O', and all the rest of them. We weren't bothered. We thought we were adding to the fun of the broad evening by ribald interruptions and bawdy variations. But there was bliss on Wee Annie's face. She was no longer the old maid Miss Partridge, wicked old witch. She was a mild and benevolent eagle, watching from her eyry the antics of the earthbound little lambs, and her beak moved in happy time with the anonymous melodies that pleased the setting sun. The moment she appeared we were silent, fearing her curse would fall upon us. We cut off our joco parodies as abruptly as you would turn off a radio when you had heard enough. We knelt on the flat roof like dumb oxen, with patient downcast eyes, listening as reverently as if we were stalled in church listening to the choir, so scared we were of Wee Annie three storeys above us, an ugly old bird hovering in the golden sky of our westering holidays.

She listened till the light thickened and the little ones were tired of dancing round in a handlinked circle. When they began to niggle at each other and toddle off in twos and threes she tutted and turned from the window, sadly rubbing her skinny elbows scraped by the stone sill. Then swiftly, craftily, she winged down the stairs to the close, hoping to catch Grace Christie on the way up. Grace was a dainty elf, a teacher's pet. She lived on the first storey. She was Wee Annie's current favourite.

Annie caught her that night as planned, on the half-landing just outside the lavatory door. She jerked to a stop, her claw at her beak as if she was alarmed at bumping into anybody at all on that dim and silent staircase, remote from the traffic on the main road, totally withdrawn from the teeming life of the city. That was her pretending she was surprised to see Grace. Then she gave herself away by showing she had been watching her all evening.

'Ach, you must be tired, my wee hen!' She stopped the child, cuddling her shoulder. 'And thirsty too, eh? After all that singing and dancing. Come on you up with me and I'll give you a nice glass of lemonade before you go to your bed. And I think I've got a cake for you. You like cakes, ee, don't you now?'

Grace stared up at her. She was a solemn thing with a pretty face, but behind her big blank eyes there was a sharp enough little brain. I think she saw through Annie right from the start and knew what was wrong before Annie herself did. Such bright children have their own intuition even though they haven't got the words for it. But she preferred to bend like a reed. She knew if she showed any alarm it would only make Wee Annie worse. Even at that age, she was about ten at the time, she knew a jealous nature when she met it. And cautious of the cruelties that go with jealousy she played safe with a passive obedience. She let the old bird pick her up and carry her off to the Partridge nest, three up the middle. Maybe it was worth suffering for the sake of the lemonade.

She was very fond of lemonade, and Annie always had the fizzy kind that tickled your nose. Grace liked that sensation. It interested her. She tried to understand it every time she got it. But it always escaped her, so she had always to try again by drinking more lemonade.

Before she got any she had to put up with being led over to the sink at the window and stuck there beside a talkative parrot in a standard cage while Wee Annie held her by the ears and looked her lovingly up and down, tenderly, more than maternally.

'Let me see your wee hands,' Annie commanded, granting what she thought was an affectionate smile. But I remember her teeth were revolting. She showed yellow canines when she grinned, and a top incisor was missing.

Grace showed her hands. She was much given to silent obedience.

'O-my-O-my! What dirty paws, you horrid little beast!' Annie gloated, cuddling them in her own. 'That's what comes of playing with all those boys. Boys! Oh boys! They're terrible, so they are.'

'I wasn't playing with boys,' Grace slipped in a footnote. In spite of her silent nature she had a stubborn tendency to correct errors of fact.

'No, maybe not tonight, but other nights, eh?' Annie tickled her ribs. 'And you know, it sticks, Grace darling, it sticks. Once you let a boy touch you – well!'

'I don't play with boys,' Grace muttered.

'You don't like boys, eh, do you?' Annie lilted encouragingly.

Grace just looked at her. She had no answer to that question at that time.

'You don't let boys cuddle you or tickle you, now do you?' Annie asked severely. 'Tell me the truth.'

She didn't wait for an answer. She didn't want one. Her pleasure lay in asking the question, and she was happy just to be blethering to the defenceless child. She lifted a flannel from a celluloid dish above the sink and went on blethering as she washed Grace's hands, fondling each in turn, rinsing away the grime of the evening under the swan-neck tap.

'Don't you ever play with the boys, Grace dear. A lovely wee girl like you is too good for boys. Boys aren't nice. You'll know what I mean when you get older, and you'll thank me for it. Boys always want to, I'll tell you some day. O-my-O-my! Just look at those knees. That's what comes of playing Kneel Down Kiss the Ground. They're all mucky, you silly wee thing.'

She knelt and washed the child's knees with the soapy flannel, travelled slowly down the sturdy legs that were in fact quite clean and up the stalwart thighs to the brief knickers. And when that was done she went over it all again, massaging the legs from knickers to ankles with a skimpy towel, lingering over each limb.

'You said lemonade,' said Grace.

When she'd got what she wanted she edged to get out. Annie pecked after her to keep her longer, but there was a rude knocking at the door. It was Grace's mother looking for her.

'Aye, I thought she was here,' Mrs Christie said sourly. She was a big woman, in whose worried face you could dimly make out the pretty features of Grace through the fog of the years. She hustled Grace outside while Annie bowed and scraped.

'I was just giving her a wee bite for her supper,' she twittered.

'She's well enough fed in her own house, thank you,' Mrs Christie broadcast over her shoulder.

'She was washing my hands and legs,' Grace remarked out on the stairhead, raising one leg and looking casually at the ankle.

'She'd do better if she washed herself.' Mrs Christie pushed Grace downstairs, ostensibly answering her but making sure Wee Annie heard her too.

It was an unfair cut, for though she was always drab Wee Annie was quite clean. She had to be, working where she did. She was the wages-clerk and despatch-clerk and answered the phone in our little local laundry before it was taken over by the big Lavanta Company.

'How many tellings do you need, girl?' Mrs Christie scolded Grace all the way down. 'It's a good skelpin you're asking for. I'm sick tired telling you to come straight up to your own house when you're done playing. You've got my heart fair roastit, the way you carry on with that auld bitch.'

Annie listened till she heard the Christies' door bang, then she closed her own door quietly, leaned against it and wept.

'All I get is insults,' she whimpered. 'And that poor wee soul, she gets no love at all.'

She used her hankie and snivelled over to the only other living thing she loved, her pet parrot, an old bird even uglier than herself. She called it Shelley. I never found out why even after she was dead. She fed it, spoke to it, listened to it, slipped down to the lavatory, came back up and made a cup of cocoa. She sipped it at the kitchen-table, sitting in peace and quiet, writing up her diary. I have it now. She had the oldfashioned copperplate style of writing, thin up and thick down.

It was a bad summer for her, that summer. Mrs Christie's insult wasn't the only one she had to thole before the dark nights came back and there was no more playing in the back green. We got an immigrant from another world, a wise man from the east, Angus Erskine, a tinkerfaced oddity in secondhand clothes and boots too big for him, a juvenile delinquent who had plunked his way through a dozen schools on both sides of the river, a vagrant who had come to our douce land as territory where his name had travelled ahead of him and ensured him respect. He was a minstrel born out of time, a joker who feared neither policeman nor teacher. The absurdity of his clothes, which should have made him a laughingstock, was appropriate to the absurdity of his character. Whatever he wore, he wore with a swagger, and nobody laughed at him because he laughed at them first. Wee Annie didn't frighten him, she amused him. He preached to us, he converted us, he brought us into his communion of irreverence. He took us over completely, he bossed us, rehearsed us, grilled us and drilled us. He taught us saucy words and used old tunes for a choral attack on Wee Annie before he had been a fortnight with us. So there we were this fine summer night, bursting to sing. And the moment Wee Annie came hanging out the staircase window we hailed her neb with a crescendo shout and exploded into a chorus that staggered jovially round the melody of 'Come ower the Stream, Charlie'.

> O funny Wee Annie
> Never sits on her fanny,
> She hings oot the windy tae gie us a fright.
> She's bandy, she's skelly,
> Aye scratching her belly,
> She gangs tae the cludgie ten times every night.

She was speechless the first time we sang it to her. She drew away from the window, gnawing her knuckles, and fluttered upstairs like a frightened sparrow. She tried to find consolation in talking to Shelley, smiling at his cheerful replies, but the dialect word *cludgie* seemed to persist even in Shelley's friendly squawking, and it went on echoing in her head, offending her primness. She was shocked, she was even wounded, at the unwarranted slight on her continence, for the cludgie was the watercloset on each half-landing, serving all the tenants on the flat above. She felt degraded enough having to go there at all. She had been reared in a superior tenement where every house had an inside-toilet. But now she was old and alone, reduced to living in a single-end, a little cell sandwiched between a room-and-kitchen on either side of her. It was a painful come-down for her, but all she could afford. She didn't mind so much having to wash her feet in the sink at the window and have a bath piece-peel, but the cludgie was a constant offence to her.

I suppose she must have got used to our chant eventually, for we serenaded her with it every night till the clocks were put back, and even the boy who delivered her milk was tipped off by Angus to whistle 'Come ower the Stream, Charlie' as he rattled at her door, so that she got it in the morning too.

The second night we sang it she brazened it out, her skimpy bosom over the windowsill in her eagerness to fight back. She aimed direct at Angus, giving him tit for tat.

'Away back to the Gorbals where you belong, you bad-mouthed wee messan!' she screeched. Then deriding him in unexpected trochaics she sang out, thumping her fists on the sill, 'Erskine? Bumskin! Canny keep yer nose clean!'

Angus just laughed it off. He didn't belong to the Gorbals. In all his wanderings he had never lived there. His last address had in fact been in a district so much worse than the decent Gorbals that it is never mentioned outside the city, like a family scandal you don't talk about to strangers. He was greatly taken with that Bumskin. Although it was so obvious, he had missed it before Wee Annie put her tongue on it, and so had we. She gave us a name for him to balance the song he had given us for her, and he liked her for it. He was broadminded. And because he liked her we learned to like her too, and once we liked her she couldn't frighten us any more.

I think that baffled her even more than the indictments that she was bowlegged, crosseyed, was always running to the lavatory, and was afflicted with lice in the pubic region. These accusations were, or could be, visibly false. But that we liked her in our own twisted way was an incontrovertible fact. And she was never happy with facts.

Playing at shops in a corner of the backgreen, with broken crockery for money and slabs of clay from the quarry as cakes and bread, Grace Christie moved lightly amidst her playmates and spared only a casual glance at us on the roof of the wash-house and then another at Wee Annie foaming over the staircase window. The flyting failed to interest her and she carried on serving in her shop. But Annie caught a ray from the child's wandering eyes and was blinded to a silence of shame and contrition. How could little Grace, three storeys below, ever admire and love her if she went on making an exhibition of herself, she asked in her diary that night. She clamped down and played the lady, de haut en bas. Her suspender burst as she leaned over, and one stocking collapsed to her ankle.

'Sing what you please,' she called down to Angus. 'Sticks and stones may break my bones, but names will never hurt me. Go on, sing away!'

He did too.

Every window looking on to the backgreen was up by this time, and the bigbosomed matrons settled their floppy busts and huge forearms on the sill. They beamed gratefully at Angus as he accepted Annie's invitation, and some of them even cheered. The front row of the choir sang with him at his signal, and the back row threw in a phrase after each line.

> Back home in Merrylee,
>   Without a shirt!
> That's where I wanna be,
>   Without a shirt!
> Right on my mammy's knee,
>   Without a shirt!

Annie had asked for that the way she was always running down our district and dragging in a mention of the time she used to live in Merrylee, a far superior area away at the other end of the city, where she claimed her Papa had a big house.

'It's as good as the Empress,' Mrs Green called down the time-chipped face of the tenement to Mrs Christie.

Annie trembled a moment or two before she screeched. Her determination to be dignified was cancelled by the applause our interjected line had earned from the tiered housewives.

'You dirty wee tinker! It's a good skelp on the lug you're needing!'

'Yer chemeese is hinging oot the windy,' Angus bawled back. 'And whit's mair, yer Paw wis a bouncer in Barra-land.'

'Go on, give him it, Miss Partridge,' Mrs Bonnar encouraged her across the building from three up the faraway, Annie's neighbour on the left and the mother of Robina, or Bobo or Bona as she was variously called, a bonnie lass of nineteen Annie didn't like at all.

'Away back where you belong, nobody wants you here, corrupting decent weans,' Annie obliged. 'Another cheep out of you and I'll be right down there.'

She was so far out the window she seemed to be hanging on by her toes.

'Bring yer granny as well,' Angus invited her cordially.

He swaggered to the very edge of the roof and gave us a solo.

O the night I took Wee Annie to the ball,
I discovered that she couldn't dance at all,
For she started to reverse and she fell and
    bumped her erse,
O the fright I got wi' Annie at the ball.

Maybe he sang another verse, but the cheers drowned the words. And poor Wee Annie! Her beak darted left to Mrs Bonnar and right to Mrs Stockwell, looking for crumbs of comfort. She clucked down to Mrs Green, widow and school-cleaner in the single-end below her own, a sharp character who backed the horses and went out to whist-drives and music-halls and told fortunes from teacups. She yammered to the rest of her neighbours, and everywhere she was mocked by screams of vulgar laughter. On the first storey there was Grace's mother, smirking away to herself, and at her right there was Mrs Blair, wife of grumfy old Daddy Blair who had the barber's shop at the close-mouth, but he was too fond of the whisky to be doing much. In the single-end between them was old

Sandy McKay, a retired Scots comic who boasted he was the first local boy to play the Empire, but he was out at the Metropole that night, getting in on his card.

The uproar put Wee Annie in a panic. She gave in and flapped upstairs on damaged wings to talk to Shelley. But Grace was still in her mind. She wanted to put herself right with Grace. She knelt at her bedside for five minutes and prayed for Grace, bidding Shelley pray with her. Then she clawed up the side of a chair to her feet and wrote a few lines in her diary before preparing to swoop down on her victim. She judged the time well enough, reaching the first half-landing just as Grace was coming up. But Grace was popular, too popular for Annie, who wanted her alone. She had three other brownies with her, wee Susan Greenwood, a chubby child with blonde hair, a little dumpling with rosy cheeks, Betty Rodgers, nebby and spectacled, an eager clype, plus Sandra Laird, too sweet to be wholesome, a hanger-on, a cipher of no value except according to whom she tagged behind. They clambered up the steep stairs together, chattering a childish quarrel. She wanted to stop them, but they simply ignored her. The fresh breeze of their passing blew her aside like an autumn leaf and she had no chance to accost Grace.

She heard them all go into Grace's house, heard the door bang behind them, and she stuck in a corner of the landing gnawing her knuckles again. That was the night she found she loved Grace. Before then, she had only been fond of her amongst other children. She had only wanted Grace to love her. Now her disappointment pushed her into an exclusive love of Grace and she was jealous of the children who came between them.

She went back to her diary, but she was too upset at losing Grace to write much. She tried her bible, a big one, and read at chance. She was a bible-lover, looking for guidance in passages that caught her eye, and she read aloud to herself in lonely fervour.

'And there came one of the seven angels which had the seven vials, and talked with me, saying unto me, Come

hither and I will show unto thee the judgment of the great
whore that sitteth upon many waters, with whom the kings
of the earth have been made drunk with the wine of her
fornication. So he carried me away in the spirit into the
wilderness and I saw a woman sit upon a scarlet coloured
beast, full of names of blasphemy, having seven heads and
ten horns. And the woman was arrayed in purple and
scarlet colour, and decked with gold and precious stones
and pearls, having a golden cup in her hand and full of
abominations and filthiness of her fornication. And upon
her forehead was a name written.'

She had only heard one or other of the seven angels
talking to her like that a few times, though it was often she
listened for them. But Papa came with his heavenly
companions and talked to her many a time in the solitude
of her single-end after midnight, just as real as Shelley
talking to her.

It was nearly one in the morning when she closed her
good book and hopped down the empty stairs for a breath
of air at the close-mouth, her bible under her oxter. She
was standing there, at peace with a world she knew was
beneath her and nothing but the silent street in front of
her, when a girl came pegging along on high heels with her
boyfriend. It was Bobo, hanging on to Duncan Ross, a
smart youth with brilliant black hair, an ex-juvenile delinquent. He had raided his granny's gasmeter when he
was ten, set fire to his headmaster's room when he was
eleven, pinched a camera from a drunk American sailor
when he was twelve, and between thirteen and sixteen he
had been charged with housebreaking, theft, obtaining
money by false pretences, and carrying an offensive weapon. But at this time he was honestly employed in looking
for a job. Dross or Drossy was his local name.

Bobo was wearing her new swagger red coat, walking
with it hanging open to show off her lownecked summer
dress. On the lapel of the coat she had a large gilt brooch
fashioned as a scrolled capital B to encourage the boys to
guess her name, though that went back to the days before

she started going steady with Dross, and round her neck she wore a golden necklace with little lockets of various shapes dangling from it, and on her ears she had pearl-coloured earrings. She was a blonde, and she made such an impression round and about that even the boys still at primary school turned to look at her. Because she always dressed to draw attention to her bust if you saw her advancing, and to her bottom if you saw her retreating, and to her hips and legs whichever way you saw her, she had a reputation, and Wee Annie was sure she was immodest.

That was Robina Bonnar, our local belle Bobo. She swayed elegantly past Annie at the close-mouth since Annie stood bang in the centre and wouldn't budge, even though Dross piped up politely, 'Scuse us, ole girl.'

'Scarlet whore,' Wee Annie said to herself, staring straight ahead without the least glimmer of acknowledgement, but unfortunately she said it aloud. 'Mother of harlots.'

Bobo and Dross braked together on the same foot as they heard her, thought better of it at once in the silent agreement of young lovers, and marched round to the back close to kiss and cuddle a good-night.

'The body is not for fornication but for the Lord,' Annie suddenly declared, turning her back on the street and addressing the close.

She couldn't see Bobo and Dross, because the close turned sharply at the foot of the stairs before it led to the backgreen. That was why Bobo used the back-close when she was entertaining Dross.

'I'll do that ole bitch yet, so I will but,' Dross muttered, delayed by that unfavourable wind from setting out on a voyage of exploration.

'Scarlet whore!' Bobo whispered. 'I like that! Declare to God, some folk think cause you wear a red coat you're a loose woman.'

Annie faced the street again, bayed to the moon above the regimented chimney stacks of the tenements, and

raised her hands as if she would claw it down from the
night sky. When she turned to go up to her parrot the
sound of scuffling and whispering from the back close
gave her a painful spasm of pure hate for Bobo, like a
dagger shoved into her middle. She halted at the foot of
the stairs, took a deep breath, and then shouted through
the close.

'O backsliding daughter, saying, Who shall come unto
me? The Lord will judge thee according to thy ways.'

She loitered a moment longer. Silence answered her or
ignored her. She laughed shrilly twice over, and satisfied
that the scuffling had stopped she soared lightly to her
eyry.

'That sorted them,' she said with a chuckling pech on
the way upstairs.

'The badminded bitch,' Bobo breathed, listening for
her going up. 'What kind of way's that to talk?'

'She has temporarily lost possession of her cranium,'
Dross smoothed her before taking new soundings for his
voyage. 'She's aff her nut. Her mind's aye on houghmagandy. Come on.'

'Get off!' Bobo pushed. 'You're not on, brother. That
one's put me out the mood.'

Three storeys above them, in her little brick box between the Bonnars and the Stockwells, Wee Annie read in
the good book again before she went to bed. She sat at her
bare table and meditated about the Fall of Babylon and
Bobo, about sin and the saving grace of the Lord. The
grace of the Lord reminded her of Grace Christie, and a
great fear came over her that Grace would grow up to be
like Bobo. She swallowed two codeine tablets to help her
to sleep and prayed for grace to deliver her from evil. At
that very moment she received the first obscure intimations of how the Lord had laid on her the task of delivering
Grace from evil, and her Papa came to advise her.

CHAPTER TWO

Donald Duthie from the Isle of Skye came up our close
that summer as a lodger. He had the front room in Mrs
Stockwell's house. He was a gangling clumsy fellow, a bit
of a gomeril, with a deep, deep voice and a Highland
accent. Most of us called him Big Tonalt, though Angus
said he was Bluebeard because his chin was always the
colour of faded ink. He had a big nose, big ears, pop eyes,
and his hands seemed all wrists. His feet would have made
any policeman's look like Cinderella's, and he wore the
same suit from the first day I saw him till the day he died.

He was an Arts student, but we got the idea he was a
Divinity student, maybe because his cousin Hugh Main
once remarked to my mother Donald would end up in the
ministry. Donald himself supported us in our error by
behaving like a minister in a Youth Club every time he
intruded on our games. When we were gathered together
in the back-green he used to come down on us like the
Holy Ghost descending on the Apostles and try to organise us. But he was far too familiar for our comfort, and
when he trotted round the circle singing *Ma pot's bilin, ma
hen's layin*, he looked just plain daft. What particularly
sickened us was a bad habit he had of calling us 'children'.
It was, 'Now children, join hands in a circle!' or 'Gather
round, children! Who knows how to play No Roost?'

We were sure we had known it before he was born, he
made us feel that much older than he was. And anyway the
first time he ever saw No Roost played was when he saw us
play it. But we let him shepherd us rather than snub him.
And all this, of course, was before he saw Bobo in her
underwear.

The girls had a great store of pity for him, but they were too young for their pity to be of much use to a grown man. I think now that when he came grinning and basso-profunding his way into our games he was practising to be a minister visiting the Sunday School, trying to obey the divine injunction, Suffer little children. The trouble was it was the little children suffered him. One thing that struck me even then was how suddenly his expression changed when his visitation was over, his tour of duty I suppose it was for him. The cheery smile of fatherly interest went out like a light and his face was unmasked in lines of invincible unhappiness, as if he knew himself the victim of that most wounding of all our childish virtues, tolerance.

His landlords, the Stockwells, were a douce Church of Scotland couple. Mr Stockwell was a retired railway worker, a shunter I think he was, and Mrs Stockwell served behind the counter in Strathdee's the baker down the street on Friday nights and Saturdays to earn a few bob. Their children were grown-up, married and scattered, and might as well never have been born for all the difference they made. So the deserted parents lived a limited, lonely life, like some primitive twin-cellular organism suspended in the fluid of daily circumstances. They would never have taken in any Tom, Dick or Harry as a lodger. It was unusual for people up a close like ours to have lodgers at all, though in fact it was the only wally close in the block, and Mrs Tumelty across the street, where they were all wally closes, once had a medical student for two years, an Indian he was I remember. But the Stockwells were finding things a bit tight on his railway pension and what she got for her part-time job in Strathdee's. They needed more money. They lived and ate in the kitchen and slept in the recess bed there, and never used the front room. But it was a well-furnished place. After all, Mr Stockwell had been in a steady job all his life. He could afford to get in some good stuff over the years. To keep the front room unoccupied seemed a waste of capital crying aloud to be invested. And a student wasn't just a vulgar lodger they took for the sake of his rent-money. He had a touch of class. He wasn't their lodger, he was 'Mr Duthie, our student'.

Keen to show himself a true Scotsman of the old school, a working man who had read a bit in his time and could debate the questions of the day and of eternity with anybody, Mr Stockwell used to keep Donald stuck at the table in the kitchen after tea so that he could get him on to a discussion of politics, morals and theology. Many a night he made capital topics of the Welfare State and the Independence of the Individual, Fornication and Teenage Morality, Free Will and God's Omniscience, Predestination and Redemption, Sin, Repentance, Faith and Good Works. Theology was his favourite theme, and it first came up because Mrs Stockwell was something of a Calvinist in the slant of her mind.

'If it's for ye it'll no gang past ye, that's what I aye say,' was her regular contribution of sympathy if anyone dared mention to her the misfortune of a neighbour, the sudden death of a husband, a diagnosis of cancer in a young mother, or the death of a child by drowning in the Canal round the corner.

Mr Stockwell was delighted the first time she said it in front of their lodger. He swooped at the chance to raise a conversational scrap into a theological principle which he could dispute with a student from the Isle of Skye. He was a simple soul, and he thought every Scots divinity student was a Calvinist. Big Donald was too shy to explain he was neither a divinity student nor a Calvinist. He was always willing to defend any position imputed to him.

'Aye, that's one of your sayings, Jenny,' Mr Stockwell pounced. 'But I must say I'm no all that sure I can see my way to accept the complications of it. It would take you on to predestination. Would ye care to gie us your opinion of predestination, Mr Duthie, sir, and I'll tell ye what I think.'

'Well, of course, God's ways are beyond us,' Donald answered shrewdly. 'Who are we to question with our puny knowledge why some are chosen and some are rejected?'

'But that's just the question I want to raise, if you don't mind an old railwayman rushing in where angels fear to tread,' Mr Stockwell took him up, happy to have shunted the conversation on the right lines. 'You take this idea of the elect. I mean them that thinks they're saved whether they sin or no. But Saint Paul said, and I must say I'm inclined to agree with him, let us remember good works lest we fall into the hands of the living God.'

'Did he now?' said Donald, quite interested.

'Och aye he did that. And my point is what's the point of good works if it's all sewn up before ye were ever born?'

'Ah well, you must beware of the errors of Romanism,' Donald shuffled. 'Faith in Christ is sufficient for salvation. That's one thing we do know.'

'Och aye, that's all very well, that's true,' Mr Stockwell granted vaguely. 'But do ye no think there's a possibility they might be deceiving themselves? Ye know, kidding themselves on I mean. That's my point. I can assure you there's naebody mair aware nor me about the dangers of Roming Catholic fallacies. But I must say I still canny agree with this idea of predestination. It's no canny.'

Wee Annie heard about these talks because Mr Stockwell in his retirement was the kind of man that did the daily shopping and he boasted in the grocer's, in the dairy, in the butcher's and baker's, and everywhere else he went.

'I had a rare argument with my student,' he used to say. 'About some difficult points in the bible, ye know. Ach, but I gave him as good as I got, believe you me.'

She suffered, she really and truly suffered did little Miss Partridge, with a great longing to take part in talks with Donald, or at least to be present in humble silence. She yearned to let him know the bible was her book too. But Donald ignored her, and the Stockwells snubbed her like everybody else in the close except my mother. My mother was sorry for her, and that's why I know so much now that I didn't know then, for Miss Partridge confided in my mother and my mother confided in me when I was older.

But within a week of telling my mother she wished Mr Duthie would talk to her about the bible and not waste his time on an ignorant railwayman, Wee Annie saw Big Donald in a different light. She caught a glint in his eye when he looked on Bobo, and she had been through too much not to recognise it. She was one of those women who deny the infinite variety of our species and insist men are all the same. And what she saw only strengthened her conviction that Bobo was bad.

It all happened because of that lavatory on the half-landing. Bobo was coming out of it one evening just as Donald left his room to go down to it, and at that moment Wee Annie opened her door. Bobo had slipped out in her petticoat, and as she came up the stairs the rude sun came in at the staircase window, beamed through the flimsy skirt, and silhouetted her thighs and pants. Wee Annie saw her grin as she passed Donald, one hand up with the fingers splayed at her halfnaked breasts, saw what Donald saw, and then saw him turn round and look back. That's when she caught what she called the light of lust in his eyes. She stood stock-still at her door and waited for Bobo to come up.

'Daughter of Babylon,' she whispered, and showed her teeth in hate.

Bobo gave her a smile and a nod.

'Get lost, darling,' she whispered back and passed on.

She couldn't stand Wee Annie at all, but she didn't mind Big Donald. He only made her laugh the way he goggled. She thought he was a silly big sumph to blush and stumble just because he saw a girl in her slip.

'It's his own bad mind,' she said when she told Dross about it. 'To the pure all things are meaningless. And I'm very particular about my underwear, as you know.'

'Aye well all right,' Dross growled. 'I'm not jealous. But don't you start giving him ideas, that's all. Students is no like you and me. They're different. They live a terrible

life, so they do. Like the monks used to. Their nose aye in
a book. Then the first time they see a woman's leg they're
away wi' it. That's why they go daft when they're let out
for Charity. You give him the nod and you'll be sorry, I'm
telling you.'

'Well, I like that! You'd think it was my fault,' Bobo
huffed. 'You're trying the mix. You want to start a fight,
then it's me that's to make it up. On your gimmee or else.
Oh, I know you, Duncan Alexander McIntosh Ross! No,
thank you.'

But Wee Annie was right, and Dross was wise to give
Bobo a warning. For Donald was caught, even before he
saw her in her petticoat. She had been growing on him like
a blind boil he fingered every day. She nudged his mind
off his lecture-notes, she lay beside him in his dreams at
night, and melted into air, into thin air, when he moved
towards her. The attempt to act always wakened him, and
he wriggled, in misery at the state he was in. The nuisance
of guilt that he had to live with was only a pinprick
compared to the longing that nagged him like toothache.
He had to find help somewhere, somehow, and for all his
Presbyterian independence he thought he might find it in
confession. He wanted to talk about Bobo, to hear her
name spoken and link his name with hers in a frank
admission of his private thoughts. He had a confessor at
hand, his cousin Hugh Main.

Main was a medical student, in lodgings over in Byres
Road near the University. He came to see Donald about
once a week, and everybody liked him. Like Father
O'Flynn he had a wonderful way with him. He was short
and rather fat, with a waddle in his walk and a smile in his
talk, and the way he looked through his thick glasses made
it seem he was observing the oddities of mankind through
two windows that protected him from all worldly hurt and
contamination, so that he had the cut of a superior goodhearted gnome. Even Wee Annie took to him. He met her
for the first time on his way upstairs to Donald, when she
was coming down with a pail of rubbish for the midden.

He bowed, smiled, went all the way back downstairs carrying it for her, chucked the rubbish in the midden and carried the empty pail upstairs again, chatting easily about who he was and what he was, and about Donald and the weather and the Isle of Skye. When he gave her back her pail he patted her elbow.

'I'll see you again I'm sure,' he beamed at her, though there too he managed to give the impression of being untouchably behind a window as he spoke.

'That's what I call a gentleman,' she told my mother. 'He knows how to treat a lady. Not one of them that do you an obligement for what they hope to get out of you.'

Bobo was another who got to know him well in his journeys up and down the stairs to Donald's lodgings, and they flirted in passing, finding their pleasure in the equi-vocal use of the tongue and the eloquent use of the eyes. But of course, like two all-in wrestlers they were too crafty to get fatally tangled. She had a cold on her once when she met Main in the close.

'Do you think I've got a fever?' she asked.

She said it to tease him, but at the same time she had half an idea he could prescribe something for her. He was only starting his final year medicine, but to Bobo he was already a doctor.

He didn't go all serious and say he wasn't qualified. That was one of her reasons for liking him. Her teasing never put him out. He gave her a professional look, felt her forehead, took her pulse and examined her tongue. The doctor's correctness of his touch was itself a thrill to her. He frowned, brooded for five seconds, and then told her she shouldn't be going out. She ought to go back upstairs and go to bed for three days.

'Och but it's dull just lying in bed,' she complained, and straightened his tie. 'And I get so lonely there.'

'Ah well, yes of course, I see,' he said without the least glimmer of joking with her. 'I know the prescription for that, but then so do you.'

That's how they carried on, and Bobo loved it. Main's

pleasant accent and superior schooling, his style in fencing
with her, and the harmless flattery of his tongue and eyes,
all gave her a different excitement than she got from the
deep caresses of Dross. Even the fact that a man who was
practically a doctor could stop and speak to her, and spare
time for what she called 'a wee bit kidding on', raised her
in her own esteem. She believed she could have made
something of him, or something out of him for herself, if
she had been his equal in education. Yet she had no great
wish to have things other than as they were. Her two feet,
in their smart shoes, were firmly planted on the pavement
of her native reality. I think in her feeling for Main she was
like a provincial football team that plays one of the big city
clubs away from home in a cup-tie. It was a rare experience. But she knew that when she coped with the familiar
passes of Dross, with his kick-and-rush and bash on for
the goal, she was on her home ground. She would put up a
good show playing against Main, but she wouldn't win.
She didn't expect to. She simply enjoyed the game.

This waddling fellow Main was an agnostic. It didn't
bother Bobo, who was one herself without knowing it,
and Miss Partridge never found out. He was so kind to
her, so tactful and understanding when she told him her
trouble with the neighbours, she took it for granted he
believed all she believed and lived by the bible. Donald
knew the truth of course, for they had grown up together.
In their adolescence they had argued and argued till the
sun went down and came up again to see them still at it.
Neither made any impression on the other. They had the
same accent, but they didn't speak the same language.
You might have expected them to stop bothering about
each other when they took different courses at the University, so clean and fixed were their differences. But a
Scotch clannishness kept them close, facing an urban
world together. I know Main visited Donald regularly,
but I don't know Donald ever took the trouble to go over
to Byres Road and visit Main. So it would seem it was
Main who gave their kinship life. Donald never evaded it,

never denied it, but never went out of his way to keep it warm.

But now he needed Main. He knew his cousin had a way with women. Bobo wasn't the only girl he had seen him get on with. There had been many a lass in Skye when they were only lads. What puzzled him was that Main never made any use of his talents. He spoke to girls, he listened to them, he laughed and joked with them, he could even go in for a bit of horseplay with them, and that was all. But when it came to Bobo Donald wasn't just puzzled. He became really curious, because for the first time he was emotionally cogged with the girl concerned. He made himself jealous. Not so much of his cousin as a person, as of his cousin's gift for pleasing Bobo, for making her shine, sparkle and glow. He put himself to the torture speculating how much Main knew about Bobo, how much he had done with her, things he himself would never know or do. He didn't even know Bobo's right name or her exact age. And when he saw her talk so long with Main at the close-mouth, or lean out the staircase window with him, blethering happily for half-an-hour on end, he was sure she would gladly give Main all he himself wanted. Maybe she had done so already.

It griped his stomach when he saw them clench hands together and wriggle and wrestle to test whose fingers and wrist were stronger. The twining that only was a game to them would have been Adam's paradise to him if he had been allowed to play it. Whenever he was forced to believe their friendship was innocent he still wasn't comforted. He simply felt a grudge against Main for not making use of his opportunities. If they had come his way he was sure he would have known Bobo biblically and then, still in biblical language, he could put her away. By long brooding, which he confused with deep reasoning, he became convinced that since his cousin wouldn't use Bobo for her right true end his credit with her ought to be transferred to himself. He was the one was ready and willing to make proper use of it. He had more of the Old Testament authority a male should have than his frivolous cousin could ever show. He knew what the Book meant when it said the woman is subject to the man, but Main was only a pagan, treating Bobo as an equal, making use of her only for conversation.

In case after all there was more between them than he thought, and to give himself the satisfaction of talking familiarly about Bobo, he tried to quiz his cousin. They always had the Stockwells' parlour to themselves when they met, and sat facing each other at a round table covered with a billiard-green tasselled cloth. He was a frantic ocean of questions that night, nearly drowning his cousin. But Main was buoyant enough for a while, until a bigger breaker than ever before stranded him.

'My goodness, man!' he laughed. 'Whatever are you after at all? You're talking like the heavy father in a Victorian mellowdrammer. You'll be asking me next if my intentions is honourable.'

'But they're not, now are they?' Donald looked down his big nose at the green cloth, avoiding the windowed eyes across the table. He trembled a little, hoping his cousin would confess he had sinned with Bobo, but owed her nothing because she was easy.

But Main wasn't with him.

'I've no intentions of any kind, honourable or dishonourable. You're talking daft, Tonalt! What would I be doing with a girl like Bobo round my neck? At my age! In my career! Can you see Bobo living in the Highlands as a doctor's wife? She'd be wanting to know where the shops were.'

In fact he never became a country doctor, though that's all he had in mind at the time. He was assistant physician in a city hospital in his middle years.

'So you're a snob then, is that it?' Donald raised his head and boomed across the table. 'Is she not good enough for you? Because she says "I seen". She has no class, she has only a body. So she wouldn't do for your career. Aw naw! You wouldn't marry her. But you make sure you—'

He flushed and pouted, and after a couple of turkey-like gobblings he tried again in prim disgust.

'But you make sure you get a good feel every time you see her. Your hands are never off her.'

'Well, that's a load of tripe for a start,' Main still laughed. 'Me cuddling Bobo? Jesus, that'll be the day!'

'You see, you don't even know you're doing it you're so used to it,' Donald triumphed over the Philistine. 'But I've seen you. I've watched you. Aye, and how much else goes on nobody sees? Tell me that now. I bet you've had her away from here. You get left alone a lot in your place, don't you? Or just the back row at the pictures? You could get to know her breasts and thighs well there. Couldn't you, eh?'

Main sat back from the round table and tangled the tassels on the fringe of the cloth.

'You're away out of your mind, Tonalt. Just because I pass a joke now and again with a sonsie young lass that's full of the joy de veever and likes a wee blether you want to make a dirty old man out of me. Well, you're wrong. I'm not all that old. Even if Bobo is only a kid to me.'

'She's not sonsie, she's gallus,' Donald corrected him. 'A bad little besom.'

'A bosom companion,' Main flippantly retorted, sketching opulent curves in front of his manly chest with a pair of languid hands. 'Fair and buxom. Whatever she is, don't you go unloading you own bad mind on to me. You never could understand it, but I can enjoy a glass of whisky and a beer without being a drunkard. I can enjoy the sun without being a nudist. And I can enjoy the company of a pretty girl without aiming to put her on her back the first time I get a chance. But not you, you bloody old Calvinist! The minute a man likes anything you make a sin out of it and give him a free travel pass to Hell. Mind you, I don't deny I'm a poor weak wicked sinner the same as anybody else. But there's a limit. Especially when it's a decent happy lass you're having me on about.'

Donald sat bolt upright, piercing space with a fanatic

eye. His cousin's humble concession rocketed him from his trance.

'I am a greater sinner,' he announced in a vibrating, ominous, pulpit voice, his Sunday best.

Main stopped tying two tassels together and jerked forward in a spasm of delight.

'You? Since when? Come on, tell Hughie and you'll feel better. Has Bobo been seducing you in the back-close at midnight?'

Donald shook his head. He was away out on a limb, and he quoted with thundering solemnity the text that had been bothering him since he saw Bobo coming up the stairs with a shaft of sunlight between her thighs.

'Whosoever looketh on a woman to lust after her hath committed adultery with her already in his heart.'

'Jesus, is that all that's bothering you?' Main asked with a tut. 'It happens to every man.'

Disappointed there was no confession of actual guilt forthcoming, he went on twining alternate tassels of the tablecloth.

'Leave Jesus out of this if you don't mind,' Donald reprimanded him and waited for an apology before continuing his statement. He had lately been finding a strange peace in adopting the position Mr Stockwell had ascribed to him, and now he came out bluntly with it. 'Saint Paul was a sinner but Saint Paul was saved. And I'm a sinner but I'm saved. I know. It's the power of God and all the elect know it within themselves.'

'Congratulations,' Main bowed across the table. 'It's a good thing to know.'

'No, don't be funny,' Donald waved a hand impatiently. 'What I mean is, you know lots of girls. You're a right ladies' man. Though you've no appearance. I'm a much better looking man than you. Couldn't you introduce me to a girl?'

'I suppose I could,' Main agreed. 'If you think it would do you any good.'

Donald fingered triangles and circles on the green cloth.

'I mean, I've been thinking. You know how my grand-mother wants me to go on for the ministry when I get my degree. I don't know that I will. But suppose I did, then would it not be advisable if ever I do get the call I should know for myself when Saint Paul speaks of those who are dead in sin what sin is?'

'Would it not be what?' Main frowned. 'I lost you there. I thought you were trying to talk to me about Bobo.'

'About that girl you call Bobo, yes. I don't know her right name. Do you?'

He spoke as if Bobo was too vulgar and familiar a name for him to use and he would have to have something more dignified and formal before he could go on.

'Robina Jemima. She hates it. I don't wonder. She told me in confidence. So don't you ever tell her I told you. She prefers Ina to Mima if it's a question of either. Some of her pals call her Bona because of her surname. I sometimes call her Bona-Roba myself. She likes that. I told her it's Italian for well dressed. But she prefers Bobo to anything else.'

'Does she really?' Donald murmured remotely. 'I wouldn't know. I've never spoken to her.'

Main gave him no help there and he had to try again.

'Will you please stop tying up the tassels like that? This girl Bobo. I wouldn't mind if it was my tablecloth, but it doesn't belong to me. It belongs to Mrs Stockwell. I have looked on her with lust. Therefore I have committed adultery with her in my heart.'

'Well, she doesn't know about it, so she won't mind,' Main comforted him. 'She'll be all right. You don't need to worry. Nothing'll happen.'

'You must help me,' Donald appealed in a small, hungry voice. 'She'll do anything you ask her.'

'Oh aye, she will, she will that,' Main smiled. 'But that's true only because she knows there are things I'd never ask her.'

'Couldn't you introduce me?'

'Damn it all, man! She stays across the landing from you. You don't need me.'

Main divorced the tassels he had joined together and kept his eyes on them as he spoke.

'You seem to be suggesting, if I follow you, that since you've already committed adultery you ought to get the chance to commit adultery. But there's a hell of a difference between ploys you get up to in your heart and the real thing, bible or no bible. I mean to say, be your age! How do you expect me to help you? Do you think I could just go across the landing and tell Bobo to come in here, you want her? You're up the wrong close if that's what you think.'

'At least you could speak to her,' Donald said with a simplicity that frightened his cousin. 'You could put in a word for me. Break the ice. She never even says hullo to me.'

'You say hullo to her then. It's as easy as that.'

'It would mean nothing to her,' Donald muttered, beyond advice. 'So much to me, and nothing to her.'

'Don't be daft,' Main scolded him. 'What do you mean? It would mean a lot more to her.'

'Not her kind,' Donald fought back.

'What kind?' Main got up and stood over him, his fingers tipped on the green cloth. He was beginning to get a wee bit angry.

'I'm not a penniless student, you know,' Donald barged on. 'I've got money. There's never a month I spend all my allowance from home. I've got a little saved. Not much. But enough for Bobo.'

'Oh my God!' Main cried to the ceiling.

'Only I'd need you to put it to her first,' Donald said at the same moment.

Main clenched his fists and banged them several times on the table before he was able to speak.

'Look, man, you're making a mountain out of nothing. Adultery in the heart be damned. A fellow your age ought to know by this time. It's a biological urge, that's all it is. Bobo would understand. She knows damn fine what she does. But she wouldn't buy your idea. Get a hold on yourself, Donald Duthie son of Isaac. It will pass. Och aye, it'll come back. So will Christmas. But don't let it get you down. Laugh, clown, laugh! It's the kind of world we're born into.'

'You could speak to her, you know you could,' Donald wouldn't let up. 'You two, you're that thick. She'd do anything for you. You could raise my name when you talk to her, you could get her to agree, and then you could bring her in here some night and you could go away. You could easy think up some excuse to leave us.'

'And the Stockwells? What do you think they would say?'

'Och, they'd trust me,' Donald answered, sincerely innocent, innocently sincere.

'Aye, maybe, but would Bobo?' Main laughed, throwing away his anger.

He ambled round the room twice, safe behind his glasses, and he glanced with a smile at the nape of Donald's horse-like neck each time he passed behind him.

'I'll do what you want,' he announced when he came to rest facing his cousin again. 'I'll speak to Bobo. I don't know what I'll say exactly. Maybe I'll tell her you're madly in love with her. She'd like that. She likes to be loved. Don't we all? Or maybe I'll just say she'd find you worth getting to know if she'd only give you the chance. She likes men. She's interested in all kinds of men. I don't know how I'll put it. But I'll think of something. I'll get the pair of you together if that's what you want, though I can hardly tell her what else you want. And then hell mend you. You've never danced in your life, have you? Well, by God, she'll lead you a dance.'

'Och now, I don't want to go dancing or anything like that,' Donald protested. 'Maybe the pictures once or twice. So as not to be too sudden. But that's about all. I don't want to give a lot of time to her, you know.'

'It won't be what you want,' Main warned him.

I met Main again many years later when I was in hospital and he turned out to be the doctor in charge of the ward. A couple of casual words that were meant to be merely polite conversation to put me at my ease before he examined me put him on to where I came from and who I was. I recognised him of course, though he didn't know me, and I made the most of the opportunity to talk to him. When he found out I had Miss Partridge's diary at home he got quite interested, even excited, but he seemed disappointed I couldn't tell him anything about Bobo, and after I was well again I had several sessions with him in his house in Scotstoun. He told me a lot I had only guessed, things even my mother didn't know.

CHAPTER THREE

Bobo and Dross got into the habit of using the Phoenix a
lot in the autumn of that year. It was about a mile away
down the main road, near the Cross. For years it was called
the Green Cockatoo, a common city pub, the property of
an Irish immigrant, Barney Geoghegan, with its outside
painted a plain chocolate brown, the bar a long straight
counter with a sawdust track, and at the rear a couple of
unhappy sitting-rooms with varnished tables in front of a
fixed settle, and an ironbarred window looking on to the
back-court. But time marches on. After a fire that temporarily closed the Green Cockatoo, the premises were
taken over from Barney by a Scottish brewery and Barney
retired to his native village in Donegal. The abandoned
baby's linen shop next door was annexed by the brewers
and the Green Cockatoo arose from the ashes as the
Phoenix. The brewers squandered a barrel of money to
modernise the enlarged premises to a fashionable modern-
antique style, and the part where Bobo and Dross liked to
drink had a low ceiling with imitation oak rafters, plastic
panelled walls, gawky little tables, and portraits of laughing cavaliers, simpering bareshouldered beauties in Louis
Quatorze dress, a Regency buck, and a coloured print of
stout men in red coats riding chestnut horses. You got into
it by going down three rubbertiled steps off the lobby
flanking the bar, because the baby's linen shop had been
floored at a slightly lower level than the old Cockatoo.
Above the lintel a neon sign blushingly whispered TUDOR
LOUNGE in simplified gothic.

Dross used the bar when he was drinking alone or with
his pals, but it was always the Tudor Lounge when he was

with Bobo. He called it the Chewed Her, but not as a joke. That was how he said it. There was often an intrusive aspirate in his speech. For 'isn't' he said 'hisn't', just as he said 'hit' for 'it'.

'I've just had about enough of Wee Annie,' Bobo, blonde and vehement in a green dress and a string of pearls, declared to him in their cosy corner. 'She was stuck on the landing like death warmed up again after I left you last night. Waiting for me to come up, that's all she was doing. And you know what she says? Go on, you'd never guess.'

There were six of them together in the Tudor Lounge that night, but she had the best seat, against the panelling with Dross at her right hand so that they could sit back twisting fingers in comfort and see all that went on, identify the regulars and criticise strangers. Two of the other four sat facing each other, and two facing Bobo and Dross, alternate male and female courtiers round the table of the king and queen. But for all their submission to the supremacy of Bobo and Dross they were liable to wander off on their own conversation and pick up only at hazard the fragments dropped across the table. By the time the three men had all bought a round nobody was sure who was listening to what, but everybody kept on talking in the feeling somebody must be taking it in, something must get over, somewhere, sometime.

The supporting quartet was made up of two smart lads known in the district as Yoyo and Yowyow with their female comforters Jean and Jess, a couple of starchers from the laundry where Miss Partridge worked. Accustomed as they were to washing dirty linen by day in the line of duty, the two girls enjoyed nothing better than washing dirty linen by night for pleasure. Their gossip was as wide-ranging and deadly as a jet-bomber. They knew not only the sins of all the girls in the laundry, but the sins of their brothers, sisters, parents and grandparents, cousins and in-laws as well. Yoyo and Yowyow were garage hands, scholars in the language, literature and history of cars. Their comradeship was fortuitous, but none the less appropriate, perhaps even inevitable from the point of view of those who believe in the preordained fitness of things or the conjunction of twin souls, destined from all eternity. For Yoyo was Alexander Jeffrey and Yowyow was Geoffrey Alexander.

Yoyo was as Glasgow as the Fair, called Yoyo because he was never at peace, a fidgety, fingerdrumming, bobbing up-and-down fellow, moody as a day in April, smiles in the morning and scowls in the afternoon, a friend in the evening and a foe at night. One minute he was all over you with a hail-fellow-well-met enthusiasm for the very fact of your existence, and the next minute he was narky and touchy, grudging you even the space you took up on earth, picking a fight with you over a straw in the wind, pinning you down with a sharp word you never rightly meant to use but now you were stuck with it. He was a little below the average height, a small dark man with his own key to the door, good features and good teeth, and unusually powerful shoulders, so broad he seemed to fill the doorway every time he came into a room. He was no Glasgow bauchle, but he carried a chip against the world that although he was dark and handsome he wasn't tall. In his black moods he was ready to go gunning after anybody for nothing, a rebel who would kneel to no gods.

Yowyow was a taller and slimmer type, a fairhaired blue-eyed boy, an immigrant who spoke a foreign language. He was English. His father was a glassblower who had come to Glasgow from London, a reversal of the normal flow of labour that made him an oddity rightaway. It seems he was given the chance of a more responsible job with a local subsidiary of his firm and bravely faced the prospect of living amongst the savages of North Britain for the sake of the extra cash. Then he went and died of a coronary before he had been manager a twelvemonth. His wife and family, a plump pleasant mate and three hungry chicks, lacked the wings to fly south again. They nested on forlornly in Glasgow and pecked for a living. After mourning a night or two for her love the widow bird went out to work as the milk-lady in a primary school, seeing to the allocation of the crates to the classrooms, and Yowyow the eldest fledgling left school and got a job in McLellan's garage I think it was, beside the rubberwork. That's where he met Yoyo.

The trivial coincidence that his real name reversed the name of his fellow-worker and friend merely convinced the natives that he was congenitally tapsieteerie to the order around him. It was rumoured he was first called Yaow-Yaow by a poor mimic who tried to imitate his cockney accent and couldn't get any nearer to it than mouthing derisively, 'Yaow, yaow, yaow, yaow'. Later Yaow-Yaow was simplified to Yowyow, and growing up in a friendly tribe Yowyow eventually picked up some of the pure vowels he heard around him, but he never quite managed to pronounce a final or median 'r', and never got 'loch' or 'Auld Lang Syne' correct. His nickname may have been influenced by the fact that Jeffrey was already known as Yoyo, so that by a malicious twist Alexander had to be called Yowyow, the southern diphthong being deliberately opposed to the pure round 'o' of the natives. Or for some other reason. After all, who knows how names are first given? When the Lord had formed every beast of the field and every fowl of the air and brought them unto Adam it must have greatly interested Him to see what Adam would call them. And why should Adam have called them whatever he did call them? It could only have been an impromptu nickname. Anyway, whatever Adam first named those two creatures, Yoyo and Yowyow were their names thereafter. They were as proper a pair as a pair of gloves or a pair of shoes. The one opposed and required the other, matched and completed him.

'You know what she says? Go on, you'd never guess!' Bobo kept on, peeved that nobody seemed very interested. They still weren't warmed up. It was only the first round on the table.

'She says, You hoor you,' Bobo told them when nobody made a guess.

'You should just have said, Hoo're you yourself,' Yoyo advised her casually, playing the piano on the edge of the table.

'You don't want to let her needle you,' Dross was cross with her. 'That auld bitch is no worth bothering about. You've got her on the brain, that's your trouble.'

'It's all very well for you, it's no you she calls names,' Bobo sulked, and twisted Dross's fingers viciously. 'I just wish she'd lay off me, that's all. If I get much more of it I'll do something to her, so I will.'

'Wot I sigh is giver a damn good fright,' Yowyow suggested vaguely. 'Tiker down a peg. Tha'll lahner.'

'You mean?' Bobo asked politely.

'Kid the breeks affer,' Yoyo explained. 'She'll soon stope annoying you then.'

'I don't know why she calls herself Miss Partridge at all,' Jean murmured dreamily. 'Dew Jess?'

'Well,' said Jess modestly, trying and failing to tug her skirt over her bright knees, 'what I do know is. It's not much. She married an American sailor when she was nineteen and went out to some wee place in Nebraska.'

'Who the hell would ever marry her?' Bobo asked the middle distance.

'Then she comes back here and calls herself miss,' said Jean. 'Bet she's got something to hide.'

'You could blackmail a dame like that,' said Jess. 'She's living under false pretences.'

'That's no false pretences,' Dross differed. 'You take folk in show business. Maybe they're married. Maybe they're married five or six times. You never know. It doesn't matter a damn. They never use their married name anyway. They've got a stage name. They're pros.'

'Like me,' Bobo muttered, still aggrieved. 'That what you mean?'

'No, what I mean is,' said Dross. 'It's quite legal. You think o' the folk you could blackmail if Jess was right. No,

I mean to say, Jess. You can use any name you like so long as that's what you use. That's show business.'

'But Wee Annie's no in show business,' Bobo reminded him.

'Naw, she hasna a leg to stand on,' Yoyo agreed, thumping the table in majestic chords.

'Scare her outa her wits is wot I sigh,' Yowyow slipped in again. 'Think up a scheme to frighten her. She'll know it's us but kent prove it. Then she'll leeve Bobo alown in kise she gets wuss.'

'Have a word with Tommy about her,' Jean suggested knowingly.

'Tommy?' Yoyo frowned a question. 'Whee's Tommy?'

'You've been using this place all this time and you don't know Tommy!' Jess admired him.

'Tommy? You mean Tommy here? Him that's charge-hand? Him wi' the funny face and big kisser? Half man and half mouth. Whit would he know?'

'Plenty,' said Jean. She fondled her glass of vodka between her palms. 'Tommy's Mr Partridge.'

'Wee Annie's wee brother,' said Jess.

Tommy came along at that moment like a genie summoned by the rubbing of the lamp he had to obey, or like an earth-spirit who had to appear once his name was spoken. Grinning from here to here was how Dross put it.

'Good evening, boys and girls,' the genie said with a blend of servility and patronage, as if he knew that although he had to obey their summons the ultimate power was his if they made one blunder and abused his obedience.

They answered him with a show of offhand courtesy, but they were pleased to have him come over. It made them feel they belonged, the Phoenix lounge was theirs, the charge-hand valued their custom. They weren't no-bodies.

'Well I never knew that,' said Yoyo.

'We did,' said Bobo and Dross together.

'I've saw him often up our close seeing her,' said Bobo alone.

'We know about her, working with her,' said Jess and Jean.

'I didn't know,' said Yowyow.

Tommy beamed down on them. He was used to his customers carrying on with their conversation after they had returned his greetings. He didn't mind hovering a couple of moments to see if they had a word for him in due time, and then he could take his smile elsewhere to pay a duty. He was no relic of Barney Geoghegan, no clod who outstayed a welcome. He knew his job from the cellar to the gantries, from travellers and police to the public. The brewers had brought him in as manager from the last dingy pub they had modernised because he had a reputation. He was 'a good man' in the trade. As so he should have been. He had spent his life in it. He served in the bar only if it was very busy. Usually he just stood by, watching and waiting, welcoming arrivals and regretting departures, telling the latest funny story to favoured customers and quick to see strangers were served promptly. He made a tour of the lounge three or four times every night to keep himself informed, to smile here and chat there, share gossip and sow hullos to reap the gain later, and at the end of the session he saw them all out from bar and lounge alternately with the routine farewell Barney Geoghegan too had used in his time like any other Scotch publican, 'Haste ye back!'

'Bobo was complaining there about your sister,' Jean said without animosity, showing her teeth in an advertisement-smile.

'What's she been up to now?' Tommy was smooth, showing off his false teeth to match Jean's own.

'Calling Bobo bad names,' Jean explained.

'She thinks I'm one of yon you know,' Bobo elaborated bitterly.

Tommy's eyes glazed a little and he swayed uncertainly between a laugh and a groan.

'Ach, be your age, don't pay any attention to her,' he rocked back. 'She's very simple. She means no harm.'

'She's batty,' said Dross.

'I wish I'd proof of that,' Bobo muttered.

'C'est tout à fait bon pour vous,' said Yoyo, who had stayed at school long enough to learn some French and spent a fortnight once at Dinard with a Youth Club Holiday Camp, 'mais pour Bobo, non!'

With shoulders shrugging and palms upturned he pretended he was a Frenchman.

'San fairy ann,' Tommy answered airily to show he could speak French too.

'Was she ever married?' Bobo asked him, coming out of her sulk. 'Jean and Jess here say she was.'

'Well, it's a long story,' Tommy shuffled behind and over them. 'And you're too young, Miss Bonnar.'

'Oh ma Goad!' Bobo fluttered ringed fingers to her throat, twittered, cast up her blue eyes to the sham oak rafters, acted overwhelmed. 'My Sunday name on a Friday night! They call me Bobo.'

'You oughta sing it,' Yowyow told her. He was the music-lover of the company. 'Si, mi chiamano Bobo.'

He sang a falsetto Mimi but nobody listened.

'She's had a hard life,' Tommy defended her, one hand on the back of Jean's chair, the other on Yoyo's, doing a little tapdancing on the spot as he spoke. 'You know how it is.'

'Come on! Give, Tommy! Give!' Bobo kept at him.

'Tell us about her husband,' Dross supported her.

'It's a long time ago,' Tommy shuffled to a standstill.

'We've got all night,' Bobo told him. She leaned to let Dross light her cigarette with the lighter she had given him for his birthday, and he took the chance to scratch the back of her neck with his heavier hand.

'She was awful young,' said Tommy. 'She didn't know her own mind and they didn't hit it off and she left him and that's the he and she of it.'

'Come on now, there was a lot more to it than that,' Jean encouraged him.

'What did she want to go and use her single name for, tell us that,' Jess quizzed. 'Sure that's not right.'

'She wanted to forget, I suppose,' Tommy offered. 'You know, start life afresh. Turn over a new grief I mean leaf. You don't want to be too hard on her.'

'She's kind of hard on other folk,' Bobo whispered, but not as if she was keeping up her grudge.

'Aye yes, I know,' Tommy heard her. 'That's true. What are you on?'

He passed on their order to a waitress and escaped. He had other duties, he had his own worries.

'Well, what are we going to do about her?' Yoyo picked up the topic. 'Play clockwork on her window at midnight?'

'Three storeys up!' said Bobo. 'Don't be daft.'

'I can just see you climbing the rone pipe,' Jean laughed.

'Monkeys like to be high up,' Jess giggled.

'And parrots like to be talking,' Yoyo retorted sourly.

'What about poisoning her parrot?' Yowyow was inspired.

'What with?' Dross asked, staring at him with patient contempt, as if any answer would be absurd.

'Put Parozone in its drinking water,' Jean suggested. 'I could easy get Parozone from the laundry.'

'Any damfool walking the street can get Parozone.' Yoyo treated her with even more contempt than Dross had treated Yowyow. 'Good God, you don't have to sign anything to buy a bottle of Parozone.'

'That's not the point,' said Dross. 'The point is how are you going to get it into the parrot's cage.'

He turned on Jean as the Parozone proposer.

'Are you on visiting terms with Wee Annie like?'

'No, are you?' Jean answered swiftly.

'Oh, the repartee's rare in this company, so it is but,' said Yoyo.

'That's your gas in a wee peep.' Jess, always on Jean's side, slapped Dross's arm.

'Wring its flippin neck,' said Yowyow. 'Jean could easy pinch a wringer from the laundry.'

'A coupla wee coamics, you and your pal,' said Jean. 'Where are you next week?'

'Tell you what we could do,' said Yoyo. 'What they used to do when there was witches. You make a wee statue you know outa clay or something like the person you're after and you stick pins in it and the person feels the pain and if you put a pin through its heart he'll die. Simple, i'n't it? It's a better idea than the bomb any time.'

'That was before modern science,' said Jess. 'You're away back in ancient times.'

'And dipped his feet in ancient times,' Yowyow hymned to her.

'Aw, cut the comedy, yous!' Dross called masterfully.

'I'm no having it,' Bobo insisted mistressfully, mistrustfully, distressfully. 'I want no part in killing a poor defenceless fowl that never done nobody any harm. Anyway, how do you think you'd ever get in to wring its neck? Wee Annie wouldn't let one of yous across the door.'

'She calls it Shelley,' said Dross.

'What does she call it that for?' Yoyo asked, but not particularly wanting an answer.

'How should I know?' said Dross. 'It was Bobo told me. She says there was a poet called Shelley or something.'

There was a moment's silence at Bobo's erudition.

'Oh, you're a right shower, so yous are,' Bobo complained. 'Not a bright idea among the lot of you. I'll away and see Mr Shanks.'

She teetered out and went round to the ladies, and on her way back along the corridor she stopped at the side-door to the bar. In a spasm of girlish curiosity she pushed it open a few inches and peeped in. Her heart, for after all she had a heart, fluttered like a sparrow pinioned in a boy's palms when she saw Main at the far end with a pint started in front of him. She strolled in elegantly, aware she had a good carriage even if she hadn't a fairy godmother, proud of her smart shoes and her new stockings.

'Hello, hello, hello!' she made a good entrance. 'Well, well, well! If it's not you, Hugh!'

'What hue?' he asked, a hand held out to hold hers.

'Bright pink,' she said, smacking it down. 'Do I do that to you?'

'Me blushing? Nonsense! I haven't been red in the face since the night I wept with rage to be born.'

'Now, now,' she scolded him. 'Don't be like that. It's gorgeous to be alive, to dance and drink and sing and kiss and make love. Water you buying me?'

'Water?' he smiled not to offend.

'What are,' she tried again carefully.

'What would you like?'

'You,' she whispered in his ear, so close he felt her lips touch it. Then she laughed and he laughed and he bought her a drink and took his pint over to sit beside her across from the bar. She was happy, the Friday night euphoria working on her with the week's work behind her and pleasure earned.

'Water what are,' she went back over it. 'What was the other ones you learned me? I remember! The valiant Italians buried their valuables in a canal in the valley. And oh yes, my father sat with his palms on the grass. Boysaboys! I'm the Duchess of Mulguy and you're Lord Muck of Glauber Castle. We'd make a hansom pair. Come on and we'll elope to Gretna Green.'

'My father took off his hat,' he reminded her.

She tried it with spirit and tittered at the result.

'Ach naw,' she calmed down. 'Ma faither tuik his haaa aff. That's the real me. I'll never be fit for high society. I'll just have to marry Dross and have a lotta wee squealers that don't talk good.'

'I was talking to one of your admirers the other day,' Main plunged into it.

'There's a place for folk that talk to theirselves,' she wagged at him.

'No, not me, you've got more than me, you know,' he wouldn't be laughed off.

He told her about Donald, straight and brief. As he expected, she wasn't shocked, only giggly.

'Yon big drip! And to think I thought he was a

gentleman. Somebody you could trust. Ma Goad, ye couldny trust him wi' your granny. And him wi' that mollicolly face like a Saint Bernard that's loast its wee thingummy o' brandy.'

'It all goes to show you there's no art,' said Main, 'to find the mind's construction in the face.'

'You can say that again,' Bobo agreed. 'Just because I use a wee bit makeup some folk get ideas. I bet Wee Annie's been talking to him. Her heid's fu' o' chowed breid. If I find out she's been spreading rumours about me I'll sue her; so help ma Holy Willy, I'll sue her so I will.'

But even there she was laughing, happy to be chattering to Main. She told him what Miss Partridge had called her.

'We was just discussing it in the lounge. Plotting revenge like, you know. Some of them was for poisoning her parrot but I wouldn't hear tell of it. Now if we could put the evil eye on her! You don't know any good Highland curses, do you? Guaranteed to kill by remote control. Her, not her parrot. So that nobody could never prove nothing. I wouldn't harm a feather of her bloody old bird, but her the old bitch I would.'

'Don't be vindictive,' Main cautioned her soberly. 'That's not like you. And she's a sick woman.'

'Oh here, it's time I was away,' Bobo panicked. 'Ta for the natter. But if Dross comes looking for me and finds me canoodling wi' you I'll get my head in my hands to play wi'.'

'But you'll give poor Donald a chance?' he detained her.

'A chance for what?' she nudged him. 'He's big and ugly enough to ask for himself. He's just a nutter.'

She sighed.

'An utter what?' Main asked, puzzled when she stopped. He didn't understand her, and she didn't always understand him, and yet they understood each other.

'Just a nutter,' she explained, baffled with him because he was by her. 'Can't he speak up for himself?'

'I'll get him to do that much I hope,' said Main. 'But I want you to say yes. Let him take you out, even just once.

He's dying to—' he paused, thought, and added politely, 'to kiss you.'

'Aye, I know fine what you mean,' she answered grimly. 'And he'd probably make a proper muckup of it too if he ever tried.'

'I'm sure he would,' he agreed. 'But you could be an education for him. That's what he needs. He'll have to learn he can't go about the world's business that way. You could do him a power of good. Civilise him.'

'All right, leave him to me, I'll learn him,' she promised.

Dross huffed at her for being so long away.

'Who were you with at the bar?' he demanded, shrewd with the inspiration of jealousy. 'I can't trust you out of my sight for a minute. Even on your way back from the toilet you get a pickup.'

'You're a right gawk, you,' she edged past him, letting him feel her thigh hard against his. 'You're getting as bad-minded as Wee Annie. I met my doctor. That was all.'

He was eased of the gripe of jealousy, though still a bit sour. He didn't mind the fellow she called her doctor. He knew there was no serious competition there.

'So that's what kept you? He's your main interest in life eh?'

He was so pleased with his little joke he tried it another way.

'You've aye got your eye on the main chance.'

He laughed to be so witty and lost his ill humour.

'We've got a rare idea for Wee Annie,' Yoyo welcomed her.

'What? Shove her in the Canal?' she asked, uninterested, still with Main.

'Ach, don't act the budgie,' Yoyo grinned at her. 'We sit here and rack our brains to avenge your good name and you sugar off and when you condescend to come back you make bloody frivolous suggestions.'

'I can't wait,' Bobo settled against Dross. 'What brilliant idea has dazzled your puny brain? Are you going to put the evil eye on her or just send her a time-bomb through the post?'

'It's a very simple idea,' Yoyo answered. 'Something even you could understand if you'd just stop talking and listen for a minute.'

'Yowyow thought of it,' Dross intervened, peacemaking. 'It was something Jess and Jean said.'

'You know how she goes for the wages every Friday morning,' said Jess.

'And she's got to go through that big long pend,' said Yoyo.

'And it's got two halfturns in it,' said Jean.

'So halfway in,' said Dross, 'you can't be seen from the street and you can't be seen from the laundry.'

'So we're gonna getter rolled,' said Yowyow.

'Oh no,' Bobo cut him off sharp. 'None of that, thank you. The cops would be at Dross's door in five minutes flat. What with Wee Annie knowing me and me knowing Dross and them knowing his record. You can stuff it. Dross has been in enough trouble already and he's promised me that's all over and done with.'

'Dross doesn't come into it,' said Yowyow.

'It's only a joke we mean,' said Yoyo.

'Some joke!' Bobo didn't laugh. 'Stealing the wages for the laundry a joke? I fail to see it.'

'Naebody's gaun to steal any wages,' Yoyo pitied her for being so dim and so grim. 'We roll her, that's all. Snatch the bag and toss it to the far end of the pend so that she just thinks she's been robbed at first. Kid her on and give her a good fright.'

'Who's doing it then?' Bobo asked, her eyes panning them all with impartial suspicion. 'I'm at work, and you and Yowyow are in the garage, and Jess and Jean are in the laundry when Wee Annie's outside. The only one not working is Dross, and you say he doesn't come into it.'

'There's none of us in it,' said Jean.

'What would we be doing in it?' said Jess. 'Wee Annie would know us a mile away.'

'And Yowyow and me's no asking for the morning off,' said Yoyo. 'But we're gonna get a big card ready and it'll be shoved up her jumper and on it it'll have—'

He pointed the words in midair with a travelling finger as he read them off in capitals.

'THE SCARLET WHORE WILL GET YOU IF YOU DON'T WATCH OUT.'

'But who?' Bobo kept on asking. 'I don't get it. Who's going to do it?'

'Friends of mine,' said Dross. 'Pals that was with me in my old school. And a good school it was too. At least it was approved. They'll do it for us.'

'You don't mean Tiger?' Bobo moved his hand from behind her knee. 'You're a nutter so you are!'

She muttered in sorrow, her word reminding her of Main and his tale of Donald.

'Aye-a-day,' Dross answered, cross with her. 'And Hardnut.'

'And Chocolate,' Yoyo gloated.

'They'll giver the scampers all right,' Yowyow yawned.

Bobo sighed, her elbow on the table, her fingers lightly splayed on her young cheek so that she showed off her long varnished nails and all her rings.

'If that's all they do,' she said.

I don't think any of them did anything to the parrot. As
Bobo pointed out, Wee Annie would never have let one of
them across the door. So they had no chance to put a
finger on him, and it's going too far to suppose they
found an operative curse or stuck lethal pins into a wax
model. Yet something happened to him that winter. The
night she managed to get Grace Christie to come in for
tea and cakes Miss Partridge found her pleasure in the
event completely spoiled by the way Shelley moped and
wheezed. She had meant him to entertain the child with a
first-class performance, and she took him through a full
rehearsal the night before. His wit and liveliness then
delighted her, but now when she wanted him to show off
and perhaps gain for her the favour of Grace by his
charming talents the poor bird hadn't a word to say for
himself, good, bad or middling.

   She had been looking forward all week to having Grace
to herself, and the pointless love she could never tell
anyone was with her sleeping and waking, longing to be
told. After the turning point when her vague affection was
clarified into an obsessive love just because Grace walked
past her on the stairs, she tried once or twice to tell her
brother Tommy, her only visitor. But he was so busy
talking trivia nonstop in his eagerness to keep her spirits
up he never let her get a word in edgeways. If she could
only have got him to listen, a confession of her love would
have done her a lot more good than listening to him. For
all his anxiety to help, Tommy was no use to her. She
carried her absurd secret as a burden God had put on her
for her salvation and found strength in silence. Yet still she

longed to tell her love, love that never should be told. And to whom better than her beloved?

'Aye, it will maybe be a hard thing for the wee one to understand,' she admitted in her single-end, where she always spoke her thoughts aloud, arguing with herself in a private debate. 'I don't deny it.'

'And it isn't very fair either, not to a wee girl.'

'I admit that as well.'

'You're not in the grocer's asking for a pound of sugar, you know. You're asking a wee girl for something beyond her.'

'Och aye, I know. It's beyond me too. But I'll feel better once I've told her.'

'And what good will that do the wee one? Tell me that.'

'Well, if she doesn't understand now she'll understand later on in life, and she'll remember me for it. She'll remember all her life whatever happens to her there was somebody loved her.'

'That's what you think. But are you right there? Will she remember? Will she even listen in the first place, will she take in what you're telling her?'

'I don't know, I just don't know. Stop nagging me. I'm going to tell her no matter what you say.'

She rinsed her cup and saucer at the sink beside the window overlooking the main road and saw not the water running from the swan neck tap but the big blue eyes and solemn face and then the light body and skipping steps of the little girl who was innocently torturing her.

'Oh dear, if I only had her all to myself! If only she was my wee girl!' she sighed, and went on sighing, unable to think what to think after that.

She got her chance of having Grace alone because at that time there were still theatres in Glasgow, and Mrs Christie often went to the old Empress music-hall with the widow Mrs Green. Miss Partridge overheard them on the stair-head landing arranging to go on the Thursday and did a little jig of joy behind the lavatory door. With the mother out of the way for the evening there was nobody to stop her getting Grace to come in for an hour. It was only the mother objected to her talking to the child. The father never bothered one way or the other. He was a zero, a pub-man, seldom at home in the evening. Grace would be left with her big sister Agnes, a stupid lump all puppy fat and pimples, addicted to wailing pop songs as she wiggled up and down the stairs, letting the whole close hear that her world had come to an end because her boy had found another friend. She also broadcast she was ready to sur-render body and soul because she was under her true love's control. The erotic confessions of a thirteen-year-old girl who had no boyfriend, nor was likely to have one till her pimples cleared away and her budding breasts ripened a bit more, irritated Miss Partridge out of all proportion. She was convinced that only a supernatural intervention, a gratuitous descent of the Divine Essence, could have given such a jumbo-calf as Agnes such a little sister as Grace.

Every word Mrs Christie and Mrs Green said came clearly through the lavatory door, and Miss Partridge loitered behind it till they parted before she dared flush and go out. She was always shy about leaving that place since Angus Erskine's song on the wash-house roof, and she didn't want Mrs Christie to guess she had heard a music-hall date fixed which would mean leaving Grace motherless for an evening. So she lingered there, ear against wood, on one foot and then on the other in that limited privacy, and her heart was exalted above the seats of the mighty as the words she was taking in resurrected an old dream. She waited for the night to come when she could make her dream come true and have Grace all to herself for an evening. She would fill the hungry with good things. Then she worried in case something would happen to prevent it.

But she managed it easily enough, for Grace was a biddable child, a mum girl who did what she was told when she was told because she was told, bending before the breezy whims of the adult world around her at school and at home, yet always keeping herself to herself, suffering no more the loss of her independence, the tearing of her roots, than the whispering green grass does before the domineering wind.

On the Thursday night Miss Partridge leaned out of her window watching till she saw Mrs Christie and Mrs Green come out of the close together and go away down the street. She felt safe then, as released as a prisoner who has earned his due remission for good conduct, and purring to herself she padded downstairs to the first storey, knocked with the glow of pleasure at the Christies' door. When Jumbo opened it with a *Romeo* in her paw she grinned and craned. Ingratiatingly she spoke:

'Oh, it's you, Agnes! Is Grace in? I was wondering could she go a message for me. I've only my slippers on or I'd go myself. It's just down to Carlo's for a fish supper for my tea.'

'Gracie!' Agnes yelled, waving her *Romeo* towards the kitchen, and Miss Partridge trembled in horror at the gross familiarity of this unsisterly earthling. 'Aw, Gracie, here's Wee – here's Miss Partridge wants you.'

Grace dawned from the kitchen, bringing brightness to the dim lobby, all legs and a brief skirt and faraway eyes, and Agnes pushed her out to Miss Partridge and slammed the door so hard that the other doors in the close vibrated in booming obedience to the rule of the Christies.

'They're aye banging doors in that hoose!' cried Sandy McKay, all alone and irritable.

'That's that big fat Aggie again,' said Daddy Blair to Mammy Blair. 'You should speak to her about that.'

'Aye sure,' said Mammy Blair, darning his socks with a beer bottle in the heels. 'I'll start a stairhead fight just to please you. You speak to her yourself if it bothers you all that much.'

'You don't mind, do you, Grace dear?' Miss Partridge panted, one wing round the girl's shoulder to lead her away.

Grace shook her head and waited for instructions.

It wasn't that Miss Partridge particularly wanted a fish supper, though Carlo's were famous in the district, but if she sent Grace for one then Grace would have to come up to her door with it, and after that it would only be natural to ask her in. She thought it a craftier way of getting the child inside than simply inviting her in for tea. Doing it that way she ran the risk of having her invitation refused, and the snub would be a wound she feared would kill her.

'I'll maybe have something nice for you when you come back, dear,' she breathed in Grace's ear, hugging her before she sent her off.

Grace nodded neutrally and skipped down the stairs three at a time, danced all the way along the street to Carlo's fish and chip shop at the end of the block, and then found a queue there as usual.

Back in her single-end Miss Partridge set the table for two. On a large plate in the centre she put cakes, fancy biscuits, and a couple of cream buns, she put clean linen over the American cloth that was left uncovered when she ate alone, and stood back hands clasped under chin, trying to gauge how the layout would appeal to a child who had a quick eye for sweet things.

Then after all the tea-party wasn't a success. Not to her anyway. Grace pleased her to begin with, she looked so clean and pretty with an alice-band in her hair, and it may be Grace had no complaints. She certainly scoffed at once most of the chips from the fish supper and made a spirited assault thereafter on the cakes and biscuits, but she had little conversation. And Shelley, who was meant to provide talk by his running commentary on the party in particular and life in general, was as silent as the backcourt after midnight. The great occasion lacked the atmosphere Miss Partridge had expected it to have; there was no intimacy, no communion, no tender preparation for her confession of love, only a wee girl eating bravely and a bird in his cage snuffling and sniffing, gasping and wheezing, watching them with a melancholy eye, bowing his head to peck at his breast, shivering and flapping to no purpose.

He couldn't even stand at peace on his perch. He kept limping round his cage in frustrated circles.

'He's almost human, isn't he?' said Miss Partridge proudly in spite of her disappointment. 'I think the poor thing's caught a cold. Shelley, Shelley, Shelley!'

She poked a chip into the cage and encouraged the ailing parrot with unhappy lovetalk.

'Is my darling not well tonight? Not a word for your momma? Nothing to say for Grace, my pet? Come, come, come! Chooky, chooky, chooky! Who loves me? Tell me true now, come on now, tell me. Shelley, Shelley, Shelley!'

But Shelley wouldn't play.

'I think there's something wrong with his foot,' Miss Partridge brooded, and with a ruthless tenderness she probed the two toes in front and the two toes behind.

'Why do you call it Shelley?' Grace asked, not very interested, just for something to say to break her boredom at the way the woman was carrying on. Casually, lightly, she lifted the first of the cream buns.

'It's not it, it's him,' Miss Partridge checked her gently. 'He's old, you know, very old. Oh, an awfully old bird. I got him from a sailor in New York years and years ago. And the sailor told me he was seventy years old then, and that wasn't yesterday. He was ill then but I took him and nursed him and I've kept him ever since. Sometimes he tells me bits of his life story when we sit in here alone together at night, just the two of us.'

'New York? That's in America,' said Grace, a knowledgeable as well as a biddable child. She stared across at the forlorn woman making love to a languishing parrot, not believing Miss Partridge had ever seen America. It was too far away. It was another world. And she knew the only world Wee Annie had ever lived in was her lonely world in this single-end on the top storey.

'Oh aye, I've been in America all right,' Miss Partridge thrust back quickly, hearing the child's distrust as an audible wave in the room. 'I'll tell you about it some time, dear. It's a long story. And you're far too young yet.

Shelley, Shelley, Shelley! Come on, sweetheart, talk to me! Say something for Grace, darling. She hasn't heard a word out of you all night. Sing her your wee song about Chesapeake Bay. Tell her how you used to live on the banks of the Gambia.'

'Why do you call him Shelley?' Grace remembered she hadn't been told. 'Miss Galloway gave us a poem by a man called Shelley last week. She said it was a good piece to say for a girl, for Ella Kewshin.'

In an explicable gush of generosity she spoke out loud and bold.

> Hailty thee, blind spirit,
> Burd thou never wert,
> That from Heaven or Neerit,
> Poorest eyeful heart,
> Fourth in prophets
> Trains of fun,

She gulped and concluded.
'Premedicated art.'

Miss Partridge was hypnotised by the childish treble of the chant. In her anxiety about Shelley she heard only what she already knew, surprised with joy to hear someone else say the words that had once been dear to her at her Papa's knee.

'Go on,' she pleaded, but softly lest she broke the spell.

'That's all I know,' said Grace. 'It's all she gave us. We're to get more of it tomorrow,' she said. 'We get poetry every Friday. Miss Galloway. We all call her Wellaway because she acts daft. She makes us learn bits of poetry off by heart. They're hard. She says we're too young to understand them now but when we're older we will, she says, like you do.'

'There's so much to understand and you're so young,' Miss Partridge said sadly.

'I'm eleven next month,' Grace corrected her. 'I'm not that young.'

A glaze moved over Miss Partridge's eyes, the remote look of the planner. A birthday party would be a good thing to arrange, even if it meant inviting others as well as Grace. She would put up with the prattling rivals who would have to come if she could put Grace deeper in her debt and strengthen her claim to the child's gratitude.

'What day?' she had to ask.

'The fifteenth,' said Grace. 'It's a Friday.'

'That's the best night for a party,' Miss Partridge was pleased. 'And this is the best season. We must have a party for you, mustn't we, dear?'

'My mother's giving me a party,' Grace warned her off. 'She always gives me a party. Ever since I was one.'

Shelley stepped on to his perch and fell off.

'Hellhellhell!' he squawked in anger. 'Damn!'

Miss Partridge hurried over to him like a mother to her injured bairn. That was when the party collapsed. Grace hovered round the cage, looking with big blue bored eyes from the stricken parrot to her frantic hostess, and Miss Partridge was distracted about Shelley. She let Grace go without saying a word of all she had meant to say.

Shelley was worse the next night and she was in a panic of worried love. Then over the week he rallied as if he was going to be all right, and she believed she was wrong to worry, the worst was over. But no. His rallies became briefer and his relapses longer and more frightening. She lay in wait behind her door, keeping it slightly ajar, to catch Hugh Main the next time he was due to visit his cousin, and she asked him to come in and look at the bird.

'It's not me you want, it's a vet,' Main told her cheerfully. 'A vet could put him right.'

But for what it was worth, and he told her it wasn't much, he gave her his opinion after he had examined Shelley with the combined skills and sympathies of a countrybred lad used to handling nonhuman life and a final year medical student not unversed in recognising the signs of mortality.

'He's in pain, isn't he?' said Miss Partridge, tears in her

eyes and her small fingers twisting each other to no purpose. 'I can see it. Oh, I can see it all right!'

'He's certainly suffering,' Main granted.

'I can't bear to see anybody suffering,' Miss Partridge moaned. 'I always think he'd be better dead. Is there nothing you could give him to take the pain away?'

'I suppose there is,' said Main, truly sorry for the skinny-legged, flatchested, greyhaired weeping little woman. 'But it wouldn't be much use, not in the long run. Frankly, Miss Partridge, I think he's dying. He's rotten with rheumatism and it's got at his heart. And I'd be surprised if he's not tubercular too.'

She took a pride in being brave. She straightened to her five feet two inches and looked up at him.

'You mean there's no hope?'

'I don't think there's much. But of course I could be wrong. If you'd care to call in a vet he could tell you better.'

'I can't afford any vet,' she answered at once. 'I'm quite willing to trust you, Mr Main. There's an aura about you. And I've ways of knowing. When I'm alone at night the dead come and tell me things. About people often. Who's good and who's bad. But they won't come till after midnight when the whole stair's quiet, and I've got to sit and wait for them and even then they don't always come. Some nights when you're sure, nothing happens. Another night you give them up and you're nearly sleeping, and then they start whispering to waken me. Maybe you don't believe me. But it's true. I'm in touch. I've got sources of knowledge.'

Main, who would have hooted at his cousin for claiming supernatural information, wouldn't even smile at Miss Partridge. He listened solemnly, patting her shoulder, and when she stopped for breath he comforted her, 'I'm sure you have.'

'So will you put him to sleep?' she asked, blunt and bold, her eyes dry after one wiping. 'Put him out of his misery. You could get something to give him. A man in your position.'

He didn't like to ask her what she thought his position was. Instead, he frowned and pursed his lips and tried to look wise.

'Euthanasia, that's what I mean,' said Miss Partridge, hearing his sympathy as plainly as she had heard Grace's doubt that she had ever been in America.

He promised to come back with something. He had no feeling at all about the parrot. It was Miss Partridge he wanted to save from further pain. In the hospital where he was doing his final year training he got a bottle of ethyl chloride with a spray nozzle, and provided also with a rough box he had asked a joiner working in the hospital to put together for him quickly in lieu of a coffin, he went back to Miss Partridge without telling Big Tonalt what he was up to. He was sure his cousin would call it murder. Miss Partridge welcomed him gravely and went at once to the staircase window on the half-landing. She leaned out as if everything was normal in her single-end and looked into the dark backcourt, deserted in winter, while Main did what he had to do. He soaked a large bath sponge with the ethyl chloride, covered the cage with a blanket and sprayed inside it too for good measure while Shelley cowered in a corner and glared at him. He put the sponge inside the cage and made sure the blanket was firmly tucked in all round to make it airtight, and when that was done he sat in Miss Partridge's fireside chair and smoked a cigarette slowly. He had no idea how long it would take, and the first time he went to the cage and lifted the blanket to drag out what he hoped was a corpse he was stabbed in the hand by a vicious thrust of the dying bird's beak.

'Damn you, you bastard!' he cried without malice, feeling safe to call Shelley what he liked with Miss Partridge out of the room.

He laughed at his own fierce language. But it was more of an ordeal than he had expected and his nerves jittered a little when he saw he wasn't at all sure he could manage the job cleanly and silently. He put more ethyl chloride on the sponge, sprayed the cage again with the nozzle slipped under the blanket, put a table cloth on top of the blanket, shrouded the cage tightly, and waited again.

'Youth in Asia,' he joked with himself, whistling in the dark. 'Teenagers in China. Alas, my poor brother. Parricide, parrotcide. The bird is dead that we have made so much on.'

He didn't want to prolong Miss Partridge's lonely agony at the staircase window, so after the minimum patience he hauled the bird out by the neck, and feeling life still throbbing there he squeezed it steadily till the pulsations stopped. But not until he had put the dead thing in the box and nailed down the lid did he go to the door and silently signal Miss Partridge she could come back to her empty house.

She wept over the coffin, wringing her hands, rocking and keening.

'He was all I had to love and now I've nothing. What am I to do, oh what am I to do? The way he used to play with me and talk to me, aye, and listen to me! He was someone I could talk to when I came home at night. When I was happy so was he, and when I was in the dumps he used to try to cheer me up. He'd flap his wings and make funny sounds to make me smile and give me a row if I didn't, and now I'll never hear him again. Oh, we had such good times together! He had lots of wee tricks for me, and we used to fight together, but just in fun of course, my finger and his beak, and he never, never bit me, not once did he bite me. He was a good soul. He bit Tommy once, but it was Tommy's own fault, he was tormenting him. He knew I loved him. And I'm sure he loved me too. That's my share of happiness in this world over for ever. Oh, Shelley, Shelley, my own wee friend, where are you now? What's to become of me?'

She buried him darkly at dead of night, not turning any sods though for a time she thought of digging his grave in the backcourt where leaning out the staircase window she could see where he lay at peace and he would always be near her. She had the exact spot in her mind. But she knew she couldn't dig deep enough to keep him safe. The youngest children, who often sat in the backcourt excavating aimlessly with sticks and seaside spades, would turn him up in the spring. Then they would break open the plywood lid and trail the dead body round in triumph, scattering his feathers before the winds of March, and everyone would know it was her Shelley and laugh at her for burying him in so public a place and perhaps complain to the sanitary. The picture of Shelley's grave being desecrated by straddlelegged infants probing the soil of the backcourt was cruelly alive to her visionary eye, and the fear of the neighbours making a fuss and maybe getting her fined impelled her to give up the idea of burying Shelley where she could see him. She thought of a safer way, though it went against her finer feelings to give in to it. She waited till one o'clock in the morning and with the clumsy coffin under her coat she slipped downstairs, along the street and round the corner to the Forth and Clyde Canal that stagnated a hundred yards behind the block. Swaying on the bank, tempted to follow the coffin, she threw it in.

I suppose it was only to be expected (anyway she wasn't surprised, nor in the least put out, for she was too wound up about what she had to do) that she should have to pass Bobo and Dross making love at the foot of the stairs. She swept proudly on, head up, mouth tight, not even bothering to insult Bobo as usual, and Dross silently covered Bobo till Wee Annie was gone.

'What's that she's carrying under her coat?' Bobo whispered, wiggling her hips to let her skirt fall evenly about her knees. 'What's she trying to hide? You'd think she was in the pudding the way she's all stuck out in front.'

'You've got an unclean mind,' Dross scolded her amiably.

'There's something up with her,' Bobo declared. 'Come on and we'll see.'

She pulled Dross with her and they peeped round the close and watched where Wee Annie went.

'She's away to the Canal!' Bobo cried, squeezing Dross's hand in loving alarm. 'Oh ma Goad! She's gonna jump in I bet you.'

'Your granny,' Dross argued. 'She's no the kind. Come on back in the close. That dame aye interrupts me.'

'She is so the kind but,' Bobo contraried. 'I wouldn't be one bit surprised if she done herself in, the frustrated old bitch.'

She sidled into the street, drawing Dross with her, and keeping close to the shops followed Wee Annie round the corner. From a dark distance they saw her fumble at her front and then throw something into the dirty neglected water. There was a plop and a plump, and after a moment's puzzled silence a screech of eternal sorrow.

'What's up with her?' Dross fretted. 'What's she doing her nut like that for?'

'Come on quick before she sees us,' Bobo answered in distress. 'She's coming back!'

They scurried a retreat and Bobo was crafty. She led Dross into the close past her own so that Wee Annie didn't see them on her way back upstairs.

'I'm sure she was in a mood for trouble,' Bobo explained. 'She was better not to see us again. She was like somebody that had done murder. That scream, that was her conscience.'

'Ach, you're away wi' the fairies,' Dross complained. 'She was just dumping some old rubbish, that's all. An old pair of stays maybe.'

'Wee Annie doesn't wear stays,' Bobo informed him coldly. 'She's got nothing to wear stays for.'

Miss Partridge never told anyone Shelley had died and she had thrown him in the Canal, and since nobody was ever in her house except her brother Tommy and Grace Christie it was some time before the neighbours were aware she no longer had a parrot. But Bobo spread her tale around, making a mystery, and the speculations about

her secret trip to the Canal at one o'clock in the morning
were wild and various. Alone in her silence, without a
confidant or ally, Miss Partridge felt guilt go with her for a
long time afterwards. It was perhaps odd for her, but she
felt like an unmarried mother who had concealed a birth
and smothered her infant in a back-close.

Tommy Partridge always went to see his sister on Sunday. He would stay for an hour or two and he used to take off his jacket and roll up his sleeves and prepare a meal for them both with a couple of chops or bacon and eggs or sausages and liver he brought with him. He was sure it was the only square meal she had all week, and he told her so every time he served her.

'Aye, cups of tea are all very well. There's nobody fonder nor me of a cuppa. It's a habit I got in the army. But you canny live on cups of tea and a fish supper now and again. You're fading away to a skeleton, lassie. I'm telling you, if you stepped off the pavement you'd fall down a stank.'

She didn't like to hear him keep on calling her skinny, and she didn't like to see him with his sleeves up. His arms were hairy, and the anchors and mermaids tattooed on them were to her eyes an ugly emphasis of his masculine coarseness. She wanted to forget the world of matter, to escape from it, to be a disembodied spirit, hearing and seeing and thinking without being subject to the calls of nature, freed from the limitations of the flesh. To be skinny seemed to be at least part of the way there. But her brother talked as if sheer fat was one of the cardinal virtues of a good woman.

'Och sure I remember you when you were a wee rolypoly, and look at you now! If you stood sideways you'd never be noticed. Aw, come on now! Give us a smile! I'm only kidding you. You know I don't mean to offend you. You eat up this rare bitta liver and we'll sit back and talk about Papa and Mama, eh? When you and me was better off. And happier. Before we grew up into two old eedjits without a friend in the world.'

He knew she found peace in talking of the past, of her father and mother, of herself as a girl at school and a prize-winner, and him as her boneheaded wee brother who bossed and bullied her and still loved her. He had an anthology of family anecdotes, tedious they would have been to strangers, but the very substance of the 'O Sweet Mystery of Life' to him and to her, and although she knew them all she was always happy to hear them told again, and their number permitted infinite variations for each session of their familiar reminiscences. But the week after Shelley died she was in no mood for his routine of sloppy chitchat.

'Haven't you noticed anything?' she asked, hurt he plainly hadn't. 'Shows how much attention you pay to me and to the little I had to keep me going, the few times you do condescend to call.'

'Damn it all, now be fair! I'm here every week without fail, like a recurring decimal, seven places and I turn up again, as sweet as pie.'

He basted the sputtering eggs, cross with her for be-littling his loyalty.

He was so used to Shelley he had long stopped looking at him. He hadn't much patience with canaries, budgies, parrots or any other domestic pets, cats and dogs included at the top of the list, but he had found it kept him out of trouble if he pretended not to notice her absurd affection for a squawker in a cage. After years of pretending he had come at last not to need to pretend. He quite honestly didn't see Shelley when he visited his sister. But now a sob in her words and the glance she sneaked at the corner where the cage no longer stood jolted him as if he was on a bus with a bad driver.

'What's happened to your bird?' he cried with cheerful curiosity, the cheerfulness called up in lieu of sincerity. 'You know, the minute I came in I felt there was something missing.'

In his hasty attempt to put a makeshift sympathy on

parade he made two blunders that cut through his sister
like a January gale and made her more certain than ever
there was no use talking to anybody about what was near
and dear to her, because nobody understood. He called
Shelley her bird as if her loved and lost companion was
merely a nameless fowl she used to own, and he was aware
of Shelley's absence only as something missing. It made
her weep again, and he had to fuss with a hankie and
blurred phrases, trying to wipe her eyes and comfort her
while the eggs got a crinkly brown round the edges, the
liver curled and shrivelled, and the sausages went black.

She raved so much he was afraid she was going to go off
her head again.

'Shelley is with me now and for ever in eternity, but
here and now mourning and weeping in this vale of tears I
still have Grace, glory be to the Father, and I will save
Grace from the death poor Shelley had to suffer, because
all creatures must die, remember man, and not only man,
but every beast of the field, every fowl of the air, and the
fish in the rivers, even Shelley in his cage that seemed
immortal he had lived so long, he was over ninety, I'm
sure, he must have been nearly a hundred, but from the
life of sin, that's what I'll save her from, from growing old
in the world unto death. I'll make sure she doesn't grow up
to be a Bonnar girl.'

When she said she still had Grace he thought she was
using a term in theology, for he knew she had a great
interest in all religions, he knew she learned off by heart
Catholic prayers and Buddhist prayers impartially, read
the bible every day and argued with herself about the grace
of God and the eternal damnation of all sinners. But as she
rambled on he identified Grace as the little girl who lived
on the first storey, and he remembered that for many
weeks his sister had kept dragging the name into every
conversation, though she had never said anything to make
him worry about the child.

'Now, look, dear,' he said sternly. 'You keep wee Grace
out of this. Put her right out of your mind. And don't you

bother your head about Robina Bonnar, it's none of your
business what she is, and anyway you're wrong there, you
know. You're wrong! You're not ever to do that again,
what you did before, not even think about it. It's bad for
you, bad!'

He shook her like a child, and because he was shaking
her he started shouting, and because he started shouting
he got angry.

She seemed calm enough after that for the rest of the
winter and on past the turn of the year, but she got him
worried as badly as ever when he called on her one Sunday
evening in the early spring. He made it an evening visit
because he knew she always went for a walk in the Botanic
Gardens on a Sunday afternoon when the fine weather
came back. She sat at the table with her nose in her bible,
and she looked so sedate he was ready to forget he had ever
thought she was getting her daft ideas again. But when she
was drinking tea with him after they had eaten the steak
and onions he dished up, she suddenly spoke out.

'I've been reading the Gospels again and I've been
thinking. It says in the Gospel according to Saint
John—'

She took up her book, her nose almost on the page. She
ought to have been using reading glasses, but she
wouldn't. It was a little point of vanity in her, though
nobody ever thought she was particular about her appearance. She read out to him in a good clear voice.

'Greater love hath no man than this, that a man lay
down his life for his friends.'

He stroked the bridge of his nose, unsure of her purpose, and the divine words gave him a picture of a brave
soldier fatally holding off the Zulus or Fuzzy-Wuzzies
with a jammed gatling while his comrades retreated to
fight again, of a big-hearted captain giving up his place in
the lifeboat, I'll stick to the ship, lads, you save your lives,
a miner on his knees, hands flat on the ground, his broad
back taking to death the strain of a cracking roof to let his
mates crawl clear, and the voice of a schoolboy rallied the

tanks. But he didn't feel she had anything like that in mind. His fingers travelled down his nose and tapped the tip of it as he squinted across at his sister.

'Aye yes,' he said cautiously, an old fear quickening his heart. 'That's a well-known saying from the bible. It's what they put on the epitaph on the Square, isn't it?'

She gave him neither a yea nor a nay. She looked up from the text and stared at the corner where Shelley used to talk to her.

'I've been thinking. No, that's not true. It's not me that's been thinking. It's somebody thinking thoughts through me. An angel came to me on Friday night, one of the seven, and he discussed it with me. He made the point perfectly clear by heavenly logic.'

She stopped as if she had made it perfectly clear to him too and merely awaited his formal agreement.

'What point?' he asked timidly.

'Take an infant,' she said, like reading the start of a recipe. 'Baptise her. Then she dies. What happens? Unless a man be born again of water and the Holy Ghost he shall not enter the Kingdom of Heaven. But she's been baptised. And she can't have any sin on her soul. She's too young. So what will happen? She'll go straight to Heaven. Even if she's not an infant exactly. Up till when? Seven eight nine ten? So would it not be a good thing if the mother baptised her child and then killed her? Oh, I know what you'll say to that. The mother has committed murder and she'll go to Hell. But will she? Think. Maybe the law will put her to death. Then she has laid down her life for her child. Even if it wasn't her own child it would still apply.'

'That's not right,' he stood up to her bravely. 'It's not like that. That's a kind of sharp practice. You can't cheat God that way. That's not what's meant.'

'Suppose you don't kill her,' she went on through his interruption. 'The child would grow up like the Bonnar girl, destined for damnation for all eternity. Any child that grows up is doomed to damnation today. There's no faith, no religion, no morals, no piety anywhere. Zion is a wilderness, Jerusalem a desolation. And God would forgive a mother who laid down her life for her child to make sure her child entered into the life eternal because she had shown the love to do it, and greater love than this hath no man.'

He couldn't argue with her. He just stared, sitting at one end of the table with her at the other, the silent backcourt three storeys below them, silent and empty because no children dared play there on the Sabbath Day, and he knew he must do something, but he wasn't sure what.

'I often feel Grace is my child,' she said softly.

That was when he made up his mind to warn Grace's parents.

He had a bad week in the Phoenix, with a buzzer always in his head, butterflies in his stomach, and a flutter-by in his hands, so worried he was, and after his night's work he went to bed late to put off the sleepless hours, and he lay on his back and he lay on his right and he lay on his left, turn and turn about till three and more in the morning, fretting in his lonely bed about his sister. She was all he had left of his own blood, but he felt his blood was getting thin. It made him unhappy to think he would maybe be better off without her. He suffered all the guilt of disloyalty, he was hot and bothered with the shame of being a bad brother, when he lay awake knowing he wanted to have her put away again. For her own good, he answered his conscience. It would be the best thing for everybody. But he knew she was crafty and could outwit him if it came to a battle. She would never go inside willingly, and until she was quite mad and helpless she would beat any plans he made to have her certified. The least he could do in the meantime was warn the Christies not to let Grace be alone with her. And even there he would have to be careful.

'Guile,' he said to the darkness. 'I must use guile. She's clever. Well, it simply means I've got to be cleverer.'

If she saw him visiting the Christies she would guess what he was trying to do. She would be offended, she might tell him never to come and see her again, she might do something violent at once if she was afraid time was getting short. He would have to wait till the end of the week and go round on Sunday afternoon when she was out at the Botanic Gardens. That would give him an hour or two in safety. He could be up the close and down again and call on her in the evening, and she wouldn't know he had been there before. He made a dangerous mission of it, seeing himself in the dim hours before the dawn as an agent penetrating enemy territory with a message for the underground opposition.

He wasn't helped any by the week's custom in the Phoenix. Bobo and her pals were in oftener than usual because Dross had a three cross double up on a pound stake, and he heard his sister's name dropped with a frivolous clanging every time he passed. He had a feeling they were deliberately teasing him, trying to provoke him, the way they talked about her so loudly without formally identifying her. But he was sure they knew damn well he knew who Wee Annie was. He was hurt. It wasn't nice of them. Their merry allusions and flippant innuendoes every time he crossed within earshot seemed to him a childish exercise in the old addition sum about insult and injury.

He changed direction abruptly, like a soldier check-stepping in company drill, when Yowyow raised his glass and declared a toast.

'To funny Wee Annie!'

'And here's to the night we give her a fright,' Yoyo clinked.

'Right up her fanny,' Yowyow concluded and sipped.

Tommy not only heard. In the only way you ever know what people mean, he knew he was meant to hear. The buzzer in his head bossed him more busily, the flutter in his hands flitted more floatingly, and he completed his half-incline to loom over the toasting table.

The clan was surprised to see the genie appear without

being summoned. Bobo was the first to twig she must chop
him down quick before there was a clash.

'Hello Tommy, hello dear,' she gave him a blonde
welcome to brazen it out. 'We was just talking about your
sister. Why don't you get her to come in here some night
and have a drink with the girls and boys? Would do her a
world of good, so it would but.'

He was too fond of Bobo to pick with her the fight he
had meant to pick with one of them, any one of them. He
got a hold on himself.

'Oh, she'd never do that,' he answered, mild, mannerly
and managerial.

'No?' said Jean.

'Poor kwa noan?' said Yoyo.

'What for?' said Jess.

'Well, she's,' Tommy tried slowly. 'She's well, well,
she's against drink. She doesn't even like me working here.
She thinks I've let the family down.'

'Ah well, you canny look after the Lounge and the Bar
and serve the Family too,' Yoyo nipped in with parochial
wit, because the Family was the local name for the Off-
licence.

'You know how it is,' Tommy acknowledged Yoyo's
crack with a protocol smile. 'She thinks the drink's a bad
thing. She believes it's all wrong, you know.'

'There's a hell of a lot of things she thinks is all wrong,'
Dross muttered.

'Aye well, maybe so,' Tommy wouldn't argue with
Bobo's boyfriend in case he annoyed Bobo. 'But still.
You've got to make allowances. She's, you see, she's never
been used to getting out and about like, if you know what I
mean, she's all alone, poor soul. She's got nobody or
nothing. She lives too much in herself I think. Looks into
herself all the time. You know what I mean. Sees nothing
but herself like in a mirror.'

'We were talking about a wee ploy to cheer her up,' said
Jean.

'A sort of practical joke we had in mind,' explained Jess.

Tommy was puzzled. More, he was frightened.

'Nae harrum intendit,' said Yoyo.

'They've been talking about it for months,' Bobo dis-owned it.

'Leave her alone for goodness sake,' Tommy pleaded. 'Don't start any fun and games with her just now. She's not keeping well.'

They had him worried, but he shirked picking the fight he had meant to pick. If he turned rough on them they might do something quick to his sister just to show him it wasn't wise to defend her. Misgivings paralysed him, panic inhibited him. He was a man confident enough in his own job, calm in dealing with its snags, at ease in coping with its people. But the danger to his sister pressed all the spirit out of him. He hunched and huddled and stretched and sighed that night in his darkness, thinking it would be for her own safety if he could get her inside again. Loud in his troubled skull he heard the young voices jabbering, the girls squealing and the boys crowing, and the pain of their mockery was renewed in him. It was bitter in his mouth that a little clan he quite liked should laugh at his sister and want to play tricks on her just because she was a bit eccentric. Then he wasn't so sure it was only a bit, and that made him worry more about his sister than about the plans of Bobo's friends. His anxieties rankled his guts and his sleeplessness dragged on round a circle of insolubles.

I think it was during the same week that Bobo and Hugh Main had another cosy chat at the staircase window about Big Tonalt. After their chat in the Phoenix about him, she had faced Donald boldly the next time she saw him. She had no use for simpering, blushing, or making eyes si-lently. She believed in taking the bull by his horns.

'I believe you and me's to get better acquaintit,' she said for a start, and he was the one that blushed, not her.

She couldn't do much with him, but she tried to edge him on over a week or two, blethering to him on the stairs or at the closemouth instead of passing him by as she used to do. She looked for him to make some advance, willing to help him at the least sign of one, but he was handless, taking his own time.

'Yon's an awful drip,' she told Main. 'But mind you, he's funny as well. He gets that earnest, so he does. Kind of intense like.'

'He's not bad when you get to know him,' Main said to encourage her. 'The fact you even talk to him is a big help. That's what he needs, a girl to talk to, to take him out of himself. He'll learn how daft his ideas are if you just keep talking to him.'

'But he's awful hard to talk to,' she complained. 'He kinda lectures. You know, wags his finger and explains everything. I don't think he wants to rape me at all. I think he just wants to learn me.'

'Teach,' Main whispered, always gently her teacher.

'I canny get a word in edgeways once he's startit,' said Bobo. 'Yes, I know. Teach, learn. It's you does the teaching and me does the learning. But he never gives me a chance to say my piece.'

Main laughed over the windowsill, beaming at the backcourt.

'Let the woman learn in silence, subject to the man. That's what Saint Paul said. And Saint Paul is one of his favourite authors.'

'Aye, so I've gathered,' she nodded, elbow to elbow with him at the window. 'He's made it as clear as a cow's bottom. Two of a kind, him and Saint Paul.'

'I've had that from him too. But you've got to understand he's not a bad fellow, not really. He'd like to sin so as he could see himself as a justified sinner. That's all. But he can't. And he'll have to learn women weren't put on this earth just to give men the means of fornication.'

'And I'm supposed to learn him? He's like the way I imagine John Knox only without the beard.'

'You could be right there,' Main chuckled acoss at her, his hands clasped as in prayer, his wrists resting on the windowsill. 'I've often thought Knox bashed away at

Mary Stuart the way he did because he had a repressed desire to bundle her into bed. She would have been quite a change from his other girlfriends.'

'I don't know anything about "Repressed Desires",' Bobo quoted back at him with capital levity.

'Because you haven't got any. But I'm sure John Knox had. When he called Mary a lot of bad names it was because he was wishing she was what he called her. Then he might have had a chance of lifting her nightie.'

'Oh you men!' Bobo cried. 'That's all you can think of.'

'Oh you women,' said Main. 'It's all you want to talk about.'

'Not me,' Bobo gave him a rabbit punch and knocked his head down against his clasped wrists. 'It was you startit it.'

'Are your pals still out to avenge you on Miss Partridge?' he surprised her by asking when he came up again.

'Wee Annie you mean? Well, they talk and they talk, and then they talk some more. But I don't expect for one minute they'll ever do anything.'

'I knew they wouldn't,' he stroked her. 'You wouldn't let them, would you? You're too goodhearted. And it's only you she's a bit hard on at times. It's got nothing to do with the rest of them. Why should they bother?'

'Because they stand by me.'

They had shifted round after she hit him and instead of standing side by side looking over the window they were leaning face to face. She tightened his tie.

'We're all pals,' she went on. 'One for all and all for one, that's how civvy-lie-sation begun.'

'Began,' he said. 'Leave her alone. She's terribly unhappy these days.'

'It wouldn't rhyme,' she objected. 'You mean she's a sourfaced old bitch. Why these days? She's always the same.'

'She's never got over her loss since her parrot died last winter.'

'You'd think it was one of her family she lost the way

you say it,' Bobo rejected his condoling tone. 'Her and her parrot! Maybe Yoyo made a wax model and stuck pins in it after all. Not that I ever wished it any harm. It's her.'

'She's sick,' he said.

'You're a doctor, you cure her,' she retorted.

'I'm not a doctor, not yet. And even if I were, her illness isn't the kind I'd have to treat. Can't you understand, and show a little sympathy? She's lost the only creature she loved. Now she has nobody. And everybody must love somebody.'

'Oh, she'll find somebody,' Bobo threw out impulsively. 'I think she's got another wee bird lined up for loving. If you can call it love, what she's got.'

She saw he didn't quite take it in, so she hurried on before he could ask her what she meant, a little ashamed of her remark.

'She could try loving me. Everybody else does. Anyway, what's so special about her, tell me that, that I'm supposed to feel sorry for her? You're only saying what Tommy in the Phoenix says. She's no keeping well, she's sick. There's damn all wrong with her if you ask me. Why's everybody so sorry for her and nobody spares a thought for what she says about me? She doesn't deserve any sympathy the way she carries on.'

'That's a hard thing to say,' he scolded her. 'You know better than that. It's because of the way she carries on you ought to be sorry for her. It might be you in thirty years time. How are we to know what'll happen to us? I bet you she was a dainty wee thing once, and pretty too.'

'All right, I'm sorry for her, God forgive me,' Bobo answered with a swallow and an effort. Perhaps she wasn't wholly sincere, but at least she said it. To please Main. And he was pleased.

He chucked her under the chin and she caught his fingers and twisted them, and that was all they did to show they were in touch. He knew if he kissed her it would be the end of a beautiful friendship, a move over to something he didn't truly want, and he knew she knew and agreed. She didn't want anything more either, not with him. Like Britain and America they found their pleasure in believing they had a special relationship.

It was sheer chance she walked into Tommy Partridge on the Sunday afternoon that week. She was coming through the close as he came in, and she was all dressed up in her Sunday best, soaped and scented and her nails varnished, off to meet Dross.

'My, you look great!' Tommy cried, and for a moment while he looked at Bobo his sister went right out of his mind, so easily distracted by a lovely face are even the most sorrowing men. On an impulse he added, though the language was out of character, 'What the Yanks call a swell dish.'

'Och aye, I know them all right,' she muttered thrusting the fingers of one hand between the fingers of the other to tighten the fit of her beautiful white gloves. 'There was one of them sailors from the Gareloch, did you see them in the Phoenix on Friday night, and he called me a hot plate between the ladies and the gents on the way out and there was me waiting for Dross to come out the gents, believe me I damn soon froze him. They seem to think a girl's something for eating, they Yanks. They make me want to spew the way they go throwing honey about. Any man ever calls me honey he's out on his beeneck.'

'Good for you!' he slapped his hands and rubbed the palms together. He had a tendency to Yankeephobia, for he found them a bit of a nuisance in the lounge and at the bar, loud and amorous, drinking what they called Scatch as if it was lager. 'You keep them in their place!'

'I think She's out,' said Bobo. 'She's always out at this time on a Sunday. She goes to the Botanics now. I think She goes to admire the goldfish in the hothouse. Anyway I'm sure She's not in.'

'Aye, I know,' he agreed, so eager to talk to Bobo he didn't think to be secretive. 'Actually it's Mrs Christie I'm going to see. I want a wee word with her. That's why I came round now. I wanted to take the chance while She's out.'

Bobo stared hard at him and she seemed to be reading his mind as if it was as clear as a newspaper headline.

'I mean,' he started, but couldn't go on. Her blonde self-possession and her white gloves, her young perfumed purity, her well-shaped nyloned legs and her smart court shoes all intimidated him.

'Oh I know what you mean all right,' she said as if she was wise to his purpose. 'It's high time somebody had a wee word with the same Mrs Christie.'

He was too alarmed at her insinuation to make any reply, and they broke off with a wave and a smile. But his smile was gone by the time he was up the stair and knocking at the Christies' door. He was sorry he had told Bobo what he had come round for, and he wasn't happy about what he meant to do next. It seemed a mean thing to do, an act of disloyalty, and yet he was sure it was his duty to all concerned.

Mrs Christie knew him in passing. She had said 'Hullo' to him on the stairs, plus 'Lovely day' or 'Dirty weather' according to conditions, but nothing much more. She had no reason to expect him to call on her. He felt her eyes were a couple of flamethrowers searching him with suspicion when she opened the door, and he was afraid she was going to keep him standing on the stairhead and make him say at the doorstep whatever he had come to say. In which case he wouldn't. He couldn't. Perhaps she heard the pleading in his heart echoed in his voice, perhaps she gave in to the tenement convention that it's rude to keep anyone standing talking at the door. Whatever persuaded her, she straightened up after the first recoil at seeing him and invited him in as if he was a normal Sunday visitor.

When he crossed the threshold, head bowed, and stepped into the lobby, she led him to the kitchen. The kitchen and room of the two-apartment tenements are the but and ben of Scottish jargon. When a Scotsman says in song or story, 'Come awa' ben,' he is inviting you into his front room. The but is the workaday apartment, with a sink and a grate and an oven, the kitchen where he cooks

and eats his meals, performs his ablutions, sleeps in a
recess bed against the wall, and quarrels with his wife and
weans on a Saturday night. The ben is the best room,
always tidy and seldom used apart from the fact that some
of the family must sleep in the recess bed there. But she
wasn't taking him ben. He wasn't important enough. The
kitchen was the place for him.

The lobby was a dim little link between the two rooms,
traversed in half-a-dozen paces, with a gasmeter high up in
a corner and a rank of coatpegs along the wall. It had a
timid odour of forgotten clothes and weekly carbolic. The
waxcloth covering the floor was scrubbed every Friday
night by Mrs Christie, a job she would duly hand down as
a tradition to Agnes, the elder daughter, who would in the
fulness of time bequeath it to Grace.

Mr Christie, *The Sunday Express, The Sunday Mail*,
and *The Sunday Post* across his lap and round his feet as he
dozed, sprawled in an armchair hogging the fire. His
unslippered feet, in heavy grey socks with his big toe
horning through one of them, were crossed on a judi-
ciously located low stool. He hadn't a jacket on, and his
flies and waistcoat were unbuttoned, his shirt open at the
neck, and yesterday's growth still on his double chin. He
squinted up at Tommy Partridge and grunted, 'Aye.'

'Aye,' answered Tommy.

Two Scotchmen being diplomatic.

'Is there something on your mind?' said Mrs Christie,
stuck at the table that filled the centre of the room. Her
fingers kept moving round the corner of the board as if she
was a blind person discovering a right angle.

'It's about my sister,' Tommy started and stopped. 'You
know my sister? Three up the middle.'

'Och aye,' said Mr Christie. 'Of course.'

'Aye, we know her all right,' Mrs Christie admitted with
a grudge, like an accused person recognising there was no
use denying a known fact but waiting to see what could be
made of it. 'Why? What's up?'

'I just wondered could you be careful,' said Tommy,

still only a couple of steps in from the kitchen door. And nervous and miserable he was.

'Take a pew,' said Mr Christie.

'Thank you,' Tommy chimed gratefully.

He shyly lowered his bottom to the edge of a chair beside the table and couldn't go on for a minute. The Christies' Sunday dinner was over, and the table was cleared except for a bottle of milk, a bottle of HP sauce, a bowl of sugar, a jar of Heinz pickles, a pot of Robertson's jam, with the Scott Monument in jamjars on the label, a salt cellar and a bottle of pure malt vinegar.

'Whadye mean careful?' Mrs Christie, always alert to take offence.

'I don't mean it's anything you've done,' said Tommy in a hurry, equally alert to fear he was giving offence. 'I mean it's Annie my sister. If you could be careful about her I mean. She gets a bit odd sometimes you see. As a matter of fact I hate to tell you she was once put away because she tried to harm a wee girl. She's awful fond of wee girls.'

Mr Christie took his big feet off the low stool and wrestled up to a sitting position on his ruptured armchair.

'Don't get it, Mac,' he declared, ready for war. 'How do you mean she tried to harm a wee girl she's awful fonda wee girls?'

Tommy Partridge was near to tears. All eternity wouldn't be long enough to put to rights the wrong he was doing, and yet he had to go through with it because it was right as well as wrong. And anyway he had started. He knew he couldn't stop now without making bad worse. He blurted. Maybe it was because he spoke so quickly, maybe it was because what he was saying was so hard to take in, maybe it was both. Whatever the cause, the Christies man and wife gawked and gaped at him.

'She loves them so much she wants to save them. It started after she came back from America. Then she went too far. Of course it's a long time ago now you know. She took a wee girl with her, a neighbour's wee girl she was daft about, it was a kind of babysnatching like if you see what I mean, and she coaxed her into her house, she had a house away over on the south side when she came back from America, and she turned on the gas and took the wee one on her knee, she said she wanted to send her to heaven and to make sure she got there she was going to cross over with her. Luckily enough the wife next door, she was three up then like what she is now only the faraway not the middle, the wife next door was coming up the stairs with her messages and she smelt the gas and she thought to herself there's something wrong here, and the way it happened the postman was coming up the stairs at the same time, a big strong fellow, and she got him to burst the door in and it was just in time. They didn't put her in jail you understand. She wasn't a criminal. It was just her mind. They put her in a home you see. She had this idea about sending wee girls with a message to the Father and say she sent them. She said she wanted them to get across to the other side before they went bad. You know, like apples that are kept too long. That's one of the things she said to the doctor. She said she was helping them to escape to freedom across the frontier. In an express. It was her mind. You don't want to be too hard on her. It was these ideas she had. She never meant anybody any harm. She did it for what she thought was the best.'

Mr Christie flapped and slapped and tapped his Sunday paper into its original folds. Smoothed it across his knees. Glared. Stared. His Adam's apple went up and down.

'What are you telling us all this for?' Mrs Christie demanded, towering over him, glowering over him, daring him to go on.

'Smatter of fact,' Tommy muttered. 'I don't like to say it but I'm a wee bit frightened sometimes. That wee girl was called Grace too. You know, like your wee girl. Is she in? She's got this idea about God's grace and you've got to answer for it.'

'She's ben wi big Aggie,' said Mr Christie.

'Are you trying to tell us she's after our Gracie?' Mrs Christie asked at the same time as her husband spoke.

'She's very fond of your Grace,' Tommy answered bravely. 'That's what I mean. I thought I ought to warn you. Keep her away from her. Don't let her ever get her by herself. Don't let Grace go into her house.'

'You should tell the polis if it's like that,' Mrs Christie was nearly shouting. 'And if you don't I will.'

Then they were all talking at once.

'The woman should be locked up, so she should,' said Mr Christie. 'A bloody menace like that and you walk in here . . .'

'Send them across the frontier?' said Mrs Christie. 'What's that . . .'

' . . . as if it was just a wee fancy she had . . .'

' . . . meant to mean, tell me that.'

' . . . to go murdering weans.'

'She only wants to save them,' said Tommy. 'She thinks'

'Jesus Christ!' said Mr Christie. Three heartfelt syllables equally stressed.

' . . . she's being kind to them,' Tommy ended sickly.

The husband and wife nattered at him, clattered and battered and splattered at him, and he just sat there with his head bowed under the clamouring of their words. For nothing now mattered to him. He had done what he came to do.

'But I can't go to the police,' he said wearily when they stopped for breath. 'What am I to tell them? I've no proof.'

'If she's been in a home,' said Mrs Christie.

'She left it,' said Tommy. 'She walked out and nobody was there to stop her. She's been out ever since. She's as sane as you or me as far as the law goes. If I go to the police what do I say?'

'I know what I'd say,' said Mr Christie.

'Aye, but you couldn't prove it,' said Tommy. 'That's the point. And the police wouldn't thank you. I doubt if they'd listen. They've enough to bother them. And maybe she's all right now. I could be wrong you see.'

'Then what the hell are you making this fuss for?'

Mr Christie struggled out of his cosy chair and shook Tommy by the lapels of his Sunday suit.

'Frightening decent folk out their wits,' Mrs Christie pulled her husband away.

'Cause maybe I could be right,' Tommy cowered under Mr Christie's raised hand. 'I'd hate if anything happened and I'd held my tongue and never warned you. I'll try to persuade her to go in again as a voluntary patient but I haven't much hope.'

'America,' said Mr Christie, so baffled he harped back, sure Tommy was a fantastic liar. 'I never knew she was in America. She's lived here all her life. When the hell was she ever in America?'

'Oh, she was in America all right,' Tommy took him up gladly on that point. 'She married an American soldier during the war. But she dropped her married name when she came back here. Something went wrong. He was taking her to a farm in Nebraska. It was his old folks' place, oh a real sainted pair they were according to him, and they'd give her a rare welcome and then the farm would be his. He told her the tale you see but it was nothing like what he promised, and they didn't get on somehow and she came home. She's an educated woman you know, shorthand and typing and book-keeping, she can earn her living anywhere. But she'd never talk about it. About what went wrong I mean.'

They let him go with douce Scots thanks. But the thanks were as cold and lumpy as yesterday's porridge because what he had come to tell them wasn't the kind of information they could feel grateful to have. If they were to take it seriously it was a worry beyond their coping with, and if they tried to sneer it off as rubbish they were doubtful till they worried again. The idea that any woman could be so base as to murder a little girl upset the even tenor of their ways. They called Grace in from the front room. They gave her together and in turn the strictest instructions never to visit Miss Partridge, never to be alone with her, to have nothing at all to do with her. Grace listened with no

expression. She was a self-disciplined child, accustomed
to hiding what she was thinking and what she was feeling.
She was what simple folk call deep. And a contrary child
too. Her parents didn't know that from the moment the
conversation got loud she and Agnes had been listening
behind the door. They heard only the end of the dialogue,
only enough to puzzle them. And Grace thought that if
funny Wee Annie was all that dangerous and mysterious it
would be interesting, perhaps even exciting, to keep in
with her and find out what it was all about.

CHAPTER SIX

Angus Erskine, the vulgar bard who had serenaded Wee
Annie a summer earlier, was now King of the Backcourt
and All Adjacent Territories, from Ruchill Park to the
Botanic Gardens, and from the Coal Hills at Dawsholm to
the Elephant's Grave at Kelvin Bridge. He was also, by his
own creation, Earl of Angus. Having no clear idea of class
distinctions, degrees of nobility and order of precedence,
not even aware of the difference between a baronet and a
knight, he saw nothing out of place in being a King and an
Earl too. He created himself Earl of Angus one balmy
spring afternoon when Miss Galloway (requiescat in pace)
gave us a history lesson about Archibald Douglas, fifth
Earl of Angus. She told us with great dramatic effect,
suiting the action to the word, how he had hanged somebody over some bridge and that was why he was called
Bell-the-Cat. I've forgotten the details. I don't think I
followed them very well in the first place, but I can clearly
remember Miss Galloway's fingers as a rope round her
neck and her tongue lolling out between her loose dentures. We called Miss Galloway Lucy because Shoe Lur-
insky heard another teacher call her that in the corridor
one morning as the lines were tramping in to Miss
McCandlish hammering at the 'Village Blacksmith' on
the piano in the Assembly Hall. She may have been Lucy,
but she was never lucid. I have a thousand and one
pictures of gruesome facts and gay, peculiar items and
strange, stranger than fiction they were, the ants crossing
the Limpopo and lemmings drowning themselves in the
sea as she sank to the rough boards of the classroom floor,
swimming ever more and more weakly, swallows winging

south with the turn of the season, finding their way by some mysterious guidance the way she found a route from her desk to the door with her eyes shut as she flapped her hands, the greenwood of yesterday changing into the coal of today as she rolled her shoulder blades and pressed herself down to her knees with her ringed fingers splayed across her skull, but I have no certain recollection of what she was trying to prove by her various performances. Still, she was a great teacher. She died in Woodilee Mental Hospital out at Lenzie, God rest her.

When she got on to Archibald Douglas and him being Earl of Angus, our Angus in the back corner seat of disgrace for inattention and insubordination took the point at once. We turned round to give him a smile because Lucy had innocently mentioned his name. He stood up and bowed, clasped his hands above his un-trimmed thatch and made an arc of acknowledgement. Then he jabbed his chest with the index finger of his left paw, the right one out with the thumb up, and in a hoarse whisper informed us, 'Smee!'

Lucy missed it. She was at the blackboard writing out the name Cochrane. I can remember that for sure because Andrew Cochrane was our local grocer, but I've forgotten how he came into the story of the Earl of Angus. Our Cochrane had a cat, or rather the man in charge of our branch had a cat, for Andrew Cochrane himself was a superman of distant space who merely sanctified the shop with his name and the word Limited after it. Inspired by Miss Galloway's thrilling lesson Angus pinched the rib-bon from Lizzie Graham's ponytail, pinched a wee bell from a toy harness set in Woolworth's, slung the bell on to the ribbon, tied ribbon and bell round the neck of Co-chrane's big fat lazy cat, and legitimised himself as Angus Bell-the-Cat, Earl of Angus. Thereafter, history was his favourite subject, and he knew more about the Red and Black Douglases than ever I did. In his teens he read a lot about the American and French Revolutions because he had caught up on Tom Paine through looking for the

Erskines in history after he had tired of the Earls of Angus,
so oddly may an innocent teacher's words warp the mind
of the growing boy. (In case you don't know, Lord
Thomas Erskine, the youngest son of the tenth Earl of
Buchan, thought the French Revolution was a good thing
and became a great pal of Tom Paine. I didn't know, till
Angus told me.)

But he had other interests besides history. He was
interested in girls. In the light of our religion before he
came to our shores his sermons on their place in life were
downright heresy, but like a true revolutionary he obliterated the old doctrine and made his heresy the new
orthodoxy. And like a true revolutionary he bided his
time till the situation was ripe. No abortive putsch ahead
of the masses for our Angus. To begin with, he took things
as he found them. We played with the girls now and again,
especially when Big Tonalt shepherded us, and thought
nothing of it. They were just mass-produced units making
up the number required for whatever game was next.
When he began his foreign mission Angus lured us away
from them, as if to make the heart grow fonder with
abstinence. We withdrew from the backcourt and fought
for local fame as tough hombres in the badlands with him
as boss of the territory. But the withdrawal was followed
by a return when the spring came back bringing summer
at her heels. Angus abdicated his kingdom. He became a
preaching friar, spreading what was to us a novel view of
the proper organisation of our society and the most rewarding pursuits for its members. After growing up into a
warrior community, raiding our neighbours for the sheer
lust of power, and even when we were at peace with them
obstructing their journey through any close, backcourt,
street, lane or cowp we controlled, behaving like the
frontier guards of a people's democracy, happy when
we saw the timid traveller afraid of our veto on his visa,
we were converted by Angus during one joyful, glorious,
panting summer season into a band of girlchasers seeking
nightly adventures. And the girls were no longer neuter

nouns making up the complement of a team. Angus knew
their mysteries. He explained they were different.

It sorely grieved Big Tonalt. He had lost us in the long
weeks when we were away empire-building. When he saw
he had lost the girls too he floundered in loneliness, a cold
fish in a daughterless bowl. They were too busy running
from us to have time to run to him. Gone were the days
when he could call us children and play No Roost with us,
never again would he join hands with the girls singing
clockwise 'I Sent a Letter to My Love', 'She is Handsome,
She is Pretty', or 'There Stands a Lady on the Mountain',
and unsung for evermore were all their other songs of
pastoral love expressing the coiled longings of their unconscious spring. So Big Tonalt gave in. He had his own
worries that summer, and after our season of war we were
left in peace to get the right girls into ploys invented and
produced, devised and improvised, directed and orches-
trated by the talented Angus, the choreography supplied
by the girls themselves. Their footwork came back to me
some years later when I first read of that Papal Sylvia

> Who runs, but hopes she does not run unseen.
> With a kind glance at her pursuer flies,
> So much at variance are her feet and eyes.

Angus was even washing his face and hands every day
by this time, and he was strangely better dressed and
altogether smarter than he had been. He kept his dark
hair tidy with a massage of brilliantine or butter, and he
looked a real little gipsy the way one grease-flattened lock
drooped over his forehead, nearly touching his brown
eyes. The foreign cut and colour of him was especially
strong when he smiled, for he had good white teeth, an
unusual thing amongst us. Maybe that was why he turned
on a smile so often, a bright beam that lit up his tanned
face with sunshine. When lesser boys lost the head with an
enemy and got tangled in a costly battle, Angus just smiled
and by the unrelenting fixity of his smile intimidated his

opponent into unconditional surrender. For his friends he had an extra broadness to the beam, but the super one was for the girls. He treated them as if he was a gallant cavalier and they were ladies of the court. Maybe it was his interest in history affected his behaviour. For the climax of his act he had a simple little trick. He would take a girl's hand and raise it to his lips, bending over with his heels together, an absurd performance that made us think he was going sloppy the first time we saw it. But at the embarrassing moment when his lips smacked it turned out to be the back of his own hand he was kissing. He went on getting a twitter and a giggle for it even after it was familiar to the girls, and through acting the clown like that, a flippant don john, a tenement casanova, he got closer to them than any of his disciples, solemn types obsessed with the obscure implications of his doctrine, just as an unlettered saint is nearer to God than the tormented theologians who try to understand Him.

It was one of those disciples who put the ball on the slates trying to imitate Angus. That was Keechie McGibbon. But he hadn't the touch. Besides being a two-faced ape, he was a lowbrowed, pigeyed, hamfisted, unwashed nuisance with two left feet, and not in his right mind the blue and gold evening he bundled Grace Christie in a corner of the backcourt across from the midden. The usual game was all good clean fun so long as Angus was boss. He made two innings of it. The boys gave the girls three minutes start to run off and hide and then chased after them through all the closes, dunnies and stairs far and near, though to make the game playable at all we had eventually to set bounds to the territory they could fairly use. When she was captured a girl was hustled back to the den in the backcourt and kept there in charge of a guard known as the boxie till all her pals were captured too. The duty of boxie was of course given to the halt, the lame and the blind, the cissies and jessies. But all prisoners were freed if one of their side was clever enough to get to the den unseen, race through it without being grabbed by the boxie, and scream, 'Ree-leece!' Then we had to start all over again. Under the wise rule of Angus we didn't mind. Taking a struggling prisoner to the box allowed as many opportunities of wrestling and wriggling and cuddling and tickling as you cared to take, according to your temperament or your prisoner. The sun seemed to hang long in the western sky to keep a solitary eye on us in those summery evenings. Nobody else watched, except of course Miss Partridge.

We had all the girls in the box this time except the crafty Grace Christie. She was a moocher. She had a tiresome habit of lurking up some nearby close and darting out to release the rest of her team while we were combing the Garrioch dunnies down at the Kelvin for her. But a signal received at our HQ reported two runners hot on her scent and her delivery under escort could be expected any minute. So we all stayed round the den, ready to help the boxie and make sure no Grace would break through however suddenly she appeared. To entertain us Angus sported with big Lizzie Graham, a sonsy lump of unblushing girlhood as gallus as himself with a slight cast in her left eye.

They danced to each other in a paddydo they had recently invented and were still elaborating, for they were as predestined a doubleturn as ham and eggs. It was a twisted caper, by Can-Can out of Minuet and they were inspired to improvise a coda to it, producing by telepathic collaboration what Angus called a dance apacheonata, a rough and tumble that made Wee Annie scowl as she hung out the staircase window. Lizzie curtsied to her partner, the skirt of her shortsleeved summer dress held high and wide between her thumbs and forefingers, her pinkies demurely extended, and tapped a retreat on her tiptoes while Angus, with his lean gipsy belly stuck out, trotted towards her. His rigid arms moved alternately like a couple of pistons, his fingers folded into his palms and his thumbs pointing stiffly at Lizzie. When it seemed they must come together frontally because Angus was advancing faster than Lizzie was retreating, they shyly reversed and bent away from each other. The promised conjunction was made by a bump of their bottoms, with Lizzie lifting her skirt to let the jeans Angus had on meet the gym trunks she was plainly wearing. Insulted by the snub Angus whirled round like an entry cat and swung her round and off her feet. She returned to earth the fourth time round and braked suddenly on one foot, then threw him away with such nicely judged violence that he staggered drunkenly backwards, on the point of overbalancing any moment and falling flat on his seat. To compensate for the danger he lurched forward and seemed about to fall flat on his face instead. He avoided both tumbles by doing a double somersault under the friendly eye of our sinking sun, and Lizzie scampered away from him in crisscross steps, waiting in mimed alarm for his descent. He landed lightly on his feet and snatched her again, all in one movement, and she flopped like a brokenstemmed daffodil. Supporting her with one hand on the small of her back, he had her almost parallel to the ground from head to knee, her legs open, and with the other hand he tenderly stroked his own sleek hair as he gazed fiercely into her skelly eyes.

And that's how they were when Keechie McGibbon came through the close with his left fist on Grace's neck and his right fist twisting her bare arm behind her back. Shoe Lurinksy trotted alongside, clutching Grace's other arm, and Wee Annie mumped down at us all from her lonely eyry. Straddlelegged and eyes closed, Lizzie bent right back, her ponytail kissing the ground, and Angus did his burlesque of the Great Lover. He shoved one knee in between her thighs and with an explosion of his pursed lips that could have been heard across the Canal he kissed the air six inches to the left of target, while Lizzie's pouting lips hopefully searched the air on the right for the kiss that hadn't arrived.

It gave Big Keechie the wrong idea. It also gave Wee Annie the wrong idea. Angus was only acting the goat. We

knew that. But Keechie didn't get the spirit of it. He was
tone deaf. He pawed there agape, a big bawsy sillybilly,
still holding Grace by the neck under her thick brown hair.
If Angus was having Lizzie he was going to have Grace.
He shoved her past the box to the corner against the
midden and locked her against the wall. She struggled
and scuffled and wriggled and wrassled, and they fought
up and down and round and about. Looking back on it
now, I think that like Daphnis with Chloe he didn't know
what he was trying to do but Grace knew. She ducked,
kicked, elbowed and butted, and came out of it the winner
but not unwounded. She held her right wrist in her left
hand and blood was streaming down her palm, young rich
red maiden blood. Keechie stumbled on the turn trying to
keep her, fell on his knees and hit the wall.

We were already crowding round, all of us, on the point
of interference when we saw Keechie was off the rein and
Grace was shooting out her neck. She bent forward
attackingly from the hips, and her words had a good
Glasgow edge to them. This was no time for a voice that
was soft, gentle and low.

'Look what you've done!' she screamed, holding up her
bleeding wrist, her thumb across the pulse, to show the
world the blood he had shed. She was no longer the lovely
simple Grace Wee Annie loved, but a vulgar angry little
besom.

'Who do you think you are?' she howled.

It was a good question. None of us were quite sure who
Keechie was. His big sister was called Cathie Garden, an
Amazon who did him yeoman service in his many battles,
but his mother was Mrs Brown to every other missus in
the street, and the nameplate on the door brassily announced Moss, which was the name of Mrs Brown's
married sister (if she was married) who lived in the same
house. But whether Mrs Brown or Mrs Moss was the
mother of Cathie and Keechie, or if either or neither was
the mother of one or the other, nobody ever bothered to
say if they knew. Keechie himself was Garden at school,

McGibbon in the backcourt, and he had been known to use Moss as a kind of Sunday name, identifying himself as Charles Garden Moss when he had his good suit on. There was no man in the house, but many men called, especially Saturday night and Sunday morning.

Keechie didn't tell Grace who he thought he was. He scrabbled up, rubbing his paws on his haunches.

'Summa you boys is far too rough,' Grace haughtily informed his silence. 'You should get your nails cut.'

Wee Annie gloomed down on us unregarded. She had been reading her bible till on her way to the lavatory she heard us loud in the backcourt when the prisoners began to accumulate in the box, and like an unapt student she was easily distracted from her prescribed text. She just had to hang out the staircase window to see what was going on in the big wide world beneath her. She saw too much for her peace of mind. Or she saw too little. The way we swarmed round ready to separate Keechie and Grace if the first came to the worst, she lost sight of them for a bit, and when out of all the shoving and pushing and jostling and scraping Grace broke into the clear advertising her bloody wrist Wee Annie thought we had all had a hand in assaulting her pet. She was overthrown, cast down, put out, jealous and wretched. She even hated her long enough to shout rudely over the window.

'Away, ye bold wee slut! Was it just your wrist they were at?'

But not all of us heard her.

For the two or three seconds she took to conceive and utter those unhappy words she foresaw Grace already grown into what she believed all pretty little girls must become, another Bobo, or what she thought Bobo was. What she had been reading didn't help her any in that crisis. It may well have been to blame, though she of course looked on the Book as the one great comfort of her life. She didn't eat much, she never tore her dinner like a famished wolf with the veins swelling on her forehead and the perspiration running down her cheeks, she had no insatiable appetite for fish-sauce or veal-pie, but she had a great fondness for the Book of Revelation and the Pauline Epistles, and before she was distracted from her studies by hearing our voices echoing on the green she had been starting on Paul where he says to the saints at Philippi, 'Ye are all partakers of my grace'.

The sentence was still in her mind when she stopped to watch us instead of going back to Saint Paul, and it helped her to see what she thought she saw, for she had the strange belief that the words of the sacred text she came on by chance would have a direct bearing on whatever turned up next in her daily life. It made her shake against the sill in a bitter foul rage. For a handful of moments she was convinced Grace was common, and she had no harsher word for any girl. But her despair couldn't last. She had to have faith, she had to have something to keep her alive and ticking. She was pierced with sorrow for what she had shouted. She repented. She wasn't to know Grace hadn't heard her. She flew downstairs to make a quick act of contrition, scurried over to Grace, and swept her out of the ruck around her.

'Oh my pet lamb, I'm sorry!' she moaned in distress for herself and for Grace. 'My poor child! what have they done to you? Come on up with me and I'll wash and bandage it.'

She mopped the blood on Grace's wrist with a mansize hanky from the pocket of her pinny, and Grace, with innocent blue eyes staring up at her protector, curiously remembering to forget her daddy and mammy had warned her never to go there, let herself be taken upstairs to Wee Annie's single-end.

She wasn't frightened, not the least little bit. Maybe her nerves were better than mine, or maybe she had no imagination. Anyway, Wee Annie had never given her nightmares. She stood solemnfaced at the sink while Wee Annie held the ravished wrist under the running tap and she felt as safe as Snow White with any or all of the Seven Dwarfs. She even felt sorry for the woman she told me once, years afterwards, but I should say that was a retro-spective emotion, a colour cast by memory over things past.

Wee Annie put a rectangle of lint on the torn flesh and strapped a bandage round and round and blethered away. Harmless, harmless, harmless, Grace was sure. And being sure, she was disappointed.

'Long dirty nails he must have had,' Wee Annie mut-tered to the girlish wrist, 'to do that to you. Goodness knows what infection he might give you. And I told you not to play with boys. Remember? Last summer when that nasty tinker Erskine came here. Well, you can see it for yourself what like they are. They're cruel, dear. Cruel they are, and selfish.'

She cut deftly into the end of the bandage with a pair of manicure scissors, took the strips in opposite directions and tied a tender loveknot, not too tight, not too slack, and whispered, 'Boys! Ach, boys! I know what I'd do with them if I had my way.'

Grace didn't ask, and Wee Annie sat down at the empty fireplace, drew her down on to her lap and sizzled on.

'And when they're men all they can do is shed blood just to show they're men. The blood of women and children. You know, Grace, you're better dying young. It's an old saying and a true one, believe me, the good die young. When a wee girl dies she goes to heaven, and that's when she gets her real education. When she crosses over. You don't learn anything important at school. It's all got to do with the things of this world. The devil's world. And when she's made perfect in wisdom and oh, ever so much more intelligent than she could possibly be on earth if she lived to be a hundred, she becomes an angel. That's what angels are, dear. Wee girls that died young enough to go to school in heaven. The angels go God's messages. Would you like to be an angel and go messages for God?'

'Yes,' Grace granted, unwilling to say she wouldn't, for after all she went her mother's messages, and willing to give the answer that seemed to be expected.

'When I was in America, a long time ago,' Wee Annie babbled on, 'I wanted to die and go to heaven and be an angel and learn everything. Not spelling and sums or all about science. I don't mean that. They don't count, that's not real wisdom. But it was too late. And then you see there was a man. He came out of the jungle and pretended I was married to him but I wasn't, not really. And he held me back too. He had a big big farm away out in the wilds, that's what he said, but it turned out it wasn't his at all, and anyway it was only a wee place, hardly bigger than the backcourt, with some pigs I think it was he had. Not that they ever bothered me. I could have been happy enough with the birds and the rabbits. – Have you ever seen a real rabbit, not just a toy? It's lovely the way they run. Well, they don't actually run, they kind of jump and jump and jump. Without stopping. And he tried to shoot them and we used to fight about it. – But not with him, not with men. He used to come after me, this man, but I escaped. I got away and I came back here.'

Abruptly she lost interest in what she was saying. Grace slipped off her lap and wandered to the door.

'Ah well,' Wee Annie sighed. 'It's a long story and you're only a wee girl yet. Maybe some time.'

She opened the door for Grace, half closed it again and hugged her, kissing her on the brow, lightly, quickly.

'What's all the fuss about?' Grace wondered as she raced downstairs, wiping off the moist spot, and hurried through the close to catch up on us before we scattered off to prayers and bed.

It must have been the autumn of that year Bobo had her quarrel with Dross. Autumn, because the clock had been put back and instead of meeting him when the sun was sweet and low above the Old Kilpatrick Hills, the western limit of her world since she was a baby, ten miles beyond the Barracks with the Gas Works eternally visible in between from her window three up the faraway, it was already dark when she was supposed to be meeting him the night he didn't turn up. She gave him ten, twenty, thirty minutes, six times longer than she had ever waited for anybody before, and when she walked off on an impulse after swithering at half-a-dozen false departures she was fuming. She didn't usually smoke in the street, and that made another grievance. A packet that would well have lasted her through the evening and on to the next day was emptied, crushed and chucked away by the time she gave in. She swanned away on a pub-crawl on her own, not to drink, for she wouldn't drink alone, but just to inch open the door of the bar or lounge and take a quick gander round to see if he was there, alone or in company it didn't matter so long as there he was. But he never was. She tried all his likely howffs, then the possible ones, though she couldn't think why he should have gone anywhere in the huff. Not for one minute did she think anything had happened to him, run down, beaten up, lifted by the police, gone off with a married woman. She wasn't given to that kind of alarm. She was sure he had stood her up. With or without malice aforethought, deliberately or by the course of circumstance, she wasn't bothered to sort out till she knew more. Whatever they were, the circumstances would take some talking away. It wasn't the first time, but she swore on her pride as a good girl, a selfrespecting oneman decent woman, it would be the last.

Unless he had a good excuse.

The Phoenix was of course the likeliest place but she made it her last port of call because she didn't want to be seen peeping in alone where she was well known, publicising the fact that Dross had ditched her. He wasn't at the bar, so she crossed to the lounge. And she knew in advance by the intuition of pessimism he wasn't there either. But Main was. She relaxed at once. She felt she had come to a break in a tedious journey, not yet the right station but a minor halt where she could get out for a while and stretch her legs.

Always glad to see Main and sure he was always glad to see her, she daundered up on him as bright as a morning in May. He was huddled in a corner with his pipe but he wasn't alone. It didn't put a cloud over her, for the man with him had just tabled an empty glass and stood up on the point of leaving. A tall dark man with a bashed hat and a pair of kid gloves carried together by their bunched fingers in his left hand. He slapped the table with the cuff of his gloves, a man sadfaced and sufferingeyed, his miserable face creased from the wings of his eagle nose to the corners of his bleak mouth. He was on the move as she modelled forward and she pinned a smile of gratitude on him for his tact in cutting off and letting her get Main to herself.

'Who's that?'

Sitting down as if she had arrived by appointment, pleasantly, calmly, just making conversation, she whispered the question not very interested.

'Mr Wylie,' he whispered to her whisper, his pipe quiet in his hand. 'Big Tam.'

She liked the way he was always quick to take her tone, never bothered, never nosey. Any other man she knew would have been asking what she was doing in the Phoenix by herself. She wiggled three fingers in midair as a queenly greeting to Tommy Partridge hovering across the lounge.

'Who's he when he's what are you buying me when he's at home? ?'

Main moved his specs down his nose and up again to signal Tommy to serve and Tommy came along with a glass poured the moment he saw Bobo come in. He knew what she always had. And while Bobo and Tommy spent a couple of words on each other Main struck a match and fed the flame to the bowl of his famished pipe.

'Well you ought to know.'

'How?'

Bobo leaned back at peace resting her feet. At least and at last she had a man to talk to, and talk was better than loving in some moods. She delved in her handbag before she remembered she hadn't kept the empty packet to bring out as a hint to the next friend she met and she breathed a gentle dammit when she saw she hadn't got it. But nobody ever said Main was slow. He ambled over to the bar in the lounge, bought something, and waddled silently back. Filling his broad chair again with his broad bottom he planked a packet of cigarettes in front of her, the brand she smoked.

'You know how to treat a lady donchew.'

Bobo swiftly unwrapped the packet, accepting it as due tribute, and lit up for herself before Main had time to strike a match. For an obscure moment as she inhaled she wondered why he always made her feel so good all over from the crown of her head to her big toe and yet she couldn't imagine herself even kissing him.

'Do you want a box of chocolates too?' he asked politely.

'Not with a drink, kew,' Bobo answered swallowing. 'How? Why?'

'How why what?'

'Should I know him.'

It gave her pleasure to have him beside her but she was glad he wasn't trying to get closer.

'Him? Oh, him! He used to be your boyfriend's probation officer. Before your time. When you were still an innocent wee girl believing there were fairies in the back-court at midnight.'

He gave her there all the cue she needed. She brought up her grievance and leaned over to confide.

'Boyfriend? Whadyamean, boyfriend? I've no boyfriend. If you mean Dross don't talk to me about him.'

Main cuddled his glass, peered into it like a crystalgazer, and softly sang to the rim.

'Turn Edward's face to the wall, mother, don't ever mention his name.'

'My man, God help me! You know what the booger done to me tonight?'

'Nothing wrong I hope,' Main changed his tune. He saw she wanted sympathy.

'He kept me standing at the corner like a stookie. I felt such a fool. And so you know what I've been doing in case you don't think I'm daft? I've been all round here right down to the Cross looking for him. So help me holy God I feel like a pro on the prowl tapping the pubs for a man. I'm not cut out for that kind of thing, mooning about on my own at night. I'm scunnered with him, so I am. I'm willing to be a faithful wife to the man that'll marry me. I can do without nights on the town and mucking about with Tom Dicken Harry. I'm not one your loose women that would go with any man for a drink.'

She told her love, how much she'd done for him. Oh, if he had it he would spend it, like water off a duck's back and nobody one smell the better. But how often did he have it? When did he have a job last? Seldom in and usually out of one. Tell me what do I see in him. You know what I'm afraid of? He's back in his old bad company, folk I made him drop, they've picked him up again. A woman's intuition every time. Hardnut and Chocolate and that big scrubber Alec Lillie. That's why they call him Tiger, cause his name's Lillie. He broke his old man's heart the way he was never out of trouble, a decent wee Orangeman that never did no harm to anybody except one Walk when he had a half too much and kicked a Corporation bus driver on the backside because he had on a green uniform.

'There was a Rangers supporter from Milton Street was offered a Corporation house with a bit garden front and back,' Main remembered, 'and he turned it down because the grass was green. I saw it in the *Express* last week.'

'They're up to something I bet you,' Bobo went her own way. 'I know what happens to him when he gets in with his old pals and I wouldn't be one whit surprised if he was out on a job with Sammy Arnott and Toby Owen just to please Tiger.'

'So that's what's in a name,' Main got his puff-pipe puffing. 'Hardnut and Toblerone. Swiss Chocolate. Quite plain once you're told.'

It turned out she was right. Dross met her the next day at teatime on her way home from work. Right away she cast up the broken date and at once they were out of step. He was as cheery as a Christmas Party and she was as cross as a hot cross bun because she was short of sleep worrying about him in her lonely bed the night before. She drew it out of him like a dentist drawing a loose tooth tutting, at the uselessness of it, no bother at all. Yes, he was out on a job with the three she suspected when he ought to have been meeting her. But it hadn't worked out right. Lillie said he had a line on a shop near the Govan Docks that sold newspapers and cigarettes and notepaper and birthday cards and American comics et cetera et cetera and he fixed a break-in for when the weekly cigarette order had just arrived. Somehow it happened they had raided a day too soon and all they got was a few hundred fags of mixed brands and a couple of boxes of ballpoint pens.

'Four of you for that!'

Bobo was angry. It offended her sense of the right proportion of manpower to results.

'There was only two of us went in but, me and Lillie. Hardnut and Chocolate was watching outside.'

Dross held up four fingers of one hand and struck them off in twos with the index finger of the other to show he could account for the exact number. But he was always afraid of her when she was angry and he wilted under her torrid stare.

'Still four to share it,' she argued. 'Good Godman, I thought you'd chucked that kinnanon since before you left the school.'

'Lillie asked me to help,' Dross sulked with her. 'They need me, it's me's got the nerve.'

'A shop like that that's got nothing,' Bobo nagged. 'Not a big place in town that's got plenty, oh no, not for you and your friend Tiger and they other two chancers, just a wee place in a backstreet with a coupla dozen Bics and a ten Woodbine that's been lying there since your granny took your maw to Rothesay for the Fair.'

'The big shops is better in security,' Dross gave her his worldlywise act. 'Some of them's got alarums. We was misled, that was all. It was Toby's fault. He did the reckie. He told Tiger there was a delivery last night because his sister works in the baker's next door. She should have knew. Tiger's clever all right, but if you're fed the wrong facts things go aspew. You can't mark him down just because Chocolate doesn't know the day of the week.'

'Tiger?' Bobo fired at the very name. 'If he's the Brain God help the rest of you merry gentlemen. And that makes you the Brawn, I suppose. They do get you for the mug, don't they?'

'Well it was me forced the back window,' Dross was modest about it.

'You're a right nit,' Bobo told him, and hurt him by the sincere way she said it. 'You promised me you'd stopped that nonsense, you know it's not right and it's still not right even if you had got anything.'

'I needed the money,' Dross complained, too sulky to debate right versus wrong. 'We can flog the pens round the doors and we won't need to buy fags for a week or two. That'll be a saving. And money saved is money earned. You smoke too, you know.'

'That's right, blame it on me.'

'You might at least try and see my side of it. I done it for your sake. You know you like to see me with something in my pocket.'

'Aye, I know,' Bobo girned at him. 'I know I like to see you with something. But you know what it says on that wee card in the Phoenix. Anything I like is either illegal or immoral. Or fattening.'

'Hell of a funny.'

'Funny I don't see you laughing.'

Dross lost his temper at that. He was no longer the joyful Robin Hood who had stopped her, palm smacked on palm before he rubbed them together, sure of his maid marrying him one day, sure she would. He had wanted sympathy and understanding and got neither. It soured him. He snuffed and huffed, one of life's failures with a grudge against an unjust world. He swore at her and walked away.

Bobo was mad when she watched him go. But she wouldn't call him back. She thought she might as well give him up. There was no future to it.

Or was there? The moment she was sure there wasn't she thought there might be.

Still she couldn't just sit at home and hope. She had to get out at night. She told Main her troubles of course, waiting for him at the close when he was about due to visit his cousin or catching him on the stair on his way down. He talked to her to help her, he never minded talking to her, he was good at it. He was good at listening too, and she could get an hour's distraction with him at the staircase window or the closemouth. But it wasn't the same as going out with Dross. One gain she made on the side was she didn't smoke nearly so much when she had Main to talk to. Then devilment seized her.

'What's Big Tonalt doing these days? I never see him now.'

'Working away, studying hard.'

'What a way to live! Fat lotta good studying'll do him.'

'Whatever he did he'd never get fat, would he? He's the lean and hungry kind.'

Hungry reminded her.

'I wonder what happened to his crush on me. I tried kidding him on after you spoke about it. Didn't get me anywhere. Remember I told you? I remember it was that night in the Phoenix when we was all worked up to do something about Wee Annie was the first time you mentioned it. Nothing happened there either.'

'I suppose his nerve failed him. He's really awfully shy. He never came back over it with me again. I think he was sorry he had ever told me. And then when his grandmother died that might have put him off. He went home for the funeral, remember, and he's been very subdued ever since he came back. He was greatly attached to her, you know. She was paying his way. Grandma Duthie was the one with the money.'

'Did she leave him anything?' Bobo asked, quick and hopeful. She wasn't a mercenary girl but the prospect of money, however distant, always interested her. With an inheritance even Big Tonalt might become attractive.

'That I wouldn't know. She's the other side of the family, she's his granny not mine. Any money I ever get I'll have to work for.'

'Like me,' Bobo sighed. 'Dross thinks he can get it without but you can't. Do you think he's forgotten me?'

He knew that although Dross was never out of her mind and was the last she had named her question referred to Big Tonalt. He worked it out with the speed of light. She knew damn well Dross would never forget her any more than she could forget Dross and their quarrel, he was sure, would be mended before the moon changed. One or other would come round or one of their gang would crack the ice and push them both in. It could only be Big Tonalt she thought might have forgotten her. But that was why she liked talking to him. No matter how her mind skipped backwards or forwards he was always there at her landing place to pick her up.

'Impossible,' he beamed at her sideways, his back to the windowsill as Bobo mooned above the dark backcourt. A handful of schoolchildren with no homework were playing through the closes with flashlights, and from round the corner of the block, where the safe sidestreet was bright under the lamps, there came the treble of the innocents happily slaughtering a corrupt song.

> Water water well flower
> Growing up so high
> We are all maidens
> And we must all die
> Except Susan Greenwood
> The youngest of them all
> She can dance and she can sing
> And she can knock the wall down
> Cry cry cry for shame.

'You didn't stay long with him tonight,' Bobo remarked, carelessly giving away she had been watching and waiting.

'No, I know. Sometimes I wonder why I bother. I was hardly right in the door before he was telling me it was time I was away. I left him in by himself. Why don't you pop in and keep him company?'

'Could do,' Bobo smiled at the idea. 'I suppose there are worse-while occupations.'

'The Stockwells are away out to hear that American preacher at the Kelvin Hall,' Main encouraged her. 'He's a right hotdog godspiller that one. They tell me he turns the lights down and the organ plays soft music till they all get the heezyjeezies and then he says come away up front brethren and testify.'

'Steal away to Jesus,' Bobo crooned.

She whipped round startled at the sound of a foot on the stair behind her and saw what Main from his position had already seen. Big Tonalt was there, four steps above them.

'My God! Talk of the Devil!' she whispered, and clutched Main's arm.

'I was thinking I was hearing voices,' he explained shyly

with a leer that was meant to be a smile or a smile that had aborted to a leer.

'I'm just going,' Main called up quickly. 'I must get to the Mitchell tonight. I'm away behind again.'

He nodded to his cousin and waved a farewell to Bobo. 'See you again before Christmas maybe.'

Apart altogether from the fact that he had two hours hard swotting planned he didn't want to hang around and spoil her fun. He thought she was in a mood to amuse herself with Donald and he thought it would do them both good. Left alone on the half-landing of that silent top storey they looked at each other like a beast of prey and its victim, poised for the first move, ready to pounce, alert to dodge, and each was both.

'Would you care to come in for a cup of tea?' Donald jumped first.

'Oh, I don't know,' Bobo moved aside. 'I'll be getting my supper soon. I've had nothing to eat all day. Off my food somehow. Must be in love.'

'Just a chup and a wee cat.'

His face was scarlet and Bobo laughed. The man was harmless.

'A cup and a wee chat,' he glossed it, eyes down. Then the eyes wandered. Bobo felt them on her breasts, x-raying her jumper, slip and bra, felt them move wistfully down her torso and loiter at her knees. Carelessly dressed because she wasn't going out with Dross, she had on a sweater shrunk in the wash and an old skirt that was too tight and too short.

'Well, just for five minutes then,' she gave in. She was always kind to the poor and needy.

When he closed the Stockwells' door behind them she glanced slimly over her shoulder and saw the hand on the knob was all of a tremble. You'd think he had the DTs, she thought, the silly man. The state he was in made her feel awkward too. When he spoke again she heard a muted palpitation in his voice as if he was having difficulty with his breathing.

'I've a kettle on the boil, it won't take a minute, it's nearly boiling now, it won't be long, I've got the teapot ready warmed up, the kettle's nearly boiling.'

She lolled in the front room while he brewed tea in the Stockwells' kitchen, and she was more interested in the furniture of a room where the tenants had never invited her than in being alone with their lodger. She surveyed the room and the suite with an assessor's cold eye, talking away to herself because she could never stop talking even when there was nobody to hear her. Maybe it was all good stuff but it wasn't her taste at all. An enormous overmantel made her shudder. Flanking the large central mirror in it there were small mirrors behind wooden niches with postcards and snapshots stuck on the shelves.

'What a dust trap! If that was mine I'd pawn it or sell it or give it to a jumble sale. They must have got it for Queen Anne's coronation. Her with the legs. Look at that wallpaper. Oh God Almighty! How anybody could sleep with that in the room! Would howl at you all night. Ah, so that's where he sleeps. They've took the recess bed out and put a single bed in. I see. And a wee electric heater in the fireplace under that bloodigreat overmantel. Fair ridiculous. They've been trying to modernise it, God help them, and everything in it is laughing at everything else. What a room! Would gar ye grue.'

Donald came through quickly enough, but he seemed to have forgotten his invitation to a wee chat. He slouched around, as often behind her as in front of her, and she fidgeted while his eyes lingered on the back of her neck. She could feel them trying to convert sight into touch, lingering like fingering over the bright wealth of her hair.

'Aw, sit down for God's sake,' she said kindly. 'It's as cheap sitting as standing.'

He lowered his shy lankiness on to a chair at the round table, the one with the green tasselled cloth, his cup and saucer clumsily in one shaking hand. With the other he clutched a spoon and began to stir his tea daintily. He kept on stirring and stirring and stirring, his sad eyes brooding over the ripples in the cup.

'A penny for them,' said Bobo.

He acknowledged her offer with his smiling leer, his leering smile.

'If I told you you might think I'm just daft.'

'Not me. I'd never think that of somebody as clever as you. I mean a student. Anyway, what does it matter what I think? Some men are wise, some are otherwise.'

'Is that skirt not too short for you?' he asked abruptly, staring at her crossed legs that had hoisted it a goodly bit above her knees.

'Think so? Oh well, it'll just have to do. It'll be long before I get another.'

She smiled, but he didn't catch on so she tried again to amuse him.

'Would you rather I wore one like the two French towns a sailor's trousers are like, Toulon and Toulouse?'

'Ah, you're a funny girl, aren't you!'

'Haha or peculiar?'

'A wee bit both.'

He spoke into his untasted tea.

'I don't think you should talk so much to my cousin. He's a man without the torch of faith to light him through the dark ways of life.'

Bobo went over the phrase in her mind to repeat it to Main, and Donald went on speaking to his cup of tea.

'But then if you hadn't stood talking to him tonight I mightn't have the pleasure of your company now.'

'It's an ill wind they say,' Bobo commented.

'Mind you though he's a Godless man of many errors I have a special regard for him because after all he's still my cousin. His mother and my mother were sisters.'

'Yes, of course, you're bound to have. Blood's thicker than water.'

'You sound kind of tired. Are you all right?'

'I didn't sleep a wink last night. As I was saying, I must be in love.'

He looked up, but said nothing to help her.

'Well, I'll sleep without rocking tonight,' she laughed it off.

He let it go and returned to Main.

'I sometimes worry what will happen to him when his time comes.'

'Well, if he's born to be hanged he won't drown.'

'Mind you, I've been a sinful man myself in my time. But whatever I may have done in the past doesn't matter now.'

'You're right there all right. There's no use crying over spilt milk.'

'Of course we're all sinners. If it comes to that, I bet you have sinned against the Lord too.'

'Oh now,' Bobo giggled a protest. 'Don't pick me up before I fall.'

'To be quite frank with you, you know what I mean, to be honest I mean to say,' he spoke to her knees. He couldn't stop looking at them once he had yielded to the temptation and lifted his eyes from his teacup. 'Do you know, I've never kissed a girl. Would you believe that?'

Bobo tried to tug her skirt over her knees but it wouldn't come very far, and she opened the gates of her ivory castles to distract his attention from her legs.

'Live old horse and you'll get fed,' she brightly promised. 'The longer you live the more you'll see.'

He didn't take in her words, he heard only her flippant tone and he was serious, kept to his own point.

'No, now don't be funny, I mean it. You know why that is? Why I've never kissed a girl.'

'Oh well, kissing goes by favour. Maybe you haven't met the right girl yet.'

'Because I've been too busy. I've put all that aside. I've had other things to think of. But the time's coming—'

He stumbled, stopped, floundered, put his cup on the green cloth.

'So's Christmas,' she offered, to tide him over.

'I bet you've often been kissed.'

'You're a right betting man, aren't you?'

'Oh no, you're wrong there. Quite wrong. As a matter of fact, betting and gambling are against my principles. Maybe you don't believe me?'

'Oh, I believe you all right,' Bobo told him and her mind idled in longing to be engaged in conversation with Dross. Dross spoke her language, Dross went straight to the point, he was never switched to another line just because a wee joke started a passing train of thought, Dross looked her in the face when he was talking to her, and there was a rare light in his eyes when he was making love. She saw Donald's dull hands splayed on his knees, and the memory of Dross's hands, so alive and clever, sent a long ripple through her like the wind across neglected grass. She wanted to get out, to be alone in a corner and cry again the way she had cried off and on since Dross walked away, to enjoy being sentimental over a departed lover who had no future to offer her anyway. She knew full well she was being soft about it, but that was what helped her, helped to fill the vacuum Dross had left, helped to keep her heart warm for his return. But Donald was in spate about the evils of gambling.

'It's time I was going,' she slipped a warning into his sermon. 'My mother'll be having my supper ready.'

'I thought you said you were off your food?'

She was surprised he remembered she had said so. He hadn't seemed to be listening, but now he was quite cross about it. You'd think by his tone he was going to have her up for perjury.

'I'll just have to get back on to it, that's all,' she shrugged, and felt the ensuing movement of her breasts catch his eye. 'My belly thinks my throat's cut.'

Swiftly she saw from his face he was shocked to hear a young girl mention her belly, but she had spoken thoughtlessly, feeling the strain of making polite conversation.

'Ta for the tea,' she rose to him smiling.

He had no art to detain her, though she sensed he was

itching to have her stay. She didn't loiter to be shown out. She just up and went, making him follow her to the lobby, leaving unanswered his modest proposal that she should come in again some time, and when he came alongside her and stretched a long arm to open the door his mouth lurched against the rich cluster of waves above her ear. She dropped into his beggar's tin the last smile ever she gave him and wiggled out.

As she crossed the landing Wee Annie opened her door in the middle without a warning or a fumble and caught her in transit, caught Donald too at the Stockwells' open door staring at Bobo's retreating bottom as it swayed under that absurdly tight skirt.

'Be not deceived!' she announced to the stairhead, looking at neither, yet they both knew she had seen them both and they both guessed she had spied through the keyhole and seen them go in. 'Neither fornicators nor adulterers shall enter the Kingdom of God.'

Bobo darted in and home like a lightning-flash, the check key always in the door of her parents' house to save them answering a knock or ring from one of their own, and Donald rocked on the doorstep a moment. Then he too slammed inside to his corner, appalled at Wee Annie's words.

'D'you know,' Bobo said to Main the day of the funeral, 'I had one hell of a time with him that night, I can tell you that. But I never thought he'd be away out the minute I left him. He didn't even try to seduce me. I had to keep talking to get a word out of him. I felt such a fool, talking a lot of old tripe. But what could I do? I bet you've often been kissed, says he, but he'd never kissed a girl, oh no, not him! I could see damn fine where he was trying to get to, just a detail to me and glory hallelujah to him, but just because I went and said you're a right betting man, you are, he got on to betting's a bad thing. He had the chance to come it all laid on for him on a silver saliva and the poor man looked the other way. And now! Oh my, I feel such a bitch, honest I do! But it wasn't my fault, was it? I wasn't trying to send him. I wasn't even teasing him. And even supposing I'd been in the mood, supposing I'd known, supposing I'd taken pity on him? But you can't do much for pity, can you? It's not the same. It wouldn't have made any difference, would it? I mean, it's not my fault. That skirt and jumper I was wearing that night. You don't think that, do you?'

She was crying again, but not for Dross this time. After all, she was the last of the neighbours to see Donald alive. She had never got to know him well, but he was always there, she was used to him across the landing, and she was always sorry for him because he was so gawky and gormless in everything that came as easily to her as running downstairs. But for once Main didn't comfort her. He was past talking about it, silent in his own guilty sorrow.

Yet Bobo may have been to blame, just for being Bobo and letting Donald get her alone in a top back room for half an hour. He was a frustrated trembling accident of humanity when she went away, and Wee Annie's intervention didn't sober him. It made him angry. Worse, it made him want to deserve the insinuation of the words she had spoken. Then they wouldn't be so unjust. He couldn't abide their injustice. It threw coal on his fire, and he flamed. That the opportunity was lost and gone for ever only made it worse. He burned. Retrospective longing, vain regrets and imagined achievements choked him. He banged the round table in his rage, damning and helling aloud at his failure to be bold. It was like failing to pass an exam he had studied hard for. He was humiliated. If he had only tried to kiss her she wouldn't have minded, not Bobo, oh no! and he could have gone on from there. He knew only what he had heard from the bawdy talk of medicals round a coffee-table between lectures, speculative young men who pretended to know all about women. They said you could get a woman so worked up by making love the right way she was helpless and couldn't stop you. It was all a matter of technique. He had overheard the technique, and now he had gone and missed the chance to

try it. He hadn't sat down close beside her, he hadn't put
his arm round her, he hadn't looked into her eyes, he
hadn't breathed deep and caressed her patiently, he hadn't
kissed her hard till she melted, he had done nothing. He
kicked the chair she had sat in, just to think there she had
been and there she wasn't. He raised in his mind again the
short skirt showing off her thighs, he tried to repress the
memory of her breasts too big for her jumper, and he
gnawed his knuckles at the hunger she had left within him
and the frustration she had left around him. He couldn't
sit at peace, he couldn't open a book, he had no heart for
studying. But he had to do something. The Stockwells
wouldn't be back for an hour or more, and he had a few
pounds in his pocket. For the first time in his life and the
last he went out on the prowl.

He must have walked miles. In complete sincerity he
had believed his lust for Bobo would be satisfied, over and
done with, after a single indulgence. But Bobo hadn't
played her part to let him prove it, and he was left with a
lust that had no particular woman for its purpose and
would keep on coming back, he feared, perhaps till the end
of his life. The autumn chill in the night air didn't cool
him off. It quickened him. He felt alive all over, tingling
from scalp to toe. His pulses galloped. He was hardly sober
even though teetotal, but he was vigilant, a roaming lion
seeking whom he could deflower. Every girl he passed he
stared at with a plea in his eyes, and some he followed until
he lost them in a grimy tangle of backstreets. One he
actually spoke to, getting so close he could smell the
powder on her face and feel the solid roundness of her
hips, but she couldn't make out what he was saying and
glanced at him nervously as he brushed alongside, then she
crossed over in little running steps, her glamorous legs
twinkling in the starry night till they vanished round the
corner of a black scowling tenement.

He came at last to a dark deserted sidestreet still north of
the river lit by oldfashioned gaslamps where the brackets
holding the mantles were shaped like questionmarks ask-

ing him where he was going. He had no idea. Passing a pub
he heard a jabber of many drunken voices and he was
tempted to go in and see if there was a lonely woman there,
but he knew he wouldn't know how to buy her a drink. He
knew he would only be an odd stranger in hostile territory.
Two stout women came out together, not old and not
young, not well-dressed and not shabby. They whisked
along, barely steady. He might have followed either, but
not both.

Floundering deeper in a net of alleys he was in two
minds near the river. Rather than explore the south he
probed east. He had a dim feeling his prospects would be
better there. He blundered on to the London Road,
wandered off it again, and saw he was lost, quite lost,
fed up and far from home. He was weary. He slouched out
of a dead end, made three blind turns, and found he had
the Green on his right. The tide of longing for a woman
lapped weakly on the lonely shore of his fatigue. The
tingling in his scalp, the gallop of his pulses, the fire in his
loins, all faded. He wanted to go home and lie down, safe
on his own bed. Sadly, defeated, his pace slackening as he
slowly sobered, he heard the tired old Adam inside him
complain adventure wasn't meant for the likes of them. It
was a fiction for paperbacked heroes with paperdolls. The
ape in him was dying, hardly to be conjured alive by the
spell of the darkened Green or the leafy excitement of all
the demesnes that there adjacent lie. He was on the brink
of giving up. The poison in him seemed to have worked
itself out of his system. He fumbled for a route home.

Suddenly the night was torn apart by a squeal, a girl's
squeal, not a squeal of terror or even alarm, simply a
squeal of sheer abandoned female pleasure. Before it died
there was another, even more shrill in delight, but a
different girl to his ear. He plunged to the sound like a
diver to the depths. The old Adam stood erect again,
insisting adventure came to him who ventured, the dying
ape stretched his hairy limbs in exultation, assured of
gratified desire round the corner. He hurried on, eager

to complete his noctivagation and make his guilty prowling justified after all. He forgot he was weary.

They were waiting for him at the corner, two young things. Ruby was watching from the closemouth, one palm against the wall, her arm fully stretched, the other hand on her hip, one leg bent, the other straight, her pose silhouetted by the stairlight behind her. Pearl, her colleague, loitered a step away from the questioning streetlamp and welcomed Donald with an expectant smile. Jake and Jumbo had slipped into the backclose the moment they heard Donald's tired feet plod on the pavement a hundred yards away. They were the guardians of these two precious stones. The guardians, not the keepers. The kept rather. If a keeper at the zoo gets a living out of looking after the lions, it's the lions are keeping him.

Donald advanced to battle, the pleading light in his eyes again.

'Hullo darling,' Pearl greeted him brightly. 'How's it goin?'

She was sure Donald was a good man to speak to. He had a hand in his pocket as if ready to bring out some money, and the whole stamp and style and carriage of him showed he was the lone wolf on the hunt. She had seen enough lone wolves in her short time to recognise them from afar. But indeed they had all recognised Donald from afar, Ruby and herself and Jake and Jumbo. They had all heard a victim thrashing through the jungle before they ever saw him, and the sexloaded squeal of the two girls was a more arresting signal than any red light, as they well knew.

'Coming up?' Pearl asked kindly.

Donald tried to answer, but his mouth was parched and no word came. It might have been yes, it might have been no. For the first time since he left the Stockwells' front room he was frightened. It was all so new to him, he was so far from home, the street was so dark, the autumn night was so exciting. He was nervous. This was no paperdoll of a printed invention. This was a woman at last, a real woman all to himself, a woman who would let him learn. His fear was he wouldn't be clever enough. He was only a poor sheltered student, seeing every situation in terms of the vacant life he led. He feared Pearl the way he feared an examination he hadn't prepared for. With Bobo he hadn't done his best, but Bobo hadn't set him a fair paper. This was a bird of a different colour. This was an unseen. He trembled, and even while he stood there shaking Pearl cleeked him and he went with her. The touch of her hand, the light in her eyes, the smile of her lips, the smell of her body, the nudge of her hip, enticed and repulsed him. His timid mind took one step backward as his sheep's feet took two steps forward, so forward he went in the net with the forward girl.

She led him on past Ruby's close and up the next one further east. Ruby swivelled and gave the lads their cue.

'Come on up and see my granny,' said Pearl. 'She's making candy.'

But Donald was dumb.

There was a coarseness in her voice, a looseness in her manner, unpleasing to his unacquired taste, and the scabby close, so different from the wally close where the Stockwells put him up, made him limp and miserable. The dirty stairs shocked him. The peeling brown paint disgusted him. The cracked and battered doors on the first floor depressed him. His eyes were unhappy at the dimness of the gaslight on the landing and his nose was displeased by the guff of hoarded garbage. He was stifled by the squalor and depravity pressing hard against him as he went up another flight to Pearl's harbour.

She slipped a key from her coat and opened the door. This was going to be a silent customer, maybe even an awkward one. She elbowed him over the doorstep and before she followed him inside she turned to the stairs and whistled the start of 'Scotland the Brave'. Jake and Jumbo came slowly up, without a care in the world. They knew they knew their job.

Inside, faltering, the first thing Donald saw was a

kitchen table with a couple of beer cans on the naked board
and the scraps of two fish suppers in a sodden newspaper.
The stale smells of vinegar and beer made him squeamish.
He had too strong a nose for a stomach that was weak. In a
recess to his left was an untidy bed that didn't even look
clean. Two plain chairs in front of a poor fire had a pair of
knickers and stockings, a bra and a girdle, slung over
them, and the whole room was so disorderly he was sorry
he had come. He was resigned to being only the shadow of
a man if he could just get out. From cowardice he made the
great refusal. He turned back to the door, blinking to clear
the tears in his eyes. He tried to run away.

Pearl sat on the bed with her skirt off and laughed. She
didn't bother rising to stop him. She knew it was all taken
care of.

Jake and Jumbo met him on the stairs. Donald panted
an excuse me, for he was always polite to strangers, and he
thought he could go right ahead after that. But Jake and
Jumbo didn't know good manners. They pounced. Jake
grabbed Donald's right arm and twisted it so far behind
his back Donald was almost on his knees, his thighs
quivering in terror, his breast heaving. Jumbo got behind
him and thudded him callously on the neck with the edge
of his big coarse palm.

'Oh my goodness me!' Donald sobbed, and Pearl
gleamed at the door in her jumper and panties and giggled
at his feeble ejaculation.

Her handers bullied Donald alternately and together.

'Is she no guid fur ye like?'

'Hell dae ye think ye're playin at Mac?'

'Whit's the gemme insultin oor dame?'

'Whit dae ye come here lookin fur it and then renege?'

'Hivye no the pricefit ye mug?'

'Whit ur ye in a hurry fur?'

'King soon see.'

'Open up Jimmy.'

They searched him between them, exploring him, found
his oldfashioned pocketbook, a clumsy thing of real leather

inside his jacket, took his few pounds away and shoved the pocketbook back where it was. They were agreeable to let it go at that. But not Donald. Oh no, he wanted his money back. His Highland blood was up. The rest no longer mattered, but money always mattered. He snatched for it, grappled, wrestled, pleaded. Jake took him from the front and Jumbo took him from the rear.

'The silly bugger ast fur it,' was all they had to say later, shrugging off the outcome.

He was so obstinate they had to be brutal. They beat him up and they beat him down. He punched the air, weak and wild, not knowing when he was done, not seeing he was only making them lam into him worse, until Jake gave him one last kick on the right and Jumbo booted him hard again on the left. Together they sent him falling down the stairs. Eight times he bumped and rolled before he sprawled in throbbing relief on the next landing.

He got up. He must have got up. For he wasn't found there. He was found in the Saltmarket near the High Court, half a mile away. No doubt Jake and Jumbo helped him to his feet and put him on his way. They wouldn't want him fouling Pearl's lovenest. He staggered north, past the Ross Street shebeen known to sailors the world over from Glasgow to Hong Kong, weaved blindly at strange corners but still kept his aim. Like a homing pigeon he had the direction set in his wordless mind. But his spleen was ruptured by Jumbo's farewell boot. He couldn't go on. He just wanted to lie down. He tripped at the last gutter.

He fell.

He lay there.

He bled.

He died.

The official version was that a student out for a stroll in the fresh air after an evening studying had been set on by some irresponsible youths and so severely beaten he received fatal injuries. There were some five or six Letters to the Editor in the local papers over two or three days, complaining it was apparently unsafe to walk alone after dark in certain parts of the city, indignant epistles asking rhetorical questions about modern education. None of them asked what a student was up to down by the river, wandering alone where the prostitutes aren't even decent enough to give their client value for his money. I suppose the police, though too discreet to say so, had it all sorted out. But there were no arrests.

Bobo guessed all right. She knew her mother-city. She could have taken you anywhere round it. Main had no illusions either. He knew what a chaste halfhour alone with Bobo could do to Donald and the rest of that dark night was as clear as daylight to him. As for Wee Annie, she knew. She just knew. The truth was plain to her because she knew what men were like, all of them, whatever their public face.

Donald was buried from the Stockwells, and in all the comings and goings of neighbours anxious to show their sympathy at the loss of a good lodger Wee Annie easily got into the front room where the coffin was trestled in floral dignity.

'Except ye repent ye shall all likewise perish,' she declared from the back of the queue, and nobody present was prepared to turn round and deny it.

The silence encouraged her. She had her bible with her and she read it out to them, loud and bold, having a burial

service on her own before the coffin was taken to the
cemetery, her voice the voice of the preacher, slow and
canting.

'Every man is tempted when he is drawn away of his
own lust and enticed. Then when lust hath conceived it
bringeth forth sin, and sin when it is finished bringeth
forth death.'

Main drifted tactfully to her elbow as soon as she started
reading and led her out before she could go on, back into
her single-end next door, and there she thumped the bible
down on her dresser and stared up at him, defiant.

'Do not err, brethren. You know and I know.'

She spoke through him as if he was a congregation.

'God knows,' Main answered, sick and tired.

He looked at her as bitter as she looked at him. She gave
in. She sat down and wept.

'O wretched man that he was! Who will deliver us from
the body?'

'Aye, all right! All right!' Main patted her shoulder as
she wailed, for after all he had seen she loved Donald in
her own way, or at least once wanted to love him, but
Donald had never even noticed her.

Suddenly she was venomous.

'That girl put bad in his mind. I saw it in his eyes. I saw
it a long time ago. She's a bad one.'

It took him three and a half seconds to see she meant
Bobo.

'But Bobo's not bad. Sure I talk to Bobo a lot, don't I?
And you're not going to tell me I talk to bad women, are
you?'

He spoke teasingly, flippantly jostling her elbow, trying
to cheer her. But though she dried her eyes with a corner
of her pinny she wasn't to be nudged into a smile.

'She was bad with him because he was bad, or there was
bad in him, and she's bad with another man as well
because he's bad too. Oh, I know them! I know them
all. But she's not bad with you because there's too much
good in you.'

'Thanks very much. But I'm not sure I like to be called good if it means calling other folk bad. You know the old saying. There's so much good in the worst of us and so much bad in the best of us, it ill becomes any of us to talk about the rest of us.'

He jingled it out for her, but still she wouldn't smile.

It was a bad time for her. The dying year brought back the time of Shelley's death and the season returning reopened a wound unhealed. She had always the feeling that Shelley was never truly dead and gone till she drowned him in the Canal, and Donald's death by anonymous violence enlarged her anniversary misery at Shelley's death by drowning. She longed and yearned and deeply craved to soar from the earth like any astronaut, to leave the world behind and be born again in the spirit, with all things physical, gross and material as irrelevant to her newborn personality as the after-birth to the infant. She prayed for the time to come beyond time when she could live on a higher plane outside earthly space, a liberated disembodied intelligence at home among the angels in a life without end. But just as she knew there was only one way of being trapped on earth, by being born, she knew there was only one way of escaping, by dying, even though there were ten thousand doors leading to that escape and she was unwilling to open any of them while Grace was still on earth.

It was a bad time for Bobo too, the worst possible time. There she was, waiting for Dross to come back and make up. And where was he? A million miles away, waiting for her to make a move. She might well have moved first, for she was womanly weak, Dross's weekly woman, a creature of habit, and nobody else ever got the same song out of her heart as Dross did even when he wasn't trying. But she was neutralised by Donald's death, past caring. The will of her wont was paralysed. The loved body and all its joys were mortgaged to a mean estate, a condition to be paid for by sorrow. In her lonely melancholy she was more like Wee Annie than ever she knew, and in feeling she was somehow to blame for Donald's death, somehow guilty of it by being just what she was, thirtyfive, twentythree, thirtyfive, though in fact she was just turned nineteen, she justified much of what she never knew Wee Annie said to Main about her.

She lived to herself. She wouldn't even go to the Phoenix, though it was often she thought about it, wishing for the lights and the chatter and the glow of familiar spirits as she moped at home with *Woman's Own* or *Woman's Realm* or just *Woman*, thinking night and day about her man. She tried *She* but it only made her wonder what *He* was doing. Dross himself looked into the Phoenix once or twice, but of course she wasn't there. He put it down to her stuckup pride, her lack of true love, and he wouldn't demean himself to ask Jess and Jean what had happened to her. Nor could he loiter with Yoyo and Yowyow. They only annoyed him. Without Bobo he had no links with them. They were two steady lads with a trade and he was a lapsed delinquent out of a job. He soured on them. The old crowd, Bobo's crowd, was useless. He wouldn't even hang around for a chat with Tommy Partridge. It might have saved him from the upshot. Tommy was born to be the intermediary between two warring powers, a true Red Cross type. But Dross knew nothing of the conventions and probings of poker-faced diplomacy or the channels of neutral compassion. He hardened against making up. He looked elsewhere for his nights and found nowhere to go but back to Tiger. He did another job for him. And then another. And another. In a few weeks it became a way of life he seemed to have led for ages. The raid that upset Bobo was only an accident to him, a simple ploy agreed to for the immediate thrill of it as much as for the sake of putting money in his pocket. He never meant to do it again. It was just something he could boast about to Bobo to show what a devilmaycare fellow he was, out for a spot of excitement in life. He thought it would keep her in love, keen to reform him. Now he had to go about with Tiger to spite her.

'Know what I'd like to do?' he told a blurred Tiger at the bar. 'I'd like to walk right up to her and say, See that post office do was in the papers last night? See! See me? It was me done it. Me and my mates Tiger and Chocolate.'

He wrapped an arm round Tiger's neck and an arm round Chocolate's neck, swaying between them while they waited for Hardnut, and away down deep inside him he wished both arms were round Bobo's lovely neck.

'Wheesh, ya goat,' Tiger growled.

But Dross was well away, a pintman not used to the large whisky that was Tiger's milk.

'Ach, tell with the moll,' he waved his arms wide. 'There's nay shoppers here.'

He aimed a hand at the glass in front of him and pounced just in time before it shifted right and left at once.

'Bloody denna thieves this place. Just take a ganner. Stupit buggers anyway keepin a wee post office open below an empty hoose. The whole buildin's to come doon. They ast furrit, they folk, so they did.'

Entered then Hardnut, former apprentice to a joiner in a building site, an undersized ned, but tough, strong and humorous, a wee comic. He was the one that had never been caught, the one who tidily cut a hole in the floor above the post office, knowing exactly what to do and how to do it, where to start and where he'd land when he dropped through.

Dross raised an arm high to summon the barman.

'Glashnapine furma frenhere.'

He was happy when Hardnut turned up. He liked him. He was good fun. He could make a crack in one word that gave you a better laugh than ever you got from Yoyo and Yowyow trying to be clever. And as for Bobo, she was welcome to those two clowns. This was a man's world. Standing at the bar drinking the hard stuff in the right company was a sight better than sitting in a sloppy lounge listening to a lot of rot. This was the real world, not the weans' world of the Phoenix with Yoyo and Yowyow and their two bits popping corny jokes all night. When he strolled down town on an idle afternoon, welldressed, wellfed and wellpleased with himself, he wanted to stop people in the street and tell them just who he was.

'See me? I'm the bloke they're looking for. That job on the front page last night that was me. I'm not one of your common nits. I've got the old grey matter under the tiles. I can live without clocking in.'

But what had they got from the wee post office? The postal orders were no use to them and there wasn't all that much cash. Less than a hundred. And four into a hundred didn't leave you with much once you kept something to put in the pocket of the suit you bought. That was one of Tiger's rules. Don't blow it, don't bet, don't gamble, don't drink it all the next day. Set yourself up first. Look smart, buy good stuff. Specially shoes. He was always laying it off about good shoes. It suited Dross. He loved the latest styles. But after the post office they had to find another place. So they did a wee pub next. Then a wee dairy, and then a wee draper's. Always the wee shops. The shops in the old tenements south of the river, with a window in the backcourt or a side door in the close.

'Maybe not much at a time,' said Tiger. 'But still and all. It builds up.'

'Every little helps,' said Chocolate.

'As the wee boy said when he peed in the sea,' said Hardnut.

'Small profits quick returns, that's my motto,' said Tiger. 'That's how Cochrane and Lipton started. And see where they are the day.'

'Dead,' said Hardnut.

'Aye, but before they died they were worth a couple of bob at least I bet you.'

'You're not on,' said Hardnut.

Chocolate did the reckies. He had the seeing eye. He picked up in his wanderings the shops that were taking the money. From them he sorted out the shops that closed too late to bank it. Then he cut it down to the shops where the takings were left on the premises overnight. Hardnut was the acrobat, the gymnast, first in if entry was awkward. Tiger was the bossman with scores of keys, jig keys, hall keys, keys as trig as his head, the born leader and the brains. Dross was only the brave one, ever ready with the trusty blade of his strong right arm if they had to knock anybody out. They were a team. They boasted they were organised.

But now Lillie, Alexander, was sighing for new worlds to conquer. He wanted to do a snatch. Hardnut didn't. He said breaking and entering was his street. He felt safe and sound in it because he always made sure beforehand what he was breaking in for and where it was. He always knew how he was going to get in and how he was going to get out. Nothing elaborate. Just a wee sweetie shop here and a wee paper shop there would do him. S.P.Q.R., he quoted back at Tiger.

'Maybe a snatch'll get you mair but I don't see myself. Honey, you stay in your own backyard, dat's what dem white folk say. And that's my motto. We get in, we know what we're looking for, we get it, we get out. Wur time's wur ain. We've all got a job. Could do it with wur eyes shut. Could walk oot. Nay hurry. But a snatch! Who does the snatchin? And whit aboot the resta us? We canny just walk away either. If you have a snatch you're bound to have a hue and cry as well.'

'Hugh and who?'

That was Dross, glasseyed, remembering Bobo, reminded of Main.

HARDNUT: Ach belt up ya ignorant bastart. Tiger knows whit I mean.

TIGER: Ay well but. When we get a snatch fixed we can easy fix how we blow. Wan thing at a time. Anyway Dross can drive.

HARDNUT: Drive what? He couldny even drive a pram if you havny goat a pram.

Chocolate finished his whisky and reached to his pint. Raised it. His mates bowed in reverent silence. He sipped. He lowered. He thought before he spoke.

CHOCOLATE: Don't like a snatch.

HARDNUT: That's two of us.

TIGER: Bloody rebellion. I'm no sayin we must. I'm only sayin it's worth a thought.

They thought.

HARDNUT: Well but.

CHOCOLATE: Aye, sa thought.

TIGER: Of course if yous two huvny the nerve. Dross has. Huvent you, Dross?

Dross was anxious to contribute his mite. But he made a joke of it in case they laughed at the very idea. Behind the idea was Bobo. He had to talk about Bobo even if it was only in the shape of an idea. She bobbed in his liquid mind like a cork on the waves, up and down and up and down, but never drowned, never even washed away, insoluble, and he found comfort in saying her name, but grinned to disown what he was afraid wasn't worth the telling.

DROSS: Funny yous talkin about a snatch. We had the idea for a snatch once, just in fun it was, it was when I was gaun wi Bobo and there was this auld dame, she's the wages clerk in a laundry, was always callin Bobo names. Oh she had a wicked tongue, the batty auld bitch! calling Bobo a hoor, she little knew Bobo. Bobo? Bobo might do it for love but she'd never do it for money, not Bobo. I got the idea for it one night in the Phoenix when Bobo was that bloody mad at this auld dame she appealed to us and we were all kiddin Bobo we would roll her in the pen when she was comin back, she goes to the bank every Friday morning as regular as a wean's bum, comin back wi the wages through the pen to the laundry, and snatch them just to give her a fright, just in fun you know, to learn her to lay off Bobo but Bobo wouldn't hear tell of it. Smatter of fact I even kidded Bobo I was goin to get yous to do it for us. Christ you should have seen Bobo's face the minute I mentioned your name and of course the resta them was just makin a cod of it anyway but mind you even at the time I thought to myself there could be something in it if it was done right only I wasn't seein so much of yous in they days and I never thought of it again till there the now.

TIGER: Give us that again.

Dross sobered a little when he saw Tiger was taking him seriously. He answered questions. The name of the laundry. The location. The size. The address of the bank. The time of collection. The road Wee Annie took there and back again.

TIGER: She knows you?

DROSS: She's saw me often enough. Every time I was nearly there wi Bobo she turned up.

TIGER: That's you out then. Chocolate'll tail her for a couple of weeks.

CHOCOLATE: What's it always got to be me for?

TIGER: She doesn't know you.

CHOCOLATE: She doesn't know you and Hardnut either.

TIGER: That's why Dross will be the driver.

HARDNUT: Drivin what? That's what I was askin you.

CHOCOLATE: Drivin me crazy.

TIGER: I'll get something.

HARDNUT: Six months.

TIGER: Hawnaw, it won't be like that. This is gonna be takin toffy affa wean. It's the same every Friday. Jist you look at the papers on a Friday night. They send kids, lassies o seventeen and boys jist oot the school, or else it's some auld wabbit spinster. The same road the same time every week. To pick up the wages. Nutta soul wi them, nutta hander even on the way back. Then they wonder why they lose the lot. Ma heart bleeds fur them.

They wandered round the town on a pubcrawl, exploring mean dens in dim streets from the Hangman's Rest in the Fruit Market to the Homos' Bar in Hope Street. It was Tiger's idea. He had a joke he liked to make. He stood back from the bar flanked by Dross and Chocolate with Hardnut behind him and declared, 'Gentlemen, let us observe the proprietaries.'

Then he would survey the gantries to see the whiskies available before he gave his order. Leaving aside the single-malt whiskies there are over a thousand proprietary blends and Tiger had the fantastic ambition of sampling them all. The singlemalts he frankly admitted he couldn't take.

When they met again sober, Dross had forgotten but Tiger remembered. Every word, every detail. That's why he was the boss. His head was always clear, no matter what he had been drinking. Chocolate was willing after all and Hardnut agreed to agree.

'Am no prepared to be the odd wan out if yous are for it,' he explained magnanimously.

'There's all the time in the world,' Tiger said to him over their snooker. 'Let it lie. It'll be all right. Don't worry, don't hurry.'

Dross had to take Chocolate over the route and point out Wee Annie to him, lurking together in a close across the street. Then one Friday Chocolate trailed her alone. Another and another, and he was still tailing and timing her and Tiger was still trying to borrow a car for Dross to drive. They paced the pend with Hardnut late one wet and windy night when the laundry was closed and they satisfied themselves that at the bend where they meant to jump her they were covered from the street and from the yard in front of the laundry. Chocolate and Hardnut would wait there and Tiger himself would follow Wee Annie in, not too far and not too close behind her. They worked it out often at one o'clock in the morning in Hardnut's backclose. Dross acted Wee Annie and Chocolate practised the sudden push that would knock her off her feet, Hardnut where the cosh would land and Tiger the lightning coincidental snatch. Dross, the supposed strongarm man, was bored to be only the driver waiting round the corner.

'Don't be too hard on her,' he said peevishly. 'She's only a shauchly wee thing. A good fart would blow her over.'

'What do you think we're going to use, chemical warfare?' Hardnut asked.

He was joco. He could handle it. He knew where to strike with the haft of a coal hammer so as to leave her paralysed long enough to let them get out of the pend and into the car.

'That skelf'll no give us any bother,' he laughed. 'It's in the bag, Mac.'

They took a month to get ready to stage it, drinking to it every night at the bar, rehearsing their silent parts in Hardnut's backclose, enjoying their conference like actors discussing a new dramatist's first play. This was the life. This was their craft. This was their lively art.

Tommy Partridge was worried again that winter. Fraternally, miserably, friendlessly, morbidly worried. Every Sunday he went to see her she was worse. To take her back to the happy days when they were brother and sister growing up together in trust and affection with a wonderful world waiting for them the day after tomorrow, he tried calling her Anna again, the name she liked when she was young and pretty because Annie sounded too plain, too common, ill-suited to her dainty frills and laces, buttons and bows and flimsy petticoats, her first nail varnish and lipstick, but she wouldn't go back to those green times with him. She couldn't. She had long forgotten those seasons and dressings. She was looking forward now, prophesying war and evil. She made him a spectator standing on the touchline, watching a game that would have bored him and made him want to go home to his own fireside out of the cold if it hadn't been his own sister was out there, and to her he knew it was no game. She was in earnest, taking on herself to judge a wicked world.

The misgivings that had driven him in the spring to speak to Grace's parents were overlaid by a new and different anxiety. He feared for Grace less and more for his sister. He could maybe prevent her harming Grace. But he didn't see how he could stop her harming herself. Provoked, or in a panic, he might just have managed to talk to her straight about Grace and tell her to leave the child alone, though he knew she would say he was the mad one to think she would hurt Grace. She never meant harm, only good, till the fit came over her, and then she didn't know what she was doing. But in cold blood to ask her not to commit suicide was altogether too absurd.

He thought of working round to it by talking to her about Grace. But he knew that if he ever did dare remind her of the danger she was in by getting too fond of the girl she would hate him for breaking the understanding that they were never to say she had once been put away. She might show him the door, banish him for ever in anger. He couldn't have that. He couldn't leave her to die alone. She was still his sister. The only kin he had.

And anyway it wasn't Grace he was so much worried about now. It was months since she had made much of Grace in conversation, and he thought the child had lapsed in her wandering affections. But still she had him sore upset. He couldn't put his finger on it, couldn't say precisely what was wrong with her that made him think she was ready to end her life by her own hand. When he tried to make sense of the way she talked he felt he was going mad too. Time and again he was on the point of hinting to her that she should go inside again as a voluntary patient for her own good, but his nerve always failed him.

He was wrong about her of course, quite wrong. He thought she had forgotten Grace and was concerned only with her own way out of a sinful world. But Grace was never out of her mind. It was herself was out of her mind. When she spoke to him of the world as an evil place where no sane person would willingly linger he thought she was thinking of herself. That's where he was wrong. She was still thinking it was Grace had to be liberated, deserved to be, ought to be.

'What's the state of the world got to do with you?' he tried to laugh her out of her black moods, basting the eggs because she liked them fried unturned. 'You take life so serious so you do. Some folk let it prey on their mind till they get that low they do themselves in. What use is that? Things are as they are, you won't alter them. If it's got to be it's got to be. Why worry? Worrying'll not get you anywhere. Cheer up, Anna dear. Enjoy yourself. There's nothing you can do about it.'

'I haven't the slightest intention of doing myself in,' she answered him primly, quoting his phrase in a tone that disowned its vulgarity. Her nose wrinkled at the very smell of it.

He took the denial as a poor attempt to hide the truth.

'It's not myself I'm worried about,' she spoke on to herself, sitting back in her little chair in front of the winter fire and letting him make her a mixed grill as usual because he was always the handy one, the practical one, and she was the clever one, the one who had read a lot in her time, the thinker. 'There's a greater love than selflove.'

'Come on and have a bite,' said he.

She slipped from her chair like a gnome from a toadstool and went to the table, small but straight, her voice big.

'For what we are about to receive O Lord make us truly thankful.'

'Aye, all right, that's fine,' Tommy responded, sitting quickly, hungry. 'Come on now, eat up, you're at your auntie's.'

He fought the liver and sausages and bacon and eggs and fried tomatoes and black pudding and potato scone with a rapidly flanking knife and fork, winning all the way, talking through his eating.

'Remember Auntie Kate? That was her saying. She used to give us a rare tuck-in remember. We took the bus all the way to her big house on a Sunday. The bus journey was half the fun. Those good old Scotch Sunday dinners. You can't beat them. She fed us well. She fairly looked after us when Papa and Mama died. You can't deny it, Anna.'

'Yes, we've a lot to be grateful to Auntie Kate for,' she agreed, bowing to him like a judge on the bench bowing to counsel. 'But not to her family.'

'Aye, some cousins they turned out to be. They showed that when she died. We were just the poor relations, that's all we were. You know, we've been awful unlucky you and me I often think. First Papa and Mama and then Auntie Kate, the only aunt we had.'

'Mama died of a broken heart. You'll never persuade me otherwise. She loved him so much. Of course there was nobody like Papa. A woman could respect a man like Papa, so manly, so kind, so good.'

'You could have gone to the University if Papa had lived. You were clever enough. Remember he used to give you riddles and you always solved them and he called you his pretty little witch. You could easy have been a teacher. You were always fond of children.'

He misforked a piece of liver, so flustered by his clumsy tongue his hands were clumsy too. But she saw no offence. He hurried on.

'Even Auntie Kate if she had lived, she would have seen you through.'

'It's as God wishes. We had our happiness as children together when Papa and Mama were alive. Nothing can take that away. It was a good home we came from.'

'It was that all right! Papa had a good job all his days, a better job than ever I had. The pity was when he died the money died. He had nothing to leave us and we've had nothing since.'

'We've always managed,' she scolded him, kniving to one side the crumby remnants of her black pudding. 'We've nothing to complain about.'

'Maybe not. But I was always sorry you had to leave the school when Papa died and just another year and you could have got your Highers. You were that good at English. I used to marvel the way you and Papa could read poetry to each other. Was over my head. I remember there was that poet you were fond of with a kind of French name, de la mer or something.'

Anna bowed silently. Tommy was too old to save.

'But you were wise to go to that Commercial College and get your diploma in book-keeping and shorthand. It gives you a living.'

'That was Auntie Kate's kindness, she paid for that,' she always admitted the debt.

'It's as well Cousin Rab never found out, he'd have wanted the money back,' Tommy muttered through his chewing.

'I was sorrier for you,' she spoke nicely to him.

'Ach, I was never clever at the school. I just wanted to leave. Took whatever job came, jack of all trades that's me. Then I finish up as public-house waiter. Still even at that I'm in charge now as you know. I've done not bad for myself.'

'If Papa had lived he would have found you a good job. He had influence.'

'Oh aye, he had influence all right had Papa. Him working in the City Chambers he met them all. It was Councillor McFearson was one of Papa's best friends that got you your first job. Yes, Papa was respected, even after he was dead, people remembered him.'

'But I couldn't stay in it. That bad man. And I was only seventeen at the time. Luckily Papa never knew. Then I made my own mistakes. Led astray by the weakness of the flesh. Well, I learned my lesson.'

'Ach well, you can always say you've been to America, you've travelled a bit in your time,' he made a joke of it.

And that, or something like it every Sunday, was all they ever said of her marriage. But they were happy eating together, recalling old times, sharing each other's sorrows, sharing each other's joys, comrades.

'It was good of you to take me in when I got out after I came back,' she said.

That's how she always thanked him, never saying where she got out from or why she had been in, and he never made it any more precise.

'Specially when you had your own troubles,' she went on thanking him. 'I often wish I had met your Ella. It's sad to think she died just when I went in. If I had only got in touch with you when I first came back I would at least have seen her. Everyone we had is dead.'

'Ah well, that's life,' said Tommy, unwilling to put even a toe in such chilling waters.

'To think you lost Ella and the baby too. It would make you believe there's a curse on our family. We've been made to pay for the happy childhood Papa and Mama gave us. Still, it was good of you to give me a roof over my head.'

'It was only for a couple of months till you found a job,' he shrugged it off. 'After all, I'm your wee brother. Remember me?'

'But I hope you weren't offended,' she nagged at it as she always did, 'when I didn't take your offer to stay on with you. I just wanted to be alone once I found work. Best for both of us.'

'Oh, I know you were biting your nails to get away. I could see it. You wanted your own corner. You always had your own corner from you were a wee girl with a white frock every Sunday. That reminds me, tell me how's the laundry doing.'

'Doing fine,' said she. 'We've a lot of contracts for schools and hospitals and we're growing. Do you know, I'm drawing over five hundred pounds every week in wages now? They're well paid and they're well looked after. They've got their own Welfare and they've even got a Social Club.'

'You can't beat these old family firms,' said Tommy. 'I worked in an old family pub for years once. It made all the difference.'

'Oh yes,' said she. 'They've a touch about them, a decency. The old man himself doesn't come in very often now but his son Mr Alan, he's in every day and anybody can speak to him and he doesn't think it cheeky. That's the kind of man he is.'

'That's a good thing,' said he. 'I like a man that can take a wee bit kidding even if he is the boss. I see you're needing a new bottle of sauce.'

'Yes, I know,' said she. 'The funny thing is he's quite young really and yet he's quite bald on top. You always did cover your food with sauce from you were a wee boy.'

'Clever men are usually bald,' said he. 'Look at Shakespeare's photo. You need a drop sauce with this kinda meal.'

'Yes, I know, but there's rumours,' said she. 'They say the Lavanta Company's going to take us over. The day's past for the wee family business I suppose. But what'll happen to me if that's true I don't know. They're so big they must have an enormous office staff, not just one poor soul on her own like me. I'll probably be what they call redundant. They mean I'll get the sack.'

'Oh no,' he checked her stoutly. 'Don't kid yourself, Anna! They can always use a person of your experience with your qualifications.'

'Remains to be seen,' she sniffed. 'But I think Mr Alan will see me all right. He knows I've been a good servant. Never grudged working late.'

He was pleased with himself that winter Sunday was Tommy Partridge. He had got her talking calmly and rationally on everyday matters. He swithered again. Maybe there wasn't much wrong with her after all, nothing that company and conversation couldn't put right.

But after the meal, while he stood at the sink with one of her pinnies tied round him to protect the trousers of his Sunday suit, she got into her pulpit again.

She preached against the Bomb that afternoon, cornering him as if he was in favour of it. A present from the Devil she called it. His gift to mankind for inviting Him to return and have dominion over them.

'It was God's mercy for a time that Hitler and his brother Stalin never had it,' she said, hands clasped, eyes up.

He was surprised to hear her harp back so far, though he knew she had taken a fanatical interest in politics when she was worrying her way out of her teens into womanhood. Himself, he never had any time for politics, even then.

'You think they might have used it?' he asked, but only to say something, to interrupt her before she got steamed up as she used to about the twin vampires of her spring-time.

'There's a special Providence in the fall of the Bomb,' she instructed him. 'Some will be saved yet so as by fire. If it wasn't then it will be later. But it will come. The madness is all. There's a good madness and a bad madness. They are all, all mad, and wicked as well. So their madness is a bad madness. So it will fall. And they that escape shall escape and be on the mountains like doves of the valley. And their hands shall be feeble and their knees weak as water and baldness on all their heads, and every island fled away and mountains will not be found. It's all in the holy bible what the Bomb will do. They will build shelters but the waters shall overflow their hiding place.'

'I never thought of that before,' he said, going back over his question, partly because he suddenly found it inter-esting, partly because he wanted to distract her from her sermon. 'Suppose those two crooks had the bomb before we dropped it. Now there's a thought! I think Hitler might have used it. Old Adolf was stark raving mad. They say he used to chew carpets when we were young. I remember seeing that in a Reader's Digest. And then Old Joe used to murder anybody that stood up to him. They musta been both mad.'

'Two men and a third to come,' she replied to him. 'Behold a great Red Dragon and the Beast like a flying Eagle. The evil that they did lives after them. Six and six, Hitler and Stalin, and a six to come, who he is I do not know, to make six six six, the Mark of the Beast, before the Devil Himself appears on a cloud of fire. Men were bad before, only the saints were good in the sight of the Lord, but the Red Dragon and the Beast like an Eagle were a new evil, preparing the way in the wilderness for worse to come, Cain accusing Abel, the Chosen of the Lord made dross in the furnace of affliction, there was never anything like it, no sins so big nor so many not even in Babylon. And it came to pass that men preached the word of the Devil as a new God. It must have been then the Devil came down upon us with a cloven tongue like as of fire. And power was given unto Him to scorch men with His fire. So it will come to pass. The Bomb will fall.'

'Oh, I don't think so,' he wouldn't have it, rinsing out the sink with hot water, the last of the greasy plates washed and dried. 'I think you're wrong there, Anna. I must bring a washer next Sunday. This tap's like a grocer's shop, it keeps dripping. I mean to say, after all, if they can do it to us we can do it to them; so what's the point? It wouldn't get them anywhere.'

'It would get the Devil where He plans to be,' she told him curtly.

They played an innocent game of cards in the evening, and when he went away she settled at the table he had cleared and wrote in her diary. Underneath it, in case she got ink on the tablecloth, she spread out the Sunday paper Tommy had left behind him. She was at peace writing in her diary. It was in fact a cash ledger she had lifted from the laundry (she lifted one a year from the office stock), and she wrote across the vertical red lines for pounds, shillings and pence in her oldfashioned thin up and thick down script, a hand that seemed to ornament as well as fill the page. Deaf to the noise in the street and all the petty traffic of the tenement, the banging of doors and the bawling of children, she wrote flowingly and clearly.

'A wintry afternoon. Long conversation with my beloved brother. In the summer he comes on Sunday evenings because I always go to the Botanic Gardens in the afternoon then, but today he came at one and stayed till nearly nine. Sleet and a gale outside but we were quite happy beside the fire. We recalled old times together and I thought of my dear Papa again with tears in my heart for he was the only good man I have ever known. But I must correct that at once. I must learn not to be so extreme in my judgements. My beloved brother is a good man too in his own simple way though he is blind to the unseen world and I think Mr Main is good at heart. I have thought so ever since the day he carried my pail downstairs for me as I remember I recorded here at the time. . . . I stopped there to turn back and find out when that was. My goodness it was over a year ago. How time flies. I have now six of these books in which I have faithfully written down my private thoughts and all the little things that have happened to me since I escaped from that horrible Home and came here to a house of my own, humble though it is, it will probably be my last dwelling place on earth. Who will ever read them? It doesn't matter. I write them for myself, and for God to read. It soothes my poor nerves to read over what I have written in the past because it takes my mind off the future for a time anyway. But I must try to remember what my beloved brother said to me and what I said to him because it will bring it all to life for me again later on if I can write down now the most important things we discussed while they are still fresh in my mind.'

Midnight crept up on her like a silent cat and the tenement fell asleep around her as she struggled to get straight who said what and in what order. The voluntary exercise in memory led her to repeat in writing what she had said about the evil in the world and the evils to come, and she became more and more agitated. Her writing flowed faster, eddying round obstructions in parentheses, till it was almost a scribble and she had to stop and hobble round the room to take hold of herself. She was frightened. She had frightened herself. She waited, her hearing alert, fidgeting, half fearing half desiring that the spectres who sometimes came to speak to her at midnight would come tonight. She listened for the least little sound, she kept an eye on the door and kept glancing at the corners. But she knew it was silly of her. They never knocked before they came in. Indeed they never came in. They were just there if they came at all.

She had been hostess off and on to four of them for a long time, though in the beginning there was only one, an occasional angel and after that her dear glorified Papa. Then two came together, free and easy, twins but different from each other though they were both the same as Papa, and so for a time she had three spectres to listen to. But now a fourth had got into the habit of turning up sooner or later in the session, and him she didn't like. He was too cynical, a vulgar knowall. They debated her problems in her lofty single-end as if they were debating in the infinite void of space throughout an endless night where earthly clocks were of no more use than a sundial on the dark side of the moon. So deep they probed, questioning her sharply in the course of their debate, she sometimes saw them not as four wise spectres patiently torturing her, cruel only to be kind, but as four tax inspectors examining her books before accusing her of fraud. The confusion in her mind about their status was shown by the fact that although her spelling was normally good she twice referred in her diary to 'the four inspectres'. Yet for all her alarm she waited for them, she put her trust in them, she looked to them to guide her, and she was in each of them and each of them was in her.

She straightened from poking the choked strength of the big fire her brother had built and three of them sat at the table where her diary lay open at the last page she had written. Papa turned the pages and gracefully read aloud extracts from earlier entries. The clock she hadn't heard all evening began to tick loudly on the mantelpiece between Rabbie Burns and Highland Mary till Papa spoke out soothingly and silenced it again.

—So you love this child?

Yet it was less a question than a statement of fact from which all the rest would proceed in due course, and from the mild tone of it she knew they weren't going to put difficult questions to her at this meeting. They weren't going to debate her reality, consider her as a candidate and decide her election or rejection, they weren't come to determine her punishment, they were just going to chat with her in one of their kinder moods, help her, advise her. Even encourage her as they had done once already, before they traced her to her single-end.

One of the twin-inspectors whose name was a secret she

wouldn't write, and who wasn't Papa, chipped in just to
show he was the equal of Papa, sitting at his right hand.

—As I loved you, with no greater love than this, you
love?

A sword pierced through her soul, and the thoughts of
her heart were revealed to them, and she was faint at the
sight of the innocent solemn sinless face of Grace in Papa's
eternal mind, in all their visiting transparent minds, a
girlchild's face floating in three mirrors with big blue eyes
above soft full lips unkissed under a little nose. She felt the
rich hair of the young unbowed head between her fingers,
heard the sparks as she combed it. Then they were echoed
and reflected in the corner near the sink where Shelley
used to chatter in his swinging cage, but now it was
Knowall's crackling smile was oscillating over the draining
board.

They spoke to her or to each other, she wasn't sure and
it didn't matter. All she had to do was pay attention and
keep at it. Sometimes they were all talking at once, sometimes they sang her a wee song, sometimes they preached.
She couldn't cope with it all. Sometimes they warned her
separately, singing together, and then of course she lost
the place completely, not knowing which of her four
columns to write in. She could only wait and try to catch
up next time round.

'Yes I do,' she said to their babble and was answered.

—Grace cometh from the Lord and to the Lord must
Grace be returned as from His hands she came.

—Which being interpreted, Knowall challenged, proud
in his corner at the sink Tommy had left clean and tidy,
means?

—Means innocent.

She saw them all offer her again the saving face of
Grace, the four reflections converging above the table
in one bright countenance with a rainbow halo where
the light was hanging.

'Then I'll have to send her back, that's all,' she corre-
sponded with them.

They passed her note from hand to hand, smiled in one approving smile and let it go for the moment. They wanted to love her, to appeal to her, to caress her, as Papa did.

> —Come my darling daughter
> Slip off for me
> Fade into the forest grim
> Cuddled on my knee.

—I bless you, and press you, Knowall sang with Papa's plea, then rambling rose and turned on the swan-neck tap beside him so that she could hear the water fall before he drank.

They argued amongst themselves before they questioned her again.

—What was that you said?

'I simply said I must send her back that's all.'

—Save her you mean.

They all sang to her, very softly in case the neighbours heard them.

> —Save Grace from the Devil
> Save Grace from the Bomb
> Send her to Heaven
> And buy Kingdom Come.

Papa groaned in spirit and was troubled.

> —Send her to Heaven to live for ever.
> —Then she must cross the Jordan river.

They lamented together, rejoicing.

—Must cross must cross the Jordan river.

—She must you know she must. It's the only way.

Papa extinguished Grace's bright face, wrapped a silk stocking round it, and put it in a little carton packed with cotton wool. He weighed it on a spring balance that

Tommy hadn't left behind him when he cleared the table, and was going to go out and post it when she stopped him.

'It's not fair. God's got the answers at the back of the Book but all they've brought is the problem and you're leaving it to me.'

—What's your problem? Write to me

—all ye that labour.

—A child born? A child dead!

She couldn't say it straight out. It pierced her again with a word to admit it. But she knew what people thought. She had heard it often enough for herself. Grace's mother calling her a queer old bitch, an ugly old witch. But it wasn't her place to say more than she had said already. It was theirs to tell her to do it and then it would be right. She could hear Papa shouting at her because she wouldn't speak.

—Dumb, my carline daughter? Flee the foe! Fly flum!

'Don't shout at me, Papa! That's the one thing I can't stand!'

So he was patient even though she was making him cross.

—We come here to help you. I told you often and often.

—Many a time and oft on each royal toe.

—This wee Piggy went to the Market, this wee Annie stayed in a home.

—Any problem set for solution can be answered on the basis of the theorems and corollaries demonstrated in Part One

—if the pupil will diligently apply herself

—to mastering subsequent lessons before preceding to the previous ones.

—Pupil's Book without Answers halfprice. Teacher's Book with Answers

—ninepence extra, Knowall laughed. But we have all the answers you know, otherwise we'd have to work it out for myself and then we'd be no better off than you, would I?

—I think what we really mean is

—a marriage of two minds.

—A Maid in Heaven.

'That's what I said,' she said.

Knowall turned off the tap and leaned against the sink. She didn't like his haircut. It came too far down on his forehead with a centre parting from a point nearly between his eyes. And she didn't like his beard and moustache. They were ridiculous. She heard the rain chatter against the pane. All that rain all day. Lord this is Glasgow Fair reedeeculous. Papa read to her from the Sunday paper Tommy had left behind him.

—I see the fares are going up again. You used to have good fun on a Sunday afternoon just going all the way for a ride on the bus.

Knowall swooshed his scarlet cloak around him and sang a folksong she loved but all she heard was

> —I wooed that maid would be my bride
> A lass who gave a neigh
> Standing room only one inside
> That's all men spend but women pay.

'No, women give,' she argued frantically. 'When you love you want to give. And look for nothing in return.'

—Blessed is he that expecteth nothing for he shall not be et cetera.

Papa paused before he led them off again in turn.

—And if you give what greater gift

—could you give Grace

—than the gift of Eternal Life?

—Grace dying now would obtain the reward that

—the eye hath not seen the ear hath not heard neither hath it entered into the heart of man

—what things God hath prepared for

—Grace kept alive

—would be Bobo all over again.

'Or me. It could happen to Grace too. When I was only seventeen that bad man. I never told you Papa I was too ashamed. My first job Mr Badman. Sweet seventeen it's time you were kissed, Papa, that's what he said and tell me is it garters you young girls wear or have you got and he tried to lift my skirt to see, suspenders. With a wife and three children and one of them a girl. Oh Papa I was nearly sick I just screamed O Papa Papa! All men are even. You Papa. I used to sit on your knee in my nightie.

—Don't forget the problem.

Mum.

Given: A girl and a river.

Required to: Get her across.

Construction: A bridge. Abridge her life.

Proof:

Mum.

Thinks: Twould take a ship to cross that river. The Ship of the Dead of a Thousand Years.

—Gas? Are there any ships go by gas?

—No. That failed once already remember.

'I don't remember' she scribbled hastily. 'I was only sending her a message.'

—Drowning? Washed ashore like poor Shelley. But in some brighter clime.

'No,' she wouldn't have that either. 'My Shelley's death was death by drowning too. Two deaths the same way would leave the linger of suspicion on me. Show my hand. There must be some other way there must.'

—Remember man that thou art Must and unto Must thou must return.

—But must it be violence then? Axe, hammer, chopper, poker, scissors, gun, knife.

—Underline the word out of place.

—Hey, Mac! There's a queue here!

Papa comforted her.

—It's all in the mind. I queue? No, thank you. You ask me? I askew.

—Now the Kingdom of Heaven suffereth violence and the wicked take it by force.

'Where would I get a gun? I'm not in America now you know.'

—At least don't make the mistake you made before.

—Don't try to come over here with her.

—That's how they managed to stop you last time.

—Send her across to me alone, I'll receive her.

—You were too slow coming up the gangway.

—Wait on the shore though you're bound to falter more.

—This time stay behind.

—Unselfishly linger till faith is destroyed, hope abandoned, charity a bygone word, and Grace returned to the Lord from Whom all Graces come.

—And stop keeping on putting it off you ugly old bitch. Post early for Christmas for Christ's sake.

—You think on the brink but you sit there and wink, and you won't do the deed, no you never would, would you? Oh no, not you! You've a kink there's always tomorrow.

—My barque leaves the harbour tomorrow to cross the wide ocean today.

—But remember you must remember. Procrastination is the thief of Predestination. The must can rust.

—The time is come.

—Time to spare is time to kill.

'And at this very moment,' she wrote tenderly, 'my darling child Grace is lying fast asleep in her little bed two storeys beneath me.'

Knowall wandered round the single-end on his own, reading above Papa's head from the book of poems Papa had left her.

—And when I crumble who will remumble that Sadie of the best cuntree? Grace in her bare scuddie, eh? That would be something to refumble! Like you played on your daddy's knee in your nightie-night-Papa. Something you'd like to retumble. And what would Mama say if she knew that Papa knew what Papa knew?

He smirked to a corner to let the rest of them get on their high horse and talk down to her.

—You can give her bread and milk

—cakes and lemonade

—but a greater gift by far would be

—the Bread of Eternal Life.

—What a sweet gift that would be!

—Sweets to the sweet. Even one little sweet.

She nodded to their nods.

'She likes sweeties the same wee girl. There'd be no violence there. Funny I never thought of that before.'

There they were, still nodding smiling to her smiling nodding. The fire was grey, choking to death. The little room was getting chilly. She straightened from poking the fire and they were away. She let them go. She couldn't stop them. Even the four walls couldn't. She was too blearyeyed to write any more. She stumbled several times undressing, got into her nightgown unsteadily, and staggered into bed like a drunk woman.

Tiger was ready to spring that week. He couldn't get a car but he had fixed the use of a plain van from a pal in the delivery line, an old mate who had lost the courage of his previous convictions, a slightly reformed character with bandy legs, who was willing to let him take it away from the coup where he parked it for half an hour some mornings while he popped round the corner for a cup of tea between runs.

'He doesn't want to know anything about it so there's nothing he can tell,' said Tiger. 'If he's ever asked. Dross takes us over the Canal bridge and we drop off before he gets to the Scheme, walk through the Park and out the far gate.'

'And what am I supposed to do?' Dross needled him. 'Drive on till I see a cop and then jump out and run away? D'you think I'm stupit? I'm no drivin it any further than I have to. Yous get out, I get out.'

'Come on and I'll show you,' Tiger stroked him.

He walked him over the route that Monday afternoon, with Hardnut and Chocolate chatting behind. Beyond the Park, just where the Scheme started, a lonely tenement, the lonely survivor of a Victorian block, stood up stained and brown like a bad tooth in the mouth of a man needing dentures.

'All this used to be good property round here,' said Chocolate.

'Flats,' said Tiger. 'Two a landing. But the rooms were far too big. No demand.'

'The Scheme done for it,' said Hardnut. 'They were that wee bit out the way here and past the Park, gave them a touch of class. Clean air. They shoved up the slum clearances right on their tail. Wham! In came the scrubbers, out went the nobs.'

'No it wasn't,' said Chocolate. 'I was brought up near here remember.'

'Dragged up,' Tiger threw over his shoulder.

'What it was,' said Chocolate, 'it was they were gonna build a factory here for tripewriters, that's why they pulled down the whole block except they two closes because it didn't come off and that's when the Scheme went up.'

'You don't half know your history,' Dross muttered sourly. 'Dyou buggers know where you're goin? Causa wishty Christ I did.'

'Sokay,' said Chocolate. 'Keep the pan. It was me showed Tiger.'

They slowed at the dark tower.

'Come on in,' Tiger invited Dross at the second close.

'See yous at the bus stop then,' said Chocolate, taking Hardnut straight on.

Dross went with Tiger, and they strolled through the close into the backgreen where a broken line of palings cut it off from a winding lane. Tiger kept talking all the way.

'Leave the van at the close, would look sif you were deliverin somethin, through here to where the palins is broke, into the lane, and here you are, on Riggins Road – and there's the bus stop.'

'Mirawculous!' Dross sneered, still sour. 'Know any mair wee tricks?'

'Sa good service too,' said Tiger. 'Mind you it goes halfway round the bloody world to get into town butsa good service just the same. And you've a bus shelter forbye if it's raining on Friday.'

Hardnut and Chocolate came sauntering from the corner, smart and cosy in their good winter coats.

'High,' said Tiger.

'Low,' said Hardnut.

'Been oot for to get some fresh air?' Chocolate asked politely.

'Just a wee dauner,' Tiger explained amiably. 'I was showing my hander a bit of a shortcut.'

'Sall very well for yous,' Dross grumbled. 'I get the point of course. I leave the van in fronta that close. It's dead quiet there. Anybody that seen it would think there was a bloke away up the stair for his dinner or deliverin Mrs McWhaccle's laundry.'

'Wheesht,' said Tiger. 'Don't mention laundry, please! We don't know a thing about laundries, do we, my leerie lads?'

'Aye, all right, cut the kiddin,' Dross wouldn't smile. He barged on, going over his instructions with a frown. 'Then I slip through the back, round the lane, out here and get a bus. That's right. I've got that. But suppose—'

'Suppose nothin,' Hardnut stopped him. 'You get your bus and we'll see you for snooker. Same place same time as any Friday the past month.'

'If there's nobody on my tail,' said Dross.

'Who could be on your tail?' Tiger tutted at him, hands out with the palms up.

'Yous could all stay in the van wi me and take the same bus,' Dross wanted to argue. 'What have yous got to get out before then for?'

'Cause,' said Tiger. 'Four of us steppin on a bus at this stop. Carryin a bag. Sasking to be remembered. Aye, and then the four of us get off at the billards room? Might as well send the jailers wur name and address. But even if you were stopped in the van, which is bloody unlikely, what've you got? Nothing!'

'Cept a van that's no mine,' said Dross.

'You'll be all right, pal,' Hardnut drawled at him. 'Sonly commonsense us splittin up as soon as we can. Us three divide the doins in the gents in the Park, dump the bag behind the rodeedendrons and on wur way.'

'Of course the job needs nerve,' said Tiger.

'But if you've got the nerve you can't miss,' said Chocolate.

'I thought we'd been through all that for weeks,' said Hardnut.

'Nobody ever said I hadny the nerve,' said Dross. 'I've got the nerve all right. It's have yous got the nerve? It's yous is doing the grab.'

'Grab?' said Hardnut. 'Nay grab there. Just take. She's only skin and bones. You said it yourself. And I've seen her often enough now, God knows. You flattered her. She's mair bones than skin.'

'Tiger just needs to make a face at her and she'll mess herself and drop the lot,' Chocolate prophesied.

'I'd like a wee shot at that van first,' said Dross. 'Before Friday. You've got to get the feel of the gears if you want to start off quick.'

'You'll get a wee shot,' Tiger promised. 'You'll get as many wee shots as you like. Damn it, man, we've got the whole bloody week in fronta us yet.'

'The bus!' cried Chocolate, full of life and happiness.

'See, I telt you it was a good service,' said Tiger.

'All aboard the Gypsy Queen!' Hardnut sang out, leaping on first, lightfooted, lighthearted.

Wee Annie was at work as usual the same morning. Sane. Normal. Yes, sir. No, sir. Good morning, Laundry speaking. Talking to Mr Alan, answering the phone, typing letters, calculating overtime, plodding away in a routine that didn't occupy her mind, until by Thursday she was uptodate and ready once more to make out the wages envelopes. She worked hard, one person unaided doing a lot, but she was used to it. That was how the firm operated, and she preferred that to being one of many or to having a junior miss round her feet or in her hair.

From Monday till Thursday, locked in herself, she chewed over what she had to do. She had always been obedient to her father, always disciplined to respect higher authority. Sunday night's conference remained with her not as a bad dream or a lone fantasy best forgotten, but as a formal session of her advisers summed up in an order she had to carry out. She knew her duty. It was quite clear, and it was quite simple. All she had to do was get a poke of sweets, poison one and only one, and give the whole poke to Grace. She didn't want poisoned sweets left uneaten to point to the cause of death. She thought the cause would never be known if all the sweets left in the poke were harmless. Or even if they did find out the cause of death they would never connect it with the sweets she had given the dead child. So she would be safe, quite safe, and Grace too would be safe once she had eaten the right sweet.

It bothered her a little that she wouldn't know just when Grace came to it. She would be in suspense till she heard Grace was dead. But the death didn't bother her at all. Dead, death, they were a couple of worn words to her, no longer engraved with grief or regret. They meant no irreparable loss. She was only sending Grace on a journey as the Powers sent a man into space. With the big difference. That Grace wouldn't come back, as the spaceman came back, to a wicked planet. More fortunate, she would reach the Isles of the Blest.

She had the laundry to herself at lunchtime, for she ate a sandwich in her little office and made tea on a gasring in the corner while the local girls rushed home and the others went to a cheap café along the street. In the summer the girls who didn't rush home-and-back squatted and sprawled on the pavement outside the pend, like the girls in Tennent's Brewery in Duke Street, and the lads from the rubberwork would come along and sit beside them for a wrestle and a tickle.

On Monday she prowled at lunchtime. She thought of lysol. Then she thought she could get her hands on some liquid chlorine. She thought of asking Main what he had given Shelley, and for a moment she even remembered that the idea hadn't come in the first place from her Sunday visitors at all but from the way Main had saved Shelley needless suffering. But she knew she couldn't speak to Main, or to anybody else. It must be secret and all her own work or the whole operation would be invalid. In the end she settled for bleaching powder. She

could use it with hardboiled sweets, the longchewing kind
she believed children liked. Teuch jeans we called them in
the vernacular at that time, and she bought a quarter-
pound. They were a tough toffee made up in small sweets
shaped like a pillow for a doll's house. She melted one
down a little, mixed in the bleach, reshaped it patiently
and left it to harden again. The experiment engrossed her.
She went to a lot of trouble to get the tampered sweet back
into the right shape, most conscientious about it, as intent
on perfecting her instrument of death as any scientist
designing a new bomb, and as unconcerned about what
the perfected instrument would do when it was finally
used for the purpose it was meant for. The only point
immediately relevant was to get the thing right in advance.

It wasn't till the Thursday night she managed to get
Grace alone, and by that time she was fully prepared. Mrs
Christie and Mrs Green, two faithful lovers of a bawdybill
show, were off to a music-hall again. She saw them go.
There was no mistake. From her high window she
watched them. She waited till they were out of sight in
the evening shadows before she drew in her head and
lowered the window. She tiptoed across her little room,
listening behind the silent door. Her heart was a hammer
in her breast and her mouth was dry.

'The time is come,' she said they said.

She knew it was. She felt the heavenly power proving
she was one of the elect pervade her bones, she felt her
pounding heart grow steady once she told it to be proud,
she felt the smile of bliss upon her lips and cast out fear,
because she knew her love was perfect and the sacrifice
was fit, an unspotted lamb.

'But how, oh how, oh tell me please God, how am I to
get her!' she panted to the doorknob in her hand, her eyes
down, her ears alert, but she heard nothing but the winter
wind whining against the top storey. 'I can't just go down
the stairs and knock at the door and ask for Grace. I don't
even know if she's in or out.'

The inspired confidence that was leading her on surged

in and out of her. Determination to complete the task laid
on her ebbed and flowed with the attacking and retreating
wind. She loitered behind her door, praying for Grace to
come her way, frustrated that the time was come and she
had the place and the power and the loved one was
missing.

'God, help me please!' she whispered her prayer to the
door panel where her head rested, 'and bring this night to
a happy ending.'

Gently, slowly, she opened her door, keeked round,
waited a few seconds, and then tiptoed downstairs. She
couldn't expect Grace to come to her, so she would have to
go looking for Grace.

'But where am I to find her?' she moaned to the pipe-
clayed stairs.

She couldn't hear the wind on her way down, and oh!
what a hush came seeping up from the close! It made her
nervous. Three doors on each landing, all shut and dead.
Three gaslit landings, and each of them deserted. All life,
if any, domestic discord and family affection, all the joys
and sufferings, the hopes and fears of the unneighbourly
tenants were withdrawn and hidden from her behind those
poker-faced doors. It was as bad as a nightmare to her
as she crossed each corpselike landing in that timeless
silence.

She came to Grace's door, never to her the Christies'
door, but solely the door that sheltered the loved one, the
beautiful child and innocent lamb that no one truly valued
except herself. She looked at the varnished wood and the
brass nameplate in an agony of not knowing, not knowing
if Grace were at rest behind them or out playing.

'Now if I was mad I'd bang on that door and scream for
Grace,' she murmured wisely as she moved past it down to
the close. 'But I'm not. I'm quite possessed and calm. I
know what I'm doing all right. Only sometimes I wonder
who I am.'

One pace above the last half-landing she heard the
lavatory there being flushed. She stopped her step,

paralysed, one little slippered foot on its toe, the other in transit. Who would come out of that vulgar place to confront her and sidle past with a grin and a nod? Friend or foe? But she had no friends she knew, and foes she must flee. It always embarrassed her to meet someone coming out of the lavatory. Would it be old Sandy McKay, the brokendown old Scots comedian with the pot belly and his fly still unbuttoned, or Daddy Blair the drunk barber or one of his heirs, or one of Grace's family, or even it could be if God was kind, and it was.

The lavatory door was slammed shut by a little girl with tousled hair, short skirts and long legs, a girl almost visibly growing, Grace herself.

'Oh God! Oh God approves!' Miss Partridge exulted in a thought as swift as a lightning flash. 'He has sent Grace to me in my hour of need.'

'Oh, hullo Grace darling,' she smiled her smile of bliss, the certainty that she was among the elect flooding through her again. 'I was just going out to get myself a fish supper but I've only my slippers on, see!'

Coyly she showed off one tiny foot in a blue slipper with a white pompom at the instep.

'I wonder would you mind running along to Carlo's dear for me? You've done it for me before, you know what to get.'

The big solemn blue eyes were cautious. Cold words came hard from warm lips soft.

'I'll have to ask my mammy for permission.'

'But your mother's – oh, all right,' said Miss Partridge. She sagged. She was defeated. The child must know her mother was out. She followed her meekly back up the stairs and waited forlorn outside the Christies' door.

'Oh God, why are you deceiving me?' she wept in her heart. 'To arrange it all for me and bring it all so near and then cheat me with the falsehood of my little one! Why do you mock me like this? Can I wrestle with Thee, O Lord? We wrestle not against flesh and blood, but against the rulers of the darkness of this world, against spiritual wickedness in high places.'

Behind the front door Grace hung the lavatory key on its appointed nail and skipped through to her big sister crouched over the kitchen fire on her daddy's footstool.

'Wee Annie caught me coming out the closet. She's wanting me to go for a fish supper for her. What do you think? You know what mammy said. Should I go?'

'Och aye,' Agnes muttered, surfacing briefly from the depths of *Romeo*. 'It wouldn't be Christian to starve the auld bitch. Getter what she wants and hurry back. Teller to wait on the stairhead for it.'

'My mammy says it's all right if I hurry back,' Grace announced without a blush to Miss Partridge waiting on the doorstep.

'You little liar!' Miss Partridge cried, but into herself. 'You know damn fine your mother's out.'

But smiling her blissful smile she handed over enough money for the errand from the few shillings she always carried in the pocket of her pinny in case the insurance man called and scuttled back doublequick to her single-end away up on the top flat in case anyone saw her. On the way up she pardoned Grace, forgave her freely for telling a lie. But the deceit made her more sure than ever it was high time to send Grace across the border to safety. The longer the child lived the more wicked she would become. Telling lies to those that loved you was only the beginning. She was getting too big. Soon it would be too late.

She left her door ajar till Grace came back, and after five or six minutes she wearied waiting. Pushed by her demon she dragged out her ledger-diary from the end drawer of the dresser and wrote quickly in it, standing at the bunker lid. She wanted it down in black and white for future reference. Perhaps these lines would defend her in the day of battle against the wicked spirits that wandered through the world for the ruin of souls. She testified she had forgiven Grace for trying to deceive her but the lie meant the journey must be made at once.

'For the doubleminded will never purify their hearts, no matter how often they are warned, their transgressions and backslidings will increase, leading them into temptation and the works of the flesh, adultery, fornication, uncleanness, lasciviousness, the wickedness and snares of the Devil, and absence from the Lord. It is now or never.'

Grace was singing on the stairs. In hurried guilt she edged the diary back into its hidingplace.

'Come in, dear,' she called sweetly welcoming the little victim when its knuckles chapped the open door.

'I had to wait,' Grace complained, slapping the fish supper down on the table. 'They weren't ready. He was just cutting uppa lotta new chips when I went in and there was a big long queue.'

She lingered, loitering. Loitering she lingered, glad to have the hot parcel off her hands but unwilling to abandon it. She couldn't resist the temptation of those vinegar-odorous chips cuddling the pipinghot haddock fried in buttercoloured batter. And because she knew her own weaknesses she hadn't told Wee Annie to wait on the stairhead in spite of what Agnes said. She knew if she went right on up and in she would get a share. She knew her Wee Annie. And so it was.

The woman and the child sat at table together, Miss Partridge at the middle of the board, Grace at one end. The fish supper was tidily decanted on to a dinnerplate so that Miss Partridge could make a knife and fork meal of it, for she had eaten little all day, with bread and butter and a pot of tea, but Grace just used her fingers because she thought the chips tasted better that way. Of course she was polite enough to wait after each raid on the margin of the plate till she was invited to have another, and skilfully, craftily, she always managed to lift three or four chips at once and those always the biggest. Miss Partridge didn't mind. It was food and drink to her to have Grace at her table again, there at her elbow for the last supper, and if it gave the child pleasure to eat up all the chips then it gave her greater pleasure to let her. She did all the talking, for

Grace remembered her manners and wouldn't speak with her mouth full, and that saved her saying anything except *Huh-huh* and *Mm-mm* between bites.

Yet to do the girl justice I should say she stayed to help her hostess with the washing-up. Miss Partridge washed and Grace dried.

'There now, that's a big job well done!' Miss Partridge chuckled at her own remark. 'One cup one saucer one sideplate one dinnerplate one knife one fork one spoon. That's the best of living all by yourself.'

'I've to wash fower times that every night doon the stair,' Grace patronised the lonely life of a spinster.

'Four times, down the stair,' said Miss Partridge, then wondered why she bothered to correct the lovable speech of a child who hadn't long to live.

For now it was time. She had been patient all evening. Deliberately patient, steadfastly refusing to rush the last most solemn gift. But now at last she could come to the point.

'I've got something for you,' she whispered.

From the tabledrawer she took the poke of sweeties.

'Good sweets, dear,' she explained. 'This is the kind we used to eat when I was a wee girl.'

'Huh-huh,' said Grace.

'I saw them in a sweetie shop near the Cross,' said Miss Partridge. 'Good chewy sweets. You'll like them. I didn't know you could still get them.'

'Mm-mm,' said Grace.

'But not tonight,' said Miss Partridge. 'Not after chips. Might make you sick. Keep them for tomorrow.'

'Huh-huh,' said Grace, holding out her hand but she wasn't given them.

A danger not foreseen suddenly reared in front of Miss Partridge.

'They're from me to you,' she said severely. 'You're not to share them with anybody. They're all yours. They're meant for you and nobody else.'

'Mm-mm,' said Grace, still waiting to get them.

'Keep them for playtime tomorrow at school,' said Miss Partridge. 'Promise!'

She looked so alarming, staringeyed and strained, holding back the poke till the required word was spoken that Grace retreated, afraid.

'Promise,' Miss Partridge repeated, advancing.

Fierce about it she was Grace saw.

'Promise,' Grace agreed.

She swallowed. Her scare passed over.

'Here, take them then,' said Miss Partridge kindly. Grace took them.

Up in the winter morning sharp, blithe and debonair, the yellow light full on and the gasring burning to heat the chilly darkness, Wee Annie sang to herself the auld Scots sangs in the braid auld Scottish tongue, the sangs her faither loved to hear, the sangs her mither sung. She made tea and toast as usual, canting away to herself. In the small hours Papa had paid a flying visit from outer space to assure her with the prescience of the immortals that Grace would keep her promise not to share the sweeties and not to touch them till playtime. Behind Papa, one at each shoulder, the co-pilot twins nodded in confirmation. Nothing would go wrong. At ten forty-five G.M.T. Grace would leave the earth, blasted off into infinite space to come to orbit in eternal salvation. So certain of the happy outcome she was, comforted that Knowall hadn't troubled to make the trip, she passed on without a tremor when on her way to the laundry through the twilight of the December morning she got a glimpse of Grace in the baker's across the street queuing for freshbaked rolls with a pint of milk in her hand and the (Scottish) *Daily Express* under her oxter. Unseen, she glanced at the sleepy-eyed child and proceeded heartwarmed to her work.

'Ah, the wee darling! She's late this morning, she'll never be at the school for nine o'clock, I'm sure. Aye, she goes all her mammy's messages, morning and night, summer and winter, but this day I'm sending her on a better message than she ever went before. Forever and forever. Today's the day she'll go away. But tomorrow and tomorrow, ten thousand tomorrows, a hundred hundred million, and she'll never come back. No transport.'

She smiled. She was so happy she could afford a wee joke. She was only doing what she was told, it was all proper and legal and totally unselfish. Her conscience was clear. Under a sky that threatened snow she plodded dutifully on, till the vision of a world without Grace halted her for a moment.

'Then who'll be next for me to love? Susan Greenwood? Sue for Grace? I must love a wee one though no one loves me, I suppose not even Grace.'

Not even Grace, normally punctual, was in time for school that morning. But then she hadn't expected to be, the way everything had worked to obstruct and delay her. Out of breath after running, she stopped a step inside the door. Miss Galloway barred her, cross, a strap dangling from her ringed fingers, a gaunt time-honouring woman.

'What kept you?'

'Please miss Ah wis gaun messages fur ma mammy.'

Grace panting, red in the face, trembling in the childish lips, so confused she forgot she wasn't supposed to use her native tongue in the classroom. Across the corridor a junior class bawled through the nine times table.

'I was going errands for my mother.' – Miss Galloway prunemouthed, prim and proper.

The teacher always teaching coiled the strap round her fist looking lovelessly down at the frightened pupil.

Nothing said Grace looking pleadingly up.

'You should get up earlier in the morning and get all your errands done in time for school.'

Always prompt with the obvious, herself scrambled in with an egg left halfeaten and two minutes to spare, the cross teacher crossed from the door to her desk. Let Grace enter. Grace hovered.

'Ach, go and sit down!'

Up with the lid of her desk, in popped the coiled strap, down slammed the lid. Stood there muttering a bitter woman.

'Every time I want to start new sums half the class is late. I'll let you off. You're just the first of many.'

The first of many things Wee Annie had to do was check the wages envelopes and then write out fair on a slip what she wanted from the bank. The number of fivers, singles, halfnotes, halfcrowns, florins and sixpences. Backchecked, downchecked, upchecked, crosschecked, made out the cheque, went through to the other office for Mr Alan's signature or the manager's. Mr Alan was in. That pleased her. She liked him because he trusted her.

'Never made a mistake in my life,' she sometimes tossed at Tommy on a Sunday if they compared their working responsibilities.

'Well, I'm no bad myself,' he sometimes batted back. 'Working in a pub you see you've got to be quick and you've got to be right. Funny thing. You might think they're drunk. But they always know their change. Never twist a customer's change no matter how much you think he's had.'

'It wouldn't be right, would it?' she despised the very idea. 'I don't know how you can even think of it in your trade. The money's not yours. In my job it's not just money pure and simple. It's something earned that's theirs not mine.'

Alone, always alone wherever she was, counting in her cubbyhole with a twobar heater, her old typewriter shoved to one side to give her more room at the small table where she worked, she remembered Tommy and felt a warmth flow over her like the warmth when she saw Grace in the baker's, for she loved Tommy too at times. But he was only her brother. He would have to save himself. He was too old for her to help.

To help Dross get the feel of the borrowed van Tiger got him an hour with it on Wednesday night.

'Seasy,' Dross concluded. 'Sthe same gears as whit I'm usety.'

'I telt ye ye whirr worryin aboot nothin,' Tiger lolled beside him, acting and feeling the chauffeurdriven bigshot.

'Sa good startin wee van,' Dross granted. 'That's the main thing. Aye, I like her. She'll do.'

'Sa good omen. Home, James.'

They picked it up again together on Friday morning, no bother at all, and made smoothly for the corner of the escape route over the Canal. A bobby on point duty halted them to let a long funeral crawl across their front.

'Hellsbells,' Tiger chewed his pinkie. 'It's high bloody time we wis there.'

'It's high time you were away.'

Mr Alan's bald head gleamed genially round the door of Wee Annie's cubbyhole.

'I'm just going, Mr Alan,' she buttoned her coat to the neck, put on her oldfashioned hat, a cloche in felt with a feather.

'Have you your rummybirella with you?' the false teeth shone above a genuine smile. 'I think it's trying to snow now.'

'I'll be all right, Mr Alan. It's a short walk really, there and back.'

'It's not a nice morning for you at all.'

It was a dreich morning for Grace too. It dragged, a proper snail. Miss Galloway was still cross with everybody and the sums were too hard. She got the first one wrong and had no idea how to do the next one. She just sat and looked at her jotter, thinking of last week's Nature Study lesson on the snail and more aware of an ache in her middle than of the figures in her book. She was hungry. But she couldn't eat her piece till playtime. She didn't even know what her mammy had put in the poke. She wondered and guessed. She sat alone in the back seat, longing for the bell.

Dross sat alone in the front seat longing for action. It was the waiting got him. He didn't like it. And he didn't like the sickness in his middle, the quivering void, a sensation resembling hunger but craving a different satisfaction. Tiger was lucky. He was out there stretching his legs, enjoying a wee dauner up and down while he was waiting. Even that was some kind of action. Even just hanging about the corner watching for Wee Annie coming back from the bank.

Coming back from the bank she thought she was being followed. Of course she was. There and back by Hardnut and Chocolate in case by chance or appointment she picked up an escort on the way. Her first misgiving came when she passed the public convenience on her left and saw an undersized young fellow standing at the top of the stairs. She thought she had seen him already, on her way in. Indeed she had. That was Hardnut. She didn't like the way he nodded past her as if he was signalling somebody. That was him giving Chocolate a flash that he had spotted Tiger at the corner and that meant the van was there. Now he crossed over and walked ahead of her to give Tiger the tictac she was coming right behind him. On her right she had the low wall of a derelict site with hard trampled earth behind it where the grass had failed to live. Perhaps someone was crouched behind the wall waiting to jump on her. But she couldn't believe it. She marched on bravely clutching the big shoppingbag with the wages, and sacked her passing fear.

'I'm in a public thoroughfare, I'm not away in the jungle where I might be pounced on by a tiger.'

Tiger loitered near the pend while Dross waited in the van round the corner. He saw Hardnut coming and silently waved the good news round to Dross. The victim was approaching. He would time it nicely to walk briskly into the pend like someone business bound and be right at her heels. Hardnut, first to enter the pend, would be joined by Chocolate who would pass her comfortably on the last lap there. They would wait where the dim light of the winter morning was dimmest, close up behind her the moment she put a foot past them. Chocolate would bundle her to Hardnut and Hardnut would give her the stick. Tiger would grab the bag when she fell in an old maid's panic, all three of them sprint to the back of the van, where the doors were drawn to but not locked, hop in and close the doors, with Dross foot on the clutch, hand on the gears, raring to go.

'Off like the hammers,' said Tiger, 'the minute I snatch.'

He saw his two pals walk separately into the pend discreetly ahead of Wee Annie. He watched and waited. He saw her come trudging along. Hands in his overcoat pockets, collar up, hair sleek, shoes shining, he strode in after her. The rehearsals were over. It was time for the play.

By playtime Grace was ravenous. As soon as she put one foot in the yard she tore open her mammy's poke. A jammy piece and two Abernethy biscuits with butter thick between them. The little lamb wolfed them and then felt better. She wiped her jammy-buttery fingers with a dainty hanky pinched from her big sister's hand-bag, and when she shoved the hanky back into her pocket her fingers met another poke. Wee Annie's sweeties. They didn't interest her for the moment. She had no appetite for them. Teuch jeans didn't go with bread-and-jam and buttered-biscuits and she was full up anyway. They would keep. She pulled her coatcollar round her neck. She didn't usually bother to put her coat on at playtime but all morning the sky had coldly rained a cruel sleet softening to snow or a hard snow sharpening to sleet, blown at an angle by a bitter wind. Snow, snow, sleet, sleet, snow. She was glad when the bell rang the end of playtime. She would thole her teacher for the sake of getting back to a cosy classroom.

'Right! Everybody up straight! Mouths closed, arms folded!'

The cross teacher, not quite so cross after tea and biscuits, returned to the attack.

The attack? The attack was a failure. There's no point trying to hide it any longer. There's no use pretending you can build up suspense when you know all the time there's nothing to get suspended about. It was bound to fail, Wee Annie being what she was, and Tiger, Hardnut and Chocolate being what they were. Chocolate had a soft centre, Tiger wasn't swift enough, and Hardnut cracked easily when it came to the bit. They were all in position right enough, right where they should be, just to the very second. But Wee Annie didn't fall when she was pushed, didn't even let go. She staggered a little, that was all. And Tiger was so barred from action by her eldritch scream he missed the moment to snatch his chance when she was off balance. The wee woman was on guard at once, hugging her bag like a babe at her breast.

Hardnut gave her a quick clip behind the ear. He should have used his hammerhaft of course, but he had been so taken up during rehearsals with practising just where he would strike he had never practised being quick to the draw. So when he fumbled in his pocket and the haft got stuck in the lining he cut his losses and used the edge of his palm instead. It served. She tottered against Tiger, fell at his feet. Tiger stooped to conquer, grabbed at the bag, gave her an oath for it and called her a stupit bitch for not giving it up. His language didn't shock her. She had been called names before. She hung on gamely and grimly for death or dear life. She wouldn't let go. It wasn't their money and it wasn't hers to give them. It was other folk's wages, girls who worked in sweat and steam, machine-minders, pressers and folders and parcellers, vanmen and vanboys, her own earned share and the manager's salary. She wouldn't, shouldn't, she couldn't let go. Hardnut kicked her on the wrist, but he kicked the hand that was holding the hand that was holding the bag, so she still didn't let go. And all the time she screamed, partly from fright, partly from the pain in her skinny wee wrist. Tiger seized her in his fierce claws and tossed her against the wall to rattle her into dropping the bag. Her cloche hat was over one ear and her grey head hit the wall and bounced off. She fell flat. But the bag was under her, and she lay deadly still. They milled round, kicking, but they were scared to move her.

'Jesus Christ!' said Chocolate softly. He was the first to go. He thought Tiger had killed her, cracked her skull or broken her neck or given her a heart attack. She looked so frail lying there, a skelf of a woman with matchstick legs sprawled out, that Hardnut ran too. And when Chocolate melted and Hardnut cracked Tiger jumped over Wee Annie and chased after them. They were all eager beavers now, keen to be first in the van.

In the van Dross had been having the fidgets. They were taking too long. He wasn't sure what he heard at first. All he was sure of was the job should take seconds, not minutes. He knew what he heard all right when he heard the second scream, and he hopped out of the van double-quick when the scream became screams. It was a case of every man for himself and no van for anybody. He hared up to the Canal bank, beetled along the waterside till he came to a path that would take him back to the streets, loped down it like a frightened rabbit, and walked calmly in safety only when he struck the main road again and mingled with the gadding crowd.

'That is not allowed,' said Miss Galloway, mellowing now she had got over the worst of the morning. 'Who's next? Spell allowed.'

Next stood up, spelled it, said it, and sat down.

'He spoke his thoughts aloud. Spell aloud.'

Grace stood up, spelled it, said it, and sat down. Smiled to her teacher, grateful. Miss Galloway was in a good mood again. That was easy.

Hardrunning Hardnut outpaced Chocolate. He was the first to reach the van. He raced to the front to warn the driver, saw the cabin empty, knew what Dross had done and what had made him do it, flourished a signal to Chocolate, who mimed it back to Tiger, and they galloped off in all directions. They knew they'd meet again, they knew where, they knew when.

When Wee Annie first screamed the girls in the laundry, like Dross, weren't sure what they heard. But like Dross they knew what it was when it went on.

'It's Miss Partridge! That's who it is! It's Farty-Party! It's our Wee Annie. Somebody's after our lolly, that's what it is.'

All tools down, everybody out. All in a scurry, bright legs twinkling, slim legs flashing, thick legs bounding, lassies in a clamour, spinsters screeching, widows wailing, gallus wenches, warrior women, all yelling to be first, fleetfooted across the yard to the pend.

With glazed eyes she saw them come, ministering angels all in white flying on wings of mercy to bear her up in their hands, blonde Sarah Finn bending over her blue-eyed and ramstam behind her Jean and Jess and all the other seraphim, hands reverently clasped at her suffering, praying for her, with others winging forward to raise her from her fallen state to be rewarded for ever in heaven for doing her duty even unto death. Last but not least, behind the angelic choir the Lord himself.

'Oh Mistralan,' she moaned, near fainting in a fog. She couldn't look up at him, it made her head ache. And hearing them sighing over her hooded eyes she bridged the years and heard in the babble of many remote voices her father reading to her before he made her read it back to him.

—Lift her up tenderly.

—Lift her with care.

'Bashed on the head she's been!'

'Our wages there?'

'Phone for an ambulance, phone for the police,' cried Mr Alan.

The manager scampered yes-sirring back to the office.

'Yes, they're all there,' she mumbled, remumbled and fumbled as they put her together again. 'That scum didn't get them. It's just that I had a wee fall. It's my wrist. Oh, my head! It's my hand and my head.'

One hand drooped limply, the palm snapped at the stem.

'Oh Father, oh Papa,' she whispered as the white angels took her aloft. Before the ambulance came she fainted at last in thickening darkness.

Darkness drifted over the city. The snow had stopped. The sleet had ceased. Mist wandered from the river, shrouded the city centre and the suburbs. Grace flew for dinner through obscure streets, a frightened sparrow. The chill and the damp and the swirling fog seeped into her mouth, searched round her teeth and whispered with malice at a molar.

'Mammy, I've got toothache,' she wailed. 'It's away at the back.'

That was the seeds of the strawberry jam on an uncrowned grinder. Like most Glasgow children at that time Grace had poor teeth, deficient in calcium because of the water from Loch Katrine the dentists said.

'You'd better get it out then, hadn't you,' said her mother casually, accepting toothache as normal in a child's life. 'Stop girning and take your dinner.'

'But I don't think I can eat,' Grace lamented. 'I can't chew with it. I think it's shoogly.'

'It's only soup,' her mother pushed her into a chair. 'You don't need to chew it. Good Scotch broth. It'll warm you up. Right to your toes. You can soak a roll in it and you won't have to do any chewing.'

On the way to afternoon school her woollen fingers met the poke of tough toffees again.

'Oh, hullo! I'd forgotten about you!'

'Aye, it's a fine thing,' they complained. 'You get us for nothing and you canny even be bothered to—'

'Well, not just now,' she interrupted, caressing them

tenderly. 'Maybe tonight. If it wasn't I've got toothache of course I would.'

'So long as you remember you've still got us,' said a big one, nearly bursting through the poke in his eagerness to be spokesman for the rest. 'And don't forget we come from Wee Annie.'

Wee Annie was whipped off to hospital. Mr Alan went with her, waited for the verdict, his heart troubled for the fate of his faithful servant, full of hate for the neds who had caused such alarm and dismay.

Alarm and dismay in the Phoenix that night. Everybody up Wee Annie's close knew inside five minutes she had been attacked, and by teatime she was dead, she wasn't dead, she had been robbed of the lot, she was quite safe and hadn't lost a penny, she had died at her post saving the wages from a bandit with a German pistol, she had saved her life by handing over the money when a masked man threatened her with a chisel, she had been set on by one man, two men, three men, four men (and a dog), she was dead, she wasn't dead, she was dying.

Jess and Yowyow, Yoyo and Jean, cornered in whispers, kept asking for Tommy Partridge. But he wasn't in. Because he lived a goodly distance from the laundry and the rumour-centre, or because he was only her brother, he was the last to get the news, and when he should have been on duty making jokes with the soaks at the bar, acting dad to each lass and her lad in the lounge, he was kicking his heels in long corridors till he could get in to see her. Bobo turned up in the Phoenix that night, the first time for four months, joined her old mates as if she had never been away, sat facing them, her back to the door, pretended to be casual without a care in the world but had to ask over the first drink if they had heard anything fresh. She couldn't explain why she was so upset, and she couldn't hide it.

'Nutta thing,' said Jess. 'We was asking too. But Tommy's not in. Oh, she was a terrible sight when we saw her.'

'Sawful, isn't it?' said Jean. 'I tell ye ye're no safe in this city nowadays. She looked that funny with her hat over one eye.'

'She was lying there sprawled out like a frog with her clothes up her legs,' said Jess. 'And the blood! Oh my, the blood!'

'They musta hit her on the head with a hammer,' said Jean. 'The blood was coming down over her eyes.'

'Have you been seeing Dross lately?' asked Jean.

The question was malicious. She knew damn fine Bobo and Dross had quarrelled months ago and never made up. A second barb of malice was the insinuation that Dross was as likely as anyone else to be mixed up in the affair, to have gone to work seriously on an idea they had all joked about long, long ago when they were all one big happy family.

'No,' said Bobo. 'I never see him now somehow. It's an awful business. I can't pretend I like her. But still and all, she's a puir wee soul. And Hugh Main always used to say I should try to understand her. I've no idea what he's doing these days.'

'Seen him last week,' said Yoyo. 'You'd think he'd won the pools the way he was dressed. Oh, a rare coat he had on! But there was no dame with him.'

'No?' said Bobo politely, past caring.

'Talking about dames,' Yoyo carried on.

'Must we?' Jean interrogated.

'Must tell yous a funny one,' Yoyo persisted, missing the malaise heavy on the rest of them. He bashed on brightly.

'Who did I see coming out the garage the other night but big Alec, him that has the Volkswagen, and you know what he was carryin? So help ma Boab, a big can of antifreeze! And him all dressed up like gaun out on a date. So I says to him, where the hell are ye gaun wi that, I says. You'd never guess what he came out with. I'm gaun to meet the girlfriend, says he.'

He looked round the cold silence, searching for a smile.

'It was the way he said it. This big can of antifreeze.'

'You're away off,' said Yowyow. 'Sorry, pal. Wrong time, wrong place.'

'Aye, all right, we get it,' said Jean. 'My God, look!'

'Look who's coming in,' said Jess.

'There's Dross,' said Yowyow.

'Talk of the devil,' said Yoyo.

Bobo sat tight, soberly refusing to let the entrance of Dross turn her head. Yet with the fourfold warning of his coming she felt flood over her the warmth of the unforgotten past, of all the familiar carefree sessions that used to be the sum and substance and irreplaceable pleasure of a Friday night.

Friday night was clean-the-house night in the Christies' room and kitchen. Grace got off lightly. All the heavy chores were left to her big sister while her mother wandered round in charge of the campaign and reassembled all the bits and pieces of furniture Agnes had moved to get cleaning beneath and behind them. To escape the menace of three females on the warpath Mr Christie faded after seven to the nearest pub. The Phoenix wasn't his howff. It was too far down the road for him, and anyway he despised it as what he called mo-dern, stressing the second syllable. He preferred the oldfashioned Canal Vaults with a sawdust track at his feet, where a man could drink a half and a beer amongst men, served by men, and none of this barmaids everywhere and uptodate lounges ladeeda. The burr of workingmen's voices the length of the bar was music after the shrill squabbling he had left behind him, and he knew his wife was happier to have him out of the way, even if he did get a little drunk.

'Lift that rug! Shift that chair!'

'I'm fair scunnered,' Agnes whined. 'Tired of slaving, fed up scrubbing.'

'Aye, we all get weary,' said her mother, 'but it's got to be done.'

Grace said nothing in case she drew attention to herself.

'Scrub out the lobby, scrub below the bed, bleach the jawbox, clean out the press.'

Mrs Christie kept them at it till they tottered punch-drunk and it turned nine.

'And I wanted to wash my hair tonight,' Agnes grieved.

'You'll have time enough for that when you've washed the windows,' her mother snapped.

Sweating on her knees Agnes scrubbed the doorstep. Luckily it wasn't the Christies' turn for washing the stairs, or Grace might have got more to do inside while Agnes was doing that job outside.

Recognising the battle was nearly over, ending in a complete victory for Scotch cleanliness in one house at least, Grace piped up warm and willing after mopping out every shelf in the press, lining each with clean paper, polishing the jellypan, doing the brasses, nameplate and doorbell, and washing the two walliedugs on the mantel-piece, 'Will I go for a fish supper?'

'Aye, when you've emptied that pail there,' her mother, pipeclaying the hearth, panted.

Grace carried the pail in one hand to the midden and her free hand wandered into the pocket of her pinny. She had put the poke of teuch jeans there, half meaning to tackle them during the tasks of the evening, half just wanting to have them always within touch. Her angry molar was calm, as calm as if it had never raged. But her nerve failed her. She feared those solid sweets. She knew they would only start her toothache off again, and after she had timmed out her pail in the midden she found the hand that had fondled the poke was pulling it out of her pinny. Without her saying a yea or a nay her hand tossed the poke into an ashcan away at the far end of the midden. The deed was done in the darkness of a backcourt in winter, and she was neither glad nor sorry. She liked jellybabies and soft chocolates and macaroons, melting caramels, turkish de-light, nougat and liquorice allsorts, but teuch jeans had never been to her liking. She just didn't want them. And she knew, of course she knew, the whole close knew, Wee

Annie was in hospital. By the time she came out she would
have forgotten all about teuch jeans. Surely. She always
asked you how you liked whatever she gave you, but this
time she would hardly ask, and so there would be no need
to tell lies.

Grace skipped back upstairs to the shining kitchen,
washed her face and hands, squabbling at the sink with
Agnes who was wanting to start washing her hair, and then
skipped down again for three fish suppers.

'Save a few chips for your dad,' said Mrs Christie when
they were all tucking in, saltily enjoying with plenty of
vinegar what they had earned by the sweat of their brow.

Proud of himself, you'd think, the way he behaved, Dross
stood over the whole company. A cold welcome he got
from them. Bobo wouldn't even look up. To the others he
was a stranger from the past, so long is an autumn absence
in the friendships of the young. He lifted over an empty
chair from another table without a do-you-mind to the
courting couple there, acting the old lordly Dross, always
master of the situation, the bigshot, the boss, and took it
round to sit straddled facing Bobo. She looked at him
straight, just looked at him.

'Anybody heard how Wee Annie is?'

The way he said it he might as well have tabled a signed
confession. He spoke too soon in the first place, and his
offhand bravado was a threadbare coat over his nervous
suit. Everybody saw he was anxious and frightened.

'Oh, have you heard about her?' Jean asked, and the
question sounded as cruel as she intended.

'We haven't heard much,' said Yowyow.

'The last we heard she was still unconscious,' said Jess.

'There's some talk of her having a fractured skull,' said
Yoyo.

'She'll maybe no live,' said Jean. 'At least that's what
they were saying.'

They knew, they all knew, and they all knew they all
knew, he was chattering with guilt as they sat and looked at

him, just looked at him. He offered cigarettes round, but
they all refused. He lit one for himself and his hand was
shaking. Bobo stared hard at that hand all the way till he
put it back in his pocket.

'Seen Tiger and his pals?' Yowyow asked. Innocent
face, innocent question.

'No, I didn't go to the, no, I haven't seen them, no.'

He stammered, changed direction. They were all silent.
Yoyo offered cigarettes round and they all took one, even
Bobo. Dross saw the snub and fidgeted, looking round the
room as if for a friendly face or escape. He sat with nothing
in front of him. By all their conventions one of them
should have put a drink up for him at once or else he
should have joined them with a glass in his hand. He had
blundered sitting down amongst them emptyhanded and
they weren't going to put it right. He rolled his shoulder-
blades to caress the nape of his neck with the collar of his
new coat.

'Howya doin, Bobo?' he tried.

'All right,' she said. Cold, clear, concise.

'There's Tommy!' Jean cried joyfully.

'He'll know,' said Dross, half out of his seat, impatient
to learn the best or the worst.

Tommy answered the queenly flutter of Bobo's raised
hand and came gently over, a gentleman in his own house,
smiling goodwill to his seated guests. Bobo spoke. They all
left it to her, respecting her anxiety.

'How is she?'

'They tell me she might live till tomorrow,' he said with
strained flippancy. 'She's a tough old bird, my big sister.
There's hope yet.'

He smirked, grinned, laughed it off to cover his suffering, blethered so vaguely they couldn't quite follow him at
times.

'And I might have been sitting waiting to see till the
cows come home if I hadn't met Mr Main. He was
coming out when he seen me in the corridor. I've left
him in the bar having a pie and a beer. He's doing his

ward practice there he was telling me. He's a real toff. Brought me back here in a taxi. Wouldn't leave till he found out about my sister once I told what I was doing there and got the doctor to have a word with me. He even got me in to see her. He's a real gentleman that fellow. Any service wanted?'

'Well, since you're here,' said Yowyow. 'To celebrate the good news.'

He ordered for the company, and for a moment it seemed touch and go if he would include or omit Dross.

''Scuse me,' Bobo murmured.

She rose elegantly, stepped highheeled past Dross, and went straight through to the bar, blonde, smart and distant-eyed. She looked for Main, saw him sitting in a corner with his half-eaten mutton pie and a bottle of Worcester sauce and a glass of beer in front of him. Flounced down beside him, her knees showing, her mouth trembling.

'That man! I don't think he knows what he's saying. Makes a joke of it. His own sister! Tell me the truth. How is she? You know!'

'What are you on about now?' Main asked, bending his lips to a precious fragment.

'You know bloody well what I mean,' she said. 'Don't play games with me. Wee Annie.'

'Miss Partridge?' he chided her with a mild question. 'I'm not playing games. I don't know what you're so het up about. She was attacked this morning coming from the bank. That's all I was told.'

'Yes, I know. I know that. Everybody knows that. But how is she? That's what I'm asking.'

'She has a fracture of the left wrist and delayed concussion. Bruises on the back and legs. Lacerations across the bridge of the nose and forehead. No internal injuries. Nothing serious. She'll be all right in a day or two.'

Bobo wept. Her head went down, her hand grubbed in her bag, but she couldn't find her hanky.

'What in heaven or earth is troubling you now?' Main muttered plaintively. She was spoiling the rest of his pie.

'You've got me beat. I don't understand you. I thought you didn't like her.'

'It was you told me to try,' she said.

'So you've tried. I'm glad. But she's all right. What are you worrying about?'

'Dross is through there,' she nodded back to the lounge.

'Then what are you doing here?'

He finished his pie, hardly interested in the answer.

'I've gone off him,' she said, finding her hanky too late and stuffing it back into her bag. 'You know you can go off people?'

'I suppose so,' said Main. 'It never occurred to me.'

'Can I sit here and talk to you for a bit?' she asked him, not Bobo the lively girl of the spring and summer who turned everyman's head, the gallus piece that Big Donald thought he had seen, but a tired lump of a lassie in a wintry season.

'Sure, if you want to,' said Main, easygoing.

'I've gone off him,' she said again, looking blankly across at the gantries behind the bar. 'I've gone right off him. For good.'

It's very hard to know where to begin now I've come to the end. That must be the end because there's nothing much more I know.

'I don't see how you could know even as much as that,' my mother objected.

She wasn't pleased. Far from it. She sat despising my skewered pages, holding them on her lap between her palms, one thumb flipping them from last to first, the other flipping them from first to last, again and again, and went off on her own.

'Oh, I remember well when she came out the hospital and I was talking to her in this very room, the puir wee soul, and she said you know it's a strange thing, she said, it was frightening too. I'd always thought I wanted to die but when it came to the pinch I found I didn't. I couldn't let go. It was like a bad tooth that hurts you, she said. You wish it wasn't there but you hate to lose it. I used to think it would be a beautiful thing to die, just to lie back and not care any more and let go and fade away, but I couldn't let go. I just hung on, she said, and it turned out it was the wages she was hanging on to.'

'She was a brave woman,' I granted. 'Or a stubborn wee besom. I don't know. But that's not the point. You mean to say you don't like it at all?'

'Not particularly. Who told you all this anyway?'

'You did.'

'Me? I never did! There's things there I never knew, and wouldn't have told you even if I did. And there's things you just couldn't know.'

'Well of course I made up the odd bit here and there.'

'So you're not pretending it's all true? You admit you made it up?'

'I didn't say that. What you told me and what I got from Wee Annie's diaries—'

'I'm sorry I ever gave you them,' my mother cut in quick.

'It all led me on. It had to be like that. Like that bloke could reconstruct a prehistoric monster if you gave him a bone.'

'Ach, give the dog a bone!' my mother sneered at my defence. She was a deeply religious woman, but a complete sceptic about what science could do. 'And I bet you the same man made a lot of blunders too with his prehistoric lobsters.'

'Monsters,' I said patiently.

'What are you trying to do to me exactly?' she asked, just as patient. 'You come here and hand me this true history all dressed up as if it was fiction.'

'I couldn't write a historical monograph on Wee Annie, could I? She doesn't rank. I had to pretend it was a story.'

'That's what I'm saying. You ask me to read a history pretending to be fiction. Hold your wheesht! Let me finish. Then you admit you made up the half of it and pretend it's all true. So it's fiction pretending to be history?'

'I never said I made up the half of it,' I corrected her respectfully. 'I never said that at all. What I said was I made up a bit here and there to connect things. Forged a few links.'

'Forged a history!' my mother took up my mischosen word. 'You're in a bit of a muddle, aren't you?'

'Not me. It's you. And you're one of my sources.'

'Do I get an acknowledgement in the preface?' she laughed at me. 'Or maybe a wee footnote?'

'You don't have to be funny about it,' I muttered, getting sour with her.

I had fully expected her to be a lot more interested than she had turned out to be. I should explain about her. In her well-earned widowhood she had become an addict of books from the public library. Of course it was me had to go and change them for her, even after I was married, while she sat alone, two up the faraway in the close where Wee Annie had lived, acting the duchess (with all the neighbours obliging and respectful because they thought her a real lady), and found fault with whatever I brought back. Yet she always read whatever I picked, because in fact I knew her taste well enough. The two things she couldn't stand were historical novels and books about archaeology. She was no fool, and I had a great regard for her intelligence, even now she was getting old and I was an educated young man. She had been in her time what we call here a nongraduate teacher. That is, she had been at school till she was in her late teens and then spent three years at a teachers' training college. That let her teach in primary schools till she married. That was her mistake. Marrying. Well, marrying who she did. Her standing insult to me was that I got more like my father every day. He had been the plague of her life for twenty years with his groundless vanity. He was an insurance salesman when she married him, earning enough to live on by tenement standards, but he had the gift of patter and he fancied himself as a freelance journalist, concocting funny bits for the local papers and comedy sketches for Scotch comics. His undoing came when a paper took a series of his humorous articles for its Saturday afternoon magazine page. It gave him ideas. Wrong ideas. He neglected his insurance canvassing. Then he chucked it altogether. He had to have a typewriter and paper. If it was a choice between our dinner and a new ribbon and a packet of quarto his new ribbon and the packet of quarto came first. The more he tried the less he got. He wrote a comic song for a Scotch comedian, a poor man's Harry Lauder, and thought it would open the doors to the Kingdom of Heaven. He was still waiting to be paid for it when he died. Scotch comics were like that then. None of the other comics who took a few pages of patter from him ever paid

much. He took to drinking to meet the right people. He
didn't. Like Shakespeare he died from a chill he got after
drinking too much. He fell coming up the stairs at one
o'clock in the morning and lay there drunk for a couple of
hours before my mother heard his groans. I had to help to
carry him upstairs. It was a blessed relief when I helped to
carry him downstairs again.

'You can't even write as well as your old dad,' my
mother would say any time I had a tenement-sketch
printed in some ephemeral Scots magazine. And in case
I missed the full venom she always added after the due
pause, 'and he couldn't write for toffee.'

'It's all very well for you to sit there and criticise,' I
complained. 'But there's more can be recovered from the
past than you think. When you consider all the sources
available today to modern scholarship.'

'Spare me,' she threw back. She couldn't be intimidated
that way. 'You're writing down what people said, aye, and
even what they thought, fifteen years ago or more. It's not
possible. You can't know the unknowable. I've told you
often, I'd rather read a life of Mary Queen of Scots than a
lot of tripe made up about her in a novel.'

'I quite agree,' said I. 'But Bobo's not Mary Queen of
Scots. And in any case, using my sources, I've still got to
mould the material, give it a shape, make it mean something, seize the essential behind the accidental. Create the
ideal form, find the objective correlative.'

'Then you ought to have made Bobo marry Hugh
Main.'

'Jesus, Mary and Joseph!' I cried. 'Spare us that! That's
you and your happy ending again. I'm surprised at you. A
woman of your intelligence.'

'Thanks,' she said, not in the least grateful. 'But I don't
know it would have been a happy ending. They'd probably
have been miserable in a year or two once Bobo got fat, and
she was always a bit lazy about the house. It's just the way
you put it you'd make people think they were all set to
discover they were in love.'

'Don't talk soft,' I got cross with her. 'I never meant such a thing. Those two could never have married. How could a doctor like Main, an assistant physician in a big hospital, marry a girl who worked in a ladies' underwear shop in Sauchiehall Street? And she never learned to stop saying I seen.'

'You're a right wee snob, aren't you?' my mother smirked at me. 'When you made up so much you might as well have made up they got married.'

'But it wouldn't have been true,' I argued. 'Dross was her man and she knew it. Lawrence's gypsy. But she thought the price too high, that was all. I'm sure she was stuck with him for all that, for a long time, in her mind. I couldn't possibly have seen her pick up with another man within the scope of my narrative. As it says in *Finnegans Wake*, tough troth is stronger than fortuitous fiction.'

'Don't tell me you've read *Finnegans Wake*!' my mother cried, popeyed incredulous. 'You like to impress folk, don't you? Well, you needn't bother trying to impress me. I'm only your mother.'

I sighed. She was a disputatious woman to talk to. She rolled my pages between her palms and shook her head.

'No, you may be right,' she said. 'But I still think I knew them better than you.'

'And you believe Main would have married Bobo?'

'I'm not saying I believe that in particular. But tell me, all those nights in the Phoenix, that last night especially. How did you know about it?'

'Tommy Partridge told me some of it. Dr Main told me bits.'

'Miss Partridge and her Papa calling on her at midnight?'

'It's in her diaries, as you very well know.'

'And how about the way poor Donald Duthie died? You were too young then to understand.'

'There's always talk. There's gossip you hear, and you take it in, and when you're older you make sense of it.'

'So gossip is one of your sources for a history essay?'

'Why not? You're just being awkward.'

'That long digression, what do they call it, a throwback? about Miss Partridge going to America and her troubles as a G.I. bride. You couldn't know a thing about that. Him being Yankee-doodle-randy and her being a Scotch prude. It was kind of tedious.'

'I could cut it out if you like,' I offered willingly. 'I don't like it myself.'

'Another thing, according to you, the holdup was all worked out in detail by Lillie and Arnott and Toby Owen. He broke his mother's heart, that one. A good-living widow with four of a family, lost her man with T.B. when they were all weans. Worked hard all her life for them. What makes you say Dross put them on to it from a joke was made about giving Miss Partridge a fright?'

'I got it from Tommy Partridge, and Dross told his probation officer, Mr Wylie, and Mr Wylie told me. I did some chasing on all this, you know.'

'Firsthand evidence,' my mother derided. 'Somebody told somebody that told somebody that told you.'

'Don't let's labour the point,' I pleaded. 'You pick any chapter you like and I'll give you my authority for it.'

'I don't doubt it,' she shrugged. 'You always were a devious little prig. A fly wee bugger as your father called you. Sitting in a corner with your nose in a book but aye listening to whatever was said, aye adding things up. But I don't trust your answers. Oh, I admit you know a lot. You even know Grace had toothache the night she threw the sweets away after cleaning out the house.'

'Naturally,' I said. 'Grace told me.'

'Aye, she would. And how is she?'

'She's fine,' I said. 'She sends her love.'

'And how's the baby?'

'Bouncing. More like you than like Grace.'

'I am the family face,' said my mother. 'I live on. And are you going to put that in too? A delicate echo of Jane Eyre. Reader, I married her.'

'No, I'm not. That's got nothing to do with it. I wouldn't have mentioned it if you hadn't.'

We sat silent awhile before I thawed enough to speak again.

'There's one thing still puzzles me. Those silly sweeties. Maybe the one she tampered with would only have made Grace sick. I don't know. But she meant to poison her. It's in the diary. What did she think when she came back and found Grace still living?'

'Oh, I can tell you that,' my mother answered gladly, pleased there was something I didn't know and she did. 'It's in the last diary, the one I didn't give you when Miss Partridge died.'

She rummaged in a drawer in the kitchendresser and read from a cash ledger.

'I was a bad, selfish, proud woman, presuming to do the work of the Lord for the Lord Himself, but the Lord giveth and the Lord taketh away, and salvation is only of the Lord, and He left Grace here on earth to light my way on my return from the valley of the shadow, and now I know my duty henceforth, to watch and pray and trust in the Lord to look after His own.'

'Give me that!' I cried snatching.

My mother held it behind her back.

'I gave you the others because Miss Partridge asked me to give you them when she died. She knew you were afraid of her. You often hurt her, you know, the way you behaved to her. She thought you might learn to understand her. But you've made such a dog's breakfast of what you got, you're getting no more. Not from me. When I'm dead you can have it.'

She planked it away in the drawer again, under a lot of other stuff, insurance policies, post-office savings, my father's manuscript gagbooks, her marriage-lines and her teacher's diploma.

'Do you want a cup of tea before you go?' she asked
pleasantly.

'Yes, please,' I said with due filial respect. I knew when
I was beaten.

And while she brewed the pot I stood at the window and
looked down on the silent backcourt. Like Wee Annie I
too had my ghosts. But they never came to me, glorified
and articulate, in a gaslit kitchen at midnight. No, they
wandered dumbly in and out my locked bedroom when I
lay awake in the small hours with a bad conscience, or they
came to me with frightened faces in unexpected nightmares, and every time I went to see my mother I remembered with sorrow a vanished culture of immemorial song
and dance and ritual play, a culture whose children had all
migrated in the endless shift of population to have children
of their own, alien offspring in mushroom suburbs. Susan
Greenwood and Angus Erskine had long since blasted off
into strange orbits. Susan had a regular part in an STV
kitchen-comedy series called *Up Oor Close*, and Angus
was on the Town Council. Wee Annie was dead on a
Sunday morning, four years after Tiger and his mates
tried to rob her, found sprawled on her door-step clutching a halfpint bottle of milk. A heart attack when she bent
to lift it. Dross went to England like all ambitious Scots-
men, last heard of in Pentonville. Bobo? I don't know. I
just don't know. The Bonnars moved out of the close and
went to the Scheme facing the Park when I was in my
middle teens, years after the Christies had gone, and I
never heard of Bobo again. She still wasn't married when
she left, and she used to talk to me quite a lot, though never
as much as she did to Main.

'Forget it,' said my mother, pouring the tea. 'You make
too much of it.'

'It's easy for you,' I said. 'But I can't forget it. Not just
like that. I still have nightmares. I'm still liable to be
chased any night in my dreams by Wee Annie.'

'Miss Partridge,' said my mother. 'You were jealous of
her because she was so fond of Grace, and you were afraid

Grace was going to get fond of her. But I expected you'd
marry Grace one day. It used to amuse me after the
Christies flitted, you couldn't keep off them. You always
dragged the conversation round to get on to Grace. And
how is she, and what's she doing, and when you were
older, has she a boyfriend. You pestered me for gossip.
You always did love gossip. And when you met her at the
university you got such a thrill. You came home here
looking as if you'd seen Venus rising from the sea.'

'I knew she was clever,' I said. 'But I didn't know she
had stayed on at school. Your gossip-service broke down,
remember? You couldn't even tell me she had taken her
Highers. You had some silly rumour she was working in
Wood and Selby's.'

'So she was for a time, a holiday job,' my mother
defended her information. 'I could see you were caught
when you came in that day. Childhood sweethearts! The
years rolled on and once again I met them, they stood
before the alter hand in hand.'

She sang and laughed.

'I could have done a lot worse,' I said loyally.

'I never said otherwise,' my mother retorted, making
the peace. 'I've nothing against Grace. A lot better her
than some of the other girls you picked up with. Do you
want me to read all this again and see if it sounds any better
the second time?'

'Don't bother, give me it back,' I said dourly. 'I'm sorry
you don't like it. But I still think that's how it was. And
with God's grace I'll write a story one day about the
tenement where I was born.'

MR ALFRED M.A.

A NOVEL

Part One

She passed for a widow when she went to Tordoch. She flitted across the river thinking nobody there would know her husband had left her. He was a longdistance lorrydriver, always coming or going and never saying much the few hours he was at home. He went to Manchester one day with a load of castings and vanished, lost and gone for ever, as untraced and untraceable as those banal snows some folk keep asking about. Not that she bothered to ask. She was a working-woman with a good overtime in the biscuit factory. She could do without his wages. The manless planet of her life moved round her son Gerald. He was Gerry to his schoolmates, but never to her. She always gave him his name in full. She thought it sounded right out the top drawer that way. That was why she chose it, though neither she nor her husband had ever any Gerald among their kin. She loved her Gerald fiercely. She loved him a lot more than she loved his little sister Senga. He was a good boy to her, but too kind and gentle perhaps, too innocent. She had always to be protecting him from the malice of the world. But that's what she was there for. He was tall for his age, blond and grinning. The girl was skinny, gingerhaired, crosseyed, freckled and nervous. She had loved her father because he used to cuddle her at bedtime. But after the row she got for asking where he was when they flitted she was afraid to mention his name again.

About a year later, say the week before Christmas, when she was turned eleven and Gerald was fourteen, he was thumping her hard because she wouldn't fry sausages for him at teatime, even after he told her twice. The anapaests of his bawling were hammered out by his punches.

'Aye, you'll do what I say and jump up when I speak for you know I'm your boss and you've got to obey.'

Eight scapular blows.

She whimpered and crouched, but she still defied him, and her mother came home earlier than expected and caught her red-eyed in the act. Gerald was glad to have a witness of his sister's disobedience and complained it wasn't the first time.

Mrs Provan stared at Senga, frightening her.

'You'd start a fight in an empty house you would,' she said. 'You bad little besom.'

She advanced speaking.

'You know damn well it's your place to make a meal for Gerald when I'm not in. I'm fed up telling you.'

Senga retreated silently.

Poised to jouk, right hand over right ear, left hand over left ear, her head sinistral, she borded the kitchensink in a defence of temporary kyphosis.

Mrs Provan halted.

Senga straightened.

'It was me set the table and made the tea,' she replied with spirit, confounding her mother and her brother in one strabismic glare. 'If he wants any more he can make it himself.'

'It's not a boy's place to go using a fryingpan,' said Mrs Provan. 'That's a girl's job. Your job.'

'It's him starts fights,' said Senga. 'Not me, It's him. Always giving orders.'

Her guard was dropped.

Her mother swooped and slapped her twice across the face, left to right and then right to left.

Gerald grinned.

Senga wept.

'I wish my daddy was here.'

Gerald chanted.

'Ha-ha-ha! Look at her, see! She wants to sit on her daddy's knee!'

'She'll wait a long time for that,' said Mrs Provan.

She put her arm round Gerald, ratifying their secret treaty, and Gerald rubbed his hip against her thighs.

Mr Alfred sagged at the bar, sipped his whisky and quaffed his beer, smiled familiarly to the jokes exchanged across the counter, and lit his fifth cigarette in an hour. His hand wavered to put the flame to the fag and his lips wobbled to put the fag to the flame. The man at his elbow chatted to the barmaid. The barmaid chatted to the man at his elbow. Propinquity and alcohol made him anxious to be sociable. He waited for an opening to slip in a bright word. After all, he knew the man at his elbow and the man at his elbow knew him. They had seen each other often enough. But neither admitted knowing the other's name, though he must have heard it countless times from Stella, who knew them all.

It grieved Mr Alfred. Sometimes he thought he was making a mistake frequenting a common pub with common customers and a common barmaid when he had nothing in common with them. In every pub he went to he recognised anonymous faces. For besides being a bachelor and a schoolmaster, a Master of Arts and the author of a volume of unpublished poems, the only child of poor but Presbyterian parents and now a middleaged orphan, he was a veteran pubcrawler. But it was his weakness to stand always on the fringe of company, smiling into the middle distance, happy only with a glass in his hand. He had been a wallflower since puberty. He wanted to love his fellow men. When he was young he even hoped to love women. Now every door seemed locked, and without a key he was afraid to knock.

Stella drew a pint. The beer was brisk. She brought the glass down slowly from the horizontal to the vertical. She was pleased with the creamy head on it, not too much, not too little. With pride she served her customer.

'There! How's that for a good top? See what I do for you!'

The man at Mr Alfred's elbow put a big hand round the pint-measure. He grinned.

'Nothing to what I could do for you.'

'Ho-ho,' said Stella. 'I'm sure.'

Her frolic smile said enough for a book on sex without fear. Mr Alfred caught a reprint tossed to him free. He jerked and fumbled for something to say. Distracted to find nothing, he missed what they said next. When they stopped laughing Stella turned to him as if he had heard.

'This man brings out the worst in me.'

Mr Alfred smiling tried again to find a mite to contribute. By the time he was ready to catch the speaker's eye she was slanted from him, sharing another joke with the man at his elbow. She ended it laughing.

'Aye, I know. The doctor says it's good for you.'

Mr Alfred meditated. Alcohol always made him meditate. His cigarette smouldered at an angle of fortyfive. There was a glow in his middle and a halo round his head. He was getting what he came out to buy. An anaesthetic between the week's drudgery behind and the week's drudgery ahead. Stella was his world for the moment. Stella and what she said and the way she said it. His daily thoughts assured him he was the victim of a coarse and even foul mind. He accepted it, as a redhaired man accepts his red hair. He was willing to believe Stella was never guilty of an equivocation and to blame himself for thinking her conversation was loaded with a wrapped freight of allusions to sexual intercourse. He wondered how he would get on if he tried to make love to her. But he had a good idea what would happen. Even if she ever gave him the chance he would muck it up somehow. He would be sitting an examination in a practical subject when all he had was a little book-learning. He drooped.

When he came out of his soulsearching the man at his elbow was turning to go.

'Good night, sir,' Stella called out, moving up from the other end of the bar to give him a wave.

'You never call me sir,' he said as she came level.

He thought his joking pretence of jealousy would amuse her.

Stella strolled down the bar again and threw him a vague smile over her shoulder. It said she heard him say something but didn't quite know what and didn't think it mattered.

He staggered out on the bell to wintry streets and shivered. Between tall tenements and down dark lanes, his cigarette out, he talked to himself. He criticised the chaste loneliness of his habits. He muttered Milton's question. He had a habit of thinking in quotations when he had a drink on him.

> Were it not better done as others use,
> To sport with Amaryllis in the shade,
> Or with the tangles in Neaera's hair?

When he recited the pleasant alternative suggested by the great puritan poet he remembered an old surmise that *with* should be *withe*, meaning *bind* or *pleat*. It seemed an idea worth lingering over. But at that point in his erotic meditation he was interrupted by a woman who had no resemblance to Amaryllis or any other nymph. She linked her arm in his.

'Coming home, darling?'

He recognised her as the reason for his wandering, and he knew the trembling of his lean body when he left the cosy pub was due less to the chill of a sleety wind than to the hope of finding her. But the moment she opened her mouth and touched him he was as empty as all the glasses he had drained. Still, with his usual politeness he answered insincerely, or with his usual insincerity he answered politely.

'Yes, of course.'

There was a public convenience, doublestaired, a dozen steps ahead. He disengaged his arm from hers with a gentlemanly apology.

'You wait here. I'll be right back.'

He descended, leaving her loitering at the top of the stairs. When he had emptied his bladder he returned to the street by the other staircase and weaved home to his single bed.

Two of Gerry's classmates collided at playtime. There were about four hundred colts running wild in a small area. Collisions and spills were common. Most often they led to nothing more than a vindictive shove and a corresponding push. But this time Gerry intervened. When the boys began their ritual snarling he jostled them. They tangled. He persuaded one of them to challenge the other. A square-go was fixed for four o'clock in the Weavers Lane. The news of the engagement circulated with a speed only slightly less than the speed of light, which is of course the maximum velocity at which any signal can be communicated in our universe, and Gerry was sure of a big attendance. He sprawled in Mr Alfred's class after playtime, dreamy with pride at being a fight-promoter. He put a pencil between his lips, took it out and exhaled.

'Is that a good cigar?' Mr Alfred asked, very sour.

He was lately finding the afternoons tiring. They sent a jangle of pain round his skull. He felt he was a foreigner trying to get across to people who didn't speak his language. The days when he enjoyed teaching seemed so far away he believed they belonged to somebody else.

Gerry rolled the cylinder between his fingers, tried to squeeze it, sniffed it, looked at it suspiciously.

'Aw sir, it's only a pencil,' he decided.

'Put it away,' said Mr Alfred.

Gerry tapped the end of the pencil on the desk as if he was stubbing a cigarette and set it down with hyperbolic care.

Mr Alfred gave him a hard look. But he had been teaching too long to go looking for trouble. He meant his glare to be enough to show he knew cheek when he saw it and wouldn't take any more.

He glanced at the textbook to check the place and resumed the lesson tabulated there for teacher and pupils. It was, in his opinion, a rather childish exercise in oral composition. But the boys seemed to find it difficult. They hadn't an answer to any question. They sickened him.

'They just sit there pandiculating,' he said to himself. 'Shower.'

From the day Collinsburn became a comprehensive school he had always been given the dullest classes. He resented it. The men who took the bright boys and girls to leaving-certificate level were all honours graduates. But he was sure he was as good as any of them, in spite of the fact he had only an ordinary degree. He was convinced he was better equipped to be Head of the English Department than the man in the job. He had read more widely. He had written prose and verse for the university magazine when he was a student. For a session he had been the magazine's most distinguished poet. He had his collection of unpublished poems behind him, and he kept up with modern poetry. Given the chance he knew he could inspire some good boys in fifth and sixth year with his own abiding love for literature. But the Principal Teacher of English, a portly man prematurely bald and Deputy Head Master, was just a dunce who had never written a poem in his life. He was only a teaching-machine during school hours, and outside them he was a non-smoker and teetotaller who read nothing.

Gerry had no loose change when it came his turn to make a donation to the begging composition. He shrugged, shook his head, and put his pencil-cigar back in his mouth.

Mr Alfred let it pass. He was thinking of the year he had to give up his honours course and settle for an ordinary degree. It was all because his father died suddenly and his mother mourned so much she became a bit unbalanced. He qualified quickly to get a job and bring some money

into the house. Then his mother went and died too. If they
had only lived another couple of years it would have made
all the difference to his status. To his prospects of promo-
tion. To his salary. To the classes he was given.

These cogitations on his misfortune occupied the back
of his mind while the front went on soliciting sentences for
the oral composition. A yelp from the pubescent anthro-
poid beside Gerry pulled the emergency cord that stopped
both trains. He stared at the startled animal.

'Hey sir, Provan stuck a pin into me.'

'Aw sir, I never,' Gerry declared.

Innocence and indignation sparkled in the young blue
eyes.

Mr Alfred walked slowly across the room, stood over
them both, glowered down, textbook canted.

'Show me,' he ordered Gerry.

'It's only a safety-pin,' said Gerald.

He opened his fist and showed it.

'It doesn't seem to have been very safe,' said Mr Alfred.
'What were you doing with it?'

'Taking it out my pocket,' said Gerry.

'Why?' said Mr Alfred.

'My braces is broke,' said Gerry. 'I was going to try and
sort them.'

'Oh yes?' said Mr Alfred.

'And McLetchie went and shoved his arm into me,' said
Gerry. 'You see, I had the pin opened, sir.'

He lolled back, smiling up.

'Wipe that smile off your silly face,' said Mr Alfred.

Gerry raised an open hand to his face and drew it down
over his nose and mouth. Took the hand away to reveal a
straight face. The bland insolence of the obedience provoked Mr Alfred. He smacked Gerry across the nape. He
knew at once he shouldn't have done it. But he damned the
consequences. It would soon be time for the peace of a
pub-crawl. He sketched an itinerary and wondered if he
should go and see Stella again or leave her alone for a bit.

Gerry rubbed the offended neck and drew back from

any further attack though none was threatened. Cowering he shouted.

'You're not supposed to use you hands. I'll bring my maw up.'

'Bring your granny too,' said Mr Alfred.

'Ya big messan,' said Gerry.

'You cheeky little rat,' said Mr Alfred, and smacked him again where he had smacked him before.

'I'll tell my maw you called me a rat,' said Gerry.

He crouched over his desk, sullenly puffing the forbidden pencil again.

'Oh, for goodness sake,' said Mr Alfred. 'Take that thing out of your mouth. Anybody would think you were a sucking infant.'

'Oh!' Gerry cried in delight. 'What you said! Wait till I tell my maw.'

The Weavers Lane was a good venue for a fight. Not far from the entrance it changed direction sharply, and twenty yards on it veered again before turning to the exit. Whatever went on between the zig and the zag couldn't be seen from either end. To make it still more suitable the centre stretch had a recess of stony soil where some dockens and dandelions maintained a squalid existence.

On one side of the lane: the back walls of Kennedy's soap factory, McLaren's garage, and Donaldson's paintworks. On the other: the palisade of the railway embankment.

But the fight was a flop. Gerry saw at once where he had gone wrong. He had matched a warmonger with a pacifist. In a minute it was no contest. McKay hit Duthie once, an uppercut wildly off target. Duthie reeled against the spectators. They shoved him back into the ring. He stumbled forward a couple of steps and stopped with his head down and his hands across his face, patiently waiting the next blow. Disgusted at the lack of style in his opponent McKay pushed rather than punched him and Duthie fell down. He lay there. He seemed to think he had done his bit and that was the show over. Gerry was annoyed.

'Get up and fight!' he shouted. 'You're yellow!'

To encourage Duthie to rise he kicked him three or four times in the ribs. He made it clear he had a great contempt for Duthie. But Duthie gave no sign of caring about anybody's opinion. He sprawled raniform in defeat and croaked upon an ugly docken. The happy boys and girls, four deep all the way round, jeered at his abjection.

Gerry sighed.

Duthie lay still, waiting and willing for death or the end of the world to come and release him from his agony. Neither event occurred at that particular moment, but his salvation came along in the shape of Granny Lyons, famous locally for the health and vigour of her old age. She used the Weavers Lane every day as a shortcut between her house and the shops, and she was never one to emulate the Levite if she saw a creature in distress. She broke the ring of fight-fans with a swing of her shopper, hoisted Duthie to his feet, and shook him alive again.

'You stupid wee fool! You should keep out of fights.'

Duthie wept.

'A skelf like you,' Granny Lyons comforted him. 'You're no match for McKay. Oh, I know him all right. And I know that Provan there too. Some bloody widow, that one's mother.'

The dispersed mob reformed at a goodly distance.

'Hey missis!' Gerry called out pleasantly. 'Yer knickers is hingin doon.'

He was hiding behind Jamieson and Crawford, and between the phrases he ducked from a shoulder of the one to an elbow of the other.

Granny Lyons measured them all with blazing eyes.

They retreated under her fire.

'Scum,' said Granny Lyons.

She paused, swinging her shopper, thinking.

'Human rubbish,' she shouted, and went on her way.

Duthie tagged behind her, though it meant he would have to take a detour home.

Gerry's disappointment with the fight stayed with him over teatime until his mother came in. Senga did nothing to make up for it. She obeyed all his orders without a word of complaint. He was a Roman slaveowner defeated by the humility of an early Christian. He tried to make her rebel so that he could batter her. She wouldn't break. She made his tea, kept the fire going, washed the dishes, cleaned his shoes, washed his socks, and switched the TV on and off and on again whenever he told her from the command-post of his armchair. He waited for his mother.

'Big Alfy hit me this afternoon,' he said before she was right in.

'Him again?' said Mrs Provan. 'He's always picking on you, that man.'

'Right across the face,' said Gerald. 'Hard. His big rough hand.'

Mrs Provan threw her handbag on a chair and hurried to him. She took his chin between thumb and forefinger and turned his face left and right, looking for a bruise.

'For nothing?' she asked like one who knows the answer.

'I bet you were giving up cheek,' said Senga unheeded.

'Yes,' said Gerald.

His mother stopped looking. She could see nothing. She was angry.

'I'll see about this. Teachers aren't allowed to use their hand. There's no hamfisted brute going to get away with striking my boy.'

'He called me a rat,' said Gerald. 'And he used a bad word. He said I was a so-and-so-king infant.'

'Oh, he did, did he?' said Mrs Provan. 'Well, I'll call him worse when I see him. And see him I will. First thing tomorrow. Some teacher him, using that language. You leave it to me, Gerald. You're not an orphan. You've got your mother to protect you.'

Granny Lyons had a room-and-kitchen near the prison. It was on the ground floor of the Black Building. She sat knitting by the fire and waited for Mr Alfred. The little clock on the mantelpiece ticked away between Rabbie Burns and Highland Mary. Often he just posted the money, not always with a letter. But once the dark nights came in he called about once a month.

'It's only a couple of days now till Christmas,' she remarked to her needles. 'He'll come tonight.'

He did. In his oldest clothes. A wilted hat on his head, a muffler round his neck, a stained raincoat hiding a jacket that didn't match his trousers, shoes needing to be re-heeled.

'You should wear dark glasses too,' she cut at him, 'and finish it.'

He smiled. Her he would always conciliate. He spoke flippantly of his appearance.

'So! You don't like my disguise? But then you never do.'

'No,' she said. 'That's a fact. I never do.'

He saw the china-poet look at his sweetheart. He imagined they were avoiding his eyes in case they let him see they didn't like the way he was dressed.

'You think your boys won't recognise you?' she asked him. 'Sure they'd know you a mile away.'

'Not in the dark,' he answered. 'And I slip round the corner quick.'

'I don't know why you bother at all if you're that ashamed,' she said.

'That's not a nice thing to say. You know perfectly well I'm not ashamed.'

'You should get a transfer to another school. Then nobody here would know you.'

'It's too late for that. It's you should never have come here.'

'I was here before you. It was the only place I could get when I lost the shop. You know that.'

They were both silent then, remembering many things. He spoke first.

'It's quite mild outside tonight.'

'Aye, it's not been bad at all today. For the time of year.'

'The street's very quiet for once.'

'You mean nobody saw you? I think your trouble is you get frightened coming here.'

'I suppose I do. But you know what they'd do if they saw me. Hide in a close and yell after me. Something obscene probably.'

'I had a feeling you'd be round tonight.'

'Well, I thought, seeing it's Christmas. I've brought you something.'

He gave her a bottle of whisky as well as the usual money.

'I know you like your dram,' he said.

'Not any more than yourself.'

She poured him a drink. The quantity showed she wasn't a mean woman.

'You have one too,' he said.

'Well, seeing it's Christmas.'

'To my favourite aunt,' he said.

'The only auntie you've got now,' she replied to his toast, unflattered.

'The only one I ever really knew. My mother's favourite sister you were. And it was you helped me when I was a student. Don't think I forget.'

'I had money then I haven't got now.'

'If you need any more you've only to tell me.'

'No, you give me plenty. You shouldn't bother.'

'I promised my mother. Anyway, I owe you it. For the time you paid my fees if nothing else.'

'Well, as I say, I had it then. It was a good shop I had before all that trouble. And there was nobody else to give it to.'

'Is your clock slow?'

'No, it's right. Are you in a hurry?'

'Not particularly.'

'Not particularly? You mean you want to get away round the pubs?'

'I'm not desperate. I was just thinking. It was you gave me my first glass of whisky.'

'I always did my best for you.'

They laughed together.

'I suppose it will be a lot of low dives tonight, in that coat,' she said.

'I suppose so. I like to mix with the common people sometimes. You know, go around incognito.'

He laughed alone.

'You still never think of getting married?' she asked suddenly.

'If a man thinks about it he won't,' he said. 'I mean, you either do or you don't. You don't think about it.'

'You think too much. You should let yourself go. Get a good woman and marry her and get out of those digs you're in.'

'I'm too old for that now.'

'A man's never too old for that.'

'I'm happier away from women,' he said.

He elevated his glass sacramentally and plainchanted.

'The happiest hours that e'er I spent were spent among the glasses-O!'

They communicated in silence after she poured another drink. The little clock went on ticking patiently because there was nothing else it could do. Mr Alfred said into himself the first line of a poem he had lately read, 'The house was quiet and the world was calm'. It called up the small hours when he used to read poetry alone in his room and write little poems for himself. He was taken back, at peace with a glass in his hand and a verse in his head.

From a distance a merry cry rocked in the street. It rode
above an advancing babble and rolled under the window.

'Haw, Granny Lyons!'

Repeated.

Chanted loudly, chanted slowly.

'Et ô ces voix d'enfants,' said Mr Alfred, 'chantant
dans . . .'

But he was frightened.

'I've been expecting them,' said Granny Lyons.

She was calm. Mr Alfred was shaking. He forgot his
whisky. There was an edge on the antiphonal voices now.

'Granny Lyons, ye auld hoor!'

'Sounds like Wilma,' said Granny Lyons.

'Why do they call you granny?' said Mr Alfred, fretting.
'I've never understood that.'

'No idea,' said his aunt, shrugging. 'They always have.
Since the day I came here. I've been old witch and old
bitch and old granny. Doesn't bother me.'

'Here!' yelled a girl outside. 'Here's your Christmas
coming up!'

'Jennifer!' said Granny Lyons. 'Quick!'

She stepped smartly to one side of the window and
signalled Mr Alfred to get to the other.

First, a hail of stones against the glass. Next, a long rude
ring at the doorbell. Mr Alfred turned to answer it.

'Don't move,' Granny Lyons whispered.

The window imploded. A half-brick landed in the
centre of the room bringing glass with it. Then the gallop
away of the colts and fillies. The whinnying faded.

Mr Alfred stared dumfouttered at the inexplicable half-
brick lying mutely on his aunt's old carpet.

'They're getting worse,' said Granny Lyons.

'Anarchy,' said Mr Alfred. 'Mere anarchy is loosed
upon the world. Things fall apart.'

He was pale with fright.

'I chased a crowd of them out the back-close last night,'
said Granny Lyons. 'Boys and girls. And still at school
most of them.'

'You know who they are?' said Mr Alfred. 'Tell me their names and I'll go to the police.'

'Don't talk soft,' said Granny Lyons. 'Do you think the police would welcome you? What could you prove?'

'But you said you were expecting them. Have they been threatening you?'

'They told me they'd be back. If you can call that a threat. I'm as broadminded as the next person but I'm not putting up with houghmagandy in my back-close.'

'I wish you'd get out of this district,' said Mr Alfred.

'Where could I go? Anyway, it's the same everywhere now.'

'I suppose so,' said Mr Alfred.

'It's my own fault,' she said. 'I ask for it. I should mind my own business. Let them take over. It's their world now. But I never learn. That fight I stopped this afternoon. I should have walked on.'

'What fight?' he asked.

She told him about it while they tacked double sheets of newspaper across the frame of the broken window.

'Some of them were your boys,' she said. 'That big lump Provan was there. One of Wilma's boyfriends.'

'He's kind of young to be anybody's boyfriend,' said Mr Alfred.

'He's her age,' said Granny Lyons. 'She's at your school. Don't you know her? Wilma Beattie.'

'Can't say I do,' said Mr Alfred. 'But then I don't take girls' classes.'

'I've chased the pair of them out that back-close more than once,' said Granny Lyons. 'Ah well! As God made them he matched them!'

Mrs Provan put on her Sunday coat and went to the school. She saw the headmaster at nine o'clock.

'I'm very angry about this, Mr Briggs,' she said. 'I don't mind anyone chastising my boy if he deserves it. But there's a right way and a wrong way.'

A ruffled hen laying a complaint and making a song about it.

Mr Briggs listened carefully. He was a judicious little man, not long promoted. His brother had recently married a widow on the town council. He was perfectly happy signing the janitor's requisitions and sending instructions round his staff in civil-service English and a neat hand. Other clerical activities were used to keep him from working and allow him to claim he had a lot to do every day. He liked talking to parents because that too occupied his time to the exclusion of less sedentary duties.

Mrs Provan ended her aria on a high note of horror.

'But to slap a boy across the face for nothing! That's something I won't have. No!'

'Ah now come, it couldn't have been for nothing, surely it must have been for something.'

The tenor responded to the soprano, and continued piano.

'I don't mean I condone striking a pupil. Oh no, on the contrary. But on the other hand, I can't believe a man walked up to a boy and suddenly hit him for nothing right out of the blue. I mean to say, it doesn't sound a very likely story. Now does it, Mrs Provan?'

His forearms on the desk, his stainless fingers laced, he leaned forward on his magisterial swivelchair as if he was the Solomon of David's royal blood who had to decide how far maternal affection could influence veracity.

'Surely the boy must have given some provocation,' he coaxed her.

'No, none, I assure you,' said Mrs Provan. 'I have Gerald's word for it. And Gerald never tells lies. He's a good boy.'

'Yes, I'm sure,' said Mr Briggs.

'And even if he did that's not the point,' said Mrs Provan.

'Even if he did?' Mr Briggs looked at her in shocked reproach. 'Did tell lies?'

'Give provocation,' said Mrs Provan. 'A teacher's not supposed to lift his hand to a boy. And to call him a rat, well! As a matter of fact it was worse than that.'

'Oh yes?' said Mr Briggs.

'He used a bad word. He called Gerald a so-and-so rat, not just a rat. Poor Gerald wouldn't even repeat the word. But you and me can guess what he said. I ask you! What kind of language is that for a man supposed to be educated?'

'The question is, what did he say exactly?' said Mr Briggs.

Always discreet he used initials only.

'Did he say a bee rat or an effing rat?'

'An effing rat,' Mrs Provan sent word down from remote control.

'I find it hard to believe,' said Mr Briggs. 'Still, if that's what you say. Leave it with me and I'll speak to the teacher.'

'No, I want to see him myself,' said Mrs Provan. 'I want an apology.'

Mr Briggs tried a weak inoculation of sarcasm.

'In writing?'

It was a mistake. It didn't take.

'Not necessarily,' said Mrs Provan. 'But I insist on seeing him for myself.'

'I'm afraid you can't,' said Mr Briggs. 'I think it would

only make things worse. You're too much upset for me to let you see anybody.'

'Of course I'm upset,' said Mrs Provan. 'So would you be upset in my place. I've had to take the morning off my work to come here. It's costing me half a day's wages. Just because of a big bully that's not fit for to be a teacher.'

'You mustn't say things like that,' said Mr Briggs. 'It could land you in trouble. He's fully qualified and very experienced.'

'Aye, so's ma granny,' said Mrs Provan.

Mr Briggs unlaced his fingers and leaned back. He saw no use discussing Mrs Provan's grandmother.

'It broke my heart to come to Tordoch at all,' said Mrs Provan. 'But I couldn't get a house anywhere else. Everybody knows it's the lowest dregs of the city lives down there. But don't you go thinking I'm from a slum like the rest of them because I'm not.'

'Nobody ever said you were,' said Mr Briggs.

He was tired of hearing parents tell him they weren't like the rest of the folk in Tordoch. He was tired of Tordoch and all its inhabitants. Once it was a lovers' walk on the rural margin of the city. Then it became a waste land of bracken and nettles surrounded by a chemical factory, gasworks, a railway workshop and slaghills. At that point the town council took it over for a slum-clearance scheme. They built a barrack of tenements with the best of plumbing and all mod cons and expected a new and higher form of civilisation to flare up by spontaneous combustion.

But the concentration of former slum-tenants in such a bleak site led in a few years to the reappearance of the slum they had left. The first native generation grew up indistinguishable from the first settlers and produced their likeness in large numbers. The fathers had no trade or profession. The mothers were bad managers, and worn out by childbearing they looked fifty when they were barely thirty. The untended children lived a life of petty feuding and thieving, nourished by free milk and free dinners at school when they weren't truanting.

There was a constant shift of population. But there too Gresham's Law operated. The scheme became a pool where sediment settled.

Further out, on the country road, there were half a dozen big houses owned by professional and retired men, and between them and Tordoch proper there were some streets of tidy new villas. Since they had never been part of any housing-scheme these people objected if anyone accused them of living in Tordoch. Regretting the present, they turned to the past. A local historian claimed to have found the name Tordoch in a twelfth-century register of bishopric rents. An amateur etymologist said the name came from the Gaelic *torran*, a hill or knoll, and *dubh* or *dugh*, signifying dark or gloomy, implicitly ascribing a touch of the Gaelic second-sight to those who had first named the place. For now indeed it was a black spot. The police knew it as a nexus of thieves and resettlers.

Mrs Provan wasn't bothered about these matters. She had her own grievance.

'It's the way that man treats Gerald,' she said. 'Like he was dirt. He's got the boy frightened for him, so he has.'

'Oh, I don't think so,' said Mr Briggs.

'I come from a good family,' said Mrs Provan. 'And I rear a good family. And that's without a husband at my back. I'm a hardworking widow I am. Not one of your Tordoch types, neither work nor want.'

'Oh no, I can see that,' said Mr Briggs.

'I'm very angry about this,' said Mrs Provan.

Duet da capo.

He got rid of her after the third time round without letting her see Mr Alfred. He never let a parent see a teacher. He knew it would only end in a slanging match. No teacher could soothe angry mothers the way he could.

By that time it was morning break. His secretary brought in coffee and a biscuit.

'My goodness, Miss Ancill, is it that time already?' he greeted her.

Over his frugal refreshment, for he never stopped working, he told Miss Ancill what Mrs Provan had said to him and what he had said to Mrs Provan, and while he spoke and drank and nibbled he sorted an accumulation of forms intended for transmission to the Director. Amongst them he saw an application signed A. Ramsay for free meals for his family, six girls and four boys. Against *Occupation* the applicant had written 'unemployed'.

'They're all unemployed round here,' he muttered through his biscuit. 'Unemployed and unemployable.'

'Well, what with the family allowance and benefit it's hardly worth their while,' said Miss Ancill.

'Should be occupation father,' said Mr Briggs, and sipped.

He read the financial statement aloud. Weekly total, twenty-one pounds seventeen shillings.

'And they talk about unearned income,' he said.

'It's not the upper ten today have unearned income. It's the layabouts. That's your welfare state for you.'

'Some folk play on it,' said Miss Ancill. 'But you can't just do away with it.'

'Aye, the poor we have always with us,' said Mr Briggs. 'Do you know, there's a child born every two seconds. I read that somewhere the other day.'

'Quite a thought,' said Miss Ancill.

'The trouble here,' he said, 'it's the men of course. They never get a trade. Or even a steady job. They work as vanboys when they leave school, then they're casual labourers. They earn just enough to start courting. Then they marry young and the children come and keep on coming. So the man sits back and stops working. They're not working-class, these people. They're just lumps.'

'You can't stop them marrying,' said Miss Ancill.

Mr Briggs changed the subject.

'Phone the police and tell them I want a policeman for the Ballochmyle Road crossing. The trafficwarden's absent.'

After lunch he reprimanded Mr Alfred for striking a pupil and advised him to be careful what he said in class. Mr Alfred denied he had used bad language, but Mr Briggs had never expected him to admit it. He smiled and nodded and let it pass.

In the afternoon Mrs Duthie came and complained that a boy called Provan had forced her son into a fight and then kicked him when he was down. She had taken the boy to the doctor. The doctor would certify the boy's ribs were all bruises. Mr Briggs said he would speak to Provan about it. He said it was a pity she hadn't called at nine o'clock. He would have found that information about Provan useful if he had known it earlier. She said she couldn't have called at nine o'clock because she had a part-time job, mornings only, in the Caballero Restaurant. That led her to tell him about her husband, who hadn't worked for ten years. He was under the doctor on account of his heart. Mr Briggs gave her his sympathy and they parted on excellent terms.

When she had gone he littered his desk with requisitions, class lists, publishers' catalogues, and the unfinished draft of a report on a probationer. He wanted to look busy if anyone came in.

Miss Ancill disturbed him with a cup of tea and a buttered scone. He told her what Mrs Duthie had been saying to him and what he said to her. He was on about the cares and loneliness of office when the bell rang. He hurried out to his car.

Miss Ancill watched him go. She knew all the little jobs that had kept him busy since nine o'clock. She counted them off to the janitor.

'A day in the life of,' she said. 'And the way he blethers to me! It's not a secretary that man wants, it's an audience.'

In the staffroom Mr Alfred raised his voice about the headmaster's bad habit of dealing with parents behind a teacher's back. His colleagues were too eager to get out to listen, and he finished up talking to the soap as he washed his hands.

He was the last to leave. Miss Ancill saw him from her window.

'That poor man,' she said. 'I felt sorry for him today. Briggs had him on the carpet. I think he's getting past it. But still. It's not right. A man like Briggs bossing a man like that. He's so kind and gentle.'

'I think he drinks too much,' said the janitor.

'He needs a woman to take care of him,' said Miss Ancill. 'Did you see the shirt he'd on this morning? Wasn't even fit for a jumble sale.'

'You can't spend your money on drink and buy clothes too,' said the janitor.

Leaving school on a fine spring evening Mr Briggs had to go home by public transport. His car was laid up. There was something wrong with the clutch. He felt devalued. It was a long time since he last stood in a bus queue with ordinary people, some of whom in this case would be merely assistant teachers on his own staff. He was in a mood to find fault with the universe. Opportunity to let off steam was waiting ahead of him. En route to the bus stop he passed the Weavers Lane. A fankle of weedy boys loitered there in a state of manifest excitement. Mr Briggs was quick to appreciate the situation. There was something in the wind, and it wasn't the smell of roses. Obviously a fight had been arranged and was due to begin as soon as the coast was clear. The guilt in the shifty eyes of his pupils showed they hadn't expected him to come along. He stopped and scowled. He knew them all. His habit of checking against his index-cards whenever a boy came to his notice had made him familiar with their names, their intelligence quotient, their father's occupation if any, and their address. He knew the good boys from the bad boys, though sometimes he believed the former category was an anomaly, as if one should speak of a square circle.

There they were. All the rascals. A dingy mob in jeans and donkey-jackets. Black, Brown, Gray, Green, White. With McColl, McKay, McKenzie, McPherson. He recognised Taylor, Slater, Wright and Barbour, Baker [and Bourne], Hall [and Knight], Latta [and MacBeath], Liddel [and Scott], Ogilvie [and Albert], Gibson, Holmes, MacDougall and Blackie. A nightmare of classroom names. And lounging blondly, somehow the centre of the shapeless crowd, was Gerald Provan. He grinned, hands in the pockets of his tightarsed jeans, kicking the kerb, radiant with the insolence of an antimath idling out his last term at school.

Sure of his power, speaking in loco parentis, since after all they were barely outside the limits of his bailiwick and the bell releasing them from his jurisdiction had barely ceased vibrating across the gasworks, he demanded the why and wherefore of their hanging about. He waited for an answer. None was offered. Sternly he ordered them to disperse.

'Get home! All of you! At once!'

Curt. Staccato.

Slowly, grudgingly, they went. He stood till they were all on the move.

He went for his bus, pleased with himself. Perhaps the universe wasn't so unjust after all. He wished some of his teachers would learn to put into their voice the same ring of authority as he had done there. The bus was prompt, he got a seat at once, and within half-an-hour he was safe and sound at home. He had a sandstone villa, with garden and garage, outside the city. Over dinner he told Mrs Briggs all the events of his day and what he had done about them.

But no sooner was he round the corner from the Weavers Lane than the scattered boys reassembled. Like birds chased from a kitchen garden they hadn't flown far.

Last to leave the school, Mr Alfred took the same route to the bus stop as Mr Briggs. He had lingered longer than usual in the staffroom to give Mr Briggs plenty of time to get away. He always found it a bore having to make conversation on the bus, especially with someone who talked shop as loudly as his headmaster.

When he came to the Weavers Lane he heard a lot of shouting. He stopped and listened. He wasn't even tempted to walk away. He was oldfashioned, and he believed without doubting it was his duty to break up any riotous assembly of schoolboys, whether in school or out of school, during hours or after hours. And anyway he was in no hurry. If he put off time he would be in the city centre when the pubs were opening. Then he could have one or maybe two before going on to his digs. For the evening he had already planned a route that would take him round some pubs he hadn't been in for a month or so.

He put on a grim face and went deep into the lane. What he saw wasn't a storybook fight with bare fists. It was a battle with studded belts that had once been part of what the army called webbing equipment. His belly fluttered at the madness of it. He was as scared as if he was in there taking part. So excited were the spectators, encouraging Cowan and Turnbull with a good imitation of the Hampden Roar, that Mr Alfred was left standing behind them in the same situation as the three old ladies locked in the lavatory. Nobody knew he was there.

Besides swinging the heavy belt in a highly dangerous manner Cowan used an unpredictable skill, not without its own vicious grace, in getting inside the range of Turnbull's equally heavy belt and endeavouring to kick his opponent in the testicles.

In one of those attempts he lost his balance, the belt arched from his hand, and he fell unarmed to the ground. The recoil of evasive action brought Turnbull over his prostrate foe. Naturally he kicked him. Then things happened so quickly Mr Alfred was never quite sure what he saw.

It appeared that Gerald Provan moved out of the mob behind Turnbull, raised his knee swiftly in a politic nudge, sent Turnbull sprawling beside Cowan. The two fighters scrambled up clinching. They wrestled into the crowd, and the crowd pushed them back into the ring. In that surge and sway Gerald Provan thrust a knife into Cowan's hand and then shoved him off to continue the duel.

At that point Mr Alfred broke out of his paralysis. Partly he had been curious to see just what the two boys would do, partly he was afraid of raising his voice too soon and not being heard above the howling of the fans. But when it was seen that Cowan had a knife there was a breathless hush in the lane that night and Mr Alfred knew his moment was come. Cowan lunged, Turnbull dodged, and Mr Alfred spoke out loud and clear.

'Stop that!'

His voice scattered most of the onlookers. They had no wish to be involved. Turnbull froze. Cowan threw the knife away and with coincident speed dissolved into the melting crowd. Provan tried to make a quick getaway by diving behind Mr Alfred. It was a blunder. Mr Alfred caught him on the turn and held him by the collar. Gerald wriggled.

'Hey, mind ma jacket, you! Ma clothes cost good money, no' like yours.'

Mr Alfred shook him and threw him away.

'I'll see you tomorrow,' he said.

He saw the knife lying on top of a docken on the margin of the arena. He picked it up and put it in his pocket. He thought it was evidence.

It must not be supposed that the boys and girls gathered in the Weavers Lane that night were a fair representation of the pupils attending Collinsburn Comprehensive, the only school in Tordoch for post-primary education. Collinsburn was a local place-name, derived from the legend that a stream once ran through that part of Tordoch formerly owned by a Collins family whose members, like the vanished burn, had long gone underground. As a comprehensive school Collinsburn harboured all kinds and ages (mental and chronological). So while Mr Alfred was shaking Gerald Provan, Graeme Roy was sitting with Martha Weipers in Ianello's cafe round the corner from the main road. It was a roomy, almost barnlike place, that sold cigarettes and sweets and ices and offered half-a-dozen stalls where the young ones could sit with a coffee or a coke and criticise the world.

Graeme Roy was eighteen, in his last year at school. Martha was a year younger and not as clever as he was. At least, that's what she thought. She even found pleasure in believing it. They should have gone straight home, but they had got into the habit of using Ianello's for half-an-hour.

They were under parental orders to stop meeting. Their daily sessions in the cafe after school gave them the satisfaction of at once obeying and ignoring the order. They no longer met in the evenings, so they were obedient. But they still managed to meet for a little while on the way home, so they evaded the full severity of the law.

She was the poor one, the eldest of seven, a bricklayer's daughter. He was an only son and well-off, a handsome youth. He had a driving licence and a car of his own. He used to take Martha out for a run in the summer evenings after the exams were over. When the quartet of parents found out what was going on they slammed down hard on the pair of them. Graeme's folks had never thought he was taking a girl out when he used his car, and Martha's had no idea she had a rich boyfriend. Nasty suspicions were aroused, some accusations were made that hurt and even shocked them, and then the forthright veto was proclaimed. Without collusion, without ever meeting, the two sets of parents reacted in the same way and came to the same conclusion. His parents said only a girl with no self-respect would accept an invitation to go out alone with a boy in his car. Her parents said no decent right-thinking boy would ask a girl to come out alone with him in his car. Unless of course, both sides conceded independently, the boy and girl were engaged. Which would be absurd at their age. Further meetings, with or without the car, were bilaterally banned. It was for their own good their parents said.

'They try to tell us we're too young,' he said.

'That's how they see it,' she said. She was a fairminded girl. 'They're so old. My dad's nearly forty.'

'But that's not the real reason,' he said. 'It's my mother. I hate to say it. But she's an awful snob. She thinks because your father works with his hands I shouldn't talk to you. I told her a surgeon works with his hands, but she wouldn't listen.'

'My dad's the same,' she said. 'He won't listen. He thinks if folks are well-off they must be on the fiddle. Because your father's got a car and could buy you one too my dad's sure he's a crook.'

'Oh, my father's honest enough,' he said. 'He wouldn't cheat anybody.'

'My dad would cheat anybody for five bob,' she said. 'For all his supposed principles. That's the funny thing.'

'My dad wouldn't,' he said. 'But then five bob's nothing

to him. It's my mother's the trouble. She's hard. A lot harder than my father. It's my mother I blame.'

'My mother doesn't count in our house,' she said, and added with a young laugh, 'and she doesn't read either.'

He smiled. He was happy. He liked to see her laugh when she was with him. He didn't like it when he saw her laugh in any other company.

They got on well. They never had any difficulty talking. There were never any silences. They tore their parents to bits, and put the bits together again with the quick adhesive of filial tolerance. They were two earnest adolescents, able to vary their solemn dialogue with a private joke. They had the same liking for the depreciatory aside, the same bias on current affairs, the same cynical tone when they talked about their teachers. Never before, in all their long experience, had they felt such affinity with anyone else.

The first time she met him he liked her. It was at the inaugural meeting of the Debating Society. Mr Briggs had started it with a view to entering a team in an annual inter-schools debate. There was a big silver cup for the winning school and a plaque for the runners-up, and he thought either would look rather well beside the football trophies in the display cabinet at the Main Entrance. Maisie Munro, a beaming jumbo of a girl with glasses, who lived near Graeme, introduced them. She was a prefect in Martha's class.

'This is Graeme,' she said. 'You know, the famous Roy.'

He was famous at that time because he had scored a goal that put Collinsburn into the semi-final of the City Cup, but Martha didn't know that. She had no interest in football.

'Tell me,' she said when Maisie left them stuck alone together in a corner, 'is your name Graham Roy or Roy Graham?'

'Not Graham,' he said. 'Graeme.'

He made one syllable where she made two. Her speech was looser than his. She was more Scotch, he was more anglified. She was apt to say fillim for film, to make no distinction between hire and higher. She could even insert a neutral vowel between the two consonants at the end of warm and learn and such words. It was the way she trilled the r made her do it. Sometimes it offended his ear, but his heart didn't mind.

'Graeme,' he repeated to her stare. 'Not Graham.'

'However you say it,' she retorted, 'you still haven't said if it's your first name or your second.'

She wasn't put out by his correction. Far from it. She was amused. He was so tidy, trim, well-dressed and superior, and spoke so correctly.

Her levity pleased him. He explained. His father's name was John Barbour Roy, his mother's name was Alison McKenzie Graeme. They had the egalitarian idea of calling him Graeme Roy, so that each would contribute their share to his name as they had already done to his existence. Later on, when he knew her better, he confessed that his mother's name was really Graham but she thought Graeme was a more stylish version.

From the night they met at the Debating Society he began to look out for her and she looked out for him looking out for her. They grew in affection with the growing season. He had to tell her everything. He wasn't boasting. He just had to tell her. He didn't want to hide anything. He told her his father was a director in an engineering firm, he told her his mother was the graduate daughter of a defunct Conservative M.P. He described the big house where he lived. It was in an old-world residential outpost, an Edwardian if not Victorian survival from the days when Tordoch was still rural. His parents weren't happy to have him attending Collinsburn. They regretted not moving him to a fee-paying school in the west end when Collinsburn changed from a local Academy to a regional Comprehensive. But he was so near his exams for university entrance it seemed best to leave him where he was.

He mentioned one of his mother's complaints. She was

brought up in a house with a maid that lived in, and now she couldn't get anything better in her own house than an unreliable daily-help, a dismal widow who scamped the work.

In class-conscious retaliation Martha gave him an account of her domestic troubles. She had to do it all herself.

'It's worst in the winter. I'm up at six in the morning. Oh my, oh my, it's that cold! And it's that dark! I've to get the fire lit and start making my dad's porridge and give him a shout but he won't get up till I've got the fire going. Then when I've got rid of him I get my three young sisters up and make their breakfast and while they're taking their cornflakes I get my two wee brothers up and after I've got them dressed and fed and got them ready for school I get Jean up and wash her and dress her. Jean's only three. And by that time I've got to get myself ready for school.'

'But what's your mother doing?' he asked.

'She stays in bed till I take her a cup of tea before I go out,' said Martha. 'She's a poor soul really. She doesn't keep well. She gets up when we're all away and looks after Jean.'

He brimmed with pity and fell in love.

But let's have no misunderstanding. Although she was Martha and not Mary she never felt sorry for herself. She never saw herself as Martha in Beth-ania, the House of Care. She was no spiritless drudge, no pallid, thinlegged, flatchested, dullfaced little skivvy, but a lively, chatty, slim, brighteyed, clearskinned young blonde, promising at seventeen to be what blondes are vulgarly supposed to be anyway, that is, lushus – if she lived long enough.

'It must be interesting,' he said, not quite insincerely. 'Being one of a big family.'

'It's a bit of a bind at times,' she said. 'You never get any peace. You're never alone. I'd love to be alone once in a while.'

They were sitting there in Ianello's, quite content, with a coffee in front of them. Sometimes their hands touched across the table as they spoke, but they never actually held hands. He made no show of affection in public, nor did she. They despised teenagers that did. They considered themselves older, more mature.

Their conversation was disturbed by the loud entrance of Gerald Provan and his company.

'See me in the morning, says he,' Gerald was shouting as he came in. 'I'll fix him, the auld grey bastard! I'll get ma maw on to him again. She sorted him last time all right.'

'Oh dear,' said Martha.

'What are you laughing at, Poggy?' said Gerald. 'Think I'm feart for him?'

'Ach, him!' Poggy shouted, shoulder to shoulder with him at the counter. 'Who's feart for him? It's a kick on the balls he needs.'

He was a big lad, Gerald's loyal bondman.

Enrico Ianello came flustered from the backshop, fluttered at them, wanting peace and quiet, good business with decorum. His parents had left Naples with similar ambitions for the unattainable. He was a smallish man, plump, darkeyed, darkskinned, a bit of a singer when he was in the mood. He had a good moustache and a double chin. Mr Alfred said he looked like Balzac. Granny Lyons had never seen Balzac, but she liked Enrico and hoped her nephew was being kind.

'Where's Smudge?' Gerald called out, turning round to face his followers.

'They didn't used to come here,' Graeme whispered.

A thin little swarthy miasmal wraith of a boy joined Gerald at the counter.

'Here, boss,' he grinned. His teeth were yellow and deficient.

'Good lad,' said Gerald.

'Did you see him pick up the knife?' Smudge shouted.

'They're taking over,' said Martha.

'I bet you he tries to say it was me had it,' Gerald shouted back.

'You'd think they were across the street from each other, the way they shout,' said Graeme.

'I'll say you never,' Poggy shouted. 'Don't worry, pal.'

'Let's get outa here,' said Martha. 'As they say on those old fillims on the telly.'

They rose at once together. They were always en rapport. They went out, backed by a medley of jeering farewells from their comprehensive juniors.

'Ta-ta, toffee-nose.'

'Wur we annoying you, blondie?'

'Gie us a wee kiss, sugar-lumps!'

Poggy knew her name. He jumped, waving to her.

'Hey, Martha Weipers! If I get a car will ye come oot wi me?'

She went red in the face.

'Hoy! Windscreen-wipers! D'ye no hear me?'

Graeme held the door open, head up, and handed her out.

They stood a while fretting at the bus stop where Mr Briggs had waited half-an-hour earlier.

'I'm not going back there,' she said. 'It's getting worse.'

'Where else can we go?' he asked.

'I don't know. But don't ask me to go back there.'

She looked so upset he made up his mind to persuade her to meet him at night as she used to do.

It probably doesn't matter, but in case you think this is all made up here are the names and ages of Martha's brothers and sisters. ['The bricks are alive at this day to testify it; therefore deny it not.']

Mary, 15.

Rose, 12 [who has her own place in this true narrative, and of whom Martha once said to Graeme, 'She's a bit dopey. Dreamy I mean. I don't think she'll ever be a great scholar. But she's quite pretty. And awfully good-natured. Do anything for anybody.'].

Christine, 10.

Angus, 8.

Billy, 6.

Jean, 3.

Martha looked after them all. Her mother was married at twenty-two, so she was thirty-six when Jean was born. She wasn't an unintelligent woman, but bearing seven children had sapped her strength, rearing them had narrowed her mind, and the hard years had discouraged her. Sometimes she felt life wasn't worth the living.

Martha's father was a big strong man who liked work and beer. He had a lot of commonsense about everything in general and anything in particular. He was very fond of Martha but he never showed it. He thought it wouldn't be decent for a man his age to embrace a girl of seventeen, so he treated her with a cold obliquity. He ignored Mary because she was at a gawky age and made a favourite of Rose.

The teachers in Collinsburn used corporal punishment. Every time somebody wrote to the papers about the wrongness of it they laughed in the staffroom and agreed about the rightness of it. An English immigrant's letter complaining about the place of the tawse in Scottish education set them off again.

'The way these folk talk,' said Mr Brown, Deputy Head and Principal Teacher of English, 'you'd think we spent our whole day belting defenceless weans.'

'You give some pest one of the strap to keep him in line,' said Mr Campbell, Principal Teacher of Mathematics, 'and they call it corporal punishment.'

'Then in the next sentence it becomes flogging,' said the Principal Teacher of Modern Languages, Mr Kerr.

He read aloud from the offensive letter.

'Hyperbole,' said Mr Brown.

'They think we're a shower of bloody sadists,' said Mr Dale, the youngest member of staff. 'They've no idea.'

'The strap is only a convention here,' said Mr Campbell. 'Up to second year anyway. You don't need it much after that. But if you abolished it altogether you'd raise more problems than you solved.'

'It's like the language of a country,' said Mr Alfred from his lonely corner. 'You've got to speak it to be understood.'

His colleagues hushed and looked at him. He seldom opened his mouth during their discussions. He seemed to think himself above them. They were surprised to hear his voice.

Mr Alfred acknowledged their attention by taking his

cigarette out of his mouth. He went on chattily as if he was giving a reminiscent talk on the Light Programme.

'I remember one school I worked in. There was a young Latin teacher next door to me. Very young he was. He wouldn't use the strap he told me. He thought the language of the strap was a barbaric language. He would speak to the natives in his own civilised tongue. He would be all sweetness and light like Matthew Arnold.'

'Hear, hear!' cried Mr Dale.

'Bloody fool,' muttered Mr Brown.

Mr Alfred smiled agreeably to them both and continued his talk.

'But when the natives found he refused to speak their language their pride was hurt. They felt he was insulting their tribal customs. They regarded him as a mad foreigner. They sniped at him till they saw it was safe to make an open attack. Within a week they were making his life hell on earth.'

'Boys can be cruel to a weak teacher,' said Mr Campbell.

'He was baited and barbed,' said Mr Alfred.

'By defenceless children,' said Mr Brown.

'Until he broke under the torture,' said Mr Alfred.

'Once they think you're soft they've no mercy,' said Mr Kerr.

'He went berserk one day,' said Mr Alfred. 'He thrashed a boy across the legs and buttocks and shoulders with the very strap he had wanted to put into a museum.'

'Probably the least troublesome boy,' said Mr Campbell.

'It usually is,' said Mr Kerr.

'It was,' said Mr Alfred. 'I heard the row. I heard the boy run screaming from the room as if the devil were after him. I nipped out in time to catch him in the corridor and managed to pacify him. I took him to the toilets and had him wash his face and calm down. I like to think I stopped what could have been a serious complaint from the parent.'

'It would never have happened if he had used the strap just once the day he arrived,' said Mr Campbell.

'Precisely my point,' said Mr Alfred.

'I always let a new class see I've got a strap and let them know I'll use it,' said Mr Dale. 'After that I've no bother. If you show the flag you don't need to fire the guns.'

'And you know,' said Mr Alfred, 'the tawse of the Scotch dominie is never wielded like the Jesuit's pandybat that distressed the young Stephen Dedalus. Not that the pandybat did Joyce any harm. It gave him material. It showed him what life is like. These letterwriters would have us deceive the boys by pretending they'll never be punished later on in life when they do something wrong. And even if a boy is strapped unjustly it isn't fatal. Life is full of minor injustices. A boy should learn as much while he's still at school, and learn to take it without whining. I admire the heroes of history who fought against social injustice, but one of the strap given in error or loss of patience is hardly a wrong on that scale.'

He put his cigarette back in his mouth and withdrew from the discussion. He thought he had said all that needed saying about corporal punishment.

'The way I see it,' said Mr Campbell, 'the strap is our symbol of authority within a recognised code. The boys know what to expect and we can get on with the job.'

'You must have something to maintain discipline,' said Mr Kerr. 'Some quick sanction. Even if you never use it.'

'No discipline, no learning,' said Mr Brown.

'But tell me this,' said Mr Dale. 'What do you do if a boy refuses to take the strap?'

'Only a stupid teacher would create a situation where that would happen,' said Mr Campbell.

'But supposing,' said Mr Dale.

'It's a case for the headmaster then,' said Mr Brown.

'I've never met many cases of a boy refusing the strap,' said Mr Campbell. 'And those I have, they all came to nothing. The boy had to submit in the end and apologise. Then of course once he gets a public apology the teacher acts the big man. He won't condescend to strap the boy. The rebel ends up looking a bit of an ass.'

'Well, I'm deputy-boss here,' said Mr Brown, 'and I've never had any boy refuse the strap. We don't seem to get that kind of stupid defiance.'

So it was an occasion for headlines when Gerald defied Mr Alfred and kept on defying him the morning after the fight in the Weavers Lane.

Before proposing to strap him Mr Alfred told the class what he had seen in the Weavers Lane. He said those who egged boys on to fight were worse than the boys who came to blows. Even a good boy might get into a fight if he thought his honour was at stake. He would fight in case his classmates jeered at him if he didn't. That was silly. Nothing was ever solved by violence. Still, it was a pardonable mistake in a young person. But few boys would fight at all if nobody talked them into thinking they had to. This was usually done by trouble-makers who took jolly good care never to risk their own precious skin. It was a far, far better thing to tell your schoolmates there was no need to fight. Our saviour said, Blessed are the peacemakers. The really wicked ones were those who were not content to start two boys fighting with their bare fists but got them to use belts and even brought a knife into it. They were not blessed like the peacemakers. They deserved a deep damnation more than a ticking off.

He spoke very well and enjoyed having the class hushed at his rhetoric. Then he said quietly, 'Come out Gerald Provan.'

He raised his strap.

'You know what I've been talking about. You know why I'm going to punish you.'

Gerald refused to hold his hand out. He said he had done nothing wrong, it was after four o'clock when he was in the Weavers Lane, Mr Alfred had no right, he was picking on him. He spoke with a rough insolence. His tongue darted between his lips and he went through the motion of spitting at Mr Alfred's feet.

Mr Alfred nearly slapped him across the face there and then. But he saw the trap. If he let himself be provoked and hit Gerald with his hand he would put himself in the wrong. His case against Gerald would be obliterated by Gerald's case against him. He knew he had blundered. He should have referred the whole business to Mr Briggs. And he was uneasy to think it was just possible he had jumped at the chance to get at Gerald Provan because he didn't like the boy. It vexed him even more that now he would have to take the matter to Mr Briggs not as something he was merely reporting but something he had failed to handle.

The class watched his defeat with placid interest.

He grabbed Gerald by the scruff and pushed him to the door.

'You come and see the headmaster,' he said.

'Take your hauns aff me,' said Gerald.

His dialect vowels were themselves a form of insolence. Normally a boy spoke to his teacher in standard English.

Mr Briggs wasn't pleased when Mr Alfred shoved Gerald in and said his piece. But he could only support his teacher. He ordered Gerald to take his punishment. He said he was sick and tired of all the feuding and fighting that was going on in the school and he was determined to stamp it out. He nearly said with a firm hand. He said he himself had told all those boys in the Weavers Lane to go home at once. If for nothing else, Gerald deserved to be punished for disobeying that order. Mr Alfred was quite right to strap him. He would do it himself if Mr Alfred wouldn't. And in order that justice would not only be done but be seen to be done, Mr Alfred or he himself would strap Gerald in front of the whole class.

Gerald was stubborn. He said Mr Alfred had a spite at him. He wouldn't take the strap from him. And he wouldn't take the strap from Mr Briggs. It was the same thing. Whoever did it, he was still being strapped for nothing. He put his hands behind his back. No, he wouldn't take it.

He had worked himself into a mood and he was stuck

with it. But he was thrilled with the stand he was making. He knew his cause was just.

'Here's the knife I told you about,' said Mr Alfred.

He put it on the headmaster's desk.

Mr Briggs glanced at it, wrinkled his nose and looked away. He didn't touch it.

'It's not mines,' said Gerald. 'I've got witnesses.'

'Mine,' said Mr Alfred.

'We're not discussing that,' said Mr Briggs. He lolled back in his swivel chair, looking at his clean nails. 'That will come later. At the moment all I'm concerned with is you were one of the boys in the Weavers Lane and you returned after I had sent you all away. You'll either take your punishment for disobedience or you'll go home and tell your mother I want to see her.'

The option was his final bluff. Ninety-nine times out of a hundred a boy capitulated rather than bother his parents. This time it failed. Gerald went home at once. He even banged the door on his way out.

'You should never have tried to strap him just for watching a fight,' Mr Briggs scolded Mr Alfred. 'You know what he's like. And his mother's worse. The knife? That won't get us anywhere. It's just your word. He'll deny it. If you had only sent him to me in the first place I could maybe have talked him into taking the strap. Even if he had defied me it wouldn't have been in front of a class. That won't do you any good with the rest of them, you know. I could have got round it somehow if it had been kept in this room. But now God knows what we've started.'

Before the week was out he found he had started plenty. Gerald turned up the next day, early and unworried. Mr Briggs spotted the fair hair in the assembly and beckoned.

'Where's your mother?'

He waited.

Gerald said nothing.

'Go away,' said Mr Briggs, 'and don't come back here without her.'

Mrs Provan came to his room at nine o'clock the following morning with Gerald by her side, her hand on his shoulder. She was angry again. She said her boy hadn't taken part in any fight. The truth was he had done his best to stop a fight. He had even brought one of the boys home with him and used his hankie to stanch the blood flowing from the boy's nose where a big bully had punched him.

'I can show you the hankie,' she said.

'And I can show you a knife,' said Mr Briggs. 'It's not just a penknife. It's more like a dagger. Just look at it. Do you allow your boy to go around with a thing like that in his pocket?'

'No, and I don't allow him to tell lies either,' said Mrs Provan. 'That's not his knife. He told you so himself.'

'Mr Alfred saw him with it,' said Mr Briggs.

'That's his story,' said Mrs Provan. 'Gerald never had a knife like that in his life. I should know. I'm his mother. Not Mr Alfred.'

'All I'm asking,' said Mr Briggs, 'is for Gerald to take the strap. There's no question of severe punishment. If he'll take even one. It won't kill him.'

'I never said it would,' said Mrs Provan. 'I'm only saying you're not strapping my boy for nothing.'

'I've got to think of the discipline of my school,' said Mr Briggs. 'The boy disobeyed an order from me in the first place. I can't just ignore it.'

'That was after school,' said Mrs Provan. 'It had nothing to do with you.'

'He also disobeyed Mr Alfred. In the classroom. Not after school.'

'Aye, but it was about something that happened after school,' said Mrs Provan. 'And that man has a spite against Gerald.'

She wouldn't give in. Mr Briggs said if the boy wouldn't accept the laws of the school he had no option but to suspend him. He told her to think it over and sent them both away.

'I've no need to think it over,' said Mrs Provan at the door. 'I'll be back here tomorrow. It's you had better think it over. I know my rights. You'll take my boy in if you're wise. You've no authority to keep him out.'

'Oh but I have,' said Mr Briggs.

'That's two days now he hasn't had his milk,' said Mrs Provan. 'He's got a right to his free milk every day. It's laid down by the law of the land. Lucky for you you didn't stop him getting his dinner here yesterday.'

'I didn't see him or I would have stopped him,' said Mr Briggs.

'He's got a ticket for free meals,' said Mrs Provan. 'I'm a widow woman. I applied for free meals for my children and it was granted. You can't stop it.'

'I can,' said Mr Briggs. 'In certain circumstances.'

'That's what you think,' said Mrs Provan. 'I know different. Not to mention the fact he's missed his education for two days through your fault.'

'Education! For that fellow!' Mr Briggs cried to Miss Ancill, giving her a line by line account of the interview over his morning coffee. 'He leaves in a couple of months. He's hardly a candidate to stay on for O levels. He has learned all he'll ever learn at school. And God knows that wasn't much.'

When Mrs Provan brought Gerald back again he offered her a compromise. He wouldn't punish the boy nor would Mr Alfred, if she would concede they had a right to punish him.

'Not for doing nothing,' said Mrs Provan.

The peace talks broke down. Mr Briggs told her to come back when she changed her mind.

She didn't. She wouldn't. She phoned the fourth estate. She knew enough to know a free press is the guarantee of liberty. Within twenty-four hours a counter-attack was organised. Gerald arrived at school in a Ford Anglia driven by a bearded reporter accompanied by a bald photographer. He got out at the gate and went straight to Mr Briggs' room while his escorts waited in the playground. Five minutes after he sauntered out smiling. The photographer had a word with him and then took his picture against the wall of the boys' urinal. By an unfortunate coincidence Mr Alfred came along at that moment. He slowed down when he saw Gerald being photographed by a bareheaded man in a sheepskin coat and saw another man, similarly clad, shepherding a jolly crowd of pupils out of the picture. He was puzzled.

'That's him,' Gerald whispered.

The man with the camera turned quickly. Mr Alfred gaped. The man with the beard stepped forward.

'Good morning, sir,' he said pleasantly. 'Would you give me your views on corporal punishment?'

The man with the camera took aim.

Mr Alfred looked round for escape. He was jostled by cheering boys and girls and confronted by this bearded stranger with the big smile and the unexpected question. He faced him fiercely, glare answering grin.

The man with the camera snapped.

'Thank you,' he sang out.

'Excuse me,' said Mr Alfred, and barged on.

When the evening paper came out there wasn't only

Gerald full length on the front page. Mr Alfred was there too, head and shoulders. A single column story under a three column headline separated the two pictures. The headline was *Teacher Has Spite Says Mum*.

Mr Brown brought in a copy next morning in case Mr Alfred had missed it.

'You look a right badtempered old bastard there,' he said.

Mr Alfred hadn't seen his picture. He seldom bought an evening paper. He was shocked. He had the same irrational disbelief as some people have when they hear their voice on tape for the first time. That wasn't him. To increase the offence, Gerald looked boyish and handsome, happy and innocent.

'Crabbed age and youth,' said Mr Brown.

'That face doesn't do our image any good, does it?' said Mr Dale.

Mr Alfred drank more than usual that night. He went on a pub-crawl in what Granny Lyons called his disguise, but he was sure everybody recognised him. He couldn't forget how his face looked in the paper. And that would be how it looked to other people, he supposed. Yet he knew he had once been tall, dark and handsome, with a profile and a moustache that made his fellow students say he looked like Robert Louis Stevenson.

When he got back to his lodgings he hunted out the typescript of his poems. It was a long time since he last looked at them. He had an alcoholic whim to read them again and enter the mind of the man he had been in the green years that had no ophidian Provan lurking in the grass. He thought he would comfort his troubled spirit by saying his own verses aloud.

He had called his poems *Negotiations for a Treaty*. He meant a treaty with the reality of philosophers, politicians, economists, scientists and businessmen. The thirty-two poems he had typed in a fair copy after countless revisions were meant to be a lyric-sequence showing the attempt to come to terms with a material world. The poet would insist on his right to live in the independent republic of his imagination. But he would let reality be boss in its territory if it gave up all claims to invade and conquer his. If it didn't he would organise his own resistance movement.

The performance fell short of the intention. He was depressed to see how weak and derivative his verses sounded after lying long unread. He felt he was a failure, a lonely provincial hearing from afar rumours of the world of letters, the only world he cared about, a world he would never be allowed to enter. And he saw his failure didn't come from an addiction to drink and idleness. It came from the whole cast and calibre of his mind. Sleep seemed impossible. He wished he had taken just one more whisky at the bar before it closed, or bought a half-bottle to carry out so that he could have another drink before he went to bed.

Undressing slowly he saw himself as a man tossed aside by a God who had given him the ambition to be a poet without giving him the talent.

Mr Briggs saw him as a bit of a fool who had brought unnecessary publicity to the school by mishandling a difficult boy. The evening paper that started the story followed it up for a week. So did the morning paper that was its stable companion. There was *Mother Demands Enquiry* on the front page with a picture of Gerald and Mrs Provan cheek to cheek like sweethearts. Then there was *Banned Boy Tries Again* on the middle page with a picture of Gerald at the school gate, like Adam outside the gates of Paradise, wearing his best suit, face washed and hair combed. But at the week-end a youth was stabbed to death in a brawl outside a dance-hall in Sauchiehall Street. His griefstricken girlfriend was a photogenic blonde who was interviewed on her thoughts about life and love. She displaced Gerald and his mother.

Although the Provan story was no longer newsworthy the papers went on drawing dividends from it. Letters to the Editor condemning corporal punishment were printed daily for several weeks and filled a lot of space. They appeared most frequently and at the greatest length in the *Herald*.

'More letters this morning!' cried Mr Brown.

He breezed in waving his paper.

'Hey, shut that door, there's a draught,' said Mr Campbell. A cross man.

'A long one from Monica Trumbell,' said Mr Brown.

He slammed the door with a backheeler and pitched an eager question at Mr Alfred.

'Have you seen it?'

Mr Alfred stooped at the staffroom table sipping a cup of strong tea brewed by a kindly cleaner forty minutes before the first of the staff arrived.

'No,' he said. 'Who is Monica, what is she?'

'One of our conquerors,' said Mr Dale. 'She's up here on loan from England.'

'She damn near names you as the villain of the piece,' said Mr Brown.

'Oh yes,' said Mr Alfred.

He sipped his tea.

Mr Brown read to him with loud gusto.

' "It is a sorry comment on Scottish education when some survivor from a prehistoric society thinks he can solve the most subtle problems of school discipline by resorting to brute force against a sensitive adolescent." '

'An excess of sibilants surely,' said Mr Alfred.

'Onomatopoeia,' said Mr Brown. 'She's hissing you.'

'Who is she, I was asking,' said Alfred.

'Monica Trumbell?' said Mr Campbell. He frowned a moment, then identified a function. 'That's that dame is always writing letters. She's the secretary of POISE, isn't she?'

'That's the one,' said Mr Dale. 'A poisonality.'

'What is poise, saith my sufferings then?' Mr Alfred enquired.

'POISE?' said Mr Brown. 'You mean to say you don't know what POISE is?'

'Not as something having a secretary,' said Mr Alfred.

'It's an acronym,' said Mr Brown. 'It stands for Parents' Organisation for the Improvement of Scottish Education. You're not keeping up! It's old models like you POISE is out to improve on.'

'There's always room for improvement,' said Mr Alfred.

He sipped his tea and glanced at the electric clock on the wall. Two minutes to the bell. He sipped his tea again.

'She's good, our Monica,' said Mr Dale. 'Mrs Monica actually. Oh Jaysus, I'd hate to sleep with her. I bet she'd tell you your way of doing it was out-of-date.'

'How is she qualified to improve anybody?' Mr Alfred asked. 'Except herself of course.'

'I told you,' said Mr Dale. 'She's English.'

'Oh I see,' said Mr Alfred.

He sipped his tea, squinting over the rim of the cup at the sinister clock.

'She's married to the personnel boss at Bunter's Ball Bearings,' said Mr Dale. 'You know, the English firm that came to the new Salthill industrial scheme. A shower of Sassenachs out there now.'

'She's from Essex actually,' said Mr Brown.

'Upminster. Here about a year. The *Herald* had an article on her last week.'

'Oh yes,' said Mr Alfred.

'On the Woman's Page,' said Mr Brown.

'Complete with picture,' said Mr Dale. 'A horsefaced old haybag.'

'A reformer,' said Mr Campbell. 'The minute she sees a pie she shoves her finger in.'

'She's got two girls at Bay,' said Mr Brown.

'Two girls at bay,' Mr Alfred turned gladly. 'I thought it was stags one had at bay.'

'Bay School,' said Mr Campbell.

'Private school for girls,' said Mr Brown.

'You couldn't send your daughter there,' said Mr Dale.

'I know,' said Mr Alfred. 'I haven't got a daughter. Not as far as I know.'

'If you had you couldn't,' said Mr Campbell. 'Not on your salary.'

'It's not a school,' said Mr Dale. 'It's an advance post of English infiltration. Hockey and an English accent. The old girl network.'

Mr Alfred glanced at the clock. The bell rang.

He swallowed the last of his tea and was first out to meet his class.

At morning break Mr Brown was still in a teasing mood. He read out further extracts from Mrs Trumbell's letter and bits from a letter supporting her. Mr Alfred wasn't amused. Mr Brown's voice jarred on him and he disliked the man's use of juvenile slang. He tried to show his disapproval by sighs and groans but Mr Brown wasn't discouraged.

'Here's a smashing argument,' he declared loud and clear.

'Must you?' Mr Alfred asked.

Mr Brown read with zest to his jaded colleagues.

' "It is surely obvious to the meanest intelligence, even amongst teachers—" '

Mr Campbell was jolted from his crossword.

'That bloody cheek!' he cried. ' "Even amongst teachers!" '

'Than whom,' said Mr Alfred.

Mr Brown read straight on through the interruptions.

' "—that a pupil refuses punishment because he is the innocent victim of certain psychical and physical strains resulting in a feeling of resentment due to his immaturity. Now whatever the child resents cannot be just and should therefore be abolished." '

'Hear, hear,' said Mr Dale. 'Let's abolish the weans as well. That'll solve it.'

Mr Brown laughed and continued.

' "This applies particularly to that curse of Scottish education, corporal punishment. Not that way will the child with a thirst for knowledge be provided with a key to wider horizons." '

'Oh ma Goad!' said Mr Dale.

'She'll be leaving no stone unturned till she nips us in the bud,' said Mr Campbell.

Mr Alfred sighed and groaned again. Mr Brown continued.

' "A system of sanctions must be devised which will not produce resentment in the child. Here is a task for our child-psychologists. Meanwhile in view of the present atmosphere of frustration which is itself an indication of a great deterioration in our much-vaunted determination to create a higher civilisation I appeal to parents of every denomination to send me their application for registration in the Parents Organisation for the Improvement of Scottish Education." '

'Damnation,' said Mr Alfred.

'Listen to this,' said Mr Brown. 'Monica's last words. "It can hardly be without significance that Scotland is the only country, apart from Eire, Switzerland and Denmark, where teachers still think it necessary to flog their pupils." '

'To what?' said Mr Campbell, pencil poised over his crossword. Clue: *What are they when John has x times as many sweets as Jean?* 'That's a bit stupid, that is.'

He entered PROBLEM CHILDREN in his crossword and snorted.

'Flogging? The bitch doesn't know what flogging means.'

The bell rang. Harsh, crude, rude, dogmatic, domineering. Tea was gulped, cigarettes stubbed, pipes knocked out, crosswords abandoned till lunchtime, and the battle-scarred troopers marched out to rejoin their unit.

CHAPTER TWELVE

Mr Alfred went to see his aunt.

It was six weeks since he had given her any money. He swithered about sending her some by post. Then he thought it would be better if he went to see her.

'You're the fine one!' she said when she let him in. 'Your picture in the paper and you never come near folk to tell them what it was all about.'

'There was nothing to tell,' he said.

She scolded him.

'I thought you had more sense than to talk to reporters. Here, have a cup of tea.'

He sat down with his coat on and his old hat on his lap.

'I don't talk to them. One of them tried to talk to me. All I said was excuse me.'

'More fool you. You're lucky he didn't put in his paper, teacher apologises. But you must have been standing talking to them if they took your picture.'

He sat across from her and stirred his tea.

'No, it wasn't like that,' he said. 'You know, it's a very odd thing but—'

'Here, I haven't sugared it,' she said. 'Don't sit there and try to tell me they snapped your face behind your back.'

She pushed a poke of sugar across to him. He scrabbled the spoon in it. The sugar was low.

'They took it before I knew. You know, it's a very odd thing. You can stop a person printing a letter he stole from you, but you can't stop him taking a quick snap at you and printing your photograph.'

'You can't call your face your own these days,' she said. 'Do you want a biscuit? Or can I fry you something?'

'Any more trouble lately?' he was asking. 'No, thanks, no.'

'Nothing much,' she said. 'You're quite sure? It would be no bother. Except I had my purse snatched yesterday. I don't know how you stay alive on what you eat. Well, my handbag it was actually, but my purse was in it. Are you quite sure?'

'Yes, quite sure, thanks. You don't know who it was?'

'No, I've no idea. It was that quick. All I saw was the turnup of his jeans. I was coming through the Weavers Lane.'

'I've told you not to use the Weavers Lane.'

'It saves me a good minute's walk to Ballochmyle Road.'

'What happened?'

'I had my shopper and my handbag in one hand and somebody came up behind me and hit my wrist with a stick or something and I dropped them and he pushed me down and kicked me and grabbed my handbag and ran away. All I saw was the turnup of his jeans. Blue. Kind of tight. There was nothing I could do. He was out the lane and out of sight before I got to my feet. The funny thing was I found my handbag at the end of the lane but my purse was missing.'

He gave her more money than he had meant to.

'You shouldn't bother,' she said. 'The price of things these days. You need it yourself. I wish you'd buy yourself a new coat. And as for that hat. It's the midden it should be in.'

'I must get you a purse,' he said. 'You only ever had the one.'

'It was my mother's. It was a good one. They don't make them like that nowadays. Handstitched leather. It was a good one.'

'Yes, I know. I'll buy you a good one.'

'When would you buy a purse? The only shops you're ever in are beershops. I suppose you'll be off round them tonight as usual.'

He didn't deny it, and she let him go after he gave her

his version of the Provan story. He kept saying at the doorstep he would get her a good purse like the one she had lost and she kept telling him not to bother.

His wandering took him to a district he hadn't visited for over a year. The pubs were all changed. More chromium and plastic, less mahogany and brass. But it was the new people in The Kivins, a bar he used to like, that spoiled his pub-crawl. He remembered it as a bright spot off the beaten track, frequented by characters he would have said Dickens rather than God created. He hardly knew the place, and he certainly didn't know the customers.

There used to be community-singing in the back-room, and many solos too, though singing of any kind was against the licensing laws. There was an Irish labourer sang 'Danny Boy', commonly known as 'The Londonderry Air', and even 'Sonny Boy', as well as 'The Rose of Tralee' and 'I love the dear silver that shines in your hair', which is the same song as 'Mother Machree', sung elsewhere by Count John McCormack. And every Saturday night a bookie's clerk sang 'I have heard the mavis singing', a fine song for a man with a good drink on him if he is a good tenor. The point of the song was that the voice of Bonny Mary of Argyll was sweeter than the song of the mavis, and a member of the audience said one night that the song was written by Rabbie Burns and that Bonny Mary of Argyll was Mary Campbell, the Ayrshire bard's Highland Mary.

His gloss aroused considerable dissension in the company and the argument flowed out of the back-room into the bar. Mr Alfred was appealed to as arbiter, his erudition being no doubt immediately recognised from his distinguished appearance and the fact that he wore a hat. He remembered the night well. He had, he regretted later, become rather didactic and after settling the controversy he had gone on to inform his fellow-drinkers that a similar mistake was often made about 'I dream of Jeannie with the light-brown hair'. Many people, he said, believed it was

written by Burns when in fact it was the work of the
American songwriter Stephen Foster who wrote about the
old folks at home etc.

It was sober shame at his occupational habit of impart-
ing information at the lowering of an elbow that inhibited
him from going back to that haven of mirth and melody.

And now! Ah, now! No couthy customers chatted at the
bar, no merry company sang the old songs through in the
back-room. A television gabbled on a high shelf at the far
end of the gantry and dazzled him with a watered-silk
effect the moment he went in. Two trios of long-haired
youths, apparently not on speaking terms, were plainly
now the established patrons. The door of the back-room
was open, and he saw a couple of bottle-blondes, haggard
professionals, sitting there with middleaged men beside
them. The waiters too were changed. Four hard-faced,
wary-eyed silent men, moving like ex-boxers, served
clumsily. They looked as if they didn't approve of drinking.

Having gone in, Mr Alfred was unwilling to turn round
and go out again. He would have one drink there anyway.
Half-way through his pint, staring straight in front of him,
wishing he had gone to see Stella, he had a subliminal
knowledge of quarrelsome voices rising, angry scuffling,
and the approach of battle. These disturbances put an end
to his meditation of Stella's bust and smile and he glanced
round with disapproval. Two youths were fankled, legs
kicking and heads butting, one of them with blood pouring
from the tap of his nose. Four others, two on each side,
tried to pull them apart, and there was a lot of bad
language being used, another thing Mr Alfred didn't like.

The six youths came wrestling and lurching down the
length of the bar, clearing all before them. Two of the ex-
boxers dashed round to break it up and Mr Alfred stepped
quickly out of their way, glass in hand. The youth who
seemed to be the aggressor was wrenched away from his
cowering foe but went on yelling threats and insults. He
was a big fellow, and he strongly resisted the invulting

arms of the grim barmen. He heaved himself free and
launched a new attack. A joint effort by the bouncers
brought him down, but in the tackle they shouldered Mr
Alfred and brought him down too. He fell against a small
table across from the bar and spilled beer all over his coat.
When he got up he felt his ankle was hurting him. He
hurried out as hastily as his newly-acquired claudication
permitted, not waiting to hear what it was all about, nor
caring.

He limped a hundred yards or so in great agitation
before a familiar rain, tapping insolently on his bare head,
told him he had lost his hat. He slowed down. Then he
hobbled on. It was an old hat. Everybody laughed at it. He
would rather spend money on a new one than go back for
it. He kept going, head down against a wind, angry at the
young ones who couldn't drink in peace.

By the time the pubs were closed the wind was worse.
He stood in a bus-shelter and a rainy draught annoyed
his legs. He felt his turnups getting soaked. He wondered why. Then he saw that the glass panels along the
upper half and the metal panels along the lower half
were all missing. He fretted as he waited. Five schoolboys across the street stopped a while and kicked at a
litter-basket till it tumbled from its post. The wind took
up their sport and played along the gutter with cigarette-
packets, bus-tickets, orange-peel, pokes, cartons, and a
vinegar-drenched newspaper that still remembered the
fish and chips it had wrapped. A Coca-Cola bottle broke
where it fell. The schoolboys slouched on to the next
litter-basket.

'Oh dear me,' said Mr Alfred.

When the bus came he went upstairs for a smoke. There
was a drunk man wouldn't pay his fare. The coloured
conductor stood over him. Tall, patient, dignified, persis-
tent. A good samaritan across the passage offered the
money.

'No, no, oh no! That will not do,' said the coloured
conductor. 'He must pay his own fare or go off.'

'Ach, go to hell,' said the drunk man, but quite pleasant about it.

He lolled unworried, a small man with a bristly chin and nothing on his head. Mr Alfred noticed the raindrops glisten on the balding scalp.

'Your fare please,' said the coloured conductor again.

'A belang here,' said the little drunk man. 'Mair than you do, mac. It's me pays your wages. Go and get stuffed.'

The bus weaved on between tall tenements.

'Pay your fare or I stop the bus,' said the coloured conductor.

'Ye kin stope it noo,' said the little drunk man. 'This is whaur A get aff.'

He swayed up as the bus slowed, palmed the coloured conductor out of his way, and slithered downstairs. Smiling. Victorious. Happy and glorious.

Mr Alfred caught the conductor's eye.

'You meet some types, don't you,' he said, anxious to show sympathy.

The conductor went downstairs without answering him.

Mr Alfred blinked drunkenly at the graffiti on the blackboard of the seat in front of him. The rexine had been torn off and on the bare wood someone had scrawled in loose capitals FUCK THE POPE. A different hand added underneath CELTIC 7–1. Most of the seats had large stretches of the rexine stripped away. The bus was as shabby as its route. Above the front window SPITTING FORBIDDEN had been changed to SHITTING FORBIDDEN.

Mr Alfred sighed.

Three young men invaded the bus. They had shiny black jackets with white lettering on the back. ZEB ZAD ZOK I LOVE THE ZINGERS. The last one on had the outline of a broadhipped female nude in yellow paint and LAW in brass studs. They were no sooner on than they rose to get off. The conductor stood in their way to collect their fares. The first shoved him aside, the second pushed past, and the third flashed a knife.

'There's wur fares,' he said. 'Ur ye wanting it?'

He rammed his knee in the conductor's testicles and went smartly on his way. The conductor straightened in time to catch him by the collar at the top of the stairs.

'Away ye big black cunt,' said the young man, kicking as he turned. 'Take yer hauns aff me or A'll do ye.'

He jerked free and did a wardance on the steps. The conductor kicked him on the thigh. He kicked back. The bus turned a corner. Rainbeads rolled down the streaming windows. White man and coloured, both fell. When they got up the passenger took another kick at the conductor. The conductor danced backwards and whipped off his ticket-machine. He swung it by the straps.

Mr Alfred jumped up to restrain him.

'Here! Don't! You'll kill him with that.'

He was frightened.

A buckle of the strap smacked him on the cheekbone and tore across the nose. The conductor's elbow thumped him on the eye in the course of a vicious parabola.

Mr Alfred clung to him.

'Let go, you,' said the coloured conductor.

Mr Alfred pulled him back. 'I'm only trying to help you,' he said. 'For your own good. You'd brain him if that thing landed.'

The passenger decamped. His mates were already off.

'Muck of the world,' said the coloured conductor. He was shaking. 'They won't pay. Every night they won't pay their fare. White bastards.'

'Compose yourself,' said Mr Alfred.

Turning to sit down again he saw a bus-inspector huddling in the back seat. He looked down on him. The bus-inspector looked up and shrugged.

'Well, what can you do with that kind?' he asked.

Mr Alfred had a black eye the next morning, a bruise on his cheek, and an abrased nose. But he wouldn't stay off work. He never did. When he turned up at school his colleagues were sure he had been in a drunken brawl.

His awkward gait showed an injured ankle was bothering him.

'He's falling apart, that fellow,' said Mr Brown to Mr Campbell. 'I'll have to get rid of him. I'm going to have a quiet word with Briggs about him.'

CHAPTER THIRTEEN

Martha was sorry for Mr Alfred.

'Not that I know him. But every time I see him in the corridor, I mean. I was never in his class. Well, he never takes girls' classes. No, it's just when I see him about the school. I don't know. He looks so neglected.'

Graeme Roy laughed. He wasn't jealous. He couldn't see Mr Alfred as a rival.

'You want to mother him? He could be your father.'

'No, he couldn't.'

'Of course he could.'

'Of course he couldn't. In the first place my mother never met him. And even if she had I doubt if. I mean, she's not his kind.'

'I mean his age.'

'Who's talking about his age? All I said was I feel sorry for him. All that stinky stuff in the papers. The poor man always gets the low boy's classes.'

'You mean the boys' low classes.'

'No, I don't. I mean the low boys' classes.'

'I wouldn't say that. He taught me once.'

'He taught you? You never told me that. You been hiding your murky past from me?'

They liked to mention their past as if they had one and make little confessions about it that they never made to anyone else.

'In third year. Before they started the comprehensive.'

'Did you like him?'

'He was all right. A bit sarcastic maybe.'

'I can't stand sarcastic teachers.'

'I don't mean he was all that sarcastic. Just sometimes.'

'Tell me anybody that's sarcastic all the time.'

'Don't nag.'

'I'm not nagging. I was only asking a question. That's not nagging.'

'The way you do it it is. And it wasn't a question. It was an order. You said, tell me!'

'Who's nagging now?'

'Not me. It was you. I was only trying to tell you about Alfy.'

'Well, go on. Tell me.'

'He was quite amusing at times when I had him. But half the things he said were quotations. We didn't know. At least I didn't know. Not till later on. He could be very cutting. Then I found out it was Shakespeare or Pope or somebody. How were we to know? In third year. I ask you.'

'Casting his pearls before swine.'

He heard it as 'perils' and counted. Three was enough. He was in no danger of trying to improve her. It was she as she was detained him.

'Put it that way if you like. But what's the point of quoting Shakespeare when nobody knows you're quoting Shakespeare? That's teachers of course. Of course some of them say, as Shakespeare said, or in the words of Pope. But Alfy never. He was wasting his time showing off to us he knew his Shakespeare.'

'Maybe he wasn't showing off. Maybe it came natural to him.'

'Shakespeare come natural? You're joking of course.'

They were happy blethering and arguing, happiest then perhaps. Certainly happier than they were later when they expected to scale the heights or plumb the depths or learn the meaning of it all. But even then they had their troubles. When they gave up Ianello's they tried other cafes near and not so near the school. None suited. They were either too small or too big, too cheap or too dear, either a pokey wee ice-cream shop for juveniles or an adult coffee-lounge where men twice their age smoked cigars. They were beaten. Graeme offered her an answer. Instead of meeting for twenty minutes on the way home from school Monday to Friday, meet one night a week for two or three hours. A return to what they did before the ban fell. Avoid suspicion by keeping it strictly to just once a week and varying the night.

'It's not the same,' said Martha.

'We'd gain on it,' he said. 'Arithmetically.'

'It's not a question of arithmetic. I'd rather see you every day, even if it's only a few minutes.'

'But this way's no good. By the time we've said hello it's time to say goodbye.'

'Don't exaggerate,' she laughed at him.

'By the time we find a place where we can talk, I mean,' he said.

He was getting a bit sulky with her.

And he didn't mean talk though he thought he did. The ambitions of a young male growing in him. The withheld nearness of her unknown body was having its effect on his blood. A demon in his ear told him he would get nowhere talking to her in a cafe or at the bus-stop. A meeting at night would let him find the place and opportunity to go further. He could use the car again. And when he found the place he would find the time. The time to seduce her. Or seduce himself. The demon left it all very vague.

Yet his imagination remained chaste. He wanted to be longer with her, closer to her. That was all. To know more. He began to have a documentary interest in the privacies of her life. He was curious about her underwear. He wanted to know what lipstick and powder she used, what earlier loves she had and how much she knew about making love. He wondered when her periods were and how much pain she suffered then. He wanted to know if she slept alone or shared a bed with a sister. He wanted to see her half-undressed for bed. He hadn't got as far as thinking of her without her clothes on. But his hands longed to learn the precise mould and strength of her flanks, her thighs and breasts.

Past that point his uninformed thoughts faltered. What he could see kept them busy enough. The sheen of her blonde hair made him want to stroke it. But he couldn't do that in a public place. Her pale hand, small-palmed and long-fingered, seemed mysteriously different from his own. He wanted to take it and make it as familiar as the square fist that was a congenital part of himself. But he knew she would be annoyed if he held her hand in public. When she laughed, and she was much given to laughing, the good teeth behind her unkissed lips made him long to be taken behind them, to enter into her. But it was a yearning for a penetration beyond physical space. So with her complexion. She was so blonde her pure skin gave him the illusion of seeing a transparency more spiritual than epidermal. There too she tempted him to dreams of passing through an insubstantial curtain and dissolving himself within her. Her nylon knees, uncovered by a schoolgirl's skirt, whispered to his unlearned hand. For a time the height of his ambition was to fondle them. But he couldn't do that either in a public place. He was tired of seeing her in public places.

'I'm not keen on it,' she was saying. 'It would mean more deceit. I hate telling lies to my mum and dad. And once you start.'

'It would be better than this.'

'It's like saying a square meal once a week is better than a sandwich every day. I don't know that's true.'

'If you're going to be crude about it,' he huffed. 'Talking about food!'

They were trying yet another cafe for the first time. A pop hit from the juke box rocked the walls. They winced together.

'If music be the food of love,' said Martha.

He wasn't amused. He was in a bad mood.

'Oh, don't start quoting Shakespeare at me,' he said. 'You're as bad as big Alfy. Maybe you'd rather go out with him. Hold his hand and stroke his fevered brow if you feel all that sorry for him.'

'Don't be ridiculous, little boy,' she said.

'I'm taller than you,' he said.

But he won in the end. She gave in. They began to meet once a week, a different night every time. Since they were both fond of their parents they felt guilty.

Gerald went back to school in triumph. Once her grievance was off the front page Mrs Provan took it to her local
councillor, who brought it before the education commit-
tee, whose members decided the suspension was invalid.
The headmaster's writ didn't run in the Weavers Lane
after four o'clock.

'It's the last time I'll—' said Mr Briggs.

'Why bother about the little bastards?' asked Mr Campbell.

'Let's face it,' said Mr Dale. 'You can't win.'

'Alfy mucked that one up,' said Mr Brown. 'He should
never have—'

'Not after hours,' said Mr Campbell. 'Once it's after
four, well—'

'They can commit murder and mayhem,' said Mr
Briggs.

'You don't get much thanks, do you?' said Miss Ancill.

'One minute after the bell, one inch across that gate, and
as far as I'm concerned they can,' said Mr Briggs.

'I'd suspend him,' said Mr Dale. 'From the bloody
rafters.'

'Surely any grownup has a right to stop boys fighting
anywhere,' said Miss Ancill.

'The position is,' said Mr Kerr, 'you have the authority
to stop fights only at the time and place when fights don't
occur, during school hours inside the school. At the time
and place where fights do occur, after four o'clock outside
the school, you have no authority.'

'Sod them all,' said Mr Dale.

Mr Alfred sipped his tea in the staffroom, stuck in a

corner silent by himself at morning-break. He felt the world was like a crowded bus speeding past the stop. It had left him behind. The daily frustrations of public transport analogised his fate. He didn't get on. Even if the bus did stop and some of the queue was allowed on board he was the one that was put off. He was always the extra passenger the conductor wouldn't take. He was without a home, wife or child, without father, mother, sister, brother or wellwisher. He hadn't even a car. He was unnecessary in the world, superfluous, supernumerary, not wanted. Nobody would miss him. He was an exile in his native land. Not that he had any love for his native land. He rated it as a cipher, of no value until a figure was put before it. But it had no figures. It existed only as terra incognita to the north of England. Hence formerly known simply as N.B. Note well. A footnote. Whereas England was where they spoke the language he taught, the language he once thought he knew. But he had been refused an immigrant's visa there many years ago when nine publishers rejected his thirty-two poems. They had condemned him to stay where he was and go on waiting at the bus-stop till a hearse came along. He had silence and exile, but no cunning.

He had long forgiven the uninterested publishers. Maybe they were right not to want his poems. After all, they were the only arbiters he respected. The praise of a friend, if friend he ever had, would prove nothing. And now he didn't know what to do. He was too old to earn a living anywhere else. He knew it was possible there was a vacancy for a scavenger in the cleansing department. But he was probably past the age limit. There was no job open to a middleaged man that would let him live in the manner to which he was accustomed. Besides the expenses of rent, food, clothing and transport, which everyone had to meet, he had additional necessities to budget for. He was a heavy smoker. He was a hardened drinker. And sometimes he bought paperbacks and even a book in hard covers. These indulgences were not to be gained on a scavenger's wages.

He suffered an unwanted memory of the way Gerald ambled into the classroom that morning wearing new jeans and an old smirk. A spasm of undiluted hatred convulsed his guts and pained his sour face. His long lean body shuddered. He knew the emotion was unworthy of a cultured man like himself. But it was there. A glow of shame as well as hate warmed his forehead.

But Gerald and his friends were in high spirits. At the school dinner they chucked spuds across the room when the teacher on duty had his back to them. They skited peas on the floor at the server's feet when she passed with a loaded tray against her big bosom. They poured salt ad lib on the sweets of the diners across the table. They rattled their cutlery with a cha-cha, cha-cha-cha accompaniment. Smudge and Poggy importuned the perambulating teacher.

'Please sir he spat on ma dinner.'

'Please sir A never. He done it on mines first.'

'Please sir he's telling lies. It was him.'

Accuser and counter-accuser waited to see what the teacher would do. He looked down on one and then the other, turned neutrally away, and went on perambulating.

They tried him again next time round.

'Please sir he put salt on m'ice cream.'

'Please sir he pinched mines.'

'Please sir kin we have mair ice-cream?'

The teacher plodded silently on.

After four o'clock they went to Ianello's for a celebration. Gerald ordered three cokes.

'And three lucies,' he added.

When Enrico served him he pretended he hadn't any money, fumbled tediously in all his pockets. Enrico had to be patient. He had always to be patient with the boys from Collinsburn. Gerald put the money out at last in slow instalments of small change. He picked up the three loose cigarettes and handed them round. Fag in mouth, lifting their coke with a straw in the bottle, they all turned from the counter and surveyed the premises.

Gerald strolled to his favourite table, drawing his sa-
tellites round him. They were bigshots with a reservation
in a posh restaurant sitting down to a drink before they
called a waiter and ordered a meal. They talked loud and
long. But they missed an audience.

'Hey, Nello!' Gerald shouted. 'Is there nae dames come
here noo?'

Enrico served a little girl with an iced lolly and ignored
him.

'Whaur's Martha Weipers these days?' Poggy bawled.

He scraped his foot on the floor like a restive stallion and
lolled his tongue lasciviously.

'Ach, her!' said Smudge. 'I bet she's been screwed by
yon toffee-nose.'

Enrico said nothing.

Gerald grinned.

Wilma and Jennifer came in, pushing each other on
their way over the threshold. They giggled. They were
chewing bubblegum, and a pink hemisphere was pro-
truded and retracted irregularly from their lips. They
joined the boys. Gerald was pleased. He welcomed Wilma
and Poggy took care of Jennifer. Smudge entertained them
with song and story. He was the court jester.

Enrico watched them. They could have been worse.
Apart from pocketing a couple of ashtrays, scratching their
initials on the paintwork, and lifting a handful of tubular-
packed sweets on their way out, they gave him no bother.
Enrico saw them steal the sweets. But he knew it was his
own fault for leaving the display-box so accessible. When
they were crossing the door he called after them.

'Tough guys, eh? Fly men! Don't want you back here!'

Gerald stopped, turned round.

'I saw you,' said Enrico. 'Next time I call the police. I
warn you.'

Gerald raised his right hand, the palm in, and jerked two
fingers forked at Enrico. Repeated the gesture, grinning.

He had only a month to go before he left school.

Tired of living unloved unloving Mr Alfred fell in love. She was only a child, five feet one, seven stone two. But you can't measure the depth of a man's love by the height and weight of its object.

It happened when he was meditating hatred rather than love. For the first time in his life he was given a class of girls. Three periods a week. Monday, Wednesday, Friday. The last forty minutes of morning school. He complained.

'Somebody's got to take them,' said Mr Brown.

'Why me?' said Mr Alfred. 'You've cut my free time.'

'I've cut everybody's free time,' said Mr Brown. 'There's a shortage of staff. Or didn't you know?'

'Girls!' said Mr Alfred. He was disgusted. A gloomy man glumly niggling. 'What am I supposed to do with them?'

'Poetry Monday,' said Mr Brown. 'Oral composition Wednesday. Debates, speech training, anything like that. Use the tape recorder. Spot of written work on Friday. Kind of diary of the week, say. Call it creative writing. Encourage them to say what they think. Self-expression. It's only three periods. You can waffle your way through.'

'Waffling's more your line,' said Mr Alfred. 'Suppose they have nothing to express?'

'Self-expression, I like that,' said the eavesdropping Mr Dale. 'Makes it sound good, eh? Dumb weans. Self-expression my arse.'

'I'm paying you a compliment,' said Mr Brown. 'These are first year girls. I wouldn't give them to a man at all if I could help it. They can be such little bitches. I certainly can't give them to any of the younger men. I'm relying on you to keep them in order. Maybe even teach them something. A man of your experience and may I say sobriety.'

'I think your last word's a bit—' said Mr Alfred.

His head was high, his voice was cold. He saw an innuendo about his private life. He thought his aposiopesis more dignified than any word.

'I mean in class,' said Mr Brown. 'You have what the Romans called gravitas. There's no danger of you joking with them. I've always found it a mistake to make a joke with a class of girls. You lose them for good. It's different with boys. You can make a joke with them and then all right – joke over! That's it. But girls want to keep it up. They won't stop giggling. The young men coming in now, flippant types, they're no use with girls' classes. But you have that special air about you. Like one of Shakespeare's grave and reverend signiors.'

'Butter,' Mr Dale chanted.

'Othello,' said Mr Alfred.

Mr Brown was quite sincere. He was sure Mr Alfred was so humourless the girls would see no use trying to lead him on. There was plainly no fun to be had from him. He was such a sourpuss they would never think he was smashing or fab or terrific or out of this world or whatever their current word was for any male who excited their silly little minds. They would regard him as a dead loss, a square, a nutter, an oldie. They would settle down and perhaps do some work. If his guess was wrong he had nothing to lose. If a first year class of dim wenches were too slippery for Mr Alfred to control he could tell the headmaster the man had trouble with girls as well as boys. Then he could renew his plea to have him shifted.

The human need to find a silver lining through the dark clouds shining made Mr Alfred look for a ray of light on the Stygian session ahead of him. He tightened his jaws till his decadent molars ached the first morning he stood at his desk and watched this strange new class flood into his room. They were all a-giggle, untidy and sweating after forty minutes in the gym, waddling, mincing, slouching, shuffling, hen-toed, splay-footed, unkempt, unclean, black-nailed, piano-legged, pin-legged, long and short, round and square, fat and thin, bananas and pears, big-breasted and flat-chested, chimps and apes, weeds and flowers, a dazzling tide of miscellaneous mesdemoiselles, twelve to thirteen years of age. Some wore nylons, some wore socks, some wore white hose to the knees, some had long hair, some had short, some had their hair styled, some wore it as it grew, some had washed their face that morning, some it seemed hadn't ever.

The ray he found was Rose Weipers. She sat down quietly on the front seat beside Senga Provan. They were conspicuously chums. But Gerald was gone. It was a new session. And Mr Alfred never believed in visiting the sins of the brother on the sister, far less on the sister's friend. When he was a political-minded young man he disliked the totalitarian countries where they proved guilt by association. He would take Senga as he found her, a person in her own right. He found her rather unattractive. Her scared strabismic face, her freckles and her ginger hair somehow embarrassed him. He avoided looking at her. But Rose was different. She was clean and tidy. She looked human, even intelligent. Before the week was out he was thinking she looked pretty as well.

He flicked through the progress-cards to find her IQ. It wasn't very high, just comfortably over the hundred. Senga's was higher. That irked him a little. He had prepared the comment that her very name showed she was backward. The rest, like the horses in the same race as Eclipse, were nowhere. He saw he had been given a giggle of the less academic girls just as last session he had been given a huddle of the less academic boys.

His only interest was Rose. He had a teacher's snobbery about IQs, a teacher's predilection for a welldressed child, a male weakness for a pretty face. When Rose came to him as a graceful trinity of good intelligence, good clothes and good looks, he had no choice. He made her his routine messenger. Whenever he had to pass on a circular from Mr

Briggs it was always Rose Weipers he sent next door with the 'please initial' document.

It didn't take him long to make her an errand girl at lunchtime too. He sent her out for a morning paper, pretending he hadn't time to get one on his way in. In fact he never bothered much about seeing a morning-paper. But it gave him an excuse to have her come back to him when the class was gone. Then he stopped going to the school dinners. He sent Rose to the local shops for rolls and cheese, rolls and gammon, a couple of hot mutton pies, anything he could take with a cup of tea in the staffroom. He didn't care what. He was never interested in food.

At first it was only when he had her in his class at the end of morning school that he sent her on an errand. But within the month she was coming along uninvited on other days to ask if there was anything he wanted. He always thought of something, because when she came back it meant he had her alone for a few minutes.

Halfway through the term they had got into the habit of meeting every day at lunchtime. He would wait in his classroom. When she came to him he didn't touch her. He told the critic at the back of his mind he wasn't getting the girl to come to his empty room so that he could cuddle her. It was her simple presence, with no one watching, gave him pleasure. Just to be alone with her. That's what he thought.

Coming back after her first voluntary shopping for him she knocked some test-papers off his desk. She was park-ing a poke with two rolls and gammon and counting out his change. The papers glided under the poke and slipped to the floor.

'That's a good start,' she said.

She picked up the papers, tutting at herself but not flustered. He noticed the way she stooped, a girl's way, bending the knees to keep her thighs from being exposed, not straddled and straightlegged like a boy. There was a certain elegant modesty about the movement that pleased him. And he loved the way she said 'start'. As if they were beginning a new life together. He believed they were.

She had a talent for making conversation. She would talk to him the way she would talk to a friend her own age. But not always. She puzzled him. She was as unpredictable as the grown women he had tried to love when he was young. One day she was chatty, the next day she hadn't a word to say for herself. It was her confiding moods made him fall in love, as when she told him about her aunt.

'I cried myself to sleep last night,' she said, alone with him at his desk.

'Oh dear,' he said. 'What happened?'

He bent to listen. He forgot he had said he would never touch her. He was only trying to show sympathy. He put an arm round her shoulder as he inclined an ear. She moved in close, telling him.

Her Aunt Beth had been staying with them for three months and left yesterday to go to Corby and get married.

'I'll miss her,' said Rose. 'She was so good to me. I was awful fond of her.'

He was no Alfred Lord Tennyson to object to her 'awful'. He squeezed her shoulder.

'But you'll see her again,' he said. 'It's not the end of the world.'

His hand wandered down her shoulder and stroked her arm.

He was sure she had an affectionate nature. Her talk was always about people she was fond of.

'My dad's been promising for weeks to take me to *The Sound of Music*,' she said. 'We were to go last night. But I didn't get.'

'You'll learn that's how life is,' he said, instructing her in banalities by occupational habit. 'You look forward to something and then it doesn't come off. I hope you weren't too disappointed.'

'Oh, no,' she said. 'I was more concerned about my dad. He wasn't well. That's why. He was sent home from his work. He's in bed. My mum got the doctor in.'

He liked the solemn way she said 'concerned'. He liked the word itself since it came from her young lips. He thought the sick man was lucky to have Rose concerned about him.

She told him of Martha's high marks in exams. She was proud of her big sister.

'Martha's clever,' she said. 'Not like me.'

He didn't know Martha, didn't want to. It was enough knowing Rose. He would have preferred her to be without a family, existing only for him. To think of her having a sister diminished her uniqueness.

Her innocent conversation made him think she liked him. He was a happy man. He teased her sometimes.

'That's a fine face you've got today! What's the matter with you? You look fed up.'

'I'm fed up,' she said, fed up. She gave him his poke and his change. 'This weather. Put years on an elephant, so it would.'

Nonstop rain and low graphite skies for a fortnight. A damp dismal world they lived in.

'Season of mists,' he said.

Rose sniffed, not hearing or not caring.

'I've got a cold,' she said.

'You stay in your bed tomorrow,' he said. It gave him a warm feeling of intimacy to mention bed to her, to think of her there.

'Dear me, look at your hair!' he cried. 'It doesn't know which way it's going.'

Emolliated with affection he stroked her hair from crown to nape, smoothed it back from her ear. Fingertip on an auricle. So tender.

'Can't do a thing with it,' she said. 'Washed it last night.'

She slanted her head away. He felt his hand rejected.

Then she made him jealous. He was waiting at his classroom door for her return from the shops. The sight of her coming along always made him love her. She looked so young, so remote from the world's slow stain, so trim and brave, so lonely and devoted, coming back to him and him alone, he was soothed to tenderness, his vanity gratified. She always seemed so much smaller outside the classroom, more of a child, he felt quite paternal.

He saw her meet the gym-teacher in the corridor. Cantering along, lightfooted in plimsolls, the gym-teacher grabbed her by the arm, birled her. Mr Simmons. A eupeptic, bigchested, broadshouldered young man.

'Hiya, Rose!' he greeted her.

He plunged his hand into her thick brown hair and ruffled it. Rose stopped, head down, accommodating the exploring hand, laughed. Mr Simmons weaved, boxing at her, clipped her lightly on the chin.

'I'll bang you,' said Rose.

She raised a miniature fist. She was pink and delighted.

Mr Simmons danced round her on his toes. Rose shaped up to him, leading with her right but handicapped by holding in it the poke with Mr Alfred's lunch. They made a palaestra of the deserted corridor. Still sparring even as they parted they both seemed pleased with the brief encounter.

'You don't get Mr Simmons for PT, do you?' said Mr Alfred dourly. He took the poke and change. He had a grudge against her for being so pretty that another man liked her. 'How does he know you?'

'Everybody knows me,' said Rose.

'Indeed?' he said, still sulky.

'I get him sometimes,' Rose explained. 'He takes the netball team for practice after four when Miss Avis can't stay.'

'But you're not in the netball team,' he challenged her. Very suspicious he was. 'At your age.'

'Not the school team, that's sixth year,' she said. She clicked her tongue at his absurd quizzing. 'The class team I mean, for the class league.'

He didn't know anything about class teams and a class league. She was helpless at his huff and left at once. So he got no conversation that day. It troubled him. He had been afraid he was in love. Now he was sure. Given the choice, he would rather have an hour with Rose than a night with Stella.

He couldn't stop thinking of Mr Simmons wrestling with Rose in the corridor. It was so natural, so harmless. Nobody could say there was anything improper in it. Rose had taken it laughing. Obviously she liked Mr Simmons. Her threat to bang him was an example of the free and easy relations between a modern pupil and a modern teacher. She would never have said it to him. But then he could never have done what Mr Simmons did. He wished he could.

He knew the trouble lay in his own bad mind. He wanted to fondle Rose. But his bad mind inhibited him. He was afraid if anyone saw him he would get the name of a lecherous old man. Even if nobody saw him Rose might be offended or frightened. She might know what evil creatures men could be. But she could let Simmons ruffle her hair and wrestle with her because she trusted Simmons. Of course Simmons was a married man with two little girls. Simmons was a man used to showing affection. Simmons had the right touch.

His bad mind kept annoying him. There was no use saying he could no more assault Rose than fly in the air, it would be against the gravity of his nature. He could imagine many things he would never do. He could imagine himself committing suicide though he knew he never would. He had come near it the day he knew his poems would never be published, and given up the idea for good. It wasn't in his nature. He could imagine himself attacking Rose to feel her breasts and lift her skirt. He knew he never would. But he knew such things were done by men his age to girls her age. His fear was that by some misconstrued telepathy Rose might suppose he intended the enormities he sadly knew were practised if he tried to play with her the way Simmons had done.

Whenever he read in the papers the story of a schoolgirl raped and murdered he was horrified at what a man could do. But it wasn't incomprehensible, it wasn't unthinkable. He could think it easily enough. He could imagine the damnable deed in all its details. But he was certain he could never do it himself. Any more than he could stick a knife into somebody, though he could imagine doing it. An indecent assault on Rose was one of the sins he knew he could never commit. Yet he longed to kiss her goodnight, to see her into bed. He longed to say he loved her. But never to love her by force. It was the lack of affection in rape that shocked him.

He was interested when he saw a story in the papers about a man of sixty marrying a girl of twenty. He worked out the difference between his own age and Rose's. It was less than that. So marrying her, however improbable, wasn't impossible. There were precedents. But at the same time as he thought of marrying Rose in a daydream future he kept thinking of her as his daughter in the waking life of his present.

The sodden autumn drained into a freezing winter. She came back carrying the quotidian poke, her hands blue with cold.

He took one. He was upset to feel it so chilled on his errand.

'Che gelida manina,' he said.

She looked up and said nothing. Puzzled. Wondering what he said.

He put the poke aside and chafed her hands. She let him do it without a word for or against, watching the operation with silent catatropia, and he was content.

After that he got into the habit of taking her hands when they were alone. He would pretend they looked cold and rub them. Then he stopped pretending. He held out his hand for hers while she was talking to him. The first time, she didn't understand what he meant. When he put his hand out she thought he was pointing to something on the floor at her feet and she looked down for something to be picked up. But the second time she saw what he wanted and gave him her hands with a kind of motherly patience.

It became a daily ritual, this holding of hands as they chatted alone at lunchtime, and he gave her half-a-crown every Friday. He called it her pocket money.

Christmas was coming. He thought he would give her a money present in recognition of the season and her services. He was all set for a tender donation when she came back with his rolls and beat him to the love scene he planned.

'I've got a wee present for you,' she said.

She smiled up at him with a child's excitement at the time of gifts and peace on earth, the holy tide of Christmas, brimming over with good-will.

She gave him a box of ten small cigars. Holly and a robin and From and To on the cardboard wrapping.

'They'll be a change for you,' she said. 'From those cigarettes you're aye smoking. I buy these for my dad at Christmas.'

He felt numbered among her clan.

'You shouldn't have done that,' he said.

He blushed as he took the nuzzer. Rose smiled.

'I was going to give you something,' he said. 'But I didn't know what to get you. You buy yourself something.'

He slipped a pound note into her drooping hand. It was a new one kept specially for her.

Rose palmed the note with a discretion equal to his. She looked up at him brighteyed and happy but didn't say thanks.

'If you were an orphan I'd adopt you,' he blurted.

He wanted to kiss her. But he was so tall he couldn't get his mouth to hers without an awkward swoop that would spoil the spontaneity of the action, and she didn't hold her face up to help him. He settled for squeezing her hand as it closed on the money.

When she went away he found he was tumescent. He argued with the man inside that it was only a desire to give her all the love he had. Not a stupid lust, but an erotic urge to an impossible act of gratitude.

He was drunk that night. He always got drunk in the euphoria of starting a holiday from school. Recognising the face in the mirror of a public-house gents he made a face at it, questioned it.

'Well, wotta ya gotta say for yourself, eh?' he asked, swaying to the glass. 'Sennimennal old fool. Wanting to kiss Rose. Rose upon the rood of time. Red Rose, proud Rose, sad Rose of all my days. Rose of the world, Rose of Peace. Far off, most secret and inviolate Rose. You want to frighten her? Stick your ugly mug into her lovely face and what would she get? A child's sense of smell. The reek of tobacco and the smell of whisky. A fine Christmas that for Rose. A merry kiss-miss. Be your age, mac!'

He had never been at parties when he was a boy. He had never played at kissing games. He had only heard of them. He thought a kiss was too serious for games. It wouldn't be right to kiss Rose. He loved her too much to snatch an old man's peck at her. He should leave her to get her first kiss from someone she loved when she was older.

Mrs Provan got Gerald a job beside her in the biscuit factory. She was never backward in asking. She kept on at the man in charge of deliveries till he started Gerald as a vanboy. There was no future in it, but it was a job. She would find him something better in due course. Gerald liked it. The work wasn't hard and the money was good. It was a carefree life, sitting in the van beside the driver, whistling and singing. He learnt his way round his native city, stopping here and there, kidding and kissing the shopgirls and getting known as Gerry. He was growing up, a handsome lad, and at the weekend he had money in his pocket. His mother let him keep most of his pay.

'He's not going to have the hard life I had,' she said to her foreman. 'I got on for years without a penny from him. I can still manage, please God. It'll do him good to have money to spend. He'll learn to look after himself.'

But she looked after him just the same as before, and Gerald's money went without either of them knowing exactly where. He never bought a suit or a pair of shoes, never a shirt or a tie, and when he had to get a haircut he asked his mother for the money. When he started shaving she bought his razorblades and shavingsoap until she got him an electric razor for his birthday. At his summer holidays he expected a bonus from her. He always got it.

He spent most of his nights in Ianello's, but time was all he spent. He never paid for his soft drinks or ices or sweets or cigarettes. He told Enrico he would see him later. He was a big, stronglooking boy, intimidating, largehanded, bold-eyed, insolent, armed. He had a knife he let people get a glimpse of when it suited him. Not the one Mr Alfred had seen. A new one, a bigger one. He challenged opposition with the glint of it to see what would happen. Nothing happened. He never used his knife. He got his own way with the show of it. Poggy and Smudge were what he called his handers. They admired him. Enrico suffered him for the sake of peace and quiet.

It was worse for Enrico when Jennifer and Wilma came in. It led to competition. The young males kept chancing their arm to prove who was the hard man. They peacocked, disputatious. The young hens egged them on, squawking and screeching. In the upshot Gerald stayed boss of the cafe. He had this knife. Enrico sighed, and settled for peace, though there wasn't much quiet with it. The jukebox he had hoped would bring in a jolly company of regular guys and dolls was monopolised by a dissident sect that kept other communicants away.

Gerald's mother never asked him where he went at night but she was always worrying about his future.

'You learn to drive that van, son,' she said. 'Never mind what your pals do. If you can drive you'll always find a job.'

'What do you think I'm doing?' said Gerald. 'I aim to get a car of my own. You've got to have a car nowadays to be anybody.'

He loved the smell of petrol and oil, the motorodour of a garage, the sights of jacks and pumps and wrenches and spanners, he loved lolling in the van and grinning at the panic-stricken pedestrians who had to scamper back or scurry across when the van came breezing through at the changing of the lights.

He bought magazines about motorcycles and cars and kept them stacked under his bed. He read them through over and over again, hoarding an enormous specialist knowledge. He could identify any vehicle at a hundred yards, make, model and year. But when he saw the price of a good secondhand car he lowered his sights to getting a motorbike first. The visceral image of the speed he could

get on a motorbike excited him. It was like the way
Jennifer and Wilma excited him when they leaned back
crosslegged in Ianello's wearing a miniskirt. He felt an
urge to get on and on. Faster and faster. Onwards and ever
upwards. He was growing up.

'They won't keep you on once you're older,' his mother
warned him. 'Once a vanboy wants a man's wage they just
sack him and get another boy. There's never any shortage
of boys.'

'I wonder why that is,' said Gerald.

He winked at Senga behind his mother's back. Senga
gave him a crosseyed snub. She was against him. She was
loyal to Rose Weipers. She loved Rose Weipers. And she
knew Mr Alfred was always getting Rose to go errands for
him. She didn't mind. There was no envy in her. She knew
Rose had the prettier face. She was ready to like any
teacher who liked Rose. But Gerald and her mother still
kept on about Mr Alfred. They told her to stand up to
him. She never found any occasion to, and kept her
opinion to herself. Once in a month or so she had her
childhood dream again, that she was sitting on her father's
knee, or some man's knee. She couldn't remember the
face. Before he kissed her she wakened up. The only
person she ever told was Rose.

Gerald wasn't bothered about her. She was only his
sister. He had a lot more on his mind than her silences. In
the yard where the fleet of factory vehicles was parked he
was learning starting and stopping, gear-changing, rever-
sing and three-point turns. Hill-starting and stopping he
learnt on Tordoch Brae on Saturday afternoons by plenary
indulgence of the driver at the end of the week's deliveries.
He found it difficult at first. But he was interested, he
concentrated, determined to learn. He was full of himself
and nobody ever said he wasn't intelligent. He was never
nervous sitting in charge of a powerful, throbbing vehicle.
He knew it was under his control. He was the lord of an
engine that slavishly obeyed the touch of his hand and
foot. He was the triumph of mind over metal. But apart

from the lessons on hill-starting the driver wouldn't let
him take over outside the factory.

His mother was passing across the yard once when she
saw him getting a lesson. A smile thawed her frozen face.
To see him sitting up there in the cabin driving the van
pleased her.

'You know,' she said to her foreman, 'it's an awful pity
his teachers took a spite at him. They taught him nothing.
Gerald could have been an engineer if he'd got the education.'

She was a patient woman, crafty, for ever planning
ahead. Well in advance of the time when Gerald would
be too old to stay on as a vanboy she was on to the
maintenance men in the firm's garage. She deaved them
how good her Gerald was, what a smart boy, quick to
learn, a willing worker. She got him started as an apprentice motor mechanic. Poggy and Smudge went into the
same line. Poggy found a job in a bus company's garage
and Smudge scraped a place in a local petrol and repair
station. They were all happy. It kept them sharing a way of
life.

In the evenings when it was boring sitting any longer in
Ianello's talking shop, they swaggered out for diversion.
They finished up on the prowl after midnight. They
kicked over the wire litter bins on the arc-lamp standards,
lifted the empty milk bottles outside a sleeping house and
smashed them on the road. They chucked stones at the
crossing beacons. When they passed a bus-shelter with
any panes still unbroken they broke them.

Tired mooching around like that, Gerald was the first to
get a bike. Always at his heels, Poggy and Smudge got one
as well. Gerald's was on monthly payments. It was new.
Poggy and Smudge got second-hand ones cheap. The
three of them overworked their bikes. Parts had to be
replaced. But they couldn't go on buying them. It cost too
much. There wasn't much they could lift where they
worked that was any use to them. So at one and two in
the morning they raided any motor-bikes parked in the

street. Sometimes they stripped a bike for the fun of it. When they had more spares than they needed Smudge sold the surplus to any motor-cyclist who used his repair shop and asked no questions about a bargain.

Smudge was the first to steal a bike. His own was past it. After all, it was in its second childhood when he bought it. He swopped the numberplates and ditched his own in the quarry behind the brickwork. They moved on to cars. Many a man in the housing-schemes had a car but no garage. He had to leave his car in the street all night. Gerald took Poggy and Smudge with him ambling round side-streets after midnight looking for vulnerable vehicles. They had a good collection of car keys. They stripped a car of its radio, its battery, raided the boot. Anything left in the back seat they lifted.

'Bugger doesn't deserve to get keeping it,' Smudge used to say when he fished out a briefcase, an A.A. handbook, a mascot, a paperback or magazine. Any trifle at all, he took it.

They had a good night in a quiet crescent of semi-detached villas far from their own territory. There were a dozen cars parked along it. They smashed the windows, forced open any door they couldn't unlock, and stole the car-seats and travelling rugs. They tossed the car-seats into somebody's front garden well away from where they got them. Poggy and Smudge shared the travelling rugs between them. Gerald didn't want one. He never took home anything that was stolen.

It was nearly two in the morning when he got home from that raid. He had been getting later and later, but this was the worst ever. His mother was angry.

'Where have you been till this time?' she shouted. 'You've had me worried stiff!'

'Ach, shut your face, you old nag,' said Gerald.

He was tired, and that made him a bit short with her. He stared hard at the bare table.

'What've you got?' he asked. 'You don't mean to say there's nothing ready for me.'

Mrs Provan was distressed. She couldn't think what to say for a moment.

'I can fry you a sausage and an egg if you like,' she said humbly.

'That'll do fine,' said Gerald agreeably. He never kept up a bad mood.

Senga, conscripted to sit up with her anxious mother, made a face unseen and slipped off silent and unnoticed to bed.

CHAPTER SEVENTEEN

Graeme Roy went to the university. He was excited but confident, a young hawk eager to swoop on a new field. Martha stayed on at school for another year to add to her leaving-certificate subjects. She liked French and German. She thought she would get a cosmopolitan job with a good degree in modern languages. They looked forward to being students together. He saw himself as the trail blazer, preparing the way for his soul mate. With a year's experience in hand he would be able to guide and advise her, take her round the scattered buildings of the university, lead her to the French and German departments and the women's union, tell her what clubs and societies she ought to join.

But he had no one to show him around. He enrolled in engineering and missed lectures in the opening weeks because he didn't know where they were being given. When he settled to the work of his classes he discovered he was a country yokel in a mob of city slickers, a flounder in a shoal of smart students. He wanted to be a technocrat. That was how he saw it, that was how he said it. But he wasn't up to it. He had poor results in the first term exams at Christmas, the Christmas Mr Alfred and Rose Weipers were holding hands. When it came to summer and the degree exams he was in a panic. He lost the place in all his subjects. He couldn't decide which one to worry about most. He worried about them all and couldn't concentrate on one in particular. When the results went up on the board he saw he had failed in them all.

It wasn't Martha's fault. Much as she liked to be with him she wouldn't meet him oftener than once a week. She encouraged him to study. She wanted to be proud of being his girlfriend. She wanted to find him established at the university when she arrived there. She wanted him to be a student who had passed all his first year exams without any bother and who would pass all his exams the same way every year until he graduated with an honours B.S.C degree in Engineering.

His total failure made her miserable. She wept in the loneliness of her bed. He was sullen after he told her he had nothing to tell her. He blamed the system. He said there had always to be so much percent of a plough, and he had fallen below an arbitrary line. He was sure he hadn't done all that badly, he surely deserved a pass in at least one of the subjects. She blamed his father for persuading him to take a degree in engineering. But only to herself. She never came out with it to him. And amid her sorrow she wasn't surprised at his failure. She had felt all along he had picked the wrong course.

His old teachers, always informed of university results, were as little surprised as Martha.

'I don't know what comes over these fellows,' said Mr Kerr. 'I advised him to take an Arts degree.'

'He should have gone in for English Honours,' said Mr Brown. 'He had a talent for English. He wrote a very good poem for last year's magazine.'

'An engineering degree is just about the hardest degree there is,' said Mr Campbell. 'There's a heavy plough every year. And Graeme Roy and engineering maths, well, I ask you! He's a nice lad all right but no head for maths. I saw that when I had him in my last class. What makes them do it?'

'They put a glamour round it,' said Mr Brown. 'An Arts degree is too common for them, thank you.'

'That's true,' said Mr Dale. 'They get this science bug. They want to be back-room boys.'

'They think the ambition proves the capacity,' said Mr Campbell.

'His whole bent was for languages,' said Mr Kerr.

'He showed me a translation he had made of a poem by Rimbaud, "le Formeur du Val". I'd never ask a schoolboy to translate Rimbaud.'

'But wasn't Rimbaud only a schoolboy when he wrote it?' said Mr Dale.

'Yes, I know,' said Mr Kerr. 'But he was Rimbaud. I would never take Rimbaud's poems with any class here. But Roy had been reading French poetry on his own, God bless him. He wanted my opinion of his translation. I said it was quite good. So it was.'

'That poem he wrote for me,' said Mr Brown. 'For the magazine I mean. It was a case of Dylan Thomas out of Swinburne. Very good as I said. But I couldn't print it.'

'Why not?' Mr Alfred enquired sharply from his corner.

Anything concerning poetry concerned him. He had never seen the poem Mr Brown was talking about nor had he ever heard before of the translation from Rimbaud. He was annoyed. He thought he should have been consulted.

'Well, in a school magazine!' said Mr Brown. 'There are limits, you know. He was only a boy of seventeen at the time. He shouldn't have been thinking the way he was, not at his age. Kind of sexy it was.'

'I see,' said Mr Alfred. 'And at what age if not seventeen should he be thinking of sex? Folk like you would have us either too young or too old.'

'You mean you still—' Mr Brown began.

'A man's never too old,' Mr Dale tactfully interrupted. 'Look at that old bloke of sixty-four in the papers yesterday married a wench of nineteen. His grand-daughter's chum.'

Mr Alfred had seen it but didn't like to mention it.

'That's all very well,' said Mr Brown. 'But there was one bit I remember. Something about, I dream in these satyric moods of nymphs' wan thighs in summer woods. I could never have printed that. What would old Briggs have said? Not to mention the parents.'

'Or our beloved Monica the All-Seeing,' said Mr Dale.

'I had him some years back,' said Mr Alfred. 'He

seemed quite intelligent, but I should never have thought there was a poet in him.'

He sat back and said no more. He was no longer interested in the conversation. It had made him think of Rose Weipers. Everything made him think of Rose Weipers. He had never seen her thighs. He tried to imagine them. He couldn't. She was always sedate, sat down like a lady, knees and feet together. Even in the playground, any time he passed and took a quick look, she managed to jump the rope in her turn without the swirling skirt and swift show of thigh that other girls flaunted. She never showed off. He had seen without interest the legs and underwear of other girls as they lolled in his room, but Rose never showed an inch above the hemline. She was a modest girl. His autumnal longing to kiss a child good-night and tuck her into bed moved through him again. He had a passionless wish, a neutral and almost clinical curiosity, to see Rose as she was, from head to toe, whole and entire.

'He had an unusual Sprachgefühl,' said an assistant German teacher. 'I told him he ought to—'

'He had a good French accent,' said an assistant French teacher. 'Before he left I said to him—'

'I warned him,' said Mr Campbell. 'I said to him you might be good at English but as far as maths are concerned you're—'

'I advised him,' said Mr Brown. 'What you should do I said is—'

'They get this craze about science,' said Mr Kerr. 'They want to be with it. But where's the culture in all these technical subjects?'

The bell rang. Nobody answered.

They went to their classes. They dropped Graeme Roy. But I can't. Not yet, anyway.

Having failed to satisfy the examiners he wanted to satisfy Martha. There at least he would prove he wasn't an impotent failure. He tried to arouse her. She wasn't aroused. She was only offended. The nearer he tried to get

the further away she moved. When he sulked and withdrew she warmed to bring him back. Her temperature
seemed to vary inversely with his own.

In the summer vacation he took her out one day in his
car. The parents had guessed they were meeting again but
didn't want to make a new fuss about an old issue. They
were prepared to tolerate though not to encourage an affair
which had persisted in spite of them. They were willing to
concede the young couple were getting old enough to
know their own mind. It might be a case of true love after
all.

They went to Helensburgh and up by Garelochhead,
then followed Loch Long north to Arrochar and lunch.
They were lucky in the weather. The sky was an unbroken
blue and the cloudless windless heat made them feel they
had wandered into a day from the legendary summers of
the past. On a lonely stretch they saw the opposite bank
reflected in the motionless water of the mirroring loch. It
was an inverted world of tall timeless trees and unpeopled
hills. Nothing moved anywhere. They got out.

'Listen!' she cried suddenly.

He smiled, she was so happy.

Obeying her he listened. He clasped her hand and
looked up at the immense sky because she was looking
there. A birdsong rose higher and higher and faded to
heavenly silence. But he could see nothing.

'The lark in the clear air,' he said.

They sat in the car a little while before going on. He
wanted to find release in her, to lean on her, to be
comforted and encouraged. Not this time as the times
he offended her, not the male determined to conquer his
woman by force, but the defeated manchild turning to the
female for motherly solace. She gave him none. Her breast
wasn't going to be his pillow. Her retreat made him
impatient. He pulled her tight against him and kissed
her harder than he had ever kissed her before. And longer.
She was so close, his alert body was aware of her heartbeat.
It was going at a terrific rate. He thought he had only to

keep at her a moment more and she would give in. But the racing throb of that necessary engine frightened him. So fast her heart was going it seemed it could only end in a crashing stop. Let it beat for ever, he prayed, let me not disturb it further. There was plenty of time. He slackened his grip. A wave of tenderness drowned him. He let her sit away from him.

She turned suddenly and kissed him gently on the cheek. Her hand was stroking the back of his neck. He felt it was a medal awarded for devotion to duty in face of the enemy.

They went from Arrochar to Tarbet. She saw the Cobbler on her left hand. It was all new to her. She was dumb with delight. Her eyes were excited, but he knew it was only by the countryside in fine summer weather, not by anything he had done to her. He grudged her taking pleasure in nature and not in him. But he put a face on it and drove chatting up Loch Lomond to Ardlui, on to Crianlarich and through Glen Dochart. He turned south into Glen Ogle and took her home by Callander, Loch Vennacher and Aberfoyle. She had never seen so much of the country outside her city. She was exhausted at the end of the long day, dazed with strange sights. The bens and glens and lochs, the sheep and highland cattle, the remote cottage and the blue sky over all, the lonely miles where there were no streets and no shops and no tenements or housing schemes, still lingered in her town-reared brain. When she closed her eyes that night in bed alone she saw them again. Without him she would never have seen them at all. She told him so. He was pleased to have pleased her, even if it wasn't the way he had meant. It was another knot in the string that tied them.

CHAPTER EIGHTEEN

Granny Lyons used Ianello's cafe nearly every day. She bought her cigarettes there. She didn't smoke a lot, but she was never without a packet. Once in a while, if Mr Alfred hadn't come when she expected him and she was short of money, Enrico let her have a packet on tick. She was fond of sweets too, and got them in the same shop. Usually it was only a half-pound of liquorice-all-sorts, a mixture she particularly liked, almost to the point of addiction. Whenever she tried to do without them for more than a week Enrico slipped her a box with her cigarettes. Then he would turn away from her, his elbow on the counter, and look up and down and all along his shelves as if he was surveying his stock and hadn't given her anything, didn't even know she was there.

They were friends. They shared the sorrow of having blundered into Tordoch when they had set sail for a different port altogether. They were bewildered and frustrated, the way Columbus was when he tripped over the West Indies instead of making landfall in Asia. They couldn't understand what had gone wrong with their navigation. Granny Lyons saw no escape. She knew it was a life sentence, at her age. Enrico was younger and so more optimistic. He said he would move to a better area soon and get a good-going shop.

She liked to hear him talk about his plans. His accent charmed her. His voice was more lively and his tone more varied than anything the natives could manage with their flat utterance of half-swallowed syllables. She was fascinated by the energetic movement of his lips and the expressive assistance of his hands and shoulders. She preferred the vigorous activity of his mouth under the drooping moustache to the slack-jawed speech of his customers who mumbled at him with their hands in their pockets.

His vocabulary too amused her. He knew all the dialect words and the local slang. He came out with the standard obscenities as fluently as anyone else in Tordoch, but he used them with an earnest innocence that made them sound decent. How was he to know they weren't? He was no student of semantics, any more than that foreign girl, the wife of some literary gent, who typed a draft of that thing Lawrence wrote. Like Enrico, she assumed the gamekeeper's tetragrams were normal usage in polite society. Naturally enough, like Enrico, she brought them into her conversation to show her command of English idiom. And naturally enough she was puzzled when her husband and his cultured friends said she must never use those words again.

Not that Enrico was limited to four-letter words. Suddenly, in the same sentence, he would get his tongue round some polysyllable as if it too was a commonplace of intercourse between a man and a woman. He often misapplied and mispronounced the big word, showing he had never heard it used, but had merely met it in print somewhere.

When that happened Granny Lyons didn't hesitate to tell him. She knew him too well and he knew her too well for any offence to be given or taken. She saw no use trying to stop him using the monosyllables he heard the natives use every time they opened their mouth. But if he was going to use big words she wanted him to get them right. He was grateful to her.

One day he spoke to her about Gerald Provan. His hands tried to help his tongue and his big brown eyes were sad.

'He's a perpernicious youth,' he ended.

'That's very good,' she commended him. 'But just say pernicious. I must tell my nephew what you said. He'll like it. He had the same opinion when he taught that boy. Aye, and there's a lot more like him he's still teaching, poor man.'

'Your nephew not happy in that school?' he lilted. Eyebrows up. Eyes popping. Polite surprise. He shrugged and answered himself. 'No, I suppose no. Who could be?'

He shook his head slowly to indicate defeat, exhaled wearily through pursed lips, and murmured inoffensively, 'Shower of fucking bastards, that's all they are. I know them.'

He was not without self-esteem. He believed he was superior to the autochthonous tribes he served.

'They come in here and they look down on Enrico,' he complained to her. 'They call me a tally. They say, hey, tally-wally! Hey, you, Nello!'

He snapped his fingers, acting customers calling him.

'Like you call a dog. I leave Naples with my father. Me? Just a baby. We come to Scotland. Then the war. My father? Taken away. His own kind, his own kind mind you, frightened him. He had to join something. I don't know what. I know politics never his care. But the police have his name. So. Internment they say. He goes down in the Andorra Star. My mother? She live. Somehow. She work hard. Brings me up. I never much go to the school. But I work. I learn by ear. My mother and me, we speak our father's language at home. I marry. I have family. I come out here. Open my own shop. Me. Enrico Ianello from Naples. I have no boss. Ianello's boss is Enrico. Poor boy makes it good. I speak their language. Can they speak mine? Speak mine? They can't even speak their own fucking language.'

'That's very true,' said Granny Lyons.

'But yet still they look down on Enrico. I ask you. Tell me. The other night I say to that Poggy one, don't be so obstreperous. Says he to me, what the fucking hell you mean, mac. Says I to him, you mac not me. All you Scotch fucking macs. Not clever there, me. He put a great big bloody brick through my window that night. That's three times in four months my window in.'

'They're getting worse,' said Granny Lyons. 'I've had mine in twice since Christmas.'

'A shop, well,' he granted. His hands moved to say there were some things you had to put up with in this world. 'But not a house.'

'But I'm on the ground floor, you know,' said Granny Lyons. 'At a bad corner too. I wouldn't mind getting a room right at the top of one of those thirty-two storey flats they're building now. Away from it all, well above them.'

'You well above them all right,' said Enrico.

He told her about his new juke-box.

'Biggest mistake of my life,' he wailed. 'Pay for itself in a month says the man. Will bring in the young ones. Oh, big deal! Yes, brings them in too damn true. And in one night they drink what? One coffee, one coke. And what do I get? The sound of noise all night. I like hear singing. I sing myself. My father too. My mother tells me. Fine voice. You know, Italian. Not what these ignorant bastards go for.'

And indeed she knew he loved the bel canto. Often in an afternoon when the shop was quiet because the boys and girls were at school, she would go in to hear him singing in the back scullery as he prepared ice-lollies for the fridge. He was Manrico singing farewell to his Leonora, the Duke singing about the nobility of women, or Cavaradossi singing that the stars were shining.

When she heard him enjoying himself like that with his untrained tenor, she was moved to affection for him and made no sound till he finished his aria. Then she would sing out and he would come and chat with her. She would put her old-fashioned handbag on the counter and rest her forearms across the straps, hardly holding them. She was at peace in a calm oasis somewhere between the desert of three and four p.m., and Enrico too was carefree.

On one such afternoon their pleasant counter-talk was interrupted by the entrance of three lanky hairy youths in donkey-jackets and tight trousers. They came in hipsway-ing as if Enrico's cafe was a saloon in a Western and they were tough hombres on the trail who had just hitched their horses to the rail outside.

'Lucky strike,' said the first.

His mates loitered behind Granny Lyons.

'Excusa-me,' said Enrico to Granny Lyons.

He attended to his strange customers. Eyebrows raised, eyes questioning.

'Lucky strike,' repeated the gunless cowboy.

Enrico's eyebrows came down to a puzzled frown.

The cowboy tried again.

'Day ye sell Lucky Strike?'

'Ah!' said Enrico. 'American cigarettes. Some I have.'

He turned to the shelves.

'But not Lucky Strike. Chesterfield, Stuyvesant. And I have—'

Even as he began naming the brands he had in stock he had a dim feeling he was being silly. But he was that bit slow. One of the cowboys behind Granny Lyons charged at her like a football-player giving away a penalty. She tottered and teetered, lost her balance and fell. Her hand-bag remained on the counter. The other cowboy snatched it. The one that had asked for Lucky Strike knocked over a jar of hardboiled sweets and threw a tray of Wrigley's PK at Enrico's face. In a split second the three bandits ran out together.

Granny Lyons clawed at the counter and got back on her feet. Enrico raced out of his shop like a whippet. Granny Lyons wept and trembled.

'Oh, not again,' she whimpered. 'Not again.'

Enrico came back, a lot slower than he had gone out.

'Hopeless,' he lamented, pulling his hair. 'They dive in a close round the corner. I see them. By the time I get there, gone. Up the stairs, across the back-court, through another close? Who knows?'

'Oh well, it might have been worse,' said Granny Lyons. Her hands quivered as she tidied her grey hairs and smoothed her coat and skirt. She felt handless without her handbag. The loss diminished her.

Enrico saw how she felt. He wept in vexation.

'It's as well I was here,' she comforted him. 'Or it might have been the till they tried. And God knows what they might have done to you if you'd been alone. Lucky it was only me. They didn't get much. My God. Let them ask for it if they're that hard up and I'll give them it.'

'I give in,' said Enrico.

He wiped his brimming brown eyes with the cuff of his white jacket.

It may have been the saying of it made him think of surrender, or he may only have been saying what he wouldn't admit before. But from that day he lost heart. He was ashamed of his shop. He hadn't the spirit to fight its invaders any longer. He was sick of non-paying customers, bullies and rioters. The booths where he had hoped to encourage a cafe society of young people discussing politics and literature and foreign affairs were an offence to the eye. The woodwork was hacked and scratched, the walls were defaced with the sprawling initials of his patrons, the floor was fouled with discarded wads of chewing-gum. The local lads and lasses had annexed his shop as a colony for revelry and disorder. They quarrelled at the drop of a joke and fights over nothing happened every night in the week. Enrico was always expecting to see blood shed but it never quite came to that.

In an attempt to get some peace and quiet he put the juke-box out of commission. Too often it caused a fight between rival fans of different singers. But without it the boys and girls made their own noise, and that was worse.

He made a last effort to get control. One wild night some laughing youths tested the solidity of the table in the back booth by kicking it from underneath and then jumping on it from the bench. They threw crisps across the cafe and poured coke into the coffees of the mixed company in the next booth. There was a lot of recrimination, and a threat

and a challenge were heard. The uproar led to some
punching and wrestling and somebody got up from the
floor with a knife in his hand and a nasty look in his eyes.
The girls screamed, some in terror, some in delight.
Enrico phoned for the police.

By the time two policemen arrived the cafe was empty
except for Gerald Provan sitting in the middle booth with
Poggy, having a quiet conversation with Wilma and Jennifer. Gerald wasn't intimidated by a phone call. He knew
Enrico knew what would happen if he named anybody.

Enrico told the policemen about the disturbance. He
said the culprits had run away as soon as they heard him
phone from the back-shop. He didn't know any of them.
The boy who had drawn a knife? He had never seen him
before. They were all strangers. Gerald sat back listening,
his face solemn and sympathetic.

'It's a shame, Mr Ianello, so it is,' he said.

The two policemen gave Gerald and his company a hard
look but said nothing. They went away. Enrico felt very
foolish. After midnight his windows were smashed. For a
week after that he had nuisance calls, sometimes at one
and two in the morning. The various speakers threatened
him and his wife and family. One call particularly alarmed
him.

'Do that again,' said the voice in the earpiece, 'and I'll
cut your throat from ear to ear.'

And then the speaker laughed at him.

He was going over some bills and his bank statement one
night after the shop was closed. His flat above the cafe was
quiet, his wife and two children were asleep. Into the hush
there moved a vague scuffling and a susurrus of hostile
voices. He looked up from his counting and listened. He
was always frightened until he located and interpreted
what he was hearing. It was youths quarrelling in the
street. He waited for them to pass. They didn't. Then his
shop door was battered and young voices were raised,
calling him. He could have thought his house was on fire,
the way they were carrying on. He tiptoed downstairs and

stood behind the door to the street. It was double-leaved, made of stout wood, double-locked and double-bolted. He felt safe enough. They would need an axe to break in. He heard his name called again.

'En-RI-co I-a-NEL-lo!'

'Who are you?' he asked, close to the wood.

There was no answer.

Upstairs, his wife and family wakened and listened, puzzled.

'What do you want?' Enrico shouted through the wood.

He tried to sound tough and abrupt, a dangerous man to annoy.

'You,' said a bass voice, no less terrifying because it was disguised.

The appalling monosyllable was followed by a crescendo of insane screeching and hysterical laughter, male and female. Enrico trembled in the dark. The assault on the door was renewed. He half expected it to come in, so fierce was the hammering and kicking. It didn't. But while he waited for signs of it cracking and shouted to his wife to phone the police, one of his windows had a brick through it. He pulled his hair and cursed when he heard the glass shatter. His wife screamed on her way to the phone. Then there was silence.

That was when he gave in. He made his surrender public and got his name in the papers. He had a nephew Gino who was a football reporter on the local evening paper, and Gino put a colleague in the news department on to it. Enrico's rambling account of his grievances was printed in an edited version.

'I cannot continue to live in this city. I must think of the safety of my wife and children. This has been building up. These people have made my life a misery with threats of violence over the phone. They have made my shop a shambles. I tried to give them service. They do not seem to want it. I am not saying where I will go. They said they will follow me if they find out.'

He went away, and nobody ever knew where, except

Granny Lyons. She missed him, but she told him to go. He tried to sell his shop with the flat above it but nobody wanted that kind of shop and house in that kind of district. The abandoned cafe became a derelict site where children played, and all the metal fittings and lead guttering were stripped by nocturnal raiders.

CHAPTER NINETEEN

In the new session Mr Alfred was given the same class of girls again for the same three periods. He made no complaint. It was what he wanted, to keep on seeing Rose Weipers. His fondness for her became egregious. It caused talk behind his back.

'I knew none of them would ever take a crush on him,' said Mr Brown. 'But I never thought he would take a crush on one of them.'

'If it keeps him happy why should you worry?' said Mr Dale.

'I don't like it,' said Mr Brown. 'A good teacher treats all his pupils alike.'

Mr Campbell took his pipe from his mouth and put down his crossword. Clue: *View an orphan hasn't got*. It was his function in the staffroom to correct the errors of his colleagues.

'I don't know that's true,' he said. 'Pupils come in different styles. The right thing is to treat them accordingly. Not all alike. That's wrong.'

A disputation started.

'You're missing the point the lot of you,' said Mr Dale. 'If it makes him human surely it's a good thing whether it's right or wrong.'

'How can it be a good thing if it's wrong?' asked Mr Brown. 'Talk sense.'

'It depends what you mean,' said Mr Campbell. 'A good thing. What do you mean by good?'

'I mean he said good morning to me on the bus this morning,' said Mr Dale. 'Shows you how love can mellow an old crab.'

'It depends what you mean by love,' said Mr Campbell. 'If you just mean a mellowing influence, then all you're saying is a mellowing influence mellows.'

'I agree a teacher should like kids,' said Mr Brown.

'If he doesn't he's in the wrong job. But for a man to get especially fond of one pupil, above all a girl and a growing girl at that, I don't think that's right.'

'But all girls are growing girls,' said Mr Dale.

'Till they stop growing. Then they're women. And what's wrong with a man loving a woman tell me.'

'Nothing,' said Mr Brown. 'I gather it's still quite common. But that's not the point. It's a teacher loving a girl in his class we're talking about.'

'Who says he loves her?' said Mr Dale. 'Maybe he just likes her. Sure we all have a Rose. I mean, you can't help liking some kids more than others. It's only natural.'

'That's what I'm saying,' said Mr Campbell.

'You've got to define your terms. Natural, for instance. You say it's only natural. What do you mean by natural? You can have unnatural affection too you know.'

Mr Alfred came in. In his right hand he carried a poke with the two rolls brought by the Rose who had just left him. He was singing softly the words of Longfellow's translation of Müller's 'Wohin', following but never quite catching Schubert's tune.

> I know not what came o'er me,
> Nor who the counsel gave,
> But I must hasten downward,
> All with my pilgrim stave.

He put the poke on the table and went through to the wash-hand basin.

'See, the big bugger's happy,' said Mr Dale.

'Would you grudge him it?'

'Too young a rose to pluck,' said Mr Brown.

They heard him sing louder as he turned on the taps.

Thou has with thy soft murmur
Murmured my senses away.

'Oh that's that thing, ich hört' ein Bächlein rauschen,'
Mr Kerr announced, recitative. 'It sounds better in the
German of course. You can't beat the Germans for lieder.'

'Yes, he does sound happy, doesn't he,' said Mr Campbell, and entered PANORAMA in his crossword.

Mr Alfred was indeed happy. He thought he had reason
to be. Before she went away Rose let him hold her hand as
usual and he stroked her hair and caressed her ear. What
was new this time was, she sat on his knee for a minute. He
was sitting sideways at his table, tired after being on his
feet all morning. When he held out his hand for hers she
was an arm's length from him. He drew her in, meaning
only she should come a little nearer. She seemed to take it
he meant more. She came right over and sat on one knee.

He felt the cheeks of her bottom pressed just above his
kneecap. He was sure he was blushing. He was uncomfortable. He put his arm lightly round her in case she fell
off, and she was so thin above the waist, she had so little
on, he thought he could have counted her ribs if he had
dared to squeeze her. But he didn't want to frighten her.
He shifted his hand and fingered the pinna of her left ear.
She drank through a straw a surplus bottle of milk left
inadvertently in his classroom, and chatted about her
father and family between imbibitions.

So soon does the new become a habit that in a week,
when she came at lunchtime with his rolls or pies or
sandwiches, she sat on his knee as a matter of course
for five minutes and talked to him. She did it without
any shyness, no fuss and no comment, did it calmly and
casually. He was the one who felt guilty. He got into a drill
of waiting for her at the door to his room and locking it
swiftly when she came in. She would walk past him,
slender, unsmiling, slightly splay, put the poke on the
table and count out his change. By that time he had
reached his chair and sat down, ready to receive her.

She perched herself on his left knee, her toes just touching the floor. He was sure there must be a more comfortable position, and he was always uneasy. Yet he was disappointed any day she didn't do it.

One day she sat right across his lap. It may have been the way he was sitting or it may have been her angle of approach. But there she was. He believed her voluntary session sanctioned him to show more affection. Her legs and knees were convenient to his gangling hand, her slightly-parted thighs were settled trustingly across his. He imagined his hand moving over the unseen limbs. He would be gentle and loving. But his nerve failed. He couldn't. He thought it would be wrong. He put his arm round her waist and his hand stroked her lean flank.

'Oh Rose! I do love you!' he whispered, his mouth against her ear.

He felt at once he was silly to have said it. He tried to unsay it.

'But don't tell anybody,' he added, smiling as if it was only a joke.

He put his finger on her nose and followed the line of it down to her nostrils. To make it clear he was only teasing, he tenderly flipped a fingertip at her chin. She smiled.

Then an impulse beat him. Sitting across his lap, she was so accessible in a way she had never been when they were standing up together that he plunged at her. He kissed her, not on the mouth but on the forehead, somewhere above the right eye. It was a shot badly off target, but he felt he had done something tremendous.

Like all that had gone before the kissing too became a habit, with all the necessity of a habit. At first he kissed her only when he gave her a halfcrown at the end of the week for doing his errands. He looked forward to Fridays as payday. He was sour if anything happened to prevent his rite, as when some leech of a classmate came back with her and hung around. Usually it was Senga Provan, and he came near to disliking her as much as he had disliked her brother. To make up for those unkissing Fridays he began to kiss Rose during the week whenever he got a chance, whenever she didn't seem in a hurry away, for he needed time to create the dialogue of lovers' talk that was properly ended in a parting kiss.

Sometimes he worried over what he was doing. He was afraid she would tell her mother or a classmate. It would make him look ridiculous. Her mother might think it worse than ridiculous. She might think he was trying to entice Rose on to something wicked.

He went over it every night between waking and sleeping, recalling how his love had been born, in her sudden burst of confidence, unexpected and unpredictable, when they first met. Nobody had ever spoken to him like that before. It was she who had started their love affair by the way she chatted to him, by her rare trusting smiles. It was all her fault. How could he refuse to love her when she urged him to it? But he believed that what she urged him to was a father's love. She was no precocious miss just trying to provoke him. She spoke to him like a daughter, and his kisses were chaste, like a father's kisses.

He loved her very name. Rose Weipers seemed no less worthy than Rose Aylmer to appear in a poem, and she herself no less possessed of 'every virtue, every grace' than that earlier Rose. But he never found time to write a poem to or about her, though he kept on intending to consecrate some faultless lines to his love for her. He settled for making her name his talisman, a pious and even apotrapaic ejaculation in moments of temptation. When he was accosted after the last pub of his nightly crawl was closed, or when he found himself in Blythswood Square or Hope Street, not drunk and yet not sober, he remembered Rose and said her name aloud to the darkness. He believed she would be shocked, or at least disappointed, if she saw him go off with a woman who had to be paid. The fact that she couldn't know what he did made no difference. She was to him like God, who knows and sees all things, even our most secret thoughts. So he never went with even the youngest prostitute he met. Rose was the only person he wanted.

Day and night he was the victim of his autumnal love, a love that seemed at one and the same time to exclude and include the possibility of sexual pleasure. Rose, its only object, had to be female or he could never have fallen in love with her. He could never have loved a boy her age. The idea disgusted him. He knew boys too well. He thought pederasty ugly. But Rose had a girl's face, not a boy's face, a girl's body, not a boy's. That was why he could love her. Yet he had no desire to proceed beyond his constant awareness of her sex. The awareness was its own pleasure. A boy could never have interested him. His love was a heterosexual love. Therefore a normal love. To love Rose seemed natural and pure in a way that loving a boy would never have seemed to him.

He was pursuing these meditations round the alcoholic confusion of his skull one night when he was importuned on his way home after the pubs were shut. He knew he ought to have gone straight for a bus instead of wandering about to ask for encounters he didn't want.

'Looking for someone?' she said pleasantly, suddenly in front of him.

He put his palms under her elbows, rocking and beaming.

'No rose in all the world, until you came,' he sang into her powdered face.

Then dried up and lurched away.

She gaped after him. She was fed up with men who mooched round dark streets and loitered in doorways and closes and floated off when she spoke to them.

'Away hame, ya stupit big bastard!' she shouted after him.

Rose Weipers leaned against a wash-hand basin in the girls' toilet at morning-break whispering with Senga Provan. They had agreed to stop going to the playground. To walk there was like wandering across a battlefield where Amazons ignored the rights of non-combatants and blithely mowed them down. They wanted a quiet corner and the chance of a confidential talk.

'I get right fed up with the pair of them at times,' Senga was saying. 'You'd think, my goodness it's years ago now, you'd think they'd forget it.'

Wanda Clouston, a mammose wench in third year, waddled to the door of a cubicle and tore a yard of toilet-paper from the fixture. Flushed with hebetic vulgarity she draped the streamer round Rose Weiper's neck and made to kiss her on both cheeks in a gallic award.

Rose recoiled.

'Aw, for Christ's sake,' she said. 'Be your age.'

She scattered the paper with a cross hand and smacked Wanda. Wanda pulled her hair. They wrestled. Wanda broke away, getting the worst of it, and delved a hand under her blouse.

'Ach, you! You've bust ma bra, ya bitch!' she yelled.

'It's no' a bra you need,' said Rose, still cross. 'It's a couple of hammocks.'

'Think you're somebody?' Wanda asked. Bellona.

'Ignore her, Rose,' said Senga. Grave-eyed Pallas Athene, goddess of good counsel. 'I wouldn't demean myself talking to the likes of her.'

Rose looked straight into Wanda's rash eyes. A

petrifying Medusa. Wanda turned, sniffed, and waddled off.

'Think because your big sister goes wi' a toffee-boy,' she muttered vaguely.

'You see, I made a mistake,' Senga said. 'As I was saying when I was so rudely interrupted. You'd think they'd forget it. I happened to say he was all right. He could make a joke now and then. I quite liked him. You should have heard them! You'd have thought they were going to put me out the house.'

'You should never take school home,' said Rose. 'I never do.'

'But it was them raised his name first,' said Senga. 'They make me sick. Every night. How's that big dope, says Gerry. And my mother, she's not a bit better. Just because he once tried to belt her darling boy. Calls him a mean-minded big bully.'

'I could tell her he's not mean,' said Rose. 'He gives me half-a-crown every week. Sometimes more. Just for going down to the shops for him.'

'I don't like taking money from teachers,' said Senga. 'I always feel they can't afford it. Especially Alf. Did you ever look at his shoes?'

'It would hurt him if I refused,' said Rose. 'That's what I feel.'

'He's a daft big lump,' said Senga. 'Remember the morning he walked in wearing one brown shoe and one black? I bet he had a hangover. They say he's a terrible drinker. Anyway, it showed he's got two pairs of shoes. But neither of them's any good.'

'I've sometimes smelled drink on him,' said Rose.

'Can't say I have,' said Senga. 'I just know what they say.'

'It's when I go back and the room's empty,' said Rose, 'and I'm right close to him.'

'Of course,' said Senga. 'I think he likes you.'

'You know what he said to me once?' said Rose.

'No,' said Senga. 'What?'

'If I was an orphan he'd adopt me.'

They smiled together.

'O-la!' said Senga. 'I'd hate to live in the same house as a teacher.'

'When he gives me the half-crown,' said Rose, 'you know what he does?'

'No,' said Senga. 'What does he do?'

'He gives me a wee kiss,' said Rose. 'I feel right daft, the way he does it. It's not a smacker. Not even on my cheek. It's a kind of peck at my forehead. But what can I do? I'd hate to hurt him.'

'I wish somebody liked me that much,' said Senga.

'I can remember my dad used to kiss me like that at bedtime. When I was wee. But then he went away. Sometimes I don't wonder.'

'I can just see my dad kissing any of us,' said Rose. 'Mind you, he's not bad. Even when he comes in with a drink on him on a Saturday night he's not drunk. I suppose he's fond of us all right. I know he thinks the world of Martha.'

'Martha's a lovely girl,' said Senga. 'Anybody would know you two were sisters. It's just Martha's hair is different. It's really gorgeous.'

'Funny thing,' said Rose. 'Talking about kissing. You know, I've never seen my dad kiss my mum.'

The bell rang and they snailed out. Wanda slipped stealthily behind them, kicked Rose on the bottom and bounced off to her line. Rose turned to identify the assailant and sighed patiently.

She didn't mean to be disloyal when she told Senga Mr Alfred had a habit of kissing her. She didn't mean anything. She was only talking. Perhaps she had an urge to boast she had an elderly admirer, perhaps it was the intimacy induced by a tête-à-tête in the toilet made her say too much.

Whatever its reason, her casual confidence to Senga had a result neither of them expected. Senga wasn't exaggerating when she said her mother and brother were always on about Mr Alfred. They were at it again that night. She had made a mixed grill of bacon, egg, sausages and black pudding for tea, although she herself had no appetite. She was in the middle of a difficult period. She felt sick of living and eating. The only person who gave her any sympathy was Rose Weipers. She had vowed to be faithful to Rose for ever. And since Rose was Mr Alfred's favourite, she was committed to defending Mr Alfred too.

At first she said the minimum when she was asked as usual about the day's events at school. She knew they were hoping she would bring home some grievance that would let them make another complaint about Mr Alfred. Her inscrutable crosseyed face concealed how much the idea amused her, and the brevity of her answers made Gerald determined to annoy her.

'You mean to say he hasn't strapped you yet for nothing?' he said.

'That's right,' said Senga.

'It's only because he's feart,' said Gerald. 'He knows what would happen now if he did.'

'He knows better than to put a finger on a Provan,' said Mrs Provan. 'That's why.'

'Aye, we sorted that big bastard all right, didn't we, maw?' said Gerald.

'That's not a nice word,' said Senga.

'He's not a nice man,' said Mrs Provan.

'He's just as nice as anybody else,' said Senga. 'Nicer than some I could mention. Anyway, all the girls in my class like him.'

She knew she was getting heated, she knew she was liable to be provoked into some indiscreet remark if they heckled her too much, but she couldn't stop herself.

'Ho-ho, she's going to start a fan club for big Alfy,' said Gerald.

He laughed. With a lycorexia that offended her he forked bits of bacon, egg and black pudding together and bent his muzzle over his plate as he shoved them into his wide mouth.

'I don't need to start anything,' said Senga.

'Well, don't,' said Mrs Provan. 'I don't want that man's name raised in this house.'

'It's you keeps on raising it,' said Senga. 'You say he's mean. That's one thing he's not.'

'Oh?' said Mrs Provan. 'Who says so?'

'Rose Weipers,' said Senga. 'He gives her money every week. Just for going to a shop for him.'

'Oh yes?' said Mrs Provan.

'He treats her like a father,' said Senga. 'Something I haven't got.'

'That's enough,' said Mrs Provan.

'If she had no father,' said Senga, 'he'd take her home he said.'

'He'd what?' said Mrs Provan.

'Adopt her,' said Senga. 'Of course you wouldn't understand. Somebody being fond of somebody. Him kissing her, you'd think he was just a sloppy old man. The idea of affection, of anyone showing affection I mean. It would never occur to you two.'

'Kissing Rose Weipers?' said Gerald. 'Haw, maw! Did you hear that? Big Alfy kissing the girls and giving them money. The dirty old man!'

'I heard her,' said Mrs Provan.

'Ee-ya! Rose Weipers!' Gerald howled.

He gloated over the name with teenage lust, a loaded fork at his mouth.

'And who's Rose Weipers, tell me,' said Mrs Provan.

'Martha Weiper's wee sister,' said Gerald. 'You must have seen Martha, maw. She's the talk of the district. Doing a line with a toff student lives in wan o' the big hooses oot in Old Tordoch. A right wee snob, so she is.'

'She's not,' said Senga.

'She's a smashing blonde, maw,' said Gerald. 'Rose is no' a blonde but she's a good-looking wee bit. They're both sexy dames.'

'I understand,' said Mrs Provan.

Gerald leaned across the table and flicked a finger under Senga's nose to hit her plumb between the nostrils.

'I bet he doesn't kiss you,' he said.

'I never said he kissed Rose Weipers,' Senga wriggled. 'All I said was if he did what you two would think.'

'He's a dirty old man, isn't he, maw?' said Gerald.

'He's not a man should be teaching girls,' said Mrs Provan. 'And I'm the very one will let that be known.'

Senga wept.

'You keep out of it,' she wailed.

'Don't worry,' said her mother. 'I'll keep out of it all right.'

Mr Briggs read them both twice, the Director's letter and the enclosure, the one leading him to the other, forward and backward.

'Oh, my God! Not that man again!' he cried.

He handed them to Miss Ancill. She was always with him first thing in the morning. She opened his mail, gave it to him in descending order of importance, and stood by in case he needed her help while he took it in.

The senior members of his staff resented not so much the confidence he put in Miss Ancill as the confidences he gave her. They didn't mind her opening his mail if that was part of her job. What they didn't like was his habit of discussing it with her, of making her his chief counsellor in every problem and the first recipient of his intentions concerning administration and staffing. She had only a diploma in shorthand and typing, but they had an Honours degree in this and that, and some of them had double degrees in Arts and Science. They thought they had a higher claim to be consulted.

But Mr Briggs always needed Miss Ancill at his side when he dealt with his correspondence. After all, she was his secretary. She was there for him to talk to. He couldn't think unless he was talking. And in time of trouble he liked talking to a woman.

'What am I to do about that, tell me,' he said.

'There's a problem.'

Miss Ancill of course had read the Director's letter and the enclosure when she opened the mail before Mr Briggs came in. But she read them again as if she hadn't, taking her time, very slow and very serious. The Director's letter asked the headmaster for a prompt investigation and report on the charges contained in the accompanying anonymous complaint which accused Mr Alfred of giving money to girls in the school and using indecent practices with them, particularly one Rose Weipers. The anonymous letter was a rambling piece of vernacular prose without punctuation. Some words were badly misspelled. But the errors were so uncommon they seemed to arise from the writer's desire to support anonymity by bogus solecisms.

Miss Ancill wrinkled her nose the way anyone does at a bad smell.

'I don't believe it,' she said. 'Mr Alfred? Never! When could he do these,' she quoted distastefully, 'these "indecent practices"? Where? It's a piece of nonsense.'

'I can't imagine it myself,' said Mr Briggs. 'But I've got to make sure. I can't just ignore the Director's letter. I'll have to ask questions. Oh dear! The trouble that man has given me! If this gets in the papers it will put me in a fine position!'

Miss Ancill advised him to call in Mr Brown and Mr Campbell for a conference.

'I'd question the girl first,' said Mr Campbell.

'Mind you,' said Mr Brown. 'I don't believe there's anything in it. But I must say I think he has brought this on himself. He has been far too thick with one girl at least.'

'Oh yes?' said Mr Briggs.

'Rose Weipers,' said Mr Brown. 'The very one named. He has her in his room every day at lunchtime. And he locks the door. He doesn't know, but I've seen him.'

'There's your where and when answered,' said Mr Briggs sadly to Miss Ancill.

'Let's get this girl Weipers in,' said Mr Campbell. 'Get the truth out of her, and you'll get a line on the others.'

'If any,' said Miss Ancill.

'I'm not questioning any girl alone on a thing like this,' said Mr Briggs. 'That could put me in the cart too.

Improper talk alone with a schoolgirl? No, thanks. I'll
have her mother here.'

'Yes, I think you should,' said Miss Ancill.

'Or her father,' said Mr Brown.

'Or both,' said Mr Campbell.

'Just the mother, I think,' said Miss Ancill.

The attendance-officer opportunely arrived and was
immediately sent away again to tell Mrs Weipers to come
to the school at once on an urgent matter.

'All we can do now is wait,' said Mr Briggs. 'I expect
we'll have the Director or one of his Deputies out here
sometime today. I'd better have something definite for
him. Because if that letter's true, well, it's a very serious
business. There will have to be official action rightaway.'

'I've never known a teacher suspended on the spot,' said
Mr Brown. 'Quite an event, eh?'

He clapped his hands and rubbed them.

Rose's mother came in bewildered, ushered by the
janitor. Jean toddled plumply at her heels.

'I had to bring the wean,' Mrs Weipers said.

She looked at the three grave men and the single
woman. They frightened her.

'I'm sorry,' she said humbly. 'But I've no one to look
after her.'

Jean, aged three when Martha mentioned her to Graeme
Roy, was now turned five and waiting to be admitted to the
infant school when the new session started. She ambled
round Mr Brigg's room, stopped at a shelf of specimen
copies and pulled the books out one by one to use them as
building-bricks. She dropped one.

'Jean! Behave yourself, you!' Mrs Weipers said. A
worried woman. Not well.

She rose, stopped, and dragged Jean over beside her.

When they were both settled Mr Briggs resumed the
explanation Jean had interrupted. But he was so indirect
and allusive that Mrs Weipers wasn't sure if he was telling
her Rose had been assaulted by a teacher or a teacher had
been improperly approached by Rose. When she was

thoroughly confused he gave her the anonymous letter to read.

'You'll understand why I had to send for you,' he said, going on talking even as she was trying to make it out.

She was a poor reader at the best of times, with the best of print, and the scrawly handwriting, bad spelling and lack of stops made it trebly difficult for her.

'Oh my goodness,' she whispered when she took in the meaning of 'indesent praktises'.

'I'll have to question Rose,' said Mr Briggs. 'It's my duty. I can't ignore such a terrible letter. And I'm sure you'll want to exercise your right to be present.'

Rose was as baffled as her mother. When she saw the drift of the headmaster's questions she froze. At first she said she hardly knew Mr Alfred. She only got him three periods a week. Mr Briggs asked about money. She admitted Mr Alfred sometimes gave her money. Mr Briggs asked how often. She said once a week. She didn't like the way he kept glancing at a piece of pale-blue notepaper. She guessed somebody had written something that wasn't nice about her and Mr Alfred. The girls were always writing something about somebody.

'But why should he give you money every week?' Mr Briggs asked.

He pretended he was puzzled.

'It's for going to the shops for him,' said Rose.

'Just for going errands for him, you mean?' said Mr Briggs. 'And that's all? He doesn't ask you to do anything else when you come back? When you're alone.'

'No,' she said.

She was only beginning to see what he was thinking. There were tears in her eyes. Her lower lip was wobbling.

'Did you tell anybody Mr Alfred was giving you money?' Mr Briggs encouraged her to speak.

'Yes,' said Rose. 'I told Senga Provan.'

'I see,' said Mr Briggs.

He wagged his head wisely.

'It was no girl wrote that letter,' said Mrs Weipers.

Rose was just as intelligent as any headmaster. She saw it the moment Mr Briggs saw it. If that bit of pale-blue paper wasn't the usual scribbling of some girl in her class but a letter from outside she knew how it came to be written. And remembering what else she had told Senga she hurried to get her story in before she was asked any more questions about things that seemed to be known anyway.

'I told her he kissed me,' she said. 'But I just made that up.'

'Are you sure?' Mr Briggs asked. 'That's rather hard to believe. A sensible girl like you. Why on earth should you do that?'

The brimming tears overflowed. She began to cry. She knew it made her look guilty, but she couldn't help it. Mr Briggs went on probing. If she had made it up she had been very naughty, telling lies about her teacher. But was she telling the truth now? He kept at her. Was she quite sure Mr Alfred had never kissed her?

Rose blubbered. She nodded her head and shook her head, not knowing what she was doing. All she knew was she couldn't speak. Mr Briggs watched and relaxed. He had plenty of experience in asking questions and assessing witnesses. He saw through Rose. He knew why she wept. He saw the innocence in her that had heard of evil but never met it. He was convinced the charges in the anonymous letter were false. But he was curious about Mr Alfred's behaviour. He took his time. He let the mother have a word.

'Don't be frightened, Rose,' said Mrs Weipers. 'Your mammy's here. Tell the master the truth.'

Rose admitted Mr Alfred had kissed her. Yes, often.

'At first he just held my hand!' she tried to suggest how things start and then you can't stop them.

She couldn't explain it better for crying. She wept for herself and for Mr Alfred too. She hated them all, even her mother, for finding out Mr Alfred loved her.

'What kind of a kiss?' said Mr Briggs.

'Just on my brow,' said Rose. 'It was nothing. I hardly knew.'

'Did he ever lift your dress?' said Mr Briggs. 'Even once.'

Rose turned to her mother to hide her face on the breast that had nursed her.

'No, no!' she screamed.

'Wheesht,' said Mrs Weipers.

Jean began to cry and tried to hug Rose round the legs.

'Did he ever touch you?' said Mr Briggs. 'Anywhere he shouldn't, I mean.'

Rose shook her head.

'Some of these people,' said Mrs Weipers. She stroked Rose's thick untidy hair from crown to nape as Mr Alfred had often done. 'If they have anything to say why can't they come out into the open and say it? Wheesht, ma wee hen! Your ma knows you're a good girl.'

Mr Briggs apologised.

'It's an unpleasant task, Mrs Weipers,' he said. 'But it had to be done. I'm sure you would be the first to agree we can't afford the least suspicion that a girl of Rose's age could come to any harm here. Even an anonymous letter, it's got to be investigated.'

'The fire's the place for it,' said Mrs Weipers. 'Not a word of truth in it, not a scrap of evidence.'

He spoke to Mr Alfred alone later. He didn't ask him what he had been doing. He told him. He told him he had seen Rose and her mother and knew he had been kissing the girl and giving her money. He let him see the anonymous letter and gave him some fatherly advice though he was the younger man.

He sprawled back in his swivel-chair to set the tone of an informal, friendly chat. Mr Alfred sagged before him in a position vaguely suggesting a soldier standing to attention before a superior officer.

It would be a bad thing, Mr Briggs said, if one had a class with nobody in it one could like. To find that some pupils were loveable was one of the rewards of a poorly-paid profession, though one was very properly shy of mentioning love. But there must be no favouritism. It was a bad teacher that had favourites. If one found oneself becoming fond of one pupil in particular one must force oneself to give more attention to other pupils, who were probably more in need of affection. It was a bad thing to allow oneself to be emotionally involved. A bachelor was sometimes prone to do that. A man with a family would find it easier to maintain a sense of proportion. He would know girls could be little devils as well as angels. One mustn't see girls through rose-tinted spectacles. He apologised for the pun. He hadn't intended it. They could be as nasty as boys, yes, and even nastier. He could tell Mr Alfred things about girls that would shock him, things he had learnt as headmaster of a mixed comprehensive school, the things girls wrote on the lavatory walls for example. Worse than boys. It was a pity Mr Alfred wasn't married. Of course he himself and Mrs Weipers were completely satisfied there was no truth in the anonymous letter as far as Rose was concerned, and there was no other girl actually specified. The accusation that Mr Alfred was guilty of indecent practices with any girl was something neither he nor anyone else who had seen the letter believed, nonetheless . . .

He saw he had slipped there. The words 'nor anyone else who had seen the letter' made Mr Alfred wonder how many people had been shown it. Miss Ancill for one he was sure. And probably Mr Brown as Deputy Headmaster. He jerked as if prodded. He was humiliated. Once more a harsh reality had invaded the privacy of his dreams. He remembered that in the poems of his youth he had tried to negotiate with reality. But in his middle age reality was no longer open to negotiations. It was bulldozing him. It tore up the love he had hidden under the soiled surface of his public life and heaved it aside like so much rubbish that was merely in the way of new buildings. He felt destroyed. He had no idea who had written the letter and Mr Briggs gave him no clue. All he could make of

it was that Rose must have talked to somebody, somewhere, sometimes. She had wilfully made him look ridiculous.

Mr Briggs went on, man-to-man. If it came out that a
teacher was in the habit of kissing a girl in his class, that
could lead to many misunderstandings. Admittedly there
were innocent caresses and innocent kisses. Paternal or
pastoral attentions to children. But as Mr Alfred himself
must be well aware Scotch reserve looked askance on
kissing even between kin. And there were always people
eager to make trouble, like the person who had written that
malicious letter. Once they heard the word kissing they
would be only too ready to impute sexual intentions to the
teacher, especially if they heard the teacher was giving the
girl money. In a position of trust, which every teacher
occupied in regard to the pupils in his care, one must take
great care to be like Caesar's wife.

Mr Alfred felt no ambition to be like Caesar's wife. He
preferred to remain male, however inadequately. Yet
while Mr Briggs was lecturing him he felt guilty enough
of what he was charged with. There came into his mind the
Gospel text that whosoever looketh on a woman to lust
after her hath committed adultery with her already in his
heart. He didn't like that text. He thought it unfair. But he
knew how he had often looked on Rose. So the anonymous
letter could claim the support of the Gospel for what it said
about him.

He said nothing of that to Mr Briggs. He went dumbly
back to his class unfit to teach again that day. He was hot
with vexation, as if he had been surprised in an absurd
position, like being caught in his shirt-tail and long hairy
legs. His high love for Rose had been reduced to the
occasion for a condescending homily from Mr Briggs, a
man too discreet to kiss a growing girl who offered affection.

He stayed in town till the pubs opened. He wasn't
bothered about going home. His landlady was used to
his irregular returns. He drank till the pubs closed, not to

get drunk but just to brood. Still, he finished up not sober and walked the streets till past midnight.

Mr Briggs had his expected visit from the Director, who wasn't inclined to judge Mr Alfred harshly. He understood him. But because of the letter it was decided to transfer him to another school.

When he saw nothing in the papers Gerald shrugged.

'Ach, don't worry, maw,' he said. 'We'll get the old bastard yet.'

Senga heard about the letter. The whole school heard about the letter. Miss Ancill told the janitor and the janitor told the cleaners and the cleaners told the parents. But Senga knew more. She knew who had written the letter, though the writer never mentioned it.

Having made her own good guess, Rose wouldn't speak to Senga for a week. She walked past her in the street. She changed her place in class. But Senga was too articulate to let it go on. Her hurt was great, but it would be less if she was forgiven. She waylaid Rose and had her say. She didn't waste time suggesting the writer could have been anybody. She wouldn't make a mystery where they both knew there was none. She admitted her share. She explained how a few unwise words had been picked up by Mr Alfred's enemy. She couldn't tell how sorry she was.

Her unhappiness made her eloquent. The affection that had been dammed for a week overflowed in her eyes. Rose was hard. But she couldn't quarrel. She couldn't rant and rave and accuse and denounce. She hadn't the voice for that kind of part. She listened. She gave in. They became friends again.

Still a bitterness stayed with Senga. She had sued for peace with Rose, but she waged a civil war at home. The cause of it was never alluded to by either side, though both knew what the other was thinking. The week she was in disgrace with Rose she went on a modified hunger strike to annoy her mother. It comforted her to refuse food from an adverse party. She never missed a chance to be sarcastic. She had come to have a sharp tongue, and she used it to cut those who wounded her. Perhaps it was guilt kept her

mother from using heavy artillery to discourage these
bayonet charges. Anyway she got away with them. Even
Gerald had nothing much to say for a time. Senga didn't
enjoy her victories. They were too easy. She wanted stiffer
opposition, then she would really show what vengeance
could be.

She criticised Gerald's clothes and the shoes he wore.
She derided his haircut, even his walk. She mocked the
way he spoke. His enunciation was poor. He swallowed
half his words, he used a glottal stop, and he spoke so
quickly that every sentence came over like one enormous agglutination of syllables. It pleased Senga to
make him repeat what he said the few times he dared
speak to her.

'Pardon. What did you say?'

She gave a demonstration of clear speech in her very
question.

'We'll have less of your airs, madam,' said her mother.
'Don't you try and make a monkey out of Gerald.'

'If people can't speak properly they can't expect to be
understood,' said Senga.

'Feudcleanyurears,' said Gerald.

'Pardon,' said Senga.

'Do you think there's nothing wrong with the way you
speak?' said her mother, crushing her with tone and glare,
ironing handkerchiefs for Gerald. 'You should hear yourself sometimes. But we're not good enough for you. Oh no!
You're that superior.'

'To him and his pals anyway,' said Senga.

She was loaded with venom, ready to strike.

'There's nothing wrong with Gerald's pals,' said her
mother.

'Not much,' said Senga. 'Crowd of apes.'

'Hoosapes?' said Gerald.

'And he's in a gang,' Senga tossed at her mother.

'Hoosnagang?' Gerald shouted.

'You are,' Senga turned, shouting back.

'Oh, hold your tongue, you little besom,' said her

mother. 'You're aye nagging. What shirt do you want to wear tomorrow, Gerald?'

'Mayella,' said Gerald.

'You don't like the truth,' said Senga. 'Either of you.'

'Gerald sees his friends after a hard day's work,' said her mother. She flattened the last handkerchief, stacked the lot. 'They go out and enjoy themselves, and you choose to call it a gang.'

'Because so it is,' said Senga. 'He's in a gang all right. I'm telling you. You'll find out.'

'What gang?' her mother demanded. Voice raised. Angry. 'You let your imagination run away with you, you do.'

'Just ask him,' said Senga. 'Ask him what they call his gang.'

'Amnoinanygang,' said Gerald.

He rushed across the kitchen with fist raised to thump his sister as he used to do. Senga hurried to a corner, turned her back to him, hands at her ears, reverting to her childish kyphosis at the threat of assault.

'She's not worth it, Gerald,' said the mother. 'Just ignore her.'

But Gerald was in a gang. It was called the Cogs. Nobody knew why.

Gangs were no novelty in the city. Between the wars they did some shopbreaking and demanding money with menaces, but that was only on the side. They were never started for criminal purposes. They had no big boss in the background planning even petty crime. They were the local expression of religious sympathies amongst the irreligious. Their main activities were mutual aggression and breach of the peace. Like ancient Constantinople, the city had its factions of Blue and Green, his devotion to either depending solely on the adherent's accident of birth. There were gangs that had a special loyalty to the memory of William Prince of Orange for beating the papishes at the Boyne in 1690. There were gangs that professed a particular reverence for the Holy Father and a great dislike to King Billy. It was a matter of complete indifference to both sides that the Pope and the Orangeman were allies in that famous victory.

But now instead of the gangs that flourished in the slump, the Norman Conks, San Toy, Billy Boys and Sally Boys, Cheeky Forty, Calton Entry and Baltic Fleet, all with explicit or latent support for the Orange or the Green, there were the gangs of the affluent society, the Toi, Tong, Peg, Monks, Fleet, Gringo, Goucho, Cody, Cumbie, Town and many others.

Orange and Green no longer mattered very much, though even in a period of ecumenicity colour prejudice couldn't be entirely obliterated. It could still be heard at some football matches, where the fans believed King Billy supported the Rangers and the Pope supported Celtic. But with the decline of religion the new gangs had merely secular loyalties. They were the result of a rationalisation of production in keeping with a technological society. Instead of a district manufacturing two gangs with different colours each district turned out one gang with no colour.

The members lived like bushmen, treating anybody from a different part of the forest as if he belonged to a different species. Strangers were stopped and challenged, assaulted with boot and knife, and killed if they resisted. If no aliens turned up they went out to look for them. They went by bus and train in the summer season to the seaside resorts and county towns, travelling in the autumn as far south as Blackpool, where the natives deserved to be beaten up for not belonging to Glasgow. Between vacations they invaded each other's territory. They fought in dance halls, pubs, the Queen's highway, discotheques and corporation parks.

The Cogs were in the news a fortnight after Senga named them. They were the budding talent of Tordoch, and it was thanks to Gerald they got headlines and Wilma got her name in the papers.

It all started at a party in Jennifer's house.

Jennifer and Wilma were amongst the dozen or so girls in the Cogs. If nothing was cooking it was the girls lit the gas. When they went dancing they would either pick a quarrel in the powder-room with any dame that looked sideways at them or they would tell the Cog-commander they had been insulted by their escort. If it came to a battle they played their part. The only weapon they used was a steel comb.

Of course nobody expected any trouble the night of Jennifer's party. They weren't out on the town looking for anything. They were all tadpoles in their own pond. Jennifer's parents were away at Ayr for the week-end visiting relatives, and Jennifer fixed a record-session. She invited a mixed company, mostly Cogs. Everyone knew she kept open house on such an occasion, and some of the boys and girls brought other guests. There must have been forty or fifty young ones in that four-roomed council house that night.

It was never found out who brought Alec McLetchie, but brought he was. He was a darkeyed boy of Gerald's age, with long chestnut hair down to the collar of his newstyle jacket. He had a broad face and a big hanging-lipped mouth. He looked just like a pop singer or one of a beat group. At least that's what Wilma thought. She was thrilled with the cut of him. She was getting tired of Gerald. His blond head seemed shallow beside the dark depths of Alec's rich waves.

The trouble was Wilma liked boys of any colour. She liked to make up to boys, to lead them on and then tease them by wriggling out of it. She was amused when she saw they were excited. It always surprised her to see how easily a boy got excited. She wanted to see if Alec was easily excited. She called him Alec rightaway to put him at his ease, because it gave her the giggles if a boy was stiff when she spoke to him. If he wasn't easily excited he might be her true mate instead of Gerald. She sat beside him on the settee when the first record was being played and clasped his hand between her left thigh and his right. She felt switched on, she felt a higher voltage coming through, she began to glow.

Jennifer's guests had brought cans of beer and bottles of coke. A young syndicate, with a simple theory of seduction, had clubbed for a bottle of vodka to go with the coke. Jennifer was disc-jockey as well as hostess. She had a good line of patter at each record and everyone was happy. The liquor flowed, the guests were all keen to show they were sophisticated in spite of the burden of being young, and the party was swinging.

Alec solemnly nuzzled Wilma and Wilma played with his chestnut hair in a five finger exercise. The fetching of drinks and the parking of empty glasses caused some irregular rising and sitting and changing of seats. After one of those moves Wilma found she was being crushed to one end of the settee by an extra occupant who shouldn't have been there. She took the chance to sit on Alec's lap. He fondled her knees and put his hand up her miniskirted thighs a little distance. Not eagerly, but rather as if going through a drill expected of him. He still looked solemn, kind of faraway, his big mouth drooping with the weight of the lower lip. But in Wilma's opinion he was smouldering like a dross fire that would burst into flame at the least touch. She put one arm round his neck, then both. Robust they were and shapely, naked from the shoulders of her sleeveless blouse. She bent her face to his, silently asking. They kissed.

Across the room at the same time Gerald was kissing Davina Gordon. She was a chubby girl he had never met before. When they were introduced he chanted as a joke, 'A Gordon for me!' He was stuck with her after that. But he wasn't annoyed. He didn't mind what he did because she didn't. It was her first time at one of Jennifer's parties and she wanted to get invited back. But Gerald was too much for her. She was too untrained to have the stamina for his long kiss. She had to come up for air. So Gerald was idle while Wilma and Alec were still busy. He saw them mouth to mouth as if they were stuck together by a new super-adhesive. He was shocked. Her infidelity offended him. Wilma caught the dagger of his glare in a corner of her eye as she squinted to see how other lovers were getting on. She palmed Alec away, smacked his hand and lifted it from her thigh. She pulled down her skirt.

Gerald wasn't the boy to let it be smoothed over as easily as that. His honour demanded satisfaction. When the party was starting to break up at two in the morning he slipped out ahead with Poggy and Smudge and a couple more of his handers. He knew Wilma was fixed to stay overnight to keep Jennifer company and he told his mates what the situation demanded. When McLetchie came round the corner alone he was ambushed and beaten up. No weapons were used. Just five pairs of ringed fists against one, five pairs of sharp shoes on one huddled body. McLetchie went home a bruised and bloody mess and told his big brother.

And who was his big brother? He was Peter McLetchie, known as Big Paw, one of the Fangs from the Auchenglass scheme. Gerald was furious when he got the buzz.

'Who the hell brung a Fang's kid brother to Jenny's?' he asked his assembled company.

No one answered. They were all troubled in spirit. But the threat of invasion and the slogan 'Cogs!' raised them to the high pitch of dare-and-die required for battle. All they lacked was a claymore and kilts and someone to play the bagpipes. They fought long and bravely when the Fangs attacked them in the Ballochmyle Road, the main pass into the highlands of Tordoch. Gerald was working late in the garage that night and was sorry he missed it he said, but he couldn't get away. Even without him the Cogs managed to drive the Fangs away in a late rally. The buses on Ballochmyle Road were held up for twenty minutes before the fighting ended, but the police got there in time to pick up some warriors who were slow in leaving the battlefield. That was when the Cogs got headlines. SIXTEEN HELD AFTER COGS FIGHT. Wilma's turn came a few days later.

The defeat of the invasion didn't discourage Big Paw. He knew it was hard, if not impossible, to conquer someone else's territory. And he was an old hand at drag-fighting. He sent a challenge by under-ground. Let any one of those who had given his brother a doing come out on Sunday morning and he would take him on, all in. A signal was returned by the same route. Message received and understood.

Big Paw came into the Weavers Lane from the Ballochmyle Road with a posse of grim hombres. Poggy came in from the Tordoch Crescent end, with Gerald and Smudge and half-a-dozen anonymous backers behind him. Poggy enjoyed the limelight. The sun was shining. He walked slowly to Big Paw and Big Paw walked slowly to him. High Noon in the peace of a Scotch Sabbath.

'G' on, Poggy, take him,' said Gerald.

Poggy stopped, chest out, and waited. The captain's hand on his shoulder smote.

'Easy meat,' Gerald whispered. 'You can do him.'

'Fancy yer chance, day ye?' Big Paw drawled.

'Could take you anyway,' Poggy said, and spat at Big Paw's feet. 'Any time.'

It started mildly enough, just a rough-house warm-up, until Big Paw got Poggy on the ground and gave him a kicking. Poggy fumbled to get at a knife in his waistband before rising. Big Paw drew smoothly from his braces, ready for him. To save time Gerald bent quickly and shoved his own knife into Poggy's shaking hand and Poggy scrambled up with it clenched in his right fist. But Big Paw had his chisel out. And while Poggy was still trying to get balanced on his feet and make up his mind where and when and if to strike, Big Paw struck first. It was a swift, savage, powerful thrust. The whole weight of his body sent it in and down. Poggy fell down again, bleeding. Big Paw and his posse let it go at that and ran off to get a bus on the Ballochmyle Road. They knew when it was the end of a programme. No point waiting for the commercials.

Poggy pulled at his shirt. It was his best shirt. He always wore his best shirt on Sundays. It was soaked with blood. His hand was red to the wrist. He was amazed. He gasped an appeal.

'Gerry, help! Help me! That bastard, he's got me, so he has!'

But Gerald was in as big a hurry as the other fellow.

'Yill b'aw right,' he shouted over his shoulder. 'Hang on! Ah'll phone fur a namblance.'

He decamped with Smudge and the rest of the backers.

Poggy died alone there in the Weavers Lane that quiet Sunday morning under a clear sky. The only person who got any pleasure out of the business was Wilma. When the pressmen came into Tordoch looking for a story she gave them one. She said Poggy had been her boyfriend. She told them she had foolishly tried to make him jealous by letting another boy kiss her at a party. The two boys had gone and had this fight over her. She was heart-broken it ever happened. She would never forget Poggy. He was a kind, gentle boy.

'IT'S ALL MY FAULT' said the thirty-two point caption above a picture of her smiling pretty face. She cut it out and kept it with a bundle of holiday-snaps in her handbag.

Part Two
The Writing on the Wall

Mr Alfred didn't like his new school. The old journey to Collinsburn was long enough, but this was twice as long. He had to change buses in the city centre, and if he missed one by a few seconds he had a long wait for another. It meant he had to rise a lot earlier to allow for delays. He soldiered glumly on, suffering life patiently.

He was still in mourning for the loss of Rose. Even before he left Collinsburn she was taken from him. There was a quick alteration made in his timetable and someone else was given her class till his transfer came through. He gained free time by the adjustment, but that was no compensation. He still felt she had treated him badly, and yet he wanted to see her again. He hoped for her every day, but she never came near him.

Rather than tell his aunt the truth he said he had asked for a transfer.

'You were always saying that's what I should do,' he reminded her.

'It took you a long time,' said Granny Lyons. 'And why so sudden? Are you sure there's not something behind it you're not telling?'

'No, nothing,' he said. 'I just got fed up with Tordoch. That's all. Collinsburn used to be a good school, but not any longer.'

He changed the subject. He was afraid he would give himself away if he said any more.

The transfer made his visits to her less frequent than ever. If any of his old pupils saw him in Tordoch any night they would think he was looking for Rose. That's how he saw it, for he believed his love was common knowledge.

He believed a rumour of it had preceded him to his new school. He knew his very appearance when he entered the staffroom for the first time would make him seem an oddity. He was sure the teachers already there saw him as a tall, grey, haggard old man who came sidling in unsociably. And he was sure they talked about him behind his back and said a man of his age wouldn't be shifted from one school to another unless he was no use at his job.

He took more and more to drink in the evenings. He found he had to drink more to get the right effect of not worrying about anything. He drank in different parts of the city, in a kind of judicial assizes, to observe the customs and customers in a variety of bars. To prevent any barmaid seeing how much he took he never spent the whole night in one pub. His circuits helped him to get over Rose. He recovered as from an illness, with diminishing relapses.

It wasn't just the tedious journey to an outlying housing scheme made him dislike Waterholm Comprehensive, called Watty Compy by its pupils, with an *ah* and a glottal stop in the Watty. It was also the boys he had to teach. They frightened him. He had never been frightened in a classroom before.

It started the day he arrived and came to a climax at four o'clock. He left promptly because he wasn't sure about the times of the buses. He never left promptly again. A mob of boys at the stop outside the school tried to board the first bus that came. A score of them jammed the platform and the staircase to the top deck. The rest milled between the bus and the pavement. The Pakistani conductor was angry. The boys were merry. Especially to have made the conductor angry. The driver came out of his cabin and announced he wasn't going on till the surplus boys got off. The boys wouldn't get off. They were in good spirits. They jeered at the driver, they called the conductor nigger boy, they argued with the passengers.

Mr Alfred was shocked. He hated disorder and bad manners. He raised his voice. He told the boys to line up quietly in a proper queue. Nobody bothered. Nobody knew him.

'You're wasting your time, mac,' said an old-age pensioner watching the world go by from the kerb. 'The young ones the day! They'll no' listen to anybody.'

A fresh wave of boys surged on to the platform, leaping joyously on their schoolmates' backs.

'Come on, get off!' the submerged conductor shouted. 'Some of you get off.'

The adults already on the bus grumbled at the hold-up. They said the conductor should put the boys off. They said the driver should drive on. They said they didn't know what the world was coming to. They made remarks about modern education when the boys gave in and the bus moved off.

'Makes you wonder what they learn them at the school nowadays,' said a stout lady with a labrador under the seat.

'It's all these free travel passes,' said the conductor. 'They should take them from them. Make them walk. All I get is cheek.'

A squad of boys ran alongside the departing bus, chanting.

'Watty Compy! Cha-cha-cha!'

They straggled behind when the bus gathered speed, and one of them picked up a stone and threw it at the conductor who was leaning from the platform giving them the v-sign Gerald had given Enrico.

Mr Alfred walked on to the next fare-stage to get away from the remnants of the mob. He was in a bad temper. He saw why he was the only teacher who had waited with the pupils for a bus. Most of his new colleagues had a car, and they had given a lift to those who hadn't. Nobody had offered him a lift. He didn't mind that, but he thought somebody should have warned him what he would walk into if he went to the stop outside the school.

He tried to settle down in Waterholm. It seemed an ugly place. He was familiar with the pupillary scribblings that raped the virgin flyleaves of textbooks. He had seen them

countless times in Collinsburn and he wasn't surprised to
see them in Waterholm. There was nothing new in the
otiose curves intended to represent the female breasts,
waist and hips, in the crude sketches of the male organ,
and certainly nothing new in the four-letter words whose
use in print was sometimes supposed to prove the author
had a literary talent never attributed to the boys who wrote
them in their schoolbooks. What was new was the sheer
quantity of obscene scribbling. And the quantity became
quality. It gave Waterholm a peculiar aura, increasing his
dislike and fear of it.

What was also new, and what puzzled him, was the
frequent occurrence of the word 'Hox'. He saw it everywhere in Waterholm. In textbooks, in exercise books, cut
on the desks, scratched on the twelve-inch rules, pencilled in the corridors. The janitor told him it was in the
lavatories too, chalked on the walls, scrawled in the
cubicles, chiselled on the doors. Sometimes it was 'Yung
Hox'.

He unfroze far enough to ask what it meant when he was
alone in the staffroom with a brighteyed tubby little man
known to the boys as Wee Bobby. This was Harry Murdoch, a man of Mr Alfred's age. Though unknown to Mr
Alfred he had been his contemporary at university, and
like him had taken an ordinary degree in Arts and trained
for teaching. The day Mr Alfred arrived at Waterholm he
recognised him as the student who had been famous for
the amount of poetry he contributed to the university
magazine. Murdoch had found the poems unreadable,
but in middle age he was willing to be pleasant to a
contemporary. He laughed agreeably at Mr Alfred's question.

'Hox?' he said, echoing Mr Alfred's precise rhyming of
it with Box and Cox. 'It's really Hawks. That's our local
mob.'

'Mob?' said Mr Alfred, disliking the word.

'Gang,' said Mr Murdoch. 'The boys here call themselves the Young Hawks. All these gangs, they put their

name up. There's hardly a blank wall anywhere now. Haven't you noticed?'

'Can't say I have,' said Mr Alfred.

'You must know the Cogs,' said Mr Murdoch.

'Cogs?' said Mr Alfred.

'Don't tell me you don't know the Cogs,' said Mr Murdoch. 'You must have seen the name on the walls when you were in Tordoch.'

Mr Alfred said he hadn't.

'They were in the papers not long ago,' said Mr Murdoch. 'A lad was knifed in a Cog fight. It happens every day. There's always somebody knifing somebody now. You should keep up with current affairs.'

He wanted to drop the topic and ask Mr Alfred if he still wrote any poetry. But he was afraid the question might sound derisive instead of friendly. And he wanted to be friendly, but Mr Alfred's face put him off. So he said nothing. At the same moment Mr Alfred wanted to ask him why the boys called him Wee Bobby when his name was Harry. But he didn't want to seem nosey. So he said nothing either. Yet in their silence there was the respect of one old soldier for another.

CHAPTER TWENTY-FOUR

Mr Alfred took Harry Murdoch's advice. He tried to keep up with current affairs. He began to read a morning paper, which was more than he had done when Rose brought him one every day at lunchtime. Buying something she used to get for him was only one of the many trivial acts that resurrected her. It made him wish he could go back over the script of his life and rewrite the dialogue. But he knew he had no option. He had to read the part he had been given.

Travelling across the city on a route not yet stale to him he would glance from his paper to see where the bus was going. Every day from the top deck he saw another gang name on the walls and hoardings. Every day he read of another boy of seventeen knifing a boy of eighteen or vice versa. His route and his paper told him he had been missing all Murdoch took for granted.

He saw a new rash break out on the scarred face of the city. Wherever the name of a gang was scribbled the words YA BASS were added. The application of the phrase caused some dispute at first. Nobody doubted YA BASS meant YOU BASTARD. But the grammarians who discussed it were undecided about its vocative or apostrophic use. Some said COGS YA BASS meant O COGS! YOU ARE BASTARDS! Others said it meant WE ARE THE COGS, O YOU BASTARDS! A fifteen-year-old boy charged with assault and breach of the peace, and also with daubing TONGS YA BASS on a bus-shelter, said in court that YA BASS was an Italian phrase meaning FOR EVER. But the sheriff didn't believe him.

Some of the intelligentsia seemed to believe him. Following a fashion, as the intelligentsia often do, they wrote the names of miscellaneous culture heroes in public places and added YA BASS. Thus soon after the original examples of COGS YA BASS, TOI YA BASS, TONGS YA BASS, FLEET YA BASS, and so on, which were plastered all over the districts where those gangs lived, a secondary epidemic occurred on certain sites only. SHELLEY YA BASS suddenly appeared in the basement of the University Union. In a public convenience near the Mitchell Library MARX YA BASS was scrawled in one hand, LENIN YA BASS in another, and TROTSKY YA BASS in a third. When *The Caretaker* was put on at the King's Theatre PINTER YA BASS was pencilled on a poster in the foyer. BECKETT YA BASS, later and more familiarly SAM YA BASS, was scribbled on the wall of a public-house urinal near the Citizens' Theatre the week *Happy Days* was on. When the same theatre presented *Ghosts* somebody managed to write IBSEN YA BASS in large capitals on the staircase to the dress circle.

In bus shelters, railway stations and tenement closes, on factory walls and shop fronts, on telephone boxes, junction boxes, police boxes and pillar boxes, outside churches, libraries, offices, schools and warehouses, on the back of the seats upstairs on the buses, with the rexine ripped off to show plain wood, wherever there was a wall or a hoarding, a gang name and YA BASS were flaunted. Always in big clumsy capitals, in white paint, in yellow paint, in green pencil, in blue pencil, in black ink and purple ink. The more recently a surface was cleaned or repainted the more immediate the writing.

Mr Alfred was puzzled.

'When do they do it?' he asked. 'What do they use?'

'A paint spray,' said Harry Murdoch. 'Or a felt pen.'

'I'm surprised nobody is ever caught doing it,' said Mr Alfred.

'Maybe it's leprechauns. Or monsters from outer space. You know, psychological warfare. Demoralise us before they invade in force.'

Murdoch laughed at his passing fancy but Mr Alfred wasn't amused. The rash seemed to him so mysterious he was ready to believe anything. It upset him. He used his pubcrawls to make a perlustration of the city, north and south of the river, east and west of the Square. He began to compile a list of what he saw. The words weren't inspired graffiti. They weren't the poetry and pathos photographed and commented on by two young Londoners to make up a book at a couple of guineas. They weren't political or surrealist, they weren't witty or comic. They were only the monotonous evidence of a civic battology. He brooded over the inexplicable words that turned up irregularly alongside YA BASS. He noted FUZZ, JOEY, DOTT, PEEM, MUSHY, BUNNY, ETTIE, CLAN, BIM and forty more. Sometimes the gang name was followed by OK instead of YA BASS, sometimes it was preceded by YY, but he couldn't find out what YY meant.

He became obsessed with the unending defacement of the city. He was angry nobody seemed to care, nobody did anything about it. The correspondence columns of the papers were filled with debates about the need for comprehensive schools and a technological education in a twentieth-century Britain, about the duty of adults to hand on a moral code and maintain the nation's cultural heritage, about the prevalence of bad language in television plays. But never a word about the writing on the wall. He made himself irritable, worrying. Harry Murdoch laughed at him. He said 'Ya Bass' was a contribution to Scottish literature. It was even used as a joke in one of the pantomimes.

'There's a housing-sketch about the multistorey flats,' he explained. 'And the dame does a solo piece in the old panto couplets. Something like,

> If you're a stranger in Auchenglass
> Just shout the password, Fangs ya bass!
> It brings the house down they tell me.

Mr Alfred was shocked.

Meanwhile, his attempt to make the best of Waterholm and forget Rose wasn't very successful. He couldn't get much work done with the classes he was given. They seemed barely literate. He had Murdoch's registration class for two periods every day and he risked a comment since Murdoch was the only man on the staff he cared to talk to.

'I'm finding it hard to do much with your fellows,' he said. 'I can't get anywhere.'

'Don't worry, old boy,' said Murdoch. 'Neither can I. We're out of date, you and me, with our M.A. Ordinary. After thirty years in the job we've no future. We don't rank in a Comprehensive, so we get the worst classes.'

He smiled. He wasn't bitter. He did what he could to teach some maths, went home, and put the school out of his mind. He had his garden in the spring and summer, his classical records in the autumn and winter, and golf when the mood and weather suited.

Mr Alfred was different. He had no garden and no hobbies. He worried. Anxious to get on good terms with the boys he tried chatting to them paternally with his hands in his pockets. He would be patient and pleasant. He wouldn't get rattled. He gently discouraged a forward youngster who always wanted the limelight, he wagged a hushing finger at another who kept answering out of turn. He had seen enough to know a class could be goaded into insurrection by tyranny, clammed to sullenness by sarcasm. He wanted to be benevolent without being a despot. He wanted to be friendly and get communication. But there were no dividends from his policy. Only idleness, noise and bad manners. That was what frightened him. He saw something uncivilised in their eyes, something rude in their smirk, something savage in their slouch. They were foreigners. They didn't speak his language. They were on a different channel and he couldn't switch over. He believed that like animals they would sense he was afraid and turn on him. He tried to hide his fear, to conquer it by a kind of auto-suggestion. He put on a free and easy manner, pretending they didn't frighten him. He failed.

Then on a Thursday morning came what he had always thought impossible. Mr Murdoch's class came to him the first period, lads of fourteen and fifteen. The team they supported had won a European Cup match the night before. Mr Alfred had seen the result in the paper, but it meant nothing to him. He didn't appreciate it was a glorious victory. So he didn't expect the entry of a choir singing the song the fans had sung the night before. He bawled at them. They went on singing. Some sat down sideways with their long legs stretched out. Others hunched round the hot pipes, fondling the warm metal, and argued with a nonconformist who said their team was lucky. Somebody played a party tune on a mouth-organ. Two upstanding boys, as big as Mr Alfred himself, quarrelled about whose seat it was in the back row.

'Sit down there!' he roared. 'Be quiet!'

The edge on his voice made him even angrier than he was already. He knew he was getting himself worked up, but he couldn't stand the noise. The insult of an uproar in his classroom maddened him.

'Sit down! Be quiet!' he roared again.

'Sit down! Be quiet!' echoed a mocking soprano.

So sudden it was, so unexpected, he failed to pin the source. He walked in among them, up and down the passages. Young eyes looked at him with calm insolence, mouths grinned but said nothing. Feet stamped when he passed.

'Sit down there! Be quiet!' a parrot-voice squawked.

It came again. And again.

'Be quiet! Sit down! Sit down! Be quiet!'

Always from behind his back. Bass, baritone and tenor. All bogus. Putting the impossible challenge to spot who it was.

He fired glares right, left and centre. He was at bay, and he knew it. He trembled. He was ripe for murder. There came into his mind the question a colleague in Collinsburn had once put to him.

'What would you do if a whole class started kidding you?'

'It wouldn't happen,' he had answered then. 'Not to me. I wouldn't let it.'

'No, it wouldn't happen to you because they know you here,' his friend said. 'But suppose they didn't know you. Suppose it did happen. What would you do? What could you do?'

'I don't know,' he admitted. 'I can't imagine it happening to me.'

And now it had. They were jeering at him, and he could do nothing to stop them. The row they were making recalled the class that had baited the young Latin teacher next door to him a long time ago. He was humiliated to be a victim where once he had been only an observer.

At that point Mr Murdoch came in. He had heard enough outside. He knew his class as a man knows his warts or corns. He picked on one conspicuous boy even as he crossed the door.

'Hey, Jumbo! Pipe down! And get back to your seat or I'll skelp your big arse hard, so I will.'

'It's no' me, Bobby,' Jumbo shouted back. 'Ah'm daying nothing. It's him.'

He put the finger on the boy nearest him, shoved him accusingly. But he sat down. Grudgingly. Still, he sat. The class hushed in waves of gathering peace.

Mr Murdoch, brighteyed and tubby, strolled up and down the silent passages. He whispered an auricular threat here, gave a nuchal smack there, padded to the front of the class and gave Mr Alfred a wink the boys couldn't see.

'Let it rest,' he whispered on the way out. 'They won't do it again.'

In the staffroom later he told Mr Alfred not to worry. It was only because he was still a stranger. This class always chanced its arm with a new teacher, no matter how old he was. The only answer was to hit somebody hard right away. Rough justice for these fiery particles. Show them who's boss.

'But even that's failing,' he elaborated sadly. 'It used to be boys took a pride in taking the belt. They'd boast how many they got. They used to despise a man couldn't use the strap. Ach him, they'd say, he canny draw it! But now they want to argue. It wasn't me, it was him. They're yellow. They know their rights. We can't do this and we can't do that, but they can do what they like. They're outside the law. It's all this child-cult. They're starting to defy me even. I had a reputation here. Handed down. God, I taught their fathers! There was a time no boy ever dared look sideways at me. But not now. I'm losing ground. There's no respect now for tradition. I've got to act the clown, speak their lingo, to keep on the right side of them. But there are limits. I'm telling you, it will be hell let loose when they raise the leaving age.'

Mr Alfred didn't need advice about showing who was boss. He didn't need a lecture on the change for the worse in the attitude of the pupils. He didn't need gloomy prophecies about the future. He knew all that. He had said it himself, often. Platitudes didn't stop his belly quivering with anger. He was ashamed that his class had been silenced only by a colleague's intervention. He was furious he hadn't had revenge. He wanted to hit out and assert himself. He wanted to terrorise them so much they wouldn't dare mock him again. But when Murdoch left the room all he could do was get on with his lesson, and a poor one it was. He was sick with frustrated passion. At the morning break he went to the staffroom toilet and vomited in the wash-hand basin.

He wasn't displeased when Waterholm was raided one night in what the papers called an orgy of destruction. Gang slogans were painted on the walls and blackboards, bottles of glue were emptied on the classroom floors, textbooks and exercise books were torn up and scattered, fire hoses were turned on, flooding four classrooms, and the secretary's room and the gymnasium were damaged by fire. But the main attack was on a recent acquisition greatly valued by the headmaster. It was what he called the Language Laboratory, where a classroom had been converted into a number of cubicles with tape-recorders, headphones, and some French and German conversation on tape. The cubicles were wrecked and the sound equipment was smashed beyond repair.

Mr Alfred used the break-in to justify his dislike of the pupils of Watty Compy, for nobody doubted some of them were the culprits.

'I'm not surprised,' he said. 'That's the kind of people you have here. I thought Tordoch was bad, but I see I was transferred from the Ostrogoths to the Visigoths. That's all.'

'Ah, now!' said Harry Murdoch. 'Be fair! It could happen in any school.'

CHAPTER TWENTY-FIVE

The love affair between Martha Weipers and Graeme Roy
was over. Mr Alfred read about them in the paper at a
quarter to five one evening the week before Christmas. He
bought a paper in the city centre when he changed buses.
Sleet was falling and the bus windows were misty. He
couldn't see through them. All he could do was read his
paper. It was the name Weipers caught his eye and gave
his heart a knock. But it wasn't Rose. It was Martha. She
was found dead in Graeme Roy's car at 8 a.m. She must
have died in the small hours of the morning. Graeme Roy
was dead beside her. He was in the driver's seat and she
was leaning against him with her head across his chest. His
left arm was round her shoulder. The car was in the garage
at the side of his father's house. They had been at a latenight dance in the University Union and Roy's parents
were asleep at the time he was expected home.

Mr Alfred went to see his aunt. It was his first visit for a
long time. She knew he hadn't come just because Christmas was near. She too had seen a paper. She knew he
wanted to hear what they were saying about it in Tordoch.
But she knew he wouldn't ask. He would never admit he
liked gossip.

'I see your old school's in the papers again,' she said.

'So long as it's not on television,' he answered her.

He spoke lightly, pretending he didn't know what she
was talking about and didn't care, implying she ought to
know he wasn't interested in anything to do with his old
school.

'Former dux-girl at Collinsburn,' she read from the
paper. 'She looks such a happy girl in that picture. You'd

wonder how the papers get hold of these old photos. I thought you might have seen it.'

'No,' he said.

His lie meant he had to read the report as if he hadn't seen it before. He was ashamed of his deceit. But its purpose was to hide his true feelings. He kept thinking of Rose. He wanted to comfort her.

'You see the police think it was fumes poisoned them,' said Granny Lyons.

'That would be carbon monoxide,' said Mr. Alfred. 'If the engine was running and the doors closed. It doesn't say. Or does it?'

He acted a second reading of an account he knew by heart.

'They're saying here it was suicide,' said Granny Lyons. 'The pair of them together. Because she was in trouble.'

'There's always folk want to gossip,' said Mr Alfred. 'Folk that like to think the worst.'

'Did you know them?' asked Granny Lyons.

'I didn't know her,' he said. He wouldn't mention Rose. 'I taught the boy once. A very intelligent boy as far as I remember.'

'He couldn't have been all that intelligent,' said Granny Lyons. 'It was the girl was clever. See what it says. Prizes for French and German. But see what it says about him. He gave up his studies at the university a year ago. He must have been a right failure, him.'

'Many a boy good at school fails at university,' said Mr Alfred. 'I've known highly intelligent boys had to give it up. Not their bent.'

'Well, that wasn't very intelligent,' said Granny Lyons. 'What he did. If all they say is true.'

'If all they say is true,' said Mr Alfred. 'Suppose it is. Perhaps he loved her.'

'He took an odd way of showing it,' said Granny Lyons.

'He was young,' said Mr Alfred. 'They were both young. Perhaps they thought love was all. How can a

man die better than with his loved one dead beside him?
Maybe that's what he thought.'

'A strange kind of love,' said Granny Lyons, 'to want to
die together. They had their whole life before them.'

'But if they saw no future?' said Mr Alfred.

The way he saw it, the death wish was in them. He
remembered he had known it himself when he first saw he
would never get his poems published. But he had drawn
back from suicide. Graeme Roy hadn't. That was the
difference between them. What he didn't know, and knew
he couldn't know, was the temptation Graeme Roy had
met and what had led him into it, how great the despair
imposed by age and circumstance, what defeat or resistance he had suffered from Martha, who may have chosen
to die in the flesh rather than die in the Elizabethan sense.
Perhaps he had lost heart because he was a university
failure. Perhaps his parents had forbidden any talk of
marriage till he qualified for some profession. Or even
forbidden him to see Martha at all because she lived in the
worst street in Tordoch. Then it was a worldly ban had
made him choose eternity and take Martha with him.

He brooded over them. Over Martha too young to die
and over Roy persuading her death was life's high meed.
Dying together was one kind of communion. He thought he
understood them. He sorrowed for them. How could any
love or beauty live in Tordoch? Only weeds could survive
there, like the flat ugly dockens in the Weavers Lane.

He knew his meditation proceeded on the assumption
that the local talk of a suicide pact was the truth. But he
knew he couldn't be sure about that. He longed to speak to
Rose, to encourage her to live, whatever had happened. It
was unthinkable that nobody should ever break the curse
of Tordoch and grow up to a proper life. And who more
deserving salvation than Rose?

An alcoholic whim took him back to Tordoch between
two pubs one night. There was a decent interval since
Martha's death. If Rose came along the meeting would
seem accidental and he could talk to her of Martha without

appearing ghoulish. He slipped into the scheme through the Weavers Lane. On the wall of Donaldson's paint works he saw REAL COGS RULE ALL, on the back of McLaren's garage was COGLAND, and leaving the lane he saw COGS RULE HERE chalked on Kennedy's soap factory.

He loitered in a closemouth. It was raining. It had been raining all day. Across the dark street the windows of a fish-and-chip shop and a general stores stared through the downpour with a flood of inane brilliance. He would see Rose silhouetted there if she passed. He would know her walk and figure at once. He waited and waited, wearing an old coat and a waterproof cap as his disguise.

A big puddle in the gutter reflected the building opposite him, making it plunge into the ground as much as it reared above it. He knew it was madness. There was no reason why she should come. He knew she lived just round the corner. That's why he was waiting where he was. But where would she be going or coming from at that time of night with the rain lashing down? His feet were cold. He felt the damp seep into his bones. He gave it up and went back to his pubcrawl.

The papers had an epilogue to their story of the young lovers. Roy's parents had no comment. But there was an interview with Martha's father plus his picture. He wanted to make a statement he said. He had a grievance. People were saying his daughter was pregnant when she died. He and his wife wanted to have it publicly declared there was no truth in the rumour. After that there was nothing more in the papers, and the Weipers moved quietly from Tordoch two months later.

Mr Alfred too let it drop out of mind. He was having worries of his own. Before the session ended he was transferred to a primary school. Mr Charles Parsons, M.A. (Hons.), B.Sc., Ed.B., FEIS, saw him out with a smile and a handshake.

'I should very much have liked to have kept you here. But you understand you were only standing in for Mr Auld till he recovered from his operation. Now he's back

I've no time-table for you. It's a pity. But I'm sure you'll enjoy teaching in Winchgate Primary. It's a fine modern school. It was only opened a year ago.'

'Oh yes,' said Mr Alfred.

He knew he had lost face at Waterholm, but he had never expected to be sent to a primary school.

'You've always taught post-primary, haven't you?' Mr Parsons asked as if he didn't know.

'Yes,' said Mr Alfred. 'I've been teaching secondary classes for—'

'Then this will be a challenge to you,' said Mr Parsons. He was smooth and quick. He didn't want Mr Alfred talking back. 'I always say teaching is a job that's full of new challenges. One must accept the challenge.'

'Yes, I know,' said Mr Alfred. 'But I—'

'Children are delightful to teach at that age,' said Mr Parsons. 'So innocent, so keen to learn. I've taught primary classes myself, you know. I'd love to get back into the classroom and do some solid teaching, instead of all this admin. I'm sure you as a graduate will find it most rewarding to work with primary children.'

'Yes, I'm sure,' said Mr Alfred.

CHAPTER TWENTY-SIX

When he got to Winchgate Primary he was told his class was in an annexe a mile from the main building.

Mr Chambers, the headmaster, received him in a pleasant office with picture windows, central heating, a fitted carpet, a modern desk with matching chair, glass fronted book-cases, a coffee table and a jar of mixed flowers. He had two phones on his desk, a master-radio and an intercom panel behind him, and four lounge chairs for his visitors.

Mr Lauder, the deputy head, hovered respectfully. Mr Alfred recognised him as a type rather than an individual. A deferential man, useful to his superiors, discreet and stonefaced, conspiratorial if need be, and all the time taking care of his own interests. Never without a paper in his hand to make him look busy.

'I'm sorry I've got to put you in the annexe,' said Mr Chambers, smiling broadly. 'But I can't send an established member of staff down there to make room for you here. You'll have to sort of thole your assizes in the outposts of empire till there's a vacancy in the main building. It's the curse of a primary school, an annexe.'

'There's hardly a primary school without one now,' said Mr Lauder.

He raised sad eyes from a sheaf of foolscap held by a bulldog-clip.

'Some have two,' said Mr Chambers. 'Sandy Logan over in Clachanwood, he has three, poor man.'

'He must be getting on now, old Sandy,' said Mr Lauder. 'He's about due to retire I should think. And did you see wee Jimmy Rae died yesterday?'

'Yes, I saw it in the *Herald*,' said Mr Chambers. 'All that superannuation and he never lived to draw a penny of it.'

'That means a new head wanted for his place,' said Mr Lauder. 'There's bound to be a call-up soon. There's only two left on the reserve list.'

'You'd better get busy,' said Mr Chambers. 'If you want your own school.'

'There's nothing I can do,' said Mr Lauder. 'I don't know anybody.'

He lowered his head, darted a tick at the top sheet of his clip and turned it over.

Mr Alfred waited silently.

'Ah yes,' said Mr Chambers. 'Well, yes, now.'

'Yes,' said Mr Alfred.

The annexe he was sent to was a row of six classrooms in prefabricated huts. They were shoved up thirty years ago as temporary accommodation to take the overflow from the old school till the new one was built, and they were still needed because the new school was too small even before it was opened. They were drab lairs with hardboard walls and wooden floors. At the end of the row was a cell used as a staffroom. It had a deal table and no tablecloth, five hard chairs, a gas-ring and a two-bar electric fire, a tiny toilet round the corner and a wash-hand basin with no hot water. Mr Alfred sighed and tightened his jaws till his decadent molars ached again.

He was uneasy in his new job. He had no idea how to talk to children ten years old. They might have been ten months old for all he knew about people so young. They seemed babies, and like Mr Briggs he thought there were already too many babies in the world. He had never had boys and girls in the same room before. He had never had forty-eight pupils in the same room before. He had never worked through the day without a change of class or a period off before.

'You'll be all right here,' said Mr Lindsay, senior resident and cynic, an older man. 'Nobody bothers us.

Up in the main building you've always got the boss
breathing down your neck. I prefer it down here. I don't
like these new schools they're putting up. This is what
I'm used to. That's why I volunteered to stay here. You
can be independent. Nothing to worry about. Old Chamber-pot, he won't put any class in the annexe for more
than six months. So they come and they go and I stay.
Suits me. Never see wee Lauder either. Can't stand that
man. That's why I asked out of the main building. And
they can't pin a thing on you when you've had the class
less than six months. You'll like it here, an old hand like
you.'

Mr Alfred didn't like it. He wanted to teach. But nobody wanted to learn. He knew it was his job to make
them. He tried. He failed. It was like talking into a phone
with nobody at the other end. His troubled conscience
found a line of defence. He took the progress cards for
every pupil in his own class, in Mr Lindsay's class, and in
two other classes. He listed the intelligence quotients
recorded there and worked out the average. It was
ninety-two. The mean was ninety.

'No wonder we can't do much,' he said. 'They just
haven't got it. Do you think it's possible there are more
stupid children now than there were in our time?'

'Now, now!' said Mr Lindsay.

He raised a censorious finger and grinned. A man as
earnest as Mr Alfred amused him.

'What do you mean – now, now?' said Mr Alfred.

'You must never say a child is stupid,' said Mr Lindsay.
'There are no stupid children, just as there are no bad
children.'

'But there are,' said Mr Alfred. 'Whether you believe in
original sin or believe in evolution, you can't deny there's
wickedness and stupidity in the world.'

'You know that and I know that,' said Mr Lindsay. 'But
the top brass won't admit it. They've never worked nine
till four, Monday to Friday in a classroom. They talk as if
there was only a shower of little Newtons and Einsteins

who haven't had a fair chance because you didn't teach them right.'

'I see,' said Mr Alfred.

'And if the boy is a thief, a liar and a coward, it's not his fault. It's yours for not giving him enough love.'

'It's a very attractive theory,' said Mr Alfred. He turned it over and looked at it. 'No child is bad. Then all children are not bad. Does that mean good? No child is stupid. All children are not stupid. Does that mean clever?'

'You're so new in primary teaching,' said Mr Lindsay, 'you don't seem to know the line. All children are equal. So why should the clever ones get prizes? Either give them all prizes like in Alice in Wonderland or give nobody a prize. If everybody can't get something it's only fair nobody should get anything. If you deprive a child of a prize you make him feel he's inferior. You might warp him for life. We've got to discourage the competitive spirit. It's a bad thing. So no more exams. Some poor sod might fail.'

Mr Alfred said the new schemes of work, and the new methods they involved, were making life difficult.

'I don't know what I'm trying to do,' he complained.

'Does anybody?' said Mr Lindsay.

'Another thing,' said Mr Alfred. 'It doesn't seem this school was ever meant for teaching in. It's more like a welfare centre. I've never met so many cases of free dinners and free clothes and getting tokens for the clinic. We feed them and clothe them and give them medical care. Next thing is we'll be putting them to bed.'

'Wouldn't be surprised,' said Mr Lindsay. 'Once you start with the idea all children are equal, next thing is you say some of them don't get a fair chance because they come from a poor home. So tomorrow or the day after we'll be having legislation for equal environments. We'll have the mums and dads in barracks and all the weans brought up together in one bloody big comprehensive sleeping-and-feeding-centre.'

'Back to Sparta,' said Mr Alfred.

'It's bound to come,' said Mr Lindsay. 'You can have liberty or you can have equality. You can't have both.'

'What about fraternity?' said Mr Alfred.

'Haven't seen it since I left the army,' said Mr Lindsay.

'No, I suppose not,' said Mr Alfred.

There was a young teacher, Miss Seymour, two doors along the veranda from him, a female non-graduate, college-trained for three years. She had been teaching for a year and a bit. He thought her youth and her zest for the job might help him if he discussed the new methods with her. Inadvertently he mentioned poetry.

She boggled.

'Poetry? Oh, I never do poetry. I encourage the children to write their own poetry.'

She was airy-mannered, brisk-moving, swift-speaking, and fully fashionable. She decorated the walls of her classroom with the drawings and paintings of her pupils and pinned up the foolscap pages of a handwritten class-magazine.

Mr Alfred inspected the display, hoping to learn something.

'Wouldn't it be better to let the children see some good reproductions of famous paintings?' he asked. 'Or even coloured posters of Scotland's beauty spots. You can get them from British Railways.'

'That's no good,' said Miss Seymour. 'It's the children's own work that's important.'

'I see there's a lot of bad spelling and bad grammar in your magazine,' he said.

'Spelling and grammar don't matter,' said Miss Seymour. 'Just so long as they write something. Creative activity, that's what counts.'

'But very few folk are creative,' said Mr Alfred. 'Even those that are need examples when they're young. Shouldn't you let them see a painting by a great painter, let them learn a poem written by a poet? Instead of all this rubbish.'

She laughed at him.

'Rubbish? I like that! You're a right old fossil! What you see there is what the inspectors want. This is the day of the child-dominated classroom.'

'The child is master of the man,' he muttered.

'Pardon?' she said.

She used a pale pink lipstick, her nails were varnished silver, her hair was a long sheeny blonde, she wore fishnet tights and a miniskirt. She had pale-blue eyes, a small nose and a big bosom. But she didn't attract him. Since the day he lost Rose he had become impotent and lost interest in women. He had even forgotten Stella. He never went to her pub now.

'Don't worry so much,' Mr Lindsay patted him on the elbow. 'All this will pass. In education the experts of one generation always discover the experts of the previous generation were a crowd of bloody eedjits.'

'I don't doubt it,' said Mr Alfred. 'But I'm afraid the new fashion will last my time.'

At the lunch-hour break, to get away from it all, he went for a walk round the neighbourhood. There was a new park five minutes away, and he felt the better for a walk round it in spite of the fact that the urinal at the main entrance had GATE YA BASS daubed on the wall and YY GATE chiselled on the door of the solitary water-closet. There were two pubs, but he didn't go into either. He never touched alcohol till his day's work was over. One of the pubs was new, but the other, the Black Bull, was an old howff surviving from the days when Winchgate like Tordoch was only a village on the edge of the insatiable city. There was an old cinema, the Dalriada, dating from the Chaplin era, and behind the park a local railway line closed by Beeching. There was a public library and reading room. And further out, he was told, there was a cemetery beside the old village church. He meant to visit it some lunchtime, but procrastinated. He saw himself trying to make out the inscriptions on the weatherworn tombstones and going over some stanzas of Gray's 'Elegy' in his head. The library too he meant to visit. It would be peaceful there and in the cemetery.

But he found no peace. He got used to the janitor accosting him every Monday morning.

'Another break-in at the weekend, sir. Sorry it's your room again. But you see, it's you being at the far end. They've a clear getaway across the field and over the railway. Even if I spotted them I could never catch them.'

The first time it happened was the worst. He thought it was an attack on him as much as on the room. He thought he must have antagonised his boys somehow. All his windows were smashed and the classroom entered. Text-books and exercise books were torn to bits and the scraps scattered. The desks had been pushed about and over-turned. The walls were sprayed with paint, and chalk was stamped into the floorboards. The pupils were jubilant when they came in and saw chaos. Mr Alfred tried to settle them and sort things out, but it took a long time.

'Please sir, I still haven't got the right seat.'

'Please sir, I've got books here aren't mine.'

'Please sir, there's dirt in my desk.'

They were excited, curious to see what he would do. Mr Alfred rubbed his chin. He felt the bristles coarse under his fingertips. He never seemed to get a close shave in the morning now. He breathed in and breathed out, slowly.

His windows were broken three weeks running, but when other rooms were raided as well he stopped thinking it was his fault. The fourth weekend Mr Lindsay's room was nearly set on fire. All that was left of the register and the pupils' documents, progress cards, medical schedules and report cards, was a charred mass in a corner where the floorboards and the wall were badly scorched. The in-vaders put the water-closets out of use by stealing the chains that flushed the cisterns. The janitor tied cords to the lever in lieu of chains, but they soon disappeared too. The ceiling in the toilets had big holes caused by boys swinging from the lintel of the cubicle doors to see how high and hard they could kick. The damage was so recurrent repairs became desultory.

'I'm sick of this place,' said the janitor.

He was an old-fashioned man, impatient of children, much given to whining about the hard life he had. He spent his days moaning in the huts and his nights drinking in the Black Bull. He was there one night when his lonely wife heard glass breaking. She hurried out just in time to see three lads scampering. She was angry, and in her anger she spoke foolishly.

'I know you,' she called out in the twilight. 'I know you, McCulloch! I saw you, Baxter! Yes, and you with the red hair, I know you too!'

She told her husband. He challenged McCulloch and Baxter in the morning. He thought he would get the third boy's name by threatening them. All he got was abuse. When it was dark that night somebody threw a brick through his living-room window. At the end of the month he handed in his resignation.

'I'm not putting up with this any longer,' he told Mr Alfred. 'I'm getting a job with the Parks Department.'

He wasn't there a week before he was moaning again. Mr Alfred met him on one of his lunchtime walks.

'I've just lost eight young trees,' said the ex-janitor. 'They must have come prepared to do damage. It would have took a good axe to fell they trees. It would break your heart, so it would.'

'Oh dear,' said Mr Alfred. 'I don't understand it.'

To avoid having to listen to the ex-janitor's grumbling he stopped going to the park. He went further out to have a look at the cemetery he had long meant to visit. It was a restful plot, away from the world and divorced from time, but before he was very far in he saw two tombstones lying flat. A wizened labourer was bent on putting them up again. He straightened when he heard Mr Alfred come along. He had to tell somebody.

'But how did they manage it?' said Mr Alfred.

'They broke into my toolshed,' said the old man. 'It took a crowbar to get these stones down. I give up. Folk that'll do that, they've no respect for nothing.'

'Oh dear,' said Mr Alfred. 'I can't understand it.'

He was in low spirits at that time in any case, because Granny Lyons was in hospital. She was to have a mammectomy. He went out at midday to phone the hospital and ask about her. He didn't like to use the phone in the school in case he was overheard. He preferred to keep his private life private. He walked round and round Winchgate for an hour and got nowhere. Every phone-box he tried was out of order.

'Oh dear,' he said. 'I'll never understand it.'

Still searching peace and quiet he went next day to the local library. He liked going to the corporation's public libraries, he liked showing his spare ticket to get in, and then browsing through the catalogues and the card-index of recent additions. The librarian on duty that day was a sedate little spinster with grey hair and a cameo brooch on her blouse. When she saw Mr Alfred come in she knew at once he was a booklover. She watched him go to where the catalogues should be, watched him squint for the card-index boxes. She sighed, padded over in flatheeled sympathy. She explained the library had no catalogues. There had been a break-in through the skylight. All the index-cards and the printed catalogues had been stolen. Some of the cards had been found scattered across the old railway line, but she couldn't say yet how many were missing. The printed catalogues, bound in volumes, had still to be found.

'We'll have to recatalogue the whole library,' she said.

'Oh dear,' said Mr Alfred. 'What a shame.'

She blinked and sniffed, acknowledging his share in her sorrow.

'Fourteen thousand volumes,' she said. 'I don't know how long it will take us. We're short of staff as it is.'

'Oh dear,' said Mr Alfred. 'I don't understand. Why do they do it?'

He was glad he wasn't a cinema-goer when he saw from the bus one morning that the Dalriada was only the hollow shell of a burned-out building. But he wasn't surprised. He knew he was in a bad area. He seemed to have spent his life in bad areas. And he supposed the annexe where he taught was the prey of vandals because it was a neglected backwater lacking the amenities of the main building. It bred resentment, and resentment was expressed in destruction. That's how he explained it to Mr Lindsay.

Mr Lindsay smiled. He knew the main building was having trouble too. The climax came when a single-storeyed wing was gutted by fire. A passing motorist saw the flames at two in the morning. The wing included a dining-room, kitchen, gymnasium, and medical room. The papers said it cost more than £100,000 when it was opened. The police said entry had been gained through a pantry-window too small to admit anyone but a schoolchild. Mr Chambers had to make emergency arrangements to feed the children who used the dining-room their schoolmates had destroyed.

'I can just see old Chamber-pot,' said Mr Lindsay. 'Chasing his tail in ever decreasing circles till he disappears up his own arse.'

'Oh dear,' said Mr Alfred. 'What a school!'

'Ah now, wait a minute!' said Mr Lindsay, aggressively loyal. 'It's not just here. It happens everywhere.'

'The child-dominated school,' said Mr Alfred.

'That's not a fair thing to say,' said Miss Seymour.

CHAPTER TWENTY-SEVEN

Mr Alfred liked the weekend. He could forget school and Miss Seymour then. On a Saturday afternoon he went strolling along Sauchiehall Street. He meant to go to Boots and buy shaving-soap and razor-blades. But he was on the wrong side of the road, and when he came out of a day-dream he saw he couldn't get across. Where there should have been four lanes of one-way traffic racing from west to east, with a break at Hope Street or Renfield Street on the Cross signal, there was only a crowd of pedestrians from east and west who kept going on a collision course. He thought it rather strange so many people should be walking right in the middle of a busy road. It took him a moment or two to make out that what he was seeing was two gangs, about fifty in each, armed with axes and hammers, throwing bottles and yelling as they advanced.

He was frightened by the noise and the flourish of weapons. When the rearguards flowed from the road on to the pavement, routing neutrals there, he ran into a shop doorway. He wasn't the only one. All the shopping housewives flocked for cover, and their hysterical screams made bedlam of a battlefield already bellowing and rebellowing. He saw a scampering matron trip herself in her hurry and fall on her face just as an empty bottle crashed beside her. He was terrified, but he thought he had to be at least a gentleman if not a hero. He dashed from his shelter and tried to help her to her feet. She was fat and heavy. He couldn't lift her. He felt the sag of big flabby breasts as he grasped her round the middle and he blushed. Some women, gabbling indignantly, gave him a hand and raised their fallen sister. She got off her knees slowly, white and shaking.

When he had calmed her a little and taken her to the doorway Mr Alfred turned to watch what was going on in the street. He was still frightened, but he was interested too. He couldn't believe that two gangs had the cheek to pick Sauchiehall Street on a Saturday afternoon as the venue for a challenge match, Sauchiehall Street above all places, the city's most famous thoroughfare, its answer to Edinburgh's Princes Street, to London's Regent Street.

He looked and listened. The medley of chanting and barracking made it hard to distinguish the words, but he recognised the same warcry coming from both sides.

'Ya bass!'

'Ya bass!'

'What's it all about?' he asked in the doorway.

Nobody seemed to know. Nobody even looked at him, far less answered him. All eyes front, all mouths open.

Before the gangs were fully engaged six patrol cars and a Q car came speeding along. They barged through them and swerved to a stop in the middle of the road. A score of policemen jumped out. Mr Alfred wanted to cheer. He saw the crowd break like shattered glass, he saw youths throw away bottles and bayonets as they fled. He saw a butcher's cleaver tossed in the air and heard it clatter in the gutter. A discarded hammer landed at his feet. He gaped at it.

In the Sunday paper he read there were twenty-nine arrests. The printed story pleased him. He had to cut it out. He had to show it to Mr Lindsay in the staffroom on Monday morning.

'I saw that,' he had to say. 'I was there.'

The cutting seemed to give more reality to what he had seen, and what he had seen made the cutting more credible.

He saw another fight in the street before he was much older. Mr Lindsay, a judicious beer drinker, told him of a bar on the south side that served good draught beer. Mr Alfred said he would give it a trial. A pub-crawl in that area might be interesting. He took a bus across the river on a Wednesday night. He thought Wednesday would be a suitably quiet night for a voyage of exploration and he got off the bus with the pleasant feeling of a day's work behind him and adventure in front of him.

Between pubs he walked into trouble. Two companies of juveniles, moving against each other at the gallop, took over the whole street and made anybody who got in their way scurry into a close for safety. Mr Alfred resented having his hard-earned right to a pub-crawl obstructed. He had a drink in him, and he wasn't going to run into a close just because of a clash of minors. He stood against a shop-window and superciliously looked on. What he saw alarmed him and wiped the sneer off his face. The vicious way the fangs were bared at the scream of 'Ya bass' seemed an appalling and yet appropriate accompaniment to the thrust of the knife.

Squad cars and a dog-van bowled along and closed in as the battle rolled along Victoria Road and into Calder Street. The dogs were taken from the van but not released in pursuit. Their barking was enough to make the rioters run.

The next morning he saw in his paper there were fourteen arrests. He read it out to Mr Lindsay. Again he had to boast.

'I saw that. I was there.'

'But you found my pub all right?' said Mr Lindsay.

'Oh yes,' said Mr Alfred. 'You're quite right. It's a good beer they have there. But you know what I'm finding now? It's hard to get a good light draught beer. It's mostly heavy ale they serve now. That's what the young ones ask for. They just want to get drunk quick. You can see it. Two pints and they want to fight their pal.'

The frequency of gang-fights in the main streets of their city became a staple of conversation between them. They told each other what they had seen in town the night before, they read aloud from the paper over their cup of tea at morning break.

'Policeman stabbed in gang affray,' read Mr Lindsay.

'Five stabbed on way to dance,' read Mr Alfred.

'Boy of sixteen gets six years,' read Mr Lindsay. 'Attempted murder by stabbing.'

'Boy of seventeen gets four years,' read Mr Alfred. 'Used razor on a girl and a youth in gang-clash.'

Minor disorders they noted too.

'Shots hit buses on terror route,' read Mr Lindsay.

'Bus rowdy jailed for thirty days,' read Mr Alfred.

'Nine arrests after dance brawl,' read Mr Lindsay. 'A gang of youths entered a dance-hall shouting, "We are the little people! We've come to rule the world."'

'I like that,' said Mr Alfred. 'The little people.'

'Come to rule the world,' said Mr Lindsay.

'Surely the Second Coming is at hand,' said Mr Alfred.

'That's Yeats, isn't it?' said Mr Lindsay. 'The Second Coming. It's a poem by Yeats. Am I right?'

'Yes, you're quite right,' said Mr Alfred. 'The blood-dimmed tide is loosed. The ceremony of innocence is drowned.'

'Oh, I don't remember that,' said Mr Lindsay. 'But I know I've seen a poem by Yeats called the Second Coming.'

Mr Alfred was surprised a fellow teacher in a primary school had read Yeats. He began to like Mr Lindsay.

CHAPTER TWENTY-EIGHT

It was payday again. He was glad. He kept out of debt, but he had no savings. By the time the end of the month came round he was beginning to need money. He had his cheque in his hand by ten o'clock and cashed it locally before lunch. Money was all the armour he took on his nightly tour of dark streets and dingy pubs, in search of a castle perilous and a holy grail.

Sometimes, as he wandered, there lurked in a forgotten corridor of his mind a twin accusing him that for all his boasted love of literature he hadn't read a book right through for a long time, that the most modern poets he had read were those in fashion thirty years ago, that he had stopped there and never read anyone younger than himself.

At those moments he felt his cloak of booklover was as shabby as the old coat he was wearing. He wished he had a quiet corner where he could sit in some comfort at a big desk and resume the studies of his youth. He blamed his truancy on the lack of a house of his own. His lodgings were so cramped he could use them only as a den for eating and sleeping, and even at that he often ate out. But over the years he had put off from day to day the attempt to find a better place. Where he was had one advantage he valued. It allowed him a wide liberty of coming and going as he pleased. To move might limit his freedom and would certainly mean a new routine. The prospect didn't please him. He was a creature of habit.

'And this is a bad habit,' he said to his silent face in a bar mirror. 'This paynight binge.'

When he had a month's salary in his pocket he always

drank more than usual. The way the world looked then was part of the colour of paynight. So leaving the last pub when the bell went he knew he had enough, if not too much. Out in the street he was aware of being hungry as well as drunk.

'No, not drunk,' he said, encouraging himself to get past people without colliding. 'I won't have that. Just a bit fuddled, that's all. What I say is, anaesthetised.'

He passed a new cafeteria with broad uncurtained windows. He saw it was packed with young people shoving a latenight snack down their gullets. The sight of so much esuriency recalled to him a practice of the days when he was only an apprentice in drinking. After a night in a pub he used to go to a cheap restaurant and eat a big plate of fish and chips. His journeyman's stomach seemed to have lost the capacity for that amount of food at that time of night. For years he had gone to bed without a bite after drinking. But now a youthful craving moved in his belly and he aimed at the Caballero for something to eat.

He didn't forget he had a month's pay in his pocket, and he had taken care as usual never to be seen fumbling with a wad of notes when he paid for a drink. He always kept a few pounds loose for easy access, but the bulk of his money he kept stowed away in a pocket inside the waistband of his trousers. It was a pocket he told the tailor to put in whenever he had a new suit. He had never lost any money, never been dipped. He took great pride in that.

Outside the Caballero he made sure he had two notes handy and some loose silver. Groping to count the coins by touch alone, his fingers met a thick cylinder. For a moment he didn't know what it was. Then he remembered it was the felt-tipped pen he had taken from a boy he caught writing GATE YA BASS on the flyleaf of an atlas. He had put the pen in his pocket and forgotten about it. He slipped it aside and went on trying to add up the money in his pocket. He calculated he had enough silver to pay for anything the Caballero could offer, but he was pleased to feel notes there as well. Rather than put out in small change the exact sum required, especially when he wasn't sober, he was much given to handing over a note for each new payment and ending up with a dead weight of silver every night.

The city was full of new eating places open late, Italian, Indian, Chinese. Keen to compete, the Caballero had modernised its front and furnishings, though not its menus, since he last ate in it. The unfamiliar entrance offended him. The strength needed to push open a heavy glass door threw him off balance and he couldn't get in without a stumble and a stagger. His clumsiness annoyed him. In the abrupt brightness his eyes were slow to focus, and he took conspicuously long to spot a table to suit him. There was one four yards from him, at fortyfive degrees to his angle of incidence, but he missed it.

He loitered two steps inside the door, making a survey that was difficult for him because he was suffering from an unexpected diplopia. He blinked. Right where he was dithering a young man and his girlfriend were eating sausage, eggs and chips baptised with HP sauce. The young man was quick-eyed and kind-hearted. He wanted to show his girlfriend he was a gentleman. He put down his knife. With his right hand freed he tapped Mr Alfred's elbow and thumbed to the vacant table. He looked up. Mr Alfred looked down. The young man smiled. His girlfriend was pleased with him. Mr Alfred bowed to both smiles.

'Thank you,' he said, age respecting youth.

He heard a thickening in his speech and began to feel self-conscious. He advanced obliquely, swimming against the current of departing customers, anxious to reach the undulating table before he drowned.

The young man and his girlfriend weren't the only ones who noticed him come in. A quartet in the back corner stared, watching him all the way till he sat down. Two of the four recognised him.

'That's big Alfy,' said Gerald Provan.

'Christ so it is,' said Smudge.

'Who's big Alfy?' said Dianne McElhimmeny.

'He looks squiffed,' said Yvonne McGudgeon.

'Well away,' said Dianne. 'Who is he?'

'Yous know him?' said Yvonne.

Gerald told them big Alfy used to be his teacher.

'See! See teachers?' said Yvonne. 'Can't stand them so I can't.'

'I hated school so I did,' said Dianne.

'Imagine him coming to a place like this,' said Smudge.

'A man his age,' said Gerald. 'With what he gets paid.'

'He looks a right tramp,' said Yvonne.

'Is he one of yon?' said Dianne. 'You know what I mean.'

'A query?' said Yvonne.

'Nut hom,' said Gerald.

He told them about Rose Weipers.

'Dirty old man,' said Dianne.

'Bad wee bitch that one was,' said Yvonne. 'Letting a drip like that feel her for a couple of bob.'

'I bet you he's loaded,' said Smudge.

'Of course he's loaded,' said Dianne. 'You can see it in his eyes.'

'Not drink, money,' said Smudge.

'Christ you're right, pal,' said Gerald. 'The enda the month the day. The big bugger'll have his pay in his pocket. How about rolling him?'

'That's what I mean,' said Smudge. 'You on, chookies?'

'Wadyathink, Dianne?' said Yvonne.

'Fits okay with you sokay with me,' said Dianne.

They plotted while they waited for Mr Alfred to finish his two hamburgers and coffee. They paid after he paid, stalled a moment more, and followed him out. The girls accosted him on the pavement.

'You a teacher?' said Dianne pleasantly.

Mr Alfred was wary. He always distrusted people who stopped him in the street, especially youths who asked familiar questions.

'Gotta fag, mister?'

'Gotta light, mac?'

'Got the right time, Jimmy?'

The questions were often put to him on his way home at midnight. He didn't like them. He never liked strangers who tried to speak to him as if they were old friends. He thought it was obvious he wasn't a man to be spoken to without an introduction. In his opinion youths who asked a man his age for a cigarette or a match, or even the time, were much too egalitarian in their manners, even in a city famous for its democratic way of life, or else they were rascals. He believed if he looked at his watch to tell them the time they would find out what they wanted to know, that he had a watch. Then they would attack him and take it from him. Or if he stopped to take out a box of matches or a packet of cigarettes he would be off guard for just as long as that took, which would be long enough for them to surround him, and rob him. So he never stopped to answer a question.

But this was different. He was warmed to have two lissom lassies, one at each elbow, hanging on to him and flashing a smile. An old desire stretched in him, so long quiescent it had the thrill of novelty. He couldn't tell a lie. He had to be chatty to girls so friendly, young and pretty. He had to be gallant. He was. They smiled to his smile.

'And was you ever at Collinsburn?' said Yvonne.

'Yes, indeed I was,' he said, and lurched with good will between the pair of them. 'But I'm sorry I don't remember either of you. Of course I didn't have many girls' classes.'

He felt sure he had said clashes. He laughed to laugh it off.

'Aw, you'll no remember me,' said Yvonne.

'Nur me,' said Dianne.

'We was at Collinsburn,' said Yvonne. 'But no in your class.'

'Naw, we never got you,' said Dianne. 'Wasn't we unlucky!'

She laughed. He laughed. They all laughed.

Yvonne squeezed Mr Alfred on one arm, Dianne

squeezed him on the other. They hung on tight. They made conversation as instructed. They diverted him.

'But ma wee sister knew you,' said Dianne. 'She was in your class.'

'Oh yes?' said Mr Alfred.

The press of the girls' hands on his arms, the feel of their hips against him, the brush of their lips at his cheek as they chattered, so soothed and yet aroused him that he didn't see he was being led astray from the main road into an empty sidestreet of old tenements.

'So was mines,' said Yvonne.

'Mine,' said Mr Alfred.

'Same class as Rose Weipers,' said Dianne.

'Dyever see wee Rose now?' said Yvonne.

'She's no so wee,' said Dianne. 'You should see the boys that's after her.'

The thought of boys after Rose made Mr Alfred jealous. He suffered.

'Rose?' he said. 'Do you two know Rose?'

'Sure,' said Yvonne.

'Of course,' said Dianne.

'Does she ever,' said Mr Alfred.

He didn't get a chance to say 'mention my name'. Gerald and Smudge came up behind him and bundled him into a close. They acted quickly and efficiently. Gerald was tall and strong, Smudge was smaller but broad and tough in his teens. Yvonne and Dianne let it go with a muted cry as if they were as surprised as Mr Alfred. They watched at the closemouth while Gerald and Smudge roughed him. His head was forced down, their knees and fists were on him. They shoved him smartly into the back-close where they wouldn't be seen from the street and went to work on him. They rifled him when they had him flat and got his loose silver and the two pound notes he kept handy. But they missed the rest of his salary hidden in the waistband of his trousers.

'Was sure he'd've had more,' Gerald panted.

Mr Alfred lay groaning and writhing. He whimpered.

He was in pain. The way they had cracked his head against the wall to make him give in left him seeing flashes of lightning in a granular darkness.

'Bastard banks it quick maybe,' said Smudge. 'They toffs. Pay by cheque all the time. Fly.'

'Coo-ee,' called Yvonne.

Gerald kicked Mr Alfred again and spat on him.

'Quick,' said Smudge. 'Somebody coming.'

'He must have more somewhere,' said Gerald.

'Coo-ee,' called Dianne. 'Coo-ee.'

'Ach, leave him,' said Smudge.

He pulled Gerald away from starting another search and they joined the ladies. They returned deviously to the main road and took the first bus that came. They didn't care where it was going. In a shop doorway far from the Caballero they shared the winnings.

'Thought you said he was loaded,' Yvonne complained at the pittance allotted her.

'Ach, shut your face,' said Smudge. 'Wadyedo to earn it anyway?'

'Was us took him,' said Dianne.

'Wayamoanin aboot noo?' said Gerald.

'A'm no moanin,' said Yvonne.

'Well don't then,' said Smudge.

'Was worth it,' said Gerald. 'Just to get that big bastard. Money's not everything, you know.'

Mr Alfred stopped groaning and writhing, stopped whimpering. He lay still in the back-close of the tenement where they left him. Fatigue and alcohol and the crack on the skull and the beating and the kicking were too much for him. He gave in. He was unconscious.

His twin stood over him saying, 'I told you so. You asked for it. Going about the way you do.'

He waited in a dream to be rescued from a nightmare.

CHAPTER TWENTY-NINE

Someone shook him, but not roughly, whispered, 'Are you all right, old man?'

The voice was gentle.

Mr Alfred moaned coming round, hearing it lean over him.

'Oh, you poor old soul! How are you feeling?'

The speaker was not yet distinguished. He helped Mr Alfred up, brushed him down with judicious hands, gave him his pubcrawling cap, tidied his coatcollar, straightened his tie for him, patted his cheeks, put him against the wall. At every touch he exuded sympathy.

'Not know me?' said the faraway voice.

'No,' said Mr Alfred.

He couldn't see yet, only hear. The close was dim. Everything was dim. He wasn't sure he was where he seemed to be. His mind seemed someone else's. So did his feet when he felt himself teetering on them.

The speaker came closer. There was a slight halation of his face, but Mr Alfred could see white teeth smile. The blurred lips moved in friendly speech.

'You used to teach me. Not remember?'

'Your face I think,' said Mr Alfred. 'But your name I don't know.'

'Tod,' said the speaker. 'Not remember?'

The gentle voice changed to harsh. The speaker was hurt not to be remembered.

'No,' said Mr Alfred. 'No, I'm afraid I don't.'

He apologised. He was afraid not to. It seemed to be a youth was talking to him, and youths he knew were dangerous. They had to be spoken to respectfully.

'Do forgive me please. I didn't mean to snub you. Oh no, you mustn't think that. But see it from my side.'

The young face turned into darkness, not bothering to listen. But Mr Alfred had to explain.

'When I taught in Collinsburn I had say forty boys in a class, say three classes on my timetable every session. That's a hundred and twenty boys a year. That's one thousand two hundred in ten years. Not to mention girls. I had a class of girls once. It's too many to expect any man to remember. Two thousand four hundred boys in twenty years. Plus girls.'

Tod came into the light again.

'Good at the old mental, eh?' he said. 'I thought you was an English teacher.'

'A teacher of English,' said Mr Alfred. 'I myself am not English. But even a teacher of English can do a little arithmetic.'

'Funny old man, aren't you?' said Tod. 'I've been watching you. You've got some weird ideas, so you have.'

The voice changed again. It delivered a sneer. It became aggressive. The illumined face of the speaker moved against the unseen face of the listener.

'For the eye sees not itself,' said Mr Alfred, 'but by reflection. Excuse me. I'm too tired to reflect.'

'I know all about you,' said Tod. 'I know what you are all right. I know what you've been up to.'

Mr Alfred sagged with guilt. He waited to be accused of corrupting Rose Weipers.

But Rose wasn't mentioned.

By an abrupt transition, without hanging about for transport, he was in the house where Tod lived. It was a place he had heard of but never seen, a three-roomed house on the first floor of an abandoned tenement, condemned as unsafe, where teenagers of both sexes who had left home lived rough and slept together on the bare boards. It was called The Flat.

Tod pushed him against the kitchen sink.

'Think you're the great poet, eh?' he said. 'It's not you, it's me. I'm the one that's the poet.'

'Have you published anything?' Mr Alfred enquired. 'That's the test.'

'Of course I've published something,' said Tod.

'Where?' said Mr Alfred.

'Everywhere,' said Tod.

'What do you mean, everywhere?' said Mr Alfred. 'That's a damn silly answer.'

'Manners,' said Tod. 'You're not talking to one of your pupils now, you know. You're talking to me. Tod.'

'I'm sorry,' said Mr Alfred.

'Tell me this,' said Tod.

He sat at the derelict kitchen table, elbow on the board, a fingertip on his temple. He made it clear he was thinking.

'Tell you what?' said Mr Alfred.

'What have you with all your education ever wrote to compare with Ya Bass?'

'Your Ya Bass?' said Mr Alfred. 'You mean you wrote Ya Bass?'

'It was me thought it up,' said Tod. 'Me and nobody else. All my own work. Alone I done it.'

'Did,' said Mr Alfred. 'Coriolanus.'

'Did,' said Tod. 'An act of poetic creation so it was. Don't you agree?'

'Yes, indeed,' said Mr Alfred.

Tod stood behind the kitchen table, hands pulling lapels, and lectured.

'The careful student will appreciate the vowel music and consonantal vigour of these remarkable words. He will hear the sublime derision of the street urchin's *Yah*, a primitive ideophone, modulated into the polite plural *You*, pronounced *Ya* in the dialect of our northern poet. This striking economy of address is immediately followed by the masterly brevity of *Bass*, a monosyllable with more vehemence and malevolence than the full form *Bastard*, found in the work of the more cultured poets who wrote in the southern dialect. Only someone with a great poetic talent could have invented such language in a society as yet hardly civilised. It is from such vulgar eloquence that a great vernacular poetry arises.'

'Very true,' said Mr Alfred. 'Dante. De vulgari . . .'

He was feeling frightened again. He wanted to please the lecturer.

Tod came round the kitchen table.

'I'm glad you like Ya Bass,' he said. 'It's my best poem so far. But I've a lot more coming up.'

'I'm sure I'll like them all,' said Mr Alfred.

'You'd better,' said Tod.

'Yes, I know,' said Mr Alfred.

Tod smiled. He was pleased.

'You used to take notes wherever you saw Ya Bass, didn't you?'

'That's right,' said Mr Alfred.

'And you cut bits out the paper about all the fights I fixed, didn't you?'

'That's right,' said Mr Alfred.

'Ah, you're a great man,' said Tod. 'A real documentarian.'

'Docs, ya bass,' said Mr Alfred.

'It was just the last two words I thought up,' said Tod. 'I left the rest to the lads themselves. It only needed a few of them to start it off.'

'Then the sheep,' said Mr Alfred.

'That's right,' said Tod. 'I know mine and mine know me. It gave me variety in uniformity.'

'Unity in diversity,' said Mr Alfred.

'All the same only different,' said Tod.

'The formula is xYB,' said Mr Alfred. 'Where YB is a constant and x has an infinite number of values.'

'And xYB equals CR,' said Tod. 'Where CR is a Cultural Revolution.'

'Yes, indeed,' said Mr Alfred.

'Well, the start of one anyway,' said Tod. 'And if I've got Cogs fighting Fangs and screaming Ya Bass at each other it's all in a good cause surely.'

'What cause?' said Mr Alfred.

'Disorder,' said Tod. 'You can't have a revolution without disorder, now can you?'

'No, I suppose not,' said Mr Alfred.

'What we want,' said Tod, 'is liberty. And there's no liberty in order. And you just think for a minute. The wars of religion were fought with men screaming Ya Bass at each other. In their own language of course. The same with the wars of nationalism. All I've did is reduce human conflict to its simplest terms. My boys from the north get killed fighting my boys from the south? So what? Dulce et decorum est pro housing-scheme mori.'

'The territorial imperative,' said Mr Alfred. 'All you've done, you mean, not all you've did.'

'I'll do more before I'm finished,' said Tod. 'I'm young enough yet. Who's going to stop me? Mind you, I'm proud of what I've did so far.'

'What you've done,' said Mr Alfred. 'You have every reason to be.'

'Those intellectuals,' said Tod. 'Small fry. They misunderstood me. They wrote Brecht Ya Bass and Beckett Ya Bass. I didn't mean it that way at all. Some folk thought it meant Brecht and Beckett were bastards in my opinion. I never meant no such thing.'

'Oh no, I'm sure you didn't,' said Mr Alfred.

'I've nothing against Brecht or Beckett,' said Tod. 'Or any of the big guys. They have their place in literature and I have mines.'

'Mine,' said Mr Alfred. 'Indeed you have.'

'Another thing,' said Tod. 'The intellectuals, they only wrote it once in the one place. That was no use. They missed the whole point of the operation. I wanted Ya Bass to be ubiquitous. Like those bloody young Cratchits in that thing you read to us the week before Christmas one year. I still remember that, you know.'

'Oh, it's ubiquitous all right,' said Mr Alfred.

'Thanks to me,' said Tod. 'These things isn't accidental. It was me made it ubiquitous. Poets are the unacknowledged legislators of the world. Wordsworth.'

'Shelley,' said Mr Alfred.

'Pedantic old bastard, aren't you?' said Tod.

'I'm sorry,' said Mr Alfred.

'I'm a teacher as well as you only better,' said Tod. 'I gave a course of lectures to a few of the lads. I told them what to do. Where to do it, like. I don't mean just writing on walls everywhere. That was only the basic training. No, I mean action. I got Action Groups going. You know, like revolutionary cells. Three principles. Deride, deface, destroy. It was me suggested scattering the catalogues from a library for example. You saw that one yourself. And it was a good one, wasn't it?'

'Yes, that was a very good one,' said Mr Alfred.

'My lads,' said Tod. 'They're all nice fellows. When you get to know them. Maybe not so bright some of them. But you can teach them. You can organise them. That's what I done. I put it to them.'

He went behind the kitchen table again, arms waving, voice raised, and put it to them.

'Do you want to be nobody or somebody?'

'Somebody,' said Mr Alfred.

'Do you want to be pushed around or do the pushing?'

'Do the pushing,' said Mr Alfred.

'Do you want to have nothing or do you want to have power?'

'Power,' said Mr Alfred.

'Destroy, destroy, destroy!'

'It's quite safe,' said Mr Alfred. 'Nobody will touch you.'

'The old folks at home will blame themselves.'

'They'll say it's all their fault,' said Mr Alfred.

'It's the fault of society.'

'They must have failed you somehow, somewhere,' said Mr Alfred.

'It's not your fault, lads.'

'On my head be it,' said Mr Alfred.

'About! Seek! Burn! Fire! Kill! Slay!'

'Julius Caesar,' said Mr Alfred.

'You are the little people,' said Tod. 'You are sent to rule the world.'

'I've heard that before,' said Mr Alfred. 'Somewhere. I've forgotten.'

'I'm the new Pied Piper,' said Tod.

'So long as you're new,' said Mr Alfred. 'That's all that matters.'

'It was you taught me,' said Tod. 'Remember? In Hyderabad I freed the Nizam from a monstrous brood of vampire bats. But you know what I done when I went to Hamelin. I'll do the same here. Lead all the weans away from you.'

'I'm sure you will,' said Mr Alfred. 'What you did.'

'Don't forget I'm only starting,' said Tod. 'Every revolution is brought about by a determined minority. You take the twelve apostles.'

'Take the Bolsheviks,' said Mr Alfred. 'Lenin and Trotsky.'

'Take John Knox and the Scotch reformers,' said Tod. 'Think what they done to bonny Scotland. Nothing to what I'm doing.'

'I'm sure,' said Mr Alfred. 'What they did.'

'I've got friends,' said Tod. 'Friends in high places. You know that. You've met them. Your bosses. This is a New International, so it is.'

'We've had four already,' said Mr Alfred. 'All failed.'

'Ah, but this is the best yet,' said Tod. 'This one won't fail. From Aberdeen to Vladivostok. From Omsk and Tomsk to Kirkintilloch, you're all on the way out. All you literary bastards. It's the end of the printed word. Everything's a scribble now. The writing's on the wall. I know. I got it put there.'

'Yes, I've seen it,' said Mr Alfred.

'You wait,' said Tod.

'I've no choice,' said Mr Alfred.

'I've got a new campaign coming up,' said Tod. 'I'm starting a League Against War. I'm going to call it LAW.'

'An acronym,' said Mr Alfred. 'Like POISE.'

'I'm working on a monogram for it,' said Tod. 'Something simple the lads can slap up quick wherever there's a blank space.'

'There are still a few left,' said Mr Alfred.

'Even if there's not I can do a palimpsest, can't I?' said Tod. 'LAW everywhere. Suddenly appearing overnight. That'll fox the public, eh? For a while anyway. I'll let out later on what it means.'

'I saw LAW somewhere,' said Mr Alfred. 'A great while since, a long, long time ago.'

'Not so long,' said Tod. 'I tried it out on a couple of my fellows. But they didn't take to it. And I was too busy with Ya Bass to follow up. But I'm getting on to it again now. I'm finished with YY.'

'I never understood that one,' said Mr Alfred. 'Why YY?'

'If the world belongs to the Young,' said Tod, 'then still more it belongs to the Young Young. I get them at school. Train up a child in the way he should go, and when he is old he will not depart from it.'

'Proverbs,' said Mr Alfred.

'But I'm more interested in my League Against War now,' said Tod.

'I'm glad you're against war,' said Mr Alfred. 'That's always something.'

'I'm against everything,' said Tod. 'To end war you've got to fight. I'll get the yungins to fight against war because the aldyins are past it. You've had the war to end war. It didn't work. I'm going to give you a League Against War, a LAW to end law. Instead of Cogs and Fangs and Tongs and Toi you'll be seeing LAW everywhere you go. I'll have a new wave of destruction in the name of LAW. I'll have LAW YA BASS and LAW OK and YY LAW. The poor public won't know what's going on. They never do till it's done.'

'What good will it do you?' said Mr Alfred.

'I'm not a do-gooder,' said Tod. 'I believe in the dialectic. The unity of opposites. Law is anarchy. That's

what I'm after. I'll do it the way I done Ya Bass. Just a
scribble here and a scribble there to start with. Nobody'll
bother. But it will spread and spread till the whole city's
covered with it. That'll be something. The quantity becomes quality. You said that yourself.'

'But not necessarily a good quality,' said Mr Alfred.

'Who said anything about good?' said Tod. 'It's new.
That's all that matters. You admitted that a minute ago.
And that's how I'll get revenge.'

'Why do you want revenge?' said Mr Alfred.

'Badness is all,' said Tod. 'You made me what I am
today, I hope you're satisfied.'

'If they had slapped down Gerald Provan the first time
he stepped out of line this would never have happened,'
said Mr Alfred.

'But you don't know it was Gerald Provan rolled you,'
said Tod. 'You saw nothing, you heard nothing. They
came up behind you. You're only guessing. You've got a
spite at Gerald Provan. You're aye picking on him.'

'The way they ought to have stopped the young ruffians
in Germany,' said Mr Alfred. 'Before Hitler came to
power at all. Terrorising decent people in the street.
But no. They even said Hitler himself was all right. He
just needed sympathy.'

'The Hitlerjugend weren't ruffians,' said Tod. 'They
were good lads. They were organised. I could organise my
lads like that. As a matter of fact I'm doing something
better. Because you can't pin a thing on me. I'll destroy
Europe without a war. You wait. You won't get me in a
bloody bunker waiting for a bomb. I'll live to laugh.'

'Who do you think you are?' said Mr Alfred. 'A new
Schickelgruber?'

'Who?' said Tod.

'Skip it,' said Mr Alfred.

'You talk the slang of the thirties,' said Tod.

'How do you know?' said Mr Alfred. 'You weren't born
then.'

'Was I not?' said Tod. 'I was, I am, and I always will be.'

'You think you're God perhaps?' said Mr Alfred.

'No, the other One,' said Tod. 'The Adversary.'

'The devil seeking whom he may deflower,' said Mr Alfred. 'Der Geist der stets verneint.'

'That's me,' said Tod. 'I say No to you and your likes. I'm nibbling away at the roots of your civilisation. I'll bring it down. The felt-pen is mightier than the sword.'

'You've made my city ugly,' said Mr Alfred. 'Apart from all the stabbings and fighting in the street, this writing on the wall everywhere – it's an offence against civilisation.'

'Civilisation means class distinction,' said Tod. 'To hell with it. Life is more important than civilisation. Life is a comprehensive school. Every child is equal.'

Mr Alfred raised his hand for permission to speak.

'May I say a poem, please?'

'If you like,' said Tod. 'So long as it's not one of yon there was a young lady of things. Can't stand them.'

Mr Alfred elocuted.

'My heart sinks down when I behold the boys and girls go by.'

He stopped.

'I'm sorry,' he said. 'That is all I can remember.'

'You're getting past it, mac, that's your trouble,' said Tod. 'You should be like me. Young, keen, eager. Accept the challenge. Always learning. I've been thinking I might even learn something from China. You know, the Red Guards. They're fairly knocking the old ones. Taking over the trains. Go where they like. Causing alarm and dismay. I must ask the International Secretariat for more information.'

'You really believe you have an international movement?' said Mr Alfred.

'You can see I have,' said Tod. 'Don't you ever read the papers, mac? I can't lose. I've got a fifth column. You know that. What folk say about me and my lads, it's like what you were saying they said about wee Adolf and his lads. They feel rejected. Give them love. Treat them nice and they'll be nice. Treat them nasty and they'll be nasty.'

'It doesn't work out that way,' said Mr Alfred.

'Yes, you know that and I know that,' said Tod. 'But you mustn't ever say it.'

'They made that mistake about Hitler,' said Mr Alfred.

'It wasn't just wee Adolf,' said Tod. 'Don't forget there was Poor Old Joe as well. He was a great pop figure too in his day before folk decided he was as big a bastard as wee Adolf. You'll remember the pair of them were aye having their picture took with a wee lassie in their arms. You know, cuddling her. They were fond of wee girls, just like you.'

'Excuse me,' said Mr Alfred. 'One only, if you don't mind.'

Tod conceded the correction with a placatory bow and resumed his argument.

'They failed to conquer Europe between them because they were too crude. But see me? I'm subtle. They were there to be named. Not me. I'm nowhere.'

'Everywhere,' said Mr Alfred.

'They'll never catch me,' said Tod.

'No, they won't, will they?' said Mr Alfred.

'Those two stupid bastards wanted a State,' said Tod. 'I don't. I don't want a thousand-year Reich. I don't want a New and Higher Form of Civilisation. I don't want to be the Big Führer Brother Secretary-General. I don't want to conquer Europe. I want to destroy it. Destroy its schools and libraries and public telephones. You can fight an army invading your territory. But you can't fight me. I'm not invading you. I'm already inside. And I'm nobody.'

'Everybody,' said Mr Alfred. 'When I look at what you've done to this city!'

'Go thou and do likewise,' said Tod.

He faded rather than went away.

Mr Alfred found himself out of The Flat as abruptly as he had found himself in it. He teetered at the closemouth.

'How are you feeling now?' said the gentle voice.

'I'll be all right,' said Mr Alfred.

'Now are you sure?' said the young man. 'Are you sure you'll manage?'

'I'll manage fine,' said Mr Alfred.

'It gets worse every night,' said the young man.

'Yes, indeed,' said Mr Alfred.

'Will you get a bus all right?' said the young man.

'I can get one round the corner,' said Mr Alfred.

'I'll leave you then,' said the gentle voice. 'I go this way.'

'I go that way,' said Mr Alfred. 'Good night. And thanks very much.'

'No bother,' said the young man. 'Good night then.'

'Good night,' said Mr Alfred.

CHAPTER THIRTY

When Tod left him Mr Alfred wasn't sure where he was. He was with himself but outside himself, as if there were two of him. He looked up at the nightsky like an ancient mariner trying to take his bearings from the stars. But he couldn't see any stars in the narrow vault between the buildings. All he saw was a crescent reflector hanging in the dark void.

'A falcate moon,' he said.

He repeated the words. They seemed to promise the start of a poem, but the promise wasn't kept. He was distracted from the abortive lyric by a fear he had lost his way. When he went round the corner to get a bus there wasn't a bus to be seen. There wasn't even a bus-stop. He tried another corner and wandered into a hinterland of mean streets. He veered, and got into a tangle of lanes and pends. At that point he wasn't just afraid he was lost. He knew he was lost. He was tempted to panic, but the man with him said it didn't matter, there was always a way out.

The coffee and hamburgers he had taken in the Caballero were meant to sober him. But now he felt drunk again, and always he had the idea he wasn't walking alone. Perhaps it was the crack on the head when he was rolled in the close. Perhaps it was his alarm at losing his way. He thought of going back to the close and starting again from there. But he had zigzagged so much he didn't know if he was walking towards the river or away from it, going east or going west. He plodded on and round about and back again, looking for a main road, one man in him trying to hear the tape of a conversation another had recorded.

Yet for all his confusion he remembered his money. He

searched every pocket three or four times. But there was
no change. They were all empty. He felt he had been
insulted rather than robbed. That most of his month's
salary was still safe in his hidden pocket was only what he
expected. Had it been gone too he would have groaned in
agony. It would have meant the end of his little private
world of self-esteem, a mockery of his boast that nobody
could ever rob him. The loss of a couple of pounds and a
handful of silver was no hardship. It was the degradation
of being a victim hurt him.

Now he had a problem. Even if he found a bus going his
way he had nothing but fivers to pay his fare. It took him
some time to see a taxi was the answer. He wasn't much
given to taking taxis. But it had to be done. Instead of
looking for a bus route he began to look out for a cruising
taxi. Nothing passed.

He tripped at a dark corner and fell on his knees. He got
up shakily. He was frightened. But the other man didn't
mind in the least.

The tenements he passed looked shabby, the closes
looked slummy. Peeling paint, litter, and dim lights.
Everything was dim. Dim and dirty. He longed for the
sun and a blue sky and a clean city. He searched his
pockets again, still unwilling to believe he hadn't even
been left his bus fare. All he found in one pocket was the
thick cylinder he had felt before. The felt pen, he remembered. And a thin cylinder his fingers recognised as a piece
of chalk. He was always finding bits of chalk in his pocket.

'Talk and chalk,' he said. 'That's me. Out-of-date. The
child is master of the man. New methods. Visual aids.
Projects. Research. Doesn't matter half the bastards can't
read. Do research just the same. Discover Pythagoras'
theorem for themselves. Could you?'

He stumbled. The flagstones of the city's pavements
were seldom flush. He reeled.

'Oh no! Not again!' he cried as he lurched, head down,
arms out.

But he didn't fall. He straightened just in time and kept

going. And more and more sharply as he wandered through the empty night he was aware of being outside himself, watching himself, listening to himself, not owning himself.

He twisted and turned, corner after corner. He prayed for guidance. Suddenly he came round to shops and neon lights. Then there were hoardings on one side and on the other desolate tenements with all the windows broken, a shuttered pub left standing as the stump of a demolished block, and bulldozers parked in the backcourts of vanished closes. There was nobody about. He went on. And everywhere he went he saw it.

The writing on the wall.

The writing on the wall.

Everywhere he went he saw the writing on the wall.

The writing.

The writing.

The writing on the wall.

```
   TONGS YA BASS        GOUCHO        PEG OK
        FLEET YA BASS        YY TOI

                                  TOWN OK
                    HOODS YA BASS        CODY YYS
                              SHAMROCK LAND
                TORCH RULE OK YY HAWKS MONKS YA BASS
```

On his right in an all-night urinal COGS YA BASS.

On his left as he rocked YY FANGS OK.

Outside again, still no taxis. No buses. No people. Nothing but the writing on the wall. On every phone box, junction box and pillar box, on every shop front, bus shelter and hoarding, on every board and paling, on every bridge and coping stone there was the writing. Scrawled, scribbled, sprayed, daubed. Yellow, red, green, white, black and blue. Six, eight, ten and twelve inch letters. More writing.

```
   REBELS YA BASS    YY GRINGO        TIGERS
        BORDER RULE OK
   YY TOON        TUSKY
   UZZ RULE    YY CUMBIE    GEMY    TOI LAND
```

Some old inscriptions too he saw in passing, the weather-faded lettering chalked by children in ancient times.

FUCK THE POPE
  SHITE
    CELTIC 7–1
1690
    FUCK KING BILLY   CUNT

But since they seemed as out-of-date as himself he accepted them without complaint.

He saw a bus-stop with a route number that would suit him. On the metal frame of the windowless shelter there was slapdashed PRIESTY TOON TONGS. PRIESTY he identified as the name of a housing scheme the bus crews refused to service on Saturday nights because the passengers either showed a knife when asked for their fare or kicked and butted the conductor when they jumped off without paying. He swayed and grued.

He had an idea. He would phone the Lord Provost, the *Daily Express* and the University Principal, Mrs Trumbell, the Curator of the Art Galleries and the Secretary of State for Scotland, he would even phone the President of the Educational Institute of Scotland. He would lodge a formal protest. He assumed he could speak to them all at once on the same line. He was all set to ask them for a start, 'Do you folk know what's going on?'

But the first phone-box he went to was out of order. The phone was there in its cradle, sleeping peacefully, never to waken. The cord had been ripped away. His brilliant idea left him. He edged out of the box and waited on the pavement for something to happen. The Muse visited him and he recited aloud impromptu under an arc-lamp.

Was it the same in Carthage, Rome,
Babylon and Ephesus?
To hell! I might as well go home,
If only I could get a bus.

He moved on, wearied. He longed to see again what he had seen as a young soldier with the British Army of Liberation, the gilded buildings of Brussels, the Meir in Antwerp, the Dyver in Bruges, any handsome street in any gracious city. He was no countryman. He liked cities. He longed to live in one.

He forgot he was looking for a taxi. He didn't know where he was going. He wasn't going anywhere. He was standing still. He found that piece of chalk in his pocket again. He fumbled for it. Then he remembered the felt-pen. It was a better instrument. He took it out, unscrewed the cap, held it ready for writing. He heard Tod.

'Go thou and do likewise.'

On a wall he wrote. Carefully, a good scribe. In bold block capitals. Four inches high.

MENE MENE TEKEL UPHARSIN

He stepped back and looked at it. He looked at his work and he thought it was good. He walked along the site, looking for another empty space. But not unnoticed. Two policemen in a patrol-car had seen him. The driver stopped at the kerb. With his mate he watched. They both watched. Frowning one. The other smiling.

'The old bastard's drunk,' said King.

'A foreign bugger,' said Quinn. 'What lingo's that?'

'No idea,' said King. 'He's not a Paki, is he?'

'Doesn't look like one,' said Quinn. 'What's he up to now?'

'Go thou and do likewise,' said Mr Alfred.

He wrote on the wall again.

GLASGOW YA BASS

'Ah, now,' said King.

'We can't have that,' said Quinn.

'It's the first time I've seen anybody right in the act,' said King. 'I mean seen him write.'

Mr Alfred turned away from the wall and shouted to the sky the words he had written.

'Glasgow, ya bass!'

He shouted them so loudly he seemed to want to waken the whole sleeping city and make it listen to him. He nodded and nodded, went back to the wall and ticked off the phrase.

'Right,' he said quietly. 'Next, please.'

He held out his left hand for the next pupil's jotter, his felt-pen in his right ready for marking.

'The old scunner,' said Quinn.

'He didn't look the type to me,' said King. 'Too old I'd have thought.'

'That's the trouble,' said Quinn. 'Once it starts, every bloody fool.'

'Go and get him,' said King. 'Before he falls down.'

'Right,' said Quinn.

King sat back and waited.

Quinn eased from the car and crossed over. No hurry.

'Now, now,' he said. 'What do you think you're playing at?'

'Good evening,' said Mr Alfred.

'Now don't try and be funny,' said Quinn. 'Know what time it is?'

'Oh, I'm not being funny,' said Mr Alfred. 'There's nothing funny about it. That's my point. It's not a pantomime joke, not in my opinion.'

'You should be in your bed, old fella,' said Quinn. 'It's after two.'

'Indeed?' said Mr Alfred. 'I wondered why I couldn't get a bus.'

'What are you writing on the wall for?' said Quinn.

Mr Alfred had no answer. He felt wedged in a cleft. The writing on the wall had been done by someone occupying his body in space and time, someone not identical with himself, someone who had suddenly gone away and left him to answer for what had been done. And while he knew he wasn't responsible for all this writing on the wall he knew he had to answer for it. He didn't mind. He was willing to answer for it, if he was pushed. This young policeman could do what he liked with him. Nothing mattered any more. He had done what he was told to do. He remembered an old word cherished in his youth when a dictionary was his bedside book. Ataraxia. The indifference aimed at by the stoics. That was all he felt.

'Come on,' said Quinn. 'You've had too much I think.'

He took Mr Alfred by the elbow, led him to the car. Put him in the back seat. But gently.

Settling well back Mr Alfred muttered away.

'Since that lout defied me. Nothing but. Schools, libraries, parks, railways, buses, cemeteries. Since that day that lump. All vandalised. The child is master. All natural piety gone. Insolence, be thou my courtesy.'

His head lolled. He jolted and came up again.

'Taught them language. And the profit on it is. Caliban shall be his own master. That blonde bitch Seymour. She should say less. What the inspectors want. Do-it-yourself poetry. Matthew Arnold was an inspector too. What would he say now? Culture and anarchy. Anarchy. Every child a poet, every child a painter.'

He shook his head. He felt sleepy. But he wanted to speak.

'Insolence, violence,' he said. 'It's the black-ground of those torrible grousing-schemes.'

'I told you he was drunk,' said King to Quinn.

Mr Alfred leaned over and tapped Quinn on the shoulder.

'Do you know,' he said, 'you can pick up a lunar probe but you can't pick up a phone.'

'You're right there, pop,' said Quinn.

King braked at a red light. Mr Alfred fell back on his seat and talked to himself.

'Standards must be maintained. We must pass on our cultural heritage. The tongue that Shakespeare spoke, that Milton. Though fallen on evil days, on evil days though fallen and evil tongues, in darkness and with dangers compassed round, and solitude.'

'He's got an educated voice,' said King to Quinn.

'He looks a real scruff to me,' said Quinn to King.

Mr Alfred was comfortable in the back seat. It was

better than any bus. He thought he was being taken home in a taxi. He wondered how much it would cost. He wondered how they knew where he lived.

Quinn half-turned, speaking over his shoulder.

'What did you want to go and do a daft thing like that for?'

'Wir müssen aussprechen was ist,' said Mr Alfred.

Quinn shrugged back to King.

'I told you he was a foreign bastard,' he said.

'That's German,' said King to Quinn. 'Maybe he's a refugee from the Iron Curtain.'

'Iron curtain my arse,' said Quinn.

King drove humming along the empty road in the small hours.

Peering through the window Mr Alfred saw the writing on the wall again.

'This great warm-hearted friendly city,' he said. 'The dear green place. The corn is green. How green was my valley. A lot of balls.'

'What's that you were saying?' Quinn turned to ask.

'That it could so preposterously be stained,' said Mr Alfred.

Quinn kept turned round.

'Are you all right, pop?' he asked. 'You know, you're in trouble. Defacing property. Drunk and disorderly. A man your age. You ought to know better.'

'We all ought to know better,' said Mr Alfred.

'Eh?' said Quinn.

Mr Alfred said nothing.

'Nothing to say for yourself, eh?' said Quinn.

Mr Alfred remembered something to say. He said it solemnly.

'For nothing this wide universe I call, save thou, my Rose, in it thou art my all.'

Quinn turned back to King.

'Oh Jesus,' he said.

King took a quick glance over his shoulder.

'Steady up, old fella,' he said. 'Get a hold of yourself.'

Mr Alfred fell asleep.

CHAPTER THIRTY-ONE

Sheriff Stairs wasn't impressed by Mr Alfred. He didn't like the look of him at all. It was bad enough when irresponsible juveniles went about writing on walls, but it was intolerable when the culprit was a grown man, and above all a man in Mr Alfred's position. If he was an alcoholic he shouldn't be teaching. If he was suffering from a nervous breakdown he shouldn't be teaching. If he was a harebrained eccentric he shouldn't be teaching.

Mr Alfred had nothing to say. He had a return of his old feeling that he was the man outside somebody else. There was a man there in the dock with his face, answering to his name, but it wasn't him. It was another man he had been forced to keep company with, a fellow traveller who was getting by on a borrowed birth certificate.

Sheriff Stairs had him remanded for a medical report. The doctor found him sound in wind and limb, but noticed a recent prosthodontia which may have accounted for his pyknophrasia when he was arrested. Heart in good condition, no VD, reflexes, blood count and urine normal, weight about the average for his height and age, a slight presbyopia. He also found evidence of a femoral hernia, and arranged for a surgeon to operate within a fortnight. Until then, he passed him on to Mr Knight, psychiatrist.

Mr Knight was unofficially accompanied by Mr Jubb, a psychiatrist from England. Mr Jubb had published a paper on *Some Common Phobias of Metropolitan Man*. He had come north with letters of introduction in search of material for a supplementary paper. He found nothing in Edinburgh to detain him and cut west across country to more fertile ground. Mr Knight grudgingly let him sit in on his interrogation of Mr Alfred. Mr Jubb called it an interesting case. Duly silent, he sat in a corner with a big looseleaf notebook and a ballpoint.

'Is it because you're not happy in your work you drink so much?' said Mr Knight. 'Don't you like children?'

'Not in bulk,' said Mr Alfred. 'They frighten me.'

Mr Jubb made a note.

'You're out round the pubs every night, aren't you?' said Mr Knight.

'Oh yes, every night practically,' said Mr Alfred.

'No matter what the weather?' said Mr Knight.

'Not in fog,' said Mr Alfred. 'I hate fog.'

Mr Jubb made a note.

'I'm afraid to cross the street then,' said Mr Alfred. 'Indeed. I'm afraid to cross the street at any time these days.'

'You don't seem to have any social life,' said Mr Knight. 'Don't you like meeting people?'

'Can't say I do,' said Mr Alfred. 'I don't take to strangers easily.'

Mr Jubb made a note.

'You prefer to be alone?' said Mr Knight.

'Yes,' said Mr Alfred. 'I have a great horror of crowds.'

Mr Jubb made a note.

'I hate to feel people knocking against me, touching me,' said Mr Alfred.

Mr Jubb made a note.

'You're not afraid of anything happening to you when you wander round like that?' said Mr Knight.

'I've always had a fear of being robbed,' said Mr Alfred. 'But I take care. I've got this pocket, you see.'

He showed it. He wanted to prove he was a wise old man.

Mr Jubb made a note.

'I've never been attacked before,' said Mr Alfred. 'I was terrified. I thought I was going to die.'

Mr Jubb made a note.

Mr Alfred bit the nail of his index finger. He wasn't

given to biting his nails. But there was a ragged edge annoying him. He had felt it catch on the cloth when he was showing his secret pocket and he tried to bite it off.

Mr Jubb made a note.

'Not that I should like to live till I'm senile,' said Mr Alfred.

He smiled. Mr Knight didn't. Mr Jubb made a note.

'Did you have much to drink the night you were attacked?' said Mr Knight.

'Not much,' said Mr Alfred. 'Not really. I've had more. Often. Say seven or eight pints and seven or eight whiskies. Maybe more. But then I'm used to it. I remember one night—'

He stopped. He didn't want to tell too much.

Mr Jubb made a note.

'You've no friends apparently,' said Mr Knight. 'But have you no pets? A cat or a dog for example.'

'Oh no, I can't stand animals,' said Mr Alfred.

Mr Jubb made a note.

'Least of all cats,' said Mr Alfred. 'They give me the creeps.'

Mr Jubb made a note.

'Even insects,' said Mr Alfred. 'I loathe spiders.'

He wanted to chat to Mr Knight, to help him. He felt sorry for a man who had to ask all these questions as part of his job, with a supernumerary stuck in a corner listening in. He supposed the stranger in the corner was putting Mr Knight through a test.

Mr Jubb made a note.

'I gather you've been rather upset by new schemes of work in your profession, new methods,' said Mr Knight. 'Now why is that?'

'Well,' said Mr Alfred, very judicial. 'All that's said in their favour is that they're new. I don't like that. It's not a reason.'

Mr Jubb made a note.

Mr Knight turned the pages of Mr Alfred's dossier.

'You live in lodgings, I see,' he said.

'That's right,' said Mr Alfred. 'On the ground floor. It's an odd thing that. I've always had my digs on the ground floor and I've always had my classroom on the ground floor. Just as well. I hate stairs. I don't mean Sheriff Stairs.'

He smiled to encourage appreciation of his little joke. He got no smile back. Mr Knight in front of him looked past him. Mr Jubb behind him kept his head down and made a note. Mr Alfred was afraid he had said too much and said it too quickly. But he only wanted to let them see he was quite at ease.

'These new thirtytwo-storey flats,' he said slowly. 'I wouldn't like to live in one of them. I hate heights.'

Mr Jubb made a note.

'Why don't you take a holiday abroad?' said Mr Knight. 'You told the police you liked foreign cities, but I understand you haven't been to any of them for years. Why is that? You have a long holiday in the summer.'

'The trouble is I've got lazy,' said Mr Alfred. 'All the bother you have travelling, the customs and all that, it puts me off.'

Mr Jubb made a note.

'But if you like to be alone,' said Mr Knight, 'why do you stand in a pub every night? You're hardly alone there.'

Mr Alfred was getting rattled at the probing. He answered a bit impatiently and spoke too quickly again.

'I'm a townsman,' he said. 'I'm not keen on the wide open spaces. Mind you, I don't like to go into a pub and find nobody there. You feel too conspicuous, all that empty space at the bar. Depresses me.'

Mr Jubb made two notes.

'I like to move about where there's people,' said Mr Alfred. 'But not get mixed up with them. See what I mean?'

He moved his chair away from the radiator behind him. It was too near. He felt it scorching his bottom.

Mr Jubb made a note.

Mr Alfred saw him when he shifted his chair. He

guessed there had been notes taken all the time behind his back. The suspicion that the stranger was testing him and not Mr Knight made him angry. He spoke impulsively.

'It's all these stupid buggers I've got to work with,' he said. 'They give me nightmares. You've no idea. I hate them all. All these brainless bastards and bloody bitches.'

Mr Jubb was stuck for a moment. He turned to an index page at the back of his looseleaf notebook before he made another note.

Mr Knight sighed. He stopped for coffee. As a matter of courtesy to a guest colleague he had a word with Mr Jubb. Mr Jubb was grave.

'Do you think it's safe to let him do his own –' he paused, looked across at Mr Alfred, whispered to Mr Knight – 'pogonotomy?'

'I see no reason why he shouldn't shave himself,' said Mr Knight.

'But this fellow's not right,' said Mr Jubb. 'He's not right at all. Look at what we've found out.'

'What have we found out?' said Mr Knight.

'Children frighten him,' said Mr Knight. 'He hates fog, he's afraid to cross the street, he doesn't like strangers, he has a horror of crowds, he hates to feel people touching him, he likes to wander off on his own, he has a fear of being robbed, he was afraid of dying, he bites his nails, he wouldn't like to be senile, he drinks eight pints of beer and eight whiskies, he can't stand animals, cats give him the creeps, he loathes spiders, he doesn't like what's new, he hates climbing stairs, he hates heights, he hates travelling, he speaks too quickly, he's not keen on wide open spaces but he doesn't like empty spaces, he can't stand heat and he hates bees.'

'So?' said Mr Knight.

'Don't you see?' said Mr Jubb. 'I've got enough for another paper.'

He read off softly, softly, from his notes.

'The man's got pedophobia, homichlophobia, dromo-phobia, xenophobia, ochlophobia, haphephobia, planomania, kleptophobia, thanatophobia, he's an onychophagist, he's got gerontophobia, but notice he has no dysphagia, he's got zoophobia, gataphobia, arachnophobia, kainophobia, climacophobia, acrophobia, hodophobia, he suffers from intermittent tachylogia, he's got agoraphobia and kenophobia, thermophobia and melissophobia.'

'Poor soul,' said Mr Knight. 'He's in a bad way.'

'He's in a very bad way,' said Mr Jubb. 'You could have him committed for care and attention on this evidence.'

Mr Alfred went inside for his operation while Sheriff Stairs was still considering sentence. He might have been all right, laughed at Mr Jubb, and got back to work if he hadn't taken a bad turn towards the end of his convalescence. He wakened early one morning and saw his window welcome the sun and a blue sky outside after many grey mornings. He was glad to be alive. He rose promptly and took off his pyjama-jacket. It was his habit then to put his vest on, take off his pyjama-trousers and put his pants on. This time he lifted his pants in mistake for his vest and put his arms through the legs. He knew at once there was something wrong but he wasn't sure what. He persisted in his error, trying to achieve a victory of mind over matter by simply willing the pants to become a vest. They didn't.

A nurse found him reeling and writhing round his bed, his head hooded by his pants, his hands waving blindly through the brief legs. No matter how hard he butted he couldn't get his head through the crutch of his drawers. He was worried.

The nurse watched him. He gave up struggling and sat on the edge of his bed, defeated, resigned, waiting for release. He flapped his arms above his hidden head and giggled.

The nurse had met it before. She was quiet and tactful. She slipped the pants over Mr Alfred's head, drew the legs away from his arms and put him back into his pyjama-jacket and back into bed. Mr Alfred smiled and nodded. His hair was all tousled from his battle with the cul-de-sac of his drawers. He looked at the nurse with a show of intelligent interest. She tucked him in. His lips moved between his nods and smiles but he didn't really say anything.

The nurse went out. A doctor came in. Mr Alfred was sitting up, smoothing the turnover of his sheet. He gave the doctor a colleaguing smile.

When he showed more signs of deterioration he was put in a geriatric ward. He had attacks of amnesia and aphasia, but picked up a little now and again. He managed to say please without being able to say what it was he wanted. He could also say thank you when his want was understood and met. Since he wasn't all that old and beds in the geriatric ward were scarce, he was moved to a mental asylum. It may have been that crack on his skull when he was rolled in a back-close. It may have been a natural decay. He lived on without knowing. When he could speak again he was polite to everybody. He walked round the grounds twice every day, morning and afternoon, weather permitting. His only greeting to any fellow patient he passed was a smile, a bow, and a timid murmur.

'Turned out nice again today. No sign of children.'

He would look up at the sky like a man afraid of a sudden shower.

He was suspended between heaven and earth in peace and solitude. He forgot everything else he had ever wanted. Granny Lyons came to see him three times a week, and went away crying to herself. She brought him cigarettes at first. But he didn't use them. He had forgotten about smoking. She stopped bringing them.

News always gets around. The teachers in Collinsburn heard about him and somebody raised his name once in the staffroom.

'I hadn't much use for him,' said Mr Brown. 'But I must admit I feel sorry for the poor fellow.'

'He wasn't a bad sort really,' said Mr Campbell. 'A bit pedantic sometimes maybe.'

'A bit old-fashioned,' said Mr Dale.

'Yes he was, wasn't he,' said Mr Kerr. 'Very conscientious. Never absent. Never late.'

Other people too heard about him through devious gossip.

'Haw maw!' Gerald Provan shouted one evening the moment he crossed the door. 'Know what I heard the day?'

'Naw,' said his mother standing over the frying-pan. 'What did you hear?'

'Remember big Alfy?' said Gerald.

'I'm not likely to forget him,' said Mrs Provan.

'He's been put away,' said Gerald. 'He's in the nut-house.'

'It's where he belongs,' said Mr Provan, turning the sausages. 'Bad old bugger. He was aye mad.'

Senga at the table, waiting, listening, said nothing as Gerald gave source and details. She had left school by that time and got a job as a copy typist in an insurance broker's office. In spite of her squint she had a good appearance and a refined voice. She was skinny as a child, but now she was a slim, smart, confident Miss Provan. She had lost touch with Rose after the Weipers left Tordoch.

They met by chance in the street at the evening rush-hour. They had to stop and speak for old time's sake. Rose, once the prettier and more graceful, was thicklegged and broad-bottomed. Her face was plump and the mouth rather slack. She was a filing clerk in the Tax Offices in Waterloo Street.

Senga did her best but Rose had nothing much to say. They moved to the edge of the pavement to avoid ob-structing people and stood staring past each other after the first awkward words. Senga was going to tell Rose about Mr Alfred, just to break the silence and make conversa-tion. But she changed her mind at once. It might sound malicious to say he was in a mental hospital. And remem-bering the trouble he had caused them she thought it would be tactless to mention him at all. She tried to think of something else to say.

'I'll need to hurry,' said Rose. 'Or I won't get on a bus. I'm late.'

'Yes, I'm late too,' said Senga. 'But I'll maybe see you again sometime.'